MILLER'S CROSSING

David Clark

THE ORIGINS OF MILLER'S CROSSING

Miller's Crossing Prequel

David Clark

1

The newly drawn night brought with it a familiar friend in the form of a dense mist to the 18th century Scottish fishing town of St. Margret's Hope. One might call it fog, but fog does not soak you as you walk through it, like this did. With the disappearance of the last light of day, darkness reigned for a few fleeting hours until the rise of the full moon. The white light from their lunar visitor cast eerie shadows behind every home, stone wall, and hill. In the distance, dogs howled at the object. Other livestock, such as cows and sheep, normally never paid any attention to the moon, but tonight was no normal night.

With a fresh log on the fire, William Miller settled in for the night. Before he headed in, his animals seemed restless. Something not all that uncommon. Many times, an approaching change in the weather was to blame. When night fell, the restlessness became worse. They were not overly vocal, with long mournful calls. Their calls were short and stressed, and they were not still. From inside his stone home, he heard them, but ignored them. He told himself they would settle down, but the crash he heard out in their pen told a different story.

William slid his feet into his brown hide boots, and grabbed his grey sporran. After a long bout with wolves two summers ago, William and his neighbor, John Sanders, came up with the idea to keep a sporran packed with rocks to grab in a hurry. He pulled two rocks out to have at the ready as he threw open his door. He ran to the pen, with every expectation of finding one or two wolves roaming around, or maybe a stray dog from one of the neighboring farms. A chill went up the back of his neck, and he dropped the rocks to the ground and put his hands on his hips.

"You should be used to them by now," he said to the animals. The 'them' he spoke of were three flickering human forms that roamed across his pasture a few hundred yards away from his livestock. William watched them. Instead of moving straight across and away, they wandered and meandered here and there. The 'theres' were further away from him and his livestock, but the 'heres' brought them close.

When they reached the edge of his land, they circled back instead of crossing through. William knew this would continue for the rest of the night if he did not put a stop to it. He walked out to greet them and stopped right in their path. Two of them moved around him. The third went right through. In all outward appearance, they didn't even know he was there. The cold icy chill from being passed through was a sensation that William never got used to, no matter how many times it had happened. Feeling one's internal organs shiver and shake was as close to death he could go without dying himself.

"Now, just go on and leave. No need to cause any trouble here," William said. All three continued to walk away from him. He hadn't got their attention. Reaching into his sporran. He retrieved a single rock and then tossed it at the three specters. It passed straight through the middle one and prompted no reaction. "That never works," William said under his breath. It was true, that never worked. Simple actions, like talking, rarely did. He could count the number of times it had on one hand. But he had to hope. It was a better option than what he usually did.

"Ya! Ya!", he yelled as he ran toward them from behind. When he reached them, he zigzagged through them, over and over again. The first pass through never got their attention. They would keep moving, just as these did, but if he did it enough, they would notice and move away from him. The only question was, could he stand the ice-cold grip he felt every time he did.

On the third pass, the one on the right took notice. A weathered old gentleman, with a wrinkled face and straggly white hair, turned toward William. The empty sockets he had for eyes followed William as he danced around them in an attempt to herd them like a sheep dog. It was working. They moved straight across to the other side. William's movements cut them off each time they tried to turn. If they ignored him, he ran through them to remind him of his presence. Each time he did so, their demeanor changed. The pleasant chaps on a nice stroll through his pasture were now rather irritated. Their hollow eyes, and the scowls on their faces, watched him. The mouths moved on two of them, as if they attempted to lecture or warn him, but nothing came out.

This dance continued across his land, and across the trail that separated his and the next, but he didn't stop. He wanted to make sure they didn't come back that night. He continued on until he felt they were far enough away from his farm to cause any trouble. If they caused anyone else trouble, that was none of his concern. His goal was a good night's sleep. There wasn't much of the night left, but at least it would be peaceful.

He bid his ghastly friends adieu and bowed as they passed by. When he stood up, he came face to face with the weathered old man that had taken an interest in him. The man reached out with his flickering arm of blue mist and grabbed him by the back of the neck. Its icy touch felt like a thousand pins pricking the surface of his skin. The man leaned forward and contorted its face to twice its normal size and screamed right at him. This was a sound that William heard, there was no mistaking it. William screamed in response, and fell backwards onto the damp grass as the three continued on and disappeared into the mist.

"William, is that you?", asked a sleepy John Sanders. William's neighbor approached. He held a single candle lantern as he scanned the dark fog-covered ground with his eyes. He was two years younger than William, but had a wife and two strapping boys, ages five and seven.

"Ya, over here."

It was only a few seconds before John's lantern illuminated William's form on the ground. John extended a hand and helped his lifelong friend up onto his feet. William pulled at his shirt and kilt, now both soaked from the moisture on the ground.

"What are you doing out here, and what was all that yelling?"

"Didn't you hear it?", William asked.

"Hear what?", John responded. "All I heard was you. Screaming your bloody head off, like you were some wild dog or wolf. What was all that about?"

Still pulling the cold wet clothing away from his already chilled body, William didn't say anything. He didn't need to. The sheepish look on his face said it all.

"Again?"

"Three of them," he said, as he held up three fingers in the candlelight to drive the point home.

"Three?", asked a weary John.

A quick nod from William answered the question of his friend and neighbor.

John looked to either side of them, and then turned around to look behind him. His sleepy eyes peered into the dark, but saw nothing. "You sure?"

"Yes."

"Where are they?"

William threw his hands up, and looked at his friend. His eyebrows raised to cap the question marks in his eyes. "I lost track when I fell down."

John turned around and headed back toward his farmhouse. The circle of light that had encircled both of them receded and followed him. William found himself once again in the dark cool fog of the still night. "Go home, William. It's a good thing I have been your friend for so long and understand. Someone else might think you aren't right in the head. Chained up in some asylum is where you'd be."

William knew what he said was true. He had hidden this side of him from everyone, except John. John only knew because the truth was the only way to explain how he was acting. They were friends for as long as they could remember. Anytime they weren't doing chores, or helping out on the farm, they could be found along the simple stone wall that separated their families properties. Probably up to no good. Many a day in their younger years was spent throwing small pebbles at birds and bugs. As they got older, they graduated to talking about girls, and plans to get out of this place. Sometimes they spent the afternoon taking sips out of a swiped jug of William's father's homemade whiskey, while talking of all the girls they never had the nerve to talk to.

One early evening, after they were about a third of a jug deep, William had John hide the jug behind the wall. He'd seen a man walking toward them. John had done as he was asked, but questioned him. He didn't see the man, and insisted he wasn't there at all. John suggested William had more than his share of the whiskey. The closer the man came, the weirder William felt. He started to doubt his eyes and believed John had a point. Maybe he had had a bit too much that night. A cold sweat had developed on his neck, and pins prickled up and down his spine.

It wasn't long until William got a better look at the man. He flashed and flickered. There one second, and gone the next. Combined with the feeling that had come over his body, disbelief had set in. He rubbed both eyes hard with his hands. Each eyelid burped silently as he rubbed hard enough to force tears out the sides. When he opened them again, he was still there, and now closer than before.

William hopped down off the wall and walked out to meet him. It didn't take long for him to realize he could see straight through the man. When he reached him, he circled him as he continued to walk. The man paid no attention to William. Attempts to talk to him went ignored. When William reached out to tap him on the shoulder, he about passed out when his fingers went straight through the man's shoulder.

John accused him of putting him on, but after more and more occurrences of this with William over the years, he began to accept the truth, no matter out outlandish it was. His friend could see ghosts.

"See you in the morning, John," William called after his friend.

John held up the lantern and grunted as he continued back to his house.

William started his trek home. He took a look around every once in a while. It was just out of curiosity though; he knew he wouldn't see anything. The feeling he always had when they were around was gone. A quick hop up and over the same stone wall he and John had spent many an afternoon at when they were younger, put him back on his land. His home wasn't much further, which was good. The cold damp air, combined with his wet clothes created quite a chill in his bones. He passed his animal pen on the way to his farmhouse. They were all sleeping. No longer disturbed. That was good. William was tired, and wasn't in the mood to hear them all night.

2

The midday sun chased away the fog of night. This was a daily battle. One that both sides won from time to time. If a score was kept, the North Sea would claim victory, with many a day seeing overcast clouds or dense fog for the entirety, denying the ground the warmth of sunlight. This contributed to the lush green hills that overlooked the stone buildings that lined the coast, and made good land for farming, one of two main professions in the village. You either farmed, or fished.

William and John farmed. Partially because that was what their families did. William had two uncles that fished, and his grandfather did for a bit before settling on farming. He tried it once with one of his uncles when he was only thirteen. One shouldn't really say only thirteen. At that age you are expected to start learning your trade. The decision of what that would be was one William had not made yet. The sea called to him. It would be cliché to call its image romantic, but to him it was magical. Every day boats headed out, and every night the fog rolled in. Then, one by one, the glimmer of a lantern hanging on the bow peered through the dense marine layer as each of the boats returned with their crew and their catch. Dozens of people rushed the wharf to assist in offloading the haul. Everyone worked well past the fall of darkness, until the work was done. Then they all retired to a local pub to share in drink, food, more drink, grand stories, and even more drink.

Farmers, well, farmed.

His uncle, Logan Miller, offered to take him out with his crew to show him the ropes one day. William didn't hesitate to ask his father before he jumped at it. No concern was given to any disappointment or rejection his father may have felt for his rush to consider a different path.

It was a rather calm day, but being the first time William had ever been on a boat of any type, he had no sea legs, and struggled to keep both his balance and his last meal. The former he lost more than the latter. There was more to the profession than he had expected. Tons of preparation, handled by the two youngest members of the crew, Harris Lonston and Oliver Walling. Both a mere two months older than himself, by the calendar, but their time on board had produced two burly men. Harris, with long locks of red hair, and Oliver, with a mass of dark hair. Their job, was everything but actual fishing. They cut bait, ensured all hooks were baited and ready. When one of the four others on board called "hook", both would run to that man's side. Each stood waiting with large metal hooks in their hands. Once the fish was at the side of the boat, they reached over and thrust the points of the hooks into the shiny-scaled side of the fish. With a single move, they heaved the fish up over the railing and onto the deck. William's uncle then took control of the fish. He cut, gutted, and filleted, right there on the boat. The head and the guts were thrown back overboard, with bits reused for bait. Logan explained to William that he did this by himself, as he didn't trust anyone else not to over-cut the fish, robbing them of usable weight.

William had taken his turn at cutting bait and loading the hooks. It hadn't taken long for him to get into a rhythm, despite the smell. On one occasion, he turned, with both hands holding bits of fish for the hooks, and felt a tingle along the back of his neck. Not wanting to lose what was left of his last meal in front of everyone, he steadied his legs and swallowed hard to bury the feeling. It didn't go away. It intensified. When he rounded the main mast, he ran face to face into the image of an old white-haired man, skin weathered and waterlogged. His stare blank, and mouth mumbling without making a sound.

"Boy, you ok?", asked Finlay Leigh, a large mass of a man who spent much of the trip sharing jokes with his uncle, most of which went straight over William's head. He would have to trust the thundering laughs that erupted from each of the men as a sign that they were funny. William saw Finlay looking at him through the old man. This was not the first time William had seen a ghost, not by a long shot, but it was the worst time possible. He wanted to show he was strong and capable. These men wouldn't understand. If he tried to tell them, it would be an end to his time onboard.

"Yep," he said, as strong and stout as he could muster. Maybe even overdoing it a bit. William stepped through the man, and brushed off the cold chill so no one would notice.

As the afternoon waned, the sea showed more of its character. Storms formed along the horizon and headed their way. Just the simple task of walking took on a new challenge. The deck rose to meet, or dropped away from, every step. When he didn't have to move, he stayed clamped to the railing with his eyes locked on the center of the ship. The others moved with ease. They seemed to enjoy the extra challenge, along with the spray of water over every exterior edge.

There was no concern on anyone's face, except William's, until the boat rocked to port under the edge of a wave. The water washed over the deck sending everyone sprawling on the wooden planks. Loose buckets, line, and hooks, were last seen going over the starboard side.

"Put into the waves!" yelled Finlay.

"It is. They are coming from all sides!" responded Logan, from the helm.

From where William sat, he could confirm what his uncle had said. He felt the boat rocking forward and back in the waves, while others hit them on the broadsides, sending the boat twisting from side to side. His uncle stood stone-still and locked onto the scene ahead of them. His arms turned the wheel to trace the path his brain had mapped through each of the approaching waves. Harris and Oliver had taken up positions similar to William. The child in each of them emerged above their more mature exteriors. They trembled, eyes darting from side to side at the crash of each wave.

That was the last William saw of them, at least onboard the boat. A single crash rolled it over, the sail and mast both submerged in another wave that had approached from the opposite side. Cracks and pops thundered all around them, but it was not from the storm. Large beams of cedar were giving way under the great strain, signaling the beginning of the end.

The only other sound William remembered hearing, other than the sound of the wind, the stinging rain, and the boat breaking apart, was a single laugh and bellow from Finlay, "She's ah going to win this one fellows."

William didn't remember when he went into the water. Nor did he remember how the rest of the boat broke up. He knew the section of railing he had hung onto was still tight in his grasp when he made it to the surface. If it hadn't been for that section of wood, he was sure he would be on his way to the bottom. Instead, they both floated up to the surface and rode the waves of the tempest.

The waves outlasted the wind and rain. It was at the crest of one of those towering waves that William saw how close to the shore he was. He kicked hard, and hung on to his savior. Up and down the waves they went, until he reached a point where each of the waves rushed toward the shore, giving him a welcome push. The last crash of the wave sent him flipping head over ass onto the beach

After that day, William continued to see Harris, Oliver, Finlay, and his uncle from time to time strolling through town aimlessly. Each time he sees one of them serves as a reminder that being a farmer wasn't a bad way to make a living.

3

"William, you ready?", John yelled from outside. He was standing next to a cart hitched to his faithful burro, the most useful tool on his own farm. That burro not only pulled the cart to town, but pulled the plow in the field, hauled loads across the property, and anything else John needed him to do. William had one too, but being a bit older, it was best used for the jobs around the farm, not for trips to town.

"Yep," he said as he emerged out the door of the smokehouse with three large slabs of cured pork. "One more," he said, and dropped the meat down on an empty spot in the cart. Back into the smokehouse he went, but he re-emerged quickly, this time with two large chunks of pork belly. "Last pig of the season for me. The others have to plump up a bit." A quick look back at his animal pen caused a grunt from the three hogs that remained. It was as if they knew they were the topic of the conversation.

The two men walked to town, as they had more times than they could remember. Many times, alongside their fathers as they led a burro, or sometimes a horse, that pulled a cart behind them. For the past ten years, it was their turn to lead the cart, their responsibility, and their lives. The conversation during these trips hadn't changed much through the years. The topic was always the same, dreams. They each dreamed of something bigger.

John wanted to expand the family farm, an idea he had been pitching to his father since he was only nine. Something he felt would force his father to see him as grownup, no longer a child. Instead, his father had brushed it off as just that, a childish dream. "You don't understand how much work it takes to keep up what we have," he always said. Even now, John still dreamed of doing just that.

The dreams William had were loftier. He was a farmer, only because the other option was, well, less attractive. Farming was less likely to take his life. Of course, there are still dozens of ways you could die on the farm. The thought of leaving Saint Margaret's Hope was one he couldn't remember where it came from. No one had ever mentioned anything about leaving to him. There were no encounters with strange or mysterious individuals who told tales of the outside world. It was just a thought. One that he spent many an afternoon sitting on top of the cliff imagining. His gaze looking out over the ocean at nothing in particular, while his mind pondered what was out there.

Meadows and horse tracks gave way to sparse buildings and cobblestone walks as they crept closer to town. The shoes of the burro, and the wheels of the cart that were silent on the dirt and grass path, now clattered and clopped on the stones. The midday sun may have chased the mist away for the moment, but the cool air still hung around. The walk in did not exert either of the young men, yet William still reached up to wipe a few beads of cold sweat off the back of his neck and his brow. John noticed this, and an obvious lack of color in his friend's face. "Is one of your friends around?"

"No!", William snapped back.

"You sure? You look sick." John then followed the path of William's eyes, and said with a bit of a sneer. "Good day, Ainslee."

"Good day, John, William. Heading to town?"

John looked at William. The color was gone from his face. You would think he had seen a ghost, but that was really not something that would spook him. This situation, on the other hand, was something different. Something that petrified William. With raised eyebrows, John tried to encourage William to speak. Instead, he was a statue. Frozen expression and all. With no sign of hope that William would come around, John gave up and responded, "Yes. Market day."

"I will be in town later. Maybe I will see you around."

"Maybe so," John said. He nudged the burro in the side, and they started forward again. Out of the corner of his eye, he watched William, to make sure he didn't need to give him a nudge too. He didn't, William was moving all on his own, shoulders slumped and slack jawed.

Before they had passed the end of the stone fence that surrounded the large two story cobblestone estate, they were greeted again. This time by a middle aged man, someone who would be their fathers' age, in fact, he was a close friend of their fathers'. Deep character lines on his face hinted at the years spent at sea, but his waist coat and buckled brogues told a different story, something more provincial.

"Good day, boys. Going to market?"

"Good day, Lord McLayer," they both said.

"Yes sir. I have fresh turnips and root, you need any?", offered John.

"That I might. You two have a good day."

When the two were clear of the estate, John cut William a look. There was no doubt William saw it. There was a reply look shared between the two friends.

"What was that about?"

William returned the look again.

"You can talk to Lord McLayer, but can't utter a sound to his daughter?"

William didn't have a reply. Not one that would explain the situation. It was something he didn't quite understand either. Ainslee McLayer was their age. He and John had been around her for years. Several years ago, he found himself feeling more nervous around her than before. More aware of anything he may have done embarrassing. A comment, joke, or anything else that made him appear less refined, and more like a child, sent a dagger through his soul. John had noticed it too. It was hard for him not to. There were activities that William would not take part of when she was around. Something as simple as skipping a rock across a pond on the back acre of his father's farm was an activity William avoided when Ainslee was near. John would rib him about it in front of her, which always drew his ire in the form of a look or a comment.

All he knew was, anytime he caught her green eyes and rosy cheeks framed by her flowing red hair, every ounce of confidence drained from his body, and he hated it. She had been, was, is, a great friend. He fancied her, and at one point considered courting her. It would never be permitted though; she was royalty, and he was just a farmer. Not to mention, why would she even consider him? The life he could offer her would be so far below her station.

The two made it to town. The first stop was at the butcher's, to sell the slabs of pork and chunks of pork belly. William had promised him that sow a few weeks prior. Mr. Arlen saw it during a visit out to see William. He had done business with his father, and made a point to visit their farm, and several of his other regular suppliers to check out his future supplies. When he spied the animal during a recent visit, his hands shaped the cuts his brain was making, while his eyes took in the beauty of the beast.

The payment for the meat was a bag with a few coins, but that wasn't the most valuable to William. Not that he didn't need them. He needed to purchase the few other supplies he didn't have means to provide for on the farm. Oh, and bread. He had meal and wheat on his farm, but not the talent to create a fluffy loaf with a hard crust. His attempts always produced something that resembled a field stone. The commodity he received, that held the true value to William, was the five pounds of tender beef steak Mr. Arlen had wrapped up waiting for him. A real treat. His mouth watered just thinking about throwing a hunk of that on the fire when he returned home. The rest would be salted and hung in the cellar to dry. That would have to wait, William and John had a few other items to take care of in town first. John still needed to sell the bushels of turnips and parsley loaded in the back of the cart.

On Front Street, just along the wharf, stood a public market. There were no booths or buildings that made it anything official. Just dozens of people gathered with their goods to sell. It had started as a place to buy fish from the local fleet. One by one, farmers tested their luck and wheeled in a load of their freshest crop. No one remembers who the first one was, but it didn't take long before each of the major farms in the area were regulars. No one complained. It was a win-win for everyone.

John directed the burro into an empty space. Using a stone, he blocked the wheels to keep them from rolling down the slight incline on the road. The cart itself leaned down a little toward the back, to create the perfect display for his goods.

"Keep an eye on it?", John asked.

William just nodded. It wasn't a big ask, nor one he was unfamiliar with. This was the same routine every week. With the cart in place, William watched it to make sure it didn't roll any, while John unhitched the burro and walked him over to a water trough surrounded by green grass. This may have seemed common sense, but as with much the two of them had learned in their endeavors, they had learned this particular skill the hard way. Neither had paid too much attention to what their father's did on the trips into town. Instead, they ran through the market with their friends in town. Many times, their fathers had to waste several minutes at the end of each day searching for the whereabouts of their sons. They would be found running in the streets, sitting on the wharf as they watched the fleet come in, or at any of the three or more friends they had made in town on such previous trips.

They should have paid better attention during those many trips. Each lost their father at a young age. The winter of 1710 was a bad one. Storm after storm blew in from the coast. The wind, rain, and cold were relentless. At times it wouldn't let up for weeks. The problem with being a farmer was, neither the animals nor the crops cared about the weather. Both needed to be tended to. This invited in the other thing that blew in with the storm, the creep. That is what his mom had called it. The type of cough that crept in and stayed. Started as just a hack here and a hack there, but got worse over time, until it was all the time. Those that could afford visits to the town surgeon were given herbs and liniments. Not that they did any good. The coughing continued until life left them. First, his mother, and then, three weeks later, his father. That last week was filled with tasks around the farm, while his father directed from the house. This was the first time William was responsible for the farm. John's parents followed in the coming months. Both boys were traumatized by the loss of their parents. William more than John. John never saw the ghosts of his parents around the farm. Something William did on more than one occasion. At times it warmed his heart, but at others, it chilled it.

Of the many things their fathers had taught them during their dying days, how to secure the cart wasn't one of them. Maybe it was something they had assumed wasn't needed, since the boys had accompanied them on many trips into town. It didn't happen on their first trip in, or even their second. Something that William believed now was just dumb luck. On the third trip, they leaned the cart downward, like both boys remembered seeing their fathers do, as well as everyone else there. When John unhitched the burro, William's eyes exploded before his mouth screamed. The cart started to roll down the incline, gathering speed the whole way. Everyone stood and watched as it rolled through the market. No one laughed, even though both boys later thought the image of a cart loaded with turnips, wheat, and roots rolling down the road was humorous. It avoided any other carts and people, but caromed back and forth between a few buildings before it tipped over on its side. What remained of their crops fell onto the ground with a flop. The rest was scattered up the road, tracing their path. Even with that calamity, they still managed to sell everything they brought. William believed people bought from them because they felt sorry for them. For the loss of their parents, and their inability to do something as simple as chock the wheels of a cart.

4

With both the cart and burro secured, William left John to his bartering. There was no set price for anything, just what the buyer wanted to pay, and what the seller was willing to accept. William had no patience for such things. One reason, he wasn't very good at it. John got on him all the time for offering too much and accepting too little. Something William just waved off.

Much like he used to as a young boy, William wandered the streets. It was not an aimless wander, as he followed the same path he had for some years. The destination was always the same. It wasn't the Lion's Pub just off the corner of Front Street. a popular stop for many after a long day at the market, but not for William. His endpoint was the same as it had been since he was eight. A spot with a rock that stuck out a tad higher than all the rest. Perfect for sitting. The view was the wide open ocean. Not a view of the harbor, mind you. After his one experience, there was no pining for days out fishing. This was more pining for what else was out there. Out there beyond the dark blue expanse and cloudy skies with the occasional patch of blue. What did the rest of the world look like? Was it like here? Meadows of lush green, dotted with stone-walled homes? He didn't know. Not many in St. Margaret's Hope did. He couldn't remember the last time any visitor from anywhere else had wandered into town.

William spent hours upon hours on that rock lost in thought. Nothing distracted him. Not the white birds that swirled around hoping he had a morsel of food to share. Not the people that walked past, that at times, paused to look at him with a curious gaze. This occurred more now than it did when he was younger. It wasn't an odd sight to see a child sitting on a rock looking out at nothing, but a grown man was something different.

"Um hum," coughed a delicate voice behind him. A light shadow now shed over William's back.

"Um hum," again. William didn't stir.

This time there was no cough to get his attention, it was a tap on the shoulder that sent William spinning around and grabbing at the rock to avoid an embarrassing tumble into the water below.

"Relax," said the voice.

William steadied himself and wiped the fear created sweat from his forehead. He looked up and saw the vision of an angel standing over him. The sun haloed around flowing locks of curly red hair. The voice that asked him to relax, was the sweetest sound he had ever heard. His eyes adjusted to the sun as the angel sat on the rock next to him. Her cherub face came clearly into view. Green eyes, rosy cheeks, and perfect lips.

"Do you see what you are looking for?", asked Ainslee. Her hand met his on the rock, sending a little flutter through his heart. That would be the second time today she had done that to him.

"Nah," he said. His gaze moved from her, back to the open ocean.

"What do you think is out there? You, more than anyone I know, have dreamt of leaving."

"I honestly don't know. I just feel there is something greater planned for me than this. If there is, it has to be out there." This was something William had felt for as long as he could remember. It was also something he had once asked his father about. His father hadn't agreed or disagreed. Instead, he told William, "God has a purpose for us all. Our job is to find it and do it the best we can, in the service of our lord."

The local priest, Father Henry laughed, when the precocious ten year old boy asked him about it after a Sunday sermon. "My son, you are far too young to worry about such things. When it is time for you to know your purpose, you will know." The cheery, and cheeky, priest patted him on the head and sent him on his way to play with the other kids while he talked with their parents, but even then, William knew he was different. He hadn't seen any ghosts yet, but he had felt something. A sensation, and desire, that he couldn't put his finger on. What he did know, whatever it was, wasn't here in St. Margaret's Hope.

"Why didn't you talk to me earlier?", asked Ainslee.

"Your dad was there," William said. His head dropped, and his eyes stared at the rock next to where he sat.

Even with her face skewed into the cock-eyed expression she gave him; she was still a vision of beauty. Two quick, but soft, pats on his hand remind him of the warmth of her touch. The cold north wind invaded the space left each time she lifted her hand up. The feeling was a comfort, and he knew she meant it as such. She had done it before. Usually just before she said, and there it was, "He is just a man. He respected your father. He will, he does, respect you."

"I am just a farmer," said William. This was the same response he had given several times before.

"You need to stop that. That is honorable work."

William just shook his head. She didn't understand at all. It had nothing to do with honorable work or not. Ainslee deserved a life he knew there was no way a farmer could provide. Of course, that wasn't the biggest obstacle in his way. There was still that talk. The talk that terrified him more than any ghost he had encountered, and more than the thought of going out for another fishing trip. There was no way, Lord Sheamus McLayer, the town elder and largest landowner, would ever give his daughter's hand to a farmer.

This was a dance his mind had played over and over for years. Each time, the steps still led to the same result. Which was why neither he nor Ainslee had let John, or anyone else, know they were a little more than just two people who waved awkwardly at each other. They both understood each other, but what William also understood was, it couldn't be.

She wrapped her petite hand around his and said, "Let's take a walk."

"What? Here?", he asked. His eyes were wide open, and he scanned around for anyone that might see them.

"Sure, why not? Just up the road a bit." She wasn't taking no from him, and stood up, pulling his hand with hers. One thing William had learned, once she set her mind on something, he couldn't change it.

They walked hand in hand. She strolled confidently next to him. Their hands swung between them. William wasn't as confident. There was no denying he liked how it felt, but that was overshadowed by the worry of the wrong person seeing them. He didn't know what would happen, but he knew he didn't want to find out.

The further they walked without passing anyone, that fear melted away slightly. So much so, he didn't notice that she had led him another three streets further than just up the road, as she had said. Past the pub. Past the town center, which was still empty, and up toward the church.

In fact, William was so lost in the bliss of the moment, his skin jumped when the words, "Good day, Father," escaped out of Ainslee's lips. The fear that accompanied those words forced his head down and his eyes to the ground. At some point he would need to look up and greet her father eye to eye, he knew that. He also knew such public displays of affection, even something so simple, without the father's permission, was not looked upon with approval.

"Ainslee, William," said a comforting and aged voice.

The ball of nerves that had squeezed his insides down to a tight and painful speck the size of a pea had loosened slightly. His head rose slowly, as the tension in the muscles of his neck loosened. Black mud-stained shoes were topped by a black cassock that hung loosely on the thin man. At the top, a simple white collar stood out against the black garb. The man's wrinkled and age-spotted hands were folded neatly in front of him. His weathered face and steel blue eyes smiled at the two below his black wide-brimmed hat.

"Good day, Father," William said as he greeted Father Logan Henry.

"Nice day for a walk," he said.

Ainslee said, "Yes, it is, Father." She held up their combined hands a little higher as if to make sure he saw, and they continued down the road. There was a little more of a hop to her step than there had been.

William, on the other hand, felt his shoulders slump as they walked away, and Ainslee felt it. She also knew why. "No need to worry. He won't tell anyone. Trust me," she said, as her hand gave his two quick squeezes.

5

Flames flickered in the fire and seared the remains of the fat that dripped on the grate, while also providing warmth. The aromas of cooked salted beef still wafted around his home. William sat back in his father's chair while he drank ale from his father's tin mug. No matter how long his father had been gone, William still saw everything as his father's. Well, not everything. Thanks to a spooked goat, William had to rebuild the pen, so he guessed the pen was his. The table in the drying house was his, too. Even though it wasn't much more than a large stump he cut from a tree downed by lightning on the back corner of the farm. It had sat there for months after it fell. When William cut into a sick hen, he knew he needed a new cutting table. It was bad luck, and bad health, to use the same table again after you butchered a sick animal.

He knew how to make a table. Basic carpentry was a necessary skill his father had taught him. It was also something William enjoyed, but that was when he had the time to do it right. Time was something he didn't have an abundance of on the farm, so the tree seemed like a good solution. The time lying on the ground had allowed it to dry out, which made cutting a large section of the trunk free not a difficult task. Getting it back to the farm was a different story. Its girth was too wide to fit between the sides of his cart. Probably a relief to the horse he had attached to the front. The ground was wet, and the first attempts to drag it had done nothing more than chew up a streak of earth. Again, his horse felt a great sense of relief as he walked him back to his stall. William then faced the last option he had. With the help of the horse before he walked him back to the stall, he tipped the mass of wood up on its end. The section he cut was a three-foot-thick section of the five-foot-wide trunk, and it was round.

With a hard push, the mass of wood rocked forward and then rocked back. Another shove, this time a little harder, sent it rolling forward by about a half a rotation. A third push, a little harder, resulted in the same outcome. Push after push, some harder than the others, to get it up and over an uneven patch of ground here, or out of a hole there, and the stump rolled closer to his home. It took him a few minutes to figure out how to turn it, but he managed that as well. After several hours, he stood exhausted in front of the drying shed and faced a question. Would it fit through the door? That was a question he had never considered when he cut the massive trunk. He eyeballed it a few times and lined it up. With his eyes closed and ears braced for a crash, he gave it a mighty shove. The crash never came. Instead, it rolled forward and through the door, with no issue. William centered it in the room and then pushed it over with a thud. Even as tired as he was, he felt a satisfaction unlike any he had felt before.

He felt a little of that satisfaction as he sat there at the table drinking his ale. Was it the tasty steak he traded for in town and cooked when he got home, or was it the time he spent with Ainslee? He wasn't sure. What was clear was, any dreams or thoughts of the latter needed to be put out of his mind. There was no future there. Every attempt Ainslee made to convince him otherwise just prolonged the inevitable.

Screams, shouts, and the wild neighing of a horse invaded his deep pondering and snapped William from his momentary pleasure. He sat straight up and listened to the sounds. They were not coming from his animals. That much was clear, but he still sprang up to go check. Each were quiet in their pen, unaffected by the sounds. They were far away, but not that far. It had to be one of the neighboring farms. He peered into the darkness. There, just visible in the settling fog, were spots of light. The lanterns danced in the distance as the yelling continued. William started in that direction, to lend assistance.

As he got closer, he could make out two figures, each with a lantern, moving back and forth frantically. The yelling and shouting he heard surrounded other phrases that he was now able to make out in the distance.

"Father, I tell you...there is something ungodly around. I can feel it in my bones."

William heard no reply, but assumed the voice he recognized as his neighbor, Gerald Boyd, was talking to the other person out with him, holding a lantern. The lanterns, which had started as just specks of lights, were now globes of lights, inside William saw the figures of two men as they rushed from spot to spot around Gerald's stables. He waited until he was closer before he called out, "Gerald, everything ok?"

Both globes of light stopped in their tracks. Both figures inside the globes turned toward William as he approached. He felt the quick pinch of pins pricking the skin on the back of his neck. The sensation left, but was replaced by several beads of a cold sweat. He now felt in his bones the same thing Gerald did.

"William, is that you?"

"Yes, Gerald. Everything ok? I heard the yelling."

The globe to the left walked out to meet William, while the one to the right continued a search for something in the stable. As Gerald's face came into view, his hand jutted out to greet his neighbor. He took it and gave it a firm shake. William could feel a tremble in his friend's grip. It was also visible in his face. "What is the trouble?" he asked.

"Something has the animals spooked. I have never heard them make these sounds before."

William offered a possible cause, "Is it a fox or snake?"

That suggestion was met with a quick shake of Gerald's head. He pulled him close and said, "It is not something of this world. I know it."

"Oh, come on. I am sure it is just another animal. Let's have a look." William may have brushed the notion off, but that was just to calm his friend. He knew Gerald's feeling to be true. He felt it, and it grew stronger with every step he took toward the stable. As he walked closer, he recognized the other individual to be Father Henry. He searched the stable at a furious pace, with a disturbed look on his face.

"Father."

"William, I would stand back. Something is not right here."

William didn't heed the warning and kept walking forward.

"William," Father Henry began, before he turned his head to look at him. His eyes delivered the message more than the words, "I am serious. I would stay back."

William knew darn well he couldn't do that. Not because he was stubborn, but because he already saw the problem. There was a single flickering spirit roaming between the stalls. It looked to be that of a young girl. Her face was empty and soulless, like they all were, but something about her demeanor told him she was lost, or had lost something. Something that held a strong connection to her. He often wondered if the locations he saw them in had something to do with their past life. In this instance, maybe she gravitated to the stable because she had had a horse when she was alive. Of course, that never explained those he found just roaming around an open field, or trapped in a wall between two rooms. It was just a theory.

"Does your colt kick?" he asked, as he followed her toward a stall. He could see right away what spooked the animals. She was passing straight through them. The cold shiver he had felt in the past when that happened was enough to spook him.

"He rears up, but hasn't ever kicked with his backs before," said Gerald.

The word "before", stuck in his head. It didn't mean he never would, just hadn't yet, and William didn't really want to be around, or anywhere near him, when it happened for the first time. He kept his eyes on the beast as he reached over the wood door and undid the tie.

"William, wait!" exclaimed Father Henry.

"No time, Father. I am pretty good with animals. Just give me a second." William crept open the door with slow movements, so as to not spook the animal any more than it already had been. She was over in the corner, but headed back toward the colt. He knew if he was going to stop this, he was going to have to test the statement Gerald had made about kicking. He reached out to touch the colt and give him some comfort, and also to make sure he knew he was there behind him.

The girl flickered in and out of existence as she walked toward the horse's hind quarters. William positioned himself between them. This would either work, or he would find out if the horse kicked. The girl ran into him. The cold feeling caused his body to shiver, which ran up his arm and to the back side of the horse. It stayed calm, except for just a little jostle forward. The girl stopped and turned away from William. She flickered a few more times, and then disappeared through the wall of the stable. At that moment, the muscles in the beast behind him relaxed, and the various noises throughout the stable subsided.

William waited a few moments before he exited the stall. Father Henry and Gerald waited for him outside. They still held their lanterns, but instead of holding them up around their heads as they searched, each now let the lantern dangle at the end of their arm.

"What was that?" asked Gerald.

William shrugged his shoulders and scratched his head, "Don't know. Whatever it was is gone. He just needed help settling down. They should be fine now."

Father Henry stood there, mouth dropped open, as William walked by him and out into the stable.

He kept walking beyond the large barn door entrance to the stable, and out into the dense fog that hung above the open pasture that was between his farmhouse and Gerald's. "You should be fine for the rest of the night. Night, Gerald. Night, Father."

6

A light breeze blew across the meadow. Its strength was enough to move the coolness from the ocean inland as far as the farmlands, but that didn't help William. Sweat still dripped from his brow and arms. It was possible his horse felt more relief from it, but he didn't know. Both were out in the field, plowing up the remains of his turnip and potato crops. It was time for the late summer planting, and the soil needed to be turned and crops rotated. Where he had grown potatoes would now be turnips and snap bean vines. Where the turnips were, potatoes would be planted.

This was a three day job. William knew that. It always seemed longer each time they finished a row and turned to give him a full view of the untouched ground ahead of them. He didn't complain, neither did the horse, it was what had to be done. Not that there was anyone for him to complain to, the closest person was acres away, doing the same on their property. There wasn't anyone for the horse to complain to either, except William, but the five year old brown and white beast knew that wouldn't do any good.

The pair turned onto their sixth row of the day and started on their seventh. Both were heads down with their task. The horse pulled, while William steered the blade. Grey and white hooded crows circled overhead. Their eyes kept watch over the freshly churned ground for the sign of any insects, worms, or nice juicy grubs that may have been disturbed and pulled to the top. The rattle of the chains and the creak of the wood plow frame buried the sounds of the caws from the birds. It also blocked out the attempt of a visitor to call out to William. The individual made several attempts while he walked across the pasture, but it was only when he and the horse turned to start the eighth row, that William saw him.

"William?"

"Whoa!", William called out to the horse, though it wasn't necessary. The pressure he applied to the yoke had already stopped it. He dropped the leather straps and walked to greet Father Henry as he approached.

"Father, to what do I owe the pleasure?"

"It's that time of year. Looks like you made a lot of progress today," he said as he looked around. Father Henry was sans the normal cassock he wore in and around the church. On this day, he wore black cotton pants, a jacket with a shirt and white collar under it, and a wide brimmed black hat. His choice of footwear were the same mud-stained leather boots he always wore. It was a good thing too. The pasture he had stomped through was just barely drier than a bog, and would have no doubt ruined anything of quality.

"I have, but so much to go. Might need you to do one of those blessing of the crops you do for the Lyle's." William referred to a prayer that the priest had done at a farm over the hill three seasons ago. He had walked around and recited a prayer while he sprinkled holy water in each of the corners. Nobody knows for sure if it worked or not, but the bumper crop that season had made it a legend.

"Eh," the priest waved his hand to the side, "that was just to quiet him. It was something I made up."

William opened his mouth to point out the success they'd felt, but Father Henry held up his hand before he could begin. "Don't say it. Nothing to do with it, my boy. Nothing to do with it. That was the first year he rotated and spread manure around. Lawlyer finally figured out how to farm. That is not why I am here."

"Okay, Father, why are you here?", asked William. He used the back of his hand to wipe his forehead. Sweat continued to pour due to the exertion. Little did he know, there was a smidge of dirt on the back of his hand, and it was now smeared above his eyes. Father Henry saw it, but was way too polite to say anything.

"Last night. I am here about last night," Father Henry said. His voice wavered, and his eyes avoided contact with William's.

"What about last night?", William watched the priest shift his weight back and forth as he made every attempt to avoid eye contact with him. He gave off every appearance of a man that needed to talk about a topic he didn't want to.

"How... Well, William...," Father Henry started and stopped several times before he managed to get the question that was in his head into words. "That was some fine work last night. How did you do it?"

"I am not sure what you mean, Father. The colt was---," Father Henry interrupted William with a wave of his hand.

"Don't tell me you walked into the stall and calmed the colt down. Gerald may believe that, but I don't. Now tell me, what did you see?"

Father Henry was digging for something, William knew that. The question that remained was, what? He had an idea, but as hard as it was for him to believe he could see ghosts, it was even harder to believe someone else would even think about it.

"Let me tell you what I saw. I saw you walk into that stall, with your eyes going from the horse to the back corner. Back and forth. Then you put a hand on the horse and that was all you did to him. There was nothing said to the animal.

No stroking. No patting. I did see you shiver though. The horse did too. That is what I saw. Did I miss anything?"

Father Henry crossed his arms across his black coat and made firm eye contact for the first time. Now William was the one who shifted from side to side and avoided any eye contact. The way he was put on the spot made him uncomfortable, but that was nothing compared to the realization he had reached. It rolled over and over in his head, and his stomach did flips and somersaults as each cycle stopped at the same place, each and every time.

"Father, why don't we head up to the house and talk?"

Neither of the men said anything on the way to the house. Once inside, William motioned to his father's chair at the table. Father Henry's back stayed board straight as his upper body leaned forward and his knees lowered his tall thin frame onto the seat. William held up a glass and a pitcher, to offer some water. It was something he picked up from watching his mother as she welcomed neighbors and friends into their home. With a simple nod, Father Henry accepted, and William poured him a glass of water.

As Father Henry took a sip, William poured himself a glass as well, and gulped it down. His mouth was dry and caked with dust. Which couldn't have been from the work he was doing. The pasture was moist. There wasn't much dust kicked up by either his horse or the plow. Before Father Henry put his glass down on the table, William had already deposited his back in the sink, which he now leaned against, his arms crossed.

Father Henry's glass hit the table and both men looked at one another in dead silence. The only sound William heard was the whooshing of the wind as it raced through one window and out another. It brought a coolness that settled deeper into the corners of the house, where the sunlight couldn't reach. There was a slight shiver moving up William's neck. It wasn't a ghost this time. It was something that frightened him a great deal more. Questions.

"William, why don't you tell me what you saw last night. Did you see her?"

William took a deep swallow to try to soothe his once again parched throat. It didn't help much; his mouth was just as dry. "Her?", he asked. His mind raced. Father Henry saw the girl. How did he?

"Yes, William. I am not a total sensitive, but I have enough in me to know there was a little girl roaming around Gerald's animals. Now, did you feel her, or see her?", Father Henry asked with a blank expression. His tone of voice was very matter of fact. No inflection or waver as he discussed a topic that was not one of normal conversation.

"I saw her," confessed William.

"You did? Is it safe to assume this was not a first?"

William nodded his head.

Father Henry then asked the question that broke William, "How long?"

His body language changed. The upright, arm-crossed man that leaned against the sink became the shoulder-slouched and weak-kneed child that now stumbled for the chair across from Father Henry. There was a great sigh that came from down deep, beyond his physical form, and escaped into the world around them. It was a release. The release of a secret pent up for over a decade. The release of the stress and tension he felt because of his gift. He wasn't alone. There was someone else like him.

7

"I was twelve."

Father Henry removed his black wide-brimmed hat. The fingers of his right hand pinched the top, while the ones on his left traced the brim and made sure everything was straight. Once satisfied, he placed it on the table next to the half-full glass of water. "So, you have been dealing with this for some time now. Let me guess. It starts with a cold shiver on your neck. Maybe a few beads of sweat, and a feeling deep in the pit of your stomach you can't explain. Have I described it so far?"

Upon hearing his gift described so astutely, William straightened his shoulders and sat back in the chair. His wide-open, shocked eyes answered Father Henry's question without uttering a sound, but there was more to add. "I can't explain it, though. It doesn't take me long before I see them."

"William, what do you see? A shadow?"

"Oh, no. Father, I see them. People. I see people, glowing. They disappear and reappear, right in front of me."

The long slender fingers of Father Henry's right hand shot up to his chin and rubbed it as he stared through William. The clarification caught him off guard, and created another nervous silence in the small farmhouse. Among the breeze, William could hear the rough skin of his hand catch on the stubble as it rubbed his chin.

"They look like people to you?"

"Yes, except for the eyes. They are just black and hollow."

This answer was followed by a great deal more rubbing of his chin. William wondered which would wear through first: the stubble, or the skin on his fingers. The chair creaked as he leaned forward, but only at the waist. Father Henry's back remained straight up and down. He mumbled a few phrases to himself. William thought he heard him say, "He is more sensitive than I am," but he wasn't sure he made it out correctly. The mumbling was fast and under his breath.

His next phase was not a mumble, it was a direct question. Its tone more forceful than the previous questions, "Do you talk to them? Interact? You need to tell me."

"Oh, no. They don't respond when I try. I can yell or scream, and they never pay any notice. They only notice when they run into me."

Father Henry's gaze moves from looking through William, to straight into his eyes. There was no blinking in the icy expression, "Run into? You mean they touch you?"

"Yes, Father. Or I touch them. They usually turn or go another way," William answered his question, but grew concerned. This tone and expression was not one he had seen from the normally cheerful priest. The person in front of him had a more foreboding presence.

"And last night?"

"She was walking straight toward the horse, so I stood in between and let her hit me. When she did, she turned and walked through the wall."

"You weren't afraid?"

"I was more concerned with getting kicked by the colt," confessed William.

That answer drew a little chuckle from the grim-faced priest, and gave William the first sight of the person he knew, but it didn't last long. The chuckle and cockeyed smile disappeared. The grim stone-like expression he saw for the previous few moments once again took its place on his face. Deep in thought, his eyes once again stared straight through William. Their gaze was so strong, he could feel it drilling deep into his soul. Powering the drill was a question, a thought, a concern. William knew it. The expression on his guest's face spoke of the gravity of the question.

"William, I need you to be honest with me."

"Of course, Father."

The hands that had stroked the stubble on Father Henry's chin now relaxed to the middle of his chest and faced each other in prayer. "Have you currently, or in the past, practiced the dark arts to summon or invite a spirit, demon, or Lucifer himself into this world?"

The question was a strong right uppercut to William's chin. It knocked him up out of his chair to a stand with an explosion. His quick movements sent the chair teetering behind him before it finally settled down, with all four legs flat on the floor. Father Henry remained stoic; the only movement were his eyes as they followed William up. This was not just a curious friend, or a priest asking about something they'd seen. This was more serious. It was an inquisition, a witch hunt.

There hadn't been one in St. Margaret's Hope in several years, but there had been one in William's lifetime. He remembered it as clear as day. It was a teen girl, Mary SaintClair, if he remembered correctly. She walked around town all hours of the day and night, mumbling to herself. Animals always acted spooked when she neared. Birds seemed to follow her path overhead. Especially the black crows. Flocks upon flocks of crows followed her through town and across the meadows. As the tale goes, Father Henry and several of the town elders went out one night and found her sitting in the middle of an open field with birds all around her. The elders encircled her, and the birds, and walked in slowly and cautiously. As they moved closer to her, the birds cawed like mad before they flew off and left Mary alone in the meadow. She pointed at the elders and mumbled. Several of the elders fell to their knees while the others surrounded her and tied her hands behind her. The next day, a hearing was held. Those that had fallen to their knees testified they'd felt sick to their stomach. Others spoke of how animals had reacted around her, or how the fog parted as she walked through. The hearing was quick, short, and brutal. The sentence was just as quick, short, and brutal. After the verdict was handed down, Mary was taken outside and tied to a stake, where her soul was purged clean by fire. She continued to mumble, not scream, during the purge.

William insisted, "No, Father. This is not something I asked for. They just appear. Honestly, it is nothing more than that."

The stony expression on Father Henry's face cracked. The comforting smile he displayed to his congregation began to show through each of the cracks. Warmth returned to his eyes. Both of which calmed William's nerves. He wasn't sure if what he had said was responsible for this to be honest, he had no proof. He could imagine a similar hearing with John testifying against him, and Gerald adding in what he had seen just last night. The star witness would be Father Henry, who would give a full account of the conversation they'd just had, with a few overdramatic additions for the benefit of the judge, and the spectators.

"William. I understand. Your father was the same way." Father Henry stood up and retrieved his hat from the table. His right hand pinched it at the top, while the left hand traced the brim to make sure it was straight, before he placed it level on his head. On his way to the door he said, "It seems you now have two secrets. I must be going." Without another word or motion toward William, he left out the door. William was left standing in front of a chair with a single thought in his head, *"My father?"*

8

Weeks came and went. The pasture was plowed and planted, and the first sprigs of turnips had broken through the ground. What hadn't broken through were the many questions in William's mind. He had made many trips to town. Some to bring crops to the market. Others for shopping or just coming in for a pint with John.

Many times, he passed Father Henry, but none more frequent than the weekly Sunday holy eucharist. William expected a different look from him, now that he was aware of his secret, but there was nothing. His eyes never settled on him any more than normal when he delivered his sermon from the pulpit. On the way out, he greeted and shook his hand, just like he always had. William debated on whether to approach him himself, maybe that was what he was waiting on, but never did. His gift had made him feel different before, now there was a small side of him that felt that it made him a target, and would rather just blend in with the masses.

It was four weeks after their conversation, William had spent a day out in the field pulling weeds and adding a layer of manure to add some nutrients to the soil. To say he smelled like shit was an understatement. Even the animals moved away from him as he passed on his way to the farmhouse. A bath was in order, but it would take days to get the smell out of his hands. When he opened the door to the farmhouse, he was surprised to find two guests sitting at his table. Both of the guest were surprised by the stench that came through the door with William.

Neither guest recoiled with a repulsed look on their face. Just a little twitch of their nose, and a wider than normal opening of their eyes, were the only visible signs from the two proper men seated at the table. Each had already made themselves at home. Both with a glass of water on the table, one a little emptier than the other. Two black wide-brimmed hats sat on the table next to each glass. The men sat upright, their focus was fixed on William, who stood in the doorway, more than a bit startled by the scene in his house.

"Father?" William asked, in an attempt to seem cordial and less alarmed. Inside, his mind screamed, *"What are you doing in my house?"*

"Excuse the intrusion, William. There is someone I need you to meet. Please come in and have a seat."

William held both his hands up to remind Father Henry of his current unclean state. The saying is cleanliness is next to godliness, and there was a whole lot of godliness in the room for him to be that unclean. "Do you mind if I clean up while we talk?"

"Of course not."

William stood over the sink and used a large block of soap to lather up his hands and arms. The fat-based soap produced a nice layer of brown up to his elbow. Father Henry started to talk as William poured water out of the pitcher to rinse his arms for the first time. Based on his best guess, he would have maybe three more rinses before he would need to pump more water.

"William, this is Bishop Emmanuel. He has come a long way to meet you. He is interested in your gift."

The distinguished white-haired gentleman seated to Father Henry's left stood up. He was quite a bit shorter than both Father Henry and William. He almost gave the appearance of being frail, but when he extended his hand to William, the scars and callouses from a hard life were obvious. Instead of meeting his hand, William held up two still-stained soap and filth caked hands. The bishop withdrew his hand and looked around the room, while uttering, "Excuse`"

The word meant nothing to William, but the accent he heard meant everything. He was not from around here, not even close. It was one he had never heard before. The only way he could describe it was smooth, and pleasant to the ears. The look he gave Father Henry conveyed the question he had in his head.

"That's right, William. He is Italian."

He would have to trust Father Henry on that. There was no other option. William had never met an Italian. It would only be an assumption that he was from Italy, a place he had only heard about and seen on a map in school. That was one of those far off places that was out there. Out in the rest of the world that William had dreamed of visiting to find his greater purpose, his adventure. Now, someone from one of those far-off places stood in front of him, in his farmhouse.

"Vatican City, to be more precise," continued Father Henry.

That fact astonished William more than the first. He knew where and what the Vatican City was. He also knew what that meant, but that couldn't be. Father Murray was Anglican, a prince of the Church of England, not exactly a favored bedfellow of the Vatican. If you said they were mortal enemies, that might be considered a stretch for some, but considering the wars and lives lost, others might consider it true. The Vatican and its princes were forced out of England and the dutchy of Scotland, by King Henry the VIII because of a difference in principles. Even this long after that schism, it was still considered a crime against the crown to associate with anyone from the Vatican. William knew that, and he assumed Father Henry knew that. How could he not?

William ignored the shock and alarm that ran through his bones. His imagination had the king's guards standing outside his door, just waiting to break it down. After a swallow to clear his throat, and to push his imagination out of the way, he managed to say, "It's nice to meet you Bishop Emmanuel."

"The pleasure is mine, William," said the scratchy Italian voice. He continued, " Father Henry tells me you can see ghosts and interact with them."

"Yes, I see them. I can't talk to them."

Emmanuel looked back at Father Henry, who explained William's response. "No, he can't talk to them, but he can touch them… or… I guess the better way to say it is, they are aware of him when they come in contact with him, and move away."

Emmanuel turned back to William, and studied him, up and down. "Oh, I see. What do you feel?"

William clarified, "You mean, when they walk through me?"

The bishop merely dipped his head forward.

"Cold. Very Cold. Wherever they touch is cold as they pass through."

The two visitors shared a common inquisitive look at each other. William may have had the same look on his face. Questions filled his mind at the moment, and so far, no answers had been offered.

"William, why don't you have a seat?", Father Henry requested. Bishop Emmanuel returned to his seat; hands folded on his lap. Both men watched him as he sat, spots of unrinsed soap clung to his arms. When his weight settled on the chair, he sat and looked back and forth at both men for what was next. The problem was, neither of them verbalized a response. Instead, they once again shared inquisitive looks at each other. It was as if this was their own secret language. *Maybe it was something they were taught at seminary school,* thought William.

"William, you have a gift," explained Bishop Emmanuel. "One that very few have. Those that do, are called *sensitivo*. As you can imagine, everyone is not the same. Some people can feel their presence. Some are stronger than others. They can… read their… I mean, hear their thoughts. It is strong enough in others to catch a glimpse of them as they move in and out of our world. Some see them, but then there are the ones like you; the rarest of all. Those that can see them, and touch or talk to them. It is a very special gift bestowed upon your family by God, to have that ability."

"To put it in some perspective William, Emmanuel explained to me earlier that there are less than what… a dozen families with your ability?" Father Henry looked at his fellow visitor for confirmation, which he received with an astute and thoughtful nod.

He knew he was different, and had only ever heard Father Henry describe it as a gift. What was a gift for one person, could be considered a curse to others. To William, he also considered it more of the latter. It was something he hid from everyone; he hadn't even talked to his father about it. John was the only confidante he told, and that was because he was there once, and that was all. If he hadn't been there that one time, he would have never said anything. The same with Father Henry. There was something else, though. Another phrase that had been repeated again, for the second time. This phrase was stuck in his craw, but was surging up and forward until it exploded out of William's mouth, "You said this was given to my family. What about my family?"

"It is like a royal bloodline. Your bloodline has this ability," answered Bishop Emmanuel.

"William, I don't know for sure, but I do recall several conversations with your father about him feeling an evil wind, or something not of this world, out there," interjected Father Henry. He continued, with a hint of a warning in his voice, "Now, I could be reading something into his statements that was not real, but knowing about you, now..." His face crinkled to make a flat smile.

William knew what he meant. It was a logical leap. What struck him, though, there was nothing William could recall that would lead him to believe his father could see ghosts. He was always a strong willed and confident man, who spoke his mind. That had even cost him some friends over the years. A strong lesson his father had once taught him, not everyone really wants to hear the truth. He would just have to accept that the truth might hurt some. William and John saw plenty examples of that during the verbal fights their fathers would engage in. It always started the same way; William's father would state a truth that John's father wasn't ready to hear. They always ended the same way too. John's father walking away, convinced he had won the argument. William and his father walking away as his father stated, "He just wasn't ready for the truth". Each of them may have been covered in mud or dirt, if the argument was tense enough.

Through all those truths and speaking of his mind, William couldn't remember once where his father had hinted at this gift. Not anything that matched the comments Father Henry mentioned. It was possible that such things were not stated in mixed company. That was all in the past now, the question that sat in front of William now was, what's next? He found it hard to accept that someone came all the way from the Vatican, with the travel and the risk, just to sit in his kitchen and tell him about something he pretty much already knew.

"Well, my father never said anything about it to me, if he did have what you call is 'the gift'. Gentleman, what can I do for you?" William looked at Bishop Emmanuel. His eyes bristled with all the confidence he could muster up, "I am sure you didn't come all this way to tell me what I already knew."

Both gentlemen seem surprised, and relieved, by William's newfound confidence. It didn't shock or take them aback. If anything, it drew smiles from the two men. Father Henry's was one of pleasure and approval. William had to assume the Bishop's was the same, but it was hard to tell. It looked painful to move the weathered and wrinkled skin on his face enough to produce an expression that pushed the cheeks up on his gaunt face.

They were locked in their secret language once again, exchanging looks and an occasional mumble with one another. The uncomfortable feelings William had, were now growing into frustration. Was there a point to all this, or could it really be he was just there to explain to William about his gift? Maybe the Bishop was the first of many visitors that will show up at his door. He was now Father Henry's religious sideshow act for those in the clergy. *"Come with me and meet a man that sees ghosts,"* William could imagine him barking at a crowd of monks and priests. *"Only one of his kind in the emerald isle, come see him now!"*, would be another line. If that was it, he had picked the wrong attraction. William had more important tasks to tend to than to be a storyteller, or asked over and over if he could see a ghost in the room with them.

"Gentlemen, I am here. What is this all about? It's been a long day and I need to finish cleaning up." The stench that still hung in the room anchored his last point.

Neither man seemed flummoxed by the interruption. If anything, they appeared to understand and finished their conclave together by deciding who would talk next

"William, as we stated, you are rare. You are also valuable. Your skills are needed by the Church, to serve a greater good... a greater purpose. Bishop Emmanuel is here to offer you an opportunity to fulfill that purpose."

There was a good chance Father Henry was playing the strings inside William's heart, and he knew it. Those strings were laid out in front of him during the many conversations Father Henry and William had during his childhood, about his longing for something greater. Now was he strumming them like a minstrel, or was *this* that longing William had felt? That 'something' in his bloodline, as both men had stated, knew there was something more. That 'something' asked, "What is the opportunity?"

Bishop Emmanuel explained, "There is much more you can do with your gift, but it requires training. Training the Church is willing to provide in return for service."

"Service, you mean in the conscripts?"

"In a way, yes," Father Henry said. "Not in the military mind you. There are spots around the world that are more spiritual than others. Ghosts, or spirits," he corrected, " tend to gather in those locations. For hundreds of years, the Church has assigned those like you to be their caretaker. To tend to both the living and the dead. If you accept, you will travel to the Vatican and be trained on how to handle the spirits you encounter. At the end of your training, you will be assigned a location. William, will you accept?"

Father Henry and Bishop Emmanuel leaned forward in their chairs toward William. Both looked at him with anticipation. William wasn't sure what to say. This was his ticket to leave and see the world beyond the ocean. It could also be that greater calling he felt pull at his soul for as long as he could remember. There was no way to know without trying. If he accepted though, it meant he would leave all he has known behind, which included the farm that had been in his family for centuries. That was not a trivial thing to William. He could almost hear his descendants rolling over beneath their gravestones.

"Can I have some time to think it over?", William asked.

"I leave in four days. If you accept, you will need to return with me then."

William said, "I understand," as he sat back in his chair. He did. He understood everything, but he still didn't have a clue what his decision would be.

9

To say the question weighed on William would be an understatement. No matter what he was doing, or where he was, it was there. Whether working his crops, caring for his livestock, walking through the meadow to clear his head, or even in the outhouse trying to clear something else, the question remained clouding any other thought passing through his mind. It was always there in the front of his mind.

With two days left before Bishop Emmanuel was scheduled to depart, William made a special trip into town and sat on his rock. It was unusually clear that afternoon. The normal marine layer wasn't there. Instead of a horde of fluffy white clouds passing above the horizon line, there was a majestic blue, just a few shades lighter than the dark blue ocean below it. He needed his rock. Really, he needed the clarity he felt while sitting there and pondering, several times in the past. It was while he sat on that very rock, several years ago, that he told Ainslee how he felt. It was also there where he decided they would need to keep their feelings private. Both decisions helped him quiet a yearning, and the voices of doubt that came with it. He needed that now.

Having no clue which way Italy was, William guessed and faced that direction. It was silly, he knew. At that distance he would see nothing but the ocean. That is all he ever saw from that perch, no matter which direction he looked, but this time was different. This time he had an opportunity to go beyond the horizon and see what was out there. Maybe it was that opportunity that clouded his thoughts the most. If he turned it down now, would he ever have another opportunity? It was doubtful. Visitors didn't pass through this way often, and none with such an offer.

As good as the offer seemed, there was a great bit of fear that went with it. William still didn't know what he would really be asked to do. All Father Henry and Bishop Emmanuel had said was, he would be the caretaker for a place. They hadn't provided any description of what a caretaker did, but they had talked about training. What was there to train on? He already knew how to see and stand in front of ghosts. That was his best natural talent, no one needed to teach him how to do that. The humorous thought that maybe they wanted him to teach them crossed his mind. He pictured himself standing in front of a great hall somewhere, in a grand robe, probably red or blue, with a hat. A hundred sets of eyes focused on him as he lectured them on the art of ghost seeing. He almost chucked out loud at the thought of his lecture, *"And this is how you do it. If you see a ghost, you step in front of it. That is all there is to it."*

The humor brought a smile to his face and helped to push back the fear for a moment, but another problem was behind him, literally behind him. Everything he knew, from the day he was born to this moment, was behind him in this town. His friends, his family's farm, and Ainslee. That last one pulled at his heart a tad more than the others. The thought of never laying his eyes on her again sent a bolt of cold through his core. Not the usual warmth he felt when he thought of her, or heard her voice. A warmth that, to him, felt like the morning sun and could clear any fog or feeling of cold depression away from his soul. A warmth that now spread from his left ear across his face, as the voice of an angel, his angel, whispered, "What are you doing?"

William didn't turn toward her as she joined him on his rock. She tried a few times to have him rename it their rock, but that was a point he wouldn't yield. It was his, he saw it first, he sat on it first. In his mind, both of those defined ownership. Together, they sat on his rock. She leaned ever so slightly against him, with her right arm locked around his left, at the elbow.

"Thinking?" she asked.

"Yes," William replied, with a sigh. His gaze was still locked on the horizon in front of them.

"What about?"

He knew she would ask. She always did. Of course, this time the answer wouldn't be the normal, *"Wondering what is out there"* response. William wasn't even sure he could tell her the truth. Well, he knew he couldn't tell her the whole truth, that was for sure. "Things. I might be going on a trip for a bit."

He felt her whole body turn toward him in response. A sharpening of her breath accompanied the wide-open stare of her beautiful green eyes.

"Father Henry has a visitor from...," William almost slipped up. Ainslee's family was still royalty. He couldn't take the chance that she wouldn't tell her father, and he would feel some old loyalty to the crown. "From the mainland. He offered to take me back with him, to show me what is out there." William felt that was a plausible excuse. He knew she was aware of how strong his desire to see the outside world was. Hell, she even shared it. There was no doubt in his mind, while she might be hurt, she would understand it.

"Just like that. You are going to up and leave?", she asked.

"Yes."

His terse reply was met with several more short and sharp breaths. Was it possible? Did he have miss prim and proper in a huff? She swiveled next to him like a sign blowing in the breeze. First, she looked at him, and then back out into the ocean, then back at him, and then the ocean. This continued several more times until she stopped and faced away from him.

"It's my chance. To get out of here, you know?" Before William could finish, she asked a question, hushed, under her breath. This was no attempt to hide the question from anyone passing by. His announcement had stripped the will out of her voice as she asked. "What about me?"

"We have been through all this. Your father would never..."

"Goddamnit, William Miller," anger had replaced the will in her voice. "Stop using my father as an excuse. You have no reason to hide from him."

William peered to his side. Her eyes were fixed and watering, but fire burned in her cheeks. She had a temper; he had seen it before, in their youth. In truth, he had seen it more than once. Her reactions to some poor joke or prank he and John had pulled while on the cusp of adolescence. Girls tend to mature before boys, add in a touch of nobility and proper upbringing, and that gap increases. If you asked Ainslee, John and William had yet to grow up. This was different than those times, though. This was no stupid joke or prank. He wouldn't be letting her off the hook anytime soon to laugh while she calmed down. Her next move told him there would be no calming down.

The always outspoken, never lost for words, Ainslee McLayer stood up and walked off into the sunset. Her hair flowed in the wind as her shape was silhouetted by the setting sun. William wanted to call out to her, but couldn't muster either the voice, or the words to say. There was nothing to say except goodbye, and he hated those. No one ever left St. Margaret's Hope, unless they died. This goodbye pained him deeper than any of the deaths he could remember. Perhaps it was easier this way.

10

The night began with sleep forgetting to pay William a visit. He laid in his bed and waited, but it never arrived. Perhaps it waited for his mind and heart to join the rest of his body beneath the covers. Those were still perched on the rock that overlooked the harbor. He sat there for another hour, and waited and hoped for Ainslee to return, but when the sun dipped below the buildings, darkness was cast on his body and his hopes. As he walked away, he stopped to look back a few times, to check and see if she had come back. He knew the chance was slim, but even the slimmest of hopes was hope enough.

"This is how it had to be, " was the phrase he repeated to himself. It sounded good, and made sense, at least that is what he told himself. He wasn't sure how much he was buying that argument. What was it his father had told him that time he had gotten caught in a briar patch? *The slower he moved, the longer it would hurt, just run quick. It would hurt, but it would be over soon.* Maybe this was like that. Cutting all personal ties, quickly and completely, would make it easier to leave. No connections. Nothing to hold him back. That thought caused the heart that had just rejoined the rest of his exhausted and emotional body in bed to sink. Sleep followed the darkness he felt.

The rest wasn't long, though. Warmth radiated over William from across the room, like a raging fire. Half asleep, William thought he had left a fire burning in the fireplace. Something his father had warned him about many times. It was ok to leave the embers in the fire to supply warmth during the worst of the winter, but careless to leave anything more. A rogue ember floating in the hot air as it rose up in the house, or a shift in the stack sending an engulfed log rolling out into the room, could be all it took to burn down the farmhouse.

William pushed off his blanket to allow more of the night air to cool his body, but relief was not what he found. The source of the heat took aim at his exposed arms and legs, and began to cook them to the point of being uncomfortable, even painful. He rolled over and cracked a single eye open to check the fireplace. The fire he saw was not in the fireplace, it encompassed a shirtless man seated at his table. It had the head of a goat, with a crown made of a dried vine with large thorns pointing out from all sides. A dark brown blood oozed down its head where the thorns pierced through the fur-covered skull. Snorts of smoke accompanied every breath. The yellow centers of its red eyes peeled away at the layers of William's soul.

He blinked several times to clear what had to be a leftover nightmare that was stuck in his consciousness somewhere between asleep and awake, but each blink revealed the same creature seated there. Now both eyes were open and looked straight at the beast. His breath raced along with his pulse. Deep inside, a little voice yelled "run" as loud as it could, but the fear he felt washed the voice away. The sensation was new. William didn't fear much. Something he credited to what Father Henry and Bishop Emmanuel called his gift. Once you are used to seeing ghosts, not much else could frighten you, but this was not a ghost.

"I see you there, looking at me. I am real. Not a dream," it said in a thundering, coarse voice, that was half man and half animal.

William said nothing. He couldn't. The lump of grey matter between his ears struggled with the appearance of his visitor. Verbalizing a logical coherent thought out loud was way too much to ask. Sitting up and swinging his legs out of the bed was all he could muster.

"Don't get up. I won't stay." The creature put both hands flat on the table and pushed himself up. The flames rose high against the ceiling. William watched the path of the flames as the beast moved around the table. To his surprise, nothing caught fire as the flames passed over them, but the heat grew in intensity as it moved closer, as did the glare of the yellow-centered eyes. It leaned back against the table and crossed its cloven-hoofed feet, one over the other.

"Speaking of staying, " it continued, "you really should stay here. You have a great home, a sweet lassie, and a great crop this year and every year for the rest of your life. The envy of every farmer around, that is what you will be. Especially when you and Ainslee have those two large strapping boys to help out around here." It looked in the direction of one of the windows and said, "By the looks of it, you need to start on those boys soon, you are going to need lots of help. I have never seen a crop so full. Why don't you have a look?" It then extended its left arm and pointed with its skinny, bony finger. A line of flame shot from it and pushed the window open.

William's body didn't move. His eyes looked in that direction as far as he could, but his ass, and the rest of him, remained one with the bed. All he could see from there was the dark night sky outside, and the roofline of his slaughterhouse.

It extended its other hand toward him, and one by one curled all five fingers back into its palm. When the final finger reached the palm, William felt his feet leave the floor and his ass leave the bed. He floated first toward the creature, but before he reached it, he turned toward the window, where he was placed down on his feet. Now he had a perfect view of a clear night, with a full moon that was not expected for another ten days. The light of the unscheduled Corn Moon illuminated his pasture, the pasture he had weeded and spread manure in just days before. A pasture that was now full of lush green tops of turnips. A sight that was both too early, and too good, to be true. William had never seen a crop that good before, not on his farm, or anyone else's, to be honest.

From behind him the voice growled, "You have no reason to leave." The phrase echoed over and over as four people walked through the crops. He recognized Ainslee and himself, joined at the hand, walking. On either side them were two young men. Both were bigger than him. Everyone was laughing and smiling. They stopped to wave at the window, and then continued on their stroll.

William woke up the next morning to the sound of a rooster welcoming the dawn of a new day, a cold one at that. Even under two blankets, the chill shook his bones as he stirred awake. The remnants of a dream from his slumber hung over him. Before he opened his eyes, he turned his head toward the center of the room. Then, with one eye, and only one eye, he peeked. There was nothing there, which relieved him as well as helped to settle the question in his mind. *Was this real or just a dream?*

William swung both legs out of the bed and reached for his shirt. A stretch preceded a walk across the room to start a small fire to knock off the chill and prepare his breakfast. Two eggs sounded good to him, and a hot cup of coffee would warm him right up. The nightshirt he wore to sleep in was deposited over the chair as he put on one he had washed several days ago. He walked over and shut the window and headed across to fetch his pot for coffee, but stopped as he passed the table. There, as clear as day, were two handprints burnt into the surface.

11

William couldn't shake the events of the previous night. No matter how hard he worked in the field, it didn't distract his mind from two questions. Was it real or a dream? If it was real, what the hell was it? Neither question had an answer that came right away. Instead, it was a circular spiral. There was no way that was real, but what about the handprints? A few minutes later he would repeat the same circle. The only thought that broke the cycle from time to time was the reminder that he saw ghosts. Could it be that hard to believe he saw such a vision?

If that was true, this was no ordinary ghost. That left only one possibility, it was a demon. If that were true, it would be the first he had seen. The next question would be why? It had shown him the images of a good life, but said that would be possible if he stayed. Was he trying to keep him from leaving? If so, there was that same question again, why? Why would a demon care?

The logical side of his mind submitted another argument for consideration. This was all a figment of his imagination caused by the stress he felt over the decision to leave his farm, Ainslee, and everything he knew, behind. To him that made sense, and when he thought about the handprints, he remembered how dirty he was the day Father Henry and Bishop Emanuel had come to visit. He had sat in that exact spot, perhaps he put his hands down there.

At the end of the day, William was more mentally exhausted than physically. Tomorrow was the day. The day he would walk away and start a new adventure. He had one last task to tend to, though. He had to tell John. His friend of all of his life was sure to have questions, and not just a few. William hoped giving him his farm would be more than enough to distract him and stop some of the questions.

While the sun still peeked above the rise of the hills in the distance, William made the walk over to John's. He knocked on his door and called his name, as he always did. An act that annoyed John's wife, Mary, more often than not, especially at this time of night when she puts down their two young boys. Luckily for her, this was the last time.

He waited outside for John, who emerged from the door before William called out for him again. John came out, as he always did, hands motioning for him to keep it down, which was, in most cases, too late. The children would be awake by the second or third call. No such interruption tonight, William had only called out once, and then backed away to wait. John walked toward him and asked, "Is everything ok, William? Is there something wrong?"

William stood and fidgeted with a rock that was under his foot. On the way over he rehearsed the talk a few times, and a few ways. The way he decided to start was not any of those. Instead, he took a page from how he had told Ainslee the day before. "I am leaving tomorrow," he said.

"Leaving?", John asked. His face and posture shocked straight.

"Yes. You know how long I have wondered what else is out there. I have a chance to find out." William talked while he looked down and fidgeted with the same rock.

"Okay," John said. His tone asked a dozen questions. The expression on his face asked a dozen more. "Where are you going, and when?"

"Tomorrow. I don't know where." The rock was getting a good working on. The dirt under it had been depressed and anything loose had rolled out of the way by the constant back and forth motion caused by William's foot.

"Tomorrow?", John exclaimed. William looked up at him and then toward his door. He half expected to see Mary walk out with that look on her face.

In a calmer voice, William said, "Yep, tomorrow. The farm's yours. The crops are planted. My sow has another two or three months to go. The chickens have eggs every morning, just make sure you check them, and you already know about the cow." John's own cow became sick a few months ago and started to produce foul milk. After he put her down, William and John shared William's cow. Each took turns milking and caring for her.

William had said what he needed to say, then he added, "You have been a great friend, John," and then held out his hand. John took it, but William could tell it was more of a reaction than a willful movement. After a quick shake, William turned and walked back in the direction of his farmhouse. John stood there, hand still held out, and watched his friend of forever walk away. Before William reached the stone wall that separated the two tracks of land, John sprinted after him.

"William!", he called. The huff and puff of heavy breathing emphasized every syllable of his name. This was probably the fastest John had run since they were teenagers. William stopped, but didn't turn toward John.

When John reached him, he asked, "What is this all about?"

"It is exactly what I said."

"So, you are going to leave, just as simple as that?"

"Yes, simple as that." William didn't mince words. There was no point to. Nothing John could say would change his mind, and he didn't want to give him the chance. He said, "'Night, John. Take care," and started toward his house. He wasn't good with farewells, especially those where the person was still living.

Inside, he turned in a little earlier than usual. He intended to get up early and head straight to town to meet Father Henry and Bishop Emmanuel before dawn, to tell them his decision. For the second night, sleep failed to arrive when needed. For the second night, he felt a hole in the pit of his soul. All the memories, his childhood, the life he knew, were left out there at the break in the fence where he had walked away from John. He tried to focus on what was ahead of him, but the past always crept in. Memories of summer afternoons in the fields with John. The times they'd snuck a little of his father's whiskey out to the wall. Moments of mischief they'd got each other into, and the moments of heartache they'd both experienced with the loss of their parents, and then there was Ainslee. Vision after vision of her walking with them. The sun highlighting her auburn hair. She was the last vision he saw, as his mind gave in to the exhaustion and despair he felt. Familiar old creaks and shudders of his home were the last sounds he heard before his world descended into black.

For the second time in consecutive nights, sleep didn't last long. This time there wasn't an unbearable heat baking him in his bed, nor was there a blast of cold air chilling his bones. Instead, the room was comfortable. Embers continued to glow orange in the hearth, to produce warm air that circulated around the room. What was there was a presence. A presence behind him. One that watched him, and it was close. After what was there, or not, last night, there was no desire to turn over fast. So, he rolled his head as far as he could, with the hope of getting a glimpse out of the corner of his eye at whatever it was. All he saw was his ceiling, so he let his body shift ever so slightly to bring it into view.

Instead of a creature of flame with a goat head, there was the shape of a beautiful woman with long hair. She stood just a few feet from his bed, with her hands held together in front of her. In the darkness he couldn't see her face, but could tell she had soft features. A sense of calm tranquility filled the room, along with the scents of lavender and lilac.

12

"William Miller. Do you really think you can just walk out on me like that?" The voice, one William considers the one of an angel in normal situations, had a tad of vinegar and a heavy dose of perturbation in it.

"Ainslee, how did you get in here?", William asked as he sat up half-asleep, and rubbed his eyes. He scooted over to give her a spot to sit on the bed, but she had no intention of sitting. What William thought were hands crossed in front of her, was her hands on her hips. Her left foot tapped at a furious level, and thanks to the small ambient light the embers created, he saw she was biting her lip. Seeing that was a warning to him. Running off in a huff yesterday was just the first stage of her temper. The biting of the lip was stage four, and preceded the final explosion. The other two stages, pacing, and blowing the hair out of her face over and over again, must have taken place at her home throughout the day.

"I am waiting, Will." She ignored his question, and didn't change her stance.

"Yes, now I need some sleep. You need to get home before your father, or someone notices you are gone." William braced for the impact that he knew was brewing underneath. That was when he saw something new, another blow of her hair out of her face followed by a hair flip to remove the strands that fell from a slight, but constant, bob of her head. This was serious. If there had been more light, he was sure he would see her cheeks flushed red.

"Don't you dare try to tell me what to do, and enough about my father." The foot still tapped as she resumed biting her bottom lip. "But I will tell YOU what to do."

She paused and William got up and slipped on his boots and shirt. There didn't appear to be any hope she would leave on her own. Even if she did, he wouldn't feel right if she walked back on her own. The shirt slid over his head and he went to put an arm around her. "Let's walk you home..." he started to say, but she ducked his arm and retreated to the other side of the room. Now her arms were crossed in front of her. The bottom lip was still getting worked on.

"No. I am not going anywhere. You are going to take me with you." The statement that escaped her mouth caught them both by surprise. Ainslee was the most surprised of all, her hand shot up to cover her mouth, as if to stop the words. The biting of the lip and foot tapping stopped, and pacing began.

"Come on, let me walk you home."

She held up a single finger as she paced back and forth deep, in thought. Her left hand was on her hip, the right one soon joined it. This was different than how he had found her when he woke up. Then she was angry, now her shoulders were loose, and the wheels in her head were hard at work. Arguments and counter arguments that took place in her eyes, were mouthed by her lips. She froze, and said, "Yes, that is it. Take me with you."

"No, that is not it. Let me walk you home," insisted William.

"Why not? We have talked for years about wanting to know what else is out there. Why should you be the only one to find out?"

"This is nonsense, Ainslee. I have a big day tomorrow and need to get some sleep. Let's get you home."

There was no give in her. She stood her ground firmly. "No. It's settled. Take me with you. It actually solves two problems."

She was a woman who, once her mind was made up, there was no changing it, even when she was wrong. That was a trait that William normally found humorous and charming, but not now. He was in no mood to go around and around with her, as they had many times before, and needed to put this to a stop. "You are being silly, let's go." William knew as soon as he said it, he hadn't put an end to it, not even close. He knew the trap of calling one of her notions "silly" and he had walked right into it.

"You don't want to hear what it will solve?"

"Sure," he said. Knowing this would take a bit, and there would be no stopping her until she was finished, William walked to the table and had a seat. He reached forward into his stack of sulfur matches and flicked it on his flint stone. There was a quick spark before a small yellow flame appeared on the end. Before it went out, William pushed it into his oil lamp and lit the wick, sending flickers of light through the room. Two turns of the wheel splashed bright light across the entire room. The vision in front of him caused his heart to skip a beat. Ainslee stood there in a blue dress, with hair fixed as if she were headed to Sunday mass. The vision was one that forced his head to question his decision to leave all over again.

"Well, first," she started her pacing again, as if she were about to give a lecture in a great hall. "We both want to leave St. Margaret's Hope. It is something we have talked about since we were young. This is a point you cannot disagree with."

William resisted a roll of his eyes at her use of the full word, "cannot".

"Opportunities like this don't come around often. If either of us turn it down, there may not be another chance."

"Well, first, the offer was not made to..." William attempted to reply to her argument for point one, but she shushed him and held up a hand while she continued to pace. "No response, until I have said both points, please." He had to resist a second urge to roll his eyes.

"Second, you refuse to talk to my father and ask for my hand. "

"Now, wait a moment." That point hit William right between the eyes, and stung at that. He stood up, but she stopped his attempt to respond further.

"Uh. Uh. Uh... let me finish."

Finish, he would let her, but listen to this anymore he would not. The decision was made, and this was just a waste of time for William. It did cross his mind that this may make things easier on her, but it made it worse on him.

Ainslee continued, "As I said, you won't talk to my father. So, we leave and go live our own life and you won't have to." She paused for a moment. William thought he saw her swallow hard and the emergence of a single tear on her cheek. Another hard swallow, followed by two loud sighs, ended the pacing. She turned toward him, a second tear on the other cheek. Her look less determined, and more of a plea, with a slight pout in her lips. What fire had been there earlier was gone, in fact her cheeks looked pale, more than just her normal fair complexion. The color had been drained from them as she turned toward him. A slight shake appeared in her body. The shake progressed to a tremble.

"Ainslee, are you ok?" William got up and moved around the table to her. Taking her by the arm, he helped her to a chair at the table, where he sat her down. When he tried to release her arm, her hands reached up and grabbed his, and wouldn't let go. They felt warm to him, but the expression on her colorless face looked cold and scared. She pulled his hands closer to her cheek. The skin felt soft and cool against his hard rough hands. Her big eyes looked up and her pink lips uttered a two word phrase toward him, her voice pleading with each syllable.

"Marry me."

"What?", asked William.

Gripping his hands tighter, as if to never let go, she pleaded, "You heard me. Let's start this life together, as husband and wife. You don't even have to talk to my father. I know you have wanted to forever, you're just too afraid to ask my father. You don't have to now. You don't. It is just us. You told me you are leaving with someone here visiting Father Henry. We could have him marry us before we left. I know he would do it, and he wouldn't tell anyone. William, this is our chance. I can't let you leave. We are meant to be together. Marry me. Marry me right now."

William stood there in stunned silence, mind swimming with what she had said. He looked down at her. She looked up at him. "Okay."

13

In the middle of the night, mixed among the normal creaks and groans of Father Henry's modest timber raftered residence, was a single rhythmic rap. The nightly drop in temperatures and coastal breeze gave the single room building a voice all its own, but this new knock was not part of this voice. Every so often, what sounded like a loud tap paused before it started again. This pattern continued for several minutes before a new sound was added to the chorus of creaks, groans, and taps.

"Father Henry?", whispered a voice through the brown-stained planks of his door.

The tapping resumed before a hint of light showed through the gaps in the door. Two large clunks were heard on the other side before the door cracked open. A single candle, held by the priest's elderly hand, threw shadows on his face from below. Still half asleep and in his white sleep shirt, his weary eyes peered out at William.

"Son, everything alright?"

"Yes, Father. Well, kind of..." William moved a step to the side to expose Ainslee McLayer behind him.

Father Henry did everything but jump in surprise at the sight of her there at that ungodly hour of night. The door flung inward as he motioned with his right hand to usher them inside in a hurry. When both had entered, Father Henry stuck his head outside and looked around for anyone else, or anyone that might see these two young members of his flock coming inside. Inside there was a simple wooden table, with four chairs, in the center of the room. Along the stacked stone walls sat an assortment of furniture. A single table with a wash basin sat in the corner. A tin pitcher sat on top of the table. In the opposite corner was a writing desk. The surface sloped down, but a single ledge kept a stack of papers from sliding off; an inkwell and pen sat on the flat top. Two simple bunk-style beds were pushed up against the wall, the tossed covers in one showed which bed Father Henry had emerged from. The other's occupant still slept inside. A few snorts and snores emerged.

Over the next hour, William and Ainslee sat at the table and, in hushed tones, explained their plan to the priest. Father Henry made several modest appeals to change their minds. Each time, Ainslee was able to present a counterargument.

William never tried, or never had the opportunity to, before she jumped in when Father Henry took a breath. When he was finally satisfied, they had thought this through, he leaned back in his chair, crossed his arms over his chest, and stared at the flame dancing on the tall candle in the center of the table. Or that was what the two believed he was focused on. On the table in front of the candle was a simple black leather-bound book. Several ribbons, of various colors, protruded out, marking pages of significance. On the cover, a single gold cross. Father Henry hoped for divine guidance from the good book.

He looked up at the two who sat across from him, both looked on with rapt attention and leaned closer to the table. "This changes things, then." He pushed back from the table, and sat there for a second, lost in thought. He then stood up and said, "Wait here."

Father Henry went over and roused Bishop Emmanuel, who woke up just as disoriented as his counterpart had before he opened the door. William could see Father Henry motion in their direction, which drew an inquisitive look from the bishop. This spawned a hushed conversation between the two. A shake of the bishop's head here, another there, and several exaggerated hand motions, told William the discussion was not going well. He tried to hear what was said, but they talked too quietly, and the light was too low to allow him to see their lips. If he had to guess at the objections the bishop would be making, the rushed wedding would be top on the list. The church viewed the union between man and woman to be one of the most sacred. Anyone rushing into it was counseled against it. That was probably the conversation they were having now. How William would deal with this objection, he didn't know. He hoped the bishop would listen to their reasons.

Father Henry left the side of his compatriot, and walked back toward the table. The flat smile on his face dripped with concern. Behind him, the bishop got out of bed and headed to a wash basin, mumbling the whole way. William prepared himself to hear that the bishop objected. As he grabbed Ainslee's hand, he hoped she had the same thoughts he had had, and prepared herself too. Instead of coming directly to the table, Father Henry made a stop at a simple dressing table with a single drawer. It rattled back and forth on the wood runners as he pulled it open. After a quick search he pulled out a single piece of lace and then searched again. What he emerged with, William couldn't see. It was a small object that he held in his closed hand.

Back at the table, Father Henry laid the lace out flat on the table and used his hand to smooth out a few bumps and wrinkles. He took great care with this task. A tug here, and a tug there to straighten it, his right hand clenched into a tight fist all the while. The lace was then folded in half, and then half again, to produce a square of white lace. A square that Father Henry pulled along the table to center straight in front of him. The straight smile across his face bent upward. The fourth, and last, chair at the table slid out. Bishop Emmanuel sat, still drying his face with a towel, he seemed neither refreshed nor awake.

William prepared himself for a lecture, but it never arrived. Instead, Father Henry opened his hand to reveal two rings. He placed both on the square of lace, as if to display them. William believed he had seen these rings before, but wasn't sure where. Father Henry wore several during his services, but he assumed those were ones embossed with the crest of the Church of England. A scan of his hands, and those of the bishop, revealed they both wore several rings on both hands. Each of the rings were similar, but different. That made sense to William, since their own church and its traditions were rooted in Catholicism, much of which is the same, just with different symbols and terms.

"Bishop Emmanuel has agreed to take both of you with him, but this does complicate things. Far more than you can understand. First things first, though, let's get you two married. You will need to leave before daybreak to avoid being seen." With his look and the tone of his voice, it was obvious the last statement was meant for Ainslee. "These rings are ones I have held on to for a dear friend for several years. William, that was your father. These are your father and mother's rings. On his deathbed he asked me to hold them until you were older, and ready. I see no reason why that time is not now. With this piece of lace, we will join your hands together in union."

"A union that cannot be broken," added Bishop Emmanuel, with the hint of a wry smile.

Father Henry continued with a chuckle, "Yes, one that cannot be broken. Bishop Emmanuel will perform the ceremony. I will be the witness. I assume you both understand what that means?"

Both William and Ainslee looked at each other. With smiles plastered across both of their faces, they nodded. They would now be wed in the eyes of the Catholic Church, and have to abide by the rules therein. That wasn't a problem for William, he couldn't ever imagine a scenario where he would want to leave. He hoped she felt the same.

The bishop stood up and walked toward an empty spot in the room. He asked, "Come. Come."

They both did as they were asked, and found themselves standing hand in hand in front of a Bishop, who stood there holding a bible with two rings stacked on it. He wore a simple night shirt, instead of the normal celebratory robe he would wear for such an event. The bishop handed the bible to Father Henry for a moment while he wrapped the lace around their hands and asked them to kneel. They did so. Without opening the bible, he recited a prayer in Latin and then crossed himself. Father Henry, William, and Ainslee followed suit.

The first light of day crept over the western horizon as Bishop Emmanuel, William, and Ainslee loaded up into Father Henry's carriage. The carriage was only used to carry caskets and members of the grieving family from the church to the graveside. Outside of that, it sat beside the church and gathered dust, pollen, and leaves. It squeaked and shuddered as he signaled the horse to go. Not the most covert mode to sneak the newly-married couple and his guest out of town, but he planned to be out of town before anyone would be awake to hear the noise of the carriage. There was a good chance he could be back before anyone knew he was gone. The port town of Burwick was only six miles away.

Ainslee watched out the windows as everything she knew passed by. The grip she had on William's hand tightened as all of that slipped behind them and out of sight. They were on their way to a new life, and a new beginning. That was when it dawned on her, she didn't know where this new life took them. "So, where are we going?", she asked her new husband.

"Italy. Vatican City," said Bishop Emmanuel.

14

William and Ainslee had set off on a great adventure to see the world. For the last two weeks, all they'd seen was the ocean, with the occasional hint of shoreline in the distance, but most of the time it was water, water, and more water. Water that turned from dark blue into a light turquoise, a sign that Bishop Emmanuel said meant they were close to their destination.

The two newlyweds were inseparable. At night, they did what newlyweds did. Ainslee's presence on the voyage was not expected, but at the bishop's request, the crew had made arrangements so they would have a room all to their own. By day, they were together on the deck, basking in the sun and warmer temperatures, something that was foreign to two people who'd spent their entire lives in a land that seemed to always be covered in a layer of fog. Only the private conversations between William and Bishop Emmanuel separated them. These conversations happened twice, sometimes three times, a day. William never spoke of them when he returned, no matter how much Ainslee probed.

On the morning of their fifteenth day at sea, the two of them laid in bed like they had on the previous fourteen days. The sun snuck in through the single window and shone on the wall across the room. William was awake first, as he usually was. The clock of a farmer was firmly planted in his soul. He didn't mind. It gave him time to lay there and watch his beloved sleep, to listen to her breathe. Part of him felt like this was all a dream. Weeks ago, it would not have been possible. Even if he had worked up the nerve to ask her father for permission to court Ainslee, he had no doubt such a request would have been rejected. Lord McLayer had to have a list of more suitable suitors in mind for his daughter. Now, she was there in his arms, and their future was ahead of them. The past still made an occasional tug. He thought of his farm, his animals, John, the smell of the morning dew at daybreak. It had an almost sweet aroma to him. What he had woken up to the last two weeks, was, well... salty.

At first it seemed like any of the other previous mornings on board, but a sound caught William's attention. It wasn't the creaks and groans of the wood planks of the ship. Those were all normal, and had almost become a part of his essence and unnoticeable. Above them, on deck, there was a rush of activity. William slid out of bed and slipped on his pants. He walked out the door and up the stairs into the bright sun of the morning. His head breached the opening and he looked around.

"Mr. Miller, good morning," said Captain Leonardiz. The salty old man, with a beard as black as coal, was missing something. The scowl that always appeared plastered to his face was not there. A smile was in its place. "Welcome to Civitavecchia."

William turned toward the bow, where the hive of activity was. Men pulled ropes and dropped the sails of the foremast and mizenmast. Others loosened up the sail on the main mast, letting air out of the great white sail. In the distance, beyond the crew, there was something he hadn't seen in over two weeks. Land.

William rushed down the stairs and exploded into the room he and Ainslee shared. She was still asleep until the door slammed behind it and he exclaimed, "We are here!"

Ainslee rustled awake and looked at him from underneath the covers. With a yawn she asked, "What?"

"We are in Italy. Well, not in, but coming close. I can see it. It is close. Right out there. Ahead of us," William said, speaking faster than his betrothed could hear.

"William. What are you trying to tell me?", she asked, now leaning up on an arm as she watched her husband get dressed.

He took a breath and then tried again to explain, "We are approaching land. We are in Italy."

This statement was made as clear as a bell, one that went off with a loud dong in her head. She rushed up out of the bed and splashed two handfuls of water from the wash basin onto her face. Using the same linen she had used for the last two weeks, she pulled it across her face to remove the water and grime. No time to attempt a bath before donning the same dress she had worn since they'd left. It had been rinsed out a few times, that had removed a few stains and any smells, but it was anything but what one would describe as fresh. A quick swipe backward through her hair with a brush pushed her beautiful red locks behind her ears and shoulders. With her shoulders back, she exited the door. Her husband hopped around a few steps before his right foot slipped into his boot.

Up on deck, Ainslee rushed forward, bumping into several crew members on her way. Her face lit up like it was Christmas morn as she gazed out on the approaching view. In the distance, features began to take shape. The masts of tall ships already anchored in port stood just beyond a large stone structure. She pointed it out to William, who had joined her at the bow. The closer they came, the more features of the city came into view. It was larger than St. Margaret's Hope, much larger.

"That is Fortress Michangelo," Bishop Emmanuel said, in his rich Italian accent. William wasn't sure why, but that phrase itself sounded more sophisticated than any phrase he had heard in his life. "Pope Julius II built it over a hundred and fifty years ago to protect his fleet and the economy of the region."

"I am going to guess this is not a fishing village?"

The bishop leaned against the rail and faced William as he responded to his last statement. "No, not at all. This port is the Pope's private military fleet, and the primary exporter of alum. There is a large deposit of it just to the north."

Both William and Ainslee looked at each other. William didn't want to seem ignorant to someone who had put such great faith in him, but he had no clue what alum was. It was a substance he had never heard about. Neither of them needed to ask the question, though. Their tour guide could guess at the question by the looks on their faces. He volunteered, "It's a crystal that can be ground up and used in the tanning of leathers, as well as some medicines."

Both mouthed "oh" and acted like this was common knowledge they should be aware of.

Captain Leonardiz anchored the ship about a hundred yards offshore. From this vantage point, William and Ainslee could see everything. The Mediterranean buildings lining the shoreline. Hundreds of people moved in and around the port, which were more than either of them had ever seen in a single place before. More ships in a single place they either of them had ever seen, as well. If all the fishing boats in St. Margaret's Hope were in port at the same time, they would have to double, or even triple them, to match. Even in those numbers, they wouldn't equal this sight. Those were just small boats, what was in port with them here were great ships, with large masts and huge sails. Some just plain white. Others with various symbols on them, keys and crosses.

"Come. Come," Bishop Emmanuel said as he walked back toward midship. Three members of the crew were lowering a longboat into the water. The old and frail-looking Bishop flung himself up on the railing and then quickly descended a rope ladder into the boat waiting below. Both William and Ainslee gave the ladder a questionable look.

"You first, " said William.

The cockeyed look from Ainslee told him she disagreed.

"I mean, you go first. I will help you down from here." William reached out for her hand. She sat on the rail and swung her feet over. William held her left hand and right shoulder to steady her. "Now turn around. You need to go down facing the ship."

"What?!?"

"Put your foot down on that ledge, and turn toward me. I will hold you the whole way."

"Don't let me fall!", she warned.

William promised, "I won't."

She turned while William maintained two hands on her. Holding her right hand as he bent over the railing, Ainslee made it down the ladder and into the boat. William followed shortly after, with an attempt intended to be as graceful as the Bishop, but a misstep on the last rung sent his boot crashing down on the bottom of the long boat with a thud. Neither the Bishop nor the oarsman were amused. His wife, on the other hand, was and smirked before exploding into laughter.

In just a few minutes the oarsman delivered his three passengers to the harbor's wharf. The three departed from the boat, and two of them stood, frozen, while the third member continued walking through a grand archway. The bishop never stopped to wait for the other two, he continued through the large stone archway of the Livorno Door. Neither William nor Ainslee had seen such a thing. It was massive, with people coming in and out at a dizzying pace. The opening looked large enough to fit their church, St. Margaret's Hope's largest building, inside, spiral and all. *"How could anyone build something so tall?"*, he wondered. Did they have a tall ladder? William remembered how queasy he had felt climbing up his ladder to make roof repairs. It would shake and shudder with every step. Not to mention the one time he fell off when it slipped, he landed with an awful thud. To reach the top, you would need something ten times taller. That was a job he knew he didn't want.

William's focus shifted from the structure, to the opening itself. It was impressive, but missing something. Bishop Emmanuel. He grabbed his wife's hand and rushed through the people and then through the door. Her eyes and head craned to take it all in as her husband pulled her along. He said, "Excuse me," as they bumped into or cut people off. Each responded with a look of confusion and annoyance. Some exclaimed, using words that he didn't understand. He knew people in other countries spoke other languages, this was the first time he had experienced it, it didn't come with the sense of wonder he expected it would. Instead, he felt very small, alone, and confused.

A sigh of relief pulled some of that feeling out of him, when he spied their guide, Bishop Emmanuel, just ahead of them, next to a horse drawn carriage on a cobblestone road. A single driver, clothed in a red uniform, was mounted on the front of the solid black coach. He sat upright, with the leads in his hands. The door, embossed with two crossed gold keys, was held open by a man in a yellow and blue striped uniform, with a metal helmet adorned with a red plume. A long pike was held straight up by his other hand. The bishop entered the coach first. When William and Ainslee reached it, he held her hand again to help her inside. The coach lurched to the side a little when William entered, another instance that seemed to amuse his wife. Before he sat down, the door slammed shut behind him. There were a few lurches back and forth, which William assumed was the guard climbing up next to the driver, and then a lunge forward and they were off. Bishop Emmanuel leaned back and closed his eyes. William and Ainslee, couldn't if they tried. Each were attached to a window, taking in the sights and sounds of the city they rolled through, toward the Italian countryside.

15

The coach rumbled forward into the night. Two of its three passengers were fast asleep. Why shouldn't they be? It had been a long voyage, and a long day in the coach, but that wasn't it. William and Ainslee were used to hard work and long days. Their exhaustion was rooted in overstimulation. The world they had known all of their lives had just been put in perspective. It was miniscule, like the tip of a pin, in the grand scheme of things. There was a world full of wonders out there, unlike anything either of them could have imagined. The one person in the coach that was awake understood that. While he sat there, still, with his eyes closed. He was not asleep, but instead just relaxing and giving his two guests a moment alone, as alone as they could be in the small coach, to enjoy it together. That was why he disturbed their peaceful rest.

"Ainslee. William." He nudged each one with the softness of a parent waking a sleeping child.

Both rustled awake, stretched, and looked around in the coach, confused. Bishop Emmanuel simply pointed to direct their attention out the windows. Both turned and leaned toward the window closest to them. What they had seen of the world so far hadn't prepared them for this. Line upon line of gas lamps lined the cobblestone streets. Buildings of marble, with ornate architecture, decorated with gold, bronze, and other precious metals, were everywhere. These were no simple stone homes with thatch or wood-clad roofs. William's mind searched for the word to describe it. The one it came up with was luxurious.

"William, what is that?"

The same question echoed in his head as the coach pulled into the plaza. The sound of water bubbling down a brook accentuated the tranquil night, but there was no brook to be seen. Ainslee was fascinated by this and stood up to lean out the window to look around. When she found the sources, she reached over and tapped William, but he didn't notice. He couldn't. His eyes had caught sight of the structure in the center of the plaza, it was some sort of tower that went up as far as he could see. As fascinating as that was to him, it only held his attention for a second as the enormity of the building behind it emerged from the darkness and into view. It filled the skyline from side to side, and was highlighted by row upon row of lanterns. On the top of it was a great dome. As he took it all in, he noticed there were no other streets leading out. His mind asked, *"Were they on the steps of heaven, itself?"* If so, behind the golden doors he saw at the top of the stairs that led up from the plaza would be Saint Peter himself.

"That is the Obelisk of Saint Peter's. It was brought here from Egypt over 1700 years ago," explained Bishop Emmanuel as they passed by the large statue.

William only half heard him. The name Saint Peter resonated inside. It agreed with what his mind had thought, but that would mean one thing. They, Emmanuel, Ainslee, and himself, had passed on, but when? Maybe the ship ran into a storm and all on board had perished. The remainder of the voyage was to deliver their souls. If that were the case, shouldn't he remember the storm? William didn't consider himself an expert on the afterlife, but he did have more *experience* with it than most, if you excluded his present company. Something he realized early on was that those who had appeared to him always appeared confused. A feeling he now shared. Now, the few times he had tried to understand the what, why, and how of what he saw and could do, he was never really sure if they were confused, or if that was just how he perceived it. Not that it was something he thought about often. There was no way for him to know for sure. They never responded to him when he had tried to talk to them, so he couldn't simply ask, not that he hadn't tried enough times. If this were true, it would also explain why he hadn't seen any ghosts since they'd left, that was the longest he had ever gone without a sighting.

As William considered their fate, and Ainslee searched for the source of the water, the coach's wooden wheels clattered on the cobblestones through the plaza before coming to a stop in front of the stairs. The coach shuddered left and then right, before settling back on its springs with a few smaller bounces. The door opened, and the navy and yellow-clad guard appeared. He stood at attention as Bishop Emmanuel stepped out. He turned to the two remaining passengers and said, "Welcome to Saint Peter's Basilica, the Vatican, and your home for the next few months."

"You mean, we aren't dead?", asked William.

The pinched expression and narrow eyes on Bishop Emmanuel's face made William feel sheepish. He was not amused as he turned and continued up the stairs.

William stepped out and then helped his wife down out of the coach. Hand in hand, they followed the bishop up the stairs and through the large golden doors. Inside, they stepped on glossy marble floors. William took a few quick high steps. expecting the floor to be covered in a thin layer of water. With his eyes on the painted ceilings high above his head, this produced a stumble revealing the grace of a foal taking its first steps. Bishop Emmanuel appeared unfazed by their surroundings and continued down the hall.

They followed him as close as they could, having to jog a few times to catch up after their attention was distracted by a painting on the wall, a vase on a stand, or just the sheer beauty of the illuminated space around them. Their footsteps echoed through the halls like explosions. He turned down a hallway where the lanterns were more spaced out, creating pockets of darkness. In front of them, the bishop disappeared into one of those pockets and then reappeared, only to disappear again. An eerie unsettling feeling overcame William each time he walked through a pocket of darkness. The squeeze on his hand told him Ainslee felt it too. He squeezed back to reassure her.

It was in one of these pockets of darkness where, if it were not for the blast of light coming from the side, they would have walked right into the bishop. He stood in the center of the hall, in front of an open door, a door he directed both of them through. They entered, he did not.

The room was quaint, compared to the hallway they'd just left. A large bed sat against the far wall, which was painted white like the others. In front of a large fireplace, with a bronze mesh hanging over the opening, was a table with two chairs. Neither of which were simple wooden chairs like William had at home, both the back and seats had cushions.

"William. Get some rest. I will send for you in the morning," Bishop Emmanuel said, just before the door closed behind them.

When the door closed, Ainslee danced around the room. There was no music, but she didn't need it. She floated from space to space, looking at everything. The table. The draperies, something neither of them had seen before. William's tired body and mind were focused on the bed. It looked soft and warm, something neither his back home, nor the one they'd shared on the ship, were. A screech from the attached room sent him running. Inside the white-tiled room was Ainslee, her hands over her mouth, eyes focused on a large tub. Water ran out of a spout into the tub. William walked toward it and passed his hand through the water, his fingers played in the stream falling from the spout. Ainslee stepped forward and turned the silver handle on top of the spout, and the water stopped. She giggled like a little girl chasing a butterfly in the Scottish meadows.

William walked back out into the main room, mind wandering. His wife followed behind him and finally asked a question she hadn't asked in the two weeks since they'd left the only home either of them had ever known.

"William, why are we here?"

16

"Please tell me this is some kind of sick joke," Ainslee begged as she laid back on the bed and stared up at the ceiling above her. It wasn't a plain flat one, but a beautiful one, a work of art made of moldings and paint. She hadn't undressed before she laid down. This was not a time for sleep for her, or for William. What her husband had just explained to her had made her feel woozy, and she almost fell in the center of the room. He caught her before she hit the floor and pulled her to the bed. The lightheaded feeling she felt passed as she laid back, but the color had yet to return to her face.

"I wish it was. I had hoped for years it was, but it isn't," William said as he paced at the foot of their bed. Inside, his stomach did backflips. It would have been foolish for him to believe he could keep this hidden from her. At some point he would slip up, or she would become curious and ask about their situation, like she had now. The fact that she hadn't asked during their two-week long voyage gave him a little hope he would have more time to figure out how.

"How long has Father Henry known about your… ability?"

"Only a few weeks, but I believe my father was like me, and he knew about him. I am not sure really."

"Bishop Emmanuel is going to train you in what exactly?"

"To be honest, I'm not sure," said William. He was being truthful. During their one conversation, the bishop had never gone into any great detail in explaining what he would be training him in. He had never asked, either, which in hindsight was a more than a bit foolish. The offer to leave and pursue anything the outside world presented, had hit him in his heart, leaving his mind out of the decision. Looking back on it, the second thoughts were what probably triggered that nightmare he had had. "Something about knowing how to deal with them and to protect the living," he added.

"Ok. This must be real," she said.

William was preparing to try to explain again, but stopped mid-thought. The pacing stopped, and everything in his mind left, except one question, *"What did she just say?"*

"Look at the efforts they went through to bring you here, and look at where we are. We are in the Vatican, the center of everything that is spiritual." Ainslee was sitting up now, propped on her elbows, her color was returning, but not quite back yet. She patted the bed next to her and said, "He said you start in the morning. You'd better get your sleep, ghost warrior."

The wry smile on her face made William leery. It was one he had seen one too many times. That look always ended with him either being pushed off the wall, slugged in the arm, or the butt of her own joke. She and John had always found those jokes hilarious, William, not so much. Her sense of humor was one of the traits he loved about her, but it also cut sharp and deep. Once, when they were barely ten years old, she led him out, away from the farmland he was familiar with, and into the adjacent forest. They had gone in deep, turning here and there. William felt lost, but he wasn't overly concerned. It was obvious that Ainslee knew where she was going.

They slowed as they had reached a tree with a trunk that twisted around. She told him that the tree was magical, if you kissed someone under it, your dreams would come true. William was told right where to stand and he did, eyes closed, and lips puckered, then he heard giggling. When he opened his eyes, he saw Ainslee's hair blowing in the wind behind her as she ran away from him. He tried to follow, but his feet were stuck. Where she had him stand was a patch of moor mud. Stuff so thick and strong it could trap a horse. Being only ten, he was nowhere close to the strength of a horse.

William screamed and screamed. First for her to come back, then for anyone within ear shot. The combination of the cold damp air and his screaming had caused his voice to go raw and raspy. When it was nothing more than a whisper, she came back. Tears rolled down his cheeks. That devious wry smile was on her face then, too. He expected her to make fun of him, or to take off running again, now in the other direction. Perhaps she would leave him out there all night and only come back when forced to lead his parents to where she had left him. In truth, he hadn't known what to expect. What had happened next, wouldn't have made it on the list if he had made one. She leaned in and kissed him. Softly and warmly, her hand dangling next to his and, for just the briefest of moments, she grabbed it. When she let go of his hand, and his lips, she helped him ease his legs out of the moor mud and walked him home, soggy boots and all. There had been no apology, he didn't need one. From that point on, things had changed. Maybe that legend was true, look where they are now.

There was no further conversation for the night. Ainslee's eyes drew heavy and closed. Her breathing slowed to a restful rhythm. The sound of that soothed William and sent him off to sleep, as well. The next sound he heard was a knock on the door. At first, William laid there and didn't move. When he heard the knock for a third time, he sat up. Pools of sunlight splashed across the room, through the gaps in the draperies. It was a good thing too, the light helped him see a few things, limiting what he bumped into on his way to the door. He just missed bumping into a chair at a bureau, and a footstool at the end of the bed. As he opened it, a young girl, no more than fifteen or sixteen years old, wearing an all-white habit, stood at the door, her head looking straight down at the golden tray she held.

Before William could say, "Morning", or ask what she needed, the girl walked in through the tiny space between the doorframe and William, and proceeded to the table in the center of the sitting section of the room. She placed her tray down, and then hurried out, never looking up from the floor. He walked out behind her and watched her walk at a brisk pace down the hall, her head never coming up, her feet never making an audible sound in the cavernous hall.

He walked back in and shut the door behind him. Then looked at the tray she had placed on the table. By now Ainslee was awake and sitting up in bed. Her eyes followed her husband as he tended to the door and inspected the tray. It had an assortment of bread and poached eggs, on a plate. Two cups held a brown liquid that William thought was coffee, based on the color and consistency. When he took a sniff of the steam that rose up from it, it was tea. Strong tea. He looked back at Ainslee and said, "Breakfast."

She sprang up off the bed and rushed over to the table. They were both famished. The coach had stopped twice to water and feed the horses. The driver, guard, and occupants had taken that opportunity to stop and have a bite to eat, as well, but the excitement and nerves of the day had burned off all their energy, they needed to resupply. They sat and ate, and afterwards took turns in the large porcelain tub with the fountain running into it. For the first time in days, they felt clean. They were only able to sponge off while on the ship. There was no proper bath, just a basin with some water. Ainslee found it better for washing their clothes than washing themselves.

Cleaned and dressed, they barely had a moment to wonder what was next for the day when there was another, much firmer, knock at the door. William opened it, and found Bishop Emmanuel standing on the other side, hands held near his waist, palms pressed together. There were no pleasantries. No "Good morning" or "How did you sleep?", just a firm "Come, William. We need to start your lessons."

William started out the door, but stopped as the bishop took a step inside. He turned toward where Ainslee stood looking out the window. "Ainslee, my dear. Sister Francine will be back shortly to take the tray and show you around. For the next several weeks, this is to feel like your home. Our city has a lot to offer." He turned and walked out the door beckoning, "Come, William."

Feeling more himself than he had over the last several days, William let a bit of his unsophisticated humor show through. "When is my tour of the city?"

Bishop Emmanuel retorted, "Oh, you will have plenty of opportunities to see the city. Most of them at night, when you will be most useful."

William didn't know if he was trying to answer humor with humor, or if he was serious.

17

William's parents made sure their son could read and write. Even with the plans of him taking over the family farm, they both saw those skills as necessary to conduct business, as well as to be a contributing member of society, so bookwork didn't concern him much. What was concerning during his first meeting with Bishop Emmanuel, was the volume and the content. They had set up a makeshift classroom at a table in a large library. All day long, the bishop gave instructions to monks and scribes, in Latin, who scurried away, up and down every aisle, searching the bookcases for what he had requested. William only caught a few names here and there.

One of the scribes was named Roberto, or that is what the bishop had called him once when he had retrieved the wrong text from the shelves, and he sent the short rotund balding figure back to search again. Another was Cristobal. He was different. Unlike the others, that would go off and search for what was requested. Cristobal not only returned with what he was sent for, but always had one or two more items in hand that he and the bishop took a few moments to review before adding them to the stack. A stack that grew by the moment, and was now totaling ten books, in all. When the eleventh was put on top of it, and the twelfth, one of Cristobal's recommendations, was put down to the side of the stack, the search was done. Much to the pleasure of the old priests in the opposite corner from them, who had grown rather irritated at all the moving around and interruptions to their silence.

Pulling two books from the stack, Bishop Emmanuel asked, "I am going to guess you don't read Latin?"

"I don't."

This news seemed to upset Roberto and the two other men, whose names William had not yet caught. Each appeared to be in their early thirties, and wore simple white smocks over black gowns. Cristobal responded by saying, "Riformatore." The others seemed to understand what he said and nodded in agreement. William had no clue and sat there with a blank expression on his face as the conversation occurred above his head. At least until Cristobal explained it to William.

"Pre-reformation, everyone knew Latin. It was the language of education, law, medicine, and the church. Where you are from, they separated the church, and everything," he stopped himself to correct the statement, "well, everything you would have been exposed to is now in your common language. There is nothing to worry about. I can translate for you."

His tone was warmer, friendlier, than the others'. Everyone else had what his father would call the 'cold business tone'. They were here to do a job, and that was all. Cristobal gave the impression of someone who wanted to help, which helped William breathe a huge sigh of relief. There was also something different, his accent was richer than the others'. William wondered where he was from. That would be something he would have to ask him at some point.

Bishop Emmanuel seemed pleased, as much as the man ever showed outwardly, that the young scribe had volunteered to help. So much so, he assigned him to be responsible for his academic training. That was a responsibility he didn't bat an eye about, as he slid his chair over next to William, dragging two books with him. The others left without a word. No indication of how long this would go on, or when they would be back. William watched as they left, as his teacher began the lesson.

"William, what do you know about life and death?"

The question was a seemingly simple one, which to William meant it deserved a similar answer. "Well, you are born and live, then you get old and die."

"Okay, in its crudest terms, yes, but what happens after you die?"

William thought about this for a second and considered where he was. In the Catholic Church there could only be one answer, and it was the same as the Anglican Church. "Your soul is welcomed into the ever after."

"Heaven, is that what you speak of?", asked Cristobal.

William nodded.

"Yes and no. Well... " he paused and gave an educated giggle, like a sleuth who had caught someone in a ruse, "that is what the Church wants you to think. It is the simplest and easiest view to accept. The truth is, we don't have a clue."

The surprise of such an admission, sitting here inside the holiest of holy buildings in the world, must have been written all over William's face, because Cristobal asked, "I take it that hearing that surprises you?"

Before William could answer, he continued to explain, "What you are going to learn, for as long as you are here, is not Church doctrine, beliefs, indoctrination, or anything else you might get as part of a sermon back home, or from the Holy Father, himself. You are going to learn the truth, or the truth as we know it or believe it to be. Some will be conjecture; some is what we have learned simply by doing. Some you are going to learn right alongside us. There are no set instructions on how to do what we are asking you to do. You have to figure out what works, and apply it. So, back to life and death. If it were as simple as you live, and then you die and go to heaven or hell, then why are there spirits that are still bound to this world?"

The question was not one Cristobal expected William to answer. He ended the question by opening a book to a page with a disturbing image on it. William didn't understand what he was looking at, but he knew it was evil. "In 1320, Italian poet Dante Alighieri completed a work that contained a view of the nine circles of hell. Each circle is a level you must pass through on your way into the underworld." His finger traced the page from the top down, each image more disturbing than the last. "Now, you may be thinking he was just a poet, and this was just a poem, but this work reflected a critical belief that was growing in the Church at that time." He flipped several pages to a similar diagram, that was less disturbing. "In addition to describing what you just saw in Inferno, he also wrote of the nine levels you must travel through to reach heaven, Paradiso." His finger now traveled from the bottom of the page, up through the images, to the top. "In between both is his second part, Purgatorio, or as you know it, Purgatory. Have you heard that term before?"

"Yes, that is the place where souls sit to suffer for all eternity. They neither go to heaven or hell." The sermons Father Henry gave were rarely fire and brimstone. Most where of an enlightening message, to give those that needed it hope, but occasionally he went dark with his message and used that image to help warn those in his congregation to not slip off what he called "the slick path of salvation".

"I bet you can see where this is going. Now, if you go strictly by the text, Purgatory is a mountain you have to climb to get to Paradiso, heaven, but you don't really start on that climb until you get through the first two levels called Ante-Purgatory. Those levels are called Excommunicate and Late Repentant. The last of which has a gate as an exit to the first level of true Purgatory. That is Saint Peter's Gate."

His teacher stopped the lecture for a moment and brought his brown eyes even with William's. A smile broke across his face as he saw the lightning bolt of knowledge strike inside his student. William sat back in his chair and looked up. His eyes looked up at the imagery depicted in the great stained glass windows that existed every few feet along the walls of the top level. Then he looked up at the fresco on the ceiling. The images, one after another, lined with details of what Cristobal had just explained to him.

"If it weren't for the ability of some of us to see and experience those souls trapped, we would think this was just a work of literature and a silly belief system. For now, it is the only thing that makes sense."

William asked, "So, how do we help them climb the mountain?"

"Oh, you are going to be great at this."

18

When William returned back to his and Ainslee's residence in the Vatican, he found it empty, which suited him fine. He was sure she would have a ton of questions about his first day of "training" and at the moment, he was more exhausted than any day out in the pasture had ever made him. His body wasn't tired, though, it was his mind. The result of six straight hours, scouring book after book, most of it in Latin, which required Cristobal to explain it to him. Most William understood right away, but some of the finer points required additional explanation.

Their studies covered the theories of life and death, combined with documented studies of spirits and groups of spirits that priests, and others like William, had encountered. Each study appeared to take what they'd observed and tried to fit it into their current view. At first this was a shock to William. They, those he thought were experts, didn't have a true understanding of what they were doing. This was all just guessing, based on their current beliefs and what they had observed. What was comforting was how candid Cristobal was about it all. William had expected a member of the church to be locked and rigid about their beliefs and how things were, but he was far from it. He was almost logical and scientific in his approach. He took the time to show him the times they'd had to rethink their understanding, to emphasize that it was an ever-evolving topic. Where a high level of uncertainty existed, he pointed it out.

He walked William through the study of Friar Benedictor, a Franciscan monk that, like William, could see them. The friar had had unusual and fortunate encounters with a repeating visitor. After he encountered and contacted the same spirit, in the same spot on the grounds of the monastery, for the third time, he decided to test a theory. Each time he saw the spirit, it roamed up to the courtyard wall and turned, only to encounter the wall on the other side and then turned again. It would repeat this, over and over. Being that the monastery was holy grounds, he hypothesized that spirits are sensitive to holy objects and people. He placed objects in the courtyard, both blessed and not, as his test and control variables. Two nights later, his test subject arrived, and he watched. As always, it wandered around between the walls, but never attempted to avoid any of the objects he had placed around the courtyard, whether they were blessed or not. Concerned his test subject may not be aware of anything but the walls, the friar walked into the courtyard, toward the spirit. When he was close enough, the spirit retreated away from him, several feet. He repeated this several more times, backing the spirit into a corner of the courtyard, against the wall. The friar reached out with his hand and touched it once again, and the spirit disappeared through the very wall he believed had trapped it in the courtyard. What he learned was, they were not aware of objects that had no importance to them, whether it was blessed or not. To provide supporting details to his conclusion, he tried to determine who the spirit was, and why they might be connected to the courtyard. He didn't have to go far, just another hundred yards to the cemetery, where he found the headstone of Friar Montgomery, who died eighty years earlier, and had constructed that very courtyard wall.

The friar's findings were gathered and delivered to the Council of Zion, an eleven member board made up of clergy and cardinals, that reviewed any such findings for correctness and completeness. If any beliefs needed to be adjusted based on a report, this group made such adjustments.

Thoughts and images of his learnings danced in his head as he laid back on the lush bedding. His brain craved sleep, to recover from the day's activities, as well as to process all he had learned. His eyes closed, but the outside world was not replaced by darkness. Instead, pages of text and images raced across his vision, and around in his subconscious. His mind was too tired to make an attempt to comprehend, and let the pages fall into the emptiness below while he retreated further and further into the darkness of sleep.

William woke up minutes, or hours, later to a huge racket in the sitting area of their residence. He leaned up and expected to find Ainslee, perhaps sitting there drinking tea after her day out, but that was not the case. The heat coming off his visitor, blistering his skin, told him who was there before he opened his eyes. The flames around him seemed larger than they had back during the dream in his home. Maybe it wasn't a dream after all.

"I see you didn't listen to me," thundered the familiar coarse voice. Its yellow eyes seemed more focused and determined this time. "You really should have listened. You had such a great future ahead of you. A wonderful family. Year after year of bountiful harvests. All given up, for what? The promise of something greater, by a bunch of old men that play dress-up. The life this leads to is nothing like the one I offered. The road to their greatness is paved with pain and sorrow."

It picked up one of the teacups Ainslee had left on the table, and mimicked taking a sip before placing it back on the table with a thud, then stood up from the table. Its hooves clopped against the tile floor as it walked around the table and over to the footstool William had kicked earlier that morning. When it reached the stool, it sat and crossed one leg over the other. Its hands were placed on top of its knee as it leaned forward. Its posture mimicked one he had seen Bishop Emmanuel take once, when he was lecturing William about the responsibility he was being entrusted with, during their discussions on board the ship.

"Now, I could just condemn you for ignoring my offer, but I am not a vengeful creature. It is not too late, William. You and your cherry of a wife could return home, your real home, not this place, and have all that I offered."

"Why should I believe you?", William asked.

"You can talk. I was beginning to think you were a mute. That is a fair question. Why should you believe me?", It brought a flame-engulfed hand up to its chin and rubbed, while deep in thought. Sparks flew from its fingertips with each stroke. Then it snapped its fingers, producing more sparks. "That's right. I can do what I promise, and they can't, it is that simple."

It sat there and watched William from the footstool, its yellow eyes probing below the skin and into the essence of the man. A series of images flowed through his mind: the farm, with fields full of lush green crops; two large young boys helping him put up a new fence; Ainslee, looking on with the smile of an angel on her face. Each image reinforced the promise the creature had made. Each image also brought a sense of contentment, happiness, and pleasure to William. A fresh spring breeze, with a hint of early morning dew, replaced the heat that radiated from the flames that surrounded the creature. Chill bumps developed on his arms.

"I will come back for my answer," it said, and dissipated into a puff of steam as the door opened.

Ainslee burst in, all aglow, "You are back," she exclaimed. She was followed by the same young woman, in a white habit, that had come in with breakfast that morning. Her gaze was no longer focused on the floor but, instead, was up and confident. The plain, blank, almost subservient look she had possessed earlier was gone, replaced by a pleasant smile. Ainslee rushed over to hug and kiss her husband. Over her shoulder, William noticed that the nun had turned to give them privacy for their show of affection.

"The city is beautiful. Fountains, churches, shops, everywhere. It is like walking through paradise, with all the beautiful buildings, and ... oh, the food. I didn't eat any, mind you, but the smells that roll up and down the street are enough to make your mouth water."

While Ainslee gushed over her tour of Vatican City, and the surrounding area of Rome, her escort stood in the sitting room. The pleasant look that was on her face when she had walked in was gone. One of concern had replaced it as she walked around the table. Her eyes moved from the chair the creature had sat in, up to the ceiling, and down again. Then, as she walked toward the footstool, the look of concern grew to despair. Her eyes became jittery as she approached the stool. She passed her right hand through where the creature had sat, and then ran back to the center of the room, hand over her mouth as she gasped out loud.

19

If William's head wasn't tired and spinning after his day of reading and training, it was after Ainslee's whirlwind recap of her day in town. She took her husband on a descriptive tour of each and every street she had traveled. Some of it was just her telling him, but others were even more enjoyable for William. She bought slices of bread, cheese, and meat, rolled up in a cloth. Flowers of various sweet fragrances were rolled up in another. Sister Francine explained that people placed them in vases in their residences to add a floral fragrance to the air, and once they started to wilt you could pluck the petals and add them to your bath water to create an aromatic perfume that would stay on your skin for days. William thought it odd that a nun would be aware of such an indulgence, but just because she knew about it didn't mean she practiced it. The audible tour continued for the rest of the afternoon, until Sister Francine returned with their dinner on a tray. She carried another object on her tray, as well, a vase.

So far, the outside world was meeting, if not exceeding, her wildest dreams. William, on the other hand, had seen a ship and the inside of a library. Albeit an impressive library, as was every other room and hall he had seen in the Vatican. The food wasn't bad, either. Everything was cooked just right, and the flavors were an experience. Meat that tasted sweet, vegetables that had an oily spice to them, and the bread! The bread had a buttery flavor to it, without any butter in sight.

William's fork hit the plate for the last time, when there was a knock at the door. After another quick swig of red wine from his chalice, he wiped his mouth with a small linen that was next to his plate and pushed away from the table. When he opened the door, he saw Cristobal and Bishop Emmanuel. Behind them, two monks stood in full brown robes, hoods pulled up over their heads. Their hands crossed at the center of their body. Both held a lit lantern in their hands.

"William, you need to come with us," said Bishop Emmanuel.

"More training?", he asked.

Cristobal said, "Something like that."

William walked out the door and noticed another member of their party standing outside the glow of the lanterns. He was diminutive compared to the others, and wore a red robe. His face was hidden among the shadows, and he turned away before William could get a good look. The man walked down the hallway, ahead of the rest of the group, and always outside the glow of the light. They retraced the steps William and Ainslee had taken the night before, when they'd arrived, and descended the steps down to the plaza. At the bottom, no coach waited for them, wherever they were going, they were going on foot.

The night was quiet and cool. Only a handful of people were out walking in the streets, and the faint sound of music radiated from a few of the buildings as they walked north, away from St. Peter's Basilica. These streets were similar to the ones they'd rode in on last night, but as awe-inspiring as they were when seen from the coach, seeing them up close, like he was now, revealed them in more detail. Smooth rock walls. Ornate iron gates and railings that led to equally ornate doors, or covered the bottom half of second story windows, to create a balcony. What he didn't see were simple stone structures. With the exception of large structures, like churches and government buildings, and a few houses of the very well off, every building back home was made of simple stacked stone, or wood walls and thatched or shingled roofs. That was not the case here. Everything was an elegant stone structure, with decorative architectural features, and flat or red terra cotta roofs.

Their small leader in red broke his silence and said in a thick accent, "Non è molto più lontano."

Cristobal leaned into William and, just above a whisper, repeated what was said, but in English, "It's not much further."

"What isn't?"

20

"*Not far was right,*" thought William, as the group turned down a dark alleyway between two rows of three-story, peach-colored, stone buildings. There were no gas lanterns on poles lighting this passageway, just the ones carried by the two monks, several feet ahead of him. Which is why the appearance of stairs going down caught him a little off guard, and almost sent him tumbling, but he caught his first misstep and made it down the rest of the way without incident or embarrassment.

The stairs ended on another street much like the one they had left to go down the alley, but the lighthearted amazement William felt from his first up-close look at the city had been replaced by a familiar sense of dread, and a prickling along his neck. He knew what this was, without anyone saying a word. Knowing what he was here to do, William marched forward to take the lead and handle it, but he only made it two steps before Cristobal grabbed his arm and pulled him back to his place in line.

William looked at him with alarm, and was about to say something, when Cristobal said, "Just stand back and watch. You are not ready yet."

Those words stung a bit. This "gift" was not something William had just acquired. He had experience, a lot of it. If they didn't believe he was ready, then why did they bring him this far from home? His parents had instilled a sense of manners in their gruff and somewhat overconfident son, so he did as he was told. It would be rude to do anything other; he was their guest here.

Both William and Cristobal were cast into darkness as the two lantern-holding monks spread out to either side of their red-cloaked leader. Their arms panned the circles of light back and forth, in a slow progression. Every few swings of the light was followed by a step forward. Another few swings, and another step. This continued, but Cristobal didn't move forward with the lantern-swinging monks. He stayed put where he had stopped William from rushing forward, even as the light moved forward beyond them, he stayed, now bathed in darkness.

A low growl echoed down the narrow street. If that wasn't enough to send the hair on the back of William's neck standing on end, the fact that it came from behind them was. His fight or flight response was having an argument deep inside his mind. The urge to run was there, but why wasn't anyone else running, or even looking as if they were alarmed? Was he the only one who'd heard the growl?

He didn't give in to the urge to run, but did make an attempt to turn around and look for what was behind them.

"Don't," Cristobal warned at William's first attempt to turn. "Keep looking straight ahead, and when I tell you, clear the street."

William didn't ask for a clarification as the growl sounded again, this time closer, and this time it came with a vibration that shook the ground beneath his feet. Now he knew what Cristobal meant when he had said he wasn't ready yet. In all of his experiences, nothing had ever growled before, and definitely not shook the floor.

The growl echoed again, this time deeper, more primal, and it had company. It was not one growl, but several, contained in the same sound. A hot wind breathed on him from behind. Once again, his legs wanted to run, but he wouldn't let them. Not even when the hot breath moved back and forth across the back of his head, stirring several stray hairs. Chills coursed throughout his body. The world around him shook, causing his vision to vibrate. At first, he thought the shaking was caused by the great beast behind him moving back and forth, but his teeth chattered, revealing it was his body that shook. If William hadn't known what fear was before, he did now.

"William," said Cristobal. Each syllable strung out. There was a great pause that made William believe he was waiting on a reply. "NOW!"

Cristobal ran to the left, William's legs responded to the call and he ran to the right and pancaked himself up against the wall. The ground rumbled around them as the sound of some enormous beast snorting and running thundered past them. There was nothing there, not that William could see, but he could follow it by sound as it closed in on their red-cloaked leader. His eyes were trained on him, expecting him to get out of the way, but he didn't. The only move he made was to turn and throw off his hood, revealing the face of someone William would guess was eighty years old or more. That man's eyes squinted toward the beast, accentuating the age lines and wrinkles that dominated his face. He held up an object in his right hand and recited something, but William couldn't make out what the object was. It was too small, and the rumble beneath his feet shook his vision. The words he recited were muffled under the thundering steps of the beast, which showed no signs of slowing down as they rumbled toward and through the man, as he was thrown to the ground by a great impact.

It was at that one moment, for the briefest of seconds, that the beast came into view. It towered as tall as the three-story buildings that lined the street. Hooves the size of an entire horse, a body larger than William's farmhouse. Sitting on top of the shoulders was the head of a sneering and snorting man. The beast disappeared from sight again, but the sound of it coming to a stop further down the road and turning around was clear.

The two lantern-holding monks moved to help the man in red, but he waved them off as he stood and steadied himself in the center of the road. He turned toward the beast and began reciting something, this time louder. There was great passion in his voice as he spoke. From across the road, Cristobal translated for William

"Morax, the Great Earl, and President of Hell. You are in our world. We, under the power of Almighty God, have sole responsibility of the souls here, both living and dead. You are hereby ordered to leave this world, by the power of the Father, the Son, and the Holy Ghost."

The great beast charged again, but the man in red did not run. He steadied himself for this pass, once again holding a small object in his right hand, ready for the collision. The collision never came, not for the man in red. The beast veered off the road and gored one of the two lantern-holding monks, flinging him high into the air. The man in red leapt toward that side, not to aid the monk, but to make contact with the beast. When he did, it was visible again, as was the pain and agony it wailed about.

The man began reciting again, as the great beast was frozen in pain. The spot he touched with the object in his right hand seared its flesh.

Cristobal once again translated, this time missing parts, as much of what the man in red said was overpowered by the screams of the beast, "When Jesus had stepped out on land, there met him a man from the city who had demons. For a long time, he had worn no clothes, and he had not lived in a house but among the tombs..... He commanded the unclean spirit to come out of the man...." Cristobal stopped the translation once he recognized enough of it. "He is reciting verses from the book of Luke, chapter 8, verses 26, 27, and 28... he is continuing from the same book."

Cristobal was no longer translating, but reciting from memory, but William was no longer paying attention. The sight of the great beast engulfed in flames had taken that. It broke loose and barreled down the road, flames trailing behind it. The beast was no longer visible, but the flames that engulfed it were. It turned and charged the man again but, again, he didn't move. He waited, and as the great beast dipped its flaming head to deliver a blow to the man, he punched his right hand forward. A crack of thunder echoed through the clear sky. The beast didn't make it another inch. It dropped right there and moaned and wailed. Flames grew all over it. As the flames reached the head of a man on top of the great body, the wailing increased. A bluish smoke rose above the beast before it, the flames, and the smoke, disappeared into the darkness of the night.

The monk that had been thrown high in the air pushed himself up off the ground and retrieved his lantern before rejoining the other monk, behind the man in red. The three walked back in the direction they came from. When they reached

William, Cristobal was standing in the road. He bowed and said something too silently for William to hear. The man turned toward William and walked in his direction.

When the four men reached him, Cristobal introduced him, "William, I want you to meet Cardinal Depeche. He is our most senior paranormal advocate."

The man in red held out his hand and William took it, bowed, and said. "It is a pleasure to meet you." The bow was out of respect, and a necessity in order to reach the man's hand at his height. William was still not sure what he had just witnessed. The ghosts he had seen had never looked or reacted like that. Question after question spun around in his mind.

It was obvious the cardinal didn't understand English, as Cristobal had to translate the simple greeting to him. William knew Cristobal would undoubtedly be the source, or at least the bridge, to the answers he searched for.

"What was that?"

The old man's voice cracked, "Morax."

"Morax, the Earl of Hell. He commands a legion of demons that try to enslave those souls stuck in our world. Occasionally they also make promises to those in the living world, in exchange for their souls. The cardinal has been battling those demons for years," Cristobal explained.

"So, is it over?"

"For now. He will be back. Think about it like this. We won the skirmish."

At that moment the image of a great battle of fire, on some mountaintop high above the clouds, leapt into his mind. Both the cardinal and the demon were chained to their spot. Neither able to leave. Destined to fight for all eternity. "That reading didn't get rid of him?"

"Oh, no. The reading was just that, a reading," explained Cristobal.

It was at that moment that the cardinal stepped forward and reached up to place his left hand on William's chest. In broken English he said in a voice so weak it appeared painful to talk, "The words... they provide you focus. The power comes from here." He took his hand off his chest, and returned to the road. The two globes of light caused by the lanterns carried by the two monks soon joined him as they headed back down the road toward the dark stairs they had descended earlier. Cristobal fell in line behind them.

William joined the parade and asked Cristobal, "What is that in his right hand?"

"It's a relic. We will cover that in a few days. I understand one of Morax's legions has been visiting you."

21

The walk back to the Vatican provided Cristobal another opportunity to teach, and expose William to a world that was even more complicated then he knew. Ghosts, or spirits as his teachings called them, were one thing, they were simple. Before now, he though demons were just a creation of scripture and fear, to drive a message to the congregation. The possibility that the creatures Cristobal was describing existed in their world was hard to fathom. Creatures, here, that worked with and manipulated people to do their bidding, all for the promise of knowledge, profit, love, or any other desired possession or achievement.

Cristobal explained that William was being targeted by one such demon. Sister Francine had sensed it in his residence and reported back. She was also sensitive to such creatures, but was not able to see or interact with them. William explained how it first appeared to him, the night before he left Scotland, and then again, here. He told him of the promise it had made. The lifetime of perfect crops, and the perfect healthy family. He nodded as he listened and then asked, "Were you tempted?"

"No. The first time I thought it was just a weird dream."

That response made his teacher chuckle. He then asked, "How did you feel when it made you the promises?"

William had to think about that for a moment. Both times there was a sense of contentment and pride, as the images replayed in his head. It was the life he longed and hoped for. Seeing it there, in imagery that felt as real as life itself, made it all feel possible. The first time it happened, he wasn't aware of what it was, though, and dismissed it as a wild dream, fueled by all the time he spent over the previous few days thinking of his experiences with spirits, and Bishop Emmanuel's offer to train him. The lack of any additional details provided by the bishop about his offer left a lot of gaps for his brain to fill in. William had always had a vivid imagination as a child, something he once chalked up as the explanation for the spirits he saw. If you give that kind of imagination enough gaps to fill, of course it could create that type of imagery and sensations. Now that he knows what he knows, the encounter becomes a little more chilling. The second time, he was aware it was real, but didn't know it was a demon, or even that they were real, yet. Now that he does, it changes everything, and he confessed, "It frightens me now. Why is he coming to me?"

"We will get to that. First, were you frightened at the time?"

"No," said William.

"Why not?"

"I didn't think the first time was real."

Cristobal then asked, "And the second?"

"A little, when he first appeared."

"So, let me ask you this. A demon with the bottom half of an animal, the top half of a man, surrounded in fire, appeared to you, why were you not scared out of your skin?" Cristobal turned to look at his student and walked backwards down the road, his eyes trained on him for his response.

That was a question William hadn't considered, and it showed on his face, producing another chuckle from his teacher.

"You don't know, do you?", he asked.

William shook his head as he continued to think about it. *Why wasn't he?*

Cristobal explained, "Nobody does. The archives are full of interviews taken of those that have seen demons, and not a single person was afraid. There is a reason. Demons are master manipulators." Cristobal smacked his hands together to emphasize that point. He turned and walked side by side with William. The tone of his voice contained a weight that it hadn't had through any of their studies, nor at any time earlier in the night. "That is something you must remember. Spirits don't manipulate you. They are what you see, and that is it. Never trust what you feel, hear, or see when a demon is present." His left hand slapped William on the chest as they walked. "Tell me you understand that."

"I understand," William said. His voice trailed off a bit and had a question mark hanging at the end. That question mark was attached to the question he asked before Cristobal continued, "Then h...how do you deal with demons?"

"First, you will not deal with demons. That is a priest's job, but that is not to say you will never encounter them. You will, and when you do, you go with what we are teaching you. It will never fail you. The challenge is in forcing your mind to ignore everything else, to not be taken in by them. The images it showed you, how did you feel when it showed them to you?"

"Happy."

"I bet you felt the warm sun on your face. A beautiful scent of some type wafting through the air around you, and images of your loved ones all smiling. Does that about cover it?"

As they mounted the steps to the Vatican, William nodded his head to answer his teacher.

"Of course, and let me tell you why. If someone is afraid, they won't listen to what it has to say. They need you to feel comfortable, or whatever emotion they need you to feel, to believe what they are trying to tell you."

Cristobal stopped at the top of the steps and continued, his voice a little lighter, warmer, than before. The hard edges that were present in his words of the last few minutes were gone, as he recalled his story. "A demon once came to me. It basically promised me the world. I was dressed in a black robe, with a crucifix around my neck, standing at the rose-line of a great church. Thousands were seated in the pews, repeating the prayer that I was leading. There, seated among my flock, was my father." His voice grew quieter, and dripped with remorse, "He smiled at me." Cristobal paused and looked out at St. Peter's obelisk before he took a large prolonged breath. "The demon showed me two things that would never be. My father never approved of my choice to be here. I was to follow him as a blacksmith. He would never be sitting there smiling, and there would never be a flock for him to sit among."

William knew Cristobal was not a priest. Instead, he was some sort of scholar, but he assumed he was training and learning to become one, based on the respect and how involved he was with his own training. "I don't understand. Are you not training to be a priest?"

"Let's have a seat here on the steps. It is a nice night out and sometimes I come to sit here and gaze at the plaza and ponder. My form of meditation, I guess."

The two sat, and William understood why this was his favorite spot. The great plaza was illuminated by the flickering gas lanterns that lined its borders under a clear star-filled night sky was a sight that matched, if not exceeded, in its own way, a clear cool spring night in the highlands around his home. The glow of the lights danced on the mighty stone obelisk that appeared to be standing guard overall.

"William, I cannot be a priest. The church would never allow it. I was married and a father. I was also not a very religious man. My focus was my family." He emphasized the word family in a way that made his accent stronger than at any other time William had heard. "They were taken from me, by something I didn't understand. The search for the truth brought me here. You see, my son became ill and what I now know was a demon, approached my wife with the promise of saving our son, in return he wanted her to be his agent of mischief in our realm. First, she ransacked the community crops one night. Then she released all the livestock from our neighbor's farm. Each time, she was found where these things happened and gave the excuse that she saw what happened and was trying to stop it. She gave wild descriptions of those she had seen running through the crops, or opening the doors, but no one was ever found. One night she was caught standing with a flaming torch next to a large pile of harvested grain, at a farm on the other side of town. I wasn't even aware she had left the house. When the farmer approached her, she screamed something at him in a language he didn't know and tried to touch the torch to the grain. He tackled her to the ground and, with the help of others in the area, dragged her in to town, to the constable. What he told me later was that when he laid eyes on her, her own eyes had gone solid black, and a green liquid spewed from her mouth. Every word she screamed was not one they recognized. He ordered the mob to take her to the priest, and he came to get me. By the time I arrived, Father Perez was trying to cleanse her soul, but she was fighting back. She had bent over in half, backwards, and screamed. I still hear that scream in my nightmares. It was full of woe and pain. There were multiple voices in it, screaming, but I could hear hers. I knew she was in pain, and suffering. I begged the priest to stop it, and I meant to stop both what he was doing, and what was happening to her. He continued and her legs and arms contorted around at unnatural angles until the bones snapped. She fell, lifeless, to the ground at the feet of the priest, in the middle of the mob that had brought her. Her body was twisted in so many ways, I couldn't even recognize her. When I returned home, I went to hold our son. His body was cold, death had come for him." A single tear rolled down Cristobal's cheek as he took several broken breaths.

"In the following days, Father Perez explained this world to me, and it made sense. I, like you, can see and sense ghosts. Always could. When I thought back on the days before Josefina started acting peculiar, I remembered I had felt something, but had dismissed it. I was blinded from seeing the truth, because of my lack of knowledge of this side of it, and my feelings for her. When I realized that, I committed my life to finding the truth, and came here to learn and help others learn."

21

Ainslee laid across the bed, asleep, when William returned back to their residence. It looked like she had made an attempt to stay awake and wait for him, but had given in to the late hour and her exhaustion. Neither surprised William. It sounded like she had had a pretty exhilarating day walking around the city, he was sure that had exhausted her. His night out had exhausted him.

He studied the bed for a moment, and considered waking her up or trying to move her over himself, to make some room. She looked so serene and almost angel-like sleeping there, he couldn't bring himself to do either. Not to mention, William didn't see how he could move her without waking her, as he would have to pick her up. Instead, he surveyed the room for another area for him to lay down and get some sleep. There was a long chair, covered in what appeared to be red velvet, against the wall under the windows. It looked long enough for him to stretch out on. What he was questioning, though, was its width. If he laid on his side, it might work. If he rolled at all, he might wake up to a momentary weightless feeling before his body thudded to the floor. There was always the floor, but the tiles looked hard and cold. With all the blankets on the bed, under his wife, that was the least attractive of all options. So, the red chair it was.

To try to prevent rolling off the chair, William pressed his back against the back of the chair. That left only a few inches between his body and the edge of the seat. It was unsettling, but he was tired, and his eyelids were growing heavy. He wasn't in the mood to search for another location. His world was going dark as a delicate voice asked, "What are you doing? Get over here in bed."

With a groan, he lifted his head and opened his eyes. Ainslee was sitting up in bed and patting her hand on the side he slept on last night. His body was tired and settled, but the pain in his back from the lack of comfort in the chair spoke louder. She pulled the covers back to welcome him to bed, and wrapped her arms around him as he laid down. The warm breath he felt on his neck, now, was more welcome than what he felt earlier.

"Late studying?", she whispered into his ear.

William yawned and said through a second yawn, "Training. Forty foot demon that looked like a bull running up and down the road. An old five foot tall man took care of it."

He heard her say, "What?", but after that his eyelids won and the room went dark.

23

The morning began the same way the previous morning had. Sister Francine knocked with a polite rap on their door. William heard it, but waited a moment before he stirred. His body argued with his brain about whether it was ready to wake up. The wait must have been longer than he thought, or that Ainslee would tolerate, as she got out of bed and proceeded to the door. When she opened it, the sister brought in the tray like she had yesterday, but there was a difference. Her eyes weren't down at the floor like before. Instead, they were locked on the location William's demonic visitor stood.

As Ainslee inspected the tray, she saw William was now sitting up in the bed. "Good morning, sleepyhead," she said.

"Morning," he said, as he swung his legs out of the bed and headed to the bath.

"So, any more wild dreams last night?", she asked.

"No," he responded. He must have been exhausted, as he hadn't dreamt at all, or he didn't remember any that he had. It was a curious question, though. "What do you mean?"

"You mentioned a forty foot bull when I woke you to come to bed."

William remembered saying something about it before he fell asleep, but couldn't remember how much he had told her. It was easy for him to see how someone who wasn't there, and didn't have all the other experiences he has had throughout his life, could see that as a wild dream. There was a brief thought in his head to tell her it was just a dream and protect her from any fear that might come from knowing demons like that really existed, but that thought lasted only a few seconds. She was his wife, and part of his life now. There was no shielding her from that. "Oh, that wasn't a dream. That was real," he said.

A loud clang echoed from the other room.

"You okay?", he asked as he poked his head through the door into the main room. Being okay was a relative state. Ainslee was alive and uninjured, sitting there at the table, with a shattered coffee cup on the floor and her face frozen with her mouth and eyes wide open, but her world would never be the same.

"This is not a joke?", she asked. A hint of a quiver in her voice.

"This is not a joke. It was real. Cristobal took me out with a group of others to handle a demon called Morax," said William. He used a white linen to dry the water he had splashed on his face. He intended to take a bath, but needed to handle this first. Ignoring the cup on the floor for the moment, he spun the other chair around and sat on it backwards, facing her. His arms were crossed along the top of the chair. "Ainslee, I know this all seems and sounds crazy, but this is all true. It is not a trick. There is more to the world than you know. I have known since I was very young."

"But this?", she interrupted. "You see monsters, too?"

"Well, to be honest, from what I understand, you could see them, too."

That statement slapped her straight back in the chair. Her quick movement made the chair skip backwards. One of its legs hit a portion of the cup and sent it skidding across the floor like a demonic top.

"Cristobal told me demons appear to the living in many forms. Sometimes they appear like what we saw last night. Sometimes as a person. Every time it is for the same purpose, though. They want to manipulate you. They will make promises to make you follow them willingly, and if that doesn't work, they will possess your soul… or something like that. I am still learning."

Before William had headed inside the night before, Cristobal had explained that that was what had happened to his wife, and why she had been acting like she was. When the demon promised to save her son in return for her help, it had expected her to do exactly as it said. She had refused him that last night, so it took possession of her soul and used her body as a vessel to carry out his doings. The concept of possession was one William was not that familiar with, but he had heard Father Henry mention it during some of his sermons. The facts Cristobal shared scared him far more than any fire and brimstone point Father Henry had been attempting. Chills rolled through his body as he heard stories about people mumbling in multiple voices, in all different languages, at the same time, scratches that appeared in victims from inside out, body parts contorting to the point of snapping bones, and strange fluids dripping from every orifice in the body. As shocking as those stories were, the ones about the exorcisms Cristobal had witnessed made him want to swim all the way back to his simple life in St. Margaret's Hope, and never look back. William had to ask if he would be expected to do exorcisms. Cristobal reassured him that he wouldn't, or at least not that type. That in a way what he was doing with the spirits was an exorcism, but he wouldn't be asked to perform a real one, those were reserved for trained priests only.

"How many have you seen?"

"Two, counting last night," William answered, not pausing long enough for her to say anything else before he added, "but those are just the ones I know of. Like I said, they could take any form."

Several deep sighs escaped Ainslee as William got up and picked up the jagged pieces of the broken porcelain coffee cup. There was a small puddle of coffee just beneath the table. William was on his way to retrieve the same towel he had used to dry off his face when she sighed again and asked, "So I could be a demon?"

To say that was not the next comment he was expecting from his wife would be the understatement of the year. His back was to her when she said it, but he stopped and spun around. There she sat, on the chair, with a pool of brown coffee underneath her, and that same mischievous smile on her face that he saw that day in the woods when they were younger. "You aren't taking this seriously, are you?"

"I am," she said. A crooked smile adorned her face.

"You know they can kill you if they want," William said.

The cute crooked smile on Ainslee's face melted away into one of worry and dread. Her head dropped and she looked around the room. The air had been knocked out of her attempt to bring levity to their morning, and now she took two deep breaths to regain it.

"It's true, they can hurt or kill you, but you need to know, you are in no more danger from them now than you were before. The only difference is you know about it."

"Okay," she said, and then she said it again, "Okay." The second one softer than the first. Her eyes continued to wander around the room.

He attempted to reassure her, "Trust me, you are in no more danger than you were before. Don't worry about it."

She muttered "Okay" two more times.

He meant what he said. There was no point in her worrying about any of this. She was just as likely to encounter a demon before as she is now. In fact, the way he thought about it, she was better off knowing about them. She is now aware that they exist, and can be on the alert when one tries to manipulate her. William hoped in time she might look at it this way, along with the rest of what they would both learn about this new life. What he was sure of was, he didn't like seeing his wife so full of woe, especially not about something she had no control over.

She had just picked up the second coffee cup from the tray and started to lift it toward her mouth when William said, "I am serious. The ghosts I used to see around you back home were probably more dangerous."

The cup fell a few inches back to the table with a thud, and sloshed several drops of coffee onto the table. This time, the impact was not hard enough to crack or shatter the cup. Her face shot toward her husband, who was walking back with a towel in his hand and a wry smile on his face.

24

Wake up, head to the great library, read and study with Cristobal for 9 or 10 hours, and then return to his residence. That was the pattern William fell into for the next several days. Twice there was the extra treat of spending the last waning hours of sunlight walking around the surrounding streets and shops with his wife. They walked hand in hand through the streets and took in the sights. To two people from a sleepy farming and fishing town, Vatican City, and the surrounding city of Rome, was something neither had ever imagined existed. Their ever-present chaperone, Sister Francine, acted as a tour guide.

On the last day of their second week, she asked each of them if they wanted to walk a little further, there was something she thought they would really want to see. It was only late afternoon, with plenty of light left in the day, but that didn't factor into their decision much. The level of enthusiasm Sister Francine showed, the first sign of any emotion William had seen from her, was what convinced them. They walked southwest, away from the Vatican and out of Vatican City. She and Ainslee had gone as far as the Tiber River a few times, but never across. This time, the three of them walked across the river and continued down the home and shop-lined street.

People, friendly people, were all over the place, going about their business. Some alone, some in couples, and others as families with children. All exchanged a pleasant greeting with one another as they passed, even with Ainslee and William, people they had never met. They were strangers in a strange world, but they felt as welcome as if they had always been here. Soon they approached the Piazza del Campidoglio. Up the incline they walked and out into the Roman Forum. Sister Francine kept moving at a steady pace, but William and Ainslee fell behind. The sight of the old roman arches, pillars, and other ruins was distracting them from their walk. Their eyes gazed skyward, with their necks stretched to take in the view. They rejoined their guide at a magnificent stone archway that she told them was called the Arch of Titus.

William had seen old buildings before, even what some might call ruins, but nothing like this. Nothing over a thousand years old, and nothing so grand. "I want to thank you for taking us and showing us these wonders," he said to Sister Francine.

His statement elicited the giggle of a young girl from her. The reaction of the reserved nun confused him, or it did until she took both of them by the hand and walked them to the left, around the arch. Neither William nor Ainslee could open their eyes wide enough to take in what she had just shown them. It was enormous. The thought that man could build something so large was hard for either to fathom. Before they had a chance to ask what it was, she told them it was called "the Coliseum".

They made one trip around the structure as Sister Francine explained its history. The explanation, and the ensuing questions from both of her guests, continued all the way back to the Vatican, to their room, and even when she re-entered a short time later with their dinner. If they thought the world they'd known in their old life was small before, this made it seem minuscule.

After dinner, William had planned to take Ainslee out to the steps to enjoy the star-filled night Cristobal had shown him last week. It was a spot he had visited twice since, to ponder what he had learned, and his purpose there. Both were still hard for him to have a complete grasp of, but he was getting it. When he opened the door to walk her out, Cristobal was standing there, again with two monks holding lanterns, and another figure hidden in the darkness down the hall.

"Good evening, Ainslee. Do you mind if we borrow your husband tonight? We have some work to do."

"Of course not. More demon hunting?", she asked.

In the light cast by the lanterns, Ainslee could see the uncomfortable look upon the faces of the two monks. She looked at Cristobal, who looked at her with a stoic expression. In an attempt to recover, she asked, "Can I walk him out? We were on our way out to look at the stars."

Cristobal didn't say anything, he just smiled and bowed as she exited holding William's hand. Cardinal Depeche led the procession down the hallway, with the lantern-holding monks behind him. Ainslee, William, and Cristobal followed close behind. When they exited, the procession didn't stop. At the top of the stairs, Ainslee gave her husband a quick kiss and sat down. From there, she watched the group walk through and out of the plaza.

"So, I will ask the same question my wife did. Are we going after another demon?"

"Not tonight. Tonight, is an important night. You are to show us what you have learned," said Cristobal.

"So, I am facing it?", asked William. A sliver of trepidation set in at the thought of going to battle with a demon like he witnessed the other night.

Cristobal laughed and said, "No, not a demon. This is just a run-of-the-mill spirit." With a slap on his back he added, "You shouldn't have any trouble with this. Just go with what you have learned."

The group walked, and walked, and walked. William's legs were still feeling the long walk to and from the Coliseum. The extra miles were adding to the muscle soreness he felt, the cold brisk night wasn't helping things much either.

Deep into the night, along a tree-lined road that headed out of Rome, the group paused at a cross-street while Cardinal Depeche studied their surroundings. In front of them was a dense grove of trees. To either side were roads that lead out, away from the city, with sparse buildings positioned on what looked like farms under the pale light of the moon. The gas lamps that lit the city were non-existent here. Darkness enveloped everything that wasn't in the glow of the light from either of the two lanterns the monks carried, or the light from the full moon high above them. He acted like he was searching for a landmark to determine which road to take, but that wasn't it. William knew it, but he wasn't sure who else did either. The cold sweat and row of pin pricks on the back of his neck were his tell-tale signs that their destination was close.

A hand emerged from under the red robe and waved for someone to walk forward. Neither of the two monks moved, but Cristobal took a single step forward and nudged William to move, as well. They joined Cardinal Depeche at the front, Cristobal stayed just a step or two behind, where he could serve as a translator. Fear of what was out there didn't consume William, nor should it. He couldn't remember the last time a spirit had made him afraid, but this was different. Others were watching, judging, what he did. That terrified him.

"William, He wants you to take the lead," said Cristobal.

"And do what?" William looked back at Cristobal with his eyebrows raised.

He waved William forward and said, "Show us what you've learned." Cardinal Depeche said a phrase in Italian. Cristobal translated, "Save the Spirit." He waved him forward again, and said, "Go on."

William took a few tentative steps off the road; in the direction he knew the spirit was. The chills that radiated down his body told him it wasn't too far away, and he was right. The dense forest of majestic Mediterranean cypress trees blocked the light of the full moon, casting the group in an eerie cocoon of darkness. Overhead, the treetops swayed, and the leaves chattered in the breeze, robbing them of any sense of calm and silence. The forest floor was barren, robbed of life-giving sunlight. This allowed William to move among the trunks unimpeded. The party that followed close behind weren't impeded either. They stayed just a few feet behind him at all times. William could feel the four sets of eyes on him from behind, and the spirit that grew closer ahead of him, with every step.

The towering cypress trees gave way to a grove of gnarled cork oak. The moonlight played in between their large, twisted, and distorted branches. The movement of the branches in the wind brought them and their shadows to life.

Like a hideous beast living in hiding behind the cypress. William couldn't take his eyes off the shadows. The chill deepened inside him and a great weight landed on his shoulders. With each step, it became heavier and heavier. He felt his back and legs bending under the great force but, like Atlas, he straightened and pushed that force up, and steadied himself to support the weight of the world on his frame.

In the distance, among the old cork oaks, the flickering form came into view. The form was that of an older man. His black coat, and white shirt with ruffled cuffs, looked pristine. If it weren't for the blue flickering of the form, and the hollow eyes, one might think this were an Italian gentleman, out for an evening stroll in the light of a full moon. Make that an evening float. His legs moved as if he were walking, but they were three feet above the ground as he circled around and around the same tree.

William approached him, but he paid no attention as he circled around the tree again. Over the last three days Cristobal and William had talked about this very moment a great many times. Not the test, or whatever this was, but the moment when he would stand in front of a spirit and try to help it find its way. Based on his teachings, William had thought there would be more to it. With all the focus on why spirits remain connected to the world of the living, he expected to have to resolve or remove that connection to free them, but that was not the case. Cristobal had said they were not connected, so much as stuck, and needed encouragement to move on. During their lessons William was surprised, and disappointed, to learn there was not just one way to provide that. In fact, there are many ways, the challenge was knowing what was needed for each situation. He reminded William, no one said this would be easy, in fact, it was hard, but he was chosen to have this gift for a reason. William found it interesting no one had told him what that reason was.

Holding his hand up toward the spirit. Not being the most religious of people, William didn't have any bible verses memorized. William began, "O' heavenly Father. I request you give me the power to help this soul."

The spirit passed right by William and kept going around the tree.

He moved closer and began again, "God Almighty, help this lost soul find his way home."

Again, the spirit didn't look at him, didn't pause, and didn't stop.

Feeling a slight flush in his face more than the chills, he moved closer and put his hand up again. A strong and determined voice behind him shouted "Fermare! Fermare! Fermare!" before William was able to utter another world.

He looked around and saw Cardinal Depeche marching forward. The red-cloaked man passed by him and proceeded to a spot a few feet closer to the spirit than William had stood. He stood there with his hands crossed in front of him at his waist. No hand held up toward the spirit, or anything. In an even tone of voice, he said, "Devo confrontarti con una giornata estiva? Sei più adorabile e più temperato. I venti forti agitano le care gemme di maggio, E la locazione estiva ha un appuntamento troppo breve."

The spirit stopped in its tracks and hovered there. It turned ever so slightly in the direction of the cardinal. Without another word, the cardinal turned and walked back toward William. He stopped and tapped him dead center in his chest and said, "From here." He tapped William on the chest a final time before he walked back to join the others.

"What did he say?", asked William as he turned back toward Cristobal for guidance.

"From here."

"No. Not that. What did he say to make it stop?"

Cristobal chuckled before responding, " Shall I compare thee to a summer's day? Thou art more lovely and more temperate. Rough winds do shake the darling buds of May. And summer's lease hath all too short a date. It's Shakespeare's Sonnet #18."

If the feeling of embarrassment wasn't enough before, it was boiling over now. The cardinal had upstaged him by reading a poem. William knew it could have been worse, he could have just read his favorite recipe.

"William. Remember what we have talked about. Remember the other night in the road, and what we talked about then."

He turned back to the spirit and taking Cristobal's reminder to heart, he focused. Not on the words he would say, not on any thought of projecting something through his hand, but on believing. Believing he was there to help this soul. Believing this soul was being tormented here, and need to be freed to ascend to heaven. Believing he would be easing someone's pain. As he thought about this and reaffirmed his belief, the ground around him began to glow. The glow was not large, just a small circle, as if William were holding a single candle. At the same time, the spirit moved closer to him and stopped in front of him.

The more he believed, the wider the glow grew along the ground around him. What happened next was beyond anything William could have expected. The glow contacted the ground below the spirit, and the blue flickering haze stopped and disappeared. The spirit was still there, but it was different now. It was alive. The blue haze disappeared, leaving a person of pink and white flesh. There was even a sparkle in his brown eyes, and the light breeze blew his mane of jet-black hair. It still hovered above the ground, but the eerie figure was almost, more than almost, human.

A peaceful calm inside William accompanied the transformation. The chill he felt when spirits were around was gone and replaced by a warm feeling. A feeling of purpose. Without even thinking about it, William whispered, "You are free."

The spirit nodded and faded away into nothingness. William turned back to the group, with the hope of seeing approving and pleased looks. The ones he saw were not ones he would describe like that, though. Shocked looks were plastered across both the cardinal and Cristobal's faces. Even the two monks had broken decorum and pushed their hoods off of their heads, and shared the same expression.

25

The party returned back to the Vatican in silence. William's legs weren't silent. The euphoria he felt from his moment of success was overshadowed by the protest of his legs. Their trek to the Coliseum earlier in the day, and now this adventure at night, had taken their toll. Even the short but wide steps up the front of the Vatican were a strain for his tired muscles. He looked forward to lying down in his bed and getting some rest as they crossed through the golden doors, but that rest would have to wait. The glowing orbs of light produced by the two lanterns did not follow the sparsely lit hallway toward his residence. They didn't even turn in that direction. Instead, they continued to walk forward, through the great entryway and into a different room. William and Cristobal followed.

The sight of Cardinal Depeche descending down some stairs produced a groan inside William's mind, but he made sure to not vocalize it. He followed, legs aching with each step, down the spiral staircase. The flicker of the lanterns played against the stone block walls of the narrow passage. A cool, damp, musky air greeted the group at the bottom. The finished walls, paintings, and marble floors that decorated the floors above were nonexistent here. Replaced by stacked stone block walls and simple cobblestoned floors. Some had a green and grey moss growing on them. The passageway was as narrow as the stairs, with a few plain wooden doors with large black hinges, much like William was used to back home.

Cristobal pressed himself against the walls and slid past the two monks. There was an eagerness and urgency to his movements, and a sternness to his expression. Once he reached the front, William heard the murmur of a conversation between Cristobal and Cardinal Depeche. He couldn't hear any specific words, not that it would matter, as it was probably in Italian, but could tell one side of it was heated. The hand gestures made by Cristobal were rather animated, as was the rest of his body movements as he talked. In contrast, the Cardinal stayed a picture of calm and tranquility, as he continued to walk down the passage.

The discussion continued as the group stopped in front of one of the plain wooden doors. Cardinal Depeche turned to a large iron handle, and the clunk of the lock opening echoed up and down the passageway like a rumble of thunder. He entered the room, as did Cristobal, but both monks did not. They stepped to either side of the door, placed the lanterns they held down on the cobblestone floor, knelt, and bowed their heads. Each began praying, over and over. William watched the doorway for either Cristobal or the cardinal to return, but they didn't. Only a flicker from the lighting of a lantern emerged through the door.

"William!", commanded Cristobal from inside the room.

William entered. It was a small room, constructed with the same block walls and cobblestone floors as the passage. Wooden tables lined each wall. A cloth covered each of the tables, but they didn't lay flat. There were objects underneath the cloths. It was obvious to William the objects were placed with care, the same amount of empty space between each. It was as if they were placed on display, but that didn't make a lot of sense to him, since they were hidden from sight.

Cardinal Depeche and Cristobal were still amidst their conversation at the table opposite of where William stood. From there he could tell the cloth had been raised, exposing one of the items, but his view of the item was obscured by the cardinal. He wasn't sure if it was something that was said, or the item itself, that caused the most vehement protest by Cristobal yet. Whatever was the cause, the Cardinal put it down with a single hand gesture, and a look William could not see.

He turned to William and motioned for him to join them at the table. When he walked forward, he saw an item that was uncovered on the table. It was a simple wooden cross. It looked old, and was chipped on some of the edges. The cardinal took William's right hand and pressed it down on the cross. He was firm with the pressure as he pushed his hand on to the object.

"William," Cristobal said, then he paused. His eyes glanced around the room and he swallowed hard. An awkward silence filled the room. The cardinal nodded to him, but Cristobal didn't say or do anything. His discomfort with what he was being asked to do was almost palpable. The cardinal again gestured toward him, this time with a bit of emotion.

"Fine. Fine," he said and then continued, "William, your hand is on a cross made from wood taken from the cross Christ himself was crucified on. It was retrieved and returned to Pope Urban II during the first crusade. The wood, stained with the blood of our lord and savior, was carefully pulled apart and then crafted into a series of crosses. One is in the possession of our Holy Father, and one is in possession of the priest assigned to each of the known spiritual centers around the world. It is believed to help focus your abilities when dealing with both spirits and demons of the highest abilities. Cardinal Depeche is assigning you this cross to assist you in your duties. What you showed tonight is an ability beyond what we expected. We thought you were what we call a sensitive. One that can sense and interact with the spiritual world, but you go far beyond that. You are what we call a keeper, the first non-priest keeper we have ever met. A keeper is responsible for keeping the world of the living safe from spirits and demons."

William's mind stopped hearing what was said after he was told his hand was pressed against a cross made of wood from the crucifix of Christ. When that realization hit him, he attempted to pull his hand back, but the cardinal's grip was firm and steadfast. He didn't feel worthy of touching it. This was one of the most religious items in the world, and he was just a simple farmer. Then the irony hit him. Jesus Christ is called a prince, but in his mortal life he was not. He was a common carpenter, who made tools for simple farmers, much like William.

Cardinal Depeche released William's hand, which recoiled a few inches above the cross. He motioned with his hands for him to pick up the cross. William's hands shook as he did so. At first glance, it was a simple aged wooden cross, but at a closer look it was something more, much more. It was constructed of four distinct pieces, morticed together in the center. The chips he saw on the edges were not from damage, but were the imperfect cuts of the axes and blades that had shaped the original cross Christ was mounted on. Each of the four pieces of wood used contained spots that were darker than the others, it wasn't just darker aged wood, they were stained with something, something red, the blood of Christ.

"William," Cristobal pleaded as he walked closer to him. "You can refuse this assignment. When we talked about demons, I told you only priests challenge them. It is extremely dangerous, and should only be attempted by the most faithful and pious among us. I must admit to you openly, I am against this. I agree you have a gift, a great gift, and you can use it to be a sensitive, but a priest who is a keeper should be assigned with you. That is how it is done."

A hand emerged from under the red robe of the cardinal and he motioned for William to bend down to him. Instead, William knelt down on one knee, bringing him face to face with him. The weathered and wrinkled face of the cardinal took on a fatherly look. His eyes kind and calm as he said in English, through his thick accent, "You are the one. The one who can do this." Before William could respond or ask a question, the cardinal leaned forward and kissed him on the forehead, and then used the thumb of his left hand to draw a cross on the spot he kissed. Then the man walked out of the room, leaving him standing there with Cristobal.

"And if I choose to do this?", asked William, not that he had chosen one way or the other. He didn't know how to decide on something like this. It was not your typical, 'What do you want for breakfast?' or 'In which plot does you plant what this season'? Which were some of the more difficult decisions he had made so far in his life. The only one more difficult had been to follow Bishop Emmanuel this far. He did so because he wanted an adventure, and an adventure he had found.

"Then I will train you, but you will have to accept a life more challenging than you could ever imagine."

26

"That is what?", exclaimed Ainslee as she retreated back to their bed. On their table sat a simple wooden cross, alongside a brown leather-bound book. When he explained what the cross was, what color existed in her fair complexion drained out of her face, her hand sprang up to her mouth, and she stumbled backwards to the bed.

"The wood is from the cross Christ was crucified on," explained William, for a second time now.

"Why… Why? Did they give that to you?", she asked. Her speech stuttering every syllable as she fanned herself with both hands.

William explained to her what Cristobal and Cardinal Depeche told him. He knew she would have questions when he completed the recollection. To try to head off any questions of the "This is so hard to believe" variety, he retold her about the night he watched Cardinal Depeche battle Morax. On the way back to his residence, Cristobal had told him that the relic the cardinal possessed was a piece of cloth from the burial shroud that was draped over Christ in his tomb. It was only a few inches square, but its ability to focus the cardinal's capability was not limited by its physical size. Something William could attest to from what he saw that night. The creature they'd fought was over forty feet tall, yet that small piece of cloth had brought it howling to its knees.

"Come on over. This and the leather-bound book will be part of our lives. Don't be scared of them." William stood over the table and motioned for her to join him again, but she was hesitant. He motioned again and she got up off the bed and took several tentative steps with her lower body, toward the table. Ainslee's upper body seemed less eager to approach the objects. It leaned back about as far as it could, without causing her body to fall backward. Balls of fabric from the skirt of her simple light blue dress her and Sister Francine had bought together the day earlier were kneaded by each fist.

At the table, William picked up the cross and attempted to hand it to her, but she again recoiled. He took her hand, forcing it to release the fabric of her skirt, and placed it on it. He knew darn well what she was going through. It was the same thoughts he had experienced mere moments ago. His hand was forced on the cross, like hers was now. Thoughts flooded into his head of not being worthy of touching something so sacred. Expectations of some great feeling that would pulse through him, or an explosion of light that would radiate from it as if it were the sun high in the sky on a summer day, with a chorus of angels singing in unison but only in his head. What his hand felt was a simple wooden cross. It was nothing to be scared of. That is what he kept telling himself. The object was just an object, but its sanctified beginnings reflected the responsibility that was bestowed upon him, and that was what he was afraid of.

The resistance in her arm dissipated the longer he held her hand on it. Before long he was able to remove his hand and, she kept her hand on it before eventually picking it up and studying it. The delicate fingers of her right hand held it firmly, while the fingers of her left hand caressed every edge and surface. The fear that was on her face before had been replaced with the curiosity of a young child exploring the outside world for the first time.

"What are these darker stains?", she asked, as she attempted to smell the odor of the wood.

William considered telling her what it was right away, but his mind played the image of her dropping the cross, sending it crashing to the floor in a heap of splinters. To avoid such a disaster, he suggested, "Why don't you put it on the table before I tell you?"

The curiosity that was there was replaced by a set of perplexed eyebrows. He knew the pouty look would follow, it was predictable, and how she got her way so often.

"Ainslee, put it down and I will tell you," William suggested again. This time his voice held an air of seriousness.

The suggestion worked this time. She placed the cross down on the table, next to a simple brown leather-bound book. William also managed to head off the pouty look, but the one that replaced it bothered him more so. The dropped shoulders and eyes reminded him of how she would look when her father scolded her. A look he never wanted to be the cause of, and from this day forward he swore to himself he would never do so again. The only way he could correct it was to answer her question, so she could realize, herself, why he wanted her to put it down first.

"Those stains are the blood of Christ."

He was right to have had her put it down before he told her. Upon hearing what it was, she fell to the floor with a thud. She landed on her butt and sat there, with both arms outstretched. A look that was a mixture of fear and surprise filled her eyes as they scanned back and forth, from one hand to the other. Her lips mumbled, "I touched the blood of Christ."

"Yes, you did," William said as he extended a hand toward his bride, to help her up. No attempt was made on her end to take his hand, so William reached down and attempted to grab her right hand. It moved away from him before he was able to grasp it. The hand was spread wide, and held up toward her husband, to show him what was on it. In truth, there wasn't anything on it. It was as clean as could be. The stains were part of the wood, and didn't bleed off on your skin.

"There is nothing on your hand. Come on. Let's get you up," he said as he made another attempt to grab her hand. She avoided him again, but this time her husband outsmarted her and grabbed her left hand, pulling her to her feet. Once up, he pulled her close, but her eyes stayed on the table.

"What is the book? Is that his journal?"

"No, it's my journal, and it's empty."

27

After the excitement of the new members of their family, both William and Ainslee gave in to the late hour of the night and fell asleep. Every night William fell asleep gazing at his wife, but not tonight. His eyes stared across the room at an object that sat flat on the table. Inside, he couldn't shake the expectations his mind imagined. So much mysticism surrounded what it was, how could it just sit there and not emit a glow in the darkness of the room? Shouldn't it hum, make some noise, or levitate above the ground like Jesus when he walked on the water in the book of Matthew? The fact was, it didn't. It gave no sign outwardly that it was special, but then again, neither did William. What was there was a strong belief. Something he reminded himself of as his vision narrowed and his nose smelled the last wafts of the remnants of the jasmine bath Ainslee had taken just before bed. What William didn't know was, his wife, who usually looked at him until she fell asleep, was looking across the room at the same object he was, with very similar thoughts, until exhaustion took her under.

The thoughts that had consumed William's mind before he fell asleep dominated his dreams. Fields of flowers, under beautiful blue skies, that started light blue at the horizon and grew to a deep royal blue the higher you went up, provided him and Ainslee a paradise to explore. The warm glow of sunlight basked him in life-giving energy, while a babbling brook serenaded them in a relaxing chorus. Firmly in his hand was the cross. As he pointed it in a direction, it projected a white light so bright it was almost blinding. It did not burn or destroy anything it came in contact with, it purified them. The flowers were brighter and more fragrant. The sky more vivid.

They walked through the meadows toward the brook, the scent of each flower they passed was overwhelming to the senses. A horde of butterflies scattered as they walked through a grouping of white lilies that stood knee-high to each of them. On the other side of the lilies, they found themselves standing on the bank of the brook. It appeared shallow, very shallow. River rocks below the surface created a washboard current for as far as William could see. He took a step in, leading Ainslee with him. It was not cool as he expected. It was something he had never experienced before, it was warm. He found himself standing ankle-deep in warm water, and it was getting warmer, and deeper.

It reached his knees without him having to move an inch. Overhead, the skies clouded up as if a storm front was approaching, but instead of just turning dark, the sky had a red haze to it. "Red sky at night, sailor's delight, but red sky at morn, sailor's be warned," was a saying he remembered his uncle saying. The problem was, he didn't know whether this was morning or night. He didn't have time to worry about that now. The water reached his waist, and the temperature had become uncomfortable, sending his upper body into a flop sweat. Right before his eyes, the lilies that bordered the brook turned to dried stems and wilting petals. As he looked around at the changing scene around him, he realized Ainslee was gone. The last time he saw her was before the water had started to rise. Afraid she had disappeared below the water, he tried to turn and search for her, but his feet were locked in place in the creek bed.

The water bubbled around his body, and his skin sizzled as the water surrounded his chest. Breathing became labored and painful. His skin was scalded, and yellow pus-filled blisters covered every inch of its surface. The urge to scream was primal, instinctual, but he couldn't. Water surrounded William's throat, and the steam that rose from its surface robbed him of the necessary oxygen. All around him the sky began to bleed, from just above the horizon, down to the ground. First slight drips, and then gushing flows. When it reached the ground, it continued and raced toward him like a great tsunami of red. A ring of fire exploded in the sky over his head. Waves of fire rolled across the sky toward the blood running down the horizon. Where they met, the flame congealed into a red fluid and joined the flood of red blood rushing across the landscape. The top of his head baked, and his body boiled. Pain soared through his being, forcing his eyes closed.

When William next opened them, he was back in his residence, lying in their bed, but all was not well. The full-on body sweat might have hinted at a terrifying nightmare, but that didn't explain the river of flame that surged across the ceiling, the fingers of which turned into blood when it hit the wall. Red liquid flowed down the surface of every wall, into a foot or more of the substance already pooled on the floor. Beside him, his wife laid silently, but her body cooked from the outside in. Her flesh grew taut and cracked, like the skin of a large sow on a flame pit. Singe marks covered her face. She did not scream. She did not move.

William tried to jump up and carry her to safety, but the bed linens trapped him where he was. Another pull, and he was jerked back the few inches they gave. An attempt to scream was met with nothing but silence escaping his open mouth, as a great force pulled him down deeper into the bed.

"Now, now, William. There is no reason to scream. You knew this was coming." The voice echoed from everywhere, and nowhere, all at once. It rattled the room and sent ripples running up the waterfall of blood flowing down the walls. Above him, the color of the flames changed from orange to yellow, and then the edges of a spot of white flame came into his view. It was a small circular spot, but grew by the moment. At the center sat a dark dot that grew in size within the circle of white flames. The dot took on a shape, an oval. No that wasn't it. It was a head, and not just any head. A head with a face, with horns sticking out from each side.

The head descended to just above William, along with its upper body, which hung out of the circle of white flames. "Hi, William," said the face.

William knew this head, this face, and the voice that echoed. This would now be its third visit.

"Leave her alone," William croaked. He intended to yell that demand, but the great force pressing him into the bed restricted his lungs' ability to take the gulp of air he needed.

"I gave you a choice. You should have taken it. It was a real peachy life."

It leaned over the top of Ainslee and grinned an evil grin. William tried again to break free, but the force pressed him back into the impression his body had made in the mattress. He struggled as a long and jagged claw descended past his head. A muscular arm of molten material connected it to the creature's right shoulder socket. The creature turned to look at William, with the same evil grin, as the claw drew a line down Ainslee. A white haze shined up from the line as her skin peeled back to either side. It turned its attentions back to her as it started to dissect her inch by inch.

William jerked his body wildly to either side, in a move that resembled a turtle having a convulsion while it tried to flip itself back over on its feet. His arms flung wildly at first, gaining just inches, but worked their way free, while the creature's attentions were on his wife. Faced with the choice of reaching over and trying to stop whatever was happening to her, if he even knew how, and going for help, in a sheer moment of panic he chose the latter. He was sure either Cristobal or the cardinal would know what to do. With his arms free, he pried himself off the bed and fell to the floor. The sound of his body slamming on the solid floor got both his and the creature's attention. A question rushed into William's head. *"How do you slam in several feet of pooled blood?"*

A wiggle of his toes confirmed the answer. There was no blood. None of this was real. He hoped what was happening to Ainslee wasn't either. There was only one way to find out, he had to stop and dismiss this creature, who Cristobal had told him was one of Morax's agents. William stood up, confident and strong. His body screamed in defiance and his eyes searched for the table. The creature was alarmed by these events, and thrust its hand into what was left of Ainslee's body. It cackled a thunderous laugh that pushed William back to the ground but, once again, he didn't splash down, he crashed on the floor. Even falling backward to the floor, his eyes stayed fixed on the table.

The creature spun around and followed William's focus to the table. It hovered above the bed, frozen in place. From his vantage point, William thought he could detect a slight wrinkle of its brow, and downturn of its lips. It was fear, and he had every intention of using it.

William leapt to his feet and ran to the table. The creature was transfixed by the objects laying on the table, and never saw him approach. It never saw his hand reach into its view and grab the cross. It never saw him thrust the cross up into it. His heart was full of the belief that the object, and his faith, would send that creature back where it belonged.

In that instant, the sea of blood on the floor disappeared, and the fire above his head receded back into the circle of white flame. The creature pulled back up into the circle and, in a flash, both were gone, leaving the room bathed in the darkness of night. The only sounds were the crickets outside the open window, and the deep and restful breathing of his asleep in bed.

He watched her laying there, peaceful, as his mind tried to remove the images it had been presented just moments ago. The thought that what he had seen could have happened, shook him to his core. His thoughts went back to Cristobal's story about his own wife. Over and over, William wondered if that could happen to Ainslee. His decision to do this was putting her in harm's way, and he felt both guilty and responsible for that. She would be safe, back at home in St. Margaret's Hope, if he hadn't brought her here with him, and exposed her to these dangers. The truth was, he wasn't aware of these dangers then, but that counterargument did little to quell the fear he felt, or the gnawing feeling in his gut that he needed to send her home.

A scream, followed by a second, and more harrowing one, interrupted the internal debate waging inside William. There was no question whether this scream was real or not. The second scream woke Ainslee up with a startle. "What was…" Her question was cut off by a third scream, and the sound of other voices yelling. Neither of them could understand what was being said, but the tone contained fear and violence. Before the fourth scream had completed its course down the hall, William had raced out the door, cross in hand, his footfalls echoing in the cavernous hallway along with the others that also raced toward the scream.

28

Another scream ravaged the darkness of the hallway. This scream was different than the others. It was most definitely not human. The sound was full of pain, sorrow, remorse, and hatred: pure unrestrained hatred. Following that were the exclamations of several men, in Italian, but there was one word William could recognize as clear as anything, "No!"

Behind William, other footsteps raced down the hall. He didn't know who it was, nor was he interested in turning around to find out. The source of the screams were his focus. If others were on their way to help, all the better, but not his concern. The darkness in the hallway cast a layer of confusion on where the screams were coming from. All William could do was follow his ears, but the cavernous size of the hallway masked the source, in the endless echoes of screams and cries.

A cloud of uncertainty overcame William at an intersection of corridors. Standing in the middle, the echoes seemed to emerge out of the darkness of each. The footsteps that had trailed him down the hallway caught up as he danced between the decision of continuing straight, or taking either the hallway to the right or the one to the left.

"Which way?" asked Cristobal, who had joined William in the center, just as confused as to where the source of the screams was coming from.

"I don't know."

Both men took steps down each hallway, listening, but the echoes continued to play tricks with them. As the seconds ticked by, William felt the muscles in his body tense up. He stretched his fingers and then clenched them in a fist, before stretching them again. His weight bounced back and forth on his legs as he moved to check each of the hallways for the source of the sound. Behind him, Cristobal was checking the opposite side for the source, and let out a guttural groan of frustration. Then it hit William.

He took one step further down the hall, and on the back of his neck there was a single cold prick of a pin. Another step, and several more prickles were followed by an outbreak of gooseflesh across his neck and down his back. With one more step, he knew for sure, especially when the familiar suffocating weight settled upon his shoulders.

"This way," he said, adding to the echo, and then sprinted down the hallway. Another set of footsteps followed close behind him. They were both still searching in the darkness for a destination they did not know, nor did they know what they would find once they'd reached the source of the screams. The weight pressing down on William, and the cold he felt in his core, told him they were getting close, but he neither needed nor wanted those signs. The bloodcurdling screams and cries were getting louder, and they were also getting clearer. He and Cristobal could now hear two distinct voices behind the screams. One was not human, something they already knew. The other was a voice they both recognized, Cardinal Depeche.

Cristobal sprinted past William, taking the lead down the hall and around the corner. Not knowing where the cardinal's room was, William was content with following. When he rounded the corner, there was no question of which door it was. Both men stumbled to a stop in front of the third door down on the right. An eerie red hue glowed through the gaps along all four sides of the door, and a scorching heat radiated outward.

"Fire!" screamed Cristobal, as he reached for the door.

Before his hand touched the handle, William grabbed his wrist and yanked it back. Cristobal responded with a look of shock, but William maintained his grip on his wrist and shook his head. The screams continued behind the door. The red glow intensified along with the inhuman scream full of hatred. Cristobal's head turned slowly from William's face toward the door. His eyes opened wide as the realization of what was behind the door hit him. William had known for several moments now.

Cristobal backed away from the door. His body trembled in fear. He was not alone. William felt it, too, along with all the other sensations that used to drive great fear in him, now he was used to them. The fear was palpable, and every scream allowed more of it to ooze out the door and attach itself to them, like a great parasite that fed on them and grew deep inside, until it was able to control them. Unless they took control of it first. That is what William did. He stepped forward and, with the crucifix clearly in his left hand, he reached with his right and opened the door.

A flash of flame threw both men against the opposite wall. The impact took William's breath away for a second. He rolled back over and looked toward the doorway. The large wooden door was now lying on the floor, several feet from William and Cristobal. Through the doorway, he could see the room engulfed in flames. They roiled up each wall, and across the ceiling. The screams continued, and sent ripples across the sea of fire.

William pushed himself back to his feet and walked through the doorway with his left hand out in front of him, to ensure the crucifix entered the room first. The heat was overwhelming, but he still felt the cold pinpricks from the back of his neck to the bottom of his spine. He looked around and saw no sign of the cardinal, but his scream continued, as did the other scream, the non-human scream.

The floor was clear of any fire, which allowed William to move inward freely. His eyes traced the fire from the bottom of the wall, up to the ceiling, and across. When he reached the image, he knelt down. Cardinal Depeche's body was suspended from the ceiling. Circulating bindings of flame were wrapped around both his arms and legs, as well as his neck. His screams were cut short by fingers of flame that reached over and shoved themselves through his open mouth, stifling the sound. When the fingers retreated from his mouth, his scream started again, and was allowed to persist for only a few moments. The fingers of flame cut them off again.

Movement to the right caught William's eye. He turned and saw one of the two monks, restrained by similar bindings of flame. His skin smoldered where it contacted the bindings, and produced billows of dark grey smoke. A quick search around the room found the second monk, restrained like the others, but the heat of his bindings had already reduced his body to a smoking skeleton.

Neither of the images frightened William as much as the deep snort that rumbled above his head. Full body trembles shook his vision as he looked up. A large hump circled the cardinal in the flames, as the whole mass pulsated up and down like a heartbeat. Large puffs of smoke bubbled from the hump with each snort.

He looked back. Cristobal stood in the open doorway, and crossed himself. Sheer terror dripped from his body. His body fell rigidly to his knees, like a plank of wood falling on one end. With his hands clasped in front of him, he started a prayer, but did not bow his head. With his eyes bulged out of their sockets, and his mouth gasping for air, he kept his head up, eyes fixated on the scene from the bowels of hell itself that was before him. His lips moved, but no sound escaped. The bulge slowed its rotation around the cardinal, but the snorts continued, more frequent than before, and more visceral.

It stopped, and the puffs of smoke spiraled toward the kneeling Cristobal. The fingers of flame flooded into the cardinal and silenced the start of another scream, sending the room into an eerie silence. Only snorts, and the low rumble of raspy breaths, interrupted the silence.

In and out.

In and out.

The breathing continued, slow and hollow, like wind flowing in and out of a large empty cave. William noticed with each breath in, the flames pulsated up, and then down with the exhale. William wondered if they were inside the beast, itself.

He wasn't given a lot of time to consider that, before horns broke through the bulge and the head of a bull charged at Cristobal. His friend was frozen in place, either by fear or by the power this demon had over him. William leapt in between the kneeling scholar and the head of the bull, a head he had seen before. With his left hand, he thrust the crucifix forward. The movements were strong and firm. As was his voice as he proclaimed, "Morax, you will stop."

The demon recoiled backward, and snorted a fire and smoke-filled breath that tousled William's hair, but he didn't move. Instead, he took a step forward and closed the gap. Morax roared with the voices of a thousand dead souls, but William didn't retreat, he took another step forward. Each step filled his heart with more belief, and a glow of white light began to radiate out along the floor. Morax dipped his head to look at the light and shook his head back and forth with an uncontrolled shudder. From inside the fire, ran the demon that had visited William three times over the past few weeks. It was smaller than he remembered as it ran along the neck of the great beast, but grew with each step. It leapt from its head through the air, toward William, but his resolve was solid, like a brick foundation a great house was built on. Cristobal and Cardinal Depeche had laid that foundation, and then given him the training, and the tools, to build upon it. This was a great test, like the arrival of the first hard storm a building will face. If built with the right tools and materials, he, like the building, would not crumble under the attack.

William held his position at first, and then stepped to the side and slashed at the demon with the cross. He commanded in a voice as strong as his body, "In the name of God, I condemn you." The force of the impact was not great, but the demon was sent across the room with a thud. Its body flailed on the floor, as it whined in a high pitched hum that pierced William's hearing. Its great claws dug at the floor to try to drag itself away from the fire. A hint of blue smoke rose above it. At first it was a light haze of blue, but grew denser, into a dark grey-blue. The piercing hum ceased and the flames that danced along its body dissipated, leaving a black form on the floor that collapsed into a pile of dust.

The fire that rolled up the walls receded up to the ceiling. On one side of the room, the scorched body of one of the monks collapsed to the floor. The skeletal remains of his counterpart crashed down on the other. William stepped forward again toward Morax, the light now covered the floor. The pulsating mass of fire above him skipped a beat. Its head jerked up and the flames that dripped from its horns lost their intensity.

"You're next," said William. The white light now halfway up the walls, on the way to the ceiling. Morax disappeared back into the bulge, and then up into the ocean of fire. Cardinal Depeche was released from his bonds and dropped to the floor, and the blaze above their heads began to swirl at a dizzying pace before disappearing with a roar that reverberated through every bone in William's body. The room returned to normal, no signs of anything having been burnt. William rushed over to the cardinal, who moaned and groaned in pain. Black and crisped skin circled his wrists, ankles, and neck. With the fall from the ceiling, William was sure one or more bones were broken as well. Cristobal was tending to the monk, who had suffered similar burns. There was nothing left of the other monk to help.

29

Exhausted, William dragged himself, body and soul, back down the dark hallway, leaving the madness of the last several minutes behind him. The room he left had no appearance that matched the horror of the scene he had walked in on. There were no scorch marks on the walls or ceiling from the pulsating flames; every piece of furniture was in its place. Even the bed was just slightly tousled, but that had happened when Cardinal Depeche jumped out to fight his visitor. What was damaged were the lives and faith of every person there. The smoking skeletal remains of a monk lay on the floor in a heap, resembling William's resolve. The monk's compatriot was alive, but in pain, with burns that still smoldered in his skin. Also, alive, but barely, was Cardinal Depeche. The burns around his neck, ankles, and wrists still smoldered deep inside his skin, and appeared to continue to spread up his arms and legs. William and Cristobal had attempted to provide aid, but neither could do anything more than try to keep both men calm, something they were having difficulty doing themselves.

A feeling of relief came over William as several members of the navy and gold-clad Vatican guard arrived. Both guards stood at the door for a few seconds, to take in the scene. Neither asked questions about what had happened before they took action. William figured this was something they may have been used to, or possibly instructed to not ask and just serve. One of the two guards rushed in to help, while the other rushed away. He helped stretch out Cardinal Depeche flat on the floor. The old man, diminutive to begin with, looked like a fragile creature who was clinging to life. His hands were balled up and held close to his body, shaking uncontrollably as he moaned, even though he was unconscious. The guard showed the cardinal the respect he deserved and neatly adjusted his robe around him. Next, the guard laid the monk out straight and flat on the floor. His body twitched as his fearful eyes looked up at the ceiling, in search of the beast that did this to them. He didn't utter a sound. The guard knelt between the two men and alternated his attention back and forth.

The second guard returned with two additional guards and a man wearing a dark robe with a long white beard. All four entered, but the guards remained standing at attention as the man in black knelt over the cardinal and then sprang up and ran around to the monk. While over each, he examined the burns, placed an ear to their chests, and held his hand under their noses. A phrase and question were spoken to the monk, but the monk didn't respond at first. The phrase was uttered again, and this time the man made eye contact with his patient. This must have been the first time he realized who it was, and he held his hand up to his face as the monk attempted to open his mouth to answer the questions.

He stood up and barked a command to the guard, in Italian. The four men paired off. Two grabbed the cardinal, one under his arms and one under his legs. He winced at their touch and his moans grew louder. The other two hoisted up the monk, who also winced, but remained silent. They rushed out the door and down the hall, throwing the room into silence, with the exception of the breathing of the two men left in the room, one of which was letting out a sigh of relief and the other was taking in fast, short, panicked breaths.

William turned to Cristobal, who was still sitting on his knees on the floor. His chin was pressed firmly into his chest, his hands sat on his legs, but they were not calm. Each finger dug into the fabric of his robe, released it, and then dug into it again, squeezing it as hard as his hands would allow. Something needed to be said between them, but William didn't know what that was, so he walked out, leaving the acrid smell of burnt flesh behind.

While William may have won, he felt physically and spiritually defeated. Not from any doubt in his abilities. When challenged, he put his skills to the test, and passed. At no time had he felt his faith wane or weaken. There was no pause before he took action. In fact, he felt surprised at how he had sprung into action, like a soldier on the battlefield of a war. In truth, this was a battle, one of hundreds, or even thousands, of battles in the war between good and evil. Since he had started his training, he wondered if it was possible for one side to win this war, and if it was, what would that look like? This was something deeper, and far beyond his ability to think about. What he did know was, he would not be the one to win the war, the best he could hope for was to string together enough victories in battle to keep from losing it. Then it hit him, why couldn't he win the war? Wasn't that what he was here to do? The weight of that realization collapsed down on him, already wearing on him, to further deflate his spirit. The gravity of that realization made every step down the hall, back to his residence, laborious.

His heart sank as the images of Ainslee being ripped apart from the inside flooded into his mind. Not a one of them was real. Nothing about what had happened to her was, but that didn't change how he felt in that moment. The only way he had survived was by realizing it wasn't real and dismissing it. Only then could he see through the illusion, and take control. He was able to push aside what he saw, freeing his mind and body. It removed the shackles of concern about what was happening around him and to someone he loved, from holding him back from taking care of what he needed to do. He now knows he was stupid and naïve. The scene he just left showed that people could be hurt, and even killed, when his adversary wanted to.

Why he hadn't realized that before, or comprehended the many times Cristobal had tried to tell him, he didn't know. What he did know was, taking on this responsibility put him, Ainslee, and any future family they could have, in direct danger. More so than just being brought into a world that was full of more dangers than he ever imagined, but they had a proverbial and literal target on their chests. Any conniving demon could use them to manipulate William, or another thought that had just hit him, as if he needed anything else that night. Their kids would not only be targets to manipulate William, they would be targets, themselves, to keep them from continuing this work on their own. Could he bring a family into this world with that threat? Could he live with himself if he did? Those were all questions that weighed on his soul, but there was one heavier than the rest, what had he got Ainslee into?

There was one thing clear to him, it was the thought that was foremost to him at that moment. He needed to talk to her and explain all this. When his mind should have been thinking about how, it had already jumped hours and days ahead, as he watched her sail away to return home to St. Margaret's Hope. The pain of losing her had already become a bad taste in his mouth that made him sick to his stomach. He saw no other outcome after what he needed to tell her. If only he had known, he wouldn't have dragged her in to all this. Bishop Emmanuel was really the person to blame. He knew all this and should have stopped them. William wondered if this was why he seemed to protest so hard in Father Henry's home that night. It probably was, and neither he, Father Henry, and definitely not Ainslee, had known enough to listen to him. He shook his head and muttered, "No. No," under a heavy breath. This was not their responsibility, it was his. The danger she was in was his fault, and his fault alone.

"Something troubling you, my son?", said a voice from the darkness. The voice had a soothing and calming tone to it.

William stopped and looked around through the shadows for the source of the voice. From what he could see, it was just, and only, him. "Who's there?", he asked.

Stepping from the darkness in front of him appeared a man dressed in a white robe, with a similarly white zucchetto on his head. Where had he come from? William was sure there was nothing there before, just dark empty space. Yet, as clear as the nose on his face, stood this man. This honorable man, with a sensitive and compassionate voice, and two kind eyes he could see from where he stood. The man took several unsteady steps that hinted at his age, which William guessed had to be almost 80. As he came closer, the creases of time were clearly visible on the man's face, but his eyes were still full of life.

"You look troubled," he said again.

"A tough night," responded William, as the man walked past.

A single hand rose up from the side of the man and motioned for him to follow. "Come, Let's talk."

At that moment, William recognized His Holiness and followed him. Unsure what the proper protocol was, he stayed behind him a step or two. There was something reverent about that moment. Walking through the halls of the Vatican with the Holy Father, himself, him, just a simple farmer from a small seaside village in Scotland.

"There are perfect days, and days that are less perfect. It is part of life. You know it is how you respond to them that shape who you are. I, myself, have been pushed to what I think is my breaking point, a challenge or problem too big for me. When that happens, I pray and search for guidance from my Lord. At times, he answers," his eyes and head tipped up toward the ceiling before he continued. "Sometimes he doesn't," he said with a laugh. "Oh, yes, even me. I don't take it personally. Instead, I take it as a message in its own way. It is his way of telling me to figure it out for myself, and you know what I do? I do. I walk these halls and pull in the inspiration from these very walls and take solace in the fact that they have seen challenges greater than the ones I have faced, and yet they have survived."

William realized he had followed him through the great hall, and both men were exiting through the golden doors, out into St. Peter's plaza. His Holiness paused at the top of the stairs. He held his hand out behind him. William took it and His Holiness squatted down and sat on the top step. There was a hidden strength in his old body that surprised William. Even though the arm shook slightly as he sat, William was not what helped him down, he was merely an anchor as he lowered himself to the step.

"And this, sitting at these doors, always helps me put my problems in perspective."

William remembered the night he and Cristobal had first sat on these stairs and looked up at the stars. Cristobal had described the same feeling from the scene, and assumed this was what His Holiness spoke about. "The night sky relaxes you, too."

"It does, but that is not it. It is the doors behind us. Those doors are always open for those with bigger problems than mine. Kind of puts everything in perspective, doesn't it?"

There was nothing William could say to that, so he just nodded, while imagining a line of people filing in slowly for guidance and help with their problems.

"You and I share a gift."

Again, William didn't say anything. This statement made more sense to him than the previous. He wondered if it was a requirement to be able to see ghosts and interact with that world.

"It is not what you think it is. Yes, I can see spirits and tend to their needs, but that is not what I speak of. We both share an ability to shoulder a great burden. My service comes with a great burden, but God gave me the ability to deal with the crushing weight of it. Your service comes with a similar burden, and," he paused, "God gave you the ability to handle that burden too. That is more important than seeing spirits and demons. Without it, you wouldn't be able to survive the other gift. You have to live life to the fullest, and trust in him. He would have not saddled you with this, and brought you to us, if he hadn't prepared you to handle it."

William found himself staring up at the stars while His Holiness spoke. Well, he wasn't looking at the stars, but past the stars. Through the vast darkness of space, in search of that place the human psyche believes and desires to be there. Up there is a golden throne, from which their creator looked over them and watched as HIS master plan proceeded, day after day, from the beginning of time until the end. It is not something the eyes can see, but the heart can. The spirit can. The emotional center of the person can, and it anchors them in beliefs such as, there is a plan for everyone, and this, too, must pass. There may be times in their lives that they lose faith in the plan or, even worse, question if there even is one, but they always return back to their beliefs, because even that will pass. They must trust in the plan, and this was the plan for him.

"You ok?"

William's body jerked back from its celestial search and landed within himself on the top step. Cristobal sat down beside him as his head whirled around, looking for His Holiness. He was nowhere in sight.

"William, you ok? You look like you have seen a ghost."

"Yea, ummm," his head turned around and searched the darkness inside the doorway for the frame of the old man, but there was nothing. "I didn't hear him leave."

"Who?", asked Cristobal.

"His Holiness, the pope."

"William! He is in France, and won't return for another few weeks."

William's body went rigid and he looked right at Cristobal. His eyes searched for any hint of a joke in his friend and teacher, but found nothing. "That is impossible. I was sitting right here next to him. We were talking."

Cristobal raised his chin up and looked out of the side of his eyes at William. A smirk was draped across his face. William just sat there, stone-faced. "Huh," Cristobal said as he turned his gaze to the plaza, "it would make sense."

"What would?", William asked.

"I am sure you wouldn't be surprised to know that spirits of past popes roam these halls. We believe their duty and service pull them back here after they pass. Not so much to help the living, but to council and guide the sitting Pope. It is rare, but not unheard of, for someone other than the Holy Father to see them. I have. Others have, as well. Can you describe him?"

William explained, "Well, he was old. If I had to guess, I would say in his 80s. He shuffled a little as he walked, but still seemed full of life. He had a cheery laugh and talked plainer than I would have expected..."

Cristobal interrupted, "Let me stop you right there. The cheery laugh was a dead giveaway. I have one question. Did he talk to you in Italian or English?"

"Well, English, with only a hint of an Italian accent."

"That would make sense. William, you sat here and had a conversation with Alexander VI. He has been gone from this world for almost 100 years. I am almost sure it was him. I have talked with him before, as well. Most of those who have spent any significant time inside the Basilica have, or thought they have seen him. What is unique for you is, he granted Spain the right to explore the New World. That just happens to be where you are going."

30

Days blended into weeks, and weeks transformed into months. The passage of time brought about many things. The first hint of crisp fall air on the breeze that blew through the Vatican hallways. The migration of the swallows from the north, toward the Mediterranean to the south. The arrival of the Roman festival of Cerelia and accompanying feast, something William found he struggled to stay away from. The variety of tastes were exquisite, and overwhelming, to a man who grew up on simple meats, potatoes, and greens, with the occasional fresh catch from the North Sea. Ainslee expressed a concern that if there were many more of these festivals, they would need a bigger bed. William didn't see any possible way he was gaining weight, no matter how many meals of rich pasta and sauces he ate. Every night he, and a cavalcade of others, walked miles into the city or countryside, to tend to their flock from the spiritual realm.

The most notable event of all was a quick meeting with Pope Benedict XIV. It wasn't a conversation like the one he and Pope Alexander VI had had that night on the steps. It wasn't much of a conversation at all, just a brief shaking of hands and a momentary placing of a hand on William's head, as he said a blessing.

What didn't arrive with the passage of time was a sense of comfort and relief from the events that had happened that night in the cardinal's room, and what had happened just moments before that, in his own room. He spent many hours pondering the conversation he had on the steps that night. Even if his spiritual visitor was right, it didn't mean that his wife could bear the burden of what they were asked to do.

William took every opportunity to talk to Ainslee about what he had learned and experienced. Over dinner, long walks through the streets of Rome, or just sitting in their room. He wanted to make sure she had a clear understanding of what they were in for. He never asked her if it was too much for her, or if she wanted to go home. Inside, he hoped she would say it on her own. But with each story he told her, she responded the same way, "We will go through this together." The strength he saw in her eyes was admirable, and even added to his own, but he feared it was misguided. There was no way, even with how he had explained it, that she could have an accurate understanding of all this. It was all beyond human understanding, unless you lived it as he did.

Hearing about William's concern and fears for her, Cristobal made a suggestion and included her in several of their lessons and field work, that is what William called their trips out of the Vatican to practice. After the shock, and several fainting spells, wore off, the comprehension and understanding set in. To her credit, and William's relief, she never expressed any concern or fear. Instead, she was curious, and wanted to learn along with her husband.

The day finally came where Cristobal and William sat at a table, the same table in the library that they had sat at for the last ninety three days, and the lesson ended with no other book, no other document, nothing sitting on the table next to them. The two sat in silence for several moments before he said, "You now know all that we know on this topic. You could probably teach someone yourself, and one day, God willing, you will teach your own children."

William would admit he knew more than he had when he arrived, but an expert, oh no, he felt anything but. Another question pushed that thought aside to be handled another day. It was added to the now growing list of topics for worry and consideration later. The new question had an immediacy, "What's next?"

"Well, no more training, at least not here. You will be sent to your assigned location to, quite simply, perform your duties. For you, that location is around a small area in the Colony of Virginia in the New World. I have arranged, with the help of His Holiness, for passage on a ship of settlers leaving from a port close to my home. It departs next week. Now, they can't take you straight to the colonies, the English won't allow that, but they will take you to St. Augustine, the most northern port in the Spanish territory of Florida. The local priest that will aid you will meet you there and take you north to Virginia."

"Virginia?", William asked. The question was directed more at himself than anyone else in the room. He had heard of the colonies, who hadn't? But he didn't know any of their names.

"I think you will like it there. From what I hear, the weather is a lot like what you are used to in Scotland. The dirt is dark black and rich with nutrients, perfect for farming. In fact, a small spot of land has already been secured for your family, and a small farmhouse is waiting for you."

"For us?", he asked. He wasn't asking why they were worthy of such a gift. That was not the question. Three months. It had only been a little over three months since they'd arrived at the Vatican. How was it possible that word of them had made it to the colonies in that short period of time?

"Well, yes, in a way. The farm has been there waiting for us to find the person or family that would serve the area. That William, is you and Ainslee."

William felt dumbfounded. Their simple life of just a few months past had consisted of waking up to the sounds of a rooster's crow or cow's moo. Days spent tending to the livestock, or working in the field, was a routine that was only interrupted by a trip to town to sell produce or purchase feed. Now they are doted on like they are some kind of foreign royalty on an official state visit. Neither of them have had to prepare a meal or clean their residence since they'd arrived. Now it is taking another turn, they are heading to the New World. A term William had heard many a person back home say with a sense of wonderment and fascination, without knowing what it really was. It was the promise. The promise of a new start.

Cristobal stacked the books and documents he had referred to during today's lesson, so they could be placed back on the shelves. William sat at the table with an almost dreamy look in his eyes.

"Oh, there is one more thing," Cristobal stated.

William couldn't imagine what more there could be, so he asked, "What is that?"

"Your travel papers and land are under the name of Meyer. We changed your name so that the local governors couldn't trace you back to us in any way. They won't take well with us placing someone in the leadership of a town. Might see it as tampering."

"Wait, what do you mean by leadership?"

"You will be one of the town elders of Miller's Crossing, Virginia."

31

William sat outside on his porch. His muscles ached, but it was a good ache. From hours working rows of green leafy tobacco plants that spanned across four acres of fields. This was not a crop he had ever seen before he arrived in Virginia, but with help from the neighboring farmers, he found the native plant took quite well to the dark soil. It wasn't the only crop on his property. William and Ainslee, with the help of some hired hands, had carved out a half acre adjacent to the house and set up a livestock pen and a row of plantings, just for them, or that was how it started out. It wasn't long before William shared the greens, potatoes, and parsley he grew with everyone. A little touch from their old home, for their new home. At night, William could close his eyes and let the smell of the parsley, wafting in with the sounds of the livestock, take him back to his old farm, if only just for a moment. A moment that was often interrupted by the cry of his infant son, Carl, from the other room, or a question from his oldest, Edward. The sounds of their voices would always bring him back here, the farmhouse built for them, and transformed into their home when he and Ainslee had arrived.

Cristobal, was right about this place being similar. The trees, hills, and rolling green meadows reminded him of Scotland, but it was much warmer. Occasionally, he would wake up to a layer of fog hanging over the land, but it was not the same cool marine fog that rolled in every morning and every night back home. Not that William was complaining. He had become quite used to not feeling chilled to the bone. On summer nights like tonight, after the sun went down and the most devious demon he had encountered since arriving, mosquitoes, were gone, he found peace and solace sitting out on his porch and looking up at the stars, like he had at the Vatican. Sometimes Ainslee sat out there with him. Sometimes Edward did. Ainslee would just hold his hand and gaze along with him. Edward, on the other hand, was full of questions, but one particular question was asked more than the others. "Dad, what is out there?"

Each time William would only say, "I don't know, son." Which was the truth, no matter how many times he sat there looking into the void, and past the twinkling stars, he still couldn't see that place everyone assumed was there, or the being that created and watched over the universe. It didn't make him doubt they were there. There were plenty of examples of their presence in his life.

"Ainslee?" he called from the front porch. The screen door to the porch squeaked as it opened and the hair on William's arms stood up from the gooseflesh that had developed on his arms. When Ainslee stepped out on the porch, her husband was standing up. He leaned against the railing and peered into the darkness that surrounded their home. The sun had just gone down behind the tree line. Even the last glint of green light that occurred just as the sun crossed behind the horizon was gone, leaving just the dark of night until the light raced around the globe and came up on the other side the next morning.

"Keep the youngins inside," said William. He descended the steps off the porch as he heard Ainslee usher Edward inside. He only protested a few times, asking "why" or saying he wanted to go with his dad. William's hand reached into the pocket of his brown cotton pants and pulled out a simple cross made of wood. He held it firmly in his strong and callused hands, traces of dirt from the day's work still under his nails. He disappeared into the emptiness thinking, "One day you will, son. One day you will."

DAVID CLARK

THE GHOSTS OF MILLER'S CROSSING

THE GHOSTS OF MILLER'S CROSSING

David Clark

1

"Stop!"

"Get out of the way!" The exclamation was followed by the large thump of something slamming into a wall, and woke the sleeping seven-year-old Edward Meyer. When he went to bed under a sea of stars painted on the ceiling of his bedroom by the nightlight his mother gave him for his fifth birthday, it was quiet, and all was right with the world. The world that startled him awake was loud, and the air was soaked in fear. A war had been waged downstairs.

"No!" Edward heard his father scream woefully. "No! No! No!" His voice repeated. Each word was more pained than the first.

Edward sat up and swung his feet around, letting them hang off the bed. He sat and listened as things bumped and slammed around in the room below him, the kitchen. A deep growl sent him crawling across the bed to the corner of his room. He sat and shivered in the corner while the house around him shook and shuttered. There were more bumps and slams below him and other voices yelling, but Edward was too scared to hear them. He just sat and shook, waiting for the world around him to return to the place of tranquil peace that it was when he went to sleep.

It took several minutes, but the sounds downstairs disappeared and everything, including Edward, stopped trembling. He slid across the bed and his feet landed on the floor, where he took several tentative steps to the door. Out in the hall he asked, "Mom? Dad?" But no voice answered the scared seven-year-old. He asked again, just outside the door of their bedroom. "Mom? Dad?" Again, there was no response, and Edward peered around the doorframe and found no one in the room. Behind him, downstairs, he heard footsteps running across their hardwood floor. It sounded like whoever it was ran from the front door to the kitchen.

From the top of the stairs, Edward saw the front door was wide open. Flashes of red and blue lights cast eerie shadows against the walls. In the distance he heard talking, not the screaming he heard before. He crept down the stairs and around toward the kitchen door.

Light shone through the cracks around the door, and Edward reached out and pushed it open. In a flash, his world would never be the same. Two pools of crimson on the kitchen floor. The bodies of his mother and father laid still inside them. His father's body was twisted into an unnatural shape. His head laid feet from the rest and stared at Edward with a blank expression. A warm liquid ran down the inside of Edward's legs. The world shook and twisted around him again.

"Lewis! Grab Eddie. Get him out of here," a familiar voice commanded from across the kitchen. In an instant, Edward felt himself swept up and pulled close against the chest of a large man wearing the uniform of a sheriff's deputy. The man rushed him out the front door and placed him in the passenger seat of his police cruiser. Then he whisked Edward away. His eyes watched the image of his childhood home disappear behind him in the mirror.

2

"Doctor Law will be with you shortly."

"Thanks," Edward said and took the seat Nurse Rymer walked him to. Then he sat and waited for her to leave the room. That had been a normal routine for many of his meetings with Doctor Law throughout his years here. A nurse, usually the almost retired head nurse Sally Rymer who had the bedside manner of a bedpan, would bring him to this room, or any of the others setup identical to this one, and then leave him to wait for the doctor, alone. Or so he assumed.

"This room needs some color," Edward Meyer said to himself. The old leak stains on the white drop ceiling and scuffs on the floor were the only signs of character. The simple plastic white chair Edward sat on resembled one you might find on an outdoor patio. They sat around a stainless-steel table bolted to the floor.

He mumbled with a chuckle, "Looks slightly institutional to me," then remembered he needed to be careful. The two-way mirror on the wall never gave away the secret of who was on the other side.

Today was his eighteenth birthday, and he sat alone in a green cotton shirt, drawstring pants, and slippers. This was no birthday celebration. He was there for an important discussion with his doctor. In truth, it was more of an evaluation; one he had high hopes for.

He thought about the first time he waited, alone, in that room. The table and chair were the same, but his attire and reason for being there were different. He wore jeans and an Iron Maiden t-shirt and sat there confused as to why he was there. He was only fourteen, and things had been rough with his foster parents. OK, "rough" might not be the best word. "Horrendous," yeah, that's the correct term. He wasn't beaten or neglected. Food, care, clothes, etc... nothing was withheld. In fact, to those looking in from the outside, he'd had a great childhood with supportive foster parents that gave him all they could to make sure he had a loving home.

When he turned nine, they encouraged him to sign up for little league, which he jumped at. He loved baseball. They traveled around to every practice and game, ensuring he always saw two parents supporting him. The same for every school event. To some extent, he felt they were trying to overcompensate for him having lost both parents in a horrible tragedy at age seven.

The door clicked and Edward saw the tall, slender forty-something frame of Doctor Law enter. His nose buried in papers as always.

"Good morning, Edward." Doctor Law said. His name was always the source of a few jokes among Edward and the other patients. *With a name like that, he should be a lawyer*. But Edward's favorite was *he was the "Law" around this place*. He liked that one, because it was true, and it was his joke.

Doctor Law pulled a chair away from the table and then stopped with a bewildered look on his face. He frantically studied the folder in his hands. Without looking up, he said, "I will be right back. I have the wrong folder." He walked back out the door, flipping through the pages with the look of confusion growing the whole time.

Edward always wondered if these types of mistakes were legitimate or some kind of experiment, with someone observing the subject's reactions through the two-way portal in the wall. He played it cool, sat, and waited for the doctor to return.

The two-way mirror grabbed his attention during his first visit as well. They didn't hide what it was, just who was behind it. He remembered sitting there, focusing as hard as he could to see through it; hoping his foster parents were on the other side and would be in soon to take him home. That was not the case. Instead, only Doctor Law entered the room.

They talked for hours about many topics. He asked about his relationship with his foster mom, and then about his foster father. To both questions, Edward gave glowing answers about how close he felt to them and how great his life was going.

The conversation moved to school and friends. He wanted to know if Edward was being bullied or harassed at school. He suggested that kids sometimes single out a child who has been in a foster home or has had a traumatic past. Well, the answer to that was most definitely not. Edward had lots of friends, both in and away from school. Other than the normal ribbing you give each other during a baseball game or in the schoolyard, he remembered nothing like bullying. He couldn't think of any time he may have bullied anyone else, either.

Doctor Law asked him if any of his friends tried to get him to take or experiment with any drugs. That answer was a very loud, "Absolutely not!" His foster parents asked him about drugs once before. They even took him to the doctor for testing. Edward tried everything he could to convince them. Two days later, the results were in, and his foster parents were apologetic. They explained they heard rumors from other parents about drug use among his friends, and wanted to be sure. Doctor Law listened to his answer while consulting a file laid out on the table before him. He didn't challenge Edward's answer, or ask him any more questions about it.

Next, he asked about his real parents. Edward thought for a minute about how to answer, since he was still unsure why he was there. He could have said he never thought about them or what happened to them anymore, but that would have been a lie. He thought about it daily. Sometimes hourly. He told Doctor Law how he felt and how badly he missed them. Edward then felt the need to explain. He loved his foster parents, but he missed his real parents. Doctor Law interrupted his explanation to tell him that was normal, and they understood that. Hearing that made Edward feel less guilty, though it was not really bothering him much.

Doctor Law asked delicately about the moment he found them. Edward shifted in his seat and explained, "Something woke me up. I laid there for a few moments and heard several loud crashes coming from the kitchen. I called for my mom, and she never answered. I heard another crash, and she screamed. I walked downstairs and pushed open the door. That's when... I saw both lying on the floor." Edward sighed heavily. "Shortly after that, a police officer came in and rushed me out of the house."

That was a memory Edward wished he could lose. For months, he woke up screaming as the image of his dead parents invaded his sleep. His foster mother would storm in and hold him for hours, trying with all her might to protect him from the memory, but nothing drove it away.

Moments after Edward walked in, Officer Tillingsly grabbed and rushed him out to his patrol car. He left him there for the longest minute or two of his life. When he returned, he took Edward to the police station. The officer was a friend of Edward's father, and was always around. He could tell Officer Tillingsly was in as much shock as Edward was. He sat Edward in the chair behind his desk and gave him a soda to drink. Sitting in a chair beside him, they talked about anything and everything, including a fishing trip he'd taken with Edward and his father over the summer.

They'd been out there for hours with no bites if you didn't count the bugs. Officer Tillingsly thought he had a bite on his line once. He reeled it in close to the boat, but when he looked, he leaned over the side a little too far. Flapping his arms like a back-pedaling turkey, he hung there for a few seconds until gravity won and he entered the water with a splash. Edward remember hearing his father laughing while saying, 'Well, Lewis, if we weren't going to catch anything before, we won't now. You scared them all off."

When they got home, Edward's mother asked if they had caught anything. Edward told her, "We caught Officer Tillingsly." She looked at them like they had lost their minds. All three busted out in hysterical laughter. There was no laughter between them now. His attempt to distract Edward—both of them really—failed.

The station itself was a hive of activity. Everyone moved around from one room to another in a blur. All talking, and all giving Edward the same heartbroken look as they walked past. Some even had tears in their eyes. Everyone, and I mean everyone, knew his family in this typical small town with only one elementary, junior, and senior high school. On top of that, his father was a local legend. He was a high school All-American Quarterback. Sportswriters and scouts came from all over to meet him during his senior year. He had the pick of prime offers from the best schools, and I mean the best schools. Alabama, Penn State, and Notre Dame were at the top of a lengthy list. Even with all those great offers, he bypassed college to stay and work on the family farm.

After high school, he married his high school sweetheart. They were both active in the community, helping to run the fall festival each year, things at church, town council meetings, and the school board. With all of that, Edward's house was always full of the sounds of laughter and conversation. Most memories were happy ones, but there were a few that were not so joyous. Once or twice a month, a group of men would show up late at night and talk to his father for a few minutes before leaving. Edward would hear a car door close when he came home the next morning just before sunrise. His parents never discussed his comings and goings in front of him; all he knew was that his father kept to himself and seemed different for the next couple of days.

A click from the door gave Edward the sense of déjà vu, as Doctor Law opened the door carrying a file like he did about ten minutes ago. He hoped it was the right file that time. He sat back in his chair and watched the doctor circle around to the only other chair in the room. Edward cleared his mind; it was now time for his Oscar-worthy performance.

3

"Sorry about that, Edward. I had the wrong file," Doctor Law announced with an obvious lack of emotion while sitting down. His bedside manner always lacked warmth. "Happy birthday. Have you already put in your meal request?" he asked without looking at Edward.

The annual birthday meal was one of the few attempts to make you feel as normal as possible. In each of the previous years, Edward ordered the same thing, and this year was no different. "Thank you. Yes, I have. I am simple. No steak or lobster for me. I want three slices of deep dish six cheese pizza and a cola."

"Let me talk to them and see if we can order you a real pizza. None of that stuff the cafeteria makes. You only turn eighteen once, right?"

What the doctor said was true. You turn eighteen only once, but the pizza was not what he was after. He wanted the gift that could happen if this meeting went well.

"Shall we get started?" Doctor Law settled into his seat, opened the folder, and grabbed a pen from the chest pocket in his white coat. "How are things going for you lately? It has been what... three months since we last spoke?"

Has it been that long? Edward had lost track of the time since he and Doctor Law sat down and talked in a true evaluation setting. It was easy to do, since Doctor Law and the rest of the staff interacted with all the patients daily to check on them and observe their conditions, but he played along. "Has it been that long? I am good. How are you?"

"That is great to hear. I am well. Thank you for asking," Doctor Law said while still looking down at the folder. He examined each page before flipping to the next. "So, I see you are completely off of your medications. Feeling any side effects or relapses?"

Edward remembered when they weaned him off of his various daily medications over a year ago. At first, he felt more screwed up in the head than he did on the pills, but the staff reassured him that was natural. His body chemistry needed to readjust to life without them. They were right! It took him several weeks to feel "normal," which, to his realization, was better than he had ever felt since he walked in here. He always thought it was odd that you come to a place like this for "help," but are immediately put into an unstable situation of shock and medication. He had no clue during his first meeting with Doctor Law that his foster parents had already left, not until a nursing administrator came in to help show him to his room. When he heard that phrase and realized his family had abandoned him, he fell into a dark and frenzied panic. He tried to run down the hallway toward the door he came in through, but there was no handle on his side of it. He was trapped.

After the administrator dragged him to his room, he entered a semi-catatonic depressive state. The next week was full of random explosions of emotions, followed by a dormant withdrawn state. The only reason it didn't last longer was the medication they forced him to take. After the first week, it took hold and altered his mental state to the point of not caring about anything anymore. He became what he overheard the staff call a "neutral." Someone not happy nor sad, existing somewhere in the middle. After a few years, Edward determined the entire pattern of care depended on everyone being a neutral. Neutrals were easier to control; they accepted the treatment. Most did not know they were ill and were so emotionally disconnected from the world, they were not aware of anything going on around them. Edward differed from the others.

Unlike most of the patients in the facility, Edward was not mentally or emotionally ill. Nor was he disturbed or suffering from anything. In reality, he was highly intelligent. Just misunderstood. His intelligence allowed him to see through the treatments even while on the medications. Medications that didn't address any of the reasons he was there. The more he studied the treatment method they were using on him, the more he started understanding the game. A game he had to master to make them think he had recovered from whatever they thought was wrong with him.

"No, sir, no side effects in over a year. To be honest, Doctor Law, I have never felt better."

"What about relapses? Last time we talked, you said it had been months since you had seen any images."

It was time for Edward to submit his performance for a Best Actor nomination. In a very controlled, confident, yet casual tone, he said, "I can't remember the last time I saw the image of someone that was not there."

Edward made sure to not look up at the audience of five blue and white semi-translucent individuals gathered behind Doctor Law. They were in the room roaming around and exploring when Edward sat down. The two-way mirror was a spot of extreme fascination for all but one of them. That one stood in the corner, swaying from side to side. As they moved, they floated through each other instead of bumping into one another. Their interaction, or lack thereof, made it appear as though they were unaware of each other or anyone else in the room. Some of the figures were familiar to Edward. He saw them often, but the one in the corner was a rare visitor. She only showed up for special occasions.

The first time he saw one of his "special friends" he was nine and scared shitless. It was late at night, and he got out of bed to go to the bathroom. Before he even opened the bedroom door, he felt something. It was sitting at the end of the hallway, surrounded by a glowing fog. It had the form of an old man and was fading in and out, allowing Edward to see right through him. The sight caused Edward to freeze in his tracks as a cold prickly sweat broke out all over his body. His pulse quickened to the pace of a machine gun, which he could hear in his own ears. The feeling of an immense weight fell over him, dulling the remaining senses. A feeling he still felt every time. Sometimes it was stronger, but it did not paralyze him anymore. Over the years, he learned to control it.

Edward tried to scream, but nothing came out, like in a nightmare. But that was no nightmare. That was real. He felt a warm trickle of liquid drizzle down the inside of his thigh. He tried to scream again, and that time the sound came out full volume, summoning his foster parents, who ran into the hall to his side. Edward attempted to point out the man to them, but they could not see him. Thinking it was another one of his night-terrors, they took him to the bathroom to clean him up. He pulled against them and fought every step as they moved closer to the haunting vision. Once inside the bathroom, Edward would not take his eyes off the door the whole time he was in there. He feared that the man would come in there after them, but he didn't.

The next night, one floated over his bed as he laid down to sleep. He thought about screaming, but to what end? They would run in, but not believe him. Instead, he pulled his covers up as high as he could to hide from the image and fight the chill consuming his shaking body. He squeezed his eyes shut, trying to force himself to fall asleep, which had the opposite effect. Eventually it vanished, leading to several apprehensive moments while Edward laid there waiting to see if it would return.

That continued every night. Sometimes it was one presence; other nights groups would encircle his bed. They never moved or made any sounds. They stood, or floated, there as if they were on guard duty, or just enjoyed watching him sleep.

It took a few years before the fear subsided. He noticed he felt their presence before they showed up, which cut down on the surprise. He tried to talk to them, but they never responded. He tried to walk toward them and around them, but they never acknowledged him. It was as if they had no awareness that Edward was even there. A fact that Edward enjoyed. Over time, he noticed a few regulars, so he gave them names, and when no one was around, he would greet them. "What's up, Bob?" and "I like you, Bob. You never hide anything from me. You are completely transparent." His all-time favorite joke that his twelve-year-old sense of humor loved was, "You look boo-tiful today."

"And you understand now that what you were seeing was not real. They were not real people, or 'ghosts', as you once called them. It was all in your mind, caused by the traumatic loss of your parents, right?" Without lifting his head, Doctor Law studied Edward's reaction over the edge of his wire-framed glasses.

"Oh, yes sir. Absolutely. I was just a child when my parents died. When I walked in and saw them lying there on the floor like that, I was torn to pieces. It was that 'emotional distress,' as you call it, that caused me to see people who are not really there. As we discussed in our many conversations, the images I saw were because of my desire to see my parents again. Once I realized that, I stopped seeing them and knew how silly my outbursts were. I feel horrible about how I treated my foster parents." Edward hoped he didn't spread it on too thick. He spent years perfecting the art of the game.

"Very good. You have been very well adjusted for the last few years. It is so seldom we have such a successful breakthrough, but I am happy to see it." Doctor Law made a few notes. "With today being your eighteenth birthday, and with the great progress you have made, I believe we might have some very good news for you."

With a feigned surprised look: "Really? What is it?" In reality, Edward knew exactly what it was. He had been working toward this day for several years.

4

A frustrated father pounded on the closed door of the hotel room bathroom containing his sixteen-year-old daughter. "Come on Sarah, let's go." They had been on the road for two days, make that two long days, cooped up together in the cab of a moving truck. They had only another three hours to drive to reach their destination. The original plan was to get an early start. That plan did not include her hour-long shower and two hours of make-up artistry. Edward and his seven-year-old son, Jacob, were packed and ready to leave over an hour ago. Instead, they waited and mindlessly flipped through the few TV channels available.

After he left the facility on his eighteenth birthday, he reunited with his foster parents. Everything was great the second time around. They felt bad for leaving him there and worked hard to be the family he had needed for the last four years. He put in the effort too, and suppressed his "quirks" as much as he could. Four years later, he walked across the stage and received a Bachelor of Arts in Education with a minor in English. It still brings a smile to his face every time he thinks of how proud they were of him.

His foster father was surprised by the choice of English. Before he went away, Edward was obsessed with computers and technology. In the hospital, Edward found comfort in escaping into a good story as a buffer against what he was surrounded by day in and day out. During his years of institutionalization, he read a shocking three hundred and thirty-one books. His reading material covered every genre imaginable, but anytime he could get his hands on one of the American Masters, like Melville or Hemingway, it was heaven on earth. He found an appreciation for those works. Before that, the only reading he did was for school assignments, and even then, he waited until the last minute and tried to skim it to learn what he needed to take a test or write a report. A few times, he even just rented the movie version of the book to cram for a test. All he really crammed during those sessions was popcorn and soda. His grade on the test showed him how different the movies were from the actual books.

During the many nights he passed reading, he saw the story as a movie playing in his head, letting his imagination run wild and take him to a place far away from the clinical walls that surrounded him.

After college, he moved to Portland, Oregon to take a High School English teaching job. He had other offers that were more local, but his foster mother grew up in the Pacific Northwest and after all the years of hearing her talk about it and showing him pictures, he felt a yearning inside him that he needed to explore.

It did not disappoint. The serenity of the various nature trails surrounding the area, combined with the small-town environment with big city luxuries, felt like the perfect fit. He never thought he could be happier. That was, of course, until his third year of teaching when he saw Karen Lynwood, the new history teacher, walking down the hallway. She was a vision that took his breath away: long flowing raven hair, piercing blue eyes, a smile that would not just light up the room, but the entire skyline. Edward, never one to wait, was slightly forward, and during lunch on the first day of school, he walked right up to her in the teacher's lounge and asked her out. Edward was not socially awkward. Quite the opposite. He was outgoing, and, he had encouragement from his special friends. After she said yes, Edward asked her for her name, and then introduced himself. That became a joke they would share on every anniversary together, then at their wedding, and then every wedding anniversary after that. One their children would mock at each retelling.

A few years ago, his wife complained of feeling constantly exhausted. She was never one to slow down and take care of herself. Between all the children's activities, her teaching, and the strict fitness regimen she had followed since college, Edward was convinced she had run herself ragged. He encouraged her day after day to take a break, but she resisted. Knowing there was only one way to help, Edward stepped in and took on many of Karen's daily responsibilities with the hope she would use the time off to rest.

For the first few days, Karen resisted. She would find other ways to fill her newly freed time. Each time, Edward would intercede. It turned into a game between them that produced a laugh from time to time. But the humor soon died as the fatigue became too much for Karen to deal with. She needed to stay in bed most weekends to regain her strength for the following week.

After a few weeks, she finally gave in and went to see the doctor. Edward thought the most horrific sight he would see in his life was the bodies of his dead parents, but he was wrong. Very wrong. That didn't even come close to the sight of the look on Karen's face when she told him she had aggressive breast cancer. She had just returned from the doctors, seated in the corner of the teacher's lounge waiting for Edward, all the color gone from her face along with her sparkling blue eyes. In their place sat lifeless dark orbs that resembled pieces of expressionless coal. To say it was unexpected would be an understatement. She was so young, every prior medical exam missed it. Her family had no history of cancer or any illness. Edward kept thinking about all the plans they had for the future, all the plans they would never be able to see come true.

The next eighteen months became the source of nightmares. Endless doctor visits, surgeries, treatments promising a fraction of a hope, and disappointment after disappointment. She declined quickly. It started out with fatigue. Then she was bedridden. She eventually needed a specialized hospital bed and in-home care. Then hospice after just a matter of months. Everything in Edward and the kids' lives ceased to exist during that time.

The worse she got, the more effort Edward put into searching for a cure, but it was all for naught. On a sunny Wednesday morning, surrounded by her family and friends, the body that once contained Karen's soul took its last breath. The soul had left weeks ago; the body was just a shell of who she used to be. Edward was not sure which was harder, walking out of that facility for the last time knowing he would never be back to visit her, or walking back into their home knowing she would never be there again.

He spent the next eight months teaching and doing anything he could to keep him and the kids out of the house. He found it unbearable to be there without her. He felt guilty just sitting there, always thinking he needed to help her, even though he knew she was gone. At night, he would swear he could hear her voice whispering through the halls. Every time he jumped up and went running through the house hoping to catch a glimpse of her. Only twice he saw her walking down the hallway. It seemed very real. She was there, interacting with objects in the house, so real he thought he could reach out and touch her. She was always alone. He never saw any others when he saw her. He also never felt the normal cold shivers or tingling in the spine. She looked healthier than she had in months, exactly how he wanted to remember her. Every time he moved toward her; she would disappear before he could reach her.

When the school year ended, Edward knew he and the kids had to leave if they were ever going to feel normal again. He searched online for teaching jobs in neighboring cities, but found nothing. He widened his search nationally and came across one in his old hometown of Miller's Crossing. He applied and heard back from Principal Rob Stephens in just a few days. The interview went so well he hired him right on the spot. Edward felt relieved and hopeful. It could not have worked out any better. He had a job in his old hometown, and they even had a place to live. He would just have to face the demons he'd left that night on his family's old farm.

They packed up their lives and memories, and with just a week before the new school year began, the three of them headed out on what Edward called "A New Adventure." The drive took a few days. They took their time and saw some sights. While he tried to make the move as enjoyable as he could for his children, the anxiety inside him ramped up with every passing mile. He had not been back in his old house since the day he found his parents. Each time he tried to picture what it would look like; he only saw the image of his parents on the kitchen floor.

"OK, Dad, I'm ready."

Edward thought to himself, *thank God,* Jacob expressed the sentiment out loud. His exclamation drew a look of disgust and a light slap to the back of the head from his sister as she walked by. Jacob followed her out and tried to get a revenge shot at her before they loaded up. Edward sat there for just a second before turning off the TV and letting out a little sigh before he followed them to begin the last three hours of their trip.

5

After an uneventful three hours' drive through the scenic mountainous countryside, they reached a sign indicating their cross-country trek was just about complete.

Now Entering Miller's Crossing
Population 12,379

"Do they change the sign every time someone is born or dies?" sniped the teenager, still distraught about leaving the big-city life behind.

"Oh, stop it, Sarah." It is a good question that Edward had never considered. Did they reduce it by three when his parents died, and he left?

As they drove into town, the woods and hills gave way to sporadic houses on large lots. There were no fences separating each yard, which Sarah and Jacob had never seen. He explained things are different out here.

The houses were all different styles; no subdivisions or sprawling apartment complexes, with their resort style pools and entertainment areas. Just house after house, unchanged for generations. The only thing they had in common was a mailbox out by the street with their family's name on it.

Absent were the expansive galleria or malls, instead having just a few strips of locally owned stores in the center of the city. The closest thing to name brand stores were Walt's Hardware and Lucy's Bakery.

As they passed through the center of the town, the scene returned to cozy homes nestled back in the woods. Sounding somewhat panicked, Sarah asked, "Dad, where is the Walmart?"

"Oh honey, there isn't one here. I think there is one a few towns over."

Sarah whipped her head around with a stunned expression. "What? There isn't one? Is there a movie theater? An organic store? What about a Macy's?"

Edward thought, *there goes Sarah's weekend mall-scapades.*

While the culture shock set in on his daughter, Edward sensed a comfortable familiarity setting in. "When I grew up here, there was a movie theater out on Route 22 just before you got to Sterling, maybe a forty-minute drive away, but it only had two screens."

Just the thought of only two screens left Sarah's mouth agape.

Edward added a little more fuel to the fire. "Oh, just wait until you see the high school. It's coming up in just a few minutes down the road."

The sight of the elementary school nearly brought a tear to Edward's eye. It looked like it did when he was a student there. The playground in the front with the swings made of metal chains and rubber seats, the metal monkey bars, the slide. The flagpole with the American flag flying proudly out front. He doubted anyone here protested its display or asked to have it taken down; something that was common in the larger cities. The trees looked bigger. His mind drifted back to memories of running in through those doors trying to beat the bell, playing baseball on the simple clay diamond during the spring, and the school fall festival.

The screams of his daughter and hysterical laughter of his son interrupted his trip down memory lane. "DAD! What the hell is that? Is that Rydell High from Grease? This is not the fifties."

Just like the elementary school, Miller's Crossing High School looked like the school time forgot. The building was not modern, in any sense of the word. A large, long, two-story, red-brick, window-lined building with a simple roof over it. A large central staircase wound up the hill in the front, right up to the main doors. The sign out front underneath its own flagpole proudly flying old glory announced the start of school in four days. Behind the parking lot on the side was a large football field with metal bleachers on either side and two small scoreboards at either end, with the Coca-Cola sign in the middle of it. Of course, his parents took him to every home game; everyone in town attended them. The homecoming games were special nights that were among his fondest memories. His father dressed Edward in his old jersey and his mom wore his dad's old letter jacket. At halftime, the band formed an arch around midfield as they called out one by one the former players that were in attendance. One by one, they walked out to midfield amid the cheers of those in the stands and oh, how they cheered for his father. Edward and his mom clapped and screamed when they called his name.

"Sarah, it's a great school. You'll love it there. Plus, I'll be teaching there."

That thought hit her right between the eyes. "Ewww, you're teaching at the same school? Why aren't you at the other high school, like back home?"

"This is the only high school."

Sarah's sigh announced her disappointment at the appeal of attending the same school where her father would be teaching. That had never happened before.

A few roads past the high school, Edward took the familiar left down the grass driveway toward the old family farm. As many times as he thought about selling this place, he never could. He reached out to a local realtor once about selling, but changed his mind. The realtor put him in touch with someone who could help take care of the property until he finally made the decision. From how things looked, the thirty dollars every three months was money well spent. The mown yard and old farmland to either side of the driveway were a welcome surprise.

His anticipation grew as he maneuvered the van up over a modest hill and around the corner, giving him the first look in decades at his home. Oh yes, the caretaker's services were well worth the price. The house looked great. The screen on the wraparound front porch was still intact, none of the bushes around it overgrown. The storm shutters were off and stored, probably in the shed, like he requested a few weeks back.

He pulled to a stop next to the front door, got out, and walked to the door. There was an envelope stuck in the door jamb. Edward pulled it out and opened it.

Welcome home, Edward.

- Jim Morris

That note was one of the little pleasures of living in a small town that Edward had missed so much. When they moved to the Portland area, the neighbors watched them through the window. None of them said anything for weeks.

Edward fished the front door key out of his pocket and looked up, pausing at the image of his mother standing at the door with her arms extended as if to hug him. He stood there and talked to himself. "Steady now. You didn't see that. It's just the stress of coming back here. Come on." Her vision, now and at this place, was almost too much for Edward to handle. The encounter did not have the same eerie feeling he sometimes experienced. Instead, a warm and welcoming feeling overcame him. It invoked memories of her welcoming him home from school like she did so many days. He forced himself to hold it together, but couldn't resist quietly saying, "Hi, Mom. I'm home."

"Dad, are you OK?" Jacob asked as he walked up next to his father.

Edward steadied himself. "Yep, just thinking. Let's go in." With that, he pushed the key in, and it opened right up. There was no evidence of the lock sticking like Jim Morris mentioned. He must have squirted some lubricant into it.

When he opened the door, only a hint of stale air escaped, which came as a relief to Edward. He walked in and looked around, half expecting to see boxes all over the place. Instead, it was just as he last remembered it: the sofa with the eighties floral print, books still left on the bookshelf, the console TV that he was sure his kids won't know how to operate, the loop rug on the dark hardwood floor. All the things from his childhood were where he left them. But the one area that grabbed his attention most was the table full of family photos, all framed and sitting on display. How he wished someone had packed up even one of those and sent them with him when he left that night. He took nothing with him, just the clothes on his back. Something as simple as a family photo would have meant the world to him.

"Well, guys, this is where your dad lived when he was a little boy," he announced.

Sarah and Jacob explored the family room, inspecting everything. While Edward couldn't get over how everything was as he remembered it, his kids struggled to see past the layers and layers of dust that had built up over the years. Edward saw Sarah drawing a very distinct line in the layer while running her finger along one of the shelves.

"So, it needs a little cleaning. This will be great, guys. Some of my happiest memories happened right here on this farm." Edward ignored the customary teenage rolling of the eyes. "Let me show you guys around."

6

It was a long day of cleaning and unloading the van for Edward and his children, but finally, it was done and time for everyone to settle down and relax before falling to sleep. Edward had a feeling the sleep part would come much faster than they expected. When they stopped to eat some dinner, Jacob nearly fell asleep at the table. Edward wanted to make sure the kids were all set before the end of the day. Something about living out of a box always felt unsettling to him, and he didn't want them to have to feel that way, even for a night. To his satisfaction, he achieved his goal. Sarah was set up in his father's old office, which was larger than his old bedroom. Jacob jumped at the chance to take his dad's old room. It had what he called a "neat window" in it. The neat window was a tiny alcove created by a dormer on the front side of the house. Edward always liked that spot too. As a kid he sat on that ledge and watched for his dad to come home from work.

Edward's back felt the strain of unloading all the kids' furniture and boxes. He rubbed it as he walked up the stairs to his room for some much-needed rest. It seemed simple enough, but entering his parents' room proved more difficult than he expected. He had stacked a few boxes of his belongings in the hallway, but nothing had made it inside yet. He stood at the door for a few moments and tried to gather up the nerve to even open it, something he had not done yet. The room was their sanctuary. His mind struggled with accepting his role as head of the household in this home. With a mind too tired to battle psychological ghosts, he conceded there was always tomorrow and headed downstairs to the old comfy sofa in the family room. The same one he spent many a Saturday morning lounging on while watching cartoons.

He attempted to get comfortable but faced a realization: either the sofa has gotten smaller, or he was bigger. He used to be able to lay the entire length of his body on the sofa with room to spare; now his feet hung off unless he laid on his side in a partial fetal position. He grabbed the remote off the table next to the sofa and turned on the flat screen TV they'd placed on top of the old console model. He fiddled through the channels for a few moments. Unable to find anything, he finally just let it land on whatever channel it was on when he grew tired of changing it. It didn't matter, though. He watched it for only a few moments before falling asleep like he did so many times as a child. Unlike when he was a child, three shimmering figures loomed over him. Edward was too tired to notice. He pulled the blanket up in response to the chill.

When he woke up, there was an infomercial grinding in the background. He reached blindly toward the floor searching for the remote, which he found, and clicked it off. He had every intention of falling back to sleep in the silence, but he didn't find the silence he hoped for. At first, he thought the sound came from one of the kids' televisions. He pulled the blanket up and rolled over, but after a few minutes he sat up and listened intently. His ears were hearing something real and close by. It was the unmistakable sound of a human voice, and not just one, but several of them, and they were outside.

He reached to the table beside him and disconnected his cell phone from the charger. A quick glance at the time revealed it was only two a.m. Now the sounds of people outside might be odd, but not unheard of in the city. But not here, and not on the old family farm out in the middle of nowhere. The thought of kids using their vacant lot for an innocent adolescent late-night hangout made some sense to Edward. The house had been vacant for so long and no one knew they have moved in. A simple warning and request that they move along should end the party.

He opened the door expecting to see a few pickups and cars on the property, but he saw nothing. The voices sounded distant, but Edward couldn't tell from which direction. He stepped off the porch and walked around the house and looked out at the empty pastures. It was a cool night, a touch of fog hanging above the ground. It felt rather refreshing compared to the oppressive heat of the summer day. A chill shot down the back of his neck, followed by the appearance of a few drops of cold sweat and tingly nerves. Edward recognized the feeling and thought, *not now please* as he continued to search for the source of the sounds.

He searched for several minutes, but still saw nothing, Edward was about to give up when he noticed a quick glint of light flash toward him from the southeast corner of his property. He walked toward that area, not taking his eyes off that spot the entire way. He thought about running in that direction to scare whoever it was away, but decided to be cautious until he saw who was there.

It took Edward several minutes to get close enough to see anything. With each flash of light he saw, Edward stopped to observe for a few seconds before he started creeping forward again. Soon, though, he saw the source of the light, as multiple forms holding flashlights came into view. It appeared to be several people in a line. They walked at a casual but determined pace with their lights focused on something straight in front of them. Edward froze dead in his tracks. About fifty feet in front of the line of people, he saw *them*. They were there but not at the same time. They had a human shape and form, but solid black, lifeless eyes. They never touched the ground. The scene was all too familiar to Edward. He crouched down among the tall grass and watched.

They stayed well in front of the line of people behind them. The line yelled at them like cowboys driving cattle on a ranch. Only a few of the pursuers yelled. Each exclamation put down the protests of the two ghastly floating creatures, who complied and moved forward toward the tree line at the edge of his property.

They faded in and out as they moved through the empty field. Both appeared to be male and dressed in pants and a shirt of some type. One appeared to be holding something. He occasionally brandished it like a weapon above his head. Each time he did, one from the line behind them stepped forward, held up something small in his hands, and admonished him.

The pace of the two glowing creatures slowed down. That allowed those following to close the gap, but from Edward's vantage point that appeared to be intentional. They slowed and turned slightly, instead of heading straight forward, and eventually stopped altogether. They held their position, flickering in and out of visibility inside a light patch of fog. The largest vision glared back over his shoulder at the individuals following them, and let out a protest that sent a chill through Edward's essence. The sound was not a scream or a yell, more primal and otherworldly, and created a tremble of fear in Edward's hands to go along with the chill.

The line of pursuers stopped, which appeared to only embolden both creatures. The second one turned around completely, pointed at them, and bellowed an inhuman scream. Edward's pulse quickened as he felt a terror grow in him. A terror similar to what he felt that first time in the hallway so many years ago.

The man stepped forward again. This time in the moonlight, Edward saw he was an older man, dressed in all black. Edward leaned forward slightly to see what he held, but the distance was too great, and he didn't dare to move any closer. The mysterious man in black spoke to the creatures in a voice that pierced the cool night air. "Let God arise and let His enemies be scattered, and let them that hate Him flee from before His Face!"

Both wailed wildly again, louder than before. The man in black was unfazed and continued to preach at them. "O' Most Glorious Prince of the Heavenly Armies, St. Michael the Archangel, defend us in the battle and in our wrestling against principalities and powers against the rulers of the world of this darkness..."

They reacted as though a great force had pushed against them. Each held up their hands to shield themselves. They turned without a sound and continued toward the wood line, with the man in black following them, continuing his recitation. The line followed close behind as if to ensure they continued heading toward their destination, wherever that might be.

The duo and the glowing flashlights of those following them disappeared among the dense woods that surrounded Edward's family farm, leaving him standing in the damp cool night, confused and terrified, with the sounds of crickets replacing the voices and wails that had filled the air. He stood there for a few moments more, listening and watching for any signs of them before he turned and took several terrifying steps back toward the house, looking back at the woods over his shoulder with every sound he heard.

    Back in his house, Edward securely closed the front door and double checked each lock. He settled back onto the sofa and turned on the TV. Edward did not try to lie down, instead, he sat there thinking about what he saw over and over. The sounds of the night stayed firmly stuck in his head. There would be no sleeping for Edward for the rest of the night.

7

The alarm on Edward's phone went off at 6:30 the next morning, but he didn't need it, he was awake. Of all times to deal with only a few hours of sleep, his first day at work was the worst possible day. Not feeling the caffeine of his second cup of coffee kicking in, Edward headed upstairs. He hoped a hot shower would help.

As Edward crested the top of the stairs, he heard the bathroom door close. One of the kids beat him to it. Now all the soap and shampoo in the house was behind a closed door. He was forced to stand there and wait. Following the sound of a flush, Sarah opened the door and sleepwalked past him. Edward was unsure if all the commotion outside woke her up at some point last night, or this was the normal teenage state for that time of the morning, so he inquired, "Sarah, did you have any problems sleeping last night? Did you hear anything?"

She never even stopped, just yawned as she closed her door. He muttered to himself, "Teenagers."

After his shower, he felt more human than he did before, but he still couldn't shake the sights and sounds of the previous night. Edward mostly kept things to himself. He spent some time in college trying to research the meaning and cause of his visions, even going as far as talking to a parapsychologist once. He realized there were two schools of thought: those that didn't believe in the ability to see spirits or visions of people like that, and those that did. Each person who believed in the ability had a different theory around why. None of the theories had anything scientific backing them. Several of them theorized that a person could see the spirit or afterimage of a person they had a connection with before their death. That was the one theory Edward could dismiss without question. Over the years, the only images he'd had a prior connection with were his parents and his wife, the other thousands were just random strangers. The remaining theories, the several dozen he read about, all differed from a connection to a location, to a spiritual time vortex—which Edward could never understand—to just a random combination of events, which to him seemed more likely. What Edward knew for sure was that what he saw last night was real and not some sort of hallucination, and at least one other person saw them too. Now, what to do with that knowledge?

That would have to wait, though. He needed to focus on his first day at work. Ready to head out the door, he poked his head into Sarah's room to give her some instructions for the day. "Are you awake?"

She did not respond, so he repeated the question, louder this time, "I am heading to work. Are you awake?"

There was a single groan from the direction of the mass of covers clumped on her bed.

"Remember to make sure Jacob eats breakfast and see if you guys can do more unpacking. I want to get these boxes out of here. I should be home just after three, OK?" He waited for a response, which finally came in the form of a single hand thrust out of the covers giving a thumbs up and then a quick wave goodbye.

He closed her door, knowing they would both be asleep until ten o'clock, and headed out. The drive to work brought back tons of memories, just like the drive in. Of course, the difference was now he was driving, and, in his memories, he was a passenger sitting next to one of his parents. Edward's thoughts distracted him so much he nearly missed the turn into the high school, another place he had been many times before. For the first time though, he took a slight veer to the right into the faculty parking lot. Once parked, he sat there for a few moments in his quiet car before heading in. He needed to clear his mind.

Walking up the front walk, he realized he had never been inside the high school before. Plenty of trips to the football stadium with his parents, but never inside, so this really was a first for him. He followed the signs that directed him to the office, feeling a tad nervous about meeting with the principal, a something he found no one ever shook from their days as a student.

Edward walked into the office as two other teachers exited. They greeted him with a friendly good morning as they passed by him. To him, it felt rather welcoming, and it helped to calm his first-day nerves. So much so that he felt rather confident as he walked up to the counter that separated the office into the traditional two halves, student, and faculty. He waited there for a few seconds before a woman on the other side of the counter acknowledged him. Small picture frames covered her desk. She turned and flashed him a big smile across her cherub face and, in the most welcoming and sweetest voice, asked, "Can I help you, sir?"

"Yes, ma'am." Edward never stopped addressing people with the polite *ma'am, miss, missus,* or *mister* no matter what his or their age. "I am Edward Meyer. I am here to see Principal Stephens."

"Oh, the new English teacher. Welcome." She grabbed a stack of folders and a brown envelope from her desk and brought them over to the counter. She told Edward what was inside each as she slid them across the countertop to him. "Here is your class schedule and rosters, and of course your key. Robert is yelling at the painters in the gym; they were supposed to have the gym floor completed before today. He will be back shortly. Just have a seat. Oh, and welcome." She motioned toward a few chairs lined against the wall on his side of the counter.

Edward took a seat and looked through his schedule and class roster. He'd have five English classes each day, and it looked like each class would have just under thirty students, both a surprise and a relief. Where he taught in the past, the class sizes approached forty, and one year he had forty-three in one class. In his opinion, a class of that size hindered his abilities as a teacher and limited open class discussion and the learning of the students.

A single unfamiliar voice shot through the constant ringing of phones and chatter of people coming in and out. "Eddie?"

Edward scanned the room for the source of the voice. Having no idea what Principal Stephens looked like, and assuming no one would recognize him, he assumed that was who called him; even though he never called him Eddie during any of their prior conversations. As Edward stood up, he extended the hand toward the middle-aged man who stood before him with a big smile on his bearded face. "It is great to meet you, Principal Stephens."

A full-bodied laugh met his introduction. Edward felt a lump form in his stomach.

"Now that is a good one. I am not Robert. You don't recognize me?"

Edward studied his face. "I'm sorry, but not really."

"I'm Mark Grier. We were in the same class from kindergarten until you left in the second grade. We were even on the same baseball team twice. I heard you were coming back to Miller's Crossing. I wasn't sure I could recognize you, but with how much you look like your dad, it was easy." Mark looked at the woman behind the counter and asked, "Ms. Adams, you remember Eddie Meyer, don't you?"

She looked up from her computer monitor and for a brief second looked like she had seen a ghost. It was a face that Edward had seen himself make in the mirror a few times. The color returned to her face as a smile grew. "Oh, wow. I didn't even recognize you. I can't believe you're so grown up. I remember when you and Mark both came in and were registered for your first day of school. Welcome home, Eddie."

Edward examined her closer and a brief memory crossed his eyes: the older woman now standing behind the counter was the same young woman that basically ran the elementary school while he was there. "Ms. Adams?"

"Yes, Eddie. It's me."

"I am so sorry. I didn't recognize you either. When did you leave the elementary school?"

"It's OK, Eddie. I guess I should call you Mr. Meyer now since you are a teacher. I came over here some twenty years ago when the position opened up. I needed a change of scenery, so I drove the three hundred feet down the road for that change." She gave him a wry smile that matched the dry humor of her statement, one trait he remembered about her.

Mark asked, "So, Eddie, where is your classroom?"

"I'm not sure yet." Which was true, Edward still hasn't opened the envelope with his key in it.

Ms. Adams remembered, though. "He is in 343, just down the hall from you, Mr. Grier." She pushed her glasses down to the tip of her nose and looked at them with a sinister look. "This isn't going to be a mistake, is it? I seem to remember you two getting into a lot of trouble together when you were younger."

"Of course not. We have long outgrown putting a potato in your car's tailpipe or a whoopie cushion in your chair. I will say toilet papering your rose bushes is still not out of the question though." Mark gave Edward a light slap on the back. "Do you think Robert will mind if I take him up?"

"Not at all. I will send him up to see you as soon as he returns... and you two, stay away from my rose bushes." Ms. Adams issued that warning with a rather humorous shaking of the fingers at the two nearly forty-year-olds like they were still the same mischievous kids they were back then.

"Let's go. It is so good to see you Eddie..." and with that, Mark walked Edward out of the office and up to his classroom. The walk turned into a dizzying fast trip down memory lane, some of the memories were just as if they were yesterday, others he didn't remember at all. As Mark continued to recount their childhood, Edward took in the school and looked for any other friendly faces he might recognize. It has been thirty years since he saw any of his old friends, but there may be a chance he might recognize a few. Mark recognized him, even though he didn't recognize Mark. When he accepted the job and moved back home, he knew running into his history would be something he could not avoid. The thought both excited and terrified him.

"So where are you living?"

"Back at my parents' old farm with my kids."

Edward's response caused Mark to pause for the first time since he greeted him in the office. The thought of someone moving back into the home where their parents were murdered may be disturbing, but Edward couldn't see any other option.

Mark broke the awkward silence and asked, "Back home with your kids. Wow, you are all grown up. How old are they?"

"My daughter Sarah is sixteen and Jacob is seven."

"Sixteen, huh? So, going to school here? My son Chase is seventeen, he's the tight end on the football team, even has a few schools looking at him for a scholarship. Mostly just Division II schools, nothing like your dad, the legend, did back in his day. But hey, you can get a great education at those places and that's what matters, right?"

"Absolutely... and yes, Sarah thinks she is going to die a million deaths going to the same school I'm teaching at. This would be the first time that has happened."

A wide evil grin stretched across Mark's face. "Oh, really? Then you, my old friend, are in for a treat. First, there is the seeing each other in the hallway and they turn and go the other way. Then there are the crazy looks at home followed by the random accusations of embarrassing them by doing absolutely nothing. But the best of all... you ready for this? The looks you get from your fellow teachers for something they did."

"I see what I've been missing out on for all these years."

Mark stopped at a door and turned toward Edward. Assuming this was his classroom, he looked up and saw the "343" on the sloppily painted around room number plate. He now saw why Principal Stephens might be yelling at the painters. Edward tore open the envelope with the key but stopped as Mark reached forward and opened the door.

"Too much time in the big city. We don't lock anything around here."

He was right, Edward had spent too much time away from the small-town environment. The thought of not locking everything up from the front door at home, his car, and even the door to his classroom was completely foreign and unnerving. "I guess there is a lot I have to get used to, Mark. I spent most of my life in places where they locked everything." Edward decided not to elaborate on the last part of that statement. He was not sure how anyone would react to hearing he was locked away in a mental facility for a while.

Before he stepped into the classroom, a voice echoed from down the hallway. "Mr. Meyer, I see you found your classroom."

A mid-fifties, balding man wearing a buttoned up white shirt, black slacks, and black-rimmed glasses walked toward them. He extended his hand toward Edward, who returned the gesture. He had a firm grip, evident by the twitching muscles exposed below his rolled-up sleeves.

Going out on a limb, "Principal Stephens, it is great to meet you." Inside, Edward hoped he had guessed correctly. One moment of embarrassment today was enough.

"Call me Robert. I insist."

With confidence brimming from being right, he said, "Alright, then. You can call me Edward."

"I will unless students are around. I see Mark showed you to your classroom. So, what do you think? Not the same as what you are used to?"

With a sheepish tone to his voice, Edward confessed, "Well, actually, I haven't been in yet."

"Don't let me stop you. Let's have a look."

Edward stepped inside and returned to a simpler time. The walls were painted cinderblocks, not drywall or paneling like he was used to. Lights hung from a dropped ceiling. A real blackboard with chalk hung on the front wall. No dry erase board here. The student desks were single unit metal seats with wooden backs and desk surfaces. One detail made Edward go wide-eyed. All along the back wall and continuing along the side of the classroom under the windows were bookshelves with what looked like complete classroom sets of the classics. Melville, Wells, Bradbury, Steinbeck, Bronte, and others. He hadn't seen such a display since he was in school and even then, it was only a book or two. At his last school, a handout listing where to obtain the books at a discount was the closest he came to this.

Edward stood speechless a few feet away from his desk, next to his own overhead projector. He took it all in before uttering a single, simple word: "Perfect."

He saw a sense of surprise at his remark on the faces of Robert and Mark, so he explained. "I'm serious. This is perfect. The newer schools with all their technology and perfect modern classrooms are rather... institutional." *Not really*, Edward thought to himself, but he could not think of another word at the moment. "There are times you feel disconnected from the students in those environments. The simple experience of reading from a proper book and not some e-reader creates a more lasting memory and experience. The feel and smell of the old papers that have been flipped through by scores of students before you. And the desks, proper desks. Most of the classes I have been in had tables and chairs where many students would have their back to me. I would have to either remind them to turn around or walk around the class as I lectured and talk to make eye contact with them while losing the connection with others. This is perfect."

Principal Stephens looked rather pleased with the explanation. "Great. We still do a lot of things here the older ways. We find they still work. I will let you get settled in. The first faculty meeting of the year is at ten in the auditorium. See you there."

With the principal gone, Mark closed the door behind him. "Eddie, I need to show you one trick. Don't let Robert's nice guy act fool you too much. He has a few quirks." Mark walked to the back of the room, where a clear box hung on the wall. "He wants all classrooms kept at seventy-two degrees, but on this side of the school the sun can make things warm in the afternoon."

Mark fished a bent paperclip out of his pocket as Edward moved in for a closer view. Holding it up on display with one hand and pointing out the shape with the other. "If you bend it just right, you can push it into one of these vents on top of the box and slide the lever slightly, kind of like that." Edward heard a click followed by the sounds of the overhead air conditioner starting. A few seconds later, a slight breeze of cooler air moved around him.

Feeling there was an obvious question hanging in the air, Edward asked it. "Wait, there is a lock on the box. We don't get a key?"

"Nope, not at all. Robert has one, each of the custodians have one so they can reset them each night, and that is it." Mark held up the bent paperclip. "I have my special key. I will show you how to make one."

"Appreciate it."

Mark hung around and helped Edward set up his classroom, even though it was basically ready when he walked in. They moved the desks into neat rows. Edward's desk was in the center of the room, but he preferred to stand there during lectures, so they pushed it toward the side of the room. Edward half expected to clean most of his first day, but he found himself astonished at the cleanliness of the classroom.

While they moved things around, Mark and Edward continued catching up. Edward told him about his wife, how they met, and how he lost her, which was the catalyst to moving back to Miller's Crossing. Mark felt bad and gave Edward his heartfelt condolences. He married his high school sweetheart, someone Edward remembered as Skipping Sharon. She skipped everywhere. Down the hallway. Across the schoolyard, hell, he even remembered seeing Sharon skip across the classroom once when the teacher called her up to her desk. Skipping without a care in the world with her long brown pigtails bouncing behind her. Edward was tempted to ask Mark if she skipped through the house, but decided to leave the past in the past. Mark told Edward she sold real estate across the three towns that made up their county seat. To Edward, it sounded like Mark had a very happy and stable life with a good job, loving wife, great kid, the complete package. *Lucky bastard.*

Just before ten, they headed down to the faculty meeting. During the walk, Mark addressed Edward with a hint of cautiousness in his voice. "Eddie?"

"Yes?"

"Been meaning to ask but wasn't sure how. How are things back in the old home?"

"It has been good. I hired someone to keep up the maintenance on it while I was gone, and he did an excellent job. Need to do a little cleaning. Not too much. The kids will do more of it today, I hope. We should be able to finish the rest tonight."

"That is not what I meant."

Edward suspected that, but hoped he was wrong. He knew someone would eventually ask about it, considering the tragic circumstances that surround the last time he was in that house. "Oh, you mean...."

"Yeah, any ghosts from the past?"

Surprised by the choice of words, he hesitated before replying, "I won't lie. It felt pretty weird the first time I walked in. A little flood of memories, both good and bad. Took me a bit to work up the nerve to walk into the kitchen. Part of me was afraid they would still be lying there, but having the kids there helps. We have been busy getting settled in." Edward left it at that. No need to bring up what he saw the night before. No need to give anyone a reason to think he was odd, yet.

8

Edward stood at his front door, arms full of books and notebooks, beads of sweat on his brow. The stifling heat of the summer afternoon hit him like a blast furnace when he exited his car and walked the twenty feet to the front door, but the sweat could also be from the stress he felt. He had just under two days to plan out the entire year and review with the head of the language department. He usually used the lesson plan from the previous year as a basis to start from. Now, teaching twelfth grade English at a new school, he had to start over from scratch.

He tried several times to balance the books in one arm and open the door, to no avail. While he considered putting the books down, he took a chance and used his foot to gently kick the door three times. He stood there hoping to hear the signs of someone coming to open the door, but there was just silence. He shifted his balance to his left side one more time so he could try to knock on the door with his foot once more as the door opened.

"Not even the first day of school and you already have homework," Sarah cracked from inside.

"Let's see if you think it's funny when this is you next week. HA!"

With an unamused eye roll, Sarah walked back toward the kitchen while Edward unloaded the books on the dining room table. The table served as a makeshift office for him, much as it did for his father growing up. Edward only remembered his family using the table to eat for special occasions like Thanksgiving. The large kitchen eat-in nook served his family fine growing up. It would work fine for the three of them.

"Did you guys finish unpacking?" he asked.

"Yep, well, everything but your stuff. I even cleaned a bit more. How did you live here with all this dust?"

Hearing his daughter complain about the dust reminded him of her mother, Karen. She was a major clean freak. The sight of their first house together almost caused heart failure. When they moved in, a layer of dust covered everything. She cleaned for close to sixteen straight hours, refusing to sit down until everything was spotless.

"It wasn't this dusty when I lived here. Remember, no one has lived here for over thirty years." Overall, Edward was impressed with how well everything looked, a combination of how well Mr. Morris took care of it and Sarah's cleaning.

"Go get cleaned up. We are going over to an old friend of mine's for dinner tonight." Sarah let out a frustrated sigh, another trait she got from her mother, and stormed upstairs. Edward followed her to the bottom of the staircase and, just as he imagined his parents must have several hundred times, he yelled upstairs, "Jacob, get ready. We are going to dinner. You guys have thirty minutes."

A groan echoed down the stairs from Sarah. Edward realized he didn't tell her how long she had to get ready before that moment. *Oops.*

Just after 7:00, they pulled into the driveway of Mark and Sharon's house. Mark must have heard them drive up. He was outside to greet them. Mark waved welcomingly from the porch as Edward and his children got out of their car.

"Hey Mark, did you hear us driving up?"

"Nah, it's a great time of night. We spend a lot of time out here on the front porch."

He remembered back to all the time spent on the porch in his younger days on nights just like this, something he would never do in the city. Too much traffic noise, smog, and any other of several things that made the experience unpleasant.

Edward herded his children toward the porch and introduced them to Mark. "This is Sarah and Jacob. Guys, this is Mark, we are friends from way back, well... when I was your age, Jacob. And now we teach together at the high school."

Mark flashed a smile. "It's nice to meet both of you. Come on, come on in." He opened the front door and invited them all inside. "Sharon, Chase, our guests are here."

A few seconds later a middle-aged woman in short pigtails skipped around the corner and through the dining room. The display produced a huge laugh from Mark, and a nervous one from Edward.

"Sorry, I couldn't resist," she said. She took the hair ties out of her hair and let braids fall free; then walked up to Edward and gave him a big old country style hug. "Hi, Edward, great to see you again. Mark was right. You really haven't changed that much."

"Hi, Sharon, you haven't either." Which was the truth. Edward was usually bad with faces, but he recognized her right off.

Sharon turned toward Edward's children, extending a hand to each. "And you must be Sarah and Jacob. Sorry about that earlier. Your father gave me a nickname back in elementary school. I couldn't resist."

"Wait now." Edward thought for a minute. He didn't remember being the original source of that name. "I may have used that name, but I don't think I created it."

"Oh please, I remember. I was seven and tripped in front of everyone while skipping down the hallway..." Sharon paused as she noticed the smile forming on Edward's face.

Sheepishly, he confessed. "Guilty. I remember. You tripped, and I yelled, DOWN GOES SKIPPING SHARON."

"Yep, and I didn't care. I got right up and kept skipping."

The three adults in the room had a great laugh while Edward's two kids stared at them like each of them had three heads.

"Ah, Chase. This is Edward Meyer and his daughter Sarah and son Jacob. Edward and I were friends when we were kids, and he will be teaching twelfth grade English this year."

A specimen of a young man extended a hand and greeted him with a firm handshake, "Hi, Mr. Meyer. So, you replaced Mrs. Henson this year."

"Uh yeah, I guess so. Nice to meet you, Chase. I hear you are quite the football player."

Chase modestly explained. "I play some ball, but nowhere near what your father was. We still see his name and records posted in the locker room and around the stadium."

Chase turned his attention to Edward's children "Hi. Welcome to Miller's Crossing. Our um... little town."

The normally not shy Sarah was wide eyed in his presence and shook his hand without saying a word. Edward had seen that expression on her face before. The father in him knew exactly what it was for. *Oh boy, here we go again.*

Sharon ushered everyone into the dining room where a great spread awaited them. Edward hadn't seen a display of comfort food like this since his mother used to cook large lunches for all of their friends after church on Sundays. His mother and her friends took turns hosting these. The women would each cook a dish and the families would gather at someone's house. After everyone ate to the point of being stuffed, the wives cleaned up and sat inside gossiping while the kids went outside to play a pickup game of baseball or football. The men were always out on a porch or in a barn of some type talking privately. When the kids ran through the house, the mothers kept on talking and acknowledged the kids as they passed through, but it was not the same with the men. If you came within earshot of the porch they were talking on or into the barn, they stopped talking and urged you to move along. They were always nice about it, but it was eerie how they watched you and didn't start talking again until you were away from them.

After a great dinner, things proceeded much like those gatherings back in the day, but with a modern twist. While Sharon cleaned up, Mark and Ed were out back talking and Jacob was trying to play basketball with Chase; Sarah was just watching, well, watching Chase. Mark and Ed both tried to help Sharon clean up, but she insisted they go on outside. She even took a few dishes out of their hands. She said she had just a few things to put away and would be right out, which must have been the truth, as she joined their conversation just a few moments later. "Mark said you are living in your folks' old place."

"Yep. I never got rid of it, so it just seemed right."

"Did you have to do a lot of work to get it ready?"

"Nah, I hired someone to act as a caretaker for it. He went by every few months and checked on it and made repairs as needed."

Sharon was taken aback at the thought of someone taking care of it. Her voice quivered as she asked, "He didn't mind?"

Edward replied reassuringly, "Not at all." Mr. Morris said nothing to Edward that gave any indication he had any apprehensions about going to the house. Just like Mark's response earlier, Edward doubted that would be the last person to react to the thought. "Mr. Morris never said anything or asked questions. Not even sure he was completely aware of the circumstances around the house."

"Jim Morris? Old Man Morris?" asked Sharon.

"Yes, he was recommended by a realtor in the area."

"Oh, he knows all about what happens- I... I... mean what happened there."

"She means the tragedy around your parents." Mark shot his wife a look as he stepped in to save her from the uncomfortable conversation she wandered into.

"Mr. Morris just likes to fix things." Mark's expression changed into a youthful, devilish half smile. "Do you remember that time when we were six and playing summer ball? Tim Wischter overthrew you at first base by twenty feet and broke the window in the side of the school building."

"Oh god, I remember that. I watched it go over my head and right into the glass. Shattered it into hundreds of pieces." Edward tried to remember if Tim ever made the throw from shortstop to first that summer.

"Mr. Morris fixed that. Tim's father offered to pay him, but Mr. Morris said he was just happy to see someone on the team had an arm on him."

Edward spit out the sip of sweet tea he just took and said, "Come on, we weren't that bad."

"Ummm, we were. All year we played round robin against the other three teams, and we had more ties than wins or losses. No one could hit anything." It would appear Mark's memory of their baseball days was not as rosy as Edward's. Edward thought they were all future all-stars.

From across the way, a brief cheer erupted from the pickup game between Chase and Jacob. Jacob made his first bucket of the game. Of course, Edward believed the six-foot-three teen went easy on the seven-year-old and let him score, but to Jacob, it was still a victory.

The conversations and reminiscing moved to a lighter tone and turned into a game of "whatever happened to" with various people from Edward's past. He was not that surprised to hear that most of his old friends and classmates still lived in town. Most of those that left for college came back to settle down.

As the evening moved along, the kids tired of the basketball game and sat on the deck and talked among themselves. Well, Chase talked about football. Jacob hung on every word. Sarah hadn't stopped staring into his eyes. Edward doubted she heard anything Chase had said. A smile crept onto Edward's face. For the first time since Karen's passing, his kids looked happy and were just being kids.

Sharon leaned over, saying something to Mark, the expressions on each of their faces unpleasant. Sharon gave Edward a hug. "It's late, and I have an early morning tomorrow. It was great seeing you. We will be seeing you around." She then walked over to the kids and told them it was nice meeting them before heading back inside. Edward felt embarrassed and pulled out his phone to check the time. It was just after nine. In the city that was considered early, but this was a different world.

"Sorry about that, Mark. I didn't realize how late it was."

"Oh, it is fine. Not that late at all. You just don't want to be on the road out toward your place any later than this. It isn't safe." Mark caught himself before he finished his statement.

Hearing the warning as more than just something related to overstaying one's welcome, Edward inquired, "Why is that?"

"The roads are dark and pretty winding."

While that was true, Edward's car had headlights, and it wasn't that dangerous of a drive. Not wanting to question his friend, he called to his kids to get ready and thanked Mark for the great night. They talked about doing it again and Mark agreed. "Absolutely."

"See you at work tomorrow, Mark."

"Yep. See you tomorrow. Drive straight home and be safe."

Edward backed out of the driveway and onto the road. An uneasy feeling came over him. He was not sure if it was what Mark said to him, or how Mark watched them intently as they backed out and headed down the road.

9

During the drive home, Edward had to admit, Mark was right, it was quite dark. Streetlights created small islands of light at the intersections. The rest of the road was only illuminated by the moonlight glowing through the trees or his own headlights. Edward kept the high-beams on the entire time, having not passed a single car the whole way home. He slowed down as he passed the last intersection before his driveway; he didn't want to drive right past the opening.

Edward pulled in and through the trees and within seconds they emerged into the open pasture of the farm which was fully lit by the moon. A slight layer of fog hovered above the ground as the cool night air settled in.

Edward pulled to a stop at the back of the house. He and his kids exited the car and headed toward the house. A few steps away from the back steps, something made him stop. A familiar cold and empty chill filled his lungs and radiated throughout his body. Then something caught his attention out of the corner of his eye. A movement, not that far away from them in the fog. Edward paused for a moment to look in that direction and saw nothing at first, but then it was there again for only a second before it disappeared. It was not clear enough for him to make out what it was. He tried to convince his mind it was just a denser area of fog flowing in the air, but several aspects of that story fell flat on the logical side of his brain. First, there was no wind of any type. Second, there were no other areas in the fog that looked or behaved like that. But the most important factual detail was that there was a shape to it. With his past and what he saw the first night, he would be naïve to not consider other possibilities.

When Edward turned around to follow his kids inside, he nearly ran into Sarah standing there, fixated on the same area. "Sarah, honey. What is it?"

She did not break her gaze.

With no response, he took a step closer and grabbed her by the shoulders. "Sarah, are you OK?"

Sarah snapped out of the trance and looked at her father with a fearful expression. "Yes, daddy, I'm fine."

Her tone of voice and a term she hasn't used since she was nine alerted him to the possibility she saw the same object.

"Are you sure?"

"Yes, just tired. I am going to go in and get ready for bed." Her voice was more resolute, but still not convincing to her father.

Sarah headed inside and Edward followed her as far as the top of the stairs leading up to the porch. He stood there, looking back at the same spot for several minutes, to convince himself he either saw a spirit or something else. Unconvinced either way, Edward headed inside disturbed, confused, and feeling helpless. As a father, Edward wanted to create a safe and happy environment here. With everything they'd been through over the last year or so, his children deserved that.

At the top of the stairs, he noticed Sarah's door open. He looked inside, wanting to check on her to make sure she was OK, and found her in bed all covered up and fast asleep. Edward could be jumping to conclusions. Was it possible he misinterpreted her being tired for something else?

Maybe she saw him and turned to look too. He was not sure. He had been through a lot with his daughter and had seen that look before. That was the same expression he saw on her face the night Karen told them all enough was enough, that she wanted to stop trying. None of the four of them shed a tear at that moment. Each of them knew it was coming, even the kids who were mature beyond their years in such matters. He remembered the looks on everyone's face and the feeling of being exhausted like it was yesterday. They had been through a war. Every day was a new battle through the raw emotions. It was as much physically draining as it was emotionally heartbreaking.

Edward looked in on his daughter one last time, then flipped off the light and pulled the door shut before walking down the hall to his room.

The sounds of laser fire emerged from Jacob's room. Edward poked his head inside and found his son in an all too familiar position. Headphones on, controller in hand, and attention focused on the flashing screen of his video game. Edward thought about telling him it was bedtime, but they had just a few more days of summer vacation and let it slide and closed the door.

Feeling rather tired himself, Edward knew there was one last ghost to confront tonight. One he had put off since returning home. He stood in the doorway of his parents old bedroom holding a box and knew there was no sense in avoiding it anymore and stepped inside. Much like the seven-year-old he used to be, he stood right inside the door for a few moments before taking another step. Back then the pause was to look for his parents. Now it was to absorb the memories. All the times his father sat in the chair in the corner lacing up his shoes. Seeing his mother sitting at her make-up table; the same table still covered with assorted cosmetics. The closet still full of their clothes. After one last look around, Edward took his second and then his third step into the room and placed the box on his father's chair.

Edward stripped the bed and put on a new set of sheets and folded a corner back. Before he climbed in, he took one final look out the window. The fog had settled in thick, obscuring the pasture and the tree line from his view. There were no mysterious lights dancing in the fog tonight, No voices or haunting sounds. Just a cool night with the occasional cricket chirping its delight. The scene was peaceful. Edward cracked the window to allow in the cool night air and the rich fragrance from the wildflowers and lavender growing in the pasture. There was many a night in his youth he fell asleep just like this. Those were some of the best nights of sleep he ever had. Tonight, he could use one of those.

Edward climbed in and pulled up the covers and, as he had done every night since her passing, he thought of his wife until he fell asleep. The five clouds of vapor that circled him did not seem offended when he forgot to bid them a good night before falling asleep.

10

Edward focused on adjusting his lesson plans for the first nine weeks. He sat down the day before with Madeline Smith, the head of the English department, and reviewed his plans. He entered rather confident, hoping to impress her with how he organized his classes. Much to Edward's surprise, the lesson plans were not what she desired. Instead of criticizing and destroying his confidence, she provided feedback and suggestions, feedback that Edward was more than enthusiastic to receive.

His lessons followed the same pattern he had used throughout the years in Oregon. Lecture about a specific period of literature, then read one to two pieces from the period. All reading occurred at home, with discussion and a few quizzes about what was read each day in class to gauge comprehension. Once the assigned reading was completed, there was a multiple-choice test. Edward never liked using multiple-choice to test the comprehension and knowledge of a piece of literature. He would much rather allow the students to write an essay; so he could hear their interpretation of what they read in a form that allowed them to express an opinion and defend it. Edward was not a teacher that subscribed to the "there is only one right interpretation" school of thought. How a person viewed a piece of literature was personal, it depended a lot on their past and viewpoints. No matter how strong his belief was in that, he was forced into the multiple-choice format because of the heavy reliance on standardized tests in the larger school districts. Every test given in every class had to mimic the standardized tests that were given several times each year to allow for plenty of opportunities to practice.

Hearing Mrs. Smith voice her concerns about the value of multiple-choice tests was music to Edward's ears. She preferred the old methods of reading aloud in class and discussing as you go, followed up with essay at the end, allowing the student to voice their opinion. If her personality were friendlier, he would have run across to the other side of the table and given her a hug and a big kiss, but Edward restrained himself.

Edward opened up his lesson planner and began striking things out and writing in his adjustments. They would review his plans again today at 1:00 pm. No computer-based plans here, this was the old-fashioned lesson binder he remembered seeing teachers use when he was in school. He found the whole throwback nature of the school refreshing and energizing.

He was elbow deep in corrections for week three when there was a light knock on the door frame. Edward looked up, and after his eyes adjusted, he saw Mark leaning into his classroom door. "Hey, a group of us are heading to lunch at eleven. You should join us."

Edward quickly glanced at his cell phone and realized the time. It was 10:45. "Crap. I appreciate the offer, Mark, but I need to pass. I have to finish up these changes."

Mark responded with an exaggerated sad face.

Edward explained, "I'm way behind. I still thought it was nine something."

Mark looked up at the old-fashioned clock hanging up above the chalkboard in the classroom, a feature Edward had yet to notice, and accepted his explanation with a quick reply of "Next time," before disappearing down the hallway.

Edward called after him before he was out of earshot, "Mark, wait."

Just seconds later, his head reappeared in the door. "Changed your mind?"

"Nah, I want to apologize about overstaying our welcome last night. Just like now, I didn't realize how late it had gotten."

Mark looked bewildered by Edward's statement, so Edward tried to explain "The comments about how late it was last night."

"Oh." Mark's expression changed from bewildered to one of apprehension. He shifted back and forth in the doorframe, looking for something to focus on that was not Edward. "You guys were fine. Sharon had an early morning, and I was just worried about you guys driving back on the dark roads. Deer like to run out in front of cars in the dark and such."

"Ah, good thinking." Edward gave Mark a reluctant thumbs up, and off to lunch Mark went.

Mark just lied, and Edward knew it. During the years he spent in the hospital, he honed his human lie detector skills. After only a year, Edward could tell when a nurse, orderly, or doctor lied or withheld something. Whether it was the wandering eyes, awkward pauses, or fidgeting, the telltale signs are the same for everyone. That was a great skillset to have when teaching teenagers, and even better for being the parent of one.

He buried his nose back in his lesson plans and updated them based on the guidance he received yesterday. The next few hours sped by with a flurry of strikeouts and notes. Edward leaned back in his swivel chair, which let out a slight squeak. He folded his hands behind his head and smiled. The thirty minutes left until his meeting was just enough time to walk down and scrounge up some nourishment in the teacher's lounge's vending machines. He never liked to go into battle on an empty stomach, not that Edward expected a battle during his meeting. It was quite the opposite. He looked forward to it and to the first day with students tomorrow. His enthusiasm turned into a semi-strut as he walked out of his classroom in the direction of the vending machines.

"Edward?" echoed a voice from behind, stopping him mid-strut.

Edward turned. Upon seeing who it was he thought to himself, *only in small-town America. This would have never been allowed in Portland.* He walked back toward the visitor and extended his hand. "Father. What brings you to the school today?"

Father Murray, dressed in full black with a white collar and a crucifix dangling around his neck, took Edward's hand firmly. "Walking around before the madness starts." Father Murray's face lit up. "Nah. Actually, I just blessed the football team downstairs. I do it each year. You know... for the safety of the players. Plus, any divine guidance will help. Competition is stronger these days. Coach Holmes told me you had come home. Thought I would stop by to say hello and invite you and your family back to the church." He looked warmly at Edward. "We would love to have you. Your mother and father were very active members of our congregation." His voice dropped slightly to a more somber tone. "God rest their souls. We miss them terribly."

Of everyone Edward had run into since returning, this was the one person he truly recognized and remembered. Of course, he was in his late thirties back then, but the eyes are the same kind eyes which provided him comfort when his parents were laid to rest. The voice sounded the same, maybe a few more years on it. Now in his seventies, he still tended to his flock in the very same community.

Edward and Karen struggled to find a church that felt inviting in Portland. Both of them were from small towns and in the big city, they found the churches had an antiseptic feeling. There was no sense of community. You came, prayed, listened to a sermon, and then everyone went home. They eventually found one, but did not find it to their liking. When Karen became sick their attendance waned. Between hospital stays and all the times Edward could not leave her alone, going to church took a backseat. Not to mention the period in which Edward frequently lashed out toward God. He could not understand why HE let this happen to Karen. He even cursed Him a few times.

Without hesitation, Edward agreed. "Absolutely Father, we'll be there."

Father Murray's face lit up. "I look forward to meeting your wife and children as well, and bringing them into our extended family. Your family has been missing from our congregation for far too long."

"Oh, Father, it will just be me and my kids. My wife, Karen, passed away earlier this year."

Father Murray placed his hand on Edward's shoulder and said, "Oh, Edward, I am so sorry to hear that. We know the Lord will call our name one day, we just never know when. It is always tragic when it is so young, but I am sure he has a greater purpose for her, even if we do not understand it. We are not really meant to."

"Yes, Father, I agree. And thank you for the kind words." Just hearing that was rather comforting, more so than what Edward experienced back in Portland. The priest that presided over her funeral told him he was sorry for his loss and then said a generic prayer with the family. After the service, Edward and the kids never heard from him again.

"My office is always open for you and your children anytime you need to talk. Welcome home. I look forward to you stepping into shoes vacated by your father's tragic loss."

Edward stood there for a few seconds, watching the familiar form of Father Murray disappear down the hall and around the corner. He wondered what he might have stepped into. His stomach rumbled sending him sprinting to the lounge. He had just a few moments left to down some junk food before his meeting.

11

The school year started full of optimism. Of course, that described Edward, not his children. He had to wake Sarah up three separate times so they would not be late. Jacob was up on time, but took his ever-loving time to get ready. As Edward got ready himself, he found it necessary to walk up and down the hall like an old-fashioned barker every five minutes to shout encouragement and reminders of how much time they had left. Just as he expected, at the last minute, both of his pride and joys exited their rooms and headed downstairs.

The ride to school was completely silent. Jacob's nose was stuck in a video game on his phone; Sarah's was buried in her bookbag for a few more moments of sleep. When they arrived at the elementary school, Edward veered right out of the drop off lane and into the parking lot. He parked his car in the first visitor spot next to the walkway. Jacob slammed the door as he got out, and watched with delight as his sister jerked awake.

As Edward walked him in, Jacob seemed nervous at first about starting at a new school, but all that went away when one of his classmates walked up and introduced himself before they were even in the classroom. Edward took just a few minutes to talk to the teacher before heading off. With a final look at Jacob, a smile grew on his face as he saw his son already making new friends. Jacob took after his mother in that respect. She could walk into a room of strangers and have four or five new best friends in just a matter of moments.

When Edward opened the car door to finish the drive to the high school, Sarah greeted him with the largest over-exaggerated smile he had ever seen. It went from cute to eerie in moments. "What?"

"I was just thinking. It is such a WONDERFUL morning outside. How about you drop me off a little way before we get to the school and let me walk the rest of the way in?"

Knowing Sarah hated mornings more than anything else in existence instantly tipped her hat and he called her on it. "You just don't want to be seen getting out of the car with me, dear old dad, a teacher. Huh?"

"Oh, Dad, that's not it." She tried to give him those big eyes that usually cause him to say yes to anything.

There are bigger battles to be had, so he gave in. "Alright. I will let you out just before we get there."

"Thanks, Dad, you're the best." She threw her arm around him and gave him a half hug.

He dropped Sarah off about a quarter mile from the school with instructions to walk straight there and text him when she got there. Edward pulled into the faculty parking lot and took a spot. He grabbed his brown satchel and headed inside among the crowd of rather cheerful teenagers all arriving for the first day of the new school year. Walking into a school that didn't have metal detectors at the front, seeing students walk around being friendly and polite to the teachers and each other, and hearing the magical words "Mister" and "Missus" echo everywhere was a stark contrast to the "Yo, teach" he had heard for the last several years. The refreshing and energizing environment engulfed Edward. He stood outside his door to welcome in his first class instead of waiting at his desk, using it as a shield, as he usually did.

Students filed by him down the hallway with polite and cheerful "good morning's." He checked the time on his phone. Just a few moments left until the bell rang. Sarah walked down the hallway as close to the other wall as she could, doing everything to look straight ahead while cutting her eyes in his direction. Feeling the urge to be the annoying father, he considered yelling something across the hallway such as, "Have a great first day, sweetie." But the disruption to the now peaceful home life wasn't worth the bit of ill-timed humor it would bring him, and he let her pass peacefully.

The bell rang, a real bell sound, not some electronic tone signaling the start of class. The last time Edward heard a real school bell, he was a student in elementary school. A few students made a mad dash toward their classrooms as the doors closed. Back in Portland, half the students treated the bell as a couple minute warning, and it took an assigned member of the faculty to walk the halls and send the students to their classrooms. The hallway beyond Edward's closing door resembled a ghost town. The inside of his classroom was a picture from Norman Rockwell himself.

Edward walked to the front of his class and leaned back on his desk. Every set of eyes in the classroom focused on him. He felt a quick shiver, followed a pressing feeling on every inch of his body. He did not expect to feel nervous about addressing his classes.

He dipped his head and took a deep breath to collect himself before he addressed the class. When he looked back out, he noticed a visitor walking toward the back along the chalkboard to his left. He appeared to be a cheery older gentleman just out for a stroll, wearing a tweed jacket and a Doctor Doolittle hat.

Not now, Edward thought to himself. There was never a good time for this to happen, but a moment like this was the worst. Edward watched as the man disappeared through the back wall and then returned his focus back to his class. As he did, he caught a few students turning around as well. Their expressions were normal, not showing any fear or surprise, maybe a hint of confusion. They were probably all wondering what the weird new teacher looked at.

"Good morning. I'm Mr. Meyer. Welcome to twelfth-grade literature." Edward picked up a stack of papers and took a few shaky steps to the first row of desks, giving several pages to the student sitting in each desk. "This is the syllabus for the class. Please take one and pass the rest back. If there are any left over, please just put them on the table in the back. While we hand these out, let's go around the room and introduce ourselves." The papers disbursed backward, and he noticed students looking at them and reading them.

"Let's start here." Edward stood in front of the first desk on the left side of the room. The occupant of the desk, a curly-haired blonde wearing glasses and a simple t-shirt and jeans, laid her syllabus flat and sat up straight, and said with a tremble in her voice, "I'm Susan Parker."

Edward looked back to the gentleman sitting behind her and without hesitation, said, "Robert Lewis, nice to meet you."

The rest of the class picked up the pattern and each of the other twenty-four students took turns introducing themselves.

"I am usually pretty good with names, so there will be no need for any name cards or anything. I should remember each of your names after the next few days, but now let's get to a more important topic. Why are we here?" Edward saw many students looking down at the syllabus, expecting a read-through or review of what was handed out. "It's a more general topic than even what is on the syllabus, so you can put those down for the moment."

Edward felt enthusiastic and a bit idealistic. "We are here to learn about literature. Now, that is a very broad topic. More specifically, we will talk about the types and styles of the American classics. We will read some of those classics and talk about the styles of each author and what they try to convey to the reader with their story. But there is something else..."

The English teacher in Edward forced a pause in his speech.

"Let me try that again, using proper English." A few students in the class laughed. "We will be reading several of the American classics and talk about their style and content, BUT," he over emphasized that word on purpose, "I am after an even bigger goal. I hope to share and instill with you a love for reading like I have. So, before we begin, who reads for fun?"

Not a hand entered the air, to which Edward was not surprised. "Oh, come on, reading can be fun. Let's try this again, ignoring what you have been forced... I mean, assigned to read for school, who has read something in the last year?"

That time, about half of the hands jumped into the air. "Good. Umm... Lisa, what did you read?" Edward asked, pointing to a girl sitting in the back of the third row.

"*Origins* by Dan Brown."

"Good, and have you read any of his other books?"

"Yes, all of them."

"You enjoyed it, right?"

Lisa nodded yes, as a voice from the back commented, "Not like there is anything else we can do when the sun goes down around here."

"Well Michael, thank you for volunteering to go next. I saw your hand up earlier, what was the last book you read and enjoyed."

Without hesitation, Michael responded, "*Relentless*."

Edward clarified, "The book by Tim Grover?"

"Yes."

"Excellent choice. I have read it myself. You enjoyed it, right?"

Michael's eyes perked up when he heard his teacher had read the same book as well. He straightened up in his seat before responding, "Absolutely."

"Why?" Edward asked, looking for him to clarify with more context.

"I like sports and have always been curious about that edge that some athletes have. How someone who is as talented as everyone else find that extra something to excel further? That book gave me a look into how their minds work."

Feeling his point was made, Edward did quick summary before continuing with his plans for today's class. "See, everyone? Lisa is reading what many think of as one of the best authors of our time, at least one of the most popular, and she enjoyed it. On the other side, Michael read a self-help book. A type of book that many think can be very boring, and he found enjoyment in the topic. There really is something for everyone. I hope you each find something enjoyable in what we read this year."

Looking around the classroom, Edward felt he had the class fully engaged. "OK, so let's look at your syllabus and see where we are going to start..."

Each of his remaining five classes followed suit the rest of the day. Introductions, a quick discussion about what he hoped they get out of the class, and then into the syllabus and preparing for the first selection of the year. Well, almost. By the third class, he started noticing a look. Not a look, perhaps, but a feeling coming from the students. Not one of disrespect, but like he was an animal on display at the zoo. The feeling grew from class to class until it finally came to the surface with his last class of the day.

During the introductions and open discussion, Edward asked, "Does anyone have any more questions?" A timid hand appeared from the middle of the room. A student who was outspoken during the open discussion now appeared hesitant about asking a question.

"Mr. Meyer?"

"Yes, Jeff?"

"Is it true you live in that eerie old house at the edge of town?"

Every town had that one house that everyone tells tales about. In this town, like it or not, it was Edward's home. He had no doubt the story had grown to the level of town folklore. Probably at some point, some school-aged kids stood at the end of the driveway, just outside the tree line that separates the property from the road, daring each other to run up toward the house. The dare, of course, was accompanied with some fable about an old man that lives there that eats any child that comes close to the house.

"Well, if you mean my old family home. Yes. My family and I have moved back to it. Rest assured, none of the stories," more exaggerated than before, "no matter what you have heard..." Edward paused and leaned his head forward slightly, and looked at his class humorously out of the top of his eyes under his furrowed brow, "it is not true. The house is the same as it was when I grew up there."

There was an audible murmur circulating through the classroom as they realize their teacher was that little boy from the story they heard about.

"It isn't haunted?" a voice inquired amongst the murmur.

Edward chuckled and with a straight face replied, "Well no, Robin, I can absolutely guarantee it is not haunted."

When the school day ended, Edward packed up his things, locked his classroom, and headed out to the parking lot. His daughter, who was too cool for anyone to see her driving into school with "dear old dad," now leaned against the car waiting for her ride home.

"So how was school?" he asked as he opened the driver's side door.

"Not bad."

Edward felt fortunate. He received a two-word answer instead of a half-hearted "fine" or something to that effect. "Well, glad you survived. How are your classes?"

"Not bad. Seems I am a bit of a celebrity."

"How so?"

"I... am the girl that lives in the haunted house." She looked at him with that satirical smile he saw when she was being a smartass.

"Yeah, I got a little of that, too. Let's go pick up your brother."

12

Friday afternoon arrived, providing a quiet and normal end to the first few days back at school. Both Edward and his children settled into the rhythm of the school year, and even though they continued to complain about going to school, as all kids do, they both enjoyed it. Of course, they would never admit it.

As they pulled into the driveway, they headed inside for a quick change of clothes and then back to school for the Friday Night Football game. Edward missed that part of his life. His high school education came from teachers the State sent in to conduct classes in the hospital. Having experienced the games with his mother and father, he always felt a longing for it. Now as a father, he wanted to make sure his children did not miss out.

Sarah zipped down the hall toward the bathroom she shared with Jacob. In the breeze caused by her brisk movement he heard, "A few friends want to pick me up for the game."

Sarah appeared to have forgotten how the whole parent and child thing worked. "Is that a question asking for permission?"

Doing her best impression of a whining teenager, "Dad! It's just a few people I met at school. We'll be at the same game."

Edward knew it was safe and said, "OK, al…"

Sarah blurred past him in the hallway, interrupting his answer. The glimpse Edward caught caused a quick change of his answer. "… absolutely not."

The answer stopped Sarah in her tracks at her bedroom door. "Why not?"

"You are not wearing that out. You still have to follow the school dress code." Sarah stood in her bedroom door wearing a skirt that barely covered her butt and tube top that was missing its midriff.

Sarah slammed the door. "If I change, THEN can I go to the game with my friends?"

Settling for one victory, Edward conceded. "Sure, just text me when you get there and when you leave."

Edward took a few moments to get himself ready.

The sound of someone running down the stairs was followed by a quick yell of, "Bye, Dad," and punctuated by the slamming of the front door. Edward glanced at the clock and realized he and Jacob needed to get going, too. Unlike the games in Portland which started at 7:30 PM, the games here had always started at 5:00 PM.

Even the away games. He remembered hearing someone ask his father about the start time once. "It was a tradition."

Edward and Jacob headed to the school and joined the parade of cars and trucks lined up to turn into the football stadium parking. Surrounded by cars blasting music, pickup trucks loaded with people in the back waving pompoms, and scores of others walking past them, they inched their way toward the stadium. He rolled down the windows and the smell of hot dogs on the grill, popcorn, and the sound of two marching bands playing various tunes from their positions in the stands wafted in with a flood of memories that brought a smile to his face.

Once parked, Edward and Jacob walked toward the source of the sweet smells and growing sound. Neighboring Valley Ridge was that night's opponent. Their fans created a sea of gold and crimson walking among the blue- and white-clad Miller's fans.

They parked, bought tickets, and went inside. No large police presence or wanding here.

Knowing what was on Jacob's mind, and his too, their first stop was the concession stand. There was a small line, but not too long. It gave them a moment to look at the simple menu board with the Coca-Cola red wave emblem on it as a sponsor. He felt a quick vibration in his pocket and pulled out his phone. There was a simple message from Sarah's number that just said, "here." He took a quick glance back toward the gate and saw his daughter walking in with a group of students, smiling and laughing. That image took away any doubt he had about coming back here to start fresh. He'd made the right decision.

He and Jacob placed their order, two hot dogs with extra mustard and relish, two Cokes, a popcorn, and a pack of M&Ms. The concession workers made a few trips to bring their food to the counter and Edward handed them a ten-dollar bill and donated the change back to the football boosters. With the food in hand and the popcorn pinned to Edward's chest by the arm supporting his hotdog, they headed to the bleachers and found a seat. Both teams were out on the field warming up.

✻ ✻ ✻

The game itself was great. Miller's Crossing won 14-10, but what stuck out to Edward was how right Mark was about his son. Chase had five catches for 120 yards and was an absolute beast out there blocking. Edward tried to find Mark after the game to send Chase congratulations on such a great game, but something else drew his attention. Within minutes, the stands and parking lot were almost empty. Except for the Valley Ridge fans, it was a virtual ghost town. Thinking he might have more luck over at the gym, where the locker rooms were, he and Jacob headed that direction, but found more, or less, of the same. Less than fifteen minutes after the final whistle, the Miller's Crossing players had left with their families. The only folks roaming around were the families of the opposing players, who waited to see their sons emerge from the locker room before they boarded the buses and headed home. He and Jacob gave up and headed back to the parking lot where they found a handful of cars left, all but his adorned with the yellow and crimson colors of Valley Ridge.

There was a quick vibration from his cell phone, and he reached into his pocket to pull it out. Sarah had messaged him she was already home. Edward and Jacob headed home themselves. The drive was filled with the sounds of a father and son reliving the highlights of a great high school football game.

When they walked inside, Sarah was perched on the sofa watching television and mockingly scolded them for taking so long.

"Surprised you were home so soon."

"Yeah, me too. I thought there would be a party or something after the game like back home... but everyone said we had to get home."

13

"Daaddd!!! Do we have to go to church?"

"Yes, Jacob. We used to go all the time, and you liked it." Edward leered at both of his children via the rearview mirror. "You both did." The family was dressed in their Sunday best as they drove along beautiful country roads on the way to Miller's Crossing Catholic Church.

"But that was when Mom was with us."

Sarah was right, they had not been back to church since Karen became too sick to go, but Edward knew this would be great for them. "Come on. This will be great. This is the church I attended when I was little."

"It's the only church in town. Everyone goes here." Sarah had a knack for pointing out the obvious.

"Yes, it is the only one," Edward confessed with a somewhat irritated smile as they pull along the gravel-lined driveway leading up to the single-building country church. The white building had a high-pitched roof. The traditional steeple contained a century-old bell that Edward could hear ringing even with the windows rolled up. The rooster weathervane on top showed a slight breeze blowing out of the north.

The family walked together up the stairs and entered the traditionally styled church, with high ceilings, exposed rafters, and stained-glass windows lining each wall. There was a large stained-glass scene behind a simple aged-wood altar. The sunlight coming through the windows created a myriad of dancing spots of color on every surface. Edward studied the scenes depicted in each of the windows. In all the churches he had been in before, the glass depicted a biblical scene. As he looked at each of these, he realized none of them represented a traditional Bible scene. None of the pictures depicted a child in a manger, wise men, or Moses leading the Jews. The imagery was more contemporary, showing faceless figures walking toward a cross with light emanating from it, pictures of what looked like a Catholic priest confronting a group of the same faceless figures. He didn't remember seeing those when he was there as a child.

Music from the pipe organ in the front interrupted his study. The procession filed down the aisle from the back. A minute into the intro of the song, Father Murray and the choir walked in. The congregation stood as the processional passed them and, once everyone was up front and in place, Father Murray led a quick prayer. He then instructed his flock to be seated. The service had hymns, prayers, and two readings, one each from the Old and New Testaments.

After one more hymn, Father Murray walked over to the pulpit and climbed up the small set of stairs to his perch that overlooked the congregation.

"Good morning."

The congregation returned Father Murray's greeting. "Good morning."

"It is great to see everyone here this morning. It truly warms my heart. Today is a very special day, my friends. I was and am going to give you a sermon about helping others find their way, a topic we talk about often and exercise daily. Now, right here in our congregation, we have an example of someone finding their way back to where they belong. I would like to welcome Edward Meyer, son of Robert and Laura Meyer, and his children back to our flock. Your family has been missing from our house for far too long. It is great to see you back." A brief applause followed the many heads that turned around and looked toward Edward and his children. Each face warm and welcoming. Edward felt Jacob squirm a little in the pew next to him.

Father Murray continued his sermon. "These are trying times, but I don't have to tell you that. The world is full of pain and suffering and they don't do enough to help ease the pain. We, the faithful, have taken it upon ourselves to help ease that pain. To help guide those that are misguided to find their way in the world, and it is not an easy task. It is a calling of pain and suffering that follows the example Jesus Christ, our Lord and Savior, set for us. He suffered on the cross as a penance for the sins of man. We have suffered as our penance for our sins and the sins of all men. Like the great Benedictine monk Peter Damian, this is our path toward our own glorious salvation. Also like our Brother Damian, our pain and battle are not only one of the spirit, but one of the flesh, and it takes a toll on each of us. We should not let that toll cause us to become derelict in our duty. Any lapse, even the smallest lapse, can have life or death consequences. Consequences we have already witnessed and suffered."

Father Murray paused for a second before continuing with a lower and more compassionate tone of voice. "Consequences we do not want to repeat. It is our solemn duty to help these poor souls, both good and bad, evil and innocent, contrite and hurtful, everyone without judgment. Help them down the path of their destination, no matter the cost. By doing this task, we will bask in the light of our Lord and Savior in the afterlife."

Father Murray walked off the pulpit and stood before the congregation with his arms outstretched. "The sacrifice is yours as His was for us."

Without prompt, the voices of the congregation echoed in the rafters. "We help others find their way as he helped us."

A hymn started, and the congregation stood up and joined the choir in song. Edward looked down at the hymnal to find the right page and then looked at both Sarah and Jacob as he attempted to share the book with them. Each had a fearful look on their face, and neither tried to sing.

Following the hymn, there was a final prayer before Father Murray dismissed his flock. Even though they were seated toward the back, it took twenty minutes or more for them to reach the door. Scores of individuals stopped by to welcome each of them back to Miller's Crossing and back to the church. Most talked of how they remembered Edward when he attended with his parents and how much he looked like his father. Several of the older women gushed over Jacob and how much he also resembled Edward's father. Finally, a familiar arm draped over his shoulder and helped guide him through the crowd and out the door.

"Thanks, Mark."

"Someone had to save you from the chat gaggle. Once they grab you, you're stuck for hours."

Based on his little exposure to them, Edward didn't doubt Mark one bit.

"Glad to see you guys joining the church."

"Yeah, Father Murray stopped by the school and invited me back the other day. I thought it would be good for the kids. We went often before Karen died." Edward paused and thought for a second before making the next comment. He was concerned it may seem inappropriate, but that had never stopped him from speaking his mind before. "Mark, I need to ask you a question."

"Sure bud, what is it?"

"What was up with that sermon?"

"Oh that. Kind of intense, huh? I think Father Murray is losing it a little in his old age. The last few years the sermons have taken a more 'fire and brimstone' approach. Maybe he sees his own mortality coming, not sure. All I know is he is comforting."

No argument from Edward on that point. A honk in the distance prompted Mark to wave in its direction. "Well, Sharon is waiting in the car. We have a bunch of chores to do around the house today. I need to get going. See you at work tomorrow."

"See ya tomorrow, Mark."

Edward and his still-stunned kids found their car in the parking lot of the church and headed home. Edward was the first to break the uncomfortable and abnormal silence between the three. "So, what did you two think about church?"

Jacob said, "It's not like the one back home with Pastor Mike. His sermons used comic strips and television shows to make his point."

Sarah said, "Yeah, no Marmaduke in this one."

14

Another normal week of school, Edward and Jacob headed into the stadium for another Friday night football game. The opponents this week were the Arendtsville Hornets, the two-time defending state champions. It should be a stiff test for the hometown Lions. With their less-than-healthy food choices in tow, Jacob and his father settled in for a good game. Sarah, like the week before, came with a group of friends.

The game was as they expected, a real back-and-forth tussle between two evenly matched teams. It appeared the Hornets were just bigger and stronger, overpowering the Lions on both sides of the ball. After the first quarter, they were down by seven. Midway through the second quarter, they were down by fourteen and the groans in the crowd started as it appeared there was no answer to the power running attack of the Hornets. The other side was full of cheers, and the marching band played their fight song for any reason, not just scores. Edward even heard a few parents above him wonder aloud if they play the fight song when the starting quarterback goes to the bathroom.

Just before halftime, the coaches stopped lining up man on man and try a different tactic: speed. When the whistle blew ending the first half, the Lions were on the board with a field goal cutting the lead to eleven. The Hornets spent the second half trying to adjust to the Lions' fast paced passing and outside running attack. Their size advantage worked against them and appeared to be a step behind the rest of the game. When the final gun sounded, the final score was Lions 24 and Hornets 21.

That would be considered a signature win for the Lions in most communities, prompting hours of celebration afterward, but not here.

Just like the week before, the stands and parking lot cleared out moments after the game. Edward received a quick but surprising text from Sarah. It simply stated, "Won't be home right after the game. They want to show me something. Is it OK?" Edward agreed. A nagging second thought about being naïve, but he dismissed it.

The drive home was just like the one the prior week. Full of discussion recapping the highlights of the game and the strategy of how the Lions came back. Once home, not having had enough football for one night, Jacob and his father cooked microwave popcorn and settled in on the couch, switching back and forth between two professional preseason games on that night.

Around 10:30, Jacob fell asleep. He looked comfortable there, so Edward let him lay there until the game was over. Once it was over, he took him upstairs and tucked him into his bed. With Sarah still out, Edward wanted to stay up until she came home, so he settled down on the couch and looked for a movie to watch. With few enjoyable choices, he left it on the eighth edition of an action film he loved. He paid no attention to everyone else who joked they should have stopped after the first movie.

At 11:00 pm he texted Sarah but received no reply.

11:30 pm arrived, and still no reply.

At midnight, the text messages progressed to phone calls that were neither answered, nor went straight to voicemail. His level of worry jumped from nothing to concerned in an instant. Edward wanted to jump in the car and go look for her, but he had no idea where to start. Also, not knowing who she was out with gnawed at him, making him feel like a negligent parent.

Six more calls resulted in the same response, adding to his panic. Eventually he gave into his concern, grabbed his keys to head out and look for her, but a knock on the door stopped him before he even put his shoes on. He rushed to the door and slung it open. Edward's heart skipped a beat when he saw Sarah standing there, tears running down her face, and a blanket draped around her shoulders. His mind jumped to the absolute worst as he pulled her inside.

"Are you all right?"

She wrapped her arms around him and buried her face into his chest.

"She's fine, Eddie." The voice of Sheriff Lewis Tillingsly startled him. The sheriff walked in through the door while taking off his black wide-brim hat.

"Relax. She isn't in any trouble. None at all. I gave her a ride home, but I think we should talk privately."

Edward felt beyond confused. His sixteen-year-old daughter was just brought home after midnight by the Sheriff, but she was not in any trouble.

"Sarah, why don't you go on to your room? Your dad and I need to have a talk."

Sarah headed upstairs to her room while her father stood there with his mouth gaping wide open.

"Why don't we go into the kitchen and talk? I will try to explain everything." The Sheriff knew his way around the house and walked through the living room and into the kitchen. When Edward pushed through the door, he found the Sheriff searching through the cabinets. "Where do you keep your coffee? Your ma kept it in this cabinet."

He was right, she always kept it in the cabinet next to the refrigerator and above the coffee maker. Edward, however, had things organized a little different. "It's in the pantry. There's a box of k-cups."

"I should have asked. You don't mind, do you?"

Feeling too much in a fog to even care, Edward said, "Not at all." Then he had a seat at the breakfast table in the nook surrounded by windows.

The Sheriff walked over to the pantry and pulled out two k-cups. He then retrieved two coffee cups from the cabinet. Edward sat at the table holding his head in his hands, trying to process everything. The Sheriff made two cups of coffee and joined Edward at the table, sliding one cup over to him. "You'll need this."

There was a knock at the back door and Edward jumped, but the Sheriff put him at ease. "It's okay. Let me get it. I called him." The Sheriff opened the back door and Father Murray walked in, adding to Edward's feeling of complete bewilderment.

"I'm not sure you remember, but your father and the two of us sat at this same table many times talking when you were younger." Edward had not thought about that before now, but now that he mentioned it, it was one of the more common memories he had of his childhood. The three of them, and maybe a few others, sitting at the table drinking coffee, talking about many things from the town gossip, to sports, and politics. Edward also remembers other times they would talk, and he would walk into the kitchen. They would all go silent, and his father would ask him to move along, that they were talking about adult things.

"Father, would you like some coffee?" Sheriff Tillingsly offered.

"No thanks, Lewis. If I have any now, I'll never get to sleep." Father Murray turned his attention to Edward. He was quiet on the outside, but anything but on the inside. "Evening, Edward, how are you doing?"

Edward did not answer as Father Murray placed a comforting hand on his shoulder and took the old wooden seat next to him in the alcove It was a chair he had occupied many times in the past. It gave a familiar by haunting squeak on the floor as he slid it back from the table.

With a high level of exacerbation in his voice, Edward demanded, "Will someone tell me what is going on?"

Father Murray was first to speak. "Eddie, how much did your father ever tell you about this place?"

"What do you mean? This house? This town?"

"The town. Miller's Crossing."

"He and my mother told me lots of stories about their childhood here and I heard a lot about his high school days..."

"No, not that," interrupted Father Murray.

"Father, let me try a different question." The Sheriff took his seat at the table again and looked across at Edward. "Do you remember when I came by to pick your father up late at night?"

"I remember that happening several times."

"Did he ever talk to you about where he went and what we did?"

Edward remembered asking a few times. "He just said it was adult things."

"Lewis, he was too young. Robert would have never talked to him about any of this."

"Eddie, not to play twenty questions with you, but can you tell me if you see things?"

"Things?"

"Do you see ghosts? Spirits? Images of people and creatures you can't explain?"

This question more than stunned Edward. It was a fact he had hidden from everyone for years. The last time he told anyone about the visions, they sent him for a mental evaluation. He wondered if they knew of his past, his stay in a mental hospital, and wanted to use it. Maybe Sarah got into some trouble, and they were using this to show he was an unfit parent.

The mental argument going on within Edward was visible to both of his guests. "Eddie, you can tell us the truth. We both see them too. Most everyone in Miller's Crossing does. It is a gift and a curse of sorts."

Staring at the old priest with a blank gaze, Edward tried to make sense of what he had just heard. The Sheriff added, "Your father did as well. So did your mother."

"This town is a very important place in the spiritual world. There is no natural explanation for why or how, but this town is surrounded by a very strong energy field that attracts spirits. There are other places all around the world like Miller's Crossing. Some are more obvious once you know what they are, like Stonehenge and Peak Kailash in Tibet. Others are just towns, like here, and lakes, like Rila Lake in Bulgaria. Most of the other places are rather remote, with not that many people around them. We are the lucky exception."

He understood what Father Murray said. "So, this energy, some kind of electromagnetic field, makes you think you are seeing things? If so, I am familiar with that. I read about several studies that pointed to EM fields causing most paranormal experiences."

"Well, not exactly Edward. You don't think you see them. You really see them. They are really there. The energy attracts lost souls and simply put; we have to help them find their way."

Edward thought for a moment. Something Father Murray just said brought clarity to his confusion a week ago in church. He asked, "The sermon?"

"Yes, last week's sermon was about this responsibility we have. Those that live here. We have that responsibility to the souls that are lost to help them move along and find their way. It is a responsibility we have not been as diligent about as we should. If we don't help them, they will continue to search for all eternity at best, and terrorize us all at worst. Not all spirits are kind and gentle. Those that are kind and gentle pass through our world and do no harm. Those that aren't can be more dangerous than you can ever imagine."

"Wait." Edward shook his head while he rubbed his eyes, remembering back to the first night back in his family's home. "This isn't just a prayer-type thing, right? This is really confronting the spirits and moving them?"

"Oh yes, this is a lot more than prayer."

"Did you have to move any about two weeks ago out here?"

Father Murray looked over at Sheriff Tillingsly, who answered for the both of them. "Yes, we had two spirits that didn't want to cooperate. I thought I saw a light turn on in the house when we were out in the field. We tried not to wake you."

"So that is what I saw that night? You were helping lost souls?"

"We were there, along with others to make sure everyone in Miller's Crossing was safe that night and to ensure these souls moved on. The group you saw that night is known as the town elders. Each sworn to take this responsibility, no matter the sacrifice. Your father was one. So was your grandfather. Even your great grandfather was one. Your family is one of our town's founding members going back almost two hundred years."

"That's why my father left those nights."

Sheriff Tillingsly finished taking a sip of coffee. "Yes, Edward. Each of those nights, your father was out helping us. Tonight, we were out following a group of the less kind, but not very evil type when we ran into a group of teenagers. Your daughter was with them. Her friends assumed, because of her age and who you were, that she knew our little secret. So, they took her out hunting spirits. She wasn't ready for it. Not all female descendants are born with the gift."

Edward was about to ask a question when the Sheriff stopped him. "I don't know what or if she saw anything. It is possible she just freaked out sitting in the woods as all of her friends tried to tell her there were ghosts out there with them. I tried to talk to her a little on the ride back, but she didn't say much."

Father Murray said, "I can talk to her if you want."

"No, Father, I can handle it. I need to be the one." Edward sat back in his chair and mouthed the word "WOW."

"It is a lot to take in, and I admit it may be hard for you to believe."

"Actually, Sheriff, it is not as hard for me to believe as you think. I spent years thinking I was crazy."

Father Murray patted Edward on the shoulder. "That is my fault, my son. The sheriff and others wanted to tell you, but I thought you were too young. In most children, the gift doesn't show until the early teen years, and you were only seven. I am sorry. If I could go back and change the past, that is one of several things I would change from that night."

"It's late. I'm sure your daughter feels very confused right now. If you'd like, we can talk to her."

Edward insisted. "No, let me. Even though I still need to understand things myself, I am her father. It should be from me."

Father Murray stood up and slid past Edward while Tillingsly rinsed out his coffee cup in the sink. While grabbing his hat off the counter, Tillingsly remarked, "We should go, so you can get to that conversation."

Edward only nodded. He wanted to seem confident in his ability to speak to his daughter about this, but inside, the butterflies and self-doubt created a hurricane of nerves.

"One more thing. I would like for you to come out with us tomorrow night. Take your father's place with us."

"Lewis!!!" exclaimed Father Murray.

"No, it's OK." Edward was curious about all this and felt a strong need to understand. "I'm in."

Edward bided the two of them a good night and closed the back door behind them before going upstairs to talk to Sarah. He noticed her bedroom door was closed, and it appeared her light was off. He cracked the door open and let out a little sigh of relief when he saw her sleeping. Feeling exhausted, he headed to his room and collapsed on the bed but did not sleep much. A few minutes here and there, but that was all.

Throughout the night, his mind raced between the hundreds of visions he had seen over his life. He saw his parents several times, both trying to comfort and assure him. As he fell to sleep, he heard Father Murray's words from earlier mixed with his sermon from the previous Sunday. Words like "responsibility," "duty," and "salvation." Edward woke, sitting straight up after a few hours of restlessness and stared at the clock on the table next to his bed. It was just 3:30 A.M. and still dark outside his window. He got up and walked downstairs for a quick drink of water to soothe his dry mouth. Feeling the cool water slide down the back of his throat was very pleasurable. The only feeling more pleasurable at that moment would be drifting into a deep slumber with a calm mind, which he knows won't be possible tonight. He was so sure of that, he even uttered "yeah right" out loud. What he didn't expect was the reply.

From behind him, he heard the stable and supportive voice of his mother say to him, "No need to panic, son. This is who you are." Edward spun around. He expected to catch an image of the vision he had seen throughout the years, but he only caught a glimpse out of the corner of his eye as she disappeared.

"What do you mean?" Edward asked the empty room.

He knew asking was pointless. Through the years, he tried many times to talk to or communicate with them. Each time resulted in no response. No sign they heard him, or were even aware he was there. This was also not the first time a vision had spoken to him, but this time there was a warm emotion in her words. A feeling that stirred emotions Edward locked up years ago and now emerged as a single tear building in the corner of his left eye.

Edward stood there, focused on where her image was just a few moments ago, hoping she would reappear again. He did not say a word. For several moments, he didn't move. With no reappearance, he crossed his arms and leaned back against the countertop, still not taking his eyes off that spot. After another ten minutes, the area was still void of any presence. Edward headed off to bed feeling a touch of heartbreak, now with something new to ponder.

15

Edward awoke to the light of a new morning sneaking in around the outside edge of his window shade. Laying across his bed instead of tucked under the covers, he was unsure if he was just that tired or that restless in his sleep. He sat up on the edge of the bed to wake up. His mind raced through the events of the last twelve hours. The feeling one had when a dream lingered beyond the world of sleep consumed him.

When he pushed himself out of bed, the face of the clock showed 9:00. He opened his bedroom door, allowing in the sounds of his son and daughter talking and fixing breakfast down in the kitchen. Edward headed down to join them and, when he pushed through the door to the kitchen, he saw what appeared to be a normal morning. One look in Sarah's eyes told him it was not. The play bickering between his two children was an act by Sarah. Even the way she greeted him was forced and unnatural. Jacob may not have picked up on it, but her father did.

"Morning, sleepy head. Did you stay up watching a late movie?"

Edward knew Sarah knew what kept him up so late. Her efforts to avoid any direct eye contact with him confirmed it. Edward went along with this for now. He would need to talk to his daughter alone at some point.

Edward fixed his coffee and headed upstairs to take a shower and attempted to wash the cobwebs out of his head. When he emerged from the steam-filled bathroom, his body felt more refreshed, but his mind was more occupied than ever. While in the shower, he thought about everything he needed to get done that day. That was when the agreement he made with Sheriff Tillingsly and Father Murray came running to the front of the list. Even though he had many encounters with spirits, he had no idea of what to expect. It frightened him a touch.

The rest of the morning took on the normal routine. Edward cleaned while his children watched television or engaged in other non-cleaning-related tasks around the house. Through the entire morning, he noticed that Sarah was rather clingy around her brother, and did not want to be alone. On a normal day, she would be in her room on her laptop with the door closed or out walking the field, on her phone. He continued to look for an opening to talk to her, but so far there hadn't been one.

Around noon, Jacob headed upstairs, leaving Sarah downstairs watching the last few minutes of a movie alone. When Edward saw her sitting there alone, a lump developed in the back of his throat. Before he could open his mouth and talk, she sprung up from the sofa and headed for the stairs.

"Dad, a group of friends from school want to go walk around the town center today and look in the shops. They'll be here in a few. Is it OK?" she asked.

"That's fine. Do you have a minute?"

"Not really. I need to get ready." She continued up another step on the stairs.

"Hold up for just a second," Edward insisted with a tone of voice that caused Sarah to stop in her tracks. She did not turn around. "What happened last night?"

"It was nothing, really. I know it seemed like something because the sheriff drove me home, but it wasn't. He said he was heading this way and offered to give me a ride."

Edward had seen snowstorms in the past, but nothing like what his daughter just unloaded on him. He pulled out his mental shovel and tried to shovel through it. "You know I wasn't born yesterday. Sheriff Tillingsly may have been heading this way, and he is an old family friend, but when you came home, something really upset you. What was it?" Edward needed to hear it from her.

Her shoulders dropped a little as she sighed. "You grew up around here. They have areas out in the woods that can be really spooky. That's all." She turned around, looking at her father from the fourth step. "I got a little scared and a few of the people, instead of stopping there, they kept going and I kind of freaked out and got embarrassed." She stared into his eyes to convince him, but it did not work. "The Sheriff pulled up on us to make sure we weren't up to any trouble, and he saw me in tears. That's it."

Her eyes studied his face to see if he believed her. "Now can I go get ready?"

He did not believe her, not one bit, but didn't want to push things. If she saw what Father Murray and the Sheriff said, she had to be confused. "Sure, but be home early. I have something to do tonight." Before Edward could finish his request, Sarah sprinted upstairs to avoid any further questioning.

Edward tried to have as normal a Saturday as possible, not wanting to dwell on last night or the night ahead of him. He spent a few hours grading papers, which required complete mental focus, but a part of his mind drifted through what he had learned and events that now made sense. Later on, he and Jacob went outside to toss the pigskin out in their expansive pasture. In between throws, Edward caught himself looking over at the area where he'd seen the group weeks ago. Luckily for him, he looked back just in time to avoid being beamed in the nose like Marcia Brady.

Sarah's friends dropped her off just before dinner. She appeared to be more relaxed and more herself now, but not entirely. Edward knew he still needed to sit her down and explain things. Of course, he needed to understand things himself first. He decided it would be best to wait until tomorrow when he understood more.

The kids were watching a movie when Father Murray arrived just before ten o'clock. Edward explained that Father Murray was hosting a poker game with his friends from the old days, and that he wouldn't be back too late. At that moment, he flashed back to the times his father had made a similar excuse and walked out the door with Father Murray or then Officer Tillingsly.

16

Edward did not ask where they were headed, but the path taken by Father Murray transported him back into the mind and body of a stunned seven-year-old. They pulled into the parking lot of the Miller's Crossing police station. Edward got out and stood there for a minute, looking around. The building itself looked the same as it did the last time he was there. The sign was different, instead of an old blue painted piece of wood with white letters suspended between two four by four posts, there was a blue sheet of plastic with white illuminated letters: 'POLICE'.

He followed Father Murray inside. The station was quiet and empty this time of night except for a few men sitting on the couches in the waiting room. Each of them nodded toward or extended a greeting to their priest.

"Gentlemen, you remember Edward Meyer, Robert's boy."

An older white-haired man wearing denim overalls and a presence that matched his girth stood up and extended his hand. "Hey, Eddie. John Sawyer. I was a good friend of your pop's."

Edward looked at the man's weathered face and suppressed his shock. He remembered John Sawyer, but the man in front of him did not resemble him. The John Sawyer he remembered was an in-shape, blonde, outgoing man who always acted like a big kid.

A second man stood up and welcomed Edward as Sheriff Tillingsly walked in announcing, "Mount up boys. That was Larry Mixon. He spotted a group causing a ruckus out around mile marker 23 on route 471."

In mere moments, the room emptied, leaving Edward standing in the center. The Sheriff patted Edward on the shoulder as he walked out. "You can ride with me. You ready for this?"

Edward gave a single nod and followed him out to the patrol car.

The convoy of three workhorse pickup trucks, Father Murray's old Caddy, and a patrol car snaked down the old dark road, surrounded on both sides by old growth oak and pine trees. Edward watched as the various mile markers passed by outside the passenger window of the patrol car. Moments after they passed mile marker 22, blinding red brake lights illuminated from the back of each of the cars and trucks in front. The vehicles pulled off the side of the road and parked.

Edward took a quick look into the woods on both sides and saw nothing. The rest of the men gathered around Father Murray and the sheriff. Standing on the roadside, Father Murray stared out into the woods. At that moment, Edward felt a familiar impulse to turn and look to his right, but when he did, he saw nothing.

"Where to, Father?" one man asked.

"This way," Father Murray said as he headed in the direction that pulled at Edward seconds ago.

With Father Murray leading the way, the group that reminded Edward of an old-time posse you'd see in the Western movies followed, pushing through the deep and thick woods and underbrush. Edward felt that impulse again, stronger and colder now. To him, he felt it came from farther right of their path. Father Murray turned right as well, leading the group in that direction. What Edward felt differed from anything he had felt before. It usually felt familiar, like the arrival of an old friend. This time, there was a feeling of dread when it arrived, and the feeling grew the further in they walked.

Father Murray stopped, letting the rest of the posse close ranks behind him. Among the sounds of crickets and the occasional croak of a frog, in the distance there was something that resembled the same sound Edward heard out in his pasture that night. A sound that no animal he knew of could make. Father Murray prayed under his breath and the rest of the posse crossed themselves in unison. Edward did the same. As Father Murray took a step forward, he snatched Edward by the arm, pulling him up by his side. Above a whisper he said, "Stand by me the whole time, Eddie. Remember, this is your calling."

A few steps forward and they finally came into view. There were four of them intermingled in the forest. Unlike their pursuers, these creatures moved with ease through the dense forest and underbrush. They were unaware of the group of men until Father Murray recited Proverbs 28:9 out loud.

"Whoever turns his ear away from hearing the law, even his prayer is detestable."

All four stopped and turned toward Father Murray. He reached under his robe, searching for something. When he found it, he pulled it out and handed the rosary to Edward. "This was your father's. Hold on to it and repeat after me."

Edward took the rosary in his left hand as Father Murray grabbed him by both shoulders. The old priest glared into his eyes from under his black wide-brimmed hat. "And Edward, you must repeat with conviction. Do not let your faith wane, or it will put us in a very dangerous situation."

The old priest held up his own rosary and recited, "Glorious St. Michael, Prince of the heavenly hosts."

Father Murray paused and looked at Edward who, with a quiver in his voice, repeated the line. "Glorious St. Michael, Prince of the heavenly hosts."

"Be strong and repeat what I say, immediately after me," ordered Father Murray. He continued, "who standest always ready to give assistance to the people of God."

Edward repeated, staring straight ahead, "who standest always ready to give assistance to the people of God."

"Who didst fight with the dragon, the old serpent, and didst cast him out of heaven."

As Edward was about to repeat the line, the four visions disappeared and then reappeared inches from Father Murray. The old priest's conviction and determination did not waver. "Edward! Repeat the line."

Edward repeated, "who didst fight with the drag..." but stopped as one of them left Father Murray and appeared inches from his own face. The hollow eyes locked on him, as if Edward was his prey. Frozen with fear, Edward heard Father Murray command, "Edward! Do not give in!"

Edward started over, with fear dripping in his voice, "who didst fight with the dragon, the old serpent, and didst cast him out of heaven." As soon as Edward uttered the last word, the creature thrust its hand into Edward's chest, producing a cold and squeezing pain deep inside. The pain sent Edward to his knees. He grasped at his chest and fell over, the creature maintaining its grasp.

It climbed on top of Edward and glared while twisting its hand back and forth. Edward tried to grab its arm in defense, but his hands passed right through. With a primeval scream, it twisted its arm, increasing the pain to a level that caused Edward to grasp at his chest with both hands. The look on his face told of the agonizing pain. He looked straight up through the creature and saw visions of his parents looking down at him as his thoughts shifted to his kids.

"Thrust this up into its heart." The voice of Father Murray cut through all the thoughts.

The priest stood over Edward with something in his hand and then dropped it. It passed straight through the vision and landed on Edward's chest. Using both hands, he reached for the object and gripped the bottom arm of it. He felt an electric jolt run through his arms and into his body. The feelings of fear and despair disappeared. The agonizing pain was no more. He still sensed the four spirits, but the cold and dread he felt before became something different. He was not afraid. With both hands, he thrusted the object, a simple wooden cross, up into the heart of the spirit on top of him. The creature screamed in pain as it disappeared into a cloud of mist, only to reappear a few feet away.

Sheriff Tillingsly helped Father Murray pull Edward up. He held onto that cross with a death grip. Edward searched for answers in the men's faces.

Father Murray again grabbed him by both shoulders and said, "Focus. This is what you were meant to do. The power is inside you. Here." The old priest took his left hand off the cross and shoved a book in it. The book was already opened to a page marked by a simple red rope. "Read from here."

Edward's eyes followed Father Murray's finger to a spot on the page. He heard his voice once more. "Go on."

Edward read, "and now valiantly defendest the Church of God that the gates of Hell may never prevail against her, I earnestly entreat thee to assist me also, in the painful and dangerous conflict which I have to sustain against the same formidable foe. Be with me, O mighty Prince! that I may courageously fight and wholly vanquish that proud spirit, whom thou hast by the Divine Power so gloriously overthrown, and whom our powerful King, Jesus Christ, has, in our nature, so completely overcome; to the end that having triumphed over the enemy of my salvation, I may with thee and the holy angels, praise the clemency of God who, having refused mercy to the rebellious angels after their fall, has granted repentance and forgiveness to fallen man. Amen."

Edward's reading of St. Michael's prayer caused the creatures to scream and howl. Fixated and fearful of the cross in his right hand, they kept their distance.

Father Murray held his rosary up and walked toward the visions. "Come with me." Edward followed the priest step by step.

"With the glory and love of Christ as my sword, I command you unclean spirits to leave this world and to be condemned to the fire of Hell for all eternity."

The creatures were focused on the cross and moved backward as Edward brought it closer to them.

Father Murray spoke again. "I command you to leave this place. In the glory of God and Christ our savior, I command you. In the glory of God and Christ our savior, I command you."

The creatures faded as Father Murray continued to recite the phrase repeatedly. A blue colored haze floated where the creatures were. It descended to the ground, disappearing among the fog and cool moist night air.

"Where did they go?" Edward asked.

"Where they should be. To Hell, I hope. They were pure evil."

"How did you know?"

Father Murray explained rather calmly, "It's pretty easy. It has nothing to do with how they react to us. Even the best spirits can act like that. It is the confusion they feel. It clouds their judgement. The evil ones, you feel without question. Don't tell me you didn't feel that when we first got out of the car."

He was right. Edward felt dread the first time he sensed them.

"Let's get out of here. The bugs are biting." Father Murray turned and walked out of the woods, swatting at the swarm of mosquitoes around them. Edward didn't notice the mosquitoes until now. He followed Father Murray and the rest of the men out of the woods. His body shook with each step. When the group emerged, they were about a hundred yards away from where they parked.

John Sawyer called back at the sheriff, "Any more reports?"

"A couple of friendlies, John, but it sounds like those are all handled."

"If it's all right with you and the Father, me and the boys are going home."

Sheriff Tillingsly passed the question off to Father Murray. "Father?"

"That is fine with me, Lewis. Thank you much, John."

"See you in church tomorrow."

John and the others loaded up in their trucks and headed off. Edward quick stepped a few times to catch up with the priest. "Here," Edward said as he tried to return the cross and book to him.

The priest put his hands around Edward's and the objects. "Keep them. They were your father's, and we have a lot of training to do." With a creak, Father Murray opened the door of his Caddy. "Lewis, see you tomorrow?"

"Yes, Father."

"Good. Make sure Edward gets home safely. He has had a long night." The old priest smirked.

"Yes, Father."

Neither Edward nor Sheriff Tillingsly said much to each other on the entire ride home. Mostly just chit-chat like "the football team looks great this year" and such from the Sheriff. Edward gave simple one- and two-word answers. His mind was too occupied for normal conversation, but he recognized what the Sheriff was doing. This was the second time in his life he had tried to distract him.

Edward got out of the car and walked toward the house as the Sheriff sped off behind him. When he approached the door, a familiar chill and tingling started at the base of his neck. Instinctually he looked around. The sight he saw took his breath away. It wasn't one or two. Not even five to ten. In the layer of fog that hung above the ground, a group of glowing individuals made of vapor and soulless eyes encircled his house. There was no sound or movement. They just hovered there.

Edward thought to himself, *well, this is new,* before he headed inside.

17

Edward sat in a church pew alone after the Sunday morning service. He sent his children out to the car for a few minutes so he could talk to Father Murray alone. The events of the past few days had rolled through his mind, leading to sleepless nights. Safely tucked into his coat pocket were the book and the cross. He hadn't allowed either to leave his possession since Father Murray handed them to him the night before. He laid in his bed after returning home and studied each of them, but never felt the same confidence and power surging through his body as he did in the woods. The cross was a simple wooden cross. Nothing ornate about it. The book was a simple brown leather-bound book of aged handwritten prayers and notes. There was nothing special about either item. Had he imagined the feeling? Edward dismissed that. What he felt was real, but how? Did Father Murray have anything to do with it? He needed to find answers.

"How are you doing, Eddie?"

"Oh, I am just hunky-dory, Father. And you?"

Father Murray motioned with his hands for him to slide over and make room. "I am good."

"Last night was kind of intense."

Father Murray chuckled. "Last night was nothing. They were evil, but we were never in any danger. I knew it as soon as I felt them. That is why I had you take the lead with me. Most of what we encounter is way beyond that."

Edward questioned, "Way beyond that? No danger? That one tried to kill me."

"He felt threatened and responded, but you were never in any danger. It felt that way because of how sensitive you are to them. Many we encounter, not only can, but want to harm you."

Edward tried to wrap his head around that. The pain he felt was real to him, and he'd thought he was moments from death.

Father Murray could see the self-doubt and worry rush into Edward. He attempted to reassure him, "Don't worry, we won't take the training wheels off until you are ready. The power to do all this is inside you. You were born with it. We just have to show you how to use it. We have a lot of training to do."

"Training?" Edward questioned. An image of some mythical magical school popped into his mind.

"This ability is like a muscle. You have to train to use it properly. Last night was just… a push up. Just meant to make you believe in your capability. Before last night, how much of what Lewis and I told you did you believe?"

"Well…" Edward thought about it for just a moment, "… probably more than you will believe. I have seen them since I was a kid. So, hearing that others do didn't surprise me. What you told me about Miller's Crossing and what I saw last night, I still need to make sense of."

Edward leaned down and held his head in his hands. "So, my father and mother were like me?"

"You mean able to see spirits?" Father Murray asked.

Edward nodded.

"Yes. They were just like you," Father Murray answered.

At that moment, Edward realized how different his life could have been. "I'm not sure you know this. I don't tell most people about it and need you to keep this between us."

"Of course. I am a priest, you know."

"I was put in a crazy home when I was fourteen because of what I could see. My foster parents didn't understand me and didn't know how to deal with me. I don't fault them. If my parents had been alive, they would have understood and could have helped me understand."

"I know. There are many things that would be better if your parents were still alive. I knew about what you were going through."

"You knew?" Edward asked, surprised.

"Lewis and I kept tabs on you. We tried to help, hon- "

Edward interrupted. "You tried? I spent years, drugged every day. They treated me like I was crazy. Hell, after enough of the medication I thought they were right."

"We tried." Father Murray attempted to console Edward. "Because of who you were, Lewis and I kept track of you. Lewis attempted to talk to the doctors at your facility to help explain what you had been through, to see if that would give them some perspective. We both tried to talk to your foster parents, but they sent us away and asked us to never attempt to contact you or them again." The old priest held up a hand to stop Edward. "… and, I don't blame them. They were trying to protect you. We even talked to Tony Yates to see if there was some legal avenue we could use. There was nothing."

Edward sat speechless.

"You would have had been about sixteen when Lewis said he wanted to tell your doctors the truth. Can you imagine what would have happened then?" A wide grin stretched across Father Murray's weathered face.

Edward thought about how Doctor Law would have responded. "It's a good thing he didn't. I already had a roommate. He would have been assigned to a different room."

"Those without the gift can't understand. We tried. We owed that to your parents. When you turned eighteen, we lost track of you until about ten years ago. Thank you, social media." Father Murray looked up to the heavens with his hands pressed together in prayer.

"Social media?"

"What? You think because I'm old, I don't know about such things? I post, tweet, share pictures. This church has its own page. I may be old, but I'm not dead." Father Murray bumped Edward with his shoulder and joked, "or am I? Would you know the difference?"

"Yep. You're talking," Edward said through a slight laugh.

"Ah, well... I will teach you how you can talk to them, just like I am talking to you now."

The surprised look on Edward's face said it all.

"You just don't know how yet. It is on one of the many pages of your family's book I gave you last night. I think your great-grandfather added it. Your grandfather added a few pages, as did your father. You will too, in time."

The old priest groaned as he stood up and walked toward the front of the church. His voice echoed in the empty sanctuary. "When we found you, I came out to Portland to see you. I planned to give you the cross and book, but when I sat in my car outside your house you and your family came walking by. You seemed so happy and adjusted. I debated with myself for the next few days. On one side, you needed to know. On the other, you had been through so much. To see you happy and with a family of your own. Do I risk interrupting that? I decided then to let you live your life. You were too young to understand how important your family is in this town."

"I knew how respected my father was, but nothing else," said Edward.

"Oh, your father was special. A great man, intellectually and spiritually. Never one to turn down the opportunity to help someone, but you knew that."

Father Murray was right. Edward remembered many a weekend his father and he finished their chores on their property, only to head out to help someone on theirs.

"He was a brother to me, as was your grandfather. How much do you remember of him?"

"Not too much." Edward was only seven when he passed away. He had a few memories of his father and grandfather out working in the pasture together while he ran around helping with his plastic tools.

"For you to understand all this, you need to understand your history. Are you ready to take that journey?"

His past was a mystery to Edward. He knew more about his foster family than his real family. What memories he had, were vanishing with time.

"Dad, can we go now? It's hot in the car," Sarah demanded from the church's front door.

Walking back toward Edward, Father Murray said, "Go ahead. Take them home. Do me a favor though."

"Of course."

"Think of your home as a museum. We left everything just as you left it. Look around. Discover yourself."

"I will."

Father Murray shook Edward's hand. "I will be in touch soon. Keep those items safe. They are more powerful than you can imagine."

Edward bowed and said, "Yes, master."

"Oh, I am no master. You are. You just don't know it yet."

That thought landed the weight of the world on Edward's shoulders.

18

When Edward and his children arrived home, Sarah and Jacob ran inside to avoid melting in the heat. Edward took his time and looked at the thunderheads developing. As a kid, he would ask his father, "How long do we have today?" Meaning, how long could he play outside before the storms would force him inside. There was no such conversation with his kids. They were inside turning down the air conditioning.

Edward walked in with the ancient Greek aphorism "Know Thyself" echoing in his mind. The pile of photo albums and old books in the dining room bookcases called to him. These were off limits when he was a child. Any time his mother saw him close to them or looking at them she admonished him, "Sweetie, you can look at them, but don't touch. They are old." Those books and that one antique chair in the corner were off limits. The devious seven-year-old inside him came up with an idea. He should sit in that chair while he looked through the books.

First, Edward headed upstairs to change into something comfortable. Once changed, he found himself standing in front of the bookshelf. "Where to start?" he wondered aloud. The obvious answer was the top. He pulled the first album off, a red covered, drugstore bought photo album loaded with instant pictures pressed between the pages. Edward's younger self was the main subject in most pictures. Christmas morning, candid school shots, and him in a few Halloween costumes. He didn't remember ever dressing up as a dog. That was one picture he'd never let his kids see.

He found one picture his eyes lingered on while emotions stirred inside. It was one of a younger version of himself flanked by both his mom and dad, probably the best picture he'd seen of the three of them. Carefully he removed it from the film covered page and put if off to the side. He was sure his mom would forgive him.

Edward returned that book and retrieved a larger dust covered book. Carefully prying it open, he sensed the age of it. The pictures weathered to shades of brown, grays, and hints of faded colors. They were of his father, grandfather, and various other men. Sides of the house and the old barn appeared in several of the images. One picture showed a fresh coat of red paint on the side of the barn. His father was maybe eleven years old in that photo. Someone probably wrote a date on the back, but he did not dare attempt to check.

Page by page he flipped through. Several of the pictures showed a woman with his father. He assumed that was his grandmother. He never had the opportunity to meet or even see a picture of her before. The next picture caused a pause. His father and grandfather were standing on either side of another older man. The mystery man was holding the cross and the book, and both his father and grandfather had their hands on the objects. He studied the men in the photo. His father was only a teen, and his grandfather was maybe in his early forties. The other man could've been in his sixties or seventies. Even with the discrepancy in age, there was something familiar in all of them. They shared the same eyes. He had to be Edward's great grandfather.

He tried to pry it from its page, but the aged adhesive maintained its hold. To avoid damaging it, he used a nearby piece of junk mail as a makeshift bookmark. A few pages deeper there he was again, with his father and a large group of men sitting on hay bales the barn. The image reminded Edward of a scene he walked in on several times when he was younger. It always ended with his father ushering him out.

Edward picked up the next album. The photos were more of the same, but they took on a whole new meaning. Picture after picture of men gathered together in some sort of commune. The cross and book only appeared in a few pictures each with his father, grandfather, and who he assumed was his great grandfather.

He stacked that album off to his side on top of the others. The stack in the bookshelf appeared to be more of the same, except one book. The book on the bottom had a brown leather cover and was much thicker, about the size of four albums. He pried it from its home of the last several decades and blew off the layer of dust covering it. The cover was cracked brown leather, with a single gold leaf cross on it. He remembered the book: the family bible. When he was five, his mother sat him in her lap and showed him their family tree inside it. He opened it, and sitting folded in the inside cover just like he remembered was the family tree.

The last entry at the bottom of the tree was his name, Edward Meyer, with his birthdate July 27th, 1974. Above that appeared his father's name, Robert Carl Meyer, and his birth date, February 11th, 1951 with his mother's name written next to and the date they married. The next one was his grandfather, Carl Edward Meyer, born August 13th, 1924, with his grandmother's name written next to it. Edward continued working up the family tree. It was a single tree, with each generation only having one child, which he thought was odd until he ran into something even more peculiar. There was a line drawn across the tree two-thirds of the way up. Just below the line written on the left edge of the page was "Miller's Crossing–1719". Above the line on the same side was the text "Saint Margaret's Hope, Scotland–1719". *That must be where we settled from,* Edward thought to himself. The mystery around the line only lasted a second. The next name up replaced it with even more questions. William Miller, born December 21, 1694.

Edward let the paper fall to his lap. His family's real name was Miller, like the town. Looking back up the tree, he confirmed the name below the line was Jacob Allen Meyer. *They changed their name when they moved here, but why?*

"Dad, are you ok?" Sarah asked while looking at him perplexed.

"Yeah, why?" Edward said from his position on the floor.

"Well, you're sitting in the floor, surround by old books, and looking out into nowhere, looking all weird."

"Just looking through some old family things."

"Okay," she said with a hint of a question, and then headed toward the kitchen.

Edward called after her, "Hey Sarah, wait up." Now was as good a time as any to have that conversation.

19

Edward followed Sarah into the kitchen. She grabbed a soda from the fridge and started back toward the door.

"Come have a seat with me for a second?" Edward said and sat down at the table.

She rolled her eyes and offered the mild protest, "Why?"

"Because I want to talk to you."

Her shoulders slumped as she dragged her presence over to the table and fell into the chair across from him. Edward knew if he asked her what happened Friday night, she'd give him some other excuse besides the truth. There was one way to do it, and Edward decided to lay his cards on the table, even if it meant she might think he'd lost his mind.

"How long have you been seeing…" he took a moment to choose his word, "things?"

Sarah stopped taking a drink from the bottle of soda mid-sip. Her eyes exploded wide open, and she stared at him over the bottle pressed to her lips.

He tried to reassure his daughter. "It's OK. It doesn't mean you're crazy. Quite the opposite."

Her glare had not moved, and neither had the bottle.

"You saw something Friday night, didn't you?"

The bottle dropped, and she gave a silent yet defiant, "No."

"You have nothing to hide. The Sheriff told me what happened." Edward then threw her a life preserver. "I see things. I have since I was ten."

"You see things? What do you see?"

"Well, I see spirits." Edward searched her eyes and expression for any reaction. Her body language relaxed. The bottle lowered to the table, and she leaned forward. Her eyes blinked for the first time in moments.

"You see spirits. What do they look like when you see them?"

"It is hard to describe. They look like people, but people who are there and at the same time are not there. Does that make sense?"

"The ones you see flash?"

"The ones? So, you *did* see something?"

She leaned back in the chair, looking around the kitchen. "I didn't say that. I don't know what I saw. Whatever it was didn't flash."

"They disappear and reappear in a different spot... but you can see through them."

"Like they're made up of light?"

"Yes, exactly. Some of them have a blue hue, some white. I have even seen a few that were reddish."

"Oh god, I thought they spiked my coke with something at the game or maybe used a projector to play a cruel joke on me. When the sheriff showed up, he yelled at a few of my friends for a while before he offered to take me home. I thought we were in trouble, and that was why he wanted to talk to you."

"He wanted to explain what happened and to help me understand. It took him a while to help me believe it myself. I used to think I was the only one that could see them. You have inherited something of a family trait that is tied to this town. My father had it and his father had it. I don't know how far back it goes. I was looking through our old pictures and family tree when you saw me earlier."

"Are you sure this isn't a trick or something?"

"Trust me. I wish it were. When it first happened to me, no one believed it. They thought it was the emotional stress from losing my parents. To say I had a rough time of it would be saying it lightly."

He motioned for her bottle of soda, which she slid across the table to him. He took a quick swig and continued. "Hell, I didn't understand things until the last few days. I still don't, but I know more now than I did before. Back then I learned to accept it."

"That has to be hard to just accept," Sarah replied with a sigh.

"You ain't kidding, but it was what I had to do to stop it from creeping me out and running my life."

"So, we are the ghost whispering family. Now what?"

"Not sure. Sheriff Tillingsly and Father Murray are trying to help me figure that out."

"Figures that old creepy priest would be invol..."

Edward cut her off. "Hey, wait, he's a nice man and a long-time family friend. Yes, his sermon and ways are a little... off... but the more I learn about this, the more it makes sense."

"So, they see spirits too?"

"Yes." Edward answered.

Surprised by her father's answer, Sarah asked, "Who else? Does the whole town?"

"Some do. I'm not sure who else. What I understand is much of the town sees them, but we have something beyond just seeing. We can interact with them."

Edward slid the soda bottle back to Sarah. Her eyes were wide open, and mouth hung agape. The soda bottle came to rest next to her hand, which did not try to catch it. "What do you mean interact? Can we talk with them?"

Sarah's question was one Edward had given a lot of thought. "Well, Father Murray said we can. I don't know yet? I'm still learning. There is also a chance your abilities may stop at just being able to see them. Father Murray said something about it only passing to male members of the family. So, I am not sure yet, but we can find out together."

"Good god, I was joking earlier. WE ARE the ghost whispering family," Sarah said with a half-hearted laugh. "What about Jacob? He is probably scared shitless... I mean scared to death."

Edward gave her a look at her choice of phrase, but let it slide. "He would be scared shitless, I agree with that, but no he doesn't. At least not that I know of. Father Murray said the ability doesn't develop in anyone that young." Edward realized he was making himself sound like an expert on the subject, when at that moment he was anything but. He had learned to live with it, yes, but was still learning what IT was. "When did you first see something? Was it Friday night?"

"That is something I have thought about a lot." She took a sip from the bottle and slid it to her dad as an offer, but it stopped halfway. "For a while I have had what I would call 'eerie feelings.' I would feel cold and tingly, but saw nothing. A few nights after we moved here, I felt it again and thought I saw something when I was outside. Since then, I have felt it off and on."

"A cold sweat followed by pin pricks from the top of your neck down your spine and the feeling of something heavy pushing down on you?"

"Exactly." She was stunned that he described it so aptly.

"I know it well. I feel it every time one or more of them appear. You get used to it. I have. It doesn't faze me one bit anymore. Neither does the group of them that circle my bed when I sleep."

"No way! You're just messing with me now."

"I wish I were. Every night since the first time I saw one when I was ten."

"Did Mom know?"

"Nope. I never told her."

"That is creepy. A group of them standing there watching you two sleep."

"Yep, and they watched you and Jacob too."

"What? You saw them around our beds?"

"Oh no. I mean the times you guys slept with us. They were there then."

She shivered at the thought and then stopped. "Can they harm us?"

"So, I've been told. Father Murray will teach me how to protect everyone."

"He's getting you a proton pack and traps?"

"No. Wait here." Edward went back to the dining room to retrieve two important objects. He returned to the kitchen and said, "with these," as he displayed the cross and book to Sarah. "They told me these have been in my family for years. They ward off these spirits and send them where they are supposed to go. That is all I know at the moment."

He left the kitchen again and returned carrying the photo album. Sarah was flipping through the pages of the small book he'd left on the kitchen table. Edward laid the photo album down and opened it to the page marked by the junk mail. "Look at this picture. That is my father, and I believe this is my grandfather. The man seated must be my great-grandfather. Look at what he's holding." He pointed to the object in his hands, the object that all three men were touching.

Sarah's eyes grew wide when she recognized it. She reached over and picked up the cross. She studied it as if comparing it to the photograph and uttered, "What the..."

"I don't know. It all seems unbelievable. Father Murray said he knows the story behind all this and will help me understand. This is a part of our family's past I know nothing about."

A loud rumble of thunder rolled across the pasture and rain pelted the tin roof. Sarah got up from the table. "I need to go close my window." She headed toward the kitchen door and stopped short. "I guess we're that one family every town has that is considered weird."

"I guess we are, kiddo."

"Damn, and I was just hoping to inherit something like a fortune, not a freaky ability. Just don't go changing our phone number and buying a white hearse with flashing lights Dad."

He gave her a smirk. "I'm not making any promises."

20

"Cream and sugar?" Edward asked Father Murray.

"Just black, thank you," he answered from the kitchen table.

"Here you go. This should take the chill out of your bones." Edward put a cup of black coffee down in front of Father Murray. The rain was still falling outside, along with the temperatures.

"Say goodbye to summer, my friend. It won't be long until there is snow on the ground."

Edward remembered a few heavy storms growing up that created snowdrifts out around the barn that he could get lost in. He and several friends shoveled all day to create a snow fort. It took a week until the temperatures warmed up enough to melt it. When he moved to Portland, there was just a slight dusting of snow there once. Everyone acted like it was such a big deal, but he brushed it off and went on about his business. That was until he received the fine notice in the mail for not shoveling his walk. He had never heard of such a thing, plus the snow melted by the next day anyway.

"I talked to Sarah."

"Oh, and how did that go?"

"She admitted she saw them."

"Good. I would hate for her to keep it to herself and stay confused. Nothing good can come from that."

"She was scared when the Sheriff showed up. Said he gave her friends a good tongue lashing. She thought they were in trouble for slipping her some kind of drug or something that caused her to hallucinate."

Father Murray let out phlegm-filled chuckle. "That would be an easier explanation, now wouldn't it?" he said. "Her friends are good kids, no reason to worry when she is with them. Lewis was getting on to them for taking her out there with no warning." He sipped at his coffee. "Tony McDaniel, you remember his dad, Robbie, don't you?"

Edward sure did. His father ran the local hardware store, and every time Edward and his father went Robbie and Edward ran around, to borrow his father's term, like two chickens with their heads cut off.

"Tony assumed because of your family, she already knew."

"That brings up an interesting question that Sarah asked. How many people are like us?"

"Well, nobody else is like you. Not even close." Father Murray took another sip. "But most everyone here can see or sense the spirits passing through. Let me be more specific. The original families can. Outsiders that have moved here can't. We keep things our little secret around them." Father Murray held a single finger up to his mouth. "That is why Lewis was so upset with Tony on Friday night. He thought he was showing things to an outsider. Luckily for Tony he only took her out there because he knew who you guys were. Once Lewis realized who she was, he let them off easy and brought her home."

"They knew who we are?" Edward asked. It seemed everyone knew more about his family than he did.

"Your family is one of the founding members of this town. Back in the day, when town elders saw to the day-to-day business of the town, your family had a large seat at that table. Everyone knows who you are and what you can do."

Father Murray's answer reminded him of the family tree and photographs he saw earlier. "I want to show you something." Edward sprinted from the kitchen to retrieve both books from the other room. He returned just as quick and placed them on the table.

"You heeded my words, I see," Father Murray said with a look of approval.

Edward pulled out the family tree and opened it up. "You say my family is one of the original families. Is it possible we were the founding family?" Pointing at the line drawn across the tree, "We changed our name when we moved here. Our last name was Miller, but when we moved here, we became Meyer." Edward searched Father Murray's face for answers. Answers he was more than happy to provide.

"It's true. They named this town after your family."

"OK. Why did we change our name then? Why not just keep it Miller?"

"To protect your family's identity."

"Whoa, wait." Edward sat back in his chair. He broke the silence. "What identity?"

Father Murray grabbed the family Bible and turned it toward him. He flipped in two pages and turned it back toward Edward. "I guess you didn't find the inscription in the Bible yet."

Edward stared at the page Father Murray was showing him. There was in fact an inscription written in deep dark ink. He imagined someone wrote it with a quill and old-fashioned ink well.

This sacred Bible has been blessed and given as a gift to the family assigned to the holiest of duties. May God Bless and guide your family in its duty.

–Pope Clement XI

1718

"This Bible was a gift from the Pope?" Edward asked.

"I presume. I may be old, but not that old. That is not what I wanted you to see, though. Read it again and pay attention to the words."

Edward read it again silently and then paused on one particular word. He looked up from the book and said, "Assigned?"

"Yes. The Vatican assigned your family to this location. Assigned to do a job. Do you remember what I said about this being a sacred site?"

"Yes."

"When the early settlers arrived in the New World, they identified this site. The Vatican picked, trained, and then assigned your family as guardians over it. Each of the other sites have a similar family. Your assigned responsibility is to protect the living while serving the dead. At the time, the United Kingdom and the Vatican were not on speaking terms. So, they changed your name to avoid any chance the Crown or the local British Army regiments could discover who you are."

"Why would the British have cared?"

"I am guessing they never taught you American history in that place did they, old boy?" Father Murray said as he stood up, stretching his old bones made tighter by the cool wet weather. He reached into his jacket pocket and pulled out a tin flask. He said, "I hope you don't mind," while pouring liquid warmth into his coffee.

Edward not only did not mind, but he pushed his own toward Father Murray, who obliged.

"Protestants searching for religious freedom established the colonies. They were Puritans, Quakers, Calvinists, and Presbyterians. Not a lot of Catholics or love for the Vatican. The thought the Pope was handpicking settlers and governors of those settlements would not be looked upon kindly. It could be seen as interference, and with the wrong tempers involved, it could have started the next chapter in the many wars England had with the Vatican, along with the other countries that supported it."

He took a sip of his reinforced coffee before continuing. "Luckily, the church had sympathizers everywhere. When word got around about this place, a few of them were smart enough to get word back to the Vatican through safer channels. Mind you, back then it was not as simple as emailing under a different name or anything. They had to know who to trust. If they chose wrong, their life could be at risk. When word got back, the Pope prepared the artifacts you would need and sent a dispatch for your family."

Edward's stunned look stopped the priest mid-thought.

"Yes, the Vatican knew about your family. How? I am not sure, but I assume their local priest learned of their abilities and reported to his arch diocese, and they reported up and so on and so on... anyway, where was I? Oh yes, they sent for William and trained him on the use of the artifacts, but also how to adapt and expand them. The story your grandfather told me is that the original book only had five prayers in it. Over the last however many generations, pages have been added as new prayers were created. The skills, 'the how's and what's,' were passed down from generation to generation through extensive training that begins as soon as a child shows the ability to 'see', or what your grandfather called 'ascension'."

Father Murray took his seat across from the wide-eyed Edward. "Since your father never had the chance to pass this on to you, I will have to fill in. I will not claim to replace how he would have taught you, but upon his passing I had to take up the cause, and I think I know enough to help point you in the right direction. Now if you can fix us both another cup of coffee, I can fortify it a little and we can get started."

21

Edward prepared another cup of coffee for Father Murray and himself. The cool rain outside and the events of the last several days created an air of discomfort. The warmth of the coffee helped Edward feel a little better.

Appreciative of the second cup, Father Murray added a little of his special sauce to both and asked, "Have you read any in the book?"

"A little. It looks like a book of random prayers."

"Well, you aren't wrong. They are prayers. and they are in there in a random order," said Father Murray. "Added to for over 300 years. Tell me. Is there one tool I can give you that will do everything you need no matter what it is you have to fix?"

Edward looked back at him with a quizzical expression.

"Humor me. I have a point."

Edward considered the question. His humorous side wanted to say, "Yes, a hammer. You can bang anything into shape or destroy it to the point no one cares," but he knew what Father Murray was getting at. "No. For most jobs you need a few."

He nodded in agreement and said, "And others you need specialized tools. Now consider this: are there problems that exist today the tools of a long time ago cannot solve?"

The answer was obvious to Edward, but he lets his smart-ass answer escape. "Well, I wanted to answer the first question with... a hammer. You can use a hammer to bang anything into shape and if that doesn't work you can destroy what you are trying to fix to where you don't care anymore. Same answer could apply now. If a piece of modern technology gives you a problem, you could use a hammer to destroy it and not worry about it anymore."

Father Murray showed an amused smile. The same smile he would make at a child asking if Santa Claus visited Jesus during the Christmas Day Mass. "Well yes, I guess you could, but that isn't fixing things, is it? But I assume you got my point. Things change, and you need new solutions or... eh... new tools to solve these new problems. Just like that book. Think of that book as your toolbox. It has a prayer in there for every unique problem you face. Those before you have created new prayers and added to it when they faced problems the old ones did not handle."

Edward flipped through the book. When he looked through it on Saturday, he saw page after page of prayers in various handwritings, not one labeled with the author or purpose. That begged the question. "How do I know what prayer to use for what?"

"That's what you have me for. I think first we need to go over some rules. And these are extremely important." The stern look on the normally cheerful man drove the seriousness of the message home.

"First, never let either the cross or the book out of your sight.

"Second, never damage either of them, especially the cross. I am not sure which object is the source of most power, but I can tell you they do not work without the other. With the story of the origin of the cross, I believe it holds most of the power." Father Murray paused when he realized he omitted a detail. "I haven't told you about that yet, have I?"

"Told me what?" asked Edward.

"Where the cross came from."

"No." Edward looked at the cross while taking a guess. "Let me guess. It's made from the cross Christ was crucified on?"

Father Murray replied, "That is what they say."

Edward's body language became nervous as he placed the cross on the table with great care.

"I don't know if it's true or not. There have been rumors around for centuries that they found the cross during one of the many Crusades and the church acquired it. What your grandfather told me is they created twelve identical crosses from the wood of the crucifix and sent one to each spiritual site.

"Third, when you read from the book you must do so with purpose. Believe in what you are doing and read with conviction. That is what I was trying to force you to do last night. Just reading the words will do nothing. You must believe with your heart and spirit.

"The last rule is the most important. Edward. I cannot emphasize this enough. Not every prayer in the book worked. Some completely backfired." Father Murray opened the book and then turned it around. With the conviction of God himself Father Murray looked up at Edward and said, "Never read it turned like this."

Edward looked down at the book and realized it was upside down to him, but there was text on the opposing page right side up. He asked, "What are these prayers father?"

"These are dangerous. Not only did they not work, but they also had dangerous outcomes. We logged them in here this way, so we know what not to do." Before Edward could say anything, Father Murray said, "And yes. I made a mistake once with horrible consequences. I logged it, so I would never repeat it."

Father Murray saw Edward's eyes scanning across the lines of the prayer facing him and slammed the book shut with a slap. He reissued his warning, "You can't even read them to yourself. They are not to be messed with. Understand?"

Edward wanted to ask why again, but he saw the serious expression on Father Murray's face and answered with a simple, "Yes, Father."

"Good. Are you ready for homework?"

22

"All right. All right, everyone. Let's settle down. Who did the reading last night?" Edward scanned the class and saw many attentive faces.

"Good. Who has questions?" A few hands sprung up throughout the class. Edward picked one. "Laura."

"Is it me or is everyone insane?" Laura Robinson asked from the middle of the room.

"I hope you are talking about the book and not your classmates. Care to expand on that observation for the rest of us?"

A smattering of laughter filled the room.

"Ahab, Pip, Gabriel. Ishmael describes them as being insane," Laura explained.

"Oh, that." Edward pondered how to explain that without spoiling the entire book. Melville was not the most complicated read, but can confuse someone if they only read the words.

"Let me give a simple answer. The true answer will explain itself when you read more, but I will remind you of one thing. When you read a book told through the eyes of a single person, a narrator, you are seeing their perception. As the reader, take that into account with everything else you read as you form your opinion." Edward walked towards his desk, but turned back to the class to add, "... and no, they are not all crazy. Some are brilliant. Any more questions?"

Silence filled the classroom. No hands raised or inquisitive looks adorning the scholarly faces. Edward pulled a stack of papers from his brown cracked leather satchel and announced, "Good, then you won't mind taking this quiz, now will you?"

The hush turned into a collective groan as Edward handed the front row copies of the dreaded quiz. As many things that are different in this school, the groans were a familiar sound. He resisted the smile which tried to sprout upon his face. "You know the drill. Take one and pass the rest back. Put any extras on the back table."

Edward watched the students consider the questions his quiz posed to them. Each student was quietly focused on their own paper. No sneaky attempts to look at another student's paper. Through his career he had seen many attempts. They ranged from the covert quick glance to the obvious swapping of tests. Edward remembered one creative try that took rather sophisticated planning. Someone paid the smartest kid in class to tap his foot in code for each question. One tap for A, two for B, and so on. Another reason he hated standardized multiple-choice tests. After the fourth question he noticed the tapping, but listened for a little longer. When he noticed the pattern, he put a stop to it and collected the test. The class had an old-fashioned fill-in-the-blanks style test the next day. What always struck him about that attempt was, if they put the effort it took to come up with this into studying, they would have been able to pass the test on their own.

Several students completed their tests and place them face down on the desk. The image invoked a curious thought about the conversation he'd had with Father Murray the prior day. *I wonder if he will give me a test?* Before he'd left, Father Murray retrieved three books from his car and instructed Edward to study them.

The first book was *Spiritual Exercises of St. Ignatius of Loyola*. Father Murray said that would give him the spiritual conviction to do God's will.

The second was *The Catholic Treasury and Prayers*. Father Murray said that would be the most difficult to study. Edward was not to memorize the prayers. Instead, he was to learn their meaning and understand the why and how of the prayer. The mechanics. That would teach him the proper way to develop his own when the time came.

The third was the most surprising. Instead of an official church-endorsed text, it was just the common *Encyclopedia of Saints* that you could find in any storefront or online bookstore. Edward asked Father Murray about it, but he explained that they declared new saints all the time. He needed to keep an updated guide. Father Murray told him every saint had a purpose. He needed Edward to understand and believe in that purpose.

Edward promised Father Murray he would study every night. The intensity of his voice during the request matched the glare of his eyes. That was no ordinary or casual request. When Edward agreed, Father Murray reiterated one last time, "This is a responsibility you cannot take lightly. Too much depends on it. More than you can understand at this point."

The last student turned over their quiz. Edward walked through the rows collecting the papers. To him, quizzes were both a way to measure how much his students were retaining, but also a teaching aid. "How does everyone think they did?"

A small groan, smaller than the one that accompanied the announcement of the quiz itself, radiated around the room. He stacked them on his desk for grading later at home. "Let's see how you did," he said, and quizzed the class. The reactions he saw from some students identified questions they believe they missed, while an air of confidence grew around others realizing questions they answered correctly.

They did a quick reading of a section he picked out to reinforce the topic he planned to cover for the next few days. The whole class took part. The first few days, there were a few quiet students in each class. Eventually everyone became acclimated to his interactive approach. That was a goal of Edward's. He found everyone learned better when asking questions and talking about the topic than just listening. He hated the thought of anyone afraid to ask questions, but could honestly say that did not exist here.

He assigned that night's reading just in time for the bell to ring. The students packed up with haste and headed to their next class. Well, most of the students did. A small group of three meandered in the back. Once most of the students had left, they made their way forward with a question. "Mr. Meyer?"

"Yes, Daniel. What is it?"

"Can we ask you a question?"

"You just did." Edward's try at humor only received a half smile. "But of course. What is it?"

"We heard about the other night. So, you are the guy?"

Edward expected a question on something discussed in class or the reading. It only took him a second or two to recognize Daniel's last name, Ruten. Martin Ruten was one of the group that went out with Sheriff Tillingsly that night. Daniel must be his son.

The three boys stared at him with an idolizing gaze that made Edward uncomfortable. "Look guys. I am not sure what you heard. I'm just your teacher. That's it."

"Oh, come on, Mr. Meyer. We heard how you took care of those creatures."

A small town was a breeding ground for gossip that can build up legends or tear them down. Edward knew that and tried to temper any aggrandizing of the events. "I was there, that is all. Father Murray told me what to do. It was really all him."

Students for his next class started to come in, causing the three to take a panicked glance at the clock. They hurried for the door, but not before Christopher said, "Embrace it Mr. Meyer. Your family is famous around here."

Famous was not something Edward wanted to be. He wanted to be normal.

Once home, Edward fixed his famous hotdog surprise for dinner. It was nothing fancy, just hotdogs in oversized buns. The surprise part was just the name Sarah gave it when she was eight years old. Edward was rushing to get home one night and stopped at the store for hotdog buns. In a hurry and not paying attention, he grabbed hoagie rolls. He didn't notice until Karen announced she'd lost the hot dog in the bun when she fixed one for Sarah. They had a good laugh. Sarah said, "Surprised there is a hot dog in there," and it stuck from that point forward.

After dinner he took a moment to clean the kitchen and then settled down at his makeshift office desk. To his right, the stack of quizzes that needed to be graded. To his left, the books he promised an old friend he would learn. He picked the quizzes and worked through the repetitive task of reading the answers to the same five questions over and over.

Occasionally he heard the words of Father Murray echoing through his head as he read an answer. He forced his way through the stack. He felt both a sense of accomplishment and heavy fatigue when he checked the clock. It read just after one in the morning. He should head upstairs for bed, but he'd made a promise. He reached over and grabbed *Spiritual Exercises of St. Ignatius of Loyola* and opened to the page he'd left off reading.

23

The ringing of Edward's phone startled him, and he jerked awake, grasping at the book falling from his lap, grabbing it before it reached the floor. He slapped around on the desk for his phone and pulled it to his ear. His groggy voice answered, "H... ello?"

An agitated Father Murray responded from the other side of the call. "Edward, thank god I got you. I need you to come with me."

"What? What are you talking about Father? It's..." Edward looked at his phone. "Father, it is 2:13 in the morning."

"Yes, I know. It is an emergency. I will be there in a few minutes." The call ended before Edward could respond.

Edward got up and headed out the porch to wait on Father Murray to see what that urgency was all about. The damp chill of the night cut straight through to his bones. He turned to go inside for a jacket when Father Murray pulled up behind him.

"Get in quick!" Father Murray called through the open passenger window.

Edward jogged down the steps toward the side of the car. His children were upstairs sleeping, and he didn't want to yell back-and-forth and chance waking them.

"What is going on?"

"Come, come quick. We need to get to the Kirkland farm." Father Murray reached over and pushed the passenger door open.

"Wait, Father. Please explain what is going on," Edward insisted. The old priest was moving and talking rapidly. He ignored each plea Edward made for an explanation.

"Get in," Father Murray said while leaning across the seat of his road yacht Cadillac. He looked up at Edward and asked, "Do you have the cross and book?"

Edward answered, "No."

"Never let them out of sight! Go fetch them, right now."

He did as he was ordered and sprinted up the steps and back inside. He grabbed both objects from the dining room table where they sat next to the books he was studying when he fell asleep.

The trip into the house gave him the moment he needed. If Father Murray was here at this hour asking about the cross and book, it must be one of those kinds of emergencies. He pulled the door closed behind and locked it, then hopped into the passenger side of the Caddy. Without a word, Father Murray accelerated down the dirt drive.

24

Either the old suspension or Father Murray's ability behind the wheel caused the oversized car to wander from side to side, maybe it was both. Edward hoped his driving would improve once they reached the paved road, but that hope faded when it became more of a swerve at higher speeds.

"This will be difficult. You need to follow my lead." Father Murray's cell phone rang and interrupted him.

"Yes... yes... We are on our way. Should be there in just a few minutes. Try to stay calm." Father Murray slammed his old flip phone closed and dropped it on the seat beside him.

"The Kirklands are scared shitless. Pardon my language."

"What are we walking into?"

"Remember the other night? I said some spirits are more dangerous and malicious than others. The one we are going to fight is absolutely more dangerous. It's not lost. Oh no. This one is a type who is here to just cause trouble. Evil's little helpers is what your grandfather called them. It is ok to feel afraid when you see them for the first time. The first time your grandfather took me to go deal with one my knees almost buckled on me."

The level of concern in Edward spiked to an all-time high. Other than the first few times he saw a spirit, he had experienced nothing that struck fear into him.

"Father..." Edward started a question, but was cut off with more information.

"You cannot let the fear weaken your convictions tonight. These creatures will test you, but hold fast."

Edward pondered what he meant by "test" as they pulled into the driveway of the farm just four roads from his own. There was a group gathered outside, along with Sheriff Tillingsly.

Father Murray slid his Caddy to stop and appeared to be out the door before it even stopped moving. He instantly took control of the scene.

"Lewis, where are they?" he asked the sheriff.

In a tone showing wear from both his age and the late hour of the evening, he answered. "It's still inside."

"Just one?"

"Yes, Father. Last we saw it was in the hall. Had their youngest, Kevin, trapped in his bedroom. We tried to open his window, but... Father... it interfered." The sheriff showed great disappointment at failing to secure the child.

"It is ok, Lewis."

Father Murray made a beeline over toward the sobbing mother and father doing their best to keep their other two children calm. "Calm" at that point was just lower than hysterical crying. He was saying something to them, but Edward was too far away to hear it. They all crossed themselves and he led them in a prayer before giving a final embrace to the parents.

He started toward the front door with conviction. The town elders gathered outside took a few steps, but he stopped them. "Y'all stay out here. We need to handle this alone. It is too dangerous for everyone." He motioned toward Edward and called, "Come on. We need to hurry." Father Murray did not wait, and rushed up the steps and in through the front door. Edward followed reluctantly.

Edward stepped through the door and almost ran into the back of Father Murray, who had stopped at a table just inside the doorway. The priest removed his coat and silently blessed a red stole before putting it around his neck. He crossed Edward and then himself. He placed his right hand on Edward's shoulder and said, "In the Name of the Father and of the Son and of the Holy Ghost, Amen. Let God arise and let His enemies be scattered: and let them that hate Him flee from before His Face! As smoke vanisheth, so let them vanish away: as wax melteth before the fire, so let the wicked perish at the presence of God." He released Edward and turned toward the hallway that ran through the center of the house.

"Get the book and cross out. We will need them for this battle."

Father Murray stepped through the doorway that separated the front room from the hall. When his first foot hit the worn wood floor of the hall, the entire house gave a mighty shake that knocked Edward against the wall. In his attempt to regain his balance, he looked down to see large white particles of dust dancing across the floor. A glance forward revealed the source. There was a line of salt on the floor in the doorway.

The duo proceeded further down the hallway. Rumblings of the floor accompanied every step. Edward felt his heartbeat in his throat, and even though he was not claustrophobic, the walls appeared to be closing in on him as his breathing became shallow. A heavy darkness settled on him.

A growl emerged from behind the closed door at the end of the hallway.

Father Murray yelled at the door, "Kevin, we are coming. Just try to stay calm."

The panicking voice of a child emerged from behind the door: "Ok."

Edward asked, "Was the growl him?"

"Don't be silly. That was the creature in there with him."

As they got closer, the growling and scratching of a great beast continued. Father Murray reached for the door handle and quickly withdrew his hand. He retrieved a large vial of water from his robe and poured it over the door handle. The water sizzled on contact, producing steam. "Holy water is good for many things. Even cooling off a hot door handle." He covered his hand with his robe and gripped the door handle. A grimace of pain exploded on his face. The heat from the door handle was still hot enough to sear his hand through its covering, but he fought through the pain and turned the handle, opening the door.

At first glance, Edward only saw a crying child sitting on his bed, holding up a sheet as protection.

"Where is it?" Father Murray asked the child. Kevin pointed up above the door.

"Edward, push the cross in through the door. That should force it to move back."

Edward adjusted his grip on the crucifix and extended his arm. Before it crossed the threshold of the door, a voice entered his head. *You are not a priest. You don't belong here.*

Edward stopped and Father Murray noticed. "Ignore whatever it is. Push the cross through the doorway."

Edward heard what he said, but no longer saw a doorway. In front of him was the pasture that ran alongside his home. It was a nice spring day. He felt the warmth of the sun on his face and the smell of wildflowers wafted in the breeze. The sound of his children's laughter approached him from behind. A dog chased a butterfly among the tall grass. Edward did not remember ever getting a dog, especially with Jacob's allergies to pet dander. The dog almost caught the butterfly that time. He felt a hand grab his, but before he could look down to see which of his children was holding it, the image, the smell of wildflowers, the warmth of the sun, and the dog disappeared. Father Murray gripped his hand, forcing the cross into the bedroom.

The still calm that was the bedroom became a swirling tempest of wind and debris. The child was screaming, but the sound did not escape the room.

With no sign of fear, Father Murray entered, scanning each of the corners. His hand urgently waved for Edward to join him. With the cross still firmly extended at the end of his outstretched arm he stepped in. Edward scanned the surroundings and froze in place when he saw the mass of glowing red steam hovering just above the floor.

"Open the book." Without even looking at it, Edward opened the book, and the priest flipped through the pages. When he found the one he was looking for, he pointed to the page, like he did that night in the woods, and ordered him to read. Edward looked down at the page and recited: "O most glorious Prince of the

Heavenly Armies, St. Michael the Archangel, defend us in the battle and in our wrestling against the principalities and powers, against the rulers of the world of this darkness, against the spirits of wickedness in the high places."

"You don't believe this shit, do you little Eddie?" the voice in his head asked. The voice felt personal and strange all at the same time.

Edward ignored the voice and continued. "Come to the aid of men, whom God created incorruptible, and to the image of His own Likeness He made them, and from the tyranny of the devil He bought them at a great price."

"Come now Eddie. You have always been one of my favorites. Why are you doing this? I kept you company all of those nights God and his many disciples ignored you while they locked you away."

Edward shook his head to clear the voice out. Father Murray took notice. "Are you ok?"

"I'm fine," Edward snapped back at the Priest. A memory stirred inside him of a recurring dream he had as a teen, but he pushed it to the back of his mind and continued reading. "Fight the battles of the Lord today with the Army of the Blessed Angels."

"Angels are just a viewpoint. They are eternal good to some and demons to others. To some I am an angel. Why resist me?" At that moment, his mother appeared before him. Not the spirit of his mother that he had seen many times throughout his life. The full living breathing version of his mother. She hugged him warmly. "Oh Eddie," she said in the voice he remembered as a child. "This is too much for you. Why don't you go outside with the others and relax? You look so tired."

For a moment he felt very comforted, but the distant voice of Father Murray reminded him of where he was. Edward pushed her back and exclaimed, "You are not my mother." The figure morphed into a mass of red steam again. Edward looked closer and saw a humanlike form inside the mass of steam. The cold voice echoed in his head. "No, I am not your mother. But I knew her very well. I was there the day she died. I remember when you came running into the kitchen to find them."

Edward gasped. A flood of emotions sent him alternating between now and the seven-year-old who found his parents. "You were not there. Stop talking about my parents," he screamed.

"I was. Kevin reminds me of you that day. A wide-eyed child full of fear. You left too soon for me to introduce myself."

Father Murray rushed over and yanked the book out of Edward's hands. Edward could see Father Murray talking to him, but could barely hear him. He sounded like he was yelling at him from miles away. The only voice he heard clearly was the cold one in his mind.

Muffled in the background, Edward heard the Priest read, "As once thou didst fight against Lucifer, the first in pride, and his apostate angels; and they prevailed not: neither was their place found anymore in Heaven. But that great dragon was cast out, the old serpent, who is called the devil and Satan, who seduces the whole world. And he was cast unto the earth, and his angels were thrown down with him."

Edward felt stuck between the here and now and the past. His mind's eye only saw darkness. A dark void that the voice echoed from.

"Behold, the ancient enemy and murderer strongly raises his head! Transformed into an angel of light, with the entire horde of wicked spirits he goes about everywhere and takes possession of the earth, so that therein he may blot out the Name of God and of His Christ and steal away, afflict and ruin unto everlasting destruction the souls destined for a crown of eternal glory.

"On men depraved in mind…"

"Speaking of depraved in mind. Ever wonder what a child looks like burned from the inside out?"

The dark void Edward was entrapped in was replaced by a ball of fire. "Leave him alone," he commanded.

"Why should I?"

"Why shouldn't you? Why harm the child?"

"It is simple." The presence circled around his body like a great snake wrapping around a prey. "I have to remind you of your place and me of my place in this world. It ensures balance and fights off chaos. You wouldn't want to put the world into chaos, would you?"

In a strange way that made sense to Edward.

He felt two hands on his back give him a great shove forward, breaking him from the trance, returning him to the bedroom where he now lay face down on the floor. The push forced the cross in Edward's hand through the spirit, sending it retreating to the corner of the room. Edward forced himself to his feet as papers and toys flew into everyone in the room.

He looked at the child on the bed and saw a translucent fire engulfing him.

"Father! The boy!" he screamed.

"He is fine. I need you here with me."

Edward exclaimed, "The flames!"

"What flames?"

Through the wind, Father Murray struggled to take the two steps needed to bring him alongside Edward. He held the book in front of him. "Follow me."

"Behold the Cross of the Lord, flee away ye hostile forces," Father Murray declared in the room.

Edward followed. "The Lion of the tribe of Judah, the root of David hath conquered."

"May Thy mercy, O Lord, be upon us,"

Edward responded, "Because we have hoped in Thee."

"O Lord, hear my prayer."

"And let my cry come unto Thee."

"The Lord be with you,"

"And with thy spirit."

"You need to chase it into that corner and shove the cross right in its heart."

Edward felt a surge from within and moved toward the corner.

The voice appeared again. "Do you really want to do this? Do you really want to follow the directions of the person who released me and let me kill your parents?"

"What does that mean?"

"Now Edward! Don't stop--" A huge explosion sent Father Murray flying backwards. Edward felt himself impacting the cold wet dirt outside the house. He looked over to see terrified parents running toward their child covered in flames.

Edward felt paralyzed on the ground until a few of the elders came over to help him up. Sheriff Tillingsly helped the Kirklands' tend to Kevin while they waited for the ambulance to arrive. He suffered burns on his hands, feet, and face. The only wounds Edward suffered were mental and emotional.

Father Murray emerged from the wreckage that was once the child's bedroom. He talked to Lewis and the Kirklands first, then he approached Edward, who sat on the ground where he landed.

"You lost focus. This is serious. We are lucky that the worst that happened are the burns. People could have lost their lives tonight. This is one of those spirits I told you about. An evil demon." He threw his hands up. "You cannot lose focus while we are doing this. It is a war. And no, I am not using that word lightly. It is a war."

He walked back over to the Kirklands as the ambulance pulled up. Kevin was quickly loaded up, and it headed off with full lights and sirens, with Sheriff Tillingsly's car following behind it. The silence around Edward was a stark contrast to the debris field radiating from the shattered house.

Edward had not moved since they helped him up. He sat there pondering what the creature meant by preventing Chaos, and helping the person who killed his parents. It reminded him of the question he pondered for years: why God let something so horrible happen to his parents, people who were so good.

He stood up and walked toward Father Murray, who was leaning next to his Caddy. "I'm sorry Father. I failed."

"It's all right. We all fail. I lost count how many times I have in this life. Kevin will be fine. The burns have already started to fade. They are something the creature did to scare us, but they are not real, and will be gone in the next day or so." Father Murray pointed to the house. "Now this on the other hand. Insurance companies won't understand an explosion caused by a failed spiritual saving. Lewis will help document a gas explosion to get the house repaired. For now, they will stay with me, which is fine. I need to counsel them on what they have gone through anyway."

He opened the car door. "Come on. Let's go home. We have a lot of work to do, and you need your rest."

Edward pondered the many questions on the ride home. The mental, physical, and emotional exhaustion took a toll. He just needed sleep.

When Father Murray dropped him off, Edward walked through the spirits that encircled his home. There appeared to be more now, and they were standing closer, all facing his house as if it were a religious shrine. He passed through them on the way inside, feeling the cool chill and the familiar tingle of their presence, but paying no bother. He was too tired to and discouraged to even care.

Once inside, he locked the door and threw everything in his hands on the dining room table. Cell phone, book, cross and all.

25

Edward's walk into the school the next morning resembled the trek of a zombie. He was both physically and mentally exhausted. To say the night before took it out of him would be an understatement. His path was strangely solitary. The normal greetings he heard from students and faculty were now replaced by glares, as people move to either side of the hall, clearing his path.

His talkative classes were silent and slightly clinical. They answered the questions Edward asked during class. A few asked questions on their own, but the warmth and idle conversation he had enjoyed was gone. Instead, the students looked at him as though he had a large hairy growth on the side of his face.

Lunch in the teacher's lounge was even worse. Edward was one of the first in the lounge for that lunch period. He set up at the same table he had for the last few weeks. As others came in, they barely acknowledged him. They gathered at other tables or stood at the counter at the back. Edward could hear the murmurs of their conversations, but couldn't make out any specific words.

"Is this seat taken?"

"Sorry Mark, they're all taken," Edward responded, dripping with sarcasm.

Mark pulled out a chair at Edward's table and set out his lunch.

"Are you expecting others for lunch?" Edward eyed the multiple wrappers and containers Mark pulled out of his bag.

"Sharon hosted a bridge party for her friends last night. Tons of leftovers. Hell, I don't even know what's in some of these." Mark opened one container to reveal wings, another with potato salad, and then unwrapped an aluminum foil log with ham in it. Mark pulled out a paper plate and an extra fork and handed it to his table mate. "Dig in."

Edward looked at the spread, and then back at his sandwich. The decision was not a hard one. His sandwich found its way back into the bag it came in. He took the fork and stabbed a piece of the honeyed ham and then dolloped out a lump of potato salad.

"Thanks. You sure you want to be sitting here with me?" Edward said with a mouth half full of ham.

"The back counter is full. Nowhere else for me to sit with all this food." Mark needled his friend with his elbow. "Relax. It will pass in a few days."

"How did everyone find out so fast?"

"Simple. Small town. Just don't fart during the moment of silence anymore." Mark dug in on the wings, leaving Edward to wonder what that meant, and then it hit him.

"Oh stop. I was six." That event was a perfect example of the speed of news in a small town. He farted rather loudly during the moment of silence once in the first grade. There was a mild embarrassment at the moment caused by the half-muffled giggles, by midday nobody remembered it. When his mom picked him up that afternoon, she welcomed him with, "Hey there big guy. Heard you had a rough day." He always wondered how she found out so fast.

"To some of these people you were a superhero the minute you stepped back into town. You took a little hit last night. You will recover."

"All this still seems so strange to me."

"I bet. You haven't lived through it for over thirty years like the rest of us." Mark shoveled potato salad in his mouth. "... W... When I saw my first ghost, I was afraid to tell my parents, but it was at home and they saw it too, so they knew. The explanation they gave seemed like something out of a corny horror film. I didn't believe them at first. A few of my friends thought the town elders were putting something in the water to make us hallucinate. It took years of sighting and experiences before I got it."

Edward thought how lucky Mark was to have parents that understood. "Took me a few years in a mental institution to understand what I was seeing."

Mark stopped chewing on the piece of ham and gawked at Edward. "You're serious?"

"Absolutely. My foster parents thought I was nuts."

"I could see that. How was the looney bin?"

"Crazy."

"I bet. Seriously, how was it?"

"I spent a while trying to convince everyone I was not crazy. Then I spent time convincing myself I wasn't crazy. Eventually I learned how to play the game to make them think I was all better, so I could get out. At that point I didn't care who was crazy or not."

"Maybe we are crazy. Maybe this whole town is crazy, or something is in the water making us all see things. Could be a big government conspiracy."

"Explains why the water is a little green."

"Yes, it would." Mark chuckled. "Know you aren't crazy, and others can see them too. Don't let the weight of your family's role in this wear on you. It took me long enough to accept what my eyes saw. I never had to deal with what you are. By the way, how should I address you? My Savior? Should I bow?" Mark gave a mini bow with both hands over his head.

"You can call me a failure," Edward said, looking down at his plate.

Mark patted him on the shoulder to reassure him. "Just be Edward and take things one day at a time. You have a great support system here. Father Murray, Lewis, and others like me and Sharon."

"I feel like I failed big time last night." The image of the hysterical family circled around the child screaming in agony hadn't left Edward's mind. He wondered if he should have talked to them, instead of just sitting there on the ground. He can't help feeling responsible for what happened to their son and home, but he didn't understand what he could have done differently.

"Think of it as more of a stumble. I hear the boy is fine now and enjoying all the attention in the hospital. Larry and his family will stay with Father Murray until they repair the house. Should only take a few weeks. There is a crew out there now."

Edward was unsure if Mark was just trying to make him feel better or telling him the truth. The bell for the end of the lunch period sounded and Edward helped Mark snap the covers back on the containers scattered across the table. They filed out with the mass of other teachers out of the lounge and down the hallway to their classrooms.

26

Edward tried to keep his yawn quiet, but failed. The sound echoed through the cavernous church. Luckily, it was empty at the time.

"Keeping you up?" asked Father Murray. He had entered through a door on the left of the transept. "It's alright. I still feel last night a bit too." He motioned for Edward to join him up at the front of the church.

He'd taken a pew in the back of the church. His mood and performance made him feel unworthy of sitting any closer to the altar. He only moved because his friend insisted.

"Kevin just came back from the hospital. He is fine. They all are."

"They are? But his burns?"

"They are over in the house watching TV, waiting on pizza to arrive. His burns were not real." Father Murray walked around the front of the church, picking up some bulletins discarded on the floor by the prayer service that just left. "They were more for our benefit, or should I say yours. The creature was trying to scare you, not harm the boy."

If that's the case, it succeeded, thought Edward. Just the thought of the images he saw struck fear in him.

"Did you hear voices?" asked Father Murray.

"Yes, I heard voices. The creature spoke to me."

"He was playing a psychological game with you."

Edward thought back to the images and places the creature took him. They seemed very real, not just a psychological trick. He explained, "It was more than voices. He took me to another place. I was not in the bedroom at times. I was in a field with my kids with a warm fresh breeze blowing around us."

"Trust me. You were there standing next to me the whole time. These beings are crafty." In a tone that echoed his sermons, Father Murray explained, "Like the Devil himself, these creatures will whisper rose colored promises and produce images of deception to bend our will in their direction. We, everyone, not just you and I, must be strong in our conviction and trust in the Lord. If we give in just once, that is the door that pure evil will walk through. Look at the root of all evil in this world and you will find someone that has accepted one of those promises."

The words Father Murray said struck a chord inside Edward. It was a sermon he heard him give when he was a child. It was also a sermon he heard repeated in every church he and Karen attended in Portland. His mind struggled with the literal thought of a creature like they encountered being behind all the evil in the world. It could be an example of the eternal battle of good versus evil. It could also just be a philosophical statement, that true evil comes from acceptance of a promise that was unearned or undeserved. Like a bank robber looking for the promise of riches without working for them.

"Are you coming?" Edward looked around for the Father and saw him standing in the back of the Church, heading out the door.

"Yes, ummm. Where are we going? Edward asked, following him down the aisle.

"More training. You didn't hear a word I said, did you?"

"I did."

Father Murray didn't buy that response. He knew he didn't.

27

After an uncomfortable day of isolation at school, Edward found himself yet again in the passenger seat of Father Murray's Caddy, driving to an unknown location. The trip was more relaxed than others. Father Murray even turned on the radio which was pre-tuned to an oldies station. He hummed along to the Animals singing about "The House of the Rising Sun."

They drove through the center of town, which was still rather active despite darkness setting in.

"If you want a great apple pie, go to Ruthie's right there," Father Murray pointed out. "Have you checked Dan's newsstand? He has several shelves in the back where he keeps paperbacks of the new best sellers. That is the closest you will find to a bookstore here. The next is one of those huge things a couple of towns over. If there is a book you really want, Dan can order it for you."

Edward confessed, "I haven't had much of a chance to explore downtown yet. I've shopped a few times in the corner store for groceries and a few dinners at Len's. I remembered his fried chicken from when I was a kid."

"Doc said I have to watch that stuff for my cholesterol and my gall bladder." A mischievous look spread across his face. "Don't tell him I visit or get takeout from Len's a couple times a week."

Edward smiled. "Your secret is safe with me."

The lights of town disappeared behind them as they continued to drive for a few more minutes, then pull into a driveway of an old farmhouse. There was a single light on over the front door. A man emerged when the Caddy creaked to a stop just even with the front porch.

"Evening, Paul."

"Evening, Father."

"Is it still here?"

"Yep, o'er yonder. Just past the pump house."

"All right, go on inside. We will take care of it. Tell Molly I said hello."

"Will do. Night," the man said, and disappeared back in the house without acknowledging Edward.

Father Murray started down the driveway toward the barn at the back of the property with Edward in tow. "Paul is a good man. His wife is from a neighboring town. She doesn't see the spirits, but the thought of them being anywhere near her scares her to death. I still am not sure why they haven't moved yet."

Edward asked, "If she can't see them, how does she know they are there?"

"Paul tells her when they are around."

The two rounded the barn and Edward saw their destination, a small shed about fifty feet away. "Remember how people treated you when you told them what you saw? Imagine the reverse. You see nothing but are living in a town where everyone else does. It took a while before she accepted this was not a huge joke we were all playing on her. When she did, her fear set in. I think the fear comes from not being able to see and understand like the rest of us can."

A cold shiver traveled down Edward's neck and through his back. "Father…"

"I feel it too. That's why we're here, and I want you to take the lead."

"Are you sure?"

"Absolutely. Show me what you got."

Father Murray stopped short and to the side of the shed. Edward felt timid as he walked around the shed and came face to face with a single spirit, a man, standing there. He fumbled through his pocket for the book and cross. He found them, but while pulling the cross out he dropped it in the high grass at his feet. The spirit continued to look at the back wall of the pump shed.

Edward reached down and searched for a few moments in the damp grass until he found the cross. He held it out with his right hand toward the creature and opened the book with his left. Both objects shook from his nerves.

"Relax and breathe," Father Murray coached from the side.

Edward tried to take a deep breath, but his hands continued to shake. His voice quivered as much as the cross. He recited the prayer on the page. "Holy Michael, the Archangel, defend us in…"

Father Murray cut him off. "You can't use the same prayer every time. Feel your way through this and pick the right one."

Edward stood there, dumbfounded, and unsure.

"What do you feel?"

"I feel the same cold shiver I always do."

"Go deeper."

"I don't understand."

Father Murray asked, "Do you feel fear, Edward?"

"I am afraid to fail."

"Not that. Do you fear the spirit? Do you feel any malevolent intent from this spirit?"

Edward took a moment. "No, not like last night."

"Reach out with your feelings and tell me."

Edward closed his eyes and searched through his thoughts and sensations. He sensed the spirit. Its presence combined with an overwhelming feeling of being lost. At first Edward thought that feeling was associated with his own lack of confidence, but he soon realized it was different. "I feel unsure of what I'm doing, but I also feel something else. Someone is lost."

"That feels foreign to you, like what you feel when you become attached to a character in a movie or book, doesn't it?"

"Yes. Exactly."

"That is the spirit in front of you. He is lost, not a threat. St. Michael's prayer is used when we go to battle. There is no reason to take hostilities against a peaceful spirit that needs help. Now look through the book. Find the right prayer."

Edward flipped through the pages and searched. All the while, he hoped Father Murray would come point out the right page to him. With his hands no longer shaking, Edward found a prayer on the sixth page that he believed to be the correct one. "I think I found one." He turned to show him. "Is this the right one?"

Father Murray held up a hand to stop him. "That is for you to decide. Go ahead and read it."

"O God, the bestower of forgiveness and the lover of human salvation, we beseech Thee, of Thy tender love, to grant that the brethren of our congregation, with their relatives and benefactors, who have passed out of this life, may, by the intercession of Blessed Mary, ever Virgin, and all thy saints, come to the fellowship of eternal bliss. Through Christ our Lord. Amen."

The spirit disappeared in front of their eyes.

Father Murray gave a light applause. "Good. This spirit was just lost. You gave him the rites needed to pass on. Come now. Let's get out of here, it's getting cold."

Curious about the scenario Father Murray just described, Edward asked, "Is that a guess?"

"Yes and no." Father Murray pulled his coat collar up to shield from the cold. "Call it experience." Father Murray turned. "Over the years I have felt many spirits and tried many prayers. Over time you hone your sense to what you feel. With the non-violent spirits you can try multiple prayers until you find the right one. With violent ones, mistakes empower them, so you must be careful. I cannot emphasize that enough." His words and expression landed on Edward with a fright. "So, what caused you to pick that prayer?"

Edward told him, "I read through the words and recognized a few terms and phrases in what you have me studying. They are ones used for redemption and reunification. It seemed like one that could reunite one with their loved ones."

"Perfect. Good use of information and judgement. Come now. Let's get out of here before we catch death and become spirits ourselves."

The normally quiet drive back was filled with story after story by Father Murray. Some involved Edward's grandfather or father. Others didn't. Each talked about what Father Murray sensed going into each scenario. All knowledge he was trying to impart on his new student.

He asked if it was the same feeling for everyone.

"I asked your grandfather that when I first arrived, and he explained that it is. Based on my experience, it is the same mostly. I felt everything like he described it, more or less. There are slight differences, but the sensations were close enough that I knew. It just takes time to learn and recognize it." Father Murray explained only stopping to laugh.

"What?"

Father Murray pointed ahead of them. "Look up yonder."

Edward looked up the crushed stone driveway of the church. A group of spirits circled both the church and his own car. "The cross draws lost souls. They can sense where it is, and where it has been."

"That would be why they circle the farmhouse now."

"They mean no harm. Kind of like a moth to a flame."

"Why don't they follow me when I carry it?"

"I don't know. Suppose they take a while to sense it. Maybe if you stand in once place long enough with it, they will."

The thought of being the pied piper for spirits tickled Edward's sense of humor. "As if any of this could get any odder."

28

Edward walked through the door and into a parallel universe. Jacob sat at the dining room table doing his homework. Sarah stood over his shoulder, helping. She wore an apron he hadn't seen in years. The sound of the front door closing caused both kids to turn around and look at him.

Sarah put her hands on her hips and attempted to tap her foot while asking, "Where have you been, mister?"

"I had a school meeting. Remember? We talked about it this morning and you agreed to start dinner." Edward did not make a habit of lying to his children, but at that moment he felt he needed to.

"Yes, and dinner is in there covered in foil. Jacob is almost done with his homework." Sarah took off the apron. She handed it to her father.

"Nice apron." He noticed her very non-school-dress-code-compliant-outfit and asked, "Going somewhere?"

"I found it hung on a nail on the backside of the pantry door. I didn't want to mess up my outfit. And yes, Charlotte will be by to pick me up soon. She wanted me to come over to watch a movie together and... before you ask, I won't be out late. I know it's a school night."

Sarah gave him a quick kiss on the cheek and a "Thanks Dad" on her way up stairs.

Edward took over her position behind Jacob, looking at his homework. She was right. He was almost done. With a quick glance it appeared Jacob had answered them correctly. No modern math here, everything just as he learned it years ago.

"Is it good?" Jacob asked while looking up at him.

Edward picked up the page. "Yep, everything looks right. Exceptionally good."

"Are you sure? Mom was always better at math."

"I am sure." Edward then pulled out the chair next to him and had a seat. "You miss her, don't you?"

"Yeah. Sometimes more than others."

"Like now?"

"She always helped me with my homework.

"I know. I miss her too. Just know she is looking down on us."

"Like an angel?" asked the precocious seven-year-old.

"Exactly. She watches over us."

"Even here? Does she know we moved?"

"Especially here. She came with us. We take her everywhere we go in our heart."

"Cool."

He handed the page back to Jacob, who put it in his math folder and slid it into his backpack. "Thanks," Jacob said and then headed upstairs. Edward knew he was off to declare war on a mythical world in the digital universe. The rule in the house was homework first and then video games.

That was more Karen's rule, and one he helped Jacob break a few times. His video game habit was actually Edward's fault. During college, Edward got his first exposure to video games, and he was hooked. When he and Karen started living together, she gave him a little grief about his childish hobby. When she walked in and found Jacob sitting in Edward's lap being taught how to play, she rolled her eyes and walked out. Edward still enjoyed them with his son from time to time. Some fathers and son play catch, some build things, not Edward and Jacob. They bond while hunting people down in a digital playground. The aromatic smell coming from the kitchen reminded Edward he was hungry.

Edward yelled up the stairs, "Hey Jacob, let me eat something and I will be up."

"You will just die a lot."

Edward conceded, "That's fine." Inside though he had other plans.

He placed his bag on the dining room table, along with the book and cross, and made his way to the kitchen. Sarah had a plate on the table in his spot covered with foil. He was impressed. She cleaned up afterwards too.

Edward looked at the balled-up apron in his hand. His mother wore that apron every time they cooked cookies together. Briefly he held it to his nose hoping to detect a familiar smell. To his surprise, even after all the years, a hint of it still existed. Edward un-balled the apron and straightened it out. Feeling like the seven-year-old he was the last time he opened the pantry door, he neatly hung it back on its nail.

The front door slammed. Edward sat down to enjoy his dinner. A smile and a warm feeling came over him. Despite everything that had happened to him and his family, moments like that one made him realize life was good.

29

"H... ello?" Edward said. He was not sure if he was awake or dreaming. His body had acted on instinct, reaching for his phone when he heard it ring, like Pavlov's dog. There was no answer coming from the phone, so Edward said, "Hello, Father?" The entire room was still and silent. There was no vibration from the old boiler fan. The wind blowing outside when he went to bed was now calm.

"Hi, Edward," the creature responded, not from the phone, but from the foot of his bed. Edward sat up in bed confronted by the same red steam he saw in Kevin Kirklands' bedroom. The steam slowly morphed into a form that was both human and not human. There were arms and legs and a head, but the proportions were off. Its legs were too long, and its arms were too short. They ended with hands made up of fingers that appeared to be three times too long. Its head was round, with two dark orbs where eyes should be, and no mouth.

"I like what you have done with this place."

Edward glanced quickly at his night table, but remembered the cross and book were sitting on the dining room table downstairs.

"They are not there. It is just us. Let's have a talk."

"What is your name?"

"You have been watching too many movies. Oh no. I tell you my name and disappear. Like the wicked witch when Dorothy threw water on her." The creature appeared to grow larger on its perch as the dark soulless eyes showed a hint of flames. "It doesn't work that way. Father Murray should have told you that. There is much he should tell you."

"What do you want?" Edward asked.

The creature leaned back, appearing almost relaxed. "I want to be your friend. I am not the enemy here. Not by a long shot."

"I have read about your type. You make promises to convert people."

"More propaganda from a guy that walks around wearing a robe and a white hat. I know, I am supposed to promise you love, success, knowledge of the future, money... all that jazz, or you could listen to your favorite song backwards and hear my best hits. Let me ask you this question."

Edward tried to get out of bed, but his covers pulled against and restrained him. "Sit still. We will be done soon. I have no promises to make you. No fortunes to throw your way. What I can offer you is the truth."

"I don't want your version of the truth," Edward yelled at the creature.

"Now, now. There is no reason to raise your voice at me. I know that they have brainwashed you, and I will not battle that. I offer you a more personal type of truth. One that Father Murray is hiding from you. One you need to know."

The creature, glowing with a reddish hue, got up and strolled toward the bedroom door. "You should ask Father Murray to tell you the truth about him, about you, and about me. We go way back." As it faded into nothing, Edward heard the haunting voice come from above his bed: "He is still on the phone for you..."

30

"Are you there?" Father Murray's voice screamed through Edward's cell phone. The creature that was there a moment ago was nowhere to be seen. His covers released him. A stiff breeze blew at his window and the heater vent chattered as air passed through it.

Edward answered, his voice shaking. "Yes, Father. What is it?"

"I am on the way to get you. We must hurry." Father Murray, irritated, mumbled, "Lewis should have come straight away to get you and not wait for me in this case. There is no time to waste. No matter..." His voice trailed off as he hung up. Edward believed the last bit was a rant Father Murray was making out loud, and not meant for him to hear.

Edward got out of bed and looked around the room for any sign of his visitor before moving about. There was nothing. The bed covers didn't even show signs of anyone sitting on them.

He threw on some clothes and, recalling how cool it was outside earlier, he grabbed his coat before heading into the hall. A quick check on both Sarah and Jacob, who were both sound asleep, put his mind at ease before he headed downstairs.

He stepped off the stairs as the lights of Father Murray's car flashed through the windows. Edward fetched his wallet and keys, expecting the cross and book to be right there. He placed them together on the table earlier. A quick search located them on the other side of the table, by his books. A fleeting thought of the creature moving them ran through his head as he hurried out to Father Murray's car.

Father Murray was on the phone when Edward got in. He sped off, steering with one hand when Edward closed the door. Without a seatbelt on yet to secure him, Edward was tossed around as they speed down the dirt and rock driveway.

Father Murray yelled, "No Lewis! Don't go in yet. We will be there in five minutes at the most." He hung up the phone, dropping it to the seat beside him. It bounced to the floorboard.

"We are heading to the Reynold's farm on the other side of town. This is bad."

"You told the Sheriff we would be there in five minutes at the most."

"I lied. Sue me. I had to keep him from going in," Father Murray said, annoyed.

He drove his oversized car with reckless abandon down the deserted country roads. His speed was only matched by the fire engine and two ambulances that passed them just before the edge of town. Edward noticed red lights flashing on top of the light poles as they darted through town. The original thought was these were to alert aircraft to the poles. The realization that no aircraft would be that low caused him to search for another purpose.

"Father, what are those flashing red lights?"

"What lights?"

Edward pointed one out as they sped by. Father Murray uttered, "Oh my god" and rolled down the windows on both the driver and passenger doors. The nerve shattering sound of a klaxon horn flooded into the car with the cold evening air.

Edward had heard that sound in the movies and asked, "Is that what I think it is? A tornado warning?"

"In most towns, yes. Here it's for something different. Those sirens have only sounded a few times since you were born." Father Murray reached around blindly on the seat beside him.

"It bounced into the floorboard."

The level of annoyance in Father Murray's face increased. "Agh... we will be there soon enough."

He was right. In just a few minutes they pulled into a scene more chaotic than the other night. It appeared every police car in town was there blocking the roads. Lights from the fire trucks and ambulances created blinding flashes. The doors of the ambulances were open. Several people sat on their tailgates, being tended to by the paramedics.

John Sawyer ran up to the Caddy as it slid to a stop. "Father, you need to come quick. Lewis took the boys in back."

"Damn it. I told him to wait," Father Murray exclaimed as he got out.

"A couple of the boys have come back. They are being tended to. Nothing serious."

"I heard the sirens coming through town. Is it what I think it is?"

Edward joined Father Murray on the driver's side of the car and saw the fear in John Sawyer's eyes as he said, "Yes. It is the worst I have ever seen."

Father Murray turned to Edward. "Did you read anything from the book tonight?"

"No. Not since we were together earlier," Edward replied.

"Are you absolutely sure? Not even just to yourself."

Edward confirmed. "Yes. I am sure."

Father Murray's stared sternly at Edward and then asked, "John, which way did they head?"

"Back around the house."

Father Murray took off running into the darkness and summoned Edward to follow.

They rounded the house and entered a dark empty field. The lights and sound of the hectic scene were replaced by the sounds of crickets and frogs and their own movements through tall grass. As they walked further into the darkness, an eerie silence replaced the crickets and frogs. A silence that was only pierced by men yelling and something howling and screeching.

Three forms, backlit by the creatures they were trying to hold at bay, came into view. Father Murray chastised the Sheriff. "Lewis, I told you to wait."

"Sorry, no can-do, Father. People were getting hurt."

"You're not equipped to handle this. Where is it?"

The Sheriff looked confused at the question. There were many spectral beings right in front of them, but at his request, he gave him a situation report, "Three out over there to the right. They have been quiet. Another four or five over to the left over here. They are the troublesome group. I think the one that bit the girl is in that group."

"No. Where is it?" Father Murray demanded while peering into the darkness.

"That depends on which IT you mean. I haven't seen your old friend, but I suspect he is out here. If you are talking about the other, you are right. There is one open. Follow me. I will get you as close as we can get."

The sheriff moved deliberately through the tall grass, watching every step.

"Edward, get up there with the sheriff and hold out the cross. That should keep the path clear."

Edward moved up next to the sheriff and held the cross out at the end of his stiff right arm. He took timid steps in the darkness, unsure where they were heading and what was out there.

Sheriff Tillingsly asked him, "You don't believe that piece of wood will protect us, do you?"

Edward answered without hesitation, "Yes."

"Good, I wouldn't want you out here unless you believed it. Too dangerous for all of us if you don't."

"Lewis wasn't much of a believer when he was..." Father Murray struggled with a memory of yesteryear. "How old were you the first time you went out with Carl?"

"Twenty-two."

"That is right... still wet behind the ears. Ronald was tending to a crash out on Maple Crook Road, I think. You responded to what they called in as a trespassing."

"Yeah, the old days where we used code words over the radio to avoid scaring anyone listening in."

"When Carl and I got there, Keith Lloyd told us you wouldn't wait and headed on back. We got back there, and you were frozen stiff…"

"Is this the best time for a story?" Sheriff Tillingsly said, sounding both annoyed and embarrassed.

"I don't know what he was trying to do. She was just a lost little girl. Carl took out the cross and Lewis kind of scoffed at it. I think he said something like, 'what is a piece of wood going to do?' He saw what it did. The girl settled down and let Carl kneel next to her. I still remember your eyes when you watched him whisper the prayer into her ear and she disappeared."

Still sounding embarrassed, "It's not much farther."

Edward felt the familiar chill and tingles, then the repressive weight settled in. His ears filled with a vibration that resembled static. It grew louder with each step, disorienting at first, and then painful.

"Brace yourself," Father Murray said from behind.

Then it came into view. A spinning black void, darker than the night sky. The cyclonic motion created a ring of distortion around the edge.

Edward asked, "What the hell is that?"

"You used a proper word there. It is a portal."

"To where?"

Father Murray took a few steps closer to the void. "Now that is the good question. They say to hell, but we don't know for sure. What I know is nothing good has ever come through one of those things."

"Now Father, that is not nice," echoed a voice Edward was all too familiar with. All three men tensed up and become alert. Each searched the darkness for the creature. Edward spun around, pointing the Cross in all directions.

Father Murray demanded, "Show yourself, vile creature."

"Is that anyway to speak to an old friend? Hi, Edward. I see you have your little cross now."

"Face us," Father Murray demanded again.

"I wasn't born yesterday," replied the creature. Its voice boomed among the static and vibrations, everywhere and nowhere all at once.

"Behind you," said Sheriff Tillingsly. Father Murray turned around in time to avoid a demonic creature charging at him. It caught his long peacoat in its jaw as it ran by, ripping it off.

Father Murray pulled a vial of holy water from a chain that hung around his neck. He prepared for another charge, but the creature just stood there.

Sheriff Tillingsly let out a painful shriek. Edward spun in his direction and saw a ghastly arm extending through the front of Lewis's chest. Agony on his face as he struggled to breathe. Instinctually, Edward pulled the book out of his pocket and searched through the pages. A sudden silence appeared in his head. There was no static, no vibration, just emptiness. Or so he thought. He sensed there was someone there in the silence with him. A presence he felt and could almost sense its thoughts. Not wanting to wait, Edward seized control.

"I know you are there. You can't hide from me," Edward yelled.

"You are right. I can't hide from you, but then again, why would I want to?"

"You're scared of me. You know…"

A maniacal laughter echoed in Edward's head. "Scared of you? I am here to help you. You keep placing your trust in the wrong people."

"You are pure evil," Edward retorted.

"Am I? I am truth. Face it. I am the only one who will tell you the truth. Father Murray is lying to you. The honorable Lewis Tillingsly is lying to you. You don't want to accept that."

"What truth are you talking about?"

"Oh Edward, Edward, Edward. It is right in front of you. You were handed a piece of wood and an old book and told to go save the world. They sent you out into the world ill-prepared, and to be honest, dangerous."

"I am not dangerous. I am not the one out here hurting people. That would be you."

"Are you so sure? Do you know what page to flip open to make me go away? I think not. You have no idea how dangerous it is for you to pretend you know what you are doing. You are messing with a power you can't understand, and you aren't the first, and won't be the last. You need to stop before someone else gets hurt."

"You are just trying to trick me into stopping," Edward challenged.

"Stop yes, but not by tricking you. I am trying to help you realize you are not prepared for this. One mistake can have horrible results. It happened tonight, and it happened about forty years ago."

Edward asked, "What happened tonight?"

"Oh, come now. The portal was opened. Something I cannot do. Only someone reading the wrong page from the book. Maybe a child experimenting with friends, as they might with a Ouija board."

A hazy image of a kitchen, his kitchen, replaced the darkness. Edward was floating in the air above the scene, as a small boy walked in and screamed. Edward looked at what the child saw, and there was his mother lying in a pool of her own blood. Multiple stab wounds covered her body. Each appeared to have come from the inside. His father's body was on the other side of the island lying in a similar pool. His head separated from his body.

"Wait…" Edward exclaimed as a realization hit him like lightning. "You said a something about a child experimenting. I didn't read from the book. I didn't even know about the book. You are wrong there."

"I said a child was behind tonight. Look closer," the voice said. Edward didn't want to, but he had no choice. That scene was burned into his head. It now rotated below him as a young Lewis Tillingsly burst through the door and quickly scooped Edward up. It paused for just a second and zoomed in on his face. Before he left with Edward, Lewis stopped and glared at something or someone that was outside of Edward's view. Edward tried to turn to see more, but the scene did not respond to his movement. The creature controlled the scene. Now it rotated below him, bringing in to view a figure dressed in black, weeping on his knees, with a familiar cross and book on the floor in front of him. Edward's mind couldn't believe what it was seeing. He whispered, "Father Murray."

"Yes. Your trusted family priest."

Edward didn't remember him being there that night, but he also didn't remember looking anywhere but at his parents. Edward asked, "What is he doing there?"

"Search for the truth, and be careful who you trust," the voice said, now sounding distant.

The scene faded, and the vibration returned to Edward's ears. The chill he felt from panic was replaced by the coolness of the evening air. His eyes cleared and a new scene appeared before him. Sheriff Tillingsly was lying face down on the ground. Father Murray was on his side in the grass. The dark void was closing, and in the distance behind it Edward saw a dozen or more figures disappear into the darkness of the night. As the final glimpse of the void disappeared Edward heard the familiar voice: "Be careful who you trust."

31

Father Murray rolled up to his knees. Edward rushed over and helped him to his feet. Without saying a word, they both ran to Sheriff Tillingsly's side. He was unresponsive, and Edward could only find a weak pulse. The two men picked him up and carried him back in the direction of the house, screaming for help the whole way. It took several minutes before anyone heard them, and a few more before two paramedics and another deputy reached them.

Edward stood there helpless over his lifeless body as the paramedics administered aid. He heard one of them mention it appeared he suffered a severe cardiac event before one of them began CPR. The other took off and returned with a gurney. Edward helped them load him on the gurney and then rush to the ambulance.

The sirens wailed as Sheriff Tillingsly was rushed to the hospital. The last remaining paramedic crew was tending to the many people injured. They attempted to check Father Murray several times, but he brushed them off each time.

Edward stood in the middle of the chaotic scene of light and sounds as people rushed around. He felt numb to all of it though, like he was watching it all from the outside.

Father Murray brushed off another try to tend to several scratches across his face. He approached Edward very agitated. "You can't just freeze like that. Lewis could have died. We both could have." His tone of voice snapped Edward back to the here and now. A heavy disdain for himself settled on his shoulders. It was fueled by the disappointment he felt in himself and that coming from everyone else that passed him. He was supposed to know how to handle these situations. Or was he? Edward tried to explain. "I had no control over it. That thing took me someplace else. It took me back to the day someone killed my parents."

"Took you some place? What the hell are you talking about?" He turned and walked away from him.

"I couldn't see you or the sheriff. I was some place dark and silent. It was just me and it."

"I told you this the first day. You have to be strong in your convictions. It detected weakness in you and took advantage of it. That is why he went after you and not Lewis or me. You were the weak link he could exploit, and he did." He walked away again, shaking his head. "This is my fault. You are not ready for this."

"That is what it said, too," Edward said.

"See, that is what I am talking about. It knows."

Following a few feet behind the Father, Edward said, "It was more than that. Something about trying to tell me the truth." Edward struggled to remember the details. Like a dream he woke up in the middle of, he remembered a few feelings and words, but specific details dissipated from his mind.

"What truth can that thing possibly offer you? Think about it. The Devil and his minions are creatures of lies and promises. Scripture teaches us that. I don't want to hear anything else about it. WE have a disaster to clean up."

Edward remembered one vague detail he felt compelled to share. "It said something about a child opening something."

At first Father Murray ignored what Edward said, but hesitated for a second and asked, "What did it say about a child?"

Edward tried to remember more details, but he could only come up with disjointed phrases. "Something about an opening and a child playing with something like a Ouija board."

Father Murray looked around at the people leaning against cars and sitting on the ground. His attention focused on Charlotte Reynolds, sitting on the back step of the remaining ambulance. The medics were tending to what looked like a bite wound on her face. Father Murray walked toward her, quicker than before. He approached Carol Reynolds, her mother, who was standing beside her, and placed his reassuring hand on her shoulder. "How is everyone doing over here?" he asked.

Carol turned toward the Father and Edward, tears streaming down her face. "We are ok. Once they are done here, we will head to the hospital, so they can stitch her up."

"How are you holding up Carol?" Father Murray asked.

"I am a mess. What happened here? I have never seen so many, and they were aggressive. They chased us down." At that moment, Edward ignored the fearful look in her eyes and caught sight of the claw marks on her arms. These were all real injuries, not like the flames that engulfed Kevin Kirkland. There was real pain and damage here.

"I am not sure Carol, but trust in me. We will protect you," Father Murray said in that consoling tone of voice he had used many times to comfort people in times of need for the last several decades. Edward thought there must be magic in that tone. They did not protect anyone tonight, but Carol ignored all the pain her and her family had suffered and accepted his promise. "Thank you, Father."

"Before you take Charlotte, I need to talk to her for a few minutes, if that is ok?"

Carol did not question why and agreed. "Of course."

Father Murray took off his large black brimmed hat and settled on the step next to Charlotte. "I thought you would have given it a good upper cut before it got you."

A smirk showed on the young girls face as she replied, "I got a few good blows in."

"That's my girl. Can you tell me what happened?"

"I was asleep when they appeared. These are not like the ones we usually see. Those pay no attention to us. These were here, in our world... and they ran after us, yelling and growling the whole time."

Not finding any helpful details, Father Murray probed further. "What about before you went to sleep? Did you notice anything, or did something happen?"

The girl's body language changed, and she stared at a spot on the ground in front of her.

"Come on, Charlotte. Can you tell us anything that might help us?" Father Murray said as he looked at Edward.

"We just watched a movie. She went home, and I went to bed."

Father Murray had the look of a man who knew he was just lied to. Before he could try another question, Edward jumped in. "Sarah, my daughter. Is that who you were watching a movie with?"

"Yes, Mr. Meyer. We were just watching a movie. We didn't mean to cause any problems," Charlotte said with a quiver in her voice.

"What did you do?" her mother asked.

"Sarah showed me a book. She said it was THE book. We didn't read anything out loud."

Father Murray mouthed "the book," in Edward's direction. "It is important that you answer me truthfully. Did you read anything at all? Even just to yourself?"

"No. I just looked at the outside and flipped through it."

Father Murray looked up at her mother as he said, "Thank you. Everything is going to be ok."

He got up and put his hat back on.

"Come, Edward. We need to go talk to your daughter." Father Murray sprinted toward his Caddy.

32

Father Murray sped down the dark country roads with reckless abandon. Edward's mind raced just as fast, searching for answers. Sarah had never had the book or the cross. Even if she did, how would she even know what to do? Then he remembered. When he rushed out to meet Father Murray, the book and cross were not where he left them. Had she taken them when she went to Charlotte's? That was the only explanation.

"Edward, what is it?"

"Huh?"

"What's wrong? You yelled 'Jesus'."

Edward was unaware of the utterance. It must have been a subconscious reaction to the realization. "Sarah must have grabbed the book before heading to Charlotte's. I noticed when I came to meet you it was not where I left it." Edward was not sure if he could let his priest down any more than he already did, but he had now proven that wrong. "I am sorry. I know I shouldn't have let it out of my sight."

"Don't be silly. You were at home. How could you have known?" His words were meant to reassure Edward, but his tone told a different story. "The important thing now is to find out which page she read from." Edward then heard Father Murray say under his breath, "I think I already know."

As they sped through town, the streets were vacant. The siren wailed and the red lights flashed. Edward struggled with his thoughts, trying to piece together what he was shown and what he saw. The line separating both was rather fuzzy. The word "portal" repeated in his head several times.

"It said someone opened a portal. A portal to where?" Edward asked.

"Where? I don't know. No one does. Here is a way to think of it... or how I think of it. The common thought in the church about possession is you have to invite and accept the demonic spirit. The portal is a doorway opened to accept or invite them in. Whether it is a doorway to some spiritual place..." Father Murray yanked the wheel to the left and then back again. The tires squealed in response, trying to maintain traction on the road surface. "Damn deer, the spirits must be spooking them. Anyways... we are not sure if it's specific to some realm or just a general doorway to all spirits. What I know is every time one is opened, nothing good comes through, and we need to close it."

"There is a page for that?" Edward asked. He hoped for a simple "yes."

"More than one page. We will have to try many things and we may need help. Until then we will have our hands full."

"Wait, help? Help from who?" Edward asked.

"The Church has people I can call who specialize in this kind of thing. But I am hoping we can act quickly enough that won't be necessary. We have to close the portal, and fast. That will limit how many creatures come through. GOD knows, we will have our hands full dealing with what already has."

Edward's mind pictured the swirling disk of black with creatures coming through it. "Why don't we force them back through or open another portal to push them back through?"

Father Murray glared at Edward and said, "No! Clear that thought out of your mind."

Father Murray swerved his Caddy onto Edward's driveway. In just moments it came to a stop in front of the door. Both men exited and raced through the spirits encircling the farmhouse. Edward noticed a few red entities in the grouping, but continued in without a word to Father Murray. He continued up the stairs to wake Sarah, while Father Murray stayed in the living room. Edward returned moments later with a sleepy teenager following behind him asking, "Dad, why did you wake me?"

Father Murray spoke before Edward could answer his daughter. "Sarah darling, we need to talk to you, and you need to be very truthful. You are not in any trouble. Tonight, when you were with Charlotte, what did you guys do?"

The look of someone wide awake and trapped replaced the sleepy look in Sarah's eyes. "We watched a movie, why?" she said.

"Sarah, you need to tell us the truth," Edward pleaded. Father Murray waved his hand in Edward's direction. Edward gave him a curt node.

"Sarah, a demonic portal opened behind Charlotte's house tonight. Several creatures came through. One bit her on the face. Others attacked her mother. I need you to tell me what page you read from tonight when you were there."

Sarah dropped and sat on the bottom step of the stairs. She buried her head in her knees and sobbed.

Father Murray stepped forward and sternly, as if giving a sermon, said, "Everyone will be ok, and you aren't in any trouble. You had no way of knowing what could happen, but I need to know what page you read from so your father and I can stop it before someone else is hurt."

"I am sorry. I did not know. Everyone at school knows who I am, and they have all heard the legend of the cross and book. I get asked everyday if I have ever seen it. I didn't mean any harm. Just wanted to show it off."

"That is fine, but the page. I need to know the page."

Father Murray extended his hand toward Edward. Edward pulled the book out of his pocket and gave it to Father Murray. He knelt in front of Sarah and presented the book. "The page, Sarah. Please?"

She took the book and flipped through several pages. About two thirds through the book, she spun it around and pointed to a page.

Father Murray glanced the page and dipped his head. Without moving he said, "Thank you. You can go back upstairs. Your father and I will handle this."

Sarah stood up, tears streaming down her cheeks. Guilt filled her eyes. In between sobs, she said "Daddy, I am sorry. I am really sorry."

Edward said, "It's ok. Go on back to bed." Edward was not sure if everything was ok. He was trying to shield his daughter from what that was. From the body language of Father Murray, he sensed things were a long way from being ok.

After a few moments of silence between them, Father Murray stood up and walked toward the kitchen. "I will need some coffee," he said while pulling a familiar flask out of his pocket. "I suggest you have some too."

Edward followed him into the kitchen. He took his familiar seat at the table while Edward prepared the base for their liquid courage. Edward delivered the steaming hot cups of caffeine to the table and Father Murray opened the flask and poured a generous amount into his coffee. Father Murray extended it over Edward's cup and paused for Edward to nod permission.

"So now what?" Edward asked.

"It is not Sarah's fault. What she read was in Latin. I am sure it sounded fancy and impressive to her, but she didn't know what the words meant."

"What did they mean?"

"She asked Satan to grant her the power to open a doorway for his army of darkness."

Edward had just picked up his coffee cup when Father Murray explained the prayer. He dropped it the inch back to the table. It landed with a thud. Coffee sloshed over the edge and onto the table. "Why would a prayer like that be in the book?" he asked.

Father Murray sighed and sat back. "Well, do you want to hear the complex answer or the simple answer?"

"Just an answer."

"In all conflicts, there are two sides. The dark and the light. Good and Evil. At some point someone on the side of the light always considers trying to harness the powers of the dark to aid them. There are several prayers or readings in the book that attempt to do that. They were enticed by the power they perceived to exist."

Edward bluntly asked, "My relatives were Devil worshipers?"

"Absolutely not. Your family is one of the most prestigious and religious families in the world. They tried to use these dark passages to aid them in their duties. How can I explain it? It is like someone who is against violence and guns, resorting to violence to further their cause." Father Murray thought about it for a second and then said, "That didn't help clear it up, did it? Just understand your family is an honorable family. They understand the responsibility of their duty and the power that exists on both sides. Along the way, they made a few bad decisions about how to use those powers to fulfill their duties."

"So, what do we do? I assume there is a page that counters this spell."

"Not exactly. I need to call someone. This is above both you and me. I tried once before and failed. I won't take that chance again."

Father Murray's final word crossed into Edward's ears as a loud vibration built inside. The room around him faded to black. There was no chill or tingling forewarning him of the presence, but in just moments he was back in a familiar vacant place, and he was not alone. That same presence was in there with him.

A voice boomed through the blackness. "Remember what I showed you."

The black void gave way to the scene of his parents lying on the floor in the kitchen. Their arms were moving, pointing toward the table, pointing toward Father Murray. He was on his knees weeping.

"Search for the truth, Edward. Search for the truth."

"Edward. Edward, can you hear me?" The image of his kitchen cleared, and he was once again sitting at the table across from Father Murray.

Edward responded, "Yes, Father. I can now. It was here again."

"You must block him out of your mind. Strengthen the conviction of your faith. I will help you learn to battle it."

As Father Murray explained, Edward's mind pondered what it was just shown. The phrase still echoing deep in his thoughts forced a question to the surface. Edward exploded, interrupting Father Murray. "Why were you here the night my parents were killed?"

Father Murray was taken aback by the question. Edward considered the possibility he wasn't there, and the creature was showing him a false story. The expression in the eyes of the person sitting across from him said something different.

"That was the worst day of my life, in so many ways." He took a tentative sip of coffee, his hands shaking the entire time. "I didn't know you saw me."

"Why were you here?"

"We were trying to save you and your mother, but were too late. Your father... your father rushed in before I got there."

Father Murray's words contradicted the story he'd been told. They told him it was a break in, and the cops believed his parents heard a sound and went downstairs to check it out. When they walked into the kitchen, they startled the burglar and he killed them before they had a chance. There was obviously more to the story, and Edward wanted to know it all. He demanded, "Tell me what happened. Not the story you all told me about a burglar. Tell me the truth."

Father Murray swallowed and took a deep breath. "You should know the truth, but let me say I am so sorry. I didn't understand as much as I do now. We were in the middle of an extremely bad and violent period of spiritual activities. Your father and I were trying everything we could to keep things under control and some days we did, and others were not so good. We were desperate and tried something. Just once. We thought we could keep it controlled, but it got away from us."

"What did?"

"We were out in the pasture just on the edge of your property. One of the creatures took off toward the house. Remember I told you they're drawn by the energy of the book and cross. Your father left the cross inside, and that one was going for it. I heard your mother scream before your father reached the porch. Then I heard your father screaming prayers and commands. I entered the backdoor just as your father fell to the floor. The book and cross both crashed on the floor and slid toward me."

"What did Father?" Edward questioned again, louder, insisting on an answer.

"Before I could do anything it was gone. Your parents were dead, and you were standing in the kitchen doorway. We called Lewis earlier when we headed out into the pasture to deal with it."

Edward slammed his fist on the table, causing coffee to spill from both cups. "Father, you said something got away from you. What did?"

"You have to understand. We were running out of options."

"Tell me. Tell me the truth."

"Your father and I discussed it over and over and we agreed." The expression and body language of the old priest became defeated by a great weight he had carried for decades. Edward felt his temper growing inside and opened his mouth to unleash on his friend.

Before Edward could utter a sound, Father Murray confessed. "We… or I, tried to use a dark prayer to battle the demons." He looked straight at Edward and tried to explain. "It was something we discussed over and over. Things were out of control, and people were getting hurt. We thought if we could gain control of it, we could send them back to where they belong. I even consulted a fellow priest on the matter. We both agreed under the circumstances. I made a mistake. I used one I didn't fully understand. The same one Sarah read tonight. A portal opened outside, letting in several creatures. We had it controlled. Your father tried to force one back through the portal, but a creature emerged. The creature you have encountered several times. It took control and turned everything against us."

Edward's temper had control of his senses. His mind stopped hearing the words coming out of Father Murray's mouth after he admitted to using a dark prayer to battle the demons. He leapt to the next logical conclusion. A conclusion that had shattered his confidence in the man sitting before him and brought the tragedy from so many years ago back front and center. He stood up and walked away, Father Murray still pleading at table behind him.

In a moment of anger and clarity, Edward turned and walked back to the table. Father Murray was still talking, but Edward did not hear him. Instead, he slammed both the cross and the book on the table in front of the old priest. He jumped in shock. "Father, your actions killed my parents. You destroyed my life in so many ways... and you hid the truth from me. You created this problem. YOU released these monsters. This is your problem. I came here with my family for a fresh start, not to continue a tragedy. I will protect my family, but as for this great responsibility you speak of. It is yours to deal with."

"But Edward..." pleaded Father Murray.

"There is no 'but' anything. I am done. You created this. You have done fine without me for so long. Now take those things and get out of my home."

Edward walked over and opened the backdoor. "You will be leaving now, and will not return."

Father Murray reluctantly stood up and paused for a second, searching for the words to say, but nothing came to him. He walked to the door and left.

Neither man said a word to each other as Edward closed the door. Edward took a seat back at the table and had a few more sips of his coffee. His mind and heart bled at the realization of what really happened to his parents. There was no robbery or aggressor. It was a careless mistake by someone his father trusted, the cruelest crime of all.

33

Edward slept little the rest of the night. There were no disturbances or interruptions. At least not outside of his own mind. The scene of his parents in the kitchen played over and over in his head, much like it did when he was younger. There was just one difference now. He had filled in the missing pieces. The more he saw, the more his anger developed toward Father Murray. He wondered who else was involved. Was the sheriff? Was his father aware of the danger? He responded to each question with the same answer. His focus was his family and kids and that was it. The others were all on their own.

He turned over in the bed, trying to get comfortable and clear his mind. He needed to get some rest. Instead, he spied the time on the alarm clock on the bedside table. One minute before his alarm was scheduled to go off, the cruelest trick of all.

Edward forced his tired body and exhausted mind out of the bed and toward the shower. He was hoping the hot water would wake him up. It only took a few minutes for him to realize that hope was full of hot air. He dressed and finished getting ready before he started down the hallway to make sure his children were up and getting ready for school. There was a brief consideration of letting Sarah stay home from school, but he heard her up and heading into the bathroom to get ready.

Jacob met his father downstairs sitting at the table, already showered, and dressed for school. It looked like it would be one of the easy mornings, and Edward was thankful for that. "What'll you have for breakfast, champ?" he asked his son.

"Cereal."

With a choice of four varieties in the pantry, Edward gave his son a look that asked for clarification. Jacob's reply was also non-verbal, as he pointed in the air, directing his father's hand until it hovered in front of the right box. Edward pulled down the box of sugar covered morsels and poured Jacob a bowl and then covered it with milk.

Edward leaned back against the countertop while he downed a cup of coffee. He wanted to get two in him before he went to work. Sarah emerged through the door and walked over and gave her father a hug. She whispered "Sorry" in his ear and then fixed herself a cup of coffee. He wanted to let some of his anger loose on her and tell her that sorry didn't come close to even covering it, but he stopped.

She did not understand what she was doing or even how bad things were. Edward wanted to keep it that way and protect his family.

He started on his second cup and wondered if there would be any reaction at work today to what happened last night. He remembered how surprised he was at how fast things got around after the first time. It was almost a guarantee people would know. The last drop of his second cup hit his lips and he checked the time on his watch. They should have left five minutes ago, but he was too tired to panic. He said, "Let's go. We're late." Neither kid resisted nor hesitated. They grabbed their things and headed straight for the door.

Jacob hopped out of the car at his school and shut the door. Edward pulled off and headed toward the high school. His drive was mostly on auto pilot. He sat there looking straight forward. Sarah was too. She broke the silence. "Charlotte texted me earlier. She is all stitched up and feeling much better, but won't be back to school for a few days."

"That is understandable. How is her mom doing?"

Sarah said nothing. Instead, she looked down at her phone and typed feverishly. About a minute later there was a ding. "Her mom is doing fine. Father Murray is with them now."

Edward wanted to say, "Tell them not to trust that old goat. He is more dangerous than helpful," but he held it to himself. Instead, he said, "Ok, good."

Sarah said nothing and appeared to be waiting for her Father to start a lecture about what happened last night, but he didn't. He left the tension sitting there above them both and pulled into the parking lot at the school. He parked and turned off the car. She sat there, still waiting for the lecture of a lifetime. Edward opened his door, exited, closed the door, and walked into the school, leaving his daughter sitting there bewildered.

Edward felt the looks and glares of others as he walked down the hallway. The level of disappointment hanging in the air was heavier than before. He half wanted to respond, but also half didn't care what anyone else thought. Luckily for everyone, the second half won.

He walked into his classroom, which was half full of his students. It was quieter than normal. No pre-start of class chatting going on. Each student was sitting at their desk, staring at him.

These kids are too young to understand, thought Edward. Instead of saying anything, he returned the same cold welcome back to them and unpacked his bag to prepare for the day.

Each class took a few minutes to warm up, but eventually the discussion on the lessons picked up to close to the normal level. That was all Edward could ask for. He didn't know what people thought of him or his actions, and he didn't want it to affect his effectiveness as a teacher. The discussion also helped him stay awake through the first few classes.

After his fourth class, he packed up a few things and prepared to pull out his lunch. He did not feel he would be welcomed in the teacher's lounge today. A voice from the door called him. "Mr. Meyer." He turned, expecting to see a student with a question, but saw a young man in a deputy uniform standing in his doorway with his hat in his hands. Tillingsly introduced him once, but Edward was currently drawing a blank trying to remember his name. He thinks it is Mike, but he is not sure of his last name.

"Mike?"

"No. Marcus, Marcus Thompson," the deputy said.

"Oh, that's right. We met at the Kirklands' farm last week. I am so sorry."

"Yes sir, we did. It is ok. We only met once. Do you have a moment?" he asked.

Edward motioned for him to come in. "The sheriff asked me to check in on you and make sure you are all right."

"I am just fine, Deputy Thompson. How is the sheriff? He is the one I am worried about."

"Well, he is not doing too well. The doctors said he had a pretty serious heart attack. He will be out for a few weeks."

Edward's remorse hit him tenfold. As much as he tried to convince himself he was not totally responsible for what happened, it didn't work. "Next time you see him, tell him I am sorry. Will you do that for me?" Edward asked. He wanted to go see him, but felt now was the wrong time.

"He said you would say that, and asked me to tell you not to worry about it. None of this was your fault. He also gave me a list of things to tell you. If you know the sheriff, you know he may be out of service for a while, but he will still run the department from the hospital bed. There was this one time he stepped in a hole out possum hunting with old man Rickers out on route 142. He snapped his ankle in two, but that didn't stop him, oh no..." The deputy looked at Edward and cut his story off. Either the mood in the room or the look on Edward's face told him this was the wrong time for a story. "The sheriff asked me to tell you to not be too hard on Father Murray. You three need each other. He also said to tell you that I am at your disposal while he is out."

It seemed the deputy was correct. Sheriff Tillingsly was still trying to control and manage things right from the hospital bed, and had named someone to be his eyes and ears. That made Edward wonder something, so he asked, "Deputy Thompson, do you know what that last bit means?"

The deputy looked around and fidgeted. "Yes, sir."

"Are you sure?" Edward asked while walking toward the deputy. "You are ready to go to war with the supernatural. To fight against an evil as old as the world itself. One we cannot physically fight against, but can only use mystical blessed relics and words. Are you really ready for that?"

"I am ready to do what you need me to do."

Edward was less than convinced by the deputy's tone, so he asked, "Have you seen a spirit before?"

"Not up close, but a few out in a field or across the road," he said.

"Have you heard the sound they make when you fight them?"

He did not respond. Edward pressed again, "Have you felt their cold touch as they reach in and squeeze your heart? Or how about when they enter your mind and play with your thoughts?"

The visibly shaken deputy swallowed deep and answered, "Mr. Meyer, I am here to do whatever you and Father Murray need me to do."

The deputy's reaction confirmed Edward's assumption. "Let's be honest, Marcus. You aren't. None of us are. We can say we are ready for this, but we aren't. I know the sheriff trusts you, or he wouldn't have sent you here to see me. If I need anything, I will call you. You are the sheriff now."

"No sir, he is the Sheriff. Only an election can change that. I am just standing in for now."

"My mistake. I thank you for stopping by. Please give the sheriff my best."

"I will, and you take care. Call me if you need anything." The deputy donned his hat on his way out of the door.

Edward had no intention of taking him up on his offer. Deputy Thompson had no clue what they asked him to step into. It was bad enough with neither Father Murray nor himself knowing what they were doing. Taking him out with them would only put him in danger.

No matter. Edward was out of all this anyway. His children were his only focus. A glance at the clock changed that focus for just a second. He was starved, and only had a few minutes before students would file in for his next class.

34

 Edward settled in at his dining table turned desk. Exhausted but determined to grade at least two classes' worth of essays, he pulled the stack from his bag and started to read. The quiet calm of the house wasn't helping his fight against exhaustion. Thinking some background music might do the trick, he reached for his phone to start up the music app. The phone vibrated and danced across the table before he could grab it. The display listed the familiar number of Father Murray.

 He checked the clock on his phone; it was just after eleven at night. That was not a social call, not at this hour. Not that he would have answered a social call from that man at the moment. He must need help. Out of both fear and anger, he used his thumb and swiped left to reject the call.

 The display changed to his screen saver and Edward unlocked the phone and opened his music app. He selected his favorite eighties playlist and dove back into the essays. Thirty seconds into the first song a ding interrupted the music. Edward had no intention of stopping to listen to the message. At least not yet. The music started again, and Edward found where he left off in the essay.

 Two essays in and the music stopped, again alerting Edward to a new text message. At this hour it could be only one person. His hand reached for the phone in reaction to the tone, but he stopped it halfway. There was a small voice in his head telling him to read the text. The hurt and anger yelled that voice down.

 He graded another five essays before the phone rang again. Edward threw his hands up and let out a frustrated sigh. He gave up and stacked the papers back in his desk, declined the call, and headed upstairs to bed.

 The next day Edward encountered the same looks and avoidance as he walked into school, but he didn't care. There was a slight feeling of being an outcast, but his subconscious combated every look or glare with the thought, *you don't understand anything.* His students were still standoffish, but not as much as yesterday. They engaged during classwork-related discussions. There were no such casual talks or students coming in early or after class to say "hi."

 At lunch he ventured into the lounge to get a drink from the vending machine. As he walked through the door, conversations stopped, and everyone looked at him. Their eyes watched him as he crossed the room toward the machine. As he turned his back to them to make his choice, he felt their gaze burning a hole through him. He wanted to turn around and yell something like, "go ahead and hate me, not like I care." But he didn't care enough to cause a career limiting scene. This was where he worked. He needed to work past this.

He made the perp walk back across the lounge and out the door. Mark got up and followed him out. Edward heard footsteps following him, but did not stop. He continued to his classroom.

"Edward," Mark called when he walked through the door of his classroom.

"Hi, Mark. Aren't you worried what the others will think if they saw you talking to me?"

"Not really. See, they elected me to talk to you," Mark responded with a wry smile.

Edward was not in the mood to take the humorous bait. "That so?"

"Yea, it is. Most of us know about what happened. We don't know all the details, just pieces of what is going around. What happened in that field that night would have shaken anyone up. To be honest, I don't know how you do it. I still get scared when I see them. It must be something in your DNA. You have to know what happened to Lewis was not your fault, and none of this is your daughter's fault either. She didn't know. Neither did Charlotte. Hell, that creature has been running around for years."

Edward sat there at his desk, listening to his friend's impassioned plea.

Mark changed his approach.

"What I am trying to say is, you can't give up. We, everyone, need you and what your family does. Times have been rough here for a long time. Many of our old friends left because of it. I can't blame them. I thought about it myself a few times. We need you. Don't lose confidence."

Mark stopped and looked at his friend for a reply. Edward sat in silence for several moments, calculating his response. His mind stewed on how out of touch everyone was. He was not sure how much to say, but the built-up frustration got the better of his judgement and he unloaded. "Confidence? Is that what you guys think this is about? I lost confidence?"

"Well maybe not confidence. What happened would have shaken anyone."

"Stop right there." He stood up and walked to the end of his desk and leaned against it. "That is not it. There is so much more to it. Did you know the great Father Murray is only guessing at what to do? There is no science to this stuff."

Mark looked at Edward with a confused look.

"Oh yea. You didn't know THAT, did you? The magic book is just a bunch of prayers with no explanation of when or how to use them. You have to," Edward made air quotes, "'feel your way through things.' You can just as easily make a mistake than make the right choice. Oh, and these mistakes can kill. I should know. Father Murray made a mistake years ago that killed my parents. You didn't know THAT either, did you?"

A look of unspeakable shock crossed Mark's face. Edward had just exposed one of Mark's heroes as a fraud.

"His guesswork, his mistake, killed my parents. He wasn't even man enough to own up to it. He only admitted it after I asked. That… that thing roaming around out there… that thing he released, told me. I will protect my family, but I am not doing it anymore Mark. I am not going out there with him and making another mistake that will cost someone else their life. Nope. That will not happen."

Mark remained standing there stunned, looking at his friend.

"You can hate me, but I have my reasons. I am a father first. This stuff cost me my parents. I won't risk my kids or let them go through what I did. I don't care if anyone understands."

"That makes sense. I understand, and I might do the same in your shoes. Not sure how many others will. Things have been rough here for a while. You were a sign of hope."

The last statement Mark said rubbed Edward the wrong way, but he stayed silent. He was no sign of hope. Everyone was on their own.

"You and the kids should come over to dinner again," Mark offered.

Edward's first reaction was to decline, but he realized Mark may be the only person in town that didn't hate him, so he answered in a non-committal fashion. "We'll see. Right now, I want to stay at home."

35

The next few days at school were the same. Edward felt isolated, like a leper, but the urge to respond or make a scene had been diminishing. The interaction in his classes was mostly back to normal. It was not as social as they had been before, but it was a good learning environment.

That day was exam day, so the classes were silent. He'd spend the weekend grading each exam in the five rubber banded stacks, one stack for each class. In fact, he'd start tonight. He was skipping the football game. No reason to expose himself to the ire of the entire town.

As he gathered up the stacks of exams, his phone rang from inside his bag. His first instinct was to dismiss it, like he had most calls recently. Those calls had been at night, and he knew who they were from. It was just after three in the afternoon, and odd time for Father Murray to call him. Edward retrieved the phone to check. The number was not one he recognized. He answered. "Hello."

"Hey Edward, hope I caught you at a good time," Sheriff Tillingsly said.

"Sheriff, how are you feeling?"

"Not too bad. The doctors are still poking around on me. They are trying to tell me I need to cut back on the greasy food, red meat, and alcohol. I just say yes sir every time they read me a list of things I can't have anymore. I also need to exercise more, they say. I think I will take up walking. You can walk with me since you put me here."

The sheriff laughed loudly, but Edward did not feel the humor. "Sheriff, I feel just horrible."

The sheriff cut Edward off before he could continue apologizing. "You stop that. I was joking. I intend those walks to be times to catch up while I smoke a big cigar, something else I am not supposed to have anymore. This is not your fault. This could have happened whether you were there or not."

Edward was not sure how to respond, creating an awkward silence on the call.

"The Father told me what happened between you and him."

"I am not in the mood for a lecture. I feel everyone's disappointment in me, so you can save that talk," Edward said.

"Oh, you misunderstand me. I am not calling to give you a lecture. That is all between you and him, but I have to think about what is best for the rest of Miller's Crossing. If you don't want to put yourself and your family at any risk, not that they aren't already, that is your choice. I won't try to convince you otherwise, but... I do need to ask you a favor. There is a gentleman heading over to your home with Father Murray. I need you to meet with him."

"This is not a good night. I have exams to grade, and I am not in the mood to talk to anyone else that will try to sway or convince me to change my mind."

"This is not that. This is someone from the Vatican that will try to help Father Murray close the portal and try to restore order to things here. He wants to interview you about your encounters. Can you do that for me?"

"Yes," Edward begrudgingly agreed. He might as well get it over with.

"I thank you. I will be in touch about those walks, though. Would like to catch up with you."

The call disconnected before Edward could convey the same sentiment. Edward still had much to learn about his family. The sheriff could help fill in the gaps for him.

36

When Sarah, Jacob, and Edward arrived home, they found Father Murray's Cadillac parked in front. Next to the car stood two men, Father Murray, and another, both dressed all in black. Both men watched as Edward drove up and parked.

"Who is that?" Sarah asked.

"That is a friend of Father Murray's that I need to talk to for a few minutes."

Sarah looked concerned and asked, "Is it about Charlotte?"

Not wanting to lie to his daughter, Edward said, "Sort of. He wants me to talk to him about what I saw there so he can help Father Murray with it. Why don't you two go on inside? See if your brother needs help with his homework while I talk to them."

Sarah ran past the two men, only pausing to say, "Good afternoon, Father."

Father Murray returned the pleasantry. "Afternoon, Sarah."

Jacob just smiled as he bounced up the front steps.

Edward walked over to the two men and politely nodded and greeted Father Murray.

Father Murray nodded back.

Edward extended his hand to the stranger, who was wearing a black overcoat over his black pants, black shirt, and white collar. The man looked at him from under the brim of his black hat and greeted him while firmly taking his hand. "Mr. Meyer. I am Father Lucian. It is a pleasure to meet you." Father Lucian spoke with a very strong Italian accent, catching Edward off guard.

"Thanks for agreeing to meet with us," Father Murray said.

Edward snapped back, "I wasn't given much of a choice. I was told you were heading here before I was even told you were coming."

"Um... yea... sorry about that. Time is of the essence. Father Lucian has come a long way to speak with you. Can we go inside?"

"You know the way," Edward said, and all three headed toward his front steps. Father Murray walked through the spirits that still encircled Edward's house, but as Father Lucian approached them, they parted and allowed him through. Edward watched as they closed ranks behind him again before walking through himself.

Once inside, Father Murray continued on into the kitchen. Edward resisted asking him how it felt to return to the scene of the crime. Father Murray took his familiar seat at the table and Edward leaned back against the counter next to the sink. Father Lucian remained standing, holding his hat in his hands before him. His posture was upright and proper. He turned and spoke directly to Edward. "Mr. Meyer, they sent here me to assist Father Murray with the situation."

Edward was quick to interrupt and looked straight at Father Murray. "So, you brought another priest in to convince me to help you again." Father Murray shook his hands in denial the whole time.

"No, Mr. Meyer. That is not why I am here. Father Murray has explained the issue between him and yourself. That is not of my concern. I want to know about the creature. Father Murray said you had direct contact with it."

Feeling foolish about his earlier outburst, Edward responded to the visitor, "Yes, a few times."

"Can you tell me about them?"

"Well, the first time would be at the Kirklands.' It took me out of the room, showed me images of this room from when I was a child and the dead bodies of my parents, and said he was trying to show me the truth. That is pretty much all I remember."

"He took you from the room? Where did he take you?" Father Lucian asked.

"First it was someplace empty, dark. It was just him and I, but I couldn't see him. I could only hear his voice." Edward suddenly remembered a field with his children and mumbled, "Then a field with warm sunlight." He paused for a minute, trying to remember more before continuing. "I am sorry. A lot of the details escape me, like a dream after you wake up. It seemed we kept alternating between the dark space to other places he wanted to show me, like the field, and my kitchen."

"You keep saying 'he,' but you said you never saw it."

"His voice was masculine, plus I saw it once. Not that night, another time."

Father Murray asked, "How many times have you encountered it?"

"Three. At the Kirklands,' and the other night at the Reynolds'. Both times were similar. The black empty space and showing me this kitchen. The whole time he offered to tell me the truth, which he showed me." Edward glared past his visitor at Father Murray. "Then, just before you called me to help at the Reynolds,' he appeared in my bedroom."

Father Murray and Father Lucian both appeared shocked at the revelation that the creature appeared to Edward. "Can you be more specific?" asked Father Lucian.

"The phone rang. I thought it was Father Murray. When I tried to answer it, he or it was sitting there at the foot of my bed."

"What did he look like?"

Edward described the creature for the two men. They exchange a few interested looks while Edward gave his description.

"You say it kept talking of truth. Did it tell you what truth?"

Edward looked past Father Lucian and straight at Father Murray seated behind him. "No, he never told it to me directly. He kept telling me Father Murray was lying or hiding things from me. Told me I was putting my trust in the wrong person. But every image it showed me led me back here to the part Father Murray played in the death of my parents." Edward looked Father Lucian in the eyes. "I am sure your friend told you about that."

"He did. Was there anything else? Did he try to get you to harm anyone or join him?"

"No, he said he was trying to help me find the truth and avoid committing similar mistakes."

Father Lucian turned to Father Murray. "Abaddon? Did you release him?"

"I don't know who I released, but it sounds like him. It would explain his more leadership type of actions. He tries to manipulate us and sends other spirits to do his work."

"Will someone tell me what you are talking about?" Edward demanded, feeling more than a little confused.

"You hadn't taught him yet?" Father Lucian asked Father Murray.

"We were starting on prayers and their meaning first. I thought I might have more time before he needed to know demonology."

Father Lucian appeared to disapprove of his fellow priest's method. "The sower of discord. The angel of the abyss, or as Revelation 9:11 says, 'whose name in Hebrew is Abaddon, The Angel of Death'. In other religions they call him 'The Destroyer.' It would appear he is building an army. What better place to do it than one of the most spiritually sensitive sites in the world?"

He turned his attention back to Father Murray. "You should have called sooner. Not waited a day, a month, and definitely not decades. You have put everyone at risk."

"Wait a minute. An army?" Edward asked. The explanation provided by Father Lucian both confused and frightened him.

"Mr. Meyer, take a walk with me please."

37

The two men strolled together, one next to the other, out into the pasture beside the main house. Father Lucian looked around and took in the fresh cool air and the lasting orange glow of the setting sun. Edward watched two geese flying to the south. That was the peacefulness he sought when he returned home. So far it came only in fleeting moments.

Father Lucian said, "Beautiful home you have."

"Thanks."

"It is not uncommon for nature to use true beauty to hide significant dangers."

"I don't catch your meaning."

"Nature often disguises the dangerous creatures and places. To the uneducated eye, no one would ever guess what really goes on here."

"If you tried to explain it to a true outsider, they would think you're nuts."

"Ah, true. There are many non-believers out there. Truly faithful believers would know they are being told the truth."

Edward's common sense disagreed on the surface, but considered there maybe deeper meaning to his statement.

"I didn't come here to talk to you about this..." Father Lucian said as he gestured toward the horizon line. "Mr. Meyer, can I speak completely freely... honestly to you?"

"Of course, Father."

"Father Murray means well, but he is not able to deal with what goes on here. His training does not cover this. The Vatican hand selects, trains, and assigns the priests for these sites. None, and I mean none, of the training involves how to handle the demons or spirits. We look for priests with a certain level of faith and personality. They are to be trusted allies and confidants to the Primaries assigned. To help sure up and deal with their spiritual and mental health. He has had none of the training your family has."

"Is the training you are talking about knowledge handed down through our family?" asked Edward.

"Yes and no. That is part, but once a child in the Primary family ascends, they undergo formal training at the Vatican."

Edward looked at Father Lucian with a quizzical expression. "Ascend?"

"Oh yes, you were probably too young to have heard that term. Think of it as a coming of age when a child first shows an ability. You lost your parents and disappeared from our view before you ascended. Your father was seventeen when he ascended, and like all before him, he came to the Vatican for one year for training." Father Lucian's stoic expression now showed a hint of a smile. "He was an inquisitive one."

"You knew my father?" Edward asked.

"Yes, very much so. His training was my responsibility."

"So, you taught him which prayers to use and when."

"We talked about the prayers a little, but I left that to his father. He was more familiar with the book than I. Actually, until Father Murray showed it to me earlier today, I had never seen it. My training was more around an ability. Do you know why the church selected your family as the Primary for this location?"

Edward answered with confidence. "Because we can see the spirits."

"Wrong. Most every family here can see spirits. Father Murray can see them. I can see them. Not that unique of an ability. Most can, they just need to accept it. There is something more to your family. You were too young for anyone to tell you about it, but you have felt it. You felt the surge flowing through you before, haven't you?"

Edward remembered the conversations he and Father Murray had about the importance of his faith and conviction. That must be what Father Lucian was talking about, so Edward guessed, "The surge? You mean a feeling of faith?"

Father Lucian shook his head. "No, my son. Not everything I speak of is about faith. It is a power flowing through you. A strength from within you."

"Wait!" Edward exclaimed wide-eyed.

"So, you have?" Father Lucian asked.

"I think once. The first-time Father Murray took me out. A spirit was on top of me. He had me thrust the cross up into it while reciting a prayer."

"What did you feel?"

"It is hard to explain."

"Try."

"Power. Confidence. Strength."

"You felt it coming from within you and projecting out, right?"

"Yes. Have you felt it before?"

"No. It is not something I nor Father Murray would ever experience. It is something deep inside you, your family, and the few families like yours around the world."

That left Edward speechless.

"If that is surprising, what I am about to tell you will be... well, the relic is just a prop."

Edward tried to ask a question, but Father Lucian continued before he had the chance.

"Don't get me wrong. It works through the Cross of Christ's crucifixion, but that is not where the power comes from. The prayer book is just a book passed down from generation to generation. The power…" Father Lucian stopped walking and turned toward Edward. With his right hand he made a cross in the air and then touched the center of Edward's chest. "It is within you. It is that power, that ability that is your weapon in this war. It is that which can drive these creatures back from where they came. I can help you learn to control it, in time. But first I need your help to deal with this. Things are far worse than you know. This creature has been running loose for almost thirty years. Father Murray tells me it has killed seventeen and terrorized hundreds. I need your help to end it."

Remorse overtook Edward. He had failed to deal with that creature twice. Maybe he didn't have the true capability, or not in the way his father and the others did. "Father Lucian, I would love to help, but I don't know how. Whatever you think I can do, maybe it skipped a generation or something. I have failed now twice."

"Mr. Meyer, you do. You need help to find it and use it. What you felt that day with Father Murray was just a fraction of what you are capable of. I know you have had bad experiences and doubt things now, but that was not your fault."

"Father Lucian!!! Come quick," Father Murray yelled while running toward the two men. "It showed up at the high school and has attacked two people. We must go."

"Mr. Meyer, you must come with us. We need your help," Father Lucian pleaded.

Still full of self-doubt, Edward said, "I can't help you. I am not who or what you think I am. I am sorry."

Father Lucian passionately pleaded again, "You are. Let me show you."

Father Murray exclaimed, "Father Lucian, we must go!"

Edward once again tried to explain. "I am sorry Father. I would only put more in danger."

Father Murray exclaimed again as he reached them, "Father!"

Father Lucian looked dismayed and disheartened at Edward's refusal to help. Without further delay, he hurried with Father Murray toward his car and they both sped away.

38

Edward sat in the living room for a few moments to gather his thoughts before trying to have a normal Friday night. The thought that a special power ran through his family should've been strangely humorous to him, but living in a world of ghosts and demons opened a world of possibilities. He knew he was no superhero, and other than that one time, he had felt nothing. That moment could have been adrenaline kicking in from the stress, and the pure fear of the moment. That had to be it. "Well superhero, time to grade exams," he said to himself.

A blood-curdling scream echoed down the stairs from Sarah's room. Edward leapt off the sofa and sprinted up the stairs, taking two at a time. He knocked through the door without even turning the door handle. Standing on her bed was the creature, holding Sarah above its head. She appeared to be unconscious.

"Hello, Edward," it said to him.

Edward commanded, "Put her down."

Defiantly, it shook its head, and then spun it all the way around. "Not going to happen. Seems she has inherited the same ability you have. Can't let this continue."

The creature forced Sarah's back into an unnatural arch above its head. The sight of his daughter being broken in half caused something to snap inside of Edward. Fear, anger, or something deeper surfaced and his voice boomed through the house, "Put her down!"

The creature took notice and stopped. "I didn't think you had it in you. You don't know what to do with it, though." It bent Sarah again.

Edward felt a warmth flowing through his body. He lunged for the creature. It jumped away, dropping Sarah down on her bed. When she hit the mattress, she woke up and screamed. She clawed her way to the headboard of her bed, as far away from the creature as she could get. Edward had it trapped in the corner.

Edward wished he had the book in his hands. With no option at all, he attempted to create his own prayer. "Foul creature, you have invaded my home and my realm. I condemn you back to the depths of hell you came from. In the name of God Almighty, the protector of heaven, earth, and all that is just, I command you out." At that moment, Edward made a cross with his right hand in front of the creature. While finishing the cross, a fingertip contacted its torso, creating a burning singe they both felt. The contact created a mark on the creature. It fell to the floor writhing in pain, making the most inhuman sound Edward had ever heard, like a thousand souls screaming all at once.

"Out with you, Abaddon. Back to the bowels of hell with you." Edward pressed his right hand on the creature. Its skin felt like worn leather. In appearance it looked hot, but it felt freezing cold at first and then sizzled under his palm. The smell of burnt flesh permeated from the corner of the room and a cloud of steam developed around it. Edward continued to press while he repeated, "I command you to leave this world. I command you to leave this world."

The cloud of steam grew large and dense, obscuring the creature for a second. When it cleared, the creature was gone. Deep down Edward knew it was not gone from this world. Just gone from his daughter's room. This was not over.

Edward turned his attention to his daughter sitting at the head of her bed, still screaming hysterically. He embraced her warmly and told her she was ok. She stopped screaming, but he did not let go. He sat there holding her, rocking back and forth for several moments, telling her it was ok. Then he stopped and whispered, "I need to go. You will be safe now." She said nothing. She let go and watched him walk out of the room.

Edward pulled out his cellphone and dialed. "Father Murray, where are you?"

Over the sounds of screams and howls, Father Murray screamed, "At the high school, hurry," and the call disconnected.

Close to the school, Edward passed groups of frightened people running away. They had abandoned their cars in the road, making it unpassable. He drove as close as he could get and then stopped and ran toward the school, weaving his way through the masses.

Edward fought through the crowds and finally reached the gate of the football field. He ran through and emerged out on the field. From there he could survey the scene. There were people injured and bloodied laying on various spots of the field and surrounding track. There was a circle of red spirits and demons about thirty feet away. Father Lucian was on the ground in the center. Father Murray stood over him holding the cross. They had not noticed Edward yet.

He crossed himself quickly and silently prayed, "GOD as my protector, guide me tonight in the protection of others." He felt what he felt in Sarah's bedroom, but this time it was stronger, much stronger. There was a pulsating glow around his hands.

Edward walked toward the circle and yelled, "Leave them alone." His voice appeared to echo as if it came from above. The creatures all stopped and looked at him.

Father Murray finally saw him and pleaded for Edward to stop. "You are not ready!"

Edward ran toward the group of spirits. He felt a strength building within him. Something unlike anything he had felt before. The power surged through every fiber of his body, while inside he had doubts about how to use it. The bodies littering the ground were all he needed to convince him he had to try. Which one should he go for first? The time to think was at an end. The time to act was now. They were on top of him.

Edward ran through the horde, throwing his hands at as many as he could. Each one he contacted staggered backward. He felt a slash on his shoulder and a quick stabbing blow to his lower back. The adrenaline of the moment blocked the pain. The cold touch of a spirit trying to grab his neck caused him to leap out of the way. A demon wildly swung at Edward's head. Its claw grazed his left temple, sending a trickle of blood across his vision and down his face.

"O Father..." he started a prayer, but stopped to dodge another attack. The demon's claw ripped across his right thigh, digging into the tissue, sending Edward down to one knee. As the creature passed him, Edward hit him with his right hand, causing it to howl in pain while it retreated to the circle that had formed around him.

"Edward, here!" Father Murray yelled with both the book and cross in hand. Edward held up his hand to tell him to wait, but Father Murray threw them anyway. Edward reached to catch them, but a creature covered in scars jumped up and used its body to knock them away. It fell to the ground, limp, with a thud following the contact.

The circle closed in on Edward. Outnumbered and injured, he was running out of options. But as hopeless as he felt, the confidence and strength inside him built to a level of that made Edward want to scream and jump out of his own skin. He held up a hand and prayed, but couldn't get a word out before a small four-legged creature ripped into his forearm with a claw. Edward yanked his injured arm back and held it close to his chest. When he looked down at it, he took notice of his other hand, now on the ground supporting him. The glowing he saw coming from his hands was now radiating out along the ground. Father Lucian told him the power to deal with all of this was inside of him. Maybe he was right.

Out of options, and now a wounded prey being circled by predators, Edward placed both hands firmly on the ground. The ground below his feet and knees shook. He began, "O Divine Eternal Father, I, your humble warrior, beg your strength to cast out the forces of your greatest enemy. Send them to the darkest depths of hell, where they will be imprisoned for all eternity. Use my body as your weapon against them."

The glowing circle on the ground shot out away from him across the field. The creatures and spirits reacted violently as they came into contact with it and then froze, unable to move. Edward pushed through the pain in his right thigh and stood up. He walked through the frozen beings and touched each, one at a time, repeating "In the name of God and Christ Almighty, I condemn you to hell, foul creature." One by one they disappeared in a puff of fog.

Edward left one for last, one he knew intimately. First, he retrieved the cross from off the ground. Then he walked over to the frozen creature. Its soulless eyes watched him the whole time. Edward pressed the cross against its cold leathery flesh. Flames emerged at contact. "Abaddon, in the name of the son, the father, and the holy spirit, I condemn you to the darkest depths of hell for all eternity."

The creature did not howl or make any sounds of pain as it disappeared. From the darkness its voice made one last proclamation. "I always return. The seed has been sown."

Edward limped over to Father Murray, who was helping Father Lucian to his feet.

"Everyone ok?" he asked.

Father Lucian picked up his black wide-brimmed hat and put it back on. "I am ok."

Edward and Father Murray looked around the ground. Paramedics rushed in to help many of the injured. Others were being covered in sheets, as they had succumbed to their injuries. Father Murray lamented, "Not everyone was so lucky."

A great sadness and feeling of guilt came over Edward. He looked at both Father Murray and Father Lucian. "I am sorry. I could have prevented all this."

"No, you couldn't. This started long ago. You stopped it from getting worse," Father Murray said. "There is hope now that this darkness that has shrouded our community is coming to an end. We have you to thank for that."

Father Lucian cautioned, "Father Murray, don't be lulled into believing this. This is not over. It never is. Abaddon gave up too easy. This may be just the beginning."

DAVID CLARK

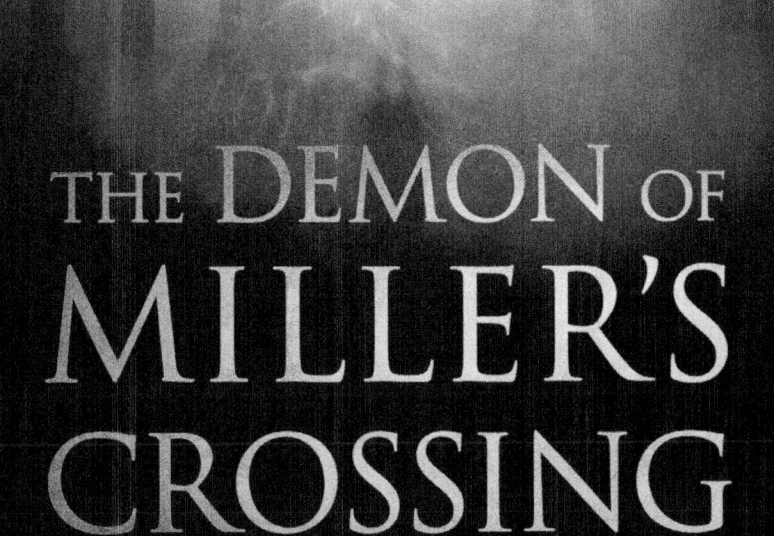

THE DEMON OF MILLER'S CROSSING

THE DEMON OF MILLER'S CROSSING

Miller's Crossing Book 2

David Clark

1

"What are you guys doing back in this dark corner, huh?", Sarah asked the two flickering figures in the back of old man Tyson's barn. He saw them run in there just before sunset and immediately called for help. There had been problems on his property for the last several days. The chickens were spooked and his cows were so upset they wouldn't produce any milk, and his wife went on and on about not feeling right. At first, he blew it off as his wife just being her odd self, but the chickens and cows were something different. If they weren't acting right, then something was wrong. He caught a glimpse of something running through his farm the night before, but he thought it had left. Today it was back, and it had a friend.

The two flickering vapors paid no attention to her as she inched closer. She held her hand out as if trying to lure a leery puppy out from under the bed with a treat. Inch by inch, she moved closer. With each step she ignored the chill that ran up her spine, and the cold sweat that gathered on the back of her neck. Those were feelings she felt almost every day and was used to them by now. The dark pit she felt in her stomach was a less frequent sensation, but unfortunately it had become more common than it should. She felt the evil within these things and knew just how dangerous they could be. Her first experience was with another very dangerous demon. These two were far weaker than that one, but her training taught her you never let your guard down, any of these entities can be deadly to her, and everyone around.

"Come on. Can I show you what I have in my hand?", she asked, holding her right hand out further. Both entities were still ignoring her presence, or were they? One glanced in her general direction a few times, with the beady black orbs he had for eyes. They felt it, and she knew it. They always felt it, and the closer they were to it, the feeling, the fear, became stronger.

The barn door behind her opened with a loud creak and squeal of the rusty metal wheel and hinge. Sarah looked back at the door, as did both entities. Father Murray poked his head through the door and asked, "Sarah," he stopped and coughed twice, "do you need any-".

Both entities screeched and howled as they turned and rushed toward the door.

"God dammit!", Sarah exclaimed. She opened her palm, exposing the old wooden cross hidden in it. As the entities reached her, she swung it out at the end of a cord she had looped around it and exclaimed, "Be gone, foul beast. You are not the image of God and not permitted in his realm." The cross contacted one, sending the creature away in a cloud of vapor. She pulled the rope in just as the second entity took a swipe at her. A quick duck and forward roll kept her from being hit. The creature moved past her and headed to the door. She pulled the cross into her hand and then threw her own punch, connecting with the side of the great beast. Flames burst from its side, and it fell to the ground in pain. It screamed and howled with a sound that raped the silence of the night air.

Sarah circled around it. The cross was in her right hand and extended toward the beast at all times. "You need to go, too. Go follow your friend to the bowels of hell. Never to return to this realm." Her voice was forceful, not a tad of fear in it, as her left hand retrieved a small vial of water from her pocket. With her thumb she flipped the top off and splashed it on the beast in the shape of a cross. The water froze on contact with the beast. "With this, I seal your fate. You are banished from this world, never to return."

The creature shuddered and moaned on the floor. The flickering sped up until it was not there, more than it was. Eventually, it disappeared altogether, with just a layer of red fog where it had originally laid. The fog soon dissipated, and Sarah walked toward the door.

"I said I had it," she said as she passed Father Murray standing at the door.

Father Murray wiped his nose with the red paisley handkerchief he had tucked tightly in his left hand. He pulled his collar up to guard against the damp night air and followed Sarah. "Oh, I know," he said. "Just was there in case you needed some help."

"I don't need any help. As you saw, I had it under control until you antagonized them."

"Well.. um.. yeah..," responded Father Murray. "Why did you banish him for all eternity? You can't use that kind of prayer haphazardly. We still don't know enough about the afterlife. Maybe we are reincarnated, and that poor soul will never be allowed back."

Sarah kept walking, now ten feet in front of Father Murray. "Nothing to worry about there. Neither of them were human. Even you should have been able to see that. They were not one of God's creatures. At least not ones he planned for this world."

Father Murray struggled to keep up with her pace as she trounced through the high grass, out toward the driveway and her car. The severe cold he had didn't make things any easier. "Sarah, you can't play God," he pointed out. "Some of those decisions are not yours to make."

Sarah stopped and spun around, startling the old priest. "You are the wrong person to lecture me about playing God. Those two were one of your doings. Not ones I released. I can feel how long they have been in this world, and those had been here a while." Her words were harsh, but her tone was harsher, which she realized and stopped to wait for him. Father Murray was a well-meaning family friend, and they both shared a bond, which some might consider a scar or branding. "Look, we both have enough blood on our hands from our mistakes. I am committed to fixing mine." She threw an arm around the old priest's shoulder's and said, "Now, let's get you out of here before the night air makes a ghost out of you. I don't want to have to send you out of here."

Sarah helped Father Murray to her two seat hatchback. She threw the car in reverse and sped down the driveway. Once out on the road, her pace didn't slow down at all. Even when she passed Sheriff Thompson's patrol car. Her foot didn't even twitch to come off the gas. He never went after her anyway, so what was the point? She hung a left, without slowing down an iota, and flew through the opening in the trees, down the dirt covered drive, up and over the rise to her dad's family farm. They slid to a stop in front. She got out and went around to the back, opening the hatch.

"Need any help?", Father Murray asked, halfway to the house.

"Nah," she said. The hatch sprang open, and she reached in and grabbed the Tupperware bowl of homemade chicken noodle soup that Mrs. Leonard had made for them earlier. She said it was an old family recipe, perfect for getting rid of the creepy crud. "Go on inside and to the kitchen. I will have this warmed up quickly."

She was carrying the bowl inside, marching toward the kitchen, when she heard the shuffling of papers off to her side. "Dad, what are you doing?"

Positioned behind two stacks of papers at the dining room table was her father, dripping with sweat, but wearing a sweater and a jacket. Dark circles had made a home under his eyes, and several coughs interfered with his attempt to respond. He took a sip from his cup of hot tea and lemon, to clear his throat, before he could finally explain, "I have papers to grade. I feel fine."

"You look like shit."

"Sarah, language please," Edward said, trying to sound parental in between coughs and sneezes.

"Oh, she has been a real sailor tonight. Don't think I didn't notice you took the lord's name in vain back at the farm. Oh, I noticed," said Father Murray, from the kitchen.

Sarah stuck her tongue out at the kitchen door, and Edward smirked.

"Come on, Dad. Mrs. Leonard sent this. She said it would have you two right as rain, whatever that means."

Edward got up from the table and followed Sarah into the kitchen. She put the bowl down on the counter and pulled out a large pot that she placed on the largest burner on the stove. She turned the burner on high and poured the contents of the bowl into the pot.

Edward walked past the stove and looked inside the pot on his way to the table. "What's in it?"

"Chicken, chicken broth, vegetables, noodles, and something green. Maybe that is the special ingredient she talked about."

"Sounds good, I wonder what that ingredient is," said her father. He took another sip of his tea.

"Probably pot," remarked Sarah, which caused her father to choke on his tea. She realized, he was not ready for that response.

Father Murray added. "Eh, that wouldn't surprise me. She always has been a little too happy."

The three of them had a good chuckle at that. Sarah watched the pot and once it started to steam, she spooned out two bowlfuls of the soup and delivered them to the table. "Okay, you two eat up. And no more chasing things when it is pouring rain and thirty degrees out. Do that a few more times and you guys will be ghosts, yourselves." She stood over the two men for a few seconds with her arms crossed. Her scolding look produced the same response from both men, "Yes ma'am."

"Okay, good. I am going to go talk to Jacob about ordering a pizza or something. There probably is pot in that stuff."

2

"Jesus," Sarah muttered, the collar of a pink sweater pinned under her chin, while her hands worked at a furious pace to fold the sleeves against the back. Once in position, she let go with her chin and allowed the top to flip naturally across where she held, into the perfect fold before placing it back on a display table. That was one down, and a dozen or more to go. It was the same every afternoon. School let out and droves of junior and senior girls stormed through to shop with their eyes.

This wasn't the local mall or soda shop, something that was still popular in small town America. At least it was in Miller's Crossing. Ralph's had been open since... well, before the birth of anyone still alive. They passed it down from generation to generation. The inside had seen everything from the radio reports of the battle on the beaches of Normandy, to the internal strife of the civil rights, not that Ralph's ever had separate entrances or places for people to sit based on the color of their skin. Fred Ralph didn't believe in that stuff, and when anyone made a comment he always said, "The only colors I care about is the green of a dollar, and the whites of someone's teeth when they smile and laugh."

No, this wasn't Ralph's. This was the place next door to it, one of the three clothiers in the Crossing. All three, like Ralph's, were family-run stores that have spanned generations. Myrtle's dress shop had a problem none of the others had. God didn't bless Myrtle Sanders and her husband, Larry, with children. Though they tried. Lord knows, they tried, and faced heartbreak on two occasions. When people would tell them how sorry they felt for her, she would tell each of them, "God granted me a large family. Every child here is her child." In a way, she was right. If you needed jeans and work clothes, you could go to The Miller's Crossing Haberdashery. The sign outside was as gaudy as it sounded. Inside, only the back corner, with suits, hats, and finer clothes, qualified as haberdashery-ish. The rest of it was just run-of-the-mill jeans and work clothes. A-Stitch-in-Time was its female equivalent. Before the large conglomerate stores had opened down the road in Waynesboro or Valley Ridge, that was the one and only destination for back-to-school shopping for every girl from kindergarten to high school seniors. If you needed something nicer, church clothes, a Christening dress, something to wear to Aunt Mabel's funeral, or for homecoming or prom, it was Myrtle's. She had seen it all, for every child in town, from their baptisms through to the measuring and ordering of their wedding gown, only for the cycle to repeat with the next generation.

When Myrtle became ill, Sarah stepped up from her part-time job and ran the store. This was a temporary situation, or was supposed to be. During the winter of the third year after Sarah's graduation, she took a turn for the worst. By spring, she was gone, and Sarah continued to run the store. Larry Sanders's stopped by the Meyer's farmhouse on a Friday afternoon to talk to Edward. Something that wasn't too odd, as he came over often to talk to Edward about his father and the "good ole days". Edward enjoyed those lengthy chats while sitting out on the porch. They felt comfortable and like home, and brought back memories from his childhood. This visit was different. The smile on his face wasn't the normal cheerful expression that brightened his cheeks and brought light into his eyes. It wasn't a grim expression either, like the one he had seen when Myrtle passed.

He said he had something to talk to him about and, like their conversations before, they sat on the porch and talked. This time without sweet tea, or a batch of Larry's home brew. Larry had an idea, and he wanted Edward's honest opinion. He was old and didn't have the energy his wife had had. In seeing how Sarah was running the store, he proposed making an arrangement to sell her the store. As payment, he would withhold 5% of her pay for the next ten years. Edward did the math, and it seemed fair.

The two of them drove together to the store to discuss it with Sarah, who jumped at it before they finished laying out the conditions of the deal. First, she couldn't change the name, and second, she couldn't change what it was. It still needed to be everything it was for the community that it had been. When Larry had slowed Sarah down enough to talk through the conditions, she didn't hesitate.

In the five years since, both conditions had been honored. Myrtle's name was still up on the front outside, now freshened up with a fresh coat of bright red paint, an honor to the bright red lip stick she had always worn. The surrounding building was white shiplap siding, with a green and white canvas awning over the front window and door. At first, Edward had concerns if she could satisfy the second condition. Not that he discounted his daughter's ability to continue to serve everyone how Myrtle had, but this was more than a shop. This was a place people stopped to talk. A place people went to walk around, just to be seen, and to find out what was going on in town. Edward had never considered his family as celebrities in the Crossing. For the longest time he felt it was the opposite. He believed they were notorious for his and Sarah's part in what people now referred to as the "Reaping". It took most of the eight years since for him to realize that no one viewed him as that, instead the town viewed him as the savior that stopped it. They cast Sarah in a similar light, after she returned from her training at the

Vatican, with most stopping to thank her for handling a visitor they had had on their property. This meant the shop was never at a loss of people stopping in to shop, browse, or just talk.

With homecoming two weeks away, throngs of teenage girls invaded the shop daily, all coming in to spy the perfect dress, which they would now spend a few days trying to sell their parents on. While in, they indubitably treated the shop as their personal room and picked up various articles of clothing to check the size, the fit, or just to hold up against them to see if it made their eyes pop in one of the two banks of mirrors in the dressing room. This lasted for an hour or two right after school, with most rushing home in time for dinner or to beat the fall of darkness, which arrived early during the autumn. Sarah never complained about the aftermath. Instead, she maintained a cheery appearance as she re-shelved clothes and prepared for the next day. She remembered when she was their age, which wasn't that long ago, and left clothes around for Myrtle to have to put away. It was all part of the repeating pattern of life. Much like the turning of the leaves before fall, then the snow and frost of winter, followed by the blooming of the flowers of spring, and then the long summer nights, which slowly cool again, and the leaves turn once more`.

"Is the storm clear?"

Sarah looked up from the stack of yellow sweaters and smiled in greeting as the third ding from the bell attached to the door echoed around the store. This bell was the same bell that had announced the arrival of every friend, everyone was a friend, and customer since the store first opened. It also reminded Sarah of the past. "Temporary reprieve. Still have two more weeks until homecoming."

The first friend Sarah made after what she thought was a move to a social desert, Charlotte Stance, formerly Reynolds, asked, "Were we ever this bad?"

Sarah cocked her head and retorted, "Myrtle told me once that this was revenge for all the times we did the same." She put the sweaters down long enough to hug her friend and then placed a gentle kiss on the smiling and cooing baby girl on her hip. "And, one day, it will be your turn to run through the store." Sarah gave her friend an evil look, "And your mommy will be nice enough to come help me refold everything."

"And, I will tell auntie Sarah, she has a better chance of getting me to hunt ghosts with her," Charlotte said, with an equally evil look on her face. "How was last night?"

"Wet. Cold. But easy. Neither gave me any trouble."

"I ran into Mrs. Martsen in the salon today, to hear her talk about it, you would think they were from the devil himself, here to suck her soul out through a straw."

"Just small town gossip. She's a local, but still goes on and on, and... Wait! We were supposed to go together on Saturday." Sarah dropped the long flower printed skirt she was refolding. It landed like a parachute covering the table of matching skirts.

"Oh, I can still go with you. Dan's mom was already watching her while I ran some errands in town. I saw an empty chair when I passed by. I had to do something with these ends. I still need to do something about this color."

That color was something Sarah had always been jealous of, the perfect shade of auburn. Not red, not orange, like the leaves of autumn, but an auburn that contained a touch of brown to soften the red.

"Seriously, I am still going with you Saturday. 3:00 PM, right?"

"Yep," Sarah said, her attention was back on the floral print skirt. This was the last table to straighten before closing.

"Good, I can bask in the glow of your fame. Gives me a feeling of what it is like to be around a celebrity A-lister. A break from mommy world."

Sarah sighed. She seriously doubted any celebrity A-listers went through what she did when she was out around town. Ruthie Day, a woman who did not give the appearance of having the skill to help others look good, owned the salon, Perm and Clips,. Her hair was still a fifties style beehive that had some serious altitude. Layers of eyeshadow stood guard over her face against the elements of the world, a battle the elements didn't stand a chance of winning. Just like any salon in any small town in America, Perm and Clips was one of the very centers of town gossip.

Ironically, Ruthie's family had an extensive history of being in the gossip business. When the phone lines were strung through town in 1904, her great grandmother, Ruth, not Ruthie, was the first phone operator. That put her in the cat-bird seat for every morsel of town news, with the latest advancement in technology to distribute that news.

On a normal day, two or three of the five cushioned rotating chairs would be filled by someone with some cream in their hair, foil wrapped, being assaulted by a blow dryer and brush, or looking nervous while being orbited by a woman with scissors clipping away as fast as she smacked on her gum. Ruthie, who hadn't touched a strand of hair since before Sarah had arrived in town, would be holding court for those in the waiting room, who most of the time weren't waiting for a seat and were just there for the show. Delores, Crystal, and Pam were there every day to take care of the customers. Lauren and Lisa were part-timers that were only there a few days during the week, both would be there on Saturday, but probably not on the clock.

When Sarah had an appointment, the waiting room was standing room only, with overflow into any unused rotating chair. All five hairdressers would be there, even though only two were working. Instead of being mobbed by paparazzi photographers trying to catch her with hair dye in her hair, or other embarrassing predicaments, they peppered her for stories and questions. Everyone and anyone wanted to hear a harrowing tale of chasing some devilish horned creature through a swamp, or a battle for someone's soul against dark forces. Her first few visits, including her first when Sharon took her thinking it might be less awkward than her father taking her, she resisted talking much about it. In truth, she wasn't involved in things much back then. Her father and Father Murray handled most of it, and neither talked much about what happened. When she returned back from the Vatican, she became more involved and realized most situations were not that interesting. To appease the adoring fans, she embellished slightly. Even pulling from popular culture movies and books, neither of which anyone in attendance would recognize.

That was always curious to her. This was the one place in all of America, that she knew of, where people not only believed in ghosts, but knew for a fact there were aspects of the spiritual world in ours. A place where it was a part of everyday life, but there was no great curiosity in it. No one spending any significant time reading or studying about that world. Instead, they avoided it. There was the natural love for horror movies most high schoolers shared, but as people became older that seemed to wane. Was it because it was too close to reality for them? That was a possibility she gave a lot of credence to.

With every rule, there is an exception. In Miller's Crossing that exception was eighty-three-year-old Edith Wickerson. A source of stories herself. Many that Sarah found fascinating, as they gave a window into her own grandparents' lives. She was more than interested in the world of the spiritual. It was not the "whys" and "whats" that fascinated her. It was the "who". During every story Sarah would tell, Edith asked for a description of the spectral visitor. She wanted to know if it was someone she knew.

3

Wind whipped the first signs of autumn down State Road 32, or what the residents called Main Street. Red and orange leaves rode the wind like a surfer on a majestic blue wave. They fell to the ground as the brisk breeze passed them by, only to be picked up by the next draft. A cold briskly steely feeling blew in with the winds; the first sign that winter was on their doorsteps, and this was its official knock to let you know it was coming in. Sweaters, sweatshirts, hoodies, and jackets, replaced short sleeves for function, not just a fashion statement.

Sarah opted for both as she walked out of Myrtle's and down the three blocks to the Perm and Clips. No less than a dozen people greeted her by name during her walk. All were people she either went to school with, saw at the shop, or met around town. In a town this small, there was no such thing as not knowing someone. Even in the rare instance you didn't, the learned response still kicked in the same as if it were your best friend. Each time she had to loosen up her arms to let a hand free to wave, but as soon as the wave was done, she folded her arms up as tight to her body as possible to keep the chill from penetrating to her core.

Charlotte was doing the same as she walked up from the other direction. She hunched down and turned her head slightly, to let the cloth of her hoodie take the brunt of the wind. "Global warming my ass," she said as she reached for the door handle to open it. She held it open just a moment, to allow Sarah, who was now jogging stiff-legged the last several feet. Sarah went in first, and Charlotte followed. "When I get home, my daughter will get ice cream out of these things."

Sarah rolled her eyes at the nursing humor, one of Charlotte's favorite subjects to make jokes of. She doesn't see the humor, but everyone tells her to just wait, she will.

"Close tha door, you're letting the cold in!", cried Ruthie. The cold air that snuck in didn't keep her from rushing both of them and giving them a hug before they were barely inside the door. As she released Sarah, the fragrance of the rose-scented perfume she bathed in hung in the air and mixed with the putrid chemical smells of dyes, perms, shampoos, and coffee. Coffee was a must for anyone that walked in the door. Not that it was a must for the person, it was a must for Ruthie. Before a person's butt hit their chair, Ruthie had a cup of coffee in a proper cup, on a proper saucer, ready for them. No Styrofoam here. Sharon told Sarah on her first visit to the salon that no one had ever turned her down. Just take it and say, "Thank you." If you drink it, great. If you don't, great too. Sarah always wondered what would happen if someone turned it down.

Ruthie turned around and bent over the counter where the cash register sat. Her artificially gold-colored blond hair seemed exceedingly tall and brushed the shelf above the counter as she bent down. It disturbed none of the hair products displayed on the shelf. She turned around with a smile plastered on her face and a cup of coffee balanced on a saucer in each hand. Charlotte was the first presented with coffee, which she eagerly accepted, and took a sip of the warm liquid. With a hand free now, she handed the other cup to Sarah, while she guided her to an open chair. "Come right this way. We are all set up for you."

They walked past the counter and register, to the first workstation. Crystal was still blow-drying high school senior, Megan Flink's, hair. Ruthie stopped short and gave both a look of disapproval while she tapped her foot. "Ummmm," she said slightly, below a yell, but loud enough to be heard above the hum of the blow dryer. Crystal turned, saw the expression on Ruthie's face, and turned off the dryer. Megan looked back now and saw the two people standing there, waiting on the chair. With no direction from Crystal, she sprang up from the chair and said, "Hi, Miss Miller," as she moved to the next chair over. No matter how many times this had happened, it still embarrassed Sarah.

While all this was going on, Pam stepped forward and took Charlotte back to the fourth chair, the same chair she sat in for her trim a few days before. The color job was saved for today. It took a while to set, and experience had taught her that salon appointments with Sarah were never quick.

"What we doing today, darling?", asked Delores. The mid-forty-year-old petite woman stood behind her and ran her fingers through her hair. Her fingers were stiff with arthritis and years of work, but the pain didn't slow her down. Once the scissors were on, she was a performer which was why Sarah liked her. Of everyone in the salon, she was the only one who had the appearance that she knew what she was doing. She was also the only one without a fancy certificate from a fancy sounding salon school. All she had posted at her station, which was really the one next to where Sarah sat, was her license from the state of Virginia. She acquired her skills through home-schooling. Her grandmother did hair, her mother did hair, her aunt did hair, and now it was her turn. Handed down from generation to generation. All worked for Ruthie from time to time. When not working for Ruthie, they worked out of their kitchens, trading their services for something else of value.

"Take about an inch off, and can you give me something else?", asked Sarah.

"Something else?"

"Yeah, a little wave, texture or something. I don't want tight curls."

Delores studied her straight black hair and looked up at Sarah in the mirror. "Want something for just a few days, or something that will last a few months?"

"Just a few days," said Sarah.

Delores leaned forward and, with the tenderness of a grandmother, whispered, "What is the occasion?"

There are certain places sensitive conversations should never be had. At church, during a quiet prayer. A quiet movie theatre. A quiet classroom. A quiet anywhere would top that list. A beauty salon is anything but quiet. Ringing phones, a television on with a random entertainment talk show grinding, blow dryers and clippers running, and many conversations all happening at the same time. It is a miracle of modern science how, in all that, a whisper could be heard. Not just heard, completely understood, as if she whispered into the ear of every person sitting there. That miracle of modern science had just happened again, and everyone leaned forward in their seat to hear the answer.

"No occasion," Sarah said. Her head turned toward the gathered gallery to her right, to send the message loud and clear. That was a mistake. In her attempt to cover up the truth, she had forgotten a key dynamic in how women communicate with each other. The more you try to make someone believe something was not a big deal, the bigger of a deal it really was. Her attempt to hide it prompted several conversations focused on speculation of what the "it" was.

"She has a date," spouted Charlotte.

The ability to dispatch ghosts, spectral visitors, and demons with a single look was not something they taught her in her training. The look on her face when she turned toward Charlotte may have qualified her to teach her own master class on the topic. The left edge of her upper lip was furled, and twitched, as did her eyebrow, but not at the same time. Keeping her personal life, what little there was of it, a secret in a small town was a struggle as it was. Add the level and mysticism and celebrity that surrounded her family, she might as well post everything on a billboard. Who needs social media posts?

"We will ask about the boy soon. Even though I feel I know who he is," Ruthie said with a cackle as she sat down. The scene of her laughing among her groupies looked like something right out of Fried Green Tomatoes, a movie Sarah had watched several times with her mom. She wasn't sure who was Old Weezer in the group, and not sure it mattered. "So, I hear you had to take care of two vile creatures all on your own the other night."

"It's not the first time I have taken care of my dad and Father Murray."

The court erupted in laughter, causing a small spray of coffee to explode from Ruthie's mouth. That shot should make them forget about the secret

Charlotte let slip. In case it didn't, the yarn she was about to spin, about something very uneventful, would.

"Was one of them wearing a grey seersucker? Ronald passed away on Tuesday, and was wearing that in the casket," asked Edith.

4

The chilled breeze of the day gave way to the frozen gusts of night. It howled as it blew across the open fields around the Meyer's family farm. Sarah pulled her coat tight around her as she walked from her car to the front door, pausing for a moment at the door to look around behind her before she walked in. That pause was something of a family tradition, to do a final check before going in for the night. She saw nothing roaming around, didn't feel it either. She also didn't see her father's car in the driveway. At this late of an hour, it only meant one thing. He and Father Murray were out taking care of something.

When she walked in, the house was dark and quiet. The screams of the wind outside gave it an eerie feeling. A loose shutter on one of the dining-room window creaked and banged, adding to the haunted house feeling. Add in the feeling that something was there with her, watching, and she was convinced that with a little work, they could turn the house into a year-round attraction for those who enjoy that kind of thing. That was an idea she had needled her father about since the days he first told her about the book and the cross. That, and trading in the family car for Ecto-1 from Ghostbusters. Jacob had never understood that joke until she found the movie on an on-demand service and then he was all for it. He also wanted the proton-pack.

The floorboards groaned as she made her way through the house and up the stairs. That was something new, that hadn't happened before, at least not for her. Luckily neither her brother nor father were around to hear it, saving her from the snickers and jokes that would undoubtedly follow.

When her head was even with the second floor landing, she could see ribbons of light coming out around Jacob's bedroom door. She knocked to let him know she was home, but there was no response. She knocked again, and still nothing. The time on her phone said it was late, but not that late, only 11:04. There was no way this kid was already asleep. It was a Saturday night, no seventeen-year-old was in bed before midnight. She cracked the and found her explanation. Her younger, but much taller, brother was sitting in his padded gaming chair with his feet propped up on his bed. Still wearing his baseball pants from his fall league practice, and a single t-shirt, he was immersed in a battle in the digital space taking place on the screen in front of him, and in the sound transmitted via a headset straight into his ears. She had a few options of how to let him know she was home, but very few of them wouldn't result in him jumping out of his skin. A tap on the shoulder would cause him to spin around and scream. She could blow on the back of his neck until he turned around. The last time she did that, he jumped from the chair to the bed in a single move. Feeling a little evil twinge that siblings often do when it comes to causing a mild level of discomfort to one another, she had an idea and slipped out of her jacket and sent it flying in the air. It descended between Jacob and his screen. The only reaction was his head tilting to the side to keep his eyes locked on the monitor. Then one hand let go of the controller and he handed the jacket back over his head to her.

"Hey sis," he said, too loud for just the two of them.

"Dad out with Father Murray?", she asked.

"Dad is out with Father Murray," Jacob screamed over the sounds in his headset.

Disappointed, she dragged her jacket behind her to her room.

She took a quick shower to chase away the remaining chill of the night, and hopefully the other feeling with it. When she emerged from the bathroom, there were lights on downstairs, and sounds coming from the kitchen. Her father was home again, and she thought she heard the voice of Father Murray.

"Hey, Dad. Hello, Father," she said as she walked into the kitchen. "How was everything tonight?"

"Easy," Edward said as he finished fixing him and Father Murray some coffee. Seeing the two of them sitting at the table in the nook, drinking coffee, was as common as seeing a flower in the spring. Also common was watching the flask appear from inside Father Murray's overcoat, or black coat pocket, and then deposit a little into each cup. Sarah had a taste of that a few times. Why someone would add the taste of paint thinner to perfectly good coffee was a mystery to her.

"Are you sure?", she asked. There was an odor to the two of them, and it had nothing to do with their hygiene, or where they may have been. This was something only she had experienced. No one, not her father, not Father Murray, not anyone at the Vatican, or any other sensitive or keeper. She was told it was probably a way synesthesia occurred in her. Synesthesia was a rare condition where senses fire when a person sees a color, number, or hear a certain sound. It would be like seeing the color blue when you see the number two, or smelling strawberries when you see the color yellow. Neither are truly related, but somehow the synapses fire in a way to cross the senses, and it is consistent. If you see blue when you see the number two, you will always see blue. Sarah had that for certain types of spiritual presences, even the after presence that was sometimes still attached to the living that encountered them. She knew, based on the hint of lemony freshness, not coming from any kitchen cleaners, that the spirit they had dealt with wasn't just a lost soul. Those were blueberries. This was one that put up a little fight, probably charged one of them and contacted their clothing, which is where the after presence she could smell was.

"Pretty much," Edward said. He and Father Murray shared a glance. It was one they shared commonly in a similar setting. Sarah knew she was about to be put through a challenge. Both men looked back at her, with curiosity in their eyes. Edward leaned back in the chair and said, "Okay, how about you tell us how it went?"

"Okay," she said and leaned back against the center island. A single finger poised under her chin as she thought. Her eyes looked them up and down to take in the details. Her father had a love of mystery novels, a few she had picked up and read through, but much later in life than he would have liked. When she was nine, he brought home five Nancy Drew mystery books. Just a look at the covers had her laughing and walking away. In hindsight, they did seem a little immature compared to the Lifetime movies on the television. At this moment, she would humor her father and do her best impersonation of Nancy Drew, or was it Scooby Doo, when they unmasked the culprit at the end?

Her mind built a scene to go along with what she sensed. They were outdoors in a field of freshly cut grass. It was dark, not a leap for her mind, since she knew they were out there tonight. It was a single entity. A middle aged man, who had been wandering around for a long time. It was stubborn, and difficult to disperse. She saw her father making several attempts, each of which angered it. It reached a point where it charged at them. Her father got out of the way, but Father Murray didn't. Also not a leap for her mind. She smelled the contact on him.

A quick glance to checked for any visual clues that would confirm her suspicious, she homed in on the details and presented her case. "Well, I can tell by your shoes, you weren't walking around a swamp, or the woods. There are fresh clippings of grass still stuck to them, showing signs of a kept yard. Probably just cut today."

Father Murray nodded and toasted her with his coffee.

"Since both of you went, it tells me you didn't know what you were getting into, or had concerns."

"You never can be too cautious," said Edward.

Sarah dismissed the fatherly advice with a wave of a hand and, "Psh." Her analysis of the situation continued. The whole time she acted like she was putting together the story on the fly. "I can smell something, so it came in contact with…" her finger pointed in their direction and alternated between each of them. It stopped at Father Murray, "You."

"Guilty," and another nod. "You know, I have a theory about you and smells. If you don't mind indulging an old man?"

"By all means. The floor is yours, professor," said Sarah.

Father Murray took a sip from his coffee and then pushed his body up from his seat at the table. A few cracks and pops in his hips highlighted his progress to a standing position. He walked to the counter where Sarah had been standing, and she took his seat at the table. A quick sniff of his coffee cup put a sour look on her face. It had the same turpentine aroma she remembered.

"I have done a good deal of thinking about this ability of yours, and I think the answer is so easy, we have all overlooked it. To be sure, I did some studying and reading. Did you know there are more documented cases of females with psychic abilities than males? It is an overwhelming margin, when you look into it. Those that are more, what they refer to as sensitive, are by and large women. They're the majority. Throughout our folklore, more witches were women. In fact, there are very few legends of warlocks. Now, that is, if you believe in such fascinations as psychics and witches." He paused and then asked, "Be a good dear and bring me my coffee?"

Sarah got up and took him the chemical concoction that used to be coffee, and then returned to her seat at the table. The old priest took a healthy swig and put the cup down on the island behind him, before returning to his lecture, "There are stories all over the place, of mothers that could sense when something happened to their child. Example after example where the fairer gender was more in tune with the world, on every level, than us uncivilized Cro-Magnon aged men, that walk around ignoring the world around us and wage war against one another. Some may say men are one step above the ape on the ladder of evolution, but women are on their own ladder. I am sure you probably tired of hearing how you were the first female to ever show signs of this ability. There is no one close to being like you. It stands to reason, how you sense the spiritual world would differ from how your father, his ancestors, or anyone else with the gift would, and... like the psychics and others, you may feel things more intensely. We already know you are more capable than anyone Father Lucian has ever seen. Where your father needs to use the cross to focus and amplify his powers, you do not, at least not entirely."

5

"Keep your eye on it," yelled Edward. Jacob had just taken a swing with all the might his nearly six-foot frame could muster, but he failed to make contact. His father could see his eyes were closed from his seat in the bleachers. Something he had struggled with himself when he was younger. The refrain he had just yelled was something he remembered his father yelling at him too. He found it an unnatural sensation to keep your eyes open and focused on the spot of impact between two items moving at high speed. A collision that would send painful reverberations through the ash wood of the bat and into the tensed muscles of his wrists and forearms. The body's natural reaction was to clench the jaw and squeeze the eyes shut, just prior to the crack of the impact, which most of the time didn't arrive. Edward had experienced the overwhelming joy when his body did as he tried to instruct it, and ignored the instinctual reaction, remaining relaxed but powerful through impact. An impact that occurred in slow motion in his eyes, which allowed him to see the ball distort for the briefest of moments before it changed directions and traveled away. The sensation was rare, but memorable.

Jacob, on the other hand, experienced it far more frequently than his father ever had, but at that moment found himself in a slump. He tried hard, not smart, to pull himself out of the bad habits that crept in and added to the frustration. So far, this slump had lasted a little over a week. Coach Tenison, both the fall league and high school team coach, had worked with Jacob in the batting cage, focusing on his fundamentals. Edward felt the itch to add in his own advice, but didn't want to become one of those overbearing parents, so he let the coach do what he does best. Not to mention, he wasn't too sure what he could add that hadn't already been said. Both the coach and Jacob had surpassed his ability, and whatever he might say could just frustrate his son further.

Another swing and a miss sent Jacob sulking back to the dugout. Edward watched each step as he walked. The coach met him just outside the chain-link dugout and pointed up to his own eyes. Jacob nodded at the instructions and then walked in to take his place on the bench. So far, he was 0-for-3 in the game, but made decent contact with a foul ball during the bottom of the third. Even though it was foul, contact was contact. He would pull through this.

They retired the next batter up, ending the inning. The Miller's Crossing Owls held on to a two run lead heading into the bottom of the ninth. The last hint of the orange line of sunset had disappeared below the horizon about a half hour ago, five or ten minutes earlier than the day before, and five or ten minutes later than it would the next day. The days got shorter from here until the end of winter. Banks of lights high atop poles cast a weird, almost too perfect, light across the field from various angles, which didn't allow a single shadow to appear anywhere. A contrast to the long shadows of the twilight just before the sun set. Edward always enjoyed playing under the lights when he was seven, a rare treat normally reserved for the older boys. It made him feel like a major leaguer. In his mind, the simple metal bleachers with wood planks as seats, were towering stands in a stadium that reached up to the heavens. Those sitting in the stands enjoyed the lights too. They were a sign of protection, and kept what lurked in the darkness away.

An unmistakable whack of an ash bat against rawhide sent a ball flying. It took on a florescent appearance in the lights as it traveled, making it easier to see, easier to track down than during the day. Jacob tracked the fly to deep right field. He positioned himself underneath the ball and made the grab to seal the victory for his team. A few ran in with their arms raised, but Jacob jogged in, tossing the ball back and forth between his glove and his hand. The frustration was clear in his body language.

Parents and fans exited the bleachers to stand behind their team's dugout to gather their child and clear out of the park as quickly as possible. Being outside after dark made everyone uncomfortable in Miller's Crossing. The only thing that made them more uncomfortable than the mystery of what the night might bring, was seeing Edward standing in the grandstands fixated on a spot just beyond the centerfield wall. He hadn't moved yet. No attempt to join the rest of the parents behind the dugout, or to gather up Jacob and head home. Instead, he stood there, which caused a few parents to stop and watch him.

Those that watched didn't feel a sense of relief when he moved. They might have if he had joined the rest of the parents. Instead, he walked through them, slowly, his eyes never left that spot. Dozens of eyes watched as he passed the dugout and continued down the right field foul line, pausing next to the tall yellow pole at the outfield wall. His hand now searched the pocket of his tweed jacket for something. That sent all but one heading to their cars. The one left walked a few feet behind Edward. With the roar of dozens of cars starting up and racing off as fast as they could go behind them, Jacob closed the distance between him and his father.

"Dad, is everything ok?"

"Stay back Jacob."

"I will. I feel it too. It's different," Jacob said, his voice strained.

Different was right. There was the normal chill, cold sweat, and pricks of needles up his spine, but there was something else there. Just above the silence of the night, in the void left by the crickets who, on most nights, would be in full chorus by now. It was a hum, buzz, or a drone. He couldn't make out which to be exact, it was too silent, but there was no mistaking it, it was there. He could hear it, feel it, and even taste it. It was bitter and repulsive, causing waves of nausea. Something about it reminded Edward of the sound he had heard the first time he had witnessed a portal, but different. It pulsated up and down. Not a tremendous difference in volume between the peaks, but enough to hear it. Enough to have a purpose. Enough to seem alive.

Edward took a few steps into the tree line behind center field. The hum was everywhere, and nowhere, all at the same time. A part of the fabric of time itself, deep inside his physical being, vibrating at the molecular level. The vibration disoriented his soul. There was no focus. Thoughts ran in and out, shaking as they passed through. Like being on a giant tilt-a-whirl at the fair, if it spun faster than the speed of light. It was directionless, further blinding Edward, who had honed his perception of spiritual visitors like an extra sense, and could lead himself by it with his eyes closed, but not this time. There was nothing but the hum as he took step after step into the woods, or what he thought was into the woods. As far as he knew, he may have just spun around in a tight circle around the same tree. With each step he took, the less he knew where to go. There were no glowing or flickering spirits in view. The spinning disk he ran into the last time he heard anything that came close to this wasn't there either. He was consumed and blind. He turned around to look for the glow of the ball field, but only found darkness. The trees weren't there either, except when he bumped into them.

A patch of cold damp mist descended into the woods and assaulted Edward. The gelatinous air was hard to breathe, and burned the surface of his skin. Pain sent his eyes lips clamping down. Where the darkness and the hum had blinded his senses in a fog of confusion, he was now lost and blind in a real fog. He dropped to the ground to get below it, and found a safe haven of a few inches between the bottom of the fog and the cold damp dead leaves that laid upon the soil. The last remaining warmth of day radiated up from the ground, becoming cooler the instant it struck the night air.

As quickly as it began, the hum disappeared from everywhere and into nothingness. It didn't recede back to its source, or travel away. It dissipated into the ether, leaving Edward lying on the ground. The burning was gone, and he could breathe again. He pushed up from the ground, and an uncomfortable feeling pierced his palm. There was something in his hand and it had sharp edges. He brought it close to his eyes, to spy what it was in the darkness. It was not an unfamiliar object, and one that had been in his hand many times. He just doesn't remember retrieving the cross from his pocket.

A quick look around didn't provide any guidance on how to exit the woods. There was no glow from the ball field, or any signs of life. He called out, "Jacob!" He listened. There was no response. He called out again, this time louder, but still nothing. A check of the ground around him for footprints, or any sign of which way he came in from, was met with confusion and disappointment. There was nothing. No footprints. No disturbed leaves. No signs of anything, except directly under his feet. It was as if someone had placed him there from above.

"Jacob!", he yelled again, but still no response. A fourth attempt to scream for his son was in the works. As he took in a great breath of air to power the scream, he remembered a modern convenience, his cell phone. He pulled it out, but it only added to his confusion. It was fully charged on the drive over to the ball field. A charge that should last him a good twelve hours on a good day, with little use, eight hours if he used it heavily. At the game, he had taken a few pictures and videos of Jacob at bat, but that was it. Mostly it had sat in his pocket. There was no way it could be dead now.

Left with one remaining option, he stared up at the sky to identify the stars. His adoptive father had enrolled him in cub scouts as a way for them to bond. The camping trips were enjoyable, but he never really paid any attention to what his den leader tried to teach them. A fact documented by the lack of badges on his navy blue shirt. Faced with a clear sky, he felt some remorse for not learning anything. He knew he couldn't stay there, and made what could be a genius decision, or one he would regret for a long time. Edward picked a direction and started walking. It must have been sheer dumb luck or divine intervention, but after only fifteen minutes, he pushed through the woods out onto Highway 32. How he got there was a mystery his mind couldn't answer. It wasn't a road that was close to the ball diamond.

Two orbs of light illuminated him from behind, and the rumble of an American V8 closed in on him. It slowed and pulled off the road behind him. The gravel and uneven ground popped under its tires.

"Mr. Meyer, is that you?"

Edward turned around and saw Sheriff Marcus Thompson closing the door on his cruiser.

"Hey, Marcus. Yes, it's me."

The young sheriff, with more energy and youth than normally goes with that title, ran up to him. His cuffs and keys clinked and jingled the whole way. "Are you ok?", he asked, eyes wide with concern and confusion.

"Yep, I am fine. Just a little turned around is all."

"I'll say. I was responding to a call from Jacob. It said you went missing in the woods almost an hour ago, but he said that was at the ball field."

"Yea, I thought I saw something behind the outfield and went to check. Got a little lost."

"A little, you are more than ten miles away."

6

"Where?"

"32. Over 10 miles from the field, according to Marcus. There is no way I walked that far," Edward said. Disbelief dripped from every syllable, and his face.

Father Murray considered the possibilities of what had happened to his dear friend. Edward had called him the night before and explained what happened to him. What he had told him was unlike anything Father Murray had ever experienced, or even heard of. He thought about it the rest of that night to make sense, or apply some sense of logic to it. Both of which rarely existed in this part of their life. He needed to reach out, but with the late hour of the night, those he could talk to would be asleep, people he would only disturb for matters of extreme importance, not that he was sure this wasn't.

The next morning he woke up, tired and groggy. His sleep was restless, as dreams of dark shadowy places with a hum dominated his mind and robbed him of a peaceful rest. He hadn't heard the hum himself, so he wasn't sure if what his mind had constructed in his dream state was anywhere close to what Edward had heard. In his experience, dreams were a mechanism for the subconscious to continue working on a problem. The solution, or insight, they may bring are not tempered by the logic of the conscious mind.

A consultation of his standard texts and notes, yielded no similar experiences. On a whim, with the need for more case studies to consult, he fired up his favorite search engine and googled "paranormal hum". The paranormal aspect of his search term was an assumption but considering who he was dealing with, and where they were, it seemed logical.

The results were anything but consistent. There were several articles on the Tao's hum, an unknown sound phenomenon in a town in northern New Mexico. Medical entries for the various causes of a hum in the human ear, the most common of which was tinnitus. Then there was the hum heard around the world on April 12, 2012. People from Sussex to Madrid, Beijing to Moscow, and everywhere in between, reported hearing a hum from the morning until the early afternoon. The explanations ranged from the paranormal, which explained why it came up in his results, to the less terrestrial. To Father Murray, this didn't seem to be related but, just in case, he made a note of it and moved on.

A few pages in, he found all the conspiracy theories of government radio waves aimed at your brain to steal or control your thoughts. If not that, then it was aliens. The first few articles, showing people wearing skull caps made of tin foil, amused him. Like a viral video of someone taking a fast ball to the crotch. You felt embarrassed and bad that this was funny to most of society, but you couldn't stop watching. There was a limit, though, the teeter totter that was Father Murray's mentality tipped over heavier to the side of embarrassment at the state of some members of our supposedly intelligent society. He couldn't go any further for his own sanity, but for the briefest of moments he wondered if the government was using radio waves to plant the alien conspiracy.

He had one source left, and picked up the phone and placed a phone call. The call lasted a good portion of an hour, but still yielded nothing. He wanted to talk to Father Lucian, someone Father Murray had grown to respect a great deal, and regarded as one of the premiere experts in the world of the supernatural. Those at the Vatican saw him in that light as well, and put him in charge of the training of Sarah, and any other sensitives or keepers. To his dismay, Father Lucian was not available, he was on assignment in Puerto Rico and could not be reached, but he did reach Cardinal Rueben, who was filling in at his post for the time being. The cardinal's English wasn't as good as Father Lucian's, and Father Murray's Italian was nonexistent. Through the communication barrier, Father Murray explained what had happened to Edward. He hoped nothing was lost in the translation. There was no immediate explanation from the cardinal. Nor were they any similar situations he could remember. He promised to search through the archives and get back to him.

"Maybe you were in there longer than you thought," Father Murray proposed as an alternative and more logical explanation.

"No way, I was only in there a couple of minutes. Even if I was, I can't cover 10 miles in an hour."

Father Murray looked at his friend, and smiled in agreement. Then he leaned back against the church pew he was sitting in. The crack and pops of the old oak back echoed among the rafters with a volume that made it sound like the entire building were going to fall down. If it weren't for the generosity of several of the local craftsmen, that thought might not have been far from the truth.

"Well," the old priest cackled, "if we were anyplace else, I would say it was all in your mind." A single finger tapped his temple. "But we are here, and it is us, so... a little investigation is in order."

"I am not sure we will find anything," Edward said. "I went back this morning and walked around just outside the centerfield fence. Nothing, just woods."

"Didn't feel anything, anything at all?"

"No."

The discovery that the event was transitory deepened the mystery. There were no other similar events recorded, and now no way to investigate their oddity. At least not until it happened again.

"How is Jacob?"

"Still dropping his elbow," said Edward.

Father Murray pushed up out of the pew and walked toward the rose line. His eyes focused on the cross, and his mind on the event that Edward had described. When he had asked about Jacob, he wasn't asking about his swing. Well, not only asking about his swing. Jacob had showed signs of the same gift his father and sister shared. Edward was trying to foster it and help him accept it, much as he expected his father would have done with him. Father Murray tried not to interfere, but was there to do his job and provide spiritual guidance, as needed. There was only so much either of them could do for him. This was, in some ways, like a father passing down a trade to his son. Not unlike plumbing or carpentry. Father Murray used this analogy to explain to Edward about his family's past. He ran through several trades as examples until he found one he felt was perfect: woodworking.

Someone can take it up as a hobby. They can even receive a little guidance to refine, maybe even the guiding hand of a father can help them learn a new shape, a new technique. It takes time with a true master, as an apprentice, to master the skill. Jacob was just now learning how to see the grain in the wood. Edward was helping him learn how to create a few rudimentary shapes. A smooth pole. A table leg. A spindle for a staircase. It was just a matter of time before it was time for Jacob to take a trip to the Vatican, like his sister had, to be refined by a master, to create some of the finest etchings and carvings the world had ever seen.

"Maybe I should talk to him. I can keep both his faith and swing on an even plane," Father Murray's mind drifted to his ten-year-old self, where the sound of the crack of a bat was as holy as the best prayer is today. Times were simpler for Sarah, Jacob, and even Edward, then. As time moved on, ages increased and life became more complex, just the nature of the world.

7

"Did a strange voice welcome you in?"

"What do you mean?", asked Edward, in between bites of the soup he had brought from home.

"Well... the story you just told me sounds like something from that old show, you know... The Twilight Zone."

"Knock it off, Mark," Edward said before downing another spoonful of soup. His friend had a point. He hadn't thought about it, but his night out in the woods did resemble something he might see in black and white on that show. Most of his life could.

"Strangest thing I have ever heard, and that is saying a lot around here," Mark Grier said out of the side of his mouth, as he chewed on the leftovers he brought. A big brick of lasagna sat steaming in the microwavable container on the table below him.

This wasn't the first time the two men had sat around a lunch table in the teachers' lounge sharing ghost stories. No one else attempted to join them, but it was obvious to both men that everyone in the room was listening. The tables closest to them were full, and quiet. Not a person said a word. You could tell, based on their body language, their ears were wide open to every word spoken.

The sharing was rather one-sided. Mark told Edward some things that had occurred before he arrived back in town, but he ran out of those stories long ago. Now, Mark dug at Edward for any new stories of his adventures out with Father Murray. Edward gave him the general details of the story in about five minutes. The remaining forty-five minutes of their fifty minute lunch period was filled with question after question, to pull out more details. Some were true. Others, Edward made up. That seemed to stop the questions. It also turned into a bit of a challenge to see what he could get past him before he realized he was being pulled along by a great storyteller. The good news for Edward, whatever his imagination could come up with, no matter how outrageous, was all within the realm of possibilities. He had once considered writing a book, using his experiences as the basis for fictional stories. Even sat down and wrote out a chapter. More like half a chapter. He was just getting going when he received a phone call and had to rush off. A firm reminder of his largest impediment to doing any writing: a serious lack of free time.

"You have been here a long time. Ever hear any weird stories about sounds out in those woods?", Edward asked.

Mark thought for a moment while he chewed and then swallowed what was in his mouth. "Nah, not a one. Not even one of those stupid ones kids makes up about creepy houses buried deep in the woods. You know we had one about your old place?"

"Oh, I heard. Trust me, I heard."

"You should ask Father Murray, or some of the other old-timers. John Sawyer is one I would talk to. He knows every old tale around here."

"I talked to the father. Nothing. Not in those woods, or anywhere else around here. Even called some of his contacts at the Vatican. Nothing."

Mark chuckled, first silently, and then louder, before partially choking on the food in his mouth. After a few coughs, and looks from the other teachers in the room, he regained his breath and said, "You are the Jacques Cousteau of the paranormal world."

The white plastic spork that Edward used to eat his soup fell from his right hand and plopped into the microwavable cup. Three drops of the brown broth exploded out, splattering on the table. The table slanted away from the men and the three drops raced in that direction. Leaving a snail trail behind them. Edward grabbed his napkin and wiped up the drops before they reached the edge, "What the hell does that mean?"

"A discovery. You are the first to experience this. This is a 'summiting Everest' moment in the ghost-busting world."

8

In the fall, darkness descended on Miller's Crossing with increasing speed. With the darkness, the coolness and the fog followed. Edward could never put his finger on it, but it was something about these nights he felt connected with. Many of them he spent sitting outside on his porch, reading while drinking a beer. How he wished this was one of those nights.

Mixed along in the fog was a cold drizzling rain. The type of rain that soaked you to the bone, if you weren't sitting up on a porch, enjoying the sound. At that moment, sitting on the porch sounded good to Edward. Sitting anywhere sounded good to him. Instead, he was soaked to the bone, through his overcoat and every article of clothing he had on. Water squished between his toes from the inside of his shoes. Leather was supposed to be impenetrable by moisture. Penetration it had accomplished, by the gallons, as he trudged through the yard outside Leroy McGlint's house.

Leroy and his wife, Gladys, looked on from inside, both dry, both warm. Edward was not alone in his discomfort. Father Murray walked beside him with his head ducked inside his jacket to stem the discomfort. His plan didn't work, either. Nothing would. Nothing, except taking care of what they were here to do, getting back into Father Murray's caddie, and hightailing it out of there.

"It's here," Edward said.

"I know, but where?"

That part confused Edward. There wasn't any place to hide here. No sheds, barns, or other structures. The tree line was way off in the distance, something the McGlint clan had taken care of several generations ago, to clear room for row upon row of tobacco plants. Plants that both Father Murray and Edward took care not to step on. The steady drizzle had soaked the planting areas, creating a muddy ooze that now joined the water squishing between his toes.

In between two of the rows of plants, Edward stopped and looked around. His eyes searched for an answer as he said, "We have made several laps around the property and nothing. It is here, but I don't see it." In the years since he had returned to Miller's Crossing, Edward had never given up on a hunt. Once he and Lewis spent two days straight tracking a spirit through the woods. Edward had felt a level of malice from it he hadn't felt since that night so many years ago, at the high school. When they had finally tracked it down, it was not of the demonic nature he expected, just a spirit with an attitude problem. Whether it was worth the two-day trek, the packed sandwiches they ate for each meal, and the few naps they took in sleeping bags on the cold ground, was up for debate.

"Maybe Leroy can remember where he saw it," mumbled Edward, as he trudged through the mud back up toward the house. The light on the back porch came to life as they approached and sixty-four-year-old Leroy, and his Budweiser can that was now re-purposed as a spittoon, appeared in the doorway. His white hair was a mess, showing evidence of hours under a ball cap during the day. The sweat stains in the tee-shirt under his unbuttoned flannel shirt told of the day he had spent in the field, tending to his plants. Several farmhands helped to work his farm, a necessity on the seventy acre farm. That didn't keep Leroy from working it alongside them though. Something he would probably do until his body wouldn't allow him to anymore.

"Cold out here," pointed out Leroy from his spot on the dry stoop, under a roof overhang.

Edward was just about to ask Leroy where he had last seen the nuisance, but held up a hand that stopped all three men in their tracks. Silence hovered in the surrounding fog, with only the music of the rain drops playing in the background. Edward's head turned. He felt something as they walked back to the house, and it was stronger there at the porch.

He backed up and looked at the roofline of the house and walked from one side to the other. There was nothing there except the drain vents and an old antenna, bolted to the side of the red brick chimney. He walked back to the back door, where Father Murray had taken a break in their search to join Leroy on the stoop under the roofline. Both men looked inquisitively at Edward as he continued to search.

Edward asked, "Leroy, do you have a door to your crawl space?"

"Yes sir, right around thar," he said as he spat into his makeshift spittoon. His right hand lifted the can to meet the stream of brown liquid and motioned around to Edward's right.

Around the corner, to the right, Edward found what he was looking for. In the brick foundation, there was an iron door, hinged into an iron frame, mortared into the bricks. He knelt down and twisted the simple handle, which moved a metal bar on the back side out of a catch. It squealed as it turned. As he pulled back, the door scraped against the frame, and the hinges resisted his attempt to open it. He pulled harder and a cloud of rust exploded from the hinges with a pop as the door squealed open. The sound sent a chill up his already tingling spine. With the flashlight he had been using all night to search the property in hand, he poked his head inside the door and then pulled out and sat, leaning against the bricks.

"What is it, Edward?"

"It's there."

"Okay, then, let's get this over with." Father Murray urged him to go on in there with both of his hands.

"With mud... and lots and lots of spiders," Edward said as he stared out into space. A panicked look was painted on his face.

"So, go on."

"I don't like spiders. I REALLY don't like spiders."

"Let me get this right. You can chase ghosts all day long, but you don't like spiders?", asked Father Murray. He crouched down and looked in through the door, into the crawl space. The land on the east side sloped toward the house, sending a flood of water underneath it, creating a bog in the cramped area. No more than fifteen feet in, sat a single spirit, a woman, just sitting there on the ground, like she was enjoying the sun in an open meadow. "Doesn't look that bad."

Edward held the flashlight out for Father Murray. He took it and directed the circle of light. He let out a great sigh and joined Edward, sitting on the ground next to the door.

"Maybe it is just a lot of webs."

Edward looked at him, crossed. Under the house, the two-by-eight floor joists were not visible behind the layer of spider webs that descended each footing to the ground.

"Well, it's in there," said Father Murray. "Explains why we could feel it all around the house."

"Yep," was all Edward could muster in response.

"Someone has to go in there and deal with it."

Edward leaned over and looked through the hole. He didn't need the flashlight. The flickering of the woman illuminated the webs around her. They appeared to dance from their attachments to the house. It could be just the wind. That would be the logical explanation. Edward's mind had a different one though. In his mind, hundreds or thousands of spiders walked along each strand, causing them to bounce, like an army walking across a bridge. His skin could feel their tiny hair-covered feet walking up his arms.

As he returned to his seat on the wet ground against the brick foundation of the McGlint house, he proposed an alternative that took only seconds to rationalize in his head. "You know, she doesn't look like she is hurting anything. We could come back tomorrow, or never."

Edward heard the unamused chuckle from his partner in crime. No other reply was necessary, and he pulled out the cross and book from his pockets, then prepared himself to enter the void. Father Murray offered him the flashlight, which Edward considered taking, but eventually refused. He hoped to find a reprieve in the logic of a small child: what he doesn't see can't hurt him.

Within the first few feet he crawled, that axiom was proven untrue. His hands and knees were caked and covered in squishy mud, and he had run into several webs with his face, no matter how low he tried to get to duck under them. They stuck to his forehead, as if they were covered in glue. He didn't see them, but he knew they were there, just above his eyebrows. Every second they felt like they fell closer to his eyes, even though they hadn't moved. In his mind, dozens of tiny spiders were now walking around in his hair. His scalp crawled in response.

He kept on toward the woman. She paid no mind of him. He held the cross toward her, and she didn't move. She sat there, not motionless. Her head moved back and forth as she studied something in her lap. There was a delicateness to her expression and motion, much like a young girl brushing the hair of a baby doll sitting in her lap.

As sympathetic as he could manage, while covered in mud, with a thousand spiders marching on every synapsis of his brain, he said, "I free you to join your loved ones in His eternal garden."

She flickered twice more before she never came back. Edward turned around and rushed out through the webs. This time, he did not try to duck under them, and resembled something more akin to Godzilla walking through a Japanese town. When he emerged through the door, he collapsed on the ground and rolled back and forth in the mud. His hands were a blur as they tried to brush whatever was in his hair, and everything that wasn't, out. When satisfied the webs, and imaginary spiders, were gone, he stood up. A random tingle on his skin, probably just psychosomatic, sent his hands rushing to chase whatever it was away. The webs were all gone, as were the spiders that never were there, but mud covered him from head to toe.

"Leroy?", called Father Murray, from where he sat along the foundation of the house.

Leroy emerged from around the corner of the house, a hand held up to shield him from the rain, his head ducking to the side to avoid the drops that made it past his hand. "Yes, Father," the annoyed man said.

"Got any plastic? Edward isn't getting into my car like that."

***

"What the hell happened to you?", Jacob asked.

"Language, son."

Jacob was lounging on the sectional couch in a pair of grey sweatpants and a Senator's t-shirt. An action film with several loud explosions played on the television. He reached down for the remote and adjusted the volume to avoid another corrective instruction from his father. He had a hand full of chips from a bowl that sat on the floor and was stuffing them into his mouth when Father Murray walked through the door behind him. A smirk was on his face.

There was no such smirk on his father's face. His expression could only be described as miserable. He was wet. Rivers of mud ran down from his hair, across his face. Drops of a thick brown fluid dripped from his coat to the floor.

"I am not cleaning that up," said Sarah. She had just returned home herself, and stood there gawking at the scene now midway between the front door and the door to the kitchen. Like Father Murray, she had a smirk on her face. Her father turned toward her to give her a full view of his expression.

"It was under a house. Your father had to crawl through the mud to get to it," explained their family priest.

"And SPIDERS!", added Edward.

"Oh, yes, we can't forget the spiders," chuckled Father Henry.

Now three of the four in the room were laughing uncontrollably.

"There were thousands of them, and they were big," pleaded Edward.

"Let me get you some towels," Sarah said in between giggles. "You couldn't hose him off before you brought him home."

"Well, I thought about that, but Leroy uses reclaimed sewage water for his crops."

Sarah stopped in her tracks and looked at the brown puddle around her father's feet. The giggling stopped, and a look of repulsion replaced it. "Please tell me…"

"That is mud. Trust me, that is mud. He didn't hose me off," interrupted Edward.

The news did little to change the disgusted look on her face as she squeezed past him and up the stairs. Jacob was still planted on the sofa, but had contorted his body to keep the attraction firmly in his view. Edward was sure this would become one of the many family moments his kids would remember and bring up years later for a good laugh.

Sarah emerged from upstairs carrying several towels in her arms.

Jacob's "How was the date, sis?" question drew her ire in the form of a rolled-up towel fired at his head.

"Oh, there is someone special?", asked Father Murray.

"Just dinner Father."

"Do we know him?", he asked.

"In this town? Would it be possible for you not? It was Kevin Steirers. No point in hiding it."

9

The light of the midday sun shone through the window in the breakfast nook and across the table, casting a large irregularly shaped shadow upon the tile floor. Its normal shadow resembled a flat table, but the one today had square items protruding from the top of it, like a distant mountain range made of a child's building blocks. The objects casting the shadows were not blocks or boxes, they were stacks upon stacks of newspapers. It wasn't time for the great paper drive, like the ones Edward remembered from his elementary school days. For those, his family would store every paper, every piece of junk mail, anything made of paper, for months, to help his class gather the most paper, by weight. Of course, that was all for a little 9-inch trophy.

Edward was not sure if they still did that at the elementary school. He wasn't sure if they still had newspapers. He couldn't remember the last time he had read one, or a current one, that was. Stacked before him were yellowed, and partially rancid smelling, copies of the Miller's Crossing Ledger from thirty years ago or more. All before Edward had left town. Father Murray had collected them and stored them in his garage, as a scrapbook. Each paper had a story about Father Murray, and either Edward's Father or grandfather, dealing with some supernatural occurrence around their small town. Now none of them documented what they were really doing. A fact that Edward found rather humorous and prompted more sighs than laughs from Jacob.

The cover stories ranged from rampaging livestock, to chickens that refused to lay any eggs, or crops that wouldn't grow. Edward's father, or grandfather, were there to provide guidance and expertise as a town elder, to help the stricken families. Father Murray, on the other hand, was there to pray for the dead crops, or spooked cow.

"Oh, look another story about a pig that won't eat," cackled Jacob.

Father Murray leapt up fast for his age and read the story over his shoulder. He reached over and snatched the paper off the stack, to look at the date, July 4th, 1954. A smile slowly crept into his eyes. Eyes that were now drifting years away into the past, as he had remembered the true story of that day. "That, my boy, was the day your great-grandfather, and me took down two while fireworks went off over our heads and everyone watched on. Not particularly challenging, at least not for him, but different. We never had an audience before. Afterward, everyone tried to offer us a piece of pie, or whatever dessert they had brought with them to the city's Independence Day picnic. It took me weeks to work off all that weight."

Jacob looked at him, his expression odd and quizzical.

"I am a man of the people. I couldn't turn them down, now could I? I sampled each."

Jacob asked, "Why aren't there stories about that?"

"Well... there are. If you read, I think they even asked me whose pie was best."

"That is not what I meant."

"Outsiders," said Edward, from the other side of the table, where he was busy reading other stories. Some were ruses like that one Father Murray was discussing with Jacob, but others were actual stories. Real insights into the town's past and his family. Outside of what Father Murray could tell him, reading a story on the sports page about his father's high school career, or quotes from his grandfather about some great issue up for debate among the town elders, were his only sources to learn about his past, and who the legendary men that had preceded him were. It was fortunate that his family played a significant enough role in the town's history to allow those stories to overlap each other, more fictionalized events, making these saved treasures a true window into his past.

Time had started to rob him of the few memories he had had from the first seven years of his life. A sign of the progression of time that Edward couldn't stop, no matter how bad he wanted to. Now, more than ever before, he wanted to remember, for him, and to tell his children. It was important to him for them to know his family. The tragedy of his childhood had taken that chance from them. A chance they needed, in his opinion, more so than most families. His children needed to know their heritage. They needed the lessons of the past. They needed to know who those family members were, that walked this path before them, and what they were like. All of this would help them handle their gift better. It had to, he hadn't had that chance, and had struggled immensely.

"Hey, Jacob, here is one on your grandfather's three touchdown game," said Edward as he tossed a paper on top of the stacks in front of his son. It fanned the odor of mildew and mold out when it landed.

What he had learned so far was, his father was who he remembered: a fiery but fair individual, with a desire to help anyone and everyone. Just like he remembered, his father and mother were involved with every aspect of community life. What was obvious was, this must have been a quality instilled into him by Edward's grandfather. Story after story presented Edward with the image of a man who was bigger than life, and this small town. The way he discussed community matters in the paper resembled a seasoned diplomat, with a lean toward being a national politician.

"The need to repave the route 281 log road might not be obvious to everyone, on the surface, yet these are the little things we need to do as a community to thrive," said Alderman Carl Meyers. "You may never drive on the route, but you do derive benefits from it. The logging companies contribute to the financial wellbeing of our town. Just last year, they hired thirty-two locals. Thirty-two jobs we would not have otherwise. The more we improve the route, the better our chances of attracting other companies into our fertile land, bring more opportunities. Not to mention, the money they spend while here, at the local diners, stores, and gas stations. It supports our local business owners and contributes to our tax coffers. Over the next week I will be working with those in opposition, to address their concerns."

Story after story, were the same. His grandfather was quoted on every significant issue, and even just town gatherings. Wherever he was, the reporters, or reporter, would find him, and he always had something great to say. At that moment, but not for the first time since he had returned home, the shoes everyone looked for him to fill felt way too large for his feet.

"Knock. Knock."

Edward looked up from the report he was reading from the annual fall festival, that occurred during the day before Father Murray and his grandfather rushed a spirit from the gazebo in the town square. "Hey, Lewis. Come on in."

The now-retired sheriff stepped in through the backdoor. A minor hitch in his giddy-up caused by a touch of rheumatoid arthritis in his left knee and hip. Something that always bothered him, and got worse in the cold Virginia winters. His red and blue flannel shirt, jeans, and "Rather Be Fishin'" hat advertised his now retired status. Walking in behind him was his younger, more able-bodied, replacement, who had moved up from deputy to Sheriff after the encounter at the portal sent him into an early retirement.

Marcus Thompson was a good sheriff. He was honest, trusted by everyone, and eager. The eagerness was something Lewis worked to temper in him while he was still his deputy, and then after during their many conversations, once he was promoted. He was a local boy, born and bred. His father was a deputy on the force before him. That probably led to some of the romantic allure that line of work held for him. One might think, with a father that was in it, he would have been better prepared. He had the skills, but started out a little too idealistic and less understanding that this was a small town, a tight-knit community. Sometimes you let little things slide. If you see two friends fighting and shoving, maybe it is best to just step in and send them on their own way, instead of slapping cuffs on their wrists and bringing them down to sit in the two jail cells they had at the station. This had happened a few times, mostly involving a few of the older residents that had had a bit too much of the homemade fire-water. Each time it happened, Lewis would unlock the doors and let both men walk out with a stern warning of, "You both should know better… now don't end up back here again." If Lewis had been the one to see them doing whatever Marcus had thought they were doing, he would have issued that same warning on the street and sent them separate ways, or given each of them a ride home to end it right there and then. He eventually learned and loosened up to become a well-seasoned law man, even if his babyface didn't look it. His clean-shaven look missed that lawman mustache that Lewis had so proudly sported throughout his entire career. He continued to sport it today, but the only thing he had been taking into custody lately were carp.

"I smell something old."

"Must I remind you, Lewis, we are about the same age," sniped Father Murray.

Lewis picked up a paper from the top and began flipping through it. Marcus did as well. "Where did you find these old things?"

"I kept them. A chronicle of sorts. Figured Edward might like to read about his family."

A deep belly laugh welled up inside of the former sheriff's rotund frame. It surged up and out and filled the room. The laugh was so large, the action of releasing it forced his arms to move and shake the paper, causing the dried and aged paper to crinkle. "We had to come up with some doozies as cover stories, didn't we?"

"That we did. I figured you and I could fill in the truth behind each of these," said Father Murray.

"I imagine we would have to, but that needs to wait for another time. My young friend is here on official business."

With that, both Father Murray and Edward put down the paper they had in their hands. Jacob kept the one he held in his hand, but looked over the top edge of it at the sheriff. Those words added a tension to the room.

"How can we help?", Edward asked, his attention now focused on the young babyfaced sheriff.

"I need to speak with Sarah, Mr. Meyer," he said. Each hand hooked on a belt buckle on the sides of his waist.

"Sarah, why? Father Murray and I can help…"

"It's not something like that," he interrupted. There was a quick glance at Lewis before he continued, "Is she home?"

"Yes, let me get her." Edward got up and headed out the door to get Sarah. She was up in her room, watching television and finishing up some laundry, before heading in to work in the boutique later that afternoon. When Father Murray had arrived with the papers, they had invited her to come take a look with them. Something Edward had hoped she would have shown more interest in. Her reply was, "No, thank you. I spend too much time dealing with things from the past."

"Sarah," he said, as he knocked on the door.

"Yeah, Dad," she replied through the closed door.

"Can you come down for a bit?"

"I told you. I am not interested in looking through a bunch of old mildewed newspapers."

"It's not that. The sheriff is here. He wants to talk to you."

There was no verbal reply. Just the sound of footsteps approaching the door, followed by the creak the door made as it opened. When she stepped out, she was timid and looked at her father inquisitively. "Why?"

Edward just shrugged and led her downstairs.

10

Edward followed Sarah into the kitchen. Sheriff Thompson was the only person still standing. He was there in his cop pose, his thumbs still hooked into the belt loops on his pants, just as Edward had left him. Plastered on his youthful face was an attempted scowl. This was not a skill he had mastered. Instead of being intimidating, he looked like he had a burrito or chimichanga at lunch that was riding low in his intestines. Lewis Tillingsly, on the other hand, had a scowl that could make the earth quake. Even with his large cookie duster covering most of his mouth. It was the eyes. The narrowing of the eyes and the lean of the eyebrows. Neither of which looked menacing on Marcus.

When Sarah saw the assembled group in the kitchen, she froze in her tracks. There was a concerned look on her face. Edward shared the same look. Even though he considered everyone there a friend, there was a slight feeling of having walked her into an ambush.

"Sarah, take my seat," Lewis said as he leaned his weight forward and pushed himself up.

When she walked toward the now vacant seat at the table, Marcus stepped in behind her, before Edward could pass, closing the proverbial door. Edward moved around and stood off to the side, next to the large marble-covered island. Sarah's lips had a tad of a quiver to them.

"Jacob, why don't you go on into the other room and let us talk to Sarah?", suggested Edward. He could tell Sarah felt uncomfortable. No need adding to it, having her little brother there gawking at her from across the table during whatever this was.

"Sarah, I need to ask you a question," began Marcus. "When was the last time you saw Kevin Steirers?"

"Um... last night. Why?"

"Where was that?"

"At Len's, we had dinner together," she said, and again looked around the room for acceptance of her answer from those assembled.

"When?", the sheriff asked, coldly.

"Well, we met there around 7 and ate. Afterward, we stood outside and talked. We were still talking when Len closed things up just after 9, but left in our own cars not long after. Why? What's up?"

"Are you sure about the time you guys left? Was it closer to 9 or maybe 10?", he asked.

This time Father Murray answered on her behalf, "Had to be closer to 9. She walked in just after we got home, and that was before 9:30." His response brought a look from Sheriff Thompson, and Father Murray clenched his mouth shut and leaned back in his chair.

Edward noticed the look, and Father Murray's response, but didn't let either deter him. "Marcus, what is this all about?"

"Just asking some questions," he said, keeping his look stern, and the lid closed on sharing any additional information.

Lewis's eyes studied his replacement and then threw the lid right off. "She's not in any trouble or anything, Edward. Kevin was found wandering around Harper's Hill Road early this morning, dazed, confused, and all scratched up. Frank Tyler passed him, loaded him up in his truck, and brought him to me. The kid seemed completely out of it. No clue where he was. No clue who he was. No clue where his car was. No clue how he ended up in the passenger seat of Frank's truck. When he was transported to the hospital, Wendy Nyles said she saw him having dinner with Sarah last night, wearing the same clothes."

"Is he okay?", Sarah asked. The quiver was gone from her lips and voice, replaced by compassion and a great deal of concern.

"Hard to say. He was still pretty out of it when I left him. Did you guys have anything to drink last night?"

"No, Len's doesn't sell any alcohol," said Sarah.

"I hate to ask, but I have to, Miss Meyer... any drugs? Maybe a little pot or something?", interjected Marcus.

Sarah's head whipped side to side as she declared, "No!"

"I had to ask," Marcus said sheepishly, as he looked at the others in the room.

Father Murray placed a comforting hand on Sarah's shoulder and asked, "Lewis, do you think this could be... unnatural?"

"Don't know, Father. The thought crossed my mind."

Marcus nodded in agreement, with a look on his face that screamed, *"I don't know!"*

Edward looked at Father Murray and suggested, "Maybe we should talk to him?"

"I wish you would," Lewis said. There was a little stir in the room, and the sound of rustling next to Edward, as Marcus shifted his weight from side to side, and then his posture, as if to remind the men in the room who was really in control of such matters. Everyone, including Sarah, noticed and focused their attention on him. Among the men old enough to be his father, he still appeared to be a child trying to make sure he had his father's attention. Regardless of his age and actions, he was the sheriff, and Edward knew this was his responsibility. If he wanted them to talk to his victim, then Marcus would have to be the one to ask. It appeared Lewis remembered that, too, "If that is ok with you, Sheriff?"

"No objections. I appreciate any help you gentlemen can provide."

Father Murray slid the chair out and squeezed past Sarah. His large black brimmed hat sat on the island in the center of the kitchen. He picked it up and placed it firmly on his head, saying, "We can take my car."

"Now?", asked Edward, with a tone of mild surprise.

"Of course. Whatever has him might not be there later, plus... if it is something like this, he could be suffering and need our help now." Father Murray headed out of the kitchen, toward the front door. Without a word, Sheriff Thompson and Lewis Tillingsly headed for the back door they had entered a few minutes earlier. This left Sarah and Edward in the kitchen, in silence. It was an awkward one, which confused Edward. Having the local sheriff in his kitchen in times of emergency was not a unique occasion. It happened more than he liked, but it was life. This was the first time one of his children was the target of questioning, though.

"Edward, are you coming?", Father Murray called from beyond the kitchen door.

"Yes, Father," replied Edward. He turned around and headed toward the door.

"I am coming, too," said Sarah. As Sarah rushed by him for the door, Edward considered stopping her. Half of him didn't think this was a good idea, but the other half knew how skilled and perceptive she was. If there was something unnatural going on here, she may be able to help in ways neither he nor Father Murray could.

The ride to County General was quiet, with no sound except the occasional squeak of the old suspension, and the odd cricket-like chirp the speedometer made as it approached 55 miles per hour, a speed well over the posted speed limit. They pulled into the parking lot of the hospital just as Lewis and Sheriff Thompson were getting out of their patrol car. They all walked in together and down the front hall, toward the Emergency Room where Kevin was still being treated.

"You guys wait here for a moment," asked the sheriff who went ahead to the nurse's desk. After a few minutes of discussion with her, he returned to the group. "Okay, he hasn't improved and is very confused. They asked that we be gentle. Father. Edward. Come with me."

Sarah moved forward with them, but Lewis brushed her arm around the elbow to catch her attention. He shook his head "No" and then looked over at a row of chairs lined up against the wall as a makeshift waiting area in the small hospital's emergency department.

The sheriff led Father Murray and Edward through a break in a light blue curtain. Behind the curtain lay Kevin Steirers, on a hospital bed, now wearing a green gown, and looking straight up at the drop ceiling. Neither his eyes, head, nor body, made any motion to acknowledge their presence. The three men gathered around the hospital bed and trained their eyes on him, much like a doctor would do to diagnose him.

"Kevin, these men are here to talk to you," said the sheriff. Kevin didn't even twitch.

"How are you feeling, Kevin?", Father Henry asked. Still nothing.

Edward didn't spend long looking at the blank expression on his face before his attention roamed to the dozens of large swatches of bandages all over the exposed area of his body. There was no evidence of blood seeping through from underneath. On his right arm, someone had removed the bandages from one of the rows of three scratches. Each was long, and several layers of skin deep. Edward didn't have a logical explanation for what had made them, but he knew whatever it was wasn't human. It could have been an animal, he thought. Lots of bobcats, badgers, and even bears in the area that could have done that to him. There was one problem with that theory. If that type of animal injured you in that way, the chances that you would get away and not be chased and eventually killed by them was slim-to-none. The injuries, themselves, were grave, no matter the source. The skin around each scratch was cut clean, like a razor blade slashed it. It showed an almost surgical precision. The gouge in between each edge was something different, something more primal and violent in appearance. It had ripped the tissue down to the muscle. Even cleaned up, it gave every appearance of being infected, with small pockets of pus leaking into the middle of the gouges, creating a river of ooze.

A nurse rushed in and squeezed in between Edward and Father Murray. In her right hand was another roll of bandages that she quickly wrapped around the exposed wounds on Kevin's right arm. She finished the wrap and tightened it. With expert precision and speed, she applied strips of paper tape along the edges of the wrapping. Both hands ran along the tape to ensure proper adhesion to both the bandage and the skin. Edward watched as she worked, and expected to see the evidence of blood and pus soaking into the bandage she applied, but it didn't. It stayed as white and pure as it had before she placed it over the wound. She left the room, but not before making eye contact with all three men. Her eyebrows drawn close together.

"Are they running blood tests?", asked Father Murray.

"Thinking drugs?", asked Sheriff Thompson.

Father Murray just nodded agreeably.

"Yep."

"Kevin. It's Father Murray, can you hear me?"

Just like before, Kevin laid there. His face flaccid, only held up by the bones underneath. Eyes looked attentively out, but not at any of them, or anything in the room. They were focused, and didn't move. Outside of the slight rising and falling of his chest, there was no movement, even when Father Murray placed his hand on his forehead.

Edward watched as the priest's thumb drew a tentative cross on the young man's forehead. He hoped for a reaction. That would make it easy. They knew how to deal with demonic presences. There was nothing, not even a flinch. This was not spiritual, or at least not some kind of spiritual control. He may have still encountered something out on the road, or in the woods, that night that had put him into shock. The scratches fit into that scenario.

"I am not sure, Sheriff. This may be completely medical," Father Henry reported, somewhat disappointedly.

"Did you see the scratches?", asked Edward.

"No. Why?"

"You need to. Can we ask a nurse to show us?", Edward asked Sheriff Thompson.

The young sheriff stood there and considered the request, before walking out of the room, his eyes still locked on the victim. It didn't take long before he returned, followed by the same nurse. Edward could tell the request didn't amuse her, but she complied all the same. She peeled back a bandage on his left arm. Edward surmised she didn't want to redo the one she had just replaced on his right. When the deep cuts and gouges came into view, Father Murray gasped, "Dear God." He moved forward to get a closer look.

Edward noticed the lack of seepage on that bandage, as well, and was astonished after seeing the amount of fluid that was underneath. This put a new target in his head for investigation, and he searched the room, finding a small bag on the floor containing the jeans and black cotton button-up shirt he had to assume Kevin was wearing when he was brought in. He slipped the clothes out of the bag to investigate, keeping his back turned to the sheriff, to hide what he was doing. There was no desire to be caught possibly tampering with evidence. The sweet Jasmine smell of his daughter's favorite perfume wafted out. That wasn't surprising to him. What was, was what was missing. His shirt was dry. With all the cuts and scratches, it should have been soaked in blood, but it wasn't. There wasn't even a single dried discolored stain around the slashes in the material. Edward quickly shoved both back in the bag and returned it to the floor.

Behind him, the nurse was securing the tape and bandage back on this skin, when Kevin's head shot toward the door. It was not a smooth turn, more of a jerk, a single move, from facing forward to facing the door, in under a second. His eyes didn't blink, but had another target to fixate on. Edward followed his gaze and saw Sarah's head poking through the door. Kevin's body quivered ever so subtly.

11

Sheriff Thompson walked the others outside to the parking lot. They hadn't learned a lot, or anything from visiting Kevin. In Edward's opinion it had equal chances of being an animal or something from the natural world, as it did of being something from another world. The scratches still stuck out to him, but Lewis told the story of someone he had once seen with similar deep cuts after a run-in with a black bear, a native to these parts. It was a possibility Edward had to consider.

"Odd, very odd," remarked Lewis, as they approached their cars to leave.

"Yep, even for here," said Marcus, who then added, "this might take over-the-top spot from the animals in my list of strangest things this week."

"What animals?", asked Father Murray.

"Oh, it's nothing, Father. A couple of hunters saw the desecrated bodies of a few squirrels hung in the trees. Their heads posted on sticks. Probably just kids, but worrisome. You know most of the great serial killers started off with something similar."

The sheriff was correct on that point. Edward had seen a few documentaries on television about Jeffrey Dahmer that talked about his bucket of "fiddle-sticks". Seems his childhood involved helping his father, a professional chemist, bleach the tissue off the bones of the rodents they caught under their house. They kept the bones in a bucket that was affectionately termed his own "rattle". While, in hindsight, his family tried to cast that off as scientific curiosity, they couldn't explain the impaled dogs' heads, or other acts that occurred in his later years.

Edward knew you could never predict who would turn into such a monster. That was always the biggest question on such shows. It was hard for him to consider someone here in Miller's Crossing being that demented. There was another explanation, outside of just doing something stupid and mischievous, which was not completely out of the range of possibilities here. That option, to him, was even a bit darker than becoming the next serial killer. That was the occult.

The locals all knew the history of this place, and what it meant. It had caused a few to become more religious than you might find in most towns. Something Edward felt was relatively natural, all things considered. He, and the others, would be naïve not to consider the chance that someone might become just as fascinated in the other side. It was a topic he had recently spent some time researching. Not out of some desire to switch sides, but to gain an understanding of the other side. It was Sun Tzu that said, "Know thy enemy."

"Where did they find them?", Edward asked, breaking his silence since pointing out the scratches to Father Murray. The four others looked at him, surprised at his interest. "There is another reason someone may have done that."

The surprised looks on the other four faces was replaced by ones of deep concern, as their eyes dropped from looking at each other, to looking at the cracked rough pavement with faded lines of yellow paint.

"Edward, you can't think it would be that. Not here?", pleaded Father Murray.

His friend's argument took aback Edward. Of all people, he expected Father Henry to have already made that leap himself. "We can't discount anything, Father," he said and then turned his attention to Sheriff Thompson. "Where abouts did they find them?"

"I can take you, if you would like?"

"Okay," Edward agreed.

"I'd best come along too," said Father Murray.

"Me too," said Sarah.

"Oh, no," objected Edward.

"If it is what you think it is, you will need me," she argued.

She had a point, and Edward knew it. She was more capable in these dealings than he was, and the formal training she had received from Father Lucian covered the occults. Edward's knowledge was what he could gleam from the internet and a few books he had downloaded on his tablet. Not wanting to seem like she had won, Edward didn't agree, nor did he provide another objection.

"Well, let's go. Just follow me, Father," said Sheriff Thompson.

Lewis rode with Marcus, and Sarah and Edward took the white-knuckled ride with Father Murray. It wouldn't be too much longer before Edward had to have a conversation with the father about giving up his driving privileges, or maybe going to something a little smaller and more modern. His old Cadillac's suspension swayed back and forth from white line to yellow line. Each of his over corrections sent the car drifting over the line. A few involved a daredevil dive toward several old oak trees that had grown close to the edge of the roadway over the decades. Many were obviously placed by the devil, himself, on the edge of the blind hairpin turn. Scuffs of paint stood as warnings of past battles with motor vehicles where the car had lost.

About six miles outside the center of town, the two cars pulled off to the side of the road. The ground was still sloshy after the torrential rain from a few nights ago, allowing the car tires to sink in slightly. It squished under each footfall as Edward followed the sheriff off into the woods. The rest followed behind them.

The underbrush was thick, which made the going rough. It would be a few weeks before the first hard freeze of the year knocked down the lush weeds and bit back some smaller plants.

Edward kept his mind clear, or as clear as he could, so he could sense if anything was out there. So far, he had felt nothing, only heard the pop of a twig or a leaf a few times. Each one he dismissed as a small animal moving about, they were in their environment. That thought sent a shiver down his spine, they had all been stupid. Bow hunting season had opened a few weeks ago, and not a single one of them had thought about putting on something brightly colored to avoid being confused as an animal. He was about to comment on that when Sheriff Thompson stopped and said, "Here it is."

Here it is, was right. Edward expected to see just a few squirrels hanging from a branch, and a head or two pushed down on a stick. The scene he just walked up on sent a shiver all the way up and down his spine, and out through his arms and legs. "Think I am off-base now?", he asked.

Father Murray replied with a hesitant and mortified-sounding, "No. Absolutely not."

As he walked around the edges of the scene from hell, he asked, "You came out and checked this, yourself?"

"Yep."

"And you didn't think to contact any of us?", Edward asked. He took his eyes off the scene long enough to look over at the sheriff who was on the opposite side of the display from him. To say he had a sheepish look on his face would be a dishonor to sheep. It was obvious he had made a judgement call as sheriff, one that is allowed by his office, but not the correct one. The look Lewis was giving his young replacement echoed that. This would probably create an abundance of false-alarm-type calls from Marcus in the future, but that was better than what could happen if he walked into a situation he couldn't handle.

"Are you seeing this, Father?", Edward asked.

"Yes."

The scene in front of them started with the bodies of six headless squirrels, hanging from strings tied up in the trees, down to about head height. The arrangement made a circle. Inside the circle, the ground had been cleared of all debris, and was immaculate. There wasn't a rock, leaf, weed, or blade of grass, anywhere. Just black dirt. Edward looked closer, and discovered how that feat was accomplished. It had been burnt.

What *was* inside the burnt circle was the most disturbing scene of all. The heads of the six squirrels were on six sticks. Each faced away from the center. The ground was stained in areas, and Edward's eyes followed the dark red stains, which he assumed was created by using the blood of the slain animals. The lines created a pentagram on the ground, with all but one stick at the points. The remaining stick, and posted head, were at the center.

"We need to destroy this, all of this!", Edward exclaimed, and he began kicking at the sticks.

"What are you doing?", asked Sheriff Thompson. His voice strained and confused.

"He is right. We have to destroy this abomination," said Father Murray.

Without waiting for permission, or any further objection, Lewis pulled out his pocketknife and began cutting down the hanging bodies. As each body hit the ground, he used his shoe to push it into a pile. Later, before they left, he used his knife to dig a makeshift grave and shoved them, and their heads, in and pushed the dirt over the top of them with his boot. Edward used his feet to kick dirt over the burnt area, covering the unholy shape on the ground.

Sarah stood and watched, a hand over her mouth the whole time.

The five of them walked out of the woods quietly, and much faster than they had walked in. Edward eventually passed Sheriff Thompson. He hoped he could remember the way back to their cars. He would have to chance it, he had to get away from that scene. As far away as he could. A cold black weight sat in the pit of his stomach, and it grew heavier with every moment they spent there. Everywhere else in the world, well, except in six other places, someone might dismiss this as misguided teens messing around, or following some example they saw in a movie or music video, if anyone still watched those. That was not the case here. He knew this was real. What whoever was messing with was as real as it gets. This would be like loading a gun and pulling the trigger, not expecting the bullet to fire, or lighting the fuse on a bomb, and not expecting it to explode, strictly out of some misguided belief. You knew damn well what you were doing in both instances. Whoever was doing this knew damn well what they were doing here too. Even if they didn't know the 'how' or 'why', they knew the 'what'. Not knowing the 'how' could be the most dangerous of all. They could stumble upon something dark and evil just as easily and summon it on purpose. That was the source of the dark weight. This was not something they could ignore.

He emerged out of the trees and marched toward the cars. When he reached them, he turned and waited for the others. Once the sheriff was close enough Edward demanded, "I need a map!"

"A what?", he asked in reply.

"I assume you have a map of the town in your car Marcus." Edward caught himself after he had said it, but didn't attempt to correct it and just let it sit out there in the air.

The sheriff popped the trunk and searched. He closed the trunk and walked around to the hood of his patrol car with a fan-folded map. His hands spread it flat on the hood, using the flashlight he had on his belt as a weight to hold one side down against the wind.

"Where are we?", asked Edward.

Lewis pointed to a spot on the map, his finger then moved a little off State Road 192. "That spot was right here."

"Where was Kevin found?", Edward asked.

"Harper Hill Road, about two miles past Walter's Creek, over here," the sheriff said, and he pointed to the spot on the map again.

Edward's eyes scanned the area between the two spots. It was a constant span of woods, not a single crossroad or house. There was an old logging road, still noted on the map, that cut into the woods about a quarter of a mile, but that was it. He then looked out further, along that same line of woods, until to the north it ran into a very familiar spot, and he placed his finger on the ball field.

"This isn't just a coincidence," he said.

12

The storm cleared, leaving devastation behind. Wind-whipped debris was scattered everywhere, as a quiet relief settled over the survivors like a blanket, but it only stayed there for a moment. The grief of what was ahead of them wiped away that respite with a slap of reality. It was a seasonal storm. One that Sarah knew exactly how to handle. It was finally homecoming, and over the past three hours, every girl between the age of fifteen and eighteen in Miller's Crossing had led a reluctant parent through the doors of Myrtle's. Each parent that entered knew what was in store for them. Their daughter would try on no less than eight dresses, most that looked very similar to each other. After each dress was on, they would complain about the fit, and then finally select one that someone else just bought the last one in their size.

Once the madness cleared, the dresses that had been shoved on and off for the last few hours were miraculously still in one piece, but discarded all over the floor, along with a rain of sequins. A single run by the vacuum cleaner would take care of that before closing, but first she needed to rehang all the dresses. To her pleasure, Charlotte had stopped by to watch the madness, a madness that she would suffer through in another fifteen years. For now, it was just a spectator sport to her, and she was kind enough to stay behind to help Sarah and her part-time clerk, Judy Spencer, clean up the mess.

Judy was a high-school junior, herself, and daughter of the town's Chamber of Commerce president of the last twenty years. Before that, there wasn't a chamber, or a Tourism Department, either, which her father was also in charge of. During a town council meeting in the mid-1980s, Walter Spencer laid out a plan to put Miller's Crossing on the map. It involved setting up a Chamber of Commerce and Tourism Office. Both of which he had to explain what they were to the council. Neither was the only topic he had had to explain to the council. There was a great debate around whether they wanted to put Miller's Crossing on the map. Most of the residents enjoyed being the little secret that no one knew about. Mostly because of the secret they all hid. Walter was persistent and, after several meetings, they agreed. They would establish both and name him president of each, but they diverted no public funding to either. That didn't stop him from putting a square of wood, with both department names on it, in front of their home, nor buying a nice new suit and a bow tie that he wore every day as he walked around greeting the same people over and over, with a cheap thousand-dollar smile. There was a rumor that had spread through whispers, that had resonated in every corner of the town, that his desire to put their sleepy home on the map, seemed to coincide with his realtor's license. No one could ever be sure.

His daughter, much like her father, saw an opportunity and took steps to grab it. She was a little better at it than he was. Judy had had her eye on a dress for weeks. A blue chiffon dress that stopped just above her knees, with a single row of silver beading around the waist. She knew what was coming and, wisely, had purchased it before the store opened, with Sarah's permission and then hid it in the back. Now she had it on and twirled and danced in front of the wall of full-length mirrors in the changing room, while Sarah worked her way from the front of the store to the back, folding the entire way. Charlotte flanked her, moving up the right side, doing the same thing. In an hour, maybe a few minutes more, they would have it all cleaned up and, if they were lucky, Judy might come out to help with the last few articles of clothes.

"Stop it," Sarah chastised her friend.

"I am serious. With the way they talk about you, I feel I should lay palm fronds down to line your path." Charlotte grabbed a green dress that was puddled on the floor and rushed around a display to lay it flat on the floor in front of Sarah. "Your majesty," she gushed, the last syllable of which was a giggle as a balled up t-shirt hit her upside the head.

"Look. I know that has everyone freaked out but I, nor my father, have done anything yet. We probably won't need to. The sheriff is trying to find who did it."

The "that" she talked about was the satanic display found in the woods five days ago. Even though they had all agreed to keep it quiet, the whole town was talking and speculating about it by Tuesday. With all the weirdness that happened here, this was a first, and it made everyone uneasy. Something that, before now, seemed to not be possible in this community.

"Marcus?", laughed Charlotte. "Please. He couldn't find them if they paraded down the road in front of his car wearing an upside down cross, with black flames shooting from their hands. We need you."

"No, you don't. This is a matter for the cops," said Sarah, who kept on folding and hanging up dresses without missing a beat.

"Sarah Meyer, that sounds like your father talking. Since you got back you have been running around town like a warrior, but now you take a step back. You have an obligation to this community. To the people who look at you like a savior."

"Jesus Christ, Charlotte," Sarah exclaimed with her back to her friend. Her hands had stopped folding and hanging clothes for the first time in the last twenty minutes. They sat, still holding a yellow silk dress that hung loosely in her grip. The long flowing skirt fluttered slightly in the air, moving through a vent in a nearby wall. "I am not Jesus, or God hims..." A loud slam and the tinkle of a little bell cut off Sarah. Both women jumped and spun around. Sarah's heart beat in her throat.

"Oh, dear me. We didn't mean to slam the door," said Eileen Connors. "The wind outside.... Well..." The late-thirties former homecoming queen stood in the door with the same surprised look on her face as Sarah and Charlotte. Her daughter, Lindsey, stood behind her and peered over her shoulder at the scene as the silence descended even deeper, going from uncomfortable to awkward. It stopped short of damaging, thanks to Eileen. "Everything all right? Are we too late? Lindsey here needs a dress."

"Not at all," Sarah said as she put down the dress she was folding and hastily moved toward the door. Her eyes cut in Charlotte's direction as she passed. She extended her hand toward Lindsey, who shied away from taking it for a few seconds, before finally accepting. "There are plenty still left, might take a bit to find it in all of this, but we will take our time to find you the perfect gown."

Lindsey was the opposite of her mother in every way. Not that she was not pretty. She was gorgeous. Red hair, blue eyes, corrected perfect smile, and just the hint of freckles to give her lily-white complexion a hint of character and glow. A picture of Americana. The 'girl next door' with that little something extra, but she was quiet. Not at all the outgoing person her mother is. To be fair, many felt she didn't have any other choice than to become a shriveled flower under the shadow cast by her mother. Her mother was the former homecoming queen, Miss Crooked Road 1997 and, as she always reminded everyone, 11th runner up to Miss Virginia 1998. She never explained to anyone how she figured out she was the 11th runner up. Only the top three are ever revealed, but few questioned her, or her stature as a local celebrity. Only her personality was larger than her stardom. She lit up a room when she walked in. Even if it was full of doom and gloom, as the shop headed toward, she pulled it out of the depths of despair. It was said around town to never have a funeral without inviting her.

For the moment, with the shop all to herself, Sarah treated Lindsey like a beauty queen, and helped her find the perfect dress. They perused the racks, and the random dresses still scattered on the floor. There was a slight murmur at the front of the store, where Charlotte and Eileen, a woman old enough to be their own mother, gossiped like two old hens at Ruthie's Perm and Clip. Sarah ignored them and kept her attention on the young girl. Well, mostly, one eye kept looking over at the two, and couldn't help but notice how they seemed to look in her direction most of the time. The volume and intensity of their gossip spilled over in her direction, causing a ball of tension to build inside of her, and it swelled and pulsate in her core.

With five dresses selected, Sarah set Lindsey up in a dressing room and then found a comfortable spot to lean against on the opposite wall, while she waited. Eileen joined her to wait and help provide her judgement on each dress, which was the only one that counted. The gossip didn't stop, it only changed locations, which now allowed Sarah to hear what they were talking about. At first, she stayed quiet and let the two keep going. This wasn't the first time, and would not be the last time, but this was different. Maybe it was the conversation Eileen and her daughter walked in on that had started the little ball of tension in the pit of Sarah's stomach, and hearing the murmur from them, with the looks in her direction gave it the power to grow. Now hearing what, exactly, they were talking about sent it bouncing up and down at a furious pace. Each bounce sent it closer to escaping up and out of her mouth. The last bounce broke out and she said, "That's enough, you two. You know I am standing right here."

Both stopped and their mouths clamped shut as they stood there, stunned. Sarah looked straight ahead at the dressing room door. "My family are people just like you, and everyone else in this town," she said.

There was no immediate reply from any of them, sending the shop into an uncomfortable silence for the second time in an hour. Just like the first one, they were saved by the opening of a door. The look on Lindsey's face said it all as she walked out in a white knee-length dress, with simple pearl beads sown in to give color and texture. Not a word was spoken by the three women as the girl turned in front of the mirror while biting her lip. Her eyes searched her reflection for anything that would change her mind, but nothing did, and it was obvious when she turned around toward the others. Her mother held out a single thumbs down, sending her daughter back into the dressing room to try on her next selection. Lindsey didn't protest, instead, she provided an affirmation, "I should have known not to select a white one." The door clicked closed.

"Sorry, Sarah," said Eileen. "It is hard for those of us that have been here for a while, and heard all the stories, not to look at your family like some kind of savior. Times were dark while your family was gone. Now, with this abomination found in the woods, everyone will be looking for you guys more."

"I get that, just don't expect too much. We are human and people just like you."

"Fair enough," she said.

"And you, don't go around spreading any kind of stories, please?", Sarah asked Charlotte, who just nodded.

"What do you think it means?"

"What do you mean?"

"That display you all found. What does it mean?", asked Eileen.

"I don't know. Most likely nothing," replied Sarah.

"Wendall Lockridge said he heard it was done by a hunter who wanted to summon a demon to help him hunt."

Sarah laughed and said, "You tell Wendall if he tries to do that, chances are the demon will hunt him."

"Jen Frye, over on Randolph Street said she heard it was a bunch of bored teens repeating something they saw in a movie," said Charlotte.

"That is probably closer to the truth than any of the other guesses I have heard over the last few days. Maybe I should tell my dad to assign more homework to solve the boredom problem."

A panicked response of "Please don't," exploded out of the dressing room, creating a moment of shared laughter among the three women.

"All I know is, we all feel better with you and your father around. You guys will keep us safe."

Sarah felt an inexplicable feeling of illness at that statement that caught her off guard. It had the taste of repulsiveness, mixed with hatred, as it climbed up her throat, but never emerged higher. A few quick swallows ensured it returned down from where it came. What had caused it was still a mystery as she said, "We will try."

Sarah was considering the possibility of the stress of that responsibility as Lindsey emerged in a low-cut, pink, form-fitting number. The smile on the girl's face told the rest what her thoughts of the dress were. Too bad, she had only made it out of the room a few feet before her mother said, "Absolutely not! Might as well just walk around with your boobs out in the open. Go back and change." Lindsey turned and stomped back in. The door slammed against its own lock and bounced back into the teen, much to the amusement of her mother.

"You must think we are all silly. You and your father have skills and abilities. There is no chance anyone who doesn't know what they are doing can really cause any trouble."

Sarah nodded her head and said, "Very true," in the best reassuring-sounding voice she could muster. The whole time, her eyes were focused on Charlotte, who had a very nervous look on her face.

13

"People believe in that stuff?", Jacob asked his father. He rarely took an interest in whatever his father was doing when he was camped at the dining room table amidst stacks of papers and books. What pre-teen and now teenage boy would take an interest in the grading of papers on Henry David Thoreau? There are cool jobs for a parent to have, and there is teaching. Jacob had adjusted to it a little better than Sarah had. His cool, what Jacob called a hobby, didn't hurt.

"Some," said his father, from behind the stack of books. This was more of his light reading on demonology and the darker subjects. Something he had looked into before but, thanks to the events of last weekend, he had found a renewed interest in. "People believe in a range of religions. Your Western Civilization class covered that, I believe."

"Yeah, but this?"

"Yeah, this. Religion is just a set of beliefs one holds so dear they worship and put above themselves. There are hundreds of them around the world. This one is no different. It just carries a stigma that most of the world either look down on or fear. When you really look at it, cannibalism and head-shrinking are forms of religion. What is sacred and acceptable to some, might disgust to others."

Jacob said, "I guess." He remembered covering the most popular forms of religion during Mr. Macey's World History class last year, and he made a similar point to what his father had. It was foreign to his brain to consider Satanic rituals the same as Communion in church. Time, and he guessed experience, was what was needed to get to the place his father was on this topic. So far, his father had shared a little of that side of the world with him, but had yet to go too in depth, or take him along when he and Father Murray headed out to handle a situation.

    Not that he hadn't asked. He had, almost every time they left, since he was thirteen. Well, except that month or so stretch during the summer two years ago. Jacob had his first full-on experience that summer. He knew he had felt them a little for years before, but nothing like this. The times before were just the feeling that something was there, or something was watching him. A feeling most people might just chalk up to getting the creeps, but something deep inside of him knew differently. Then, a late evening in June, while the last rays of sunlight still illuminated the horizon, he felt a cold chill down his spine, followed by the sensation of hundreds of needles plunging into his skin. While his body had processed those feelings, his mind struggled with the presence, or lack thereof, it felt. There was something there, but not at the same time, it was more like a void. A big dark hole, and the emptiness, brought a fear he hadn't felt before. It took him several weeks before he told his father about the incident, which prompted the second father-son talk they had. The first being about the birds and the bees. The second, about spirits and demons, was the easier of the two for Edward.

Jacob leaned back in a chair, opposite his father, at the dining room table. His attention was focused on the pages of the book he flipped through, which was just the latest of the books his father had moved from the 'to be read' pile and to the 'looked through' pile. The pages were full of satanic and occult symbology. Some were obvious, such as the upside-down cross and the pentagram, but seeing some of the symbols, such as the pyramid and all-seeing eye, which is labeled as the Eye of Horus in the book, was rather surprising to him. *"What is an occult symbol doing on our dollar bills?"*, he asked himself. His eyes continued to scan the page, and found other, similar, common symbols and then noticed a link. At least at the symbolic level. Common symbols, just oriented differently, have a new meaning in the world of the occult. He thought about this on a deeper level and understood how that would make it easy to hide occult references in common sight. To one person, the symbol meant one thing, but something different to others.

"Dad, there is a dark presence in the house," announced Jacob.

Edward's head shot up from his study, but relaxed when he heard the door slam.

"It's getting closer, and it is really evil," said Jacob.

"Funny, squirt," Sarah said, with a slap to the back of his head. She reached over and grabbed the book he was reading. "Interesting school assignment. I don't remember a class on the Occult when I was in school."

"Just doing some research. Father Murray is doing some of the same," Edward said.

"Dad, symbols are just a tool. It is the intent of the person using it that worries me," Sarah said.

Her father just nodded.

"Anyway, I am exhausted. Took forever to clean up the store. I am going to take a shower and relax."

Edward looked at his phone and then asked, "I didn't realize it was so late. What about dinner?"

"Already ate. Actually, I let Judy close up so I could grab some takeout for Kevin, and ate with him."

"How is he doing?", asked Edward. He placed the book he was looking through on the top of the pile to his right. Jacob, spying an opportunity to snag another book, grabbed it, and was now flipping through it. He was not sure if his father was done with it, but he had put it down, and that made it fair game in his book.

"Okay, I guess. There are times he doesn't seem to be himself. Still doesn't remember what happened to him."

"Dang. I still can't shake the feeling this is all related. I would like to talk to him again, when he is ready."

"Well," Sarah started using a tone that usually meant she was asking permission for something that normally would be refused. Jacob made a habit of mocking this tone every chance he could get, and then reveled in their father's refusal of whatever she was asking for, but not this time. His focus was on the book, but his ears were listening to the surrounding conversation.

"He could come over for dinner. He hasn't left his parents' house since he got out of the hospital Monday afternoon. They won't let him. I am sure they would be okay if he was coming over here."

Edward eagerly agreed, "Okay."

"Tomorrow?" Sarah asked before her father completed his reply.

"Not sure tomorrow will be good. Tomorrow is the homecoming dance. I have to chaperone, and your brother will be there. How about Sunday?"

"Tomorrow is fine, we don't need you there," Jacob said. His eyes looked at his father over the top of the book he was reading.

"Nonsense," Edward said. "It's my job." A wide smile garnished his face.

Jacob's eyes dropped back to the page. He didn't think his father would go for it, but had seen the opportunity and tried. Not that it bothered him if he was there or not.

"Okay, Sunday," Sarah agreed, reluctantly.

"Great. I will see if the father can come, too," Edward said.

"A priest... witnesses... family.. we can get them hitched before dessert," Jacob said, drawing another slap on top of his head from his sister.

14

Jacob may handle being a student at the same school as his father better than Sarah had, but that didn't mean it was something he was "cool" with in all situations. There was a hierarchy of tolerance. Sarah had it too, but the reactions that went with each tier were less severe with Jacob.

School was the first level. The avoidance Edward experienced from his daughter was replaced by the open recognition, and the occasional high-five, as he passed his son and his friends in the hall.

School events, such as football games, were level two. The group of friends all gathered around Edward, cheering and talking sports, was a departure from the avoidance of the leper he saw from his daughter. That might be a guy thing. Age and parental status seem to disappear between guys at a sporting event. Either only appear during the discussion of the various principles of the game. Most Jacob's friends are always calling for their team to pass the ball. An influence from the video game age. Unless you had a rare talent at quarterback, a solid running game was the most likely path to success at the high school level. A fact that never seemed to sink in with the younger generation, even after a disappointing loss.

The last level, and the one with the most penal reaction, was at different school events, school social events. Exhibit A, the homecoming dance. A place where parents were not only not desired, but not allowed. Hundreds of sets of eyes roll, and thousands of sighs exhale out, contributing to the level of greenhouse gases in the environment, as they tolerated parents for that ever-treasured photo of their children, and their date, all dressed up. Several die second deaths if the parents mess up the first photo and have to take a second. That is where it ended for most. Unless your parent was a teacher who had to chaperone. The torture continued throughout the night. Sometimes ground rules were put in place, which was the case in the Meyer household. When Sarah went to the homecoming dance her senior year, there was a list ten rules long. Jacob went simple, he was always the simpler child, those rules were: I won't embarrass you. You won't embarrass me. They seemed mutually agreeable, which is why Edward stayed away from the balloon-arched entryway until Jacob and his date entered.

It wasn't hard to spot them upon entry. Jacob was one of the taller students at the school, but that wasn't what caused him to stand out this time.

The turquoise and hot pink paisley print bowtie and cummerbund he had ordered online picked up stray beams from the various black lights positioned around the gym. The visual effect was not intentional. Neither was his attempt to be flamboyant. A word that should never be used to describe Jacob. His date, Molly Webster, was indecisive about her dress and changed every other day. Something her mother indulged by buying both of the dresses she had liked. To make sure they matched, Jacob ordered a bowtie and cummerbund set that contained both colors.

      For the entire evening, Edward, and an army of twenty teachers, walked around the outer ring of the gym, monitoring what happened inside their ring. Nothing was added to the punch bowl to give it a bit more punch. It seemed to just be a fixture from tradition, and not a source of refreshment anyway. The attendees opted for soft drinks, or just water, more often than anyone ladled up the sweet red syrup. The six-inch rule given birth to in the forties was just the talk of legend, not one anyone enforced. Only if there was some excessive bump and grind action going on would there be a polite tap on the shoulder, but that would be it.

      The music pounded for hours on end. Edward took a few breaks and walked outside, or into one of the adjoining hallways. The thump of the bass was still audible below the ringing that would last for hours after the dance ended. Even when the music was turned off to announce the homecoming court, there was a constant ring, and a subconscious thump of bass. With the court crowned, and no pig's blood raining down from above, the music kicked up again, the dancing resumed, as did the duties of the chaperones.

      "I never went to homecoming," Cheryl Avery leaned in and said over the sound of the music. The sophomore English teacher grew up in Miller's Crossing and had attended this very high school. "It was my bad luck, always had strep throat. Every single year."

      "Wow," said Edward.

      "Yeah, the doc thought it might have been fall allergies that started it."

      Edward felt he needed to share a story, but couldn't share the truth. To this day, only three people in town knew the truth of where he was during his high school years. This was neither the time nor the place to share, *"I didn't either. I was in a mental hospital. Not allergy related."* Still feeling the need to share he said, "I don't remember much about the dances, but the homecoming games I do."

      "What are you guys talking about?", asked Mark Grier, who was passing by on one of his hundred or more loops he had made around the gym that night.

      "Reminiscing about our homecomings," Cheryl said.

      "Well, I can say nothing we did is going on here tonight. Not a single person has tried to empty a flask into the punch bowl. Something I did twice in one year, I might add. We have found no couples in any of the dark corners that I remember from when I was a student. Seems kind of boring to me."

"I like it that way," said Edward.

Mark slapped him on the shoulder and said, "You would, old friend." Then he resumed his patrol for the night. He was one of the few that was still walking around. The night was winding down, and there was not much the chaperones had to handle during the night. A few even joined the students out on the dance floor. Something Edward had considered, but knew it would break the second of his and Jacob's two rules. So, he stood back with the other teachers and enjoyed the music as they watched a few of their colleagues attempt to reclaim their youth. The concerns of the past week were gone from Edward's mind. No images of animal heads on sticks, or pentagrams drawn in blood. Just a slice of small town America. Happiness, and the cold prick of a needle.

Edward's head whipped around the room. He saw nothing but the happy scene he had seen just moments ago. There was another needle prick, and another frantic search around, but still, nothing. Not what he expected. When the chill hit him, he looked again, and this time looked above him and caught sight of an air conditioner vent above his head. He felt a little silly, and brushed it off to being tired, the dark lighting, and the loud music.

A bloodcurdling scream rammed through the entry and into the gym, freezing those dancing. The music continued, but no one moved. Then a few teachers hurried in the door's direction. Edward took a step forward, watched, and waited. The next sight he saw at the door sent him into a full run across the dance floor, bouncing off students who didn't clear the way in time. Each step caused another pinprick, then another, and then another, until his entire spine tingled and crawled. Gooseflesh developed along the back of his neck by the time he reached Jacob, who stood at the door waving for him to hurry. Together they ran out the door that was choked off by students who stood around and gawked at the scene outside.

They pushed through into a scene that sent Edward flashing back to the football field, eight years ago. These were not ghosts, they were demons. Their bodies were a hellish cross of animals, humans, and something Edward's mind couldn't find a comparison for. Their screeches rattled the world to its core. They were poised on top of cars. With each step or stomp they took, the roofs bent or caved ominously low above the students trapped inside. The car windows muffled their screams, but the terror on their faces was visible through the clear glass.

One, larger than all the others, was positioned in the middle of the parking lot. Its placement, blocked any attempt to escape. Not that anyone had tried to drive with the others perched on top. You could run to safety, but no one in the cars or in the gym had made any attempt to escape. Fear, not the demons, trapped them.

Jacob moved toward one car, to help his friends. Edward screamed, "Jacob, no!" He stopped in his tracks as a demon hopped off the car and hissed at him. It then turned back to the car and put a single claw under it. With a simple move of its arm, it flipped the car over on its roof. Shards of blue safety glass from the windows and windshield scattered out, away from the car, letting out the screams of the teens as they rolled with the car and then landed in silence on the roof.

The larger one, with cloven hoofs and the disfigured upper body of a man, walked forward. Its gait was smooth and rhythmic, but his arm movements were gangly and awkward. Both arms were different lengths and sizes. Its head had facial features, but none of them were in the correct place, or correct size. One eye was bigger than the other. The mouth didn't fit the face at all. To Edward it looked like it was made of the various parts of different people. That also explained the sound it made when it looked up and screamed. It wasn't one or two voices. It was dozens. Each uttering a different command. Each targeted to one other, who subserviently obeyed and began ripping at the sheet metal of the car roofs they stood on.

"Stop!" yelled Edward, as he held up the cross he always carried neatly tucked in the pocket of the tweed jacket, that he wore everywhere.

Each did as he commanded and turned their attention to him. It was times like this, Edward wished he had thought things through before he took action. He had done this before, but that was just with a single spirit. Easier to handle, and no need to back down. There was a portion of him that feared for his life at this moment, and he felt his weight rock backward as his gave ground to them. A lesson Father Murray had told him once, and then was reaffirmed by Sarah, yelled back at him, and he took a step forward, and then another. A slight glow began in the center of the cross and traversed out the crossbar. Inside, Edward prayed a deep prayer. This wasn't one from the book. The book was still tucked in his pocket. It wasn't one he had memorized from the book, or anything similar to any of the ones his father, grandfather, or any other Meyer had ever used. It was his own. His own approach and spin. Something he had come up with thanks to the guidance he had received from Father Lucian, and his own experimenting. The words had yet to be written in the book. At least he hadn't written it word for word. He didn't need to. It would mislead the next holder of this responsibility. There was an addition to the book. A single blank page now had three words written on it: "Empower Your Faith!" At that moment, Edward was reciting a personal prayer to empower his own faith.

With every word he whispered, the glow became brighter. His eyes stayed locked on the creature in the parking lot. The others were not his concern, not yet. They obeyed this creature, and this creature was who he dealt with.

Edward broke his prayer and ordered, "Jacob, get back to the gym!"

"But, Dad!"

"No buts..." Edward interrupted. He needed to remove his son from harm's way before what was next. He would have to get closer to the creature and make contact with it. That was what his one and only encounter with a demonic presence had taught him. He hoped the light froze them, like before, which would make it easier, but it hadn't. The creature moved forward, curious of the cross, not afraid.

"Demon, you are not permitted here. Our Lord and Savior Jesus Christ gave his life for the forgiveness of our sins, not yours. You are a vile creature that is not allowed in the realm of our lord."

If Edward had to list the 100 different reactions he expected, what happened wouldn't even come close to making that list. The dozens of voices that had barked orders moments before seemed to laugh, not from the creature, but from above. Then it turned and jumped a hundred yards away, followed by the others. Another jump sent them into the tree line. Their screams and screeches faded to nothing but a distant echo.

The thump of the music continued behind Edward and several screams emerged as teens opened their car doors and fell out on the ground in hysterical masses of humanity.

15

The mood in the Meyer's house was as dark and dank as the weather outside. While the rain pelted the windows and side of the house, the details of the previous night beat on Edward's thoughts like the music from the dance. The wind whipped and howled outside. The screams of the teenagers replaced the dull ringing from a night of loud music. Lightning flashed and thunder boomed across the farmland. The car flipped over and over, all night long and throughout the day. Each time landing in a thunderous crunch of steel and glass.

Adding to it, not a person spoke to anyone throughout the day. All talking ceased after a brief conversation between Edward and Sarah, when she returned home after them. He explained to her what happened, wanting her feedback. Her interpretation. She was the only one of the three who was properly trained in these matters. It was something Edward would never admit openly, but he felt inferior to his daughter. It wasn't just because of the training she had. From the moment she had shown the ability, she was not only more capable, but she handled it better. There was a quiet confidence and calm that exuded from her, even in the most stressful of situations. Not a bead of sweat, or moment of tension in her voice. She was calm and cool. That was where he felt inferior. He had years on her in experience, in both life and his spiritual involvements. His past life was anything but smooth, which he always felt prepared him to handle the little bumps that appeared in the grand plan of his life. Even though some events still got to him. Still pushed his stress level to a point of distraction and self-doubt. Both were dangerous at the wrong time.

The events of the night rattled him. His story rambled back and forth, and he often stopped mid-sentence to back up and add a detail to something he had said minutes earlier. The speed of Edward's words picked up as the stress level in him increased, but he was the only one. The tone, speed, and meaning of his daughter's words remained calm and consistent, even when she corrected him. He finished recalling the details, in as vivid and lifelike detail as he could. Even his heart believed the retelling and pounded inside his chest. He sat and watched his daughter for a reaction. She had none. Was she even listening to him? Did she not hear him tell her about the demons, and the flipping of the car? What about how they reacted, or didn't react, to his presence? He wanted her take on things, her trained impression. Why wasn't she saying anything? These were the questions that bounced around inside his head during what he felt was the minutes or longer since he had finished telling her. It only seemed that way because of his excited state. Actually, it had been mere seconds.

Sarah broke her silence and asked, with the same calm demeanor Edward had become jealous of, "Nothing? They didn't move back, or act frightened of you at all?"

Confounded, Edward said, "Not even at the light."

Much to his disappointment, the rest of their conversation didn't shed any light. Nothing they taught her, or any of the cases she had studied, were like this. After half an hour, both reached the same conclusion. This was something new. To Edward, it was new and troubling.

With all the distractions rolling in his head, he had a long day of cleaning, and then cooking to prepare for a dinner that was also new and troubling. His daughter, his princess, was bringing over a guy to meet the family. This had never happened before, and Edward didn't know how to react. Should he be friendly, be the over-protective parent and sit and leer at him in judgement, or maybe study every movement the young man made?

Other than television, which he hated to admit inspired certain aspects of his parenting, his only experience in this matter was from the vantage point of the young man. Karen's father had him under a microscope from the moment he entered. The handshake lasted a little longer than Edward was comfortable with. Edward was never sure why, but human contact was something he always found uncomfortable. Without a logical explanation, he chalked it up to his years in the hospital, with the only contact occurring when blood samples were needed. This time there was a slight tightening of pressure in the grip, as if to check his. He remembered his father once saying you could tell a lot about a man by his handshake. Karen's father was trying to get the entire report out of this one. For the rest of the evening, Edward felt his eyes on him. A fact that was reinforced every time Edward looked at him. That sensation has a way of unnerving even the most confident person, not that Edward was. He became subconscious about how he chewed, placed his hands on the table, gripped his fork and, worst of all, looked at Karen. Each time he glanced in her direction he thought he heard the gruff voice of her father say, *"Keep your lust-filled eyes off of my baby girl."*

The appearance of a spectral visitor behind Karen's mother while they sat at the table drinking coffee was absolutely the worst timing he had ever experienced. Edward had to fight every instinct inside him to not look at it for longer than just a glance. There was no predicting how her father would interrupt him staring off into space. *Karen, is your date on drugs or something?* Her father was not physically intimidating. He was actually smaller in stature than Edward, balding, wore glasses, and talked with a bit of a lisp. It was his role in that engagement that created the tension.

Edward could only predict that it would be the same tonight. Kevin Stierers was a young man he was familiar with. Only seven years ago, he was a student in his class. A well-mannered boy, with a lot of pride in his schoolwork. Something Edward could tell right away. English and literature were not subjects that had an abundance of tutoring or after class requests. Not like math and science, where someone might misunderstand a formula or theorem, which can easily be corrected. They were objective. Edward's subjects were more subjective. Especially when he taught creative writing. Which made it even more curious when students stayed behind for questions. The names of those students stuck with him. Kevin was one. He had received a C- on a creative writing project. It was a 5,000 word story, on the topic of their choice. Upon receiving the paper back, Kevin stayed after class to understand the source of the grade. Edward explained, he could tell all the different breaks Kevin took while writing it. The voice changed during each. So, for an hour after school that day, they discussed the story and how it could have been written in each of the different voices.

The good impression he had of Kevin helped, but didn't change that this would be a new role, a new interaction, and it had been several years since he had last spoke to the young man, other than just a hello in passing in town. Edward also knew, while he needed to be protective of Sarah, he couldn't take it too far. He wanted Kevin to be comfortable. There was still what had happened to him that night that Edward wanted to discuss and find out more about.

The distractions in his head only led to a few mistakes while cleaning, and one while cooking, when a pot boiled over while on the stove. Both of which drew a minor explosion inside. Each time Sarah pitched in to help pick up the bag of trash he dropped, or grab the pot, while Edward kept preparing the roast. She was as calm as a cucumber.

At a quarter after seven, there was a knock on the door. The doorbell hadn't worked since Edward was a child. Edward walked out of the kitchen to answer the door, but Sarah sprinted down the stairs past him. She looked nice. This was not the half cut-off shirt and shorts that matched the definition of the word that she usually wore when going out. This was a long flowing skirt, a white cardigan sweater which Edward didn't know she owned, and flats. No boots with heels. No three inch or higher heels. His heart fluttered for a moment as she looked and moved liker her mother, minus the dark hair that she got from her father.

"Be nice," she warned both her father, standing in the kitchen's door, and Jacob, who sat on the sofa watching television.

She opened the door, and a scene out of the 1950s strolled in. Kevin, dressed in his Sunday best suit and tie, stood there with flowers in his hand. The only thing missing was a black and white hue to it, and a toothy grin on Kevin as he greeted him with a very sappy, "Good evening, Mr. Meyer." Instead, Kevin walked in and gave Sarah the flowers and a hug. Then he walked forward and extended his hand to Edward, who still stood in the doorway to the kitchen, with a dishrag in one hand.

"Hi, Mr. Meyer," Kevin said.

Edward took his hand, "Hi, Kevin. It's good to see you." The handshake was firm and confident. A good start.

"I probably look a lot different than when you last saw me?", asked Kevin.

That he did, but Edward didn't know how to respond, and must have looked as confused on the outside as he felt on the inside.

"I mean in the hospital. My family and I are thankful that you and Father Murray came and checked on me."

"Glad you are feeling better Kevin," Edward said, with a bit of relief. Kevin was not responsive when they had visited him. He was not sure if Kevin had even realized they were there. There was a chance he was talking about the change in appearance since high school. The longer haired, t-shirt wearing student was now the suit-wearing man standing in his living room, holding his daughter's hand.

"I still have a few things to finish up for dinner. Make yourself at home," Edward said.

"Thank you, sir."

Before walking back into the kitchen, Edward offered, "Can I get you a drink or something? Some soda, water, maybe coffee?"

"No, sir, I am good."

Edward pushed through the door to the kitchen, leaving them in the living room. Behind him, he heard Sarah and Kevin talking and then heard, "Heya Jake, nice game. I played a bit of fall league myself."

The four of them enjoyed a dinner that didn't stretch Edward's rather limited culinary abilities. A roast that basically cooked itself once the oven was set, with rice and vegetables that only required him to boil water. During the meal, Edward tried not to put too much of a spotlight on their guest. Conversation took to normal topics, such as his job at the local mill. Remember when's; talking about people and events from when he was in Edward's class, and sports. A given topic when there are three males sitting around a table, much to Sarah's dislike. Sarah's dislike appeared more than Edward would have expected, and it didn't go unnoticed by Kevin. To say there was an odd vibe between the two of them would be a fair description.

Simple questions such as, "So, Kevin, how long have you been at the mill?" Something any father would ask, with no ulterior motives behind it, other than making sure he could be a good provider for his baby. This simple question didn't draw a look of embarrassment, or any daggers from daughter aimed at the father. Instead, there was a visible look of stun, followed by a pause from Kevin, before he looked at Sarah for, what appeared to be affirmation or permission, before answering. That happened after every question. The deeper or more probing the question was, the more Kevin looked uncomfortable. He looked down at his lap, and then at Sarah.

When Edward asked how they met, Kevin stared down at his lap, biting his bottom lip to the point of discoloration. There was a single long exhale before he looked at Sarah with a pained expression. Their eyes met, and his mouth opened, but nothing came out. Sarah immediately jumped in and said, "It was just a random meeting two months ago. We hadn't seen each other since school and bumped into each other. I was closing up the boutique when he was walking by."

"Wow, that is a chance meeting. Didn't think anything like that could happen. Seems you bump into everyone at least once a month around here."

They shared another look. Sarah's pained and uncomfortable. Kevin's was a complete lack of confidence. "I know. I was so busy at the mill, I didn't make it to town much," Kevin said and then took a long sip of his iced tea.

As the conversation returned to topics that were less contentious, the visible level of discomfort and anxiety reduced in their guest. It melted away completely when he and Jacob engaged in a discussion about baseball, both their playing days and favorite professionals. Edward took that moment to clear the table and take the spotlight off of Kevin for a few moments. Sarah helped her father.

It was on the second trip into the kitchen when Edward asked, "Is Kevin feeling all right?"

"Yes, why?", Sarah asked, annoyed, while she scraped a plate into the trash can.

"He just seems uncomfortable."

Sarah finished rinsing off the dish and placed it in the sink. She walked to the kitchen door and pushed it open. The sound of two people in a very lively debate, filled with laughter, leaked through into the kitchen. "He seems comfortable to me." She released the door, letting it swing shut.

"Yeah, now. But not earlier when we were talking."

Over the sound of running water as Sarah rinsed the remaining plates, she explained, "Come on Dad. It is because of you. Guys are nervous when they meet their girlfriend's father. I am sure you were nervous when you met Grandpa."

Edward was nervous, but not to the level he had just seen. It could just be that, or maybe that combined with what Kevin had been through just over a week ago. That could explain it, but Edward couldn't shake the feeling Kevin wasn't being honest. His mind lingered there, doing what it does best and worst. They say your brain has two sides, a logical and a creative. One side is usually stronger than the other. Most would think, with Edward's affinity for reading, the creative would be strongest, but he was quite the opposite. He had a very strong logical side, that tried to search for explanations. The equally strong creative side always participated, resulting in some rather interesting roller coaster rides that threatened to defy logic. At this moment, his logical and creative sides were struggling to balance each other out as they formulated what might be the truth about how they met. A truth that a father might not approve of. Maybe a friend's party, where the drinking got a little out of hand, and things went a little... Edward stopped his mind from finishing that sentence. It was uncomfortable just thinking about it. He couldn't imagine how it would feel explaining that to the girl's father. In the same situation, he might come up with the same clichéd story.

16

Edward sat back down at the table with a cup of coffee. Something he had just become used to after dinner. He found it made him feel more relaxed. Not at all what you would think. To him, it was a sign that his addiction to caffeine was far stronger than he believed. Not that he would try to cut back anytime soon. Anyone that tried might have to pry his hand off his cup in the morning or in the evenings. Good luck to them if they tried.

The joyous conversation he walked in on continued for a few minutes after he sat down. He didn't try to contribute. There was no way he was as much of a baseball aficionado as Jacob was. That kid ate, slept, dreamt, and breathed baseball. Anything Edward would attempt to contribute here most likely would be wrong, leading to Jacob's embarrassment. Embarrassing one child tonight was enough. Even though there was something in Edward that liked the challenge.

The conversation volleyed back and forth between Jacob and Kevin until they ran out of topics. Kevin appeared to be much more comfortable than he had earlier. Each answer, question, and topic flowed freely. Never any attempt to check with Sarah before saying anything. Not that she could provide any affirmation on this topic, she knew less than Edward did. She spent her time at Jacob's games focused on her phone's screen.

That changed when the baseball chatter wound down, and the bottom of Edward's coffee cup appeared. There was a brief, and semi-awkward silence, signaling the end of the conversation. Edward took it as an opportunity to jump in with his own topic. One that was not nearly as lively as the prior, and guaranteed to be more uncomfortable. He asked Jacob to excuse them for a minute, telling him he wanted to talk to Kevin alone. The immature "oooo" he let out as he got up and left the table struck like a hot poker into his sister's side, but the sting didn't last long. That, or she just ignored it. She immediately asked, "Mind if I stay?" Edward saw no harm in that and agreed.

He leaned forward and rested both of his forearms on the table, with his hands cupping his coffee cup. He knew he needed to tread lightly on this topic. What happened was obviously traumatic to Kevin. Anyone with any common sense, that saw him that day in the hospital, would know that. They would also be surprised to see that same catatonic individual sitting there in front of him as if nothing ever happened. That tipped Edward's suspicion that there was more than just shock at play. That a presence, of some type, had draped that condition over Kevin. That same presence could pull it away just as quickly. What that presence was? That was the question Edward needed to know. With the proximity of where they found Kevin, and the other oddities, he would be a fool to not suspect a connection.

There was no easy way to start, so he just went for it. "Kevin, I want to ask you some questions about the other day in the woods, if that is okay?"

Edward waited for an answer. The confident and joyful young man, that had just been rambling on about baseball with Jacob moments ago, was gone. Replacing him was the sullen and shrinking person that now sat across the table. Even the color drained from his face. He looked over at Sarah and then down again. She reached over and grabbed his hand. Again, he looked at her, and she whispered, "It's okay. Just answer what you can." Edward could see she squeezed his hand as she did.

"Kevin, you don't have to. But if you can, it would help. I believe everything is related. The more I know, the more I can put things together. Do you understand?"

Kevin's eyes said no, but his mouth said, "Sure."

"What can you tell me about that night?"

Kevin sat there, with the appearance of being lost in thought, as he tried to remember. Sarah leaned in closer, as if to comfort him, as he went through a struggle both could sense. The twitches of his jaw, back and forth in rapid succession, told of his mind recalling the events of the evening in vivid detail. The detail was disturbing and took a toll. Lines formed and crinkled across his forehead. The speed of the jaw twitching increased. The eyes looked at no one and everyone, all at the same time. Muscles in his forearm jerked under the skin as he squeezed Sarah's hand and then released it. She squeezed back, and he glanced in her direction.

"Well, my car stopped for no reason. Which was strange. I had plenty of gas, and both the lights and radio were still on. I tried to call for help, but didn't have service on my phone, so I got out and started walking. I remember, coming across the bridge there at Walter's Creek, but that's it. I don't remember anything else until I got home from the hospital."

"When you were walking, did any cars pass you?", asked Edward.

"No," Kevin said, with a shake of the head, after looking at Sarah.

"Anyone else out walking?"

Again, another look at Sarah, and then a shake of the head.

"Did you fall, maybe down the embankment? That area along the bridge is pretty steep," Edward asked, knowing good and well he didn't fall down the embankment. He was reaching, trying to help Kevin remember what happened.

"No. I remember walking across the bridge, and a ways past."

"What is the last thing you remember at all that night? Even just a flash?", Edward asked, sounding half agitated. He caught himself and checked his body posture to appear friendlier. The attempt appeared halfhearted on the exterior. He had leaned back away from the table, but his posture still maintained a forward lean toward Kevin.

Again, he looked at Sarah before he answered. The answer he gave was not much of one, "Dark."

"Dark?", asked Edward.

"Dark and quiet," Kevin answered, this time without looking at Sarah first. This prompted a squeeze of his hand. He glanced in her direction and smiled. "It was quiet. Oddly quiet, Mr. Meyer. That is what I remember last. No wind. No crickets. Not even the sound of the creek, which wasn't that far behind me. And then..." he trailed off and then glanced at Sarah again.

"And then what Kevin?"

"I don't know," he said timidly, while looking down at the table. "I don't know. I don't remember anything until I woke up at home."

"Do you remember being in the hospital?"

"No sir. The bracelet on my right arm was the only thing that told me I was there for sure."

17

"So he survived?", Charlotte asked.

"Yep, he did," said Sarah after a healthy sip of red wine from her goblet.

"I remember when Dan came over to meet my family. That boy had sweat through his shirt before he got to the door. His hands were shaking so bad when he reached for my dad's, I thought he would miss."

Charlotte reached over to pour more wine in Sarah's goblet. They were sitting in her living room on the couch together doing their normal debrief after either of them went out on a date. Most of the time it was Charlotte dishing on the details over a glass or two of wine. These sessions changed when she married Dan three years ago. They still got together. They still shared plenty of wine, but the topics were different. Only recently did they return to their roots when Sarah started seeing Kevin.

"Not Kevin," Sarah said. She took another sip of her wine. "He was the perfect gentleman. Walked in, shook my father's hand. It was yes sir, all night long. Even talked with my brother. He handled everything great, even the inquisition by my father."

Charlotte gave her a questioning look.

"About what happened to him that night. My father thinks something spiritual attacked him."

"Wow," gasped Charlotte. "Makes sense. What do you think? You're the expert."

"Not sure. Anything is possible. Kevin remembers nothing from that night, so it is impossible to know for sure."

"It is amazing."

"What is? Stuff like that shouldn't amaze anyone around these parts anymore."

"No, you dork," giggled Charlotte. "His recovery. In just over a week he went from in a coma to meeting your father. Man, talk about both an amazing and traumatic week."

"He wasn't in a coma. Just not responsive, and yes... an amazing recovery."

"I know why," said Charlotte. The statement produced an immediate shocked reaction on Sarah's face. Maybe it was the giggle that accompanied it.

"You do?", asked Sarah. The look on her face changed from shocked to one that looked like she had smelled something sour. Her nose up turned and scrunched. Her eyes leered at her friend.

The reaction caught Charlotte off guard. She was trying to be humorous, but had elicited a reaction from her friend she had never seen before. Even through the years of ribbing each had given the other, never anything like this. Her original comment was setting up a joke, a joke she timidly said the punchline to, "You have him under your spell."

"What spell?", Sarah asked sternly.

Looking for an escape out of the uncomfortable moment, Charlotte considered her options. She could finish the joke and hope it landed well, change the subject, or with her foot knock something off the coffee table that sat in front of her and hope it woke Melissa in the other room to give her an out. Her daughter, Melissa, slept in the other room. It was nap time, and her mother kept her on a very strict schedule. It was good for both baby and mother. Her luck, she had the one baby in the world that could sleep through anything. The scheduled nap time was a time for her get a few things done around the home, which included vacuuming. An activity that never woke her, even when she came close to the nursery door.

That left two options, but the stare from her friend eliminated the second option. There was no way she was going to be able to change the subject, that was clear. That left just one.

"You know. The spell all women cast over men. I know once I gave it up to Dan, that was it. That man would have walked over hot coals and through a lion's den for me." She attempted to cackle, like she remembered hearing Blanche Devereaux on reruns her mom watched of "The Golden Girls." Instead of sounding mature, it came out weak and airy.

There was an uncomfortable silence that hung in the air between the two friends. It lasted long enough for Charlotte to squirm on the sofa before running out of ways to fidget with her hands. What she wouldn't give at that moment for a stack of magazines to straighten on the table, or something to pick up. Her eyes listened for the sound of her daughter in the other room, but all see heard was that silence. She reached forward and poured a little more wine in her goblet. A goblet that was already two-thirds full. She tried an innocent, "Come on, you can tell me?"

To her, Sarah looked like perplexed and conflicted. Her hands jerked for her wine goblet, stopped, then reached again. The contact made was not smooth as she gripped the stem of the glass. It produced ripples in the red liquid.

Having never seen her friend like this, Charlotte took the off ramp in this conversation and apologized, "Sorry. You know me. No topic is off limits."

"It's okay. It's not that," Sarah said.

"What is it? You know you can talk to me about anything Sarah."
"No, I mean I don't have him under that kind of spell."
"Not yet," added Charlotte.

18

"Father, are you around?" Edward bellowed. His call echoed among the rafters of the empty church's cathedral ceiling. Hearing his own voice in front and behind him was off putting. The same with hearing footsteps coming at him from all directions, knowing that he was the only one walking. It was enough to produce a little gooseflesh, even in these well-lit surroundings. He thought he was just being silly, but each time he looked around and caught a scene from one of the oddly different stained-glass windows, that was enough to send his skin crawling again. The next sound made him jump and squeal like a little girl.

"Over here, Edward."

The squeal echoed slightly as Edward composed himself and walked up to the front of the church, and then off to the right vestibule. Seated in a chair, with a rag in one hand and a silver dish in another, was Father Murray. Rubber gloves adorned both hands. The rag whipped around in a furious motion against the silver dish. A few swipes made a squeaking sound as the rag moved across the polished metal.

"What are you doing?", Edward said curiously, drawing out the "are".

"I can cleanse the soul with a prayer, but it takes elbow grease to clean the house of our Lord," he answered with a chuckle. "Once a week I sit down and polish all the silver to keep it looking nice. No fingerprints, see?", he asked, as he held the dish up for Edward to see before putting it down next to him and picking up one of several chalices that sat on the ground next to him. "What brings you by so early on a non-service day?"

"Had a conversation with young Kevin," Edward said.

"Ah, the dinner. I assume he survived dinner?"

"I think so. He walked out on his own two feet. Sarah was on pins and needles all night."

Father Murray's eyes and hands focused on the chalice, which had begun to shine, but his ears were listening, and he giggled at Edward's response. "I bet."

"He doesn't remember anything from that night, though. His car stopped for no reason, and he said his cell phone didn't have a signal."

Father Murray's hands stopped. One hand still held the chalice, and the other pressed the rag against it, but neither moved. His head was still bent down toward his work, but had cocked slightly forward. He asked, "Out of gas?"

"Nope. Said the lights worked and everything. The engine just stopped and wouldn't turn over. I called Marcus and asked, he said it started up fine when they went back to tow it the next day."

His head cocked more in Edward's direction. "No cell coverage?"

"That is what he said. He remembered walking past Walter's Creek, and that was it. Nothing for a few days, until he woke up at home," Edward reported. Before Father Murray could ask another question or make a comment, Edward added, "Oh, and get this. Said It was dark and quiet. No sounds of animals, crickets, or anything."

"There are frogs in that creek. I can hear them over my car when I drive by with my windows open," said Father Murray. The chalice was now on the ground in front of him. The rag was a ball of cloth loosely dropped inside it. The base had a nice clear shine, but the rest of it was still dull and dirty. The wooden chair he sat in groaned as he leaned forward and stood up. He walked past Edward and down the center aisle, without saying a word.

"Father?", Edward asked, confused.

"Come on. I will explain on the way."

Edward followed behind and exited the church as Father Murray closed the driver's side door of his Cadillac. Edward took his familiar position in the passenger seat and, as was common, the car was in motion before his door was closed. His seat belt finally clicked closed just before the tires transitioned off the gravel driveway to the tarmac of the road that ran along the front of the church.

"Father, do you mind telling me where we are going?"

Father Murray leaned down and looked out of the windshield to the sky, then said, "We have a bit of daylight left. We need to pick up Lewis first, and then go check those woods. Earlier today, Rick Stenson, Tom Meville, and Fred Tillman stopped by. Rick promised me a few catfish the next time they were out fishing, and had forgotten to bring them by. He made up for it by bringing a plate of his latest catch, already fried up. But before they stopped by, they were out bow hunting up and down Walter's Creek. They didn't bag anything while out. No game, that is, but came back with some really wild stories. The animals they ran into, raccoons, possums, and even the foxes, didn't run away from them. They followed them."

"Followed?"

"Yeah, followed. Tom said he kept looking behind them and saw the same group following them everywhere they went in the woods, and even back to their truck. They never left the tree line, but appeared to stand there and watch them. But that isn't even the strangest. Not by a long shot. Mind you, these are small animals. A fox is no bigger than a medium-sized dog, at best. They aren't aggressive toward humans, or shouldn't be. If memory serves me, some of those are natural predators to each other. They could have cared less about that, though; they wanted the men. Before they finally pulled off, Rick walked toward the trees to try to scare them all off. He took just three steps before he said each of the animals growled, hissed, and showed their teeth. They never left the woods, but stood their ground. Then, here is where it gets weird. The woods themselves growled and hissed at them."

"Wait. Wait. Wait. The woods, Father? What do you mean, the woods?" stammered Edward, while his body jerked around to face the driver.

"You heard me. He said it sounded like every animal in the woods, all growling at the same time. Now, you and I both know that is not possible, or shouldn't be possible. Just like we've known 99 times out of 100, those animals do everything they can to get away from us, and they most definitely do not follow us."

He was right, and Edward knew it. Considering the strange events lately, he couldn't put anything out of the realm of possibility. One possibility he was hoping for was something a little less odd, and more common. A day out hunting usually involved the consumption of more than adequate levels of alcoholic drinks. Usually of the brown ale variety. He could only hope this trip was no different, and the three men had had a bit too much, maybe even been dipping into someone's homemade shine, and that, combined with their imagination, had got the better of them.

The large white Cadillac slid to a stop in front of Lewis Tillingsly's place. It was a simple log cabin with a wraparound front porch that had two rocking chairs positioned on the longer side of the porch. A sizable place that was deceptive when you looked at it from the outside. Its square shape gave the impression it was small and cramped, but the open concept and light color scheme inside gave it a grand feel. His property was a majestic piece of rolling landscape that had been in the family for over 150 years. An old tobacco farm until the fifties when Lewis' father took to law enforcement and pulled the family out of the agricultural profession. Since he retired, Lewis had toyed around with the idea of returning it to a tobacco farm.

Edward sat still while the car's old springs groaned at the exit of Father Murray. It was the age of the springs, and not the girth of Father Murray, that produced the protest. He disappeared inside, without even appearing to knock on the screen door before going in. The windows were open, and the coolness of a fall afternoon was setting in. A constant symphony of bird calls floated on the pleasant breeze. The gentle rustle of leaves in the trees provided the percussion line under the birds.

Father Murray emerged after a few moments. Lewis Tillingsly was in tow, behind him. They got in the car, the father in the driver's seat and Lewis in the back. He slid in from the driver's side and then to the center of the backseat, then leaned forward, patting Edward on the back.

"So, what grand adventure are we off on now?", he asked.

"He didn't tell you?"

"Nah, just said he needed me to come with him."

"You often get in cars with no idea why or where you are going?", Edward asked, tongue in cheek.

"Yeah, you would think I would know better. So where to, Father?"

"Need to go check out some woods. Edward, tell him what Kevin told you."

Even though there wasn't much to tell, Edward did what he was told. The former sheriff had his law enforcement ears on and asked a few questions. Each of which Edward had asked Kevin, but he didn't have any answer for. After Edward was done, Father Murray recounted the tale the three hunters told him earlier in the day. It appeared to pique his interest, just as it had Edward's. As he explained, a hunter himself, he had had many encounters with animals out in the woods. Those woods, in particular. The animals always scurried away.

"Could they be rabid?", Lewis asked.

"All of them?", retorted Father Murray.

"Good point."

It was a twelve minute drive to Walter's Creek. Father Murray parked on the side of the road, just past the bridge, and the three men got out and carefully descended the embankment to the creek's edge. They walked along the northern edge of the creek. The current setting didn't match how Kevin had described it. There was another hour left of daylight. The silence he mentioned was full of the babbling water and the first hint of night crickets chirping their heads off in the long shadows of the fall afternoon. Every so often, Edward checked his phone and, so far he hadn't lost the signal. They turned into the woods along the old logging road Tom said they had followed. The crumpled silver beer can lay in the grass confirmed their path.

Still no loss of signal. The whole time Edward had three bars or more and, beyond that, he still had a data connection, as confirmed by the social media alerts that vibrated in his pocket every few minutes. That usually dropped first in dead zones.

"How far are we from the squirrels?", Edward asked.

Lewis looked through the woods, off to his left. "You know, not sure. Not too far, if I had to guess. Same side of the road and creek. It wasn't that much further down the road." His eyes continued to look through the woods, and then he pointed to the left, ahead of them. "It is probably that direction. I don't imagine we're past it yet."

A shiver went through Edward's body from just being close to that spot. "I guess the ball field is that way, "Edward said, and pointed ahead of them toward the north.

Lewis agreed, "Yep."

"It's no coinc..." started Edward, but Lewis let out a loud "SHHHH!" that stopped all three of them in their tracks.

"Do you hear that?"

Edward didn't have to ask what the "that" was he referred to, he did. There was something off in the woods, walking along with them. It was small. Not a person. It had four legs. Whatever it was took a few more steps after they stopped, before stopping as well. The woods were deep and thick, providing the animal great cover to stay hidden. Lewis took three steps forward, and the animal mirrored his movements. He moved toward the woods, but this time the response was not footsteps. It was a large growl from, not one, but several, animals. Some were small, but one of them was sizable, formidable, and sent Lewis and Edward stepping backward.

"That sounded like a bear," said Lewis.

Or that was what Edward thought he heard. It was hard to for him to hear anything. He heard the growl. Then a vibration, low at first, but it ramped up quickly to a full on buzz that blocked out all sounds and distorted his vision. His legs were unsteady. Either the ground was moving with the buzz, or his body was.

Lewis took another step backward and joined Edward and Father Murray. When he did, the animals emerged from their cover for the first time. A fox, two coyotes, and a small black bear cub. They moved in unison. All moved forward, but kept their distance at the same time. They were warning, not attacking. Teeth bared. A low growl came from each animal. Their heads were down low, and parallel to the ground, eyes locked on the three men. It was a warning two of the men heeded and stepped backward. Edward couldn't process what he saw. The buzz distorted it. The buzz separated him from the here and now, and locked him in a world of confusion. He felt the hand on his shoulder pulling him a step backward, but didn't know if he took the step or why. The world around him had a layer of static over every sense. No sound. No sight. No smell. No touch.

Father Murray and Lewis pulled Edward back up the logging road. Both walked backward, to keep an eye on their escorts. The creatures followed them, teeth bared the whole time, and producing a cacophony of hisses, growls, and howls. Edward's steps were clumsy at first, but became more deliberate the closer they got to the creek. The static cleared for Edward, just enough to see the creatures following them. When he took a few steps on his own, Father Murray and Lewis let go of him.

Lewis warned him, "Don't run. Move slowly and deliberate."

Edward's hands jerked up to give the universal symbol for "hold up". The creatures were not aware of that symbol and continued to follow.

They continued back up the creek toward the car, and the creatures followed as far as the edge of the woods. From the sound of it, others had joined them. The hissing was deafening. The intent was clear. It was a warning to stay out of the woods. Then, the sound increased beyond a level that Edward thought was possible. The tall pines along the edge of the road bent over them in a threatening posture, and a massive gust of foul-smelling wind sent all three men tumbling to the ground and against the side of the caddy. Edward heard the warning, loud and clear, and scrambled to his feet. All three entered the car, which quickly departed. Figuring out what was warning them would have to take place somewhere else.

19

The mood among the three men sitting stunned in a white Cadillac outside of Lewis Tillingsly's home matched the darkness that had settled in. A layer of fog formed where the remaining heat of the day met the coolness of the night. The air was still. So were the men. Cricket's chirped, but the birds were silent. As were the men.

Edward had been out of the static for a while now, but his head still felt scrambled. His senses dulled. This was like the buzz he had felt just over a week ago, but much worse. Then he was just disoriented. This time, it cut him off from the outside world, and it appeared to be just him. In one of the few exchanges between the longtime friends, neither Lewis nor the father had heard the buzz or seen the static. Only the growling and hissing. Neither sound cracked through the static. To Edward, that told him all he needed to know. This was paranormal in nature, not natural.

Lewis broke the silence and said, baffled, "We need to talk to Marcus."

Father Murray nodded his agreement.

"He is the sheriff. He needs to know," said Lewis.

"Agreed," said Father Murray, and started the car and took off, sending Lewis sliding back in his seat.

"Now?", asked Lewis with a bit of surprise. His breath still taken away by the sudden acceleration.

"Absolutely," Father Murray said decisively.

20

The three men pulled into the parking lot of the Miller's Crossing police department. Father Murray maneuvered into the first open spot and slammed to a stop. When they got out, Lewis stopped and looked at the parking job and then exclaimed, "Father?" The old white-haired priest had a one track mind and continued on to the front door, ignoring the critique of his driving skills. Edward and Lewis followed. The wheels of the Cadillac straddled the lines of two parking spots behind them.

Marcus was standing in the back, past the reception desk, leaning over his desk, with the phone planted to his ear. His speech was fast, agitated. He slammed the phone down and headed toward the three visitors that stood at the countertop used by the receptionist to separate the waiting area from the offices.

"Gentlemen, this is the wrong time for a social call," he sniped from halfway back.

"This is no social call Marcus," said Lewis. "This is official business."

"There's a lot of that going on right now. Hang here. I will send Tony up to take a report." He pushed the button on the countertop to release the door and pushed through the door. With fast, large, determined steps he walked right by them.

"I am afraid that won't do Sheriff."

"And why is that, Father?" he asked as he turned around, perturbed and annoyed. They were keeping him from something. Edward could tell. That matter would just have to wait. Edward couldn't think of much in the criminal history of Miller's Crossing over the last six years that rose to this level. The 'that dog just squatted on my yard', or a dispute over who can claim the carcass if two hunters shot the same game was some of the usual fair. Maybe a car crash or two, but those were usually handled by drivers, with a simple handshake and setting of a date to come over to one another's helping repair the damages. Drunk and disorderlies were the most common calls, and the easiest to deal with. Just had to make sure they were some place they couldn't hurt themselves or someone else. That might mean the lockup for the night, or just a ride home to sleep it off.

"There is something odd in the woods out by Walter's Creek. Animals are working together to keep us out. It is the same area they found Kevin Stierers. It is all related."

"No crap, Father. There is something strange. Fred Moultry was just brought into County General, all torn up. He and his brother were out hunting in those woods, when something attacked him. Laurence said they were separated but he could hear his screams. Now I gotta get over there. You can come along, if you want."

When they arrived and walked in, the six-foot-four-inch frame of a man, who had spent his life throwing hay bails around, manhandling cattle, and raising barns and fences, all by hand, looked small as he sat bent over with his head in his hands. Around him, a flurry of nurses and doctors ran in and out of the room. Amid the sound of orders and responses given in the care of their patient, an occasional moan or scream of pain escaped out the door. Each caused the large callused hands of the figure sitting out front to grip and squeeze the hair on his head as hard as he could, each knuckle turned white with strain.

"Laurence, how is he doing?", asked the sheriff.

Without looking up, he responded, his voice shaken, "Not sure, they won't tell me anything. I just hear what is going on, and it doesn't sound… good."

"Let me see what I can find out."

"Thanks, Marcus."

Lewis took a seat next to the man on the bench. "Hey, Laurence, can you tell us what happened?"

The man tilted his head, tears streamed down his face. "Lewis, I don't know. We were out bow hunting. He thought he heard something move and went off to track it. He wasn't gone more than a minute before I heard the first scream. I ran. He was screaming, over and over, and I needed to get to him. A coyote jumped in front of me, growling and snarling. I tried to go around it, but it snapped at me. I had to shoot it with my bow, twice, to get by. When I found Fred, he was covered in blood. Another coyote and a small bear cub were ripping at his arms and dragging him away. I yelled and charged both animals, but they didn't let go or move. Strangest thing, Lewis." The man stopped his story, and took notice of the others gathered around him. "I have never seen animals act like that. Only after I put my last three arrows through them did they stop."

Edward knelt down on one knee before the man and asked, "What did the coyote and cub look like?"

"Small black bear cub. I would guess only a few months old. Its mother had to be around, somewhere. The coyote, about the size of a medium-sized dog. Grey, with black spots."

"With a white streak on top of its head?", Edward asked.

"Yes. Yes. How did you know?"

"Lucky guess," Edward said, standing up and looking at the others.

Lewis slapped Laurence on the back and said, "I am sure he will be fine. Fred is a tough guy. Going to take more than a couple animals to take him down."

"Laurence, why don't we say a prayer for your brother?"

"I would like that, Father."

Lewis got up and gave Father Murray his seat. He took Laurence's hands in his own and prayed. Lewis and Edward walked down the hallway to let the father tend to the member of his flock.

"Same coyote and cub," Lewis whispered. Edward agreed and thought at least they were dead now. Then he wondered if that were really true.

Lewis looked over Edward's shoulder, whistled a piercing whistle, and motioned for Marcus to join them. He held up a finger and leaned down to tell Laurence something. Dread was plastered all over his face as he walked down the hall toward them.

"How is he?", asked Lewis.

"I have never seen anything like that. They tore him up something horrible. There are internal organs outside of his body. They aren't sure he is going to make it."

Both men shook their heads. The brothers, like most of those in the Crossing, were the latest generation of a family that went back to the beginning. They still lived on the same family farm their ancestors had settled on. Separate houses now, mind you. Each with their own lives, wives, and children. Living on opposite sides of the property, but managing the family farm together. Everyone knew them, not just of them.

"Laurence told us what happened. It was the same cub and coyote we saw."

"Wait... what do you mean?", asked Marcus. His head shook as if he were trying to clear a fog from his thoughts.

At the end of the story, and with the details Laurence had told Lewis added to the end, Marcus stated factually, "Rabid, that has got to be it."

"No, Marcus, it is not that," interrupted Edward. "That doesn't explain why they herded us back and followed us." Just then, it hit Edward like a lightning bolt of rational clarity. "I think they are protecting something. Protecting something out there in the woods."

"Oh, come on, Edward. What would they protect and... how they hell would animals know what to protect?", Marcus asked. Disbelief dripped from every word like cold maple syrup.

"Someone is controlling them. That satanic display we found. That would explain that buzzing that I feel when I am in that area that no one else does."

"Have you ever seen ghosts control animals?"

Edward fired back, "No, but demons can."

"Edward. I respect you and your family. We all do. But not everything that happens here is supernatural in origin. Now, I need to go talk to Laurence." Marcus made eye contact with Edward and Lewis, before he turned and returned to the victim's brother. Edward knew the eye contact was to ensure they knew he meant respect and appreciation, but it was also to drive home the fact that he didn't buy into any other explanation, outside of what was practical. Even though, around these parts, the practical sometimes included what others would consider impractical.

"I am right. I know I am," Edward said harshly under his breath. He leaned back against the wall. Jaw and fists both clenched.

"Edward, I know you are," said Lewis. "Deep down, he does too. He just doesn't want it to be that. He probably remembers how it was before you returned."

"I keep hearing people refer to those as the dark days. What happened back then?"

"Well, your father did a great job of keeping things at bay. Our spiritual visitors were shown the door quickly, and he dispatched the occasional demon to where it came from or ran it out of town where it didn't harm anyone. After his death, there was no one that could do it. Ghosts ran around scaring the crap out of everyone and really creating havoc with the farm animals. That was a bigger deal than you can imagine. Spooked cows produce sour milk. Chickens don't lay eggs. That drove Father Murray to take up the cause. He, like your family, could sense them, but never really got the hang of things. He did well enough with the simple cases. Demons, on the other hand." Lewis joined Edward, leaning against the wall halfway down the hallway from the room where Fred Moultrie moaned and writhed in pain. "Let me ask you this. How big of a murder problem do you think we have here in Miller's Crossing?"

"I didn't know we had one," responded Edward.

"Technically, we don't, but the 37 unsolved homicides and missing persons would say differently. I categorized each of them as missing and, with the help of others, concocted stories about them running off to escape the town, or something to that effect, to keep the state cops off my ass. Some of them we found remains for. Others, we never did. Some did things to hurt themselves, but some of them. God, Edward. I have seen things done to the human body I didn't know could be done. The town helps keep all this hushed, but they all know. They knew Father Murray and I were doing the best we could. It's not like anyone in town could tell anyone the truth. Who on the outside would believe them if they did?"

"Grab the crash cart!" exclaimed a nurse running out of the room down the hall. Laurence and Father Murray both sprang up from their seats as they watched doctors and nurses rush into the room where his brother laid. Father Murray rushed into the room after the flood of doctors. Laurence attempted to follow, but the father performed one last act of comfort before he entered. He turned toward the concerned brother, placed both hands over his heart, and shook his head, then disappeared into the room. The grieving brother was left standing there.

Screams and moans could be heard among the exclamations of medical professionals verbalizing orders and providing statuses. Fred was fading. In both the statuses yelled in the room, and the veracity of his outburst, you could tell. As his screams subsided. So did the orders. There were a few last-minute screams of "clear" from the medical staff. Each followed by a thunderous thud. Each thud produced anguished sobs from his brother. The moans and screams ceased.

Lewis and Edward waited outside the emergency entrance of County General, trying to stay out of the way. Father Murray stayed inside to console Laurence and the rest of the family. Edward looked on as Lewis greeted Fred's wife, hugged her, and said kind words to her. He found it hard to even look at her and her small kids, knowing how their lives had just changed, and the grief they felt. Possibly an open emotional wound from his parent's and Karen's death. Perhaps one that would never close, but some handled it better. Lewis' even-keeled approach to everything probably was the crutch that helped him in matters such as these.

Edward had tried to call Sarah several times on her cell phone, to let her know he would be home late. She never answered. He tried the boutique, only to find out she went home ill a few hours ago. With the subsequent attempts to her cell phone still unanswered, he finally called home, where Jacob answered. Sarah wasn't there, either. He told Jacob that he would be home late and was out with Lewis and the father. A message that was more common than Edward would have liked. As he hung up, Father Murray emerged out the door.

"How is everyone Father?", Lewis asked.

"As good as you can expect. Wendy is pretty shaken up. I will stay a while longer with the family. One of you can drive my car back. Marcus can drive me back to the church later."

"Of course, Father."

"He also is rounding up all the local hunters at the church, 9 AM tomorrow. He wants to go out and find those rabid animals that did this."

21

"Father! Not another word."

Father Murray held back the fire he felt burning inside. Ever since leaving the hospital he tried to explain to the sheriff that there was another explanation for what was going on. Something other than rabid animals. Each attempt resulted in a similar response, with increasing furor.

"Not everything is supernatural. Be rational, Father!"

Being rational is what Father Murray believed he was doing. His rational world included both the natural and supernatural. Could it be rabid animals? Someone who didn't know any better would believe so, or just think the animals were being aggressive. There was one problem. The sheriff didn't experience what Father Murray, Lewis, and Edward did. He didn't watch the animals working together. Working with precision to herd them back. Away from something, but from what? That was the question. That was the question that made Father Murray continue his pleadings with the young sheriff. It was not about being right. It was about protecting his flock. If a group of them stumbled upon "the what", who knew what the animals or "the what" could do to them.

"I am going with you," Father Murray stated plainly, confidently, resolute.

"Father, I said be reasonable. You are not a hunter. You would only be in the way, or a liability. I need expert trackers and hunters. We can handle this."

Father Murray considered himself an expert at tracking and hunting, just not in the arena the sheriff meant. The sport of walking through the woods, swamps, and fields toting a bow or a rifle over his shoulder, in search of an animal whose horns or antlers would be mounted on his wall, was not appealing to him. He wasn't against it. Hearing others talk about it, he could see why they might be interested. It just wasn't for him. Sitting for hours in a boat, with a line in the water. Never seeing the prey you are trying to lure in. Blindly yanking on the hook. All may make fishing seem less than invigorating to others, but it was his passion. To each his own. His feelings didn't make him shy away from enjoying the fruit of those who partake in the sport. Deer jerky ranked right up there next to a nice filet of bass baking under a dollop of butter and herbs in his book.

"Nonsense. I will be fine. I will bring Lewis along. He knows what he is doing. Does that make you feel any better?"

"I guess," said Sheriff Thompson, reluctantly. "You still aren't giving up on your supernatural theory on this, are you?"

"My boy. I have been alive a great many years. What I have seen and experienced has taught me to never discount any possibility, no matter how strange it may appear on the surface. I would be more surprised if it were something as simple as a rabid fox, but I would relieved. It would serve you well to adopt a similar attitude around this place. It might make your job easier."

"Father, with all due respect. Don't lecture me about how to do my job," sniped back Sheriff Thompson.

"I am sorry. I would never attempt to do that. I meant no disrespect," acquiesced Father Murray. "but I assume you saw the claw marks on Fred's body. They were in sets of three. Much like young Kevin's."

The silence was thick uncomfortable. Only the throaty growl of the 4.6 liter V-8 of the sheriff's Crown Victoria interceptor spoke, and it spoke volumes. Father Murray's comment had produced an impulsive depression of the accelerator that caused the modified transmission to jump into a passing gear. Unnecessary on the vacant country roads. It spoke loudly for a quarter of a mile until the pressure on the pedal was released. Sending that voice into silence.

"The bear probably only made contact with three of its claws. That is all."

"On each swipe? Now, I am no animal expert, but even that seems improbable to me."

The sheriff took his left hand off the wheel and rubbed his brow before smoothing his hair back. What he saw today, aged him several years. Violence in this town was not something he had witnessed often. His predecessor had had that responsibility. Because of the nature of it, he kept it all within. Father Murray knew the look on his face. It was one he had seen on his predecessor several times. The look told of the scene of what had happened to Fred Moultry's mangled body, lying there on the gurney in the emergency room. The blood-soaked sheets around him. Every breath, scream, and moan, followed by a gurgle as blood seeped in from any one of the many mortal wounds made to his body by the huge claws of what ever did this. The sight of the man's eyes searching for help, aid, that will never arrive. The realization that his life was ending. It's a look that sticks with you. Father Murray has given last rites more times than he can remember, but every night he closes his eyes, he sees theirs looking up at him as they realize this is the end.

Some go in peace. Some go with a last word. Fred went somewhere in between. Just after the last moan, there was a single muttered phrase. Father Murray had moved to the bed, to hold the man's hand and pray. To guide his soul home. He was there, but out of the way of those still trying to save his physical form. A skill he had learned over the years. A skill that included reading the lips of a dying person. The phrase that escaped Fred's moving lips was nothing more than puffs of air. To the untrained person, they may consider this as the final exhale, but Father Murray knew it was more. He knew the word the lips said, "Floating".

They pulled up to the church, and Father Murray opened the door. "It's possible, Father."

"What is, my son?", asked Father Henry, his back to the sheriff as he exited the car.

"The bear could have missed with the other claws, or it could have been another animal. There are others out there. Rest assured, we will find it."

"Oh, I have no doubts you will. That is what I am afraid of," Father Murray shut the door, turned, and looked in through the open passenger window. "See you at 9, Sheriff."

22

"It's just a headache," Sarah said.

"I can call Doc Robinson. I am sure he would come out. He does owe me a few favors."

"No dad. Just a headache."

Edward, heard what his daughter said, but his eyes told him more. First, there was the fact she was here. Wild horses couldn't pull her away from Myrtle's for more than just a few minutes. More than once, he had to go down there and force her to go home because she was running a high fever and never should have gone in. More worrisome was her appearance. Her hair was a tangled mess. The curls and body she had added in at Ruthie's a week earlier had already fallen out leaving her naturally dead straight hair, which she straightened every morning before she headed out. What Edward saw now, looked like a brush hadn't run through it in weeks, not just hours. There was also an ashy complexion to her skin tone that made her appear to be an unhealthy gray. Even her lips, instead of the healthy pink they always were, they looked like something out of a black and white movie. She was also in bed, covered by every sheet and blank she had, with all the lights and television off. Sarah had slept with the television on, just with the volume down, for as long as he could remember. "I think it is more, and it worries me," he insisted.

She rolled over against the wall. "It's just a headache," her muffled voice said. "I haven't been sleeping well. Work has been busy. Worried about Kevin and what happened to him, and the entire town has stopped into Myrtle's to ask my opinion about everything going on. It is just exhausting dad."

Everything she said, he understood well. His nerves felt well-worn themselves, and his sleep had been more restless than normal since the encounter with the hum. The events that had occurred since only added to it. It was plausible, but the father in him said there was more. She didn't look well, and there was that parental nagging in his head. "I get that, but I really wish you would let me call the doctor to just check. It would make me feel better."

An angry, but half muffled, moan emerged from his daughter's form. She pulled the covers up tight to her neck and rolled further toward the wall, burying the rest of her face into the pillow. This was a routine Edward had seen before, but she was fourteen the last time. Sarah went through a time when she didn't want to go to school and faked being sick. She would rollover and bury her face in the pillow and pull the covers up as high as she could as a shield against his gaze. He could only surmise that her theory was, if he didn't see her he couldn't force her to get p to go to school. It didn't work, well not entirely. The first few times, he forced her to get up and school. After a while, he realized he missed a key detail in what caused all this. It coincided with Karen starting her first bouts of chemotherapy. One day, he finally gave up and let her stay home. When he came home from work, he found his daughter curled in the bed with her mom. She was holding her mom's head, stroking her hair. It was then it all made sense. Edward let her get away with it a few more times. "Sarah?"

She pushed up away from the pillow a few inches and proposed, "Tell you what. Let me get some sleep tonight, and IF, "she emphasized the world like any great attorney making an argument in front of a jury, "I am not feeling any better in the morning I will let that old Doctor friend of yours come over."

"I don't know," he responded, not quite ready to push his immediate concern aside.

She sighed and turned over to face her father. Her eyes were still closed, when she suggested, "touch my forehead. I am not running a fever."

The low profile bed she had meant he had to lean down, which required him to brace himself with his right hand on her headboard. The palm of his left hand was placed lightly on her forehead. She was correct, no fever. Instead she was icy to the touch. "Sarah, you are freezing," he gasped.

"I know. It's cold outside, and I got chilled, why do you think I am under all these covers?", she said and rolled back over toward the wall, and once again pulled the covers up over her. "Just let me sleep. I will be fine in the morning."

"I don't know, honey," he said. His mind worried, but without evidence of a fever, he couldn't put his finger on it.

"Dad, I promise. If I'm not better in the morning, then I will see the doctor, okay?"

"Okay," he agreed reluctantly. "Let me know if you need anything."

"I will. Will you check the heat?"

"Yep," he agreed.

Edward pulled her bedroom door closed and then turned to the thermostat on the opposite wall. The screen read, 64. That explained the chill he felt when he entered the house. It also explained why Sarah felt so cold, and was covered up so much. He reached up and turned it to 68, and smiled when he heard the system click on.

23

"Did you try to talk him out of this foolishness?"

"What do you think?" Father Murray answered Edward with a perturbed look on his face. "He wasn't hearing none of it. He had thoughts of grandeur in his head. Lead a big posse out. Kill those animals and save the day. Oh, he would be a legend around these parts. The biggest fool that ever wore a badge."

Edward had seen the father frustrated in the past. Edward, himself, had been the cause many times, but never to this level. He huffed as he rattled, agitated, around the church. Picking up hymnals and putting them back in their place. Another huff, before moving on to the next book still sitting on the pew. His mission, which Edward assisted with, was to have it clean and orderly before the sheriff and his men arrived.

"Make sure you don't put two books together. One book for every slot. It's big enough for two, but that means the person on the end won't have one. One book per slot."

"Yes, Father," Edward said, as he slid his twentieth book into the wooden frame hanging on the backside of the pew in front of them. He wasn't sure who would try to put two in there. You would have to squeeze and cram them together to make them fit, even if it were possible, but it must be. Why else would he have reminded him?

The main door at the back of the church cracked open, and a voice boomed in, "Come on in boys." Sheriff Marcus Thompson strutted in, his chest puffed out, showing off the badge that looked to Edward as if it had been polished overnight. "Morning Father," he said as he continued to the front. Behind him was the who's who of the hunters in the region. All dressed in the preferred weekend hunting attire. A sea of red and black flannel, green or camo pants, orange vests, and hats, flooded in. Their old muddy boots thudding on the aged wood floor. The flood continued and flowed into the first five rows of pews. Sheriff Thompson was positioned at the front, ready to tend to his flock. That drew a look and the ire of Father Murray, who stood two pews from the back.

One member of the hunting party hung back at the door, taking in the sight. He stepped forward and leaned over the back of the last row of pews, saying to Edward, "Ever see a larger gathering of yahoos?"

Edward cut his eyes up to the front and then back to Lewis, "Looks like they are after the rascally wabbit."

Lewis had to work to hold back his laughter.

Edward gave Lewis a once over and said, "You look like you kind of fit in."

"Just here for the father. You know what I think this is."

"Yep."

"I bet Marcus spent half the night making phone calls to rally these troops. I am shocked they didn't come walking in lock-stepping like some damn army. At least they left their guns outside."

The sheriff coughed rather loudly from the front and asked, "Shall we begin?" His gaze was on the three men still wandering around in the back of the church. Father Murray stopped his 'cleanliness is next to godliness' work and put the hymnal book he had in his hand in the slot before heading up to the front. Several blue-covered books would have to wait in their spots on the pews until later.

"Okay boys. You all know why we are here. There is a pack of rabid animals out by Walter's Creek. They attacked Kevin Stierers. Messed him up real bad. Then, just yesterday, they attacked and took Fred from us. God rest his soul." Sheriff Thompson paused, crossed himself, and then looked back over his shoulder at the large cross on the back wall above the altar. From where Edward stood, he could almost see Father Murray's body recoil at the display.

He continued, "Well, I say no more. We will go out there and find those animals and kill them before they can harm anyone else. It is up to us to protect our community. Now, from what Laurence told me, there are two coyotes, a bear, and a fox, moving in a pack. That should be easy to find. One coyote is grey, with a white streak on top of its head."

"It would look real good stuffed in my cabin," said a man from three rows back. A few men patted him on the back. Marcus pointed at him and smiled. "That he might, but please don't take any chances. If you see any animals that act aggressive, you know what to do. We have lost enough as it is. Are there any questions?"

"When we going?", asked another man in the front.

"Soon," Marcus said. His hands were folded behind him as he rocked back and forth a little on his heels. Each rock forward thrust his chest out that much further, to show who was in charge. "When we get out there, we will go in the woods together and stay spaced out. Safety is my number one concern today."

"*Right*," Edward thought. This was grandstanding. He knew it. Lewis knew it. Marcus knew it, and planned it. Why? Edward wasn't sure. Perhaps he saw an opportunity to exercise his authority, and show everyone he was in control. A chance to break out from behind Lewis's shadow. Maybe even that of Father

Murray, and even Edward, to some extent. Most of the problems in Miller's Crossing were not the type that were dealt with by law enforcement.

"Father, would you like to say a few words?"

Father Murray looked stunned at the request. Edward felt stunned too.

"Maybe a blessing for our safety?", suggested Sheriff Thompson.

The priest shook off the stunned feeling and stammered as he walked to the front of the gathering, "Oh... Okay...Heavenly father. I ask that you watch over these men as they head out into the wilderness. Provide your divine guidance as they search for the creatures that have terrorized our community for the last several weeks. Keep them safe as they do your work, and bring an end to the terror. In the name of our Lord, Jesus Christ, Amen."

"Thank you, Father."

Father Murray brushed him off with a wave of his hand.

"Father, is something wrong?", Marcus asked.

"Eh, ... no. It's nothing," he responded, turning to walk back to the back and resume his task.

"Father, what is it? Something is bothering you," Lloyd Wilcox asked from the second row.

Edward watched as the town's priest turned around, out of respect and love for the members of his flock. The look on his face was still very reluctant when he looked at the sheriff.

"Father, if you have something to say, please, by all means, say it."

Father Murray sighed, and with slumped shoulders, walked toward the first row of pews. The men trained their eyes on him, just as they were during his services, when he took his spot in the center to give a sermon. As he spoke, his body and voice sounded defeated. "Men, I know what the sheriff told you is out there. I think he is wrong."

There was a murmur in the gathering, as the men looked back and forth at each other and whispered among themselves.

"Now, I mean no disrespect," he continued, with a look at the sheriff. "Edward, myself, and Lewis were out there just yesterday. Those animals are not acting like that because of rabies, or any other mysterious disease. Their actions are not natural."

The murmur grew to a louder buzz that consumed the building.

"Now," he continued, louder than before, using his hands to hush the crowd. "Now, something is out there, and it is dangerous. Very dangerous. Rabid animals are sick. These animals were acting together, protecting something. I saw it with my own eyes. They worked together, like you or I would, if we were trying to move someone away. This isn't just a fox or two, protecting a den. This was different species of animals working together in concert. That was not natural. It's anything but. I am worried that one or more of you will stumble into what, or whoever, they are protecting, and suffer a fate similar to Fred. I plead and implore that you don't go."

"Father!" the sheriff interrupted. "That is enough of that. I expected more of you, than to use fear. I sat and talked with Laurence. What he described were rabid animals, not some ghost or spectral being. Perhaps so much time spent chasing ghosts through the years has clouded your judgement, and you see every threat as some kind of wild ghost tale."

"Sheriff?", Edward asked, as he rushed forward.

"I don't remember asking your opinion."

The harshness of the admonishment came out of left-field, and slapped Edward right across the face. Sheriff Marcus Thompson had always been a friendly man. The type everyone liked, and everyone got along with. Not one of those that let the power of the badge he wore go to his head. At least, not before now. This had every sign of what had happened. This was his search, his battle, and he wasn't about to let anyone interfere. The shock of this change knocked the air out of Edward. He looked back at Lewis while he caught his breath. Lewis held up a hand and shook his head. His message was clear, and it took every ounce of self-control to not say another word.

Father Murray added to his protest, "Sheriff, you are running off on a foolhardy search and you are going to get one or more of these men killed."

"I said, that's enough. Now we need to get started." He adjusted his belt and shirt as one that had been in a scuffle might. No one had touched the sheriff, at least not physically. He pulled a folded map out of his back pocket and held it up for everyone to see. "Men, come on up here and let me assign each of you an area on the grid to search, then we can head out and get to it."

Most of the congregation joined the sheriff, up at the map, but a few men straggled around in the pews and never attempted to step forward. Father Murray headed to the back with Edward and Lewis.

"We've got to stop this!", Edward declared, looking intensely at Lewis.

"It's his show now. We will be out there with them. We just need to find it first," he responded in his normal calm and dulcet tone.

"That is too big of a risk to take Lewis. Someone is going to get themselves killed," said Father Henry. He was watching the gaggle of men at the front.

"Yes, Father, it is a risk. But we have the advantage. We have been close before, and have an idea where to start."

"Can't you speak to him?", Edward asked. He lowered his voice as several of the men filed past and out the back door.

"I would be stepping over the line. Remember, guys, I am just John Q. Public now. The same as you."

Father Murray looked dismayed as he watched men he had known their entire lives file past on their way to what he believed was their deaths. Bringing up the end of the line was Sheriff Thompson, who walked by without even casting the three men a look. The men that stood up, but never went to be assigned a grid, waited until the sheriff was out the door before they broken their confab with each other, and walked to the back. Three sets of eyes watched them as they did.

"Father, you coming too?", asked Reginald Moore. The man with a salt and pepper beard that hung down to his belly, covering most all of his face, except a little round portion of his nose and his eyes, was about halfway to the back of the church. Behind him were Ted and Able, his two sons. Both students of Edward's. The sullen expressions on their faces told Edward they didn't share the same level of fascination in their tasks the others that walked past did.

"Yes, Reg, I am."

"Good, then we are coming with you. I have hunted all my life. Seen a rabid fox before. They don't do what you say they do." He planted a mighty slap on Father Murray's back.

The six men walked out and saw the dust trail from the several dozens of cars and trucks that had just left the gravel-covered parking lot. In the distance, rhe rumble of their engines raced toward Walter's Creek. Waiting for them outside was a large man that never came in.

John Sawyer, sporting overalls, like Edward always saw him in, asked, "Lewis, Father. What do you say we get this thing on the road?"

24

The seven men arrived at Walter's Creek. Lewis pulled across the bridge and then off to the northern shoulder of State Road 192, parking behind a long line of trucks and cars. A mass of people milled around the vehicles, strapping packs, vests, and guns in place. A single person stood facing the woods. Like a great General, about to lead his troops into battle, Sheriff Thompson was in an intense stare-down with the woods. The trees, now in full autumn plumage, with much of it on the ground, didn't waver under the intensity. This was a battle, and he aimed to set the tone right now, before the first boots walked into the woods. They would be victorious, and the town would be safe again.

The men lined up, gear ready, along the road and behind the sheriff. They awaited their orders. All but seven, that was. Lewis, John, Father Murray, Reginald, and his two sons, and Edward followed the same path they had earlier, following the creek until they found the old logging road. Behind them, they could hear some great speech being given, a cheer, and then a great rustling as close to forty men pushed into the low brush-covered woods on a search.

The smaller party reached the logging road and cut in. Father Murray explained to John Sawyer and Reginald what they had seen, and where, the whole way. What Father Murray shared challenged what convictions Reginald's two sons may have possessed. Both fell back further, and moved with reluctance, until their father called them forward, "Don't straggle behind. You will be easy pickings for a bear."

Edward's eyes scanned back and forth quickly, to look for any movement, any sign of an animal, or anything out of the ordinary. At the same time, he stayed mindful to his other senses. They might tell him more than his eyes, if they were right about this. Of course, if the great hum showed up again, he would be useless to them. This was why he wanted Sarah to come along. Having another along would be a great help, but she wasn't feeling good last night. She was still asleep when he left, and decided to leave her be, than push her to come with him if she was sick.

"Father, I am not sure if it is these woods, or what you are telling me, but something is giving me the heebie jeebies," said John Sawyer. His head looking back and forth through the woods.

"Me, too," Lewis started to say, but was interrupted when he, and the rest of his party, was startled by three raccoons sprinting out of the woods, across the logging road, and back into the woods on the other side. None of the animals broke stride. None of the animals looked in their direction.

"Was that them?", Able asked. The youngest of the two boys' voice sounded fearful and hesitant, just short of a quiver.

There was a pause before any of the men answered.

"No, not likely. With all that noise and racket back there, Marcus's search party is probably chasing anything alive this way."

They were not being covert, not by any definition of the word. Edward could hear screaming and yelling back and forth, between the various groups. Not to mention the constant rustling as they walked on the leaf-covered ground.

Further down the logging road, Edward started to feel disoriented and lost. He stopped, which prompted the others to stop. He closed his eyes tightly and tried to think. Where was he? In the woods. Okay, that was good, he knew where he was, but why was he here? That answer escaped him. The further he tried to chase the answer, the more random thoughts streamed into his mind at high speed. None stayed long enough for him to enjoy or understand. Just something to take up dead space in his head. He was aware enough to know that, but not able to control it. He opened his eyes to look around his surroundings, and saw the group of men standing there around him, silent. Seeing them didn't answer any questions, instead, it gave him more to ponder. Which, when he tried, the hum started, and the static appeared in his vision.

Edward tried to take several deep breaths, to clear both from his senses. That didn't work. His hands rubbed at his eyes, but the static was so dense, he never saw them. Covering his ears didn't block the hum, it intensified it. The more he fought to gain control, the deeper he fell. His whole body, and soul, vibrated. He was not in the world anymore. He was not anywhere. Trapped in a vague, blank, existence; blocked from any external stimulus by the vibrations that he now felt in his teeth. There was pressure on his body, but from what, he wasn't sure. It roamed around his physical form. Pushing. Probing. Then, it stopped and left him there, with only the vibrations and nothing else.

Edward called out, but his voice didn't pierce through the vibrations. He attempted to raise his arms, but he felt them remain limp at his sides. His feet were no longer on the ground. There was no sensation of floating, not that he would know what that really felt like, having never bungee jumped or skydived. There was nothing under his feet. Nothing to press against. No way to run or jump. A twist of his upper body, to try to roll one way or the other, produced no movement at all. Where was he? Who was he?

That was a new question. He couldn't remember who he was. Another question was, what was he? Was he just a thought, or something physical? Something that existed, or just a whimsical thought of someone's, or a dream that will disappear just as fast as it appeared? What is this thing called a dream he had just thought of? The only fact he was sure of, was he was sure of nothing at all.

The static changed from grey to a light green. Why, he didn't have a clue, but found it pleasant. Calming and tranquil. Was that the purpose of the change in color? If so, who changed it? The color pulsed, like waves. Some areas were darker than others, but all were still shades of the same calming green color.

In front of him, a white speck of light appeared in the waves of green. It grew larger and larger and then exploded past and through him. Edward found himself clear of the static, lying on the ground of the logging road. The other six members of their party were all rolling along the ground. Reginald, and his son, Tom, were thrown off the road toward the trees. The trees around them whipped back in recoil, as if blown one way by a horrendously strong gust of wind. The recoil sent them back in the opposite direction, to the point of almost breaking. In Edward's right hand was the cross. Someone had reached into his pants pocket and placed it in his hand. The static and hum were gone. The creaking of a thousand trees and screams had replaced it. The screams were human and coming from the woods. Without hesitation, Edward turned and headed into the woods, toward the screams. Lewis, John, and Father Murray got up, still out of breath from the great force that had pushed them down, and followed. Reginald and his sons hesitated for a moment, before joining the others.

Bushes and branches scratched and scraped at his arms and face as he pushed through, without pause. The sounds of pain were coming from everywhere ahead of him, but he focused on what sounded like the closest group. He pushed through another thicket of brush and into a clearing in time to see a man thrown from the ground, up high against a tree, where his body was crushed and torn to pieces. His arms and legs continued to fly past the tree. What was left of the torso crashed to the ground at its base. Around him, four more men were thrown into the air and suffered the same fate. Others held onto trees they were close to. Their feet dangled in the air. Their arms wrapped around the trunks of the great pines and oaks, holding on with all their might. Mouths gaped open as screams for help escaped. The trees, bent and shook as if they were trying to shake them loose.

A thunderous sound approached Edward from behind. He turned and saw a great wave moving through the trees, pushing them down, parallel to the ground, only to release them and allow them to whip up and back in the other direction as it passed by. Father Murray and John steadied themselves low to the ground as it approached. It thundered like a freight train toward them. Edward held firm where he stood. The ground around him and his friends had a sheen to it. The wave passed by him, and the others that stood close to him, with the gentleness of a spring breeze. All around them, it roared through, sending the treetops down to the ground before letting them go. Men holding onto the trees, lost their grip and were thrown into the air. Edward watched as some hit trees, pulverizing their flesh into mush. Others flew off into the distance on the wave of air.

Another wave developed behind them. This one appeared larger, stronger, based on the sound and the shake each of the men felt in the ground.

"Let's get out of here!", exclaimed Lewis.

None of the men argued or agreed, they ran and rushed forward through the woods, back toward the road. The wave gained on them from behind. Edward looked back and saw the trees falling to the ground, this time not whipping back up. Everything, as far as he could see, was knocked flat, like dominoes. "Move it!" he yelled, and they all picked up their pace.

Through the trees they saw the road just ahead. Just behind them, trees crashed to the ground as an invisible wave rolled over and pounded the landscape. They ran past Sheriff Thompson, impaled on a branch midway up a tree. A tree that fell to the ground moments after they passed. The four men breached the tree line as the front edge of the wave pushed them, sending them rolling along the ground to the shoulder of the road. It stopped. Behind them was a scene of devastation none of them could have imagined. An entire section of woods, flattened. Trees laid flat on the ground. No sign of the search party. No signs of any life at all, unless Edward looked hard in the distance, where a single grove of trees still stood. It appeared to be the center of the devastation. Trees were laid out away from it, like rays of sunlight projecting from the sun. Surrounding that grove were animals. They encircled it and were facing out, like guards.

Edward, still on his knees on the ground, reached over and tapped Lewis. Lewis was brushing the dirt and grass from his face when he looked up at what Edward was now pointing to.

"What the hell?"

25

Lewis raced back to town as fast as his old '73 Plymouth could go.

They passed people standing outside of their homes, looking in the direction that they just came from. He turned onto State Road 32, Main Street, without pausing at the flashing traffic signals. The tires of the large four-door squealed as they struggled to maintain traction with the tarmac. People flooded the sidewalks on Main Street, standing, looking. Everyone had heard the devastation that occurred in the woods, and they all shared the same confused expression.

"We need to get to the church," Father Murray said determinedly.

Just as determined, Lewis responded, "No. Sorry, Father. We need to get to the police station. I can have someone drive you back." There was no badge on his chest, nor hat on his head, but Edward saw he had transitioned back into Sheriff Lewis Tillingsly.

They pulled into the police station, and rushed to keep up with the long, fast steps Lewis took up the walk and into the building. The normally calm and quiet police station, for this small town, was now a hive of activity. Phones were ringing. Every available deputy was on a phone already. Each had the same frantic look on their face as they tried to calm and reassure the caller on the other end of the line. From the appearance of things, someone needed to calm and reassure them, first.

"Have you seen Marcus?", Wendy Tolliver asked from the dispatch desk. She was the person who normally took the calls and then dispatched one of their four deputies out to it.

Lewis, said stonily, "He's dead."

The buzz in the room ceased. Unanswered phones continued to ring. Voices begged for information from the handsets pressed against the heads of Wendy and the three deputies that were there.

"Tell them you will call them back, and put the phones down," Lewis said, as calmly as he could.

Behind him, Edward was frantically trying to get ahold of Sarah. He needed her help with this. She was not at home, or the boutique. It surprised him to learn from Jacob she left just after he did. It also dismayed him to hear from Jacob that he had heard the rumbles all the way back at their home. Their home was as far from Walter's creek as you could get. He called her cell phone, it rang four times before going to voicemail, sending a vibration of worry through him.

In the distance, the rumbles continued. Like a thunderstorm several counties away. It rolled closer and shook the ground, then stopped. Minutes later, it started again.

"Guys, there is something out there. We don't know what it is. It flattened the woods around Walter's Creek."

"Flattened?" asked Russ Hamilton, a 22-year veteran of the force, eyes wide and mouth agape. A look replicated on the face of the others that stood there listening to Lewis.

"Every tree, and," Lewis swallowed before he continued. Edward watched as he delivered the news, amazed at how the dead-stone concentration in his eyes never wavered. "It killed everyone in the hunting party Marcus took out there. We barely escaped, and I bet Edward's trinket had something to do with that."

Two phone handsets crashed to the desk. Another tumbled out of a hand to the floor, pulling the phone off the desk.

"There is no other way to say it, this has been a devastating day. It's not over, as you can hear." Lewis pointed a finger in the air as another rumble rolled in the distance.

Edward looked around the room. It dripped in fear. Law Enforcement was about catching speeders dragging on Main Street, or kids skipping school. Dealing with the apocalypse was not in their job description. It was a better fit in Edward's job description, if such a thing were written. Even then, he didn't have a clue how to handle this.

Wendy asked, reluctantly, "What do we do, Chief?"

That was the question Edward had no answer to and froze at the realization that Lewis may turn and look to him for advice. He was the "expert" in the room. That moment never arrived. He never turned around to ask Edward, he didn't turn to anyone, flinch, or miss a beat. He made a quick wipe across his thick mustache and steadied himself.

"Our focus is protection. Where is Tony?"

"He was out on patrol," Wendy said.

"Get him on the radio."

Wendy sat down, put the headset on, and keyed up her radio. Her movements were slow and deliberate. She had worked dispatch every day for the last 29 years. A fact she began every embarrassing story with at Lewis's retirement party. Making a call is something that should be second nature, but there was a pause before and after each movement. Almost like she was double checking.

"Tony, you out there?", she called, a crack in her voice.

"Yeah, I am here. Wendy, what the hell is happening? I keep hearing explosions."

Wendy's head dipped and landed in her hands. Her body shook at her desk.

"Wendy?", the voice over the speaker asked.

Lewis walked forward, past the reception desk. Edward could feel a sense of calm and confidence creep into the room and everyone in it. He leaned down to Wendy and said something softly. She took off the headset and leaned back. Tears streamed down her face.

Lewis put the headset on. "Tony, it's Lewis. Where are you?"

"On North Bluff, just past Jackson Hollow," Tony said, sounding surprised to hear his old boss's voice over the radio.

"Okay, I need you to get over to State Road 192, just East of the Walter's Creek bridge. Do not go across or get out of your car. Just tell me what you see. Got it?"

"Uh, yeah, Lewis. On my way," Tony responded.

Lewis walked back and joined Edward, Father Murray, and John, in the small waiting area.

"It will take him a few minutes to get out there. We need to know what is going on out there and keep everyone away. Everyone in town can hear that rumble. It won't be long before spouses, and family members of those that went out there with Marcus, start trying them on their cell phones. With no answer, they will ride out there to check on them."

It was clear to Edward; Lewis was in charge now. He was back in his element.

"Russ, do you know if Marcus had a list of those who volunteered with him this morning?", he asked, looking back at the stunned deputies that were now standing around consoling Wendy.

"N... No. I don't think he did."

"Father, any chance you remember everyone who filed into the church this morning?"

"I think so," Father Murray said, deep in thought. "I will start on a list."

"Put Wendy's husband, Daniel, on the list."

Father Murray walked up to the reception area, where there was a sign-in sheet and a local Fraternal Order of Police mug full of pens. He set to work on the list.

"Now what?", Lewis whispered to John and Edward.

"I don't know. I am trying to get ahold of Sarah. She can help."

Lewis nodded.

"Once the father has the list put together, do we need to start notifying people?" asked John.

Lewis nodded again, and then added, "At some point. I need to know what is happening out there. Hearing those rumbles continue has me concerned. There is no one out there for whatever to attack or force out."

A sick feeling landed in the pit of Edward's stomach. He understood what Lewis's concern was. They had left, and everyone else was dead. Why was it continuing? Was the area of devastation growing? His knees felt weak, and he needed to move before he fell right there. With his cell phone in hand, he walked out in front of the station. A click of the redial on his phone produced the same result. Four rings, and then her voicemail picked up. A call to the boutique went unanswered. Which was less worrisome. When they sped through town, everyone was outside looking. Another call, and Jacob answered. "Hey Jacob, have you heard from Sarah yet?"

"No. I tried her cell and texted her. Nothing," replied Jacob. "Dad, what's going on? The whole house is shaking." Edward hadn't heard his son's voice like this before. Not even when Karen had died.

"I don't know, Jacob. Just keep trying your sister and stay inside."

"Okay, Dad. I'm scared."

"Me, too, sport. Me, too."

26

The radio rattled to life and words fired out of it at the speed of machine-gun bullets, "Wendy! Wendy! Wendy! What the hell is this? What the hell is all this? It's all gone. Gone. Nothing."

"Calm down Tony," Lewis said. "Just breathe and tell me what you see."

"I can't describe it so you will believe, not what I am seeing. No way."

"Some of us will. We were out there when it happened. Now tell me what you see," Lewis told him. Keeping his voice calm and soothing. A contrast to the frantic tone of the deputy on the other end.

"The whole forest is laying down on the ground. Flat. From about a hundred feet south of 192, and a little further than that, across Walter's Creek heading ea…" a huge roar over the radio cut it off. When it subsided, Tony screamed, his voice several octaves higher than his usual tone. "What the fuck was that? I needed to move back. It threw my patrol car in the air and another row of trees just fell."

"Tony, pull back as far as you can while still keeping eyes on it. Understand?"

"Yes, I understand, Lewis. Am I happy about it? No, but I understand."

"Lewis," Edward called.

With the headset on, Lewis walked out to the waiting area. Edward had attempted to call Sarah several more times, to no avail. His gripped his cell phone tightly in his hand, to avoid missing any returned call or message from his daughter. As Lewis came closer, Edward shared the one concerning detail he had pulled from Tony's screaming and swearing, "It grew."

The comment appeared to hit a bell of clarity in Lewis. He snapped his fingers and rushed back closer to the radio, asking questions the whole way. "Tony, can you hear me?"

"Yeah?"

"You said another row of trees fell. Where?", he asked.

"Right next to me, and in front of me. Was afraid the damn things would fall on me, but they fell straight out."

"Tony, where were they in relation to the highway and creek?", Lewis asked, looking at Edward.

"A row or two east of the creek, and south of the road."

Lewis pressed the mute button on the headset and whispered, "Shit," and rushed to the reception desk. He fished in the various drawers for a few seconds and then yanked out a large map that he rolled out on the countertop. Edward ran to meet him. This thing grew with every rumble. Which were all at regular intervals of 1 every ten minutes or so. It wasn't breaking any speed records, but not slowing or coming to a stop.

Edward put the question of the mysterious force, and what the causes were, out of his mind and studied the map from that spot out. The map was a street-level view, based on a satellite photograph from high above. The streets and community of their small, peaceful town were clearly visible. Each house represented a resident, a family, a friend. Each wanted their slice of happy Americana. Each now lived in the middle of a nightmare. His hands immediately pointed out spot after spot on the map. Most of which Lewis appeared to have already noted with his eyes, as he motioned for Russ to come over to the desk. The spots Edward pointed out were the first homes in danger, if this continued. With no sign it was stopping, he had to assume it wouldn't. Science and math were never his strong suit and at the moment he was only guessing, but a guess was better than nothing. That guess estimated maybe two hours before it reached the first house. A house that undoubtedly contained an occupant or occupants that were scared to death. With its proximity to the source, everything in the house had to shake and rattle with every rolling wave of whatever it was. If they had not already fled, they would need to be moved to safety.

"Russ, I need you to get out to Kyle's place. Get him and Mildred out and bring them to the high school. With her health, he may try to put up a fight, but don't let him. Tell him I said so, okay?"

Russ said nothing. Just nodded and put on his brown wide-brimmed hat. He rushed past them and out the front door as Edward shifted their attention to the next spot he pointed out. A single road, with approximately 20 houses on it. They were next. His finger circled them, and Lewis said, "Yep."

He turned around slowly and looked back at the crying, wilted, woman that had been his dispatch officer for the better part of 29 years. A sigh escaped his lips before he said, "Wendy? I need you, are you okay?"

Her face was red with grief and streaked with makeup. Okay was a feeling Edward didn't think she would feel now, or anytime soon, but he watched her hands make frivolous attempts to wipe away the tears. A slight jerk up straightened her position. "Lewis, what do you need?", she asked. Her voice still quivered, but had a sense of resolve and strength.

"Get on over to the high school. Call Rob Stephens on the way and have him open the gym. We will use that as a shelter, for now. At least until we can get a handle on this," his eyes looked at Edward as he said the last statement.

"Good idea," was all she said as she stood up and went on her way.

Then Lewis turned back to the men standing on the other side of the counter. He stood up straight and, if he wore his old utility belt with a gun and cuffs attached on it, Edward would imagine this would be one of the times he hitched it up. "John. I need to deputize you. You up to it?"

"Just say the word," he replied, without hesitation.

"I need you and Terrence back there to head out to Riley's Ridge and go door-to-door. Instruct them to head to the high school. They're probably frightened, so be gentle."

"Got it," John said. "Terrence, you're with me. Let's go."

There was no hesitation by the deputy. He was up and past them, heading out the door before John could turn around and take a step.

"John?"

"Yeah, Lewis?"

"Don't dent him. He's new," Lewis responded, with as much of a wry smile as any of them could manage at the moment.

"Lewis, why don't we go with them? We can cover more ground," suggested Reginald. His two sons stood blankly behind them.

He agreed, "Good idea. Get them out of there as soon as they can, and regroup at the high school."

There were just three men left standing in the police department, with phones ringing off the hook behind them. Edward studied the map and located the next area they would need to move to get to safety. Each time he started a new search, his eyes went back to the same spot. That area on the map where a single grove of trees stood among all the devastation.

"Lewis, how can we help?", asked Father Murray.

"Well, Father. You two can figure out a way to stop it."

Both men looked at each other, and then the ground beneath their feet. Edward hoped for divine intervention as he turned his cell phone over in his hand and pled for the screen to show an incoming call or message. Then he asked for divine intervention to give him some kind of idea of what to do. Both prayers went answered. All he knew for sure was, he had to go back out there to learn more, but he didn't have any intention of going alone.

"I need Sarah. She has more training and is stronger than I am."

"She still not answering?", Lewis asked.

"No."

"Then let's go find her," he said, grabbed a walkie from the charger, walking around the counter and heading toward the door.

Edward looked back at the ringing phones, and the lack of anyone else back there to field the calls, or man the station. "What about the phones?"

"Nothing we can tell them will make anyone feel better."

Before Edward exited, he took one final look back. Phones rang. The extension lights on the old-fashioned plastic green phones flashed. No one was left to man the station. Something Lewis would never allow to happen while he was Sheriff. It was a matter of standard operating procedure. These were times that were anything but standard.

27

Back up Main Street they sped, or as much over the limit Lewis dared to go. His car didn' have lights or appeared official, in any capacity. The lack of cars on the road made it unnecessary. It bounced over the bumpy country roads. A few of the bounces had a little something extra in it as another wave of the mystery force rolled in. Shortly after the bounce, the portable radio Lewis grabbed squawked to life. Tony reported seeing another line of trees falling down in a large heap, sending up a cloud of dust. He had backed up a quarter mile down the road and parked at the apex of a curve, still giving him a full view of the events unfolding. Still too far for his liking, something he commented on several times over the radio, but the furthest he could go and still see.

Lewis, Edward, and Father Murray pulled into a diagonal spot in front of Myrtle's. A crowd had gathered on the sidewalk outside of each and every store. Everyone looked in the direction of the rumbling. Mouths hung open. A few attempted to cover them with their hand. The boutique was no different. Judy Spencer stood just outside the door, facing the common direction, with the same expression as the rest of the masses, plastered on her face. Edward got out of the passenger side door of Lewis's Plymouth and headed for the door. As he passed Judy he asked, "Sarah inside?"

"Uh huh," said the distracted teenager. Edward opened the door causing the little bell to ding. The simple sound seemed to snap Judy out of her trance. "Oh, no. Sorry. She is not here. She opened up early and then left."

Edward let the door close and asked Judy, "Where did she go?"

"She didn't say. Have you tried her cell?"

"Yes," he said frantically. "Several times. She hasn't answered."

He turned to Father Murray and Lewis, who were standing at the edge of the curb, next to the large green beast they had arrived in. "She isn't here," he said, with his hands out to his sides, exacerbated.

"Where would she be?", Father Murray asked.

Edward thought. Her not being at the store made little sense. That store was her life, her passion, her responsibility. She would never leave it alone. Not unless it was an emergency. He knew of only one, maybe two, other times she had left Judy alone, in charge of the store. Once, when she was sick, and the other was just recently. Then it hit him, and he turned back toward Judy, almost sprinting.

"Judy, do you know where Kevin lives?"

Judy thought. Her hand moved from in front of her mouth to her chin. "Yes. Yes, I do. His family lives in the brown house on Cattail Drive."

"Do you know the house number?", he asked anxiously. The ground under their feet rumbled again. A few moans escaped the gathered crowd.

"No, sorry. Sarah and I rode out there one day after we closed, to drop something off. It's the only one of that color. Just take a right off of Main. Pretty easy to find."

Edward turned and ran back to the car. He was in the passenger side before either of the other two men even opened their doors. The driver's side door opened and, without being asked, he said, "Cattail Drive."

"Good, it's close," said Lewis.

It was just two cross streets past the end of the main shopping district. A single light that hung from a cable across the road. It blinked yellow in the direction they were coming from, and red to the cross-traffic. On either side were lines of trees, like most of Miller's Crossing. No houses were visible when Lewis took the right.

"Lewis, you there?", Wendy called over the radio. He picked up the radio with one hand, while expertly turning the car with the other. "I'm here."

"People are arriving at the high school. Rob and a few other teachers have set up cots on the Gym floor."

"That's great Wendy. Nice work. Keep them as comfortable as you can."

"Will do. How many evacuees do you think we need to prepare to handle?"

Now that was a question that no one in the car knew the answer to, but Lewis didn't let the lack of an answer hang there and cause any feeling of uncertainty creep in for those in his charge. "Let's prepare for the thirty families. That should cover the areas we identified earlier. We will adjust, if needed."

"Will do."

"Keep up the good work, Wendy, and thank Rob and those other teachers for me," Lewis said. The radio dropped to the seat beside him.

A half mile down the road, the first house came into view. It was white, with black shutters. Another stretch of trees and another white house. On the opposite side of the road, surprise, another white house. Edward started questioning if the local hardware store sold any other colors. Then, it came into view. A brown two-story house, no shutters, with a matching attached garage. Nothing special, but nothing too simple.

"There!", he exclaimed.

"I see it," said Lewis as he whipped the car into the driveway and gave the brakes a stomp. His car slid to a stop, sending the occupants jostling back and forth inside.

The ground rumbled under them again. Edward got out and shut the door as the radio came alive again with Tony's latest report. He didn't wait to hear. He didn't need to. They all felt and heard the ground rumble. There was no ignoring it. The shrillness in Tony's voice just added to the terror that hung over them all. Like when the killer drags the knife across the metal pipe in the basement, just to torment his victim for a few seconds longer.

Edward mounted the steps and banged on the door. He didn't pause to see if anyone heard and was coming to the door, and kept banging the whole time. The hinges were loose on the metal screen door, allowing the door to reverberate and sound like a large cymbal crash every time he hit it. With every unanswered knock, the speed of his knocks increased. One bled into another, until it was one big noise of vibrating and banging metal, that never paused.

The large windowless wood door behind it clicked and opened. A woman in a tattered terry-cloth robe, and worse attitude, cracked the door open. Her eyes were as welcoming as a tarantula, and glassy. Her voice had the warmth of the arctic circle when she asked, "Can I help you?"

Edward didn't care about her attitude, or lack of welcoming demeanor. The location of his daughter was his focus. "Is Sarah here?"

"What?", she asked discourteously.

With his agitation at an all-time high, Edward snapped, "Sarah Meyer, my daughter. She is dating your son, Kevin."

The woman straightened herself. The scowl curled up, in both the mouth and eyes, in an attempt at a smile, which still lacked any sense of warmth. A hand reached up and attempted to comb through her hair. A finger caught a tangle and jerked it out with haste. "So, you are the ghost guy, huh? I haven't seen you around, yet. Cuter than I thought."

The ground rumbled under his feet again. Mrs. Stierers took notice and grabbed the door frame firmly with both hands and squealed, "What the fudge was that?"

"Mrs. Stierers. I really need to find my daughter. It's urgent."

"Ummm. Yeah," she stammered. Her eyes looking past Edward at the world around them. Searching for the source of the rumble and loud noise that shook her out of the hangover she suffered, from whatever she had enjoyed too much of last night.

"Sarah!", Edward shouted through the open door.

"Knock that off," she demanded. "She ain't here. Left here early this morning with my boy."

"Do you know where they were going?", Edward asked eagerly.

"Nope."

Edward threw his hands up and walked down the three steps, back toward the car.

"What the hell is going on?", she asked. Her voice shook. It was either fear, or the hangover sneaking back in.

"Don't know, Mrs. Stierers. Go back inside and stay safe," Lewis said, standing outside the car, next to the open driver's side door.

Her eyes darted in his direction. A hand jerked up above her eyes to shield them from the midday sun. "Sheriff?"

Edward yanked the car door open and got back in. It slammed behind him with a metallic rattle. Any ability to soften the sound had long left the thirty-year-old gaskets. Lewis followed, and the car rocked side to side as both men settled in.

"She isn't here. Said her and Kevin left earlier, and has no clue where they went," Edward said. There was a tone of defeat in his voice, and the air went out of the car.

"Now what?", Father Murray asked as Lewis backed out of the driveway and pulled off.

Edward looked down at his hands in his lap. His mind was blank, but his body was in motion. At some point after he entered the car, his hand reached into the pocket and fished out the familiar cross and book. The fingers of his right hand traced the edges of the cross. What used to be square edges were now rounded and worn, from centuries of being handled. The stem more worn than the crossbar. The dark, aged wood still had evidence of stains, from what, Edward didn't know. The feeling of it was familiar. The size, the shape of it, was comforting. It was more than physical. That old piece of wood stirred something deep inside of him. Clarity. Focus. It had from day one.

"I need to go back out there. I have to face it," Edward said sternly, decisively.

28

"You're nuts," Tony said over the radio, from his post a quarter-mile away.

Inside, Edward had to agree, but that didn't change the fact that he was sitting in the passenger seat of Lewis's Plymouth, driving out to Tony's position, to walk in there and confront the mysterious force. Nothing in his core felt fear. To feel fear, he would have to know what was out there to be afraid of. Fear of the unknown was not in his nature.

"Guys?"

Lewis answered the radio call from John Sawyer, "Yes, John. Go ahead."

"We just left the last home. Everyone is clear. Terrence will drop me off there with Tony. I am going in with you."

Edward snatched the radio out of Lewis's hand. He flipped it around several times, looking for the button to push to talk, like he had seen in many movies and television shows. There wasn't just one button, there were several. Lewis grabbed it back, and with one hand spun it around and pressed the button on the top left. The static that came through the speaker cut out for a second and then returned when he released the button. Then he handed it back to Edward. All without taking his eyes off the road.

"Absolutely not, John!", Edward exclaimed. His hands shook as he waited for a reply, but one never arrived.

"Father, talk him out of this," Edward turned to the back seat and said. His hand offered the radio to Father Murray, but he never took it. Just shook his head, and mouthed, "You will need the help."

Edward turned back around and let the radio fall to the seat in frustration. It bounced twice, before landing on the floorboard. Lewis never looked down at it, but his facial expression showed his displeasure. Edward leaned forward to retrieve it and watched Lewis's expression as he put it back on the seat. The frown disappeared.

The rumbling continued, still at the same intervals as it had for the last hour, but the intensity picked up the closer they got to the area. When they pulled up next to Tony's cruiser and got out, the intensity of each crash was so strong, each of them had to bend their knees to avoid falling over as the earth quaked below them. A cloud of dust rose from the area, creating an odd unnatural haze that resembled a battlefield under heavy bombardment. The only thing missing was the smell. Instead of the smell of gunpowder, or anything burning, there was a very sweet and almost pleasant pine smell in the air, from the thousands of cracked and mangled trees. It was natural, not like one of those hanging air fresheners.

Terrence's cruiser pulled up behind them and John got out and joined the others standing in front of Tony's vehicle. Terrence stayed standing behind his open door. Hands firmly planted on the door frame, and eyes taking in the scene in front of him.

The earth shook below them, again. Both cruisers, and Lewis's Plymouth, bounced on their springs. The seven men were sent staggering as the trees a few yards ahead of them fell flat, sending up a huge plume of dirt, adding to the haze.

Edward took a few tentative steps forward. The steps grew more confident. Held firmly in his hand was the old familiar cross. Father Murray followed him. John and Lewis fell in behind, with rifles over each of their shoulders.

Edward heard a twig snap behind him and turned. His heart sank as he saw his friends following him. "Stay here," he insisted. "This is too dangerous. I don't know if I can protect you."

"Nonsense. Who will protect you?", said Lewis. His hand tapped the butt of the rifle hanging over his left shoulder.

"I can't let you," Edward started to say, but John interrupted him. His voice gruff and deadpan. "Edward, we know what we are getting into. We were doing this with Father Murray before you arrived, and your father before him. This is our town, our home. Now, let's go take care of this."

Edward turned around and walked, with his friends following. He held the cross out a little further in front of him. It had protected them before, he hoped it would do the same as they walked back in. The ground around him had a yellow hue to it, which gave him a little confidence.

The path in was not as easy to walk as it was when they had entered that morning, or when they had escaped. There wasn't a clear piece of ground anywhere. They walked up and over destroyed and pulverized tree after tree. Some were just cracked trunks and limbs. Others were nothing more than sections of sawdust.

Each wave of air passed by harmlessly around them. It whipped tornados of dirt, dust, and small branches everywhere, sending them crashing back to the ground, but none of it came within six feet of the men. A cocoon of faith protected them, and Edward was at the point. The bubble didn't protect them from the shaking ground, which made each step as they traversed the downed trees treacherous.

Their target, the grove of trees, grew larger on the horizon with every step. It was a small patch of forest, maybe twenty trees wide, among the landscape of destruction. When the wind exploded out toward them, those trees in the grove didn't move. In there, it was a calm fall day. Figures moved around the edges of it. It was the animals. In particular, the fox and the wolves. Arrows, stuck out of each of them. They paced back and forth, equally distant from each other.

John Sawyer took the rifle from his right shoulder and raised it to sight in on the animals. "I can take them from here. Lewis?"

Lewis pulled the rifle from his left and did the same. "Yeah, I can, too."

"I got the wolf on the left."

Lewis, then called out, "I got right."

Both men shot. Both shots hit, dropping the wolves right there. The fox in the center didn't run off at the crack of gunshots that echoed across the flat land. It stood still until a third crack brought it down. Both men shouldered their rifles, and the party continued forward. The sulphur smell of gunpowder mixed with the sweetness of pine in the air.

As they approached the grove, another group of figures appeared. At first they moved in and out of the trees, just at the edge, hiding from view, but showed enough to be seen. Then they stepped out of the shadows, into the sun.

"Father, will bullets work against those things?", John asked. A cocked rifle was already up and pressed firmly against his shoulder.

"I don't know, John," answered Father Murray.

Those things, as John called it, were grunting, seething, and spitting creatures that were not of this world. Each the size of a very large dog, but that was where the comparisons ended. They were green, and covered in tumorous skin. Large ears adorned their pointy snouted heads. Most of the time, they were down on all four long legs, that ended in feet with long claws, but it was obvious they were just as comfortable on two when they reared up and screamed. The sound was not one Edward had heard before. It was nothing like any of the ghosts, or the few demons he had encountered. This was more primal.

Two shots rang out from either side of Edward. The shots struck two of the three creatures, but did not drop them. The bullets hit their targets, forcing both to recoil back at the impact, but that was it.

Another volley hit both square in the chest mid-scream. Again, they just shook it off. Edward heard a rustling beside him as both Lewis and John reloaded. The creatures took the pause as an opportunity and rushed at them. There was less than twenty yards separating them from the creatures.

"Hurry!", Father Murray said.

The rustling on either side of him continued, but faster. Edward looked to his side as he heard the click of Lewis loading a shot in his rifle and sliding the bolt back into the place. John had just fished a bullet out of his pocket. A blast came from Lewis's rifle, striking one creature in its brawny shoulder, causing it to stumble, but after just a few steps it shook the impact off and continued. John fired and hit the third one for the first time. The shot hit its elbow, or knee, on the front left leg, sending it down to the ground. It got back up and rumbled along with a limp.

It wasn't working. They were only ten feet away when Edward bent his head and said a silent prayer, while holding the cross out in front of his chest in two outstretched arms. The yellow hue that surrounded them on the ground grew deeper and expanded out. Edward continued to pray. Father Murray joined him. A bright white light projected from the cross, forward, hitting all three beasts, freezing them mid-stride where they were. They hung in the air.

"Try now," Edward said. His voice calm and resolute. Two volleys exploded from either side of him, ripping into the creatures. Another hit the third. All three fell limp in the air. Edward lowered the cross, and they fell into large heaps on the ground.

Edward walked around them. The smell of them was a combination of rot, blood, and a stench he had never smelled before. Lewis poked at one with his rifle. Edward watched for any movement, but there was nothing.

29

The four men stood at the edge of the grove and peered in from the outside. Even without foliage, the tall pines and oaks generated shadows. A gentle breeze above them caused those shadows to dance, creating the illusion of creatures moving around among the trees. Outside of the creaking of the swaying trees, and the crackling of leaves under their footsteps, the area was dead silent. No scurrying of animals. No rustling of leaves.

The woods were dense, forcing the men to weave in and around the trees. It also blocked their view to not much more than a few feet in front of them. With each step, they looked. Both Lewis and John held a loaded rifle at the ready. Each had a second one loaded and slung over their other shoulder. Edward lead the way, holding the cross out. Hoping it would continue to protect them, while fully expecting to be charged by another creature, with every step. The earth outside the grove rumbled again, and they heard it, but didn't feel it. Inside the grove was not affected. No quake beneath them, and no gust of wind. The trees that towered above them continued to sway in the light breeze, but that was all.

A haze formed in front of Edward. First just above ground level, and barely obscuring his vision, but as they moved in further it became denser, until it blocked his view of the ground around their feet, and it felt thick as he stepped through it. His legs felt numb at first, then he picked up the sensation of a vibration running up them.

"Are you guys seeing this?", Father Murray stuttered.

"Okay, good, someone else is seeing the fog. I was wondering if this was that static again," responded Edward.

"Edward, look up."

Edward took his focus off the dense fog that was getting denser, and the strengthening vibrations, and looked up as John asked. He was not prepared for what his eyes saw, and what he was about to come face to face with. Like the display they ran into before, there were desecrated animal corpses hanging there in the air, but this time, there were no ropes or strings that Edward could see. The headless deer, with its front legs cut off, hung there at eye level. Blood dripped down and pooled on the ground. Several feet away, another headless deer spun around slowly in the breeze.

Slowly, Edward stepped around the animal's body. Each step more uncomfortable than the previous, but his eyes stayed up, ignoring the fog. They ran into several other animal corpses hanging in the air. All headless. Some were missing their front legs. Some were missing their back legs. The intestines dangled from a few. The air took on the putrid odor of death.

"What's that?", Father Murray asked.

Edward stepped back behind a tree and watched for a charging beast, but none came. He looked around, but there was nothing.

"I see it, Father. Not sure," Lewis said. "Maybe an old hunter's shed."

"That's what it looks like to me," agreed John, and he and Lewis moved forward to check it out.

Edward looked again, but he saw nothing. Just a few trees right in front of him. A dense cloud of fog cloaked everything else. "Where is it?", he asked.

"Right in front of you," Father Murray said.

"Where?", he asked again.

"Edward, it is about ten feet in front of you, and to your right. It is pretty big, you can't miss it," said Lewis.

"I can't see anything through this fog," he said.

"What fog?", Father Murray gasped.

"You don't see this fog?"

Edward heard rustling leaves around him and then felt a hand grab the hand that held the cross and raised it higher. The immediate space around the cross cleared, allowing him to see a dirty and dilapidated shed, with a flat roof and aged wood panels, with various layers of peeling paint. The side that faced him had a four-paned window in it, each cracked or shattered. He stepped forward to investigate. A low bush stood between him and the shed, and he shifted the cross from his right hand to his left hand, to free up his right to push the bush out of the way. When he let go of the cross for the split second it took to transfer it from one hand to the other, he was thrown back into the void he had experienced before. Surrounded by a gray static that nulled each of his senses. It lasted for only a second or less, but was disorienting, all the same. When the cross touched his left hand, he was pulled back into the present and he knew what the fog was. It was the static, it was trying to consume him again, but the cross was negating it, somewhat.

When his vision cleared, he saw the window of the shed. Inside, a light flickered from side to side like the flame of a candle. The window was too high for him to see in. He pressed his ear to the wall and heard something. He wasn't sure what it was, but it wasn't nothing. There was a noise inside. "Someone is in there, I can see a light," he said urgently. "Find the door. We need to get in."

Edward ran along the wall and rounded the corner when Lewis and John found the door on the front. It was a simple, wood plank door, with a diagonal board across it for support. Large, black, iron hinges connected it to the doorframe. A single brass knob stuck out from the door, without an accompanying lock. Father Murray was reaching for the knob when there was a scream from the other side. A shape leapt from the trees at the men. It grabbed John Sawyer around the head as it jumped over them and, in a single move, yanked his head off at the neck and flung it through the woods. John's body fell slack on the ground, with blood spurting. His windpipe wheezed and gurgled as his lungs took their last breaths. The shape disappeared into the woods as fast as it had appeared.

The three men stood there in shock, looking at their dead friend. Then survival instincts set in and they turned their backs to the shed and focused on the woods around them. Edward searched the woods with his eyes and his ears but, once again, they were in complete silence. The trees around them no longer creaked in the breeze. It was still. Unnaturally still. Leaves on the ground around them began to float in the silence. First just a few, but then, all of them. They didn't move, or spin, just floated.

"My God," exclaimed Father Murray. "Fred's last word was floating. I bet he found this place, and ran into whatever that is."

Mixed in with the leaves were pebbles, branches, were shards of glass, that Edward had to assume came from the broken window. He turned, attempted to open the door to the shed. It was locked. He put his shoulder into it, hard, and the old wood planks in the heavy door cracked, but didn't open.

The scream came again, and the shape lunged out at them from the woods again. Lewis leveled the rifle he had at the ready and fired two shots into it. Unlike the creatures they ran into earlier, the shape fell and rolled around in pain. All three men had a good view of Kevin Stierers' bloodied body on the ground. He screamed and snarled with a crazed look, and his hands clawed at the ground. Lewis pulled his second rifle and, without hesitation, fired a third shot, this time right in his head. Putting an end to the screams. His body laid just feet from John's.

Edward tried the door with his shoulder again, but it still held. Lewis pushed him aside and kicked it. His large booted foot landed squarely just above the knob, sending the door exploding inward on its hinges. A gust of air exploded out, sending Lewis flying and crashing into a tree, back first. His limp form fell to the ground at the base of the tree.

Without a second thought, Edward rushed through the door, cross first, and then froze at the sight of his daughter in a seated position, floating above a pentagram drawn in blood. Black candles dotted the points of the pentagram. A chant in another language filled the room, but she was not speaking it. A cold chill resonated through his body, and the world around him vibrated. Edward moved around the pentagram on the floor, his daughter's solid white eyes followed him.

"Sarah!", he yelled.

She did nothing.

"Stop this!", he pleaded.

She held out a single hand, delicately. A single finger attempted to extend itself from the others, to touch him. There was a gentleness to this. A tenderness.

"Sarah!", he yelled again.

Her lips finally parted, and mouthed, "Help me."

A tear traced down Edward's cheek as his heart sank inside his chest. His little girl was in trouble, and he didn't exactly know how to help her, but he had to try.

Her hand turned over, with her palm upward. It reached for him to grasp it and, on instinct, he reached forward.

"Edward, don't!", screamed Father Murray. His warning was heard, but there was no way Edward planned to pay any attention to it. He was going to grab his daughter and yank her out of there, and then go after whatever had her trapped there in midair.

His fingers touched her, and a flash ran through his essence. He saw the bodies of his parents on the kitchen floor. Karen, as she took her last breath. The births of both Jacob and Sarah, and then his own death. Jacob, standing over his casket, mourning his loss. Father Murray, performing the burial rites as he was lowered into a hole next to his parents. Then, as quickly as it had all arrived, it was gone. Darkness replaced everything. It was an all too familiar void. Edward had been there before, which lessened his surprise when that same voice echoed around him, "I told you I would be back."

Outside the void and in the shed, his body flew limp and lifeless against the wall, before collapsing in a pile on the floor. The hand that clutched the cross bounced. On the rebound, the fingers opened, letting the cross slide from his grasp.

30

The constant slow breeze of air coming through the vents carried a sterile smell everywhere as Jacob sat in a chair not meant to be sat in for longer than a few minutes. His aching legs and back, attested to that fact. They had endured a marathon session of thirty-two hours straight, with only a few minutes away to stretch or visit the bathroom. The other chair in the room was more of a lounge chair, or so it seemed. The red vinyl cushioned structure had a tall back and leaned back a little, if you pushed down on the handle. Its occupant, Father Murray, had been there for about as long, minus an hour the day before, when he left to go tend to his concerned parish members who were holed up in the high school gym.

Jacob appreciated him being there. He had no one else. Lewis Tillingsly had spent the majority of his time there, but now had other responsibilities, following the death of Sheriff Marcus Thompson. The small police force had lost its leader and, due to lack of experience, or recent emotional losses, no one besides him was suitable to take that position. It wasn't official. He wouldn't wear a badge or uniform, but that didn't diminish the weight of his words. They would follow him, just as they had for years.

Lost in Marcus's search party were the sheriff, Mayor Chris Chandel, Chamber of Commerce chief Walter Spencer, two council members, and scores of husbands and sons. Forty-three, in total. Normal city operations ceased at that moment. Everything that happened from that point forward was just a reaction to the emergency. Over the next few days, the numbness of the shock would wear off, and grief would set in. Then panic and fear would follow.

The only question in Jacob's mind about the next few days was, would his dad wake up? He laid in the hospital bed that sat between him and Father Murray, with wires running to monitors, and a ventilator to help him breathe. He hadn't regained consciousness since his hand had contacted Sarah in the shed. None of the medical tests the doctors at County General had given him had found anything medically wrong with him, but their capabilities were limited. They were just a small medical center.

Father Murray and Lewis had argued for the better part of an hour the day before, about trying to transfer Edward to one of the larger cities, where the facilities were more modern. It pained Lewis, Jacob could tell the inner conflict he felt, to argue against trying to seek better help for his friend. As protective as he wanted to be of Edward, he had to be the same, or more so, to the town. If they transferred him, there would be questions. How could they explain it?

Out the window behind Jacob, just over seventeen miles away, was the only other family he and Edward had. She sat quietly in a shed, still floating above the ground, or so they believed. No one had laid eyes on her since they left. The progression of the attack had stopped nine hours after Lewis and Father Murray had pulled Edward out. Four square miles of forest were leveled flat. The trees that had once stood so proudly, were pulverized to nothing but dust and twigs. No homes were damaged, it had stopped short of them, but Lewis took a wait and see posture about letting anyone return home. Some wouldn't want to. Feeling the earth jump and shake under their feet was enough to spook them to the point of never wanting to return. Every major incident that happened in Miller's Crossing drove one or two families away. No one could blame them.

"Hey, Jake. How is he doing?", asked a head poking through the door of the hospital room.

"Still the same," Jacob said to Mark Grier.

Mark walked in and stood at the foot of the bed, looking at his friend of a long time. Father Murray was leaned back in the chair to the right, asleep. Mark kept his voice down and said, "Don't you worry. Your father is a tough man. He once broke his arm at the beginning of baseball season, and still made the last two games. How are you doing?"

Jacob looked up at his father's friend, wearily. He was tired. There was no denying that. Father Murray had dozed off a few times in the chair, but Jacob hadn't been so lucky. Not that his body hadn't tried, but his mind had other intentions. Each time his eyes fell heavy, his mind played a picture show of his father and his sister. He knew from what he had heard Lewis and Father Murray talk about that Sarah was at the center of all of this. That was something he couldn't believe, but his mind still constructed images that matched what he had heard the men talk about. It created a war in his thoughts and dreams. Images of her floating, with everything evil his mind could conjure around her. Flames of red, orange, and black everywhere. Then a kind image of her blue eyes looking at him with that same annoyed, but loving, look she always gave him. One image to battle the other. He felt alone, and scared. "I am fine, Mr. Grier."

"How long has he been here?", Mark asked as he pointed to Father Murray.

"Most of the day."

"Good," Mark said. His gaze back on his old childhood friend.

Jacob hadn't taken his eyes off his father, except for a few moments here and there when talking to a doctor, nurse, or other visitor. Every second he hoped to see his eyes open, or a hand move.

Mark backed up and leaned against a cabinet against the wall, and watched. Silence surrounded all three men. The only sound was the silent, but constant, pump in and out of the ventilator, and the occasional snore from Father Murray or the creak of the vinyl in his chair as he shifted.

They all just stood in silence for the better part of an hour before Lewis Tillingsly stopped by to check on Edward. When he walked in, he shook Mark's hand and exchanged a quiet greeting, and then took up his post against the cabinet next to Mark. There was no smalltalk, or there could have been, and Jacob never noticed. He locked his eyes on his father and didn't look anywhere else. His thoughts were there and everywhere. His state of exhaustion had now allowed the war of thoughts that had only occurred when his eyes closed to now invade his waking thoughts, ripping apart what was left of his emotional sanity. A tear and sniff escaped, but he caught them before they progressed to anything more. There was no concern in his head about anyone else noticing. There wasn't room for anything so insignificant.

"Lewis, you copy?", squawked the radio attached to Lewis' hip.

He pulled it off and stepped toward the door. "Lewis here. What is it Tony?" He stopped just short of the hallway. Far enough to muffle the conversation behind the door, but still close enough for everyone in the room to hear it. The sound rustled Father Murray awake, partially.

Over the radio, Tony reported, "She is out, and walking toward the town. She is not alone."

DAVID CLARK

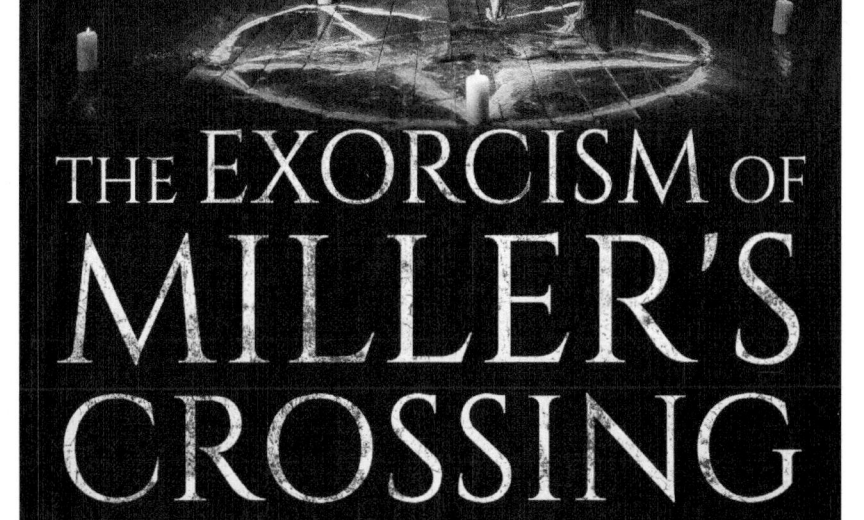

THE EXORCISM OF MILLER'S CROSSING

THE EXORCISM OF MILLER'S CROSSING

Miller's Crossing Book 3

David Clark

1

Days turned into a week in Miller's Crossing, but only the calendar recorded the passage of time. The sun continued to come up in the morning and disappear in the evening, but not even the light of day could crack through the darkness that loomed over the town. This wasn't the darkness of night or a storm cloud, this darkness was heavy and wet. Like the type you find in the furthest and deepest corner of a leaky basement, down where mold, mildew, and the fear of things that *go boo* lived. The difference here, the things that *go boo* were walking the streets.

Its citizens had taken refuge at the high school or their own homes since what they called "the event." Most only braved a daylight raid for supplies, but even that was a tentative and dangerous effort. No one moved alone or blindly. They always checked around the corner to make sure nothing was there before going further. Only a few stores remained open. Two days after the event, Ted Barton moved into the back storeroom of his local grocery and mercantile. Every morning he stepped outside and looked to see what was around and then re-locked the door; that was the only time he actually went outside. The rest of the time he stayed in the store, watching and waiting for anyone who may come in need of food or supplies. When the sun started to dip and shadows stretched across the street and his storefront, he retreated to the safety of his back storeroom. The sound from the portable television Ted had kept back there since the Cuban Missile Crisis battled against the screaming and howling outside.

Two days after the event, Lewis Tillingsly closed down the roads into and out of town under the guise of roadwork. He even went as far as sending a press release to all the neighboring towns to be read on the radio, and to the Lynchburg local news. To further sell the story, he and Frank Michaels took two farm tractors out and dug up large sections of the road, leaving piles of dirt as obstructions. To an outsider, it would look like road repair or bridge replacement. To Lewis, the new sheriff, it was a necessary protection to buy the time needed to get things under control. How much it would buy him, he didn't know. A few locals used the old grown-over logging roads to make an escape, but they knew enough to not tell.

While most of the residents of Miller's Crossing remained in hiding, unless they needed to go out, a few attempted to take a stand once their fear dissipated. Lewis had used emergency alert programs set up after 9/11 to send a specific order to every member of the town. That message stated: "Do not attempt to confront these creatures. Stay inside." Most heeded it; some did not. They headed out in patrols just after dusk, armed with whatever they had on hand: everything from hunting rifles, to farming tools, to a few homemade Molotov cocktails. Their goal was to take back their town. Their achievement was adding to the loss-of-life total.

Jacob could see the fires they set with their attacks from the window of his father's hospital room. Edward had not moved or spoken since that day. Every doctor in town took a shot at reviewing his condition. Each left scratching their head, no closer to the cause of his condition or a treatment to bring him around. Jacob had only left a few times during that time; once to take a walk and try to clear his head, which didn't work. There was a constant something there; what, he didn't really know. He mentioned it to Father Murray once, who explained it was probably him sensing the ghosts and demons that now roamed openly around town. That was possible. He had felt it a few times at first, but it had come and gone. Now it stayed and never left.

The other time he left his father's side was a move of honorable intent but foolhardy execution. Lewis had just left his father's room after receiving a radio call about another raiding party attempting to confront several demons around Westside Park, just under a mile away from the hospital. Jacob heard him order Tony to stop them before he rushed out himself to help intervene. The response from Tony told him that Sarah was with them. To Jacob's knowledge, that was only the second time she had left the shed since all this started. No one had talked to him directly about everything they knew, or had they? He had to hope they knew more about what was going on than they told him, which was nothing. What was clear was she was the key at the center of all this. If he could get through to her, he could put a stop to it, a thought he considered rather deeply as possibly the last thought his father had before what happened to him.

He ventured out and saw a sight that beat any horror film he watched late on Friday and Saturday nights. Animal-like beasts walked around on two legs, screaming, howling, and snorting. Their claws scratched against the concrete of the sidewalk in ominous screeches. At the center, his sister. Still dressed in what she wore the last time he saw her, that was all he recognized. Her eyes were wide and solid white. A cape of raven hair flew around behind her as she floated down the road and up into the park. Her arms and hands directed the creatures without a sound. They maintained a ring around her. One he couldn't find a way through. He watched as the raiding party rounded the corner, firing their rifles at the creatures. A few rushed at them, swinging axes and machetes. The flails were wild and only connected a few times, not that it made any difference. They brushed the attacks off like gnats on a summer afternoon.

Lewis's voice echoed through the loudspeaker on top of Tony's cruiser. "Stop and disperse, for your own safety." He repeated it over and over again above the screaming, but it was too late. Those were not from the creatures. They were from the men who attacked them. As a last gasp attempt, one man threw a flaming bottle at Sarah. It hit and exploded around her, but not on her. Inside that sphere of flames, her skin changed. Marks and symbols pressed through her skin from the inside while her lips moved. With a single flip of her hand, she sent those flames back at the attacker, Clay Harris. The ball of flame lifted him off the ground and up into the sky, like a shooting star rising from the ground, and he disappeared from view. Then, without warning or cause, she disappeared too, just as she had the first time she emerged from the shed. Jacob could only assume she returned to it like she had before.

That trip was last night. Lewis saw him and caught up with him halfway back to the hospital. Jacob wasn't running back like he had on his way out. Instead, he was walking, defeated, and exposed. Lewis gathered him into Tony's patrol car. There was no grand lecture on how stupid he was for doing this. Jacob merely sat in the back and cried. When he went out, he wanted to help but didn't know how. Seeing her like that cemented in him how hopeless the situation was. That was no longer his sister. She was something different. Evil. The destroyer of the world she had become part of over the last few years. Her actions killed people she had grown to call friends and family, and she didn't even hesitate. Look what she had done to her own father.

When Tony dropped Jacob and Lewis back off at the hospital, they walked in through the emergency room. Each bay around them was full of victims from tonight's encounters, either from the raiding party or those who were caught outside after dark. The fate of the victims was already sealed. That didn't stop the medical staff from trying to save them. This was a nightly occurrence.

Back up in Edward's room, Lewis called in Wendy Tolliver and placed Jacob in her care under "house arrest." Her instructions were to not let Jacob go anywhere, which she hadn't. Every time he shifted in the chair or got up to walk around the room, she took a position at the door. Even when he walked down to take a shower, she walked by his side the whole way like she was escorting a prisoner to lockup. If he had any other plans to leave, it would have to be out the window. Not an option from four stories up.

2

Jacob's excursion was not tiring physically, but it exhausted him on an emotional level, adding to the stress and strain that had built up inside him over the last week. He had spent days fighting back his body's need. A few times it won, but not for more than a few moments of respite. Each time, he shook awake to check on his dad when he realized what had happened. This time, his mind and body both gave in to the need. His head dipped once, then pulled up. Then it bobbed again. The final surrender was when his shoulders slouched, and he slid down in the chair. The mostly quiet room around him went from a place of frantic movement that appeared full of chaos to one that slid softly into a world of darkness.

The tranquil darkness didn't last. The something that had been there in his mind when this all started was still there, and it grew. It became heavier, but was familiar. It wasn't long before the darkness melted away, leaving Jacob in his room back at the family home. Something wasn't right though. It wasn't his room now. A blank wall was where his flat-screen television hung. The drapes were something straight out of some old sitcom from the eighties. He ripped them down the first day he was in that room, which explained the musky smell and the lack of anything in the room. The room was how he first saw it when he walked in through the door, which was where he now stood.

He turned around and looked down the stairs to the living room. It was much the same. Old console television against the wall. The same brown-and-orange sofa that greeted them when they walked in. A simple green loop rug under the dusty coffee table. As he descended further, the dining room looked like it did then and now. They hadn't made many changes in that room. Jacob continued walking around the house, but having accepted that this was the day they moved in, seeing everything as it was no longer surprised him. What he was looking for now was his family.

He ducked back upstairs to check his father's room. The door was closed, which it was on that day. After that, his father had always kept it open unless he was in there. Jacob turned the handle and opened it, slowly, timidly. With it cracked open, he poked his head inside. It was all wrong. This wasn't his father's room. It was the hospital room, his father still lying in the bed connected to a ventilator. Father Murray was asleep in the chair by the bed. Wendy Tolliver sat in a guest chair, her neck craned almost straight up to see the television attached to the wall. Next to her on the other side of the hospital bed was Jacob, slouched down in the chair. Each frozen in time. Not even the image on the television screen moved. He walked around and waved his hand in front of Wendy's face, but she didn't flinch. Then out of an abundance of curiosity, he walked over to himself slouched in the chair. His hand shook as he reached toward himself and then paused just above his arm. *What would happen if I touch it?* he thought. There was only one way to find out. He started to lower his hand the remaining few inches, but held up. There was something eerie about this, almost morbid. The sound of his breathing grew rapid and shallow as he extended his fingers the last bit and touched his left forearm lightly. He leapt back as the hair on his left arm stood on end and he felt the pressure of someone touching him. With a racing heart, and fear of what he didn't understand running through his mind, Jacob backed out of the room and into the hallway. The bedroom door slammed behind him, without him pulling it closed.

Across the hall stood another closed door. That was not unusual. It was Sarah's room, and she only left her door open when she wasn't home. Something about needing her privacy and having an annoying younger brother. Even as Jacob got older, it didn't change, but the time she spent in the room did. Instead of staying locked behind the door from sunup to sundown, she spent more time downstairs in the living room or sitting at the kitchen table up against the window, reading. He reached forward for her door handle and gave it a turn. It turned easily and opened. A gust of air sucked in and pulled the door handle from his grasp, sending the door slamming backward into the doorstop on the wall. The room itself was empty. None of her furniture was in there. Just a layer of dust that rose off the floor with the gust and created a cloud in the center of the room that danced in the light coming in through the window. Jacob stepped in to grab the door handle and close it, but walked into a tempest of air that pushed against his upper body and pinned him against the doorframe. It took every ounce of strength he could strain out of his seventeen-year-old athletic frame to push with both hands against the doorjamb. The shove sent him out backward, crashing into the door of his father's room. Then Sarah's door exploded shut. The window blew the hair on his head backward.

With no one upstairs, he continued his search downstairs. The living and dining rooms were both empty. A push through the door to the kitchen found a familiar scene. Sarah was sitting there, in the breakfast nook next to the window, reading. The focus of her concentration was the same little simple brown leather book his father carried around with him everywhere. She didn't acknowledge him as he entered the kitchen, and appeared frozen like those he found in his father's bedroom. He took a few more steps toward her, and her right hand jerked up and held up a palm to tell him to stop. Her face turned sideways, giving Jacob an unimpeded view of her profile. It was her again, not the white-eyed marked-up creature he saw earlier that night. She was reading, quickly, but her mouth made no sound.

She put the book down and turned toward him. Eyes cold and hostile. An expression on her face that leered whilst also attempting to be friendly. "Hey, little brother," she said. It was her voice, loud and clear, but at the same time, it wasn't. The same tone and tenor, but lacking any of the personality and warmth.

"Sarah?" he asked, unsure if it was really her or some figment in a dream.

"In the flesh." Her cold blue eyes watched as he walked around the island in the kitchen and closer to the table. They didn't blink as Jacob took the unnecessary path. He wanted to see how she reacted. To size her up.

"Is this really you?" he asked, and then felt foolish about it. If this was a dream, what answer other than yes would his mind give to itself? Then he wondered, had he ever had a dream in which he knew he was dreaming?

"Yes, Jacob. It's me. It's really me," she said as she stood up from the table and walked toward him, arms outstretched for an embrace.

Jacob stepped backward to avoid her, and her arms dropped by her sides.

"I understand. A lot has happened."

"What did you do to Dad?" demanded Jacob.

"You don't need to worry about him. He is fine. I did it to protect him. This... this thing in me wanted to kill him. If I didn't do this, he would be dead."

"What thing? What are you talking about, Sarah?"

"There is something, or someone, in me. It's hard to explain. It has been here for years, since the Reaping. For a long time, it was gone, but a few weeks back, it pushed me aside and took over. Jacob, I am not in control of my body. Not in control of my life. I can see what happens, but I can't do anything. When I try, it about kills me. Like with Dad, and with you tonight."

"Tonight, what do you mean tonight?" roared Jacob. His neck tensed and fists clenched.

"I saw you. It saw you, and it wanted to hurt you. I did what I could to hurt it to keep it from hurting you."

Hearing she could hurt it gave him an idea. "You got to stop this, Sarah. People are dying. Fight it," Jacob implored.

"I can't. It's too strong. You don't understand."

She was right, Jacob didn't understand. He still didn't know what the "it" she spoke of was. He wasn't sure if this was real or just some construct of his physically and emotionally exhausted subconscious. In fact, that made more sense than this being real. How could she be here talking to him?

"You don't understand," she continued in a mumble. Her hands covered her face, and it appeared she began to sob.

"Sarah, I don't know what this is, but tell me how to help you."

"You can't," she said.

"Is this real? Are you here talking to me?" he asked, once again feeling foolish at asking such a question.

She looked up from her hands and answered, tears streaming down her face, "Yes, Jacob, this is real. The abilities I have... the abilities I have through it let me reach out and talk to you like this. I know right now you're asleep in a chair next to Dad. I'm sitting in the shed in the woods, where it retreated when I struck out at it to save you. I can't do much more than that."

"I am coming for you!" he vowed. "As soon as I'm awake, I am coming for you."

"No! Don't!" she shrieked. "It will kill you! Stay away! Keep everyone away!" She reached out and grabbed his arms at the elbow. Her touch burned and seared the skin, causing him to pull back. The pain stopped, but gray smoke rose from soot stains on his arms. Just before he yanked away, her face changed. The shape, the color, the presence of her was evil and ominous. Yellow and red replaced the blue of her eyes. Pits of black replaced the whites. A smell of death and decay accompanied her voice. "Jacob, you can't help me."

"The cross" he whispered to himself.

Sarah heard it too. "Not even that. Dad had that in his hand when he tried." Her voice trembled, and she looked around behind her. "I gotta go."

"Sarah, tell me how to help you. There has to be a way."

"No, Jacob. I gotta go."

She frantically ran toward the back door and fumbled with the door handle. She attempted again and didn't turn it far enough before yanking on it. Finally, the door opened a crack and then stopped and slammed. Her shoulders were hunched with her head down as she turned back toward Jacob and rushed him. Strange markings, etched from the inside, scarred her skin. Yellow pupils glowed against the black pits that surrounded them. She grabbed his arms with claws.

Jacob tried to pull away but couldn't. The sharp claws dug into his skin as its evil gaze studied him. Then, with the voice of a thousand tortured souls, it screamed at him. Jacob felt something draining from him. His heart pounded in his chest as his breath left his lungs. Then something else was leaving him. He couldn't put his finger on what it was, but he was losing focus, losing himself. A white light emerged from his body. Small particles traced the path around him and then out toward Sarah. The more particles he saw, the weaker he felt. He was fading, and he knew it.

"NO!" screamed his sister's voice. It echoed around him as the claws let go, letting him fall.

Jacob landed in his chair in the hospital room. Heart still pounding and out of breath, he startled awake and stood straight up.

"You okay, Jake?" asked Wendy. "You have a bad dream?" she asked before he answered her first question. "You aren't the only one. We are all living in one right now. You're safe."

Jacob looked at his father lying still in the bed. His own hands subconsciously rubbed his arms. The area around his elbows was tender, and he rolled up the sleeves of his black sweatshirt. There were scratches and soot marks on both.

3

The first light of day cracked through the window and across the room, but the scene inside stayed the same as it had for the last seven mornings. Edward remained motionless in the hospital bed. Air cycled in and out of his lungs with the help of tubes. The rhythmic pump of the machine was no longer noticeable. It was just part of the essence of the room. Father Murray was still asleep in the recliner. He hadn't stirred much in the last several hours. Only a few snorts and moans in his sleep. Jacob was awake to hear them. His sleep came in fits. Here and there. Each time, he woke startled and searched his thoughts for any more conversations with Sarah that might have occurred while he was asleep. Nothing. Only the marks on the inside of his elbows told him it was real.

Despite the gloomy surroundings, it was a beautiful day. Cool and crisp, not a cloud in the sky. From the fourth-floor window, Jacob could see the majestic reds and oranges of fall. Out there, people should have been preparing for the great fall traditions like the carnival at the elementary school, and Halloween. Thoughts of costumes and apple bobbing should be on the mind of every child in Miller's Crossing. Instead they were trapped in their homes, while real spooks roamed the streets. Their parents only risked leaving on quick trips for the necessary supplies. From this view, though, everything looked like a normal fall day.

Jacob continued to look out the window upon the town. It was a break, one his eyes and mind needed. Once his eyes took it, the nagging concern that he might miss his father move or something consumed his mind. The thought ate at him and then became a repeated phrase over and over in his head. After enough time, the weight of the words stacked up, one on top of the other, so much he had to turn around and check on his father, just long enough to clear the thought. Then it was back to the window.

He was lost in the beauty. His mind flew like a bird across the treetops as his tired soul drifted into a daydream. The thoughts of what was behind him in the room faded. It was peaceful but brief. In the distance, screaming down Main Street, were the unmistakable flashing blue lights of a patrol car. Were they running a siren? Jacob couldn't tell from inside, but he doubted it. That would be foolish. First, who was on the road that they needed to get out of the way? Second, why attract the attention of those beasts?

With Wendy in the room behind him, watching to make sure he didn't sneak out again, it meant that was Terrance or Tony. The only remaining deputies. Jacob watched as it continued, disappearing behind trees and buildings for a few moments only to reappear. Then it turned down Oak Drive toward the hospital. The leaves of the great oaks the street was named for were all over the ground, giving him an unobstructed view through the barren branches. It was not going at high speed, just a normal drive with lights.

At the entrance to the hospital, it pulled in. That was not much of a shock to Jacob. It would only be logical for the hospital to be one of a few destinations. The first thought that exploded into his mind was that someone was hurt. He stood up to look down through the window and watch the car maneuver through the parking lot and toward the emergency services entrance, but it didn't. Instead of taking the left it needed to make, it took a right toward the main entrance.

Jacob watched as long as he could from his perch in the window. The car disappeared behind the ledge and around the corner. The flashing blue lights reflected off the cars in the lot, but even that eventually disappeared. With the curiosity gone and the fascination with the landscape subsided, he returned to his post of the last eight days and sat watching his father, with only a few glances up at the national morning news show on the television.

They were going on and on about the latest proposed stimulus bill going through the senate. One side was accusing the other of holding it up, but they had yet to request a vote. Jacob had no interest or stomach for politics. It appeared his grandfather had tinkered with it at the local level at some point, but what he saw in the old news clippings was different from this. He got things done, or tried to. From his view, no matter how many times his father tried to describe the artistry of the modern political system, it was just a bunch of old people who never learned how to share in the sandbox in kindergarten. His attention was waning when Lewis Tillingsly walked in, a familiar black hat on his head, minus the star that used to adorn it. Keeping with the old traditions, the hat was off his head before he entered the room. He held it low at his waist as he paid respects to Wendy, Jacob, and then to Edward, who wasn't in any shape to return them.

"Any change?" he asked.

Jacob just shook his head, looking glum.

"Chin up," Lewis said. "He's a fighter." Then he walked toward Father Murray, still asleep in the recliner next to the bed. He tapped the father on the shoulder, but he only rustled a bit to move away from the disturbance. This time, he reached down and shook his shoulder ever so lightly. The eyes of the old priest sprang open and searched around the room, settling on Lewis standing over him.

"Father, your guest is here," Lewis said.

The vinyl of the recliner gave a ripping sound as Father Murray hurried to his feet, and the material released its hold on the fabric of his black slacks and coat. He quickly adjusted his clothing with a tug here and a tuck there while he followed Lewis out of the room. Jacob watched as they both left without explanation. He didn't really need one. Seeing the patrol car arrive just moments ago, and now the announcement of a visitor, Jacob could piece the puzzle together, at least partially. Who the visitor was remained a mystery.

Lewis and Father Murray had been gone for over an hour when Wendy got up and announced, "I need some coffee. Want something?"

Jacob just shook his head, which provoked a concerned look on Wendy's face.

"You haven't eaten or slept much since all this happened. Why don't I walk down to the cafeteria and get you some eggs and toast?" She continued to look at him.

Jacob knew she would not take no for an answer, so he nodded, which caused her to smile for a second or two before she headed out.

Jacob was hungry, and he could think of worse things to eat, but that wasn't the driving motivation. This gave him a few minutes without the watchful eye of his guard, who hadn't left him since Lewis asked her to keep an eye on him. She hadn't even left to call home or anything, which Jacob thought was odd at first. With everything going on, you would worry about what was happening with your family. An exchange he overheard between Wendy and Father Murray explained it. The father was helping her pray and consoling her for the loss of her husband, Daniel, who had been a member of Marcus's search party. Jacob immediately felt bad. He was dead because of them—or Sarah, to be more precise. The feeling lessened as he realized she didn't appear to hold any ill will toward him or his father. She was compassionate toward them both, not something that was just a professional duty.

It was only a moment after the sound of Wendy's hard-soled shoes disappeared down the vinyl-tiled hall before Jacob was out of his chair and slinking toward the door. He stood there for a second just listening for anyone approaching. Once he was satisfied there was no one coming, he stuck his head out the door and looked around. The hall was vacant and plain; the wall color matched the floor. Only a single nurse sat behind the nurses' station, clear at the other end of the hall. At the end in the other direction was a single atrium, or so they called it. It wasn't much more than a room in the corner of the building. Windows covered the exterior walls. A simple sectional sofa that had seen better days sat under the windows. Used mostly by family members who needed to take a call in private or just a moment to gather their thoughts while visiting a loved one.

The room was occupied, as it often was, and the occupants resembled some that Jacob believed would be in there if they were delivering grim news to a family, but he knew that not to be the case. He knew two of the men and slightly recognized the third. The tall slender figure in all black wearing a black wide-brimmed hat, like the one Father Murray wore, had first visited them eight years ago.

4

The hallway remained empty, as was much of the hospital. It was a small, square building. Five floors in total, with the emergency room and several doctors' offices on the first floor. A couple of surgical suites were on the second floor, where the most common surgery was the removal of tonsils from a child with a sore throat. The recovery and medical rooms were on the third and fourth floors. They reserved the top floor for the administrative offices. On any given day there were only twenty or so patients in the complex. They referred most serious medical issues to a larger city such as Richmond where the facilities were more capable. The only exceptions were emergencies where the doctors at County General stabilized the patient while they awaited an airlift to arrive to transport them.

"Jacob, you can come on in here," said Lewis Tillingsly.

Jacob had snuck down the hallway as far as he dared to hear what the three men were talking about. His attempt to stay hidden had failed. He crept into the room, not sure what he was walking in on. All three men watched as he entered. Their gazes made him uncomfortable, but he didn't understand why. They were not leering, but looking at him with a great deal of curiosity.

Inside the door, he stood face-to-face with the tall slender man he spied from down the hall. Father Lucian stepped forward and extended his hand. In his thick accent he said, "A pleasure to see you again, Jacob. I am sorry it is under such circumstances."

Jacob shook the Italian man's hand. The first time he saw Father Lucian was about eight years ago when he stood outside their home waiting for his father. The man stood next to Father Murray as they pulled up in front. He didn't have an opportunity to talk to him much then. His father sent him and Sarah inside. After that night, they had just a brief exchange of "Nice to meet you, young man," before he left. The next time was not for another five years, when he flew over to pick up Sarah for her training. At that time, Jacob had just started to feel what his father and sister did. Father Lucian took a few minutes to talk to Jacob. His words stuck with him. "Don't be afraid of this. Embrace it. Enjoy it and live it. Your time will come soon enough."

"It's good to see you too," Jacob said. "Can you help?"

The two priests shared a look between themselves at the question. Both men looked concerned, which caused a stir in that dark pit that had settled in Jacob over the past week.

He studied each for any visual tell, but neither gave much, so he demanded again, "Can you help? You have to."

"Jacob," Father Murray started. "We will do everything we can. It's very complicated. First, we need to understand what *this* is."

"You don't know what this is? This is a possession. Like in the movies. Can't you go out and do some kind of exorcism or something and end all this?" exploded Jacob, eyes bulging and fists clenched at his sides.

"I would agree, it is a possession," said Father Lucian.

"Jacob, possessions are very difficult situations to deal with. Hollywood makes you think you sprinkle some holy water on the person, say a few prayers, and once the demon says its name, that is it, it is all over and the person gets up and walks away. It is nothing like that," explained Father Murray.

"Absolutely not. The last possession I interceded with took over three months to finally free the person, and they still aren't who they were before. But that was nothing like this. That was just a normal person who suffered from symptoms some might relate to mental illness," said Father Lucian.

"This is an all-out assault. Something that has never happened before," Father Murray added.

"Indeed, and never involving one of our own," Father Lucian said.

"What does that mean? Assault? Is this a war?"

"Yes, a war from the start of time that will continue until the end of time," said Father Lucian. "That is why they picked this place. Your sister might have just been… well, how would you say? A lucky convenience."

Father Murray invited Jacob to have a seat on the worn sofa that lined the wall. Even though it was now fall, the sun still made it up high during the middle of the day. This allowed the radiant heat to more than peer in through the windows of the sunroom, heating the cloth cushions of the ratty old green sofa. The warmth of the cushion was a welcome sensation to Jacob. The hospital itself remained rather chilly around the clock.

Over the next hour, Fathers Murray and Lucian explained to Jacob many things his father had already talked to him about. In particular, what was special about Miller's Crossing and why a demon would pick this location. They also explained what "sensitives" and "keepers" were. Both were terms he had never heard his father use. When Father Lucian explained that their family were keepers, he felt a tinge of something special. They explained that no keeper had ever been compromised before.

"Then how did this happen?" asked Jacob.

That question caused Father Murray to look down at the floor before taking a seat next to Jacob. He looked deep into the young man's eyes and explained. "I let the demon in, over thirty years ago. Something I have regretted every day since." The solemn tone in his voice continued throughout the entire explanation, which started with the day the demon killed Jacob's grandparents and ended on the football field on the night the locals call the Reaping. One detail about that night that Jacob didn't know until now was that the demon, Abaddon, had targeted Sarah before his father confronted it and sent it fleeing, or so they thought.

"I now believe it attached itself to her then, and *that* explains why she was so strong. Her abilities were beyond any we had seen from any other keeper before," interjected Father Lucian.

"So, you caused all this?" asked Jacob. There was an edge to his voice and an increase in the tension of his body. Jacob was an even-tempered kid, never losing his temper when his sister kidded him or he didn't get his way. Not to say he never got mad, he just never lost it. Never really had a teenage hormone-driven outburst, that he could remember, but this was close and getting closer. It was building up, and it wouldn't be long before it exploded.

Before the anger could boil any further, Lewis stepped in. "Now is not the time to rehash old wounds. Your father and Father Murray have already settled things. What is important is to handle what is here now. Fathers, do you have any ideas?"

"I need to see it," said Father Lucian.

Stunned looks appeared on everyone who heard the sentence.

5

"I'm going on record right now, I am completely against this," Lewis Tillingsly said. His arms crossed as he stood in front of Tony's cruiser. They had parked the black-and-white Impala at the same location every day, and most nights, since it began. He only left when the creatures Lewis assigned him to monitor left and headed somewhere in town. When they did, he followed them at a safe distance, reporting in and helping to keep others out of their way.

"He will be safe. You have my word," Father Lucian said.

"Can you even guarantee your own safety? We all saw what she did to Edward," insisted Lewis. Jacob saw his eyes dart to him when he said "she."

"I can take care of myself," Jacob said. He tried to sound confident, but inside he was a bundle of nerves on a roller coaster. How could he make such a claim when he still didn't know what this was?

"I have to agree with Lewis. We have both been out there." Father Murray provided the final vote that put an end to the discussion, and Father Lucian nodded in agreement.

Jacob considered protesting, but he knew it would be fruitless. Also, inside, a large part of him urged him to stay quiet. The fear of what was out there had taken hold, overriding his decisions. He still had seen nothing beyond what he did last night in the park, but he felt it. It had been there a week. Now, being this close to it, it was overwhelming.

From a safe distance, Jacob watched as the tall and slender priest turned away from the four men who stood at the front of the patrol car, and walked along the double yellow line down Harper Hill Road and across the bridge that spanned Walter's Creek. Each stride was the same pace and length as the previous. A board-straight back and shoulders exuded confidence as he made his approach. Once over the bridge, he stopped and pivoted at a right angle to the road and stepped across the lane. There was a brief pause when his black leather shoes hit the white line that marked the edge of the road.

A single foot raised up and stepped forward off the tarmac and onto the grass of the shoulder. At that moment, a large rumble sent Jacob and the others scurrying back behind the car. The ground didn't shake. This rumble resembled the deep throaty growl of gigantic beast. His view from his new perch was blocked, and he stood up to see Father Lucian. The ground under them was still not shaking, and the rumble had stopped several seconds earlier, but Jacob's legs felt like rubber bands. His hands braced himself against the trunk deck.

Father Lucian was unaffected and statue-straight and stiff, one foot on the shoulder, the other still on the tarmac. The second foot lifted and joined the other on the grass. Another rumble, this time louder, raced at them from the grove of trees that stood tall and strong in the center of the desolate landscape. Jacob leaned onto the car and kept his eyes on Father Lucian. The roar raised dust as it raced outward and past him. His pants legs and jacket flapped violently in the wind, but he didn't surrender any ground.

What happened next sent a shiver down Jacob like he had never felt before. Not even the death of his mother shocked him like this. He was now thankful that Lewis and Father Murray didn't let him join Father Lucian. When the gust passed by, Father Lucian took another step toward the woods. There was no roar this time in response to the step. Instead, every sliver of debris, from the smallest piece of sawdust to a branch several feet long, shot up from their resting place on the ground and hovered head high. The layer pulsated like a great ocean with waves of peaks and valleys.

On his rubber legs, Jacob walked around the cruiser to get a better view of the scene. His entire body trembled at the sight. For as far as he could see, it was the same thing. Then he looked down the road at Father Lucian, who still hadn't yielded. The priest took off his black wide-brimmed hat and carefully bent down to place it on the ground next to him. Then he stood back up, again straight and strong. His left hand reached into his coat and retrieved an object that he placed on his head. The distance and remnants of the dust cloud created by the first roar clouded Jacob's vision, and he couldn't see exactly what the object was. Father Lucian stepped forward, and the debris parted around him. As he moved in further, Jacob lost sight of him as the debris closed in around him. All they could do was wait.

And wait they did. First thirty minutes, then an hour. Dark shadows of late afternoon crept onto their position. With it, the chill of fall and a realization that Tony was the first to bring up. "What if he doesn't make it back? Are we going in there to get him?"

Lewis gave a quick shake of his head as he stared at his watch.

Jacob searched the dark feeling that had been with him for the last week for any change. Any sense of a decrease in its intensity that might signal Father Lucian had some effect. There wasn't. Nor was it stronger. There was no change, not that he was sure this was how it even worked. It was all a guess to him at this point. He wasn't even sure this feeling was related to any of this. So many emotions stirred in his head at the moment, Jacob wasn't sure what was what.

Another thirty minutes passed, and the mood of the group took another dip. Jacob had walked as far the bridge over Walter's Creek to get a better view. He searched for any sign that Father Lucian was returning. Behind him, Father Murray now sat in the patrol car, and Tony and Lewis stood quietly outside. They batted about the question Tony had asked earlier a few more times among them. It wasn't until the last time, just over five minutes ago, that Lewis put a timetable on it. They would wait an hour after the fall of darkness and then return to the safety of the police station. Tony would stay behind in case Father Lucian returned.

Darkness fell, and there was still no sign of his return. Jacob stood on top of the bridge where he had for the last hour. Now he was shrouded in complete darkness. Only the lights from Lewis's large Plymouth and Tony's patrol cruiser cast light on him from behind. His shadow stretched from the bridge down the center of Harper Hill Road and to the spot Father Lucian turned into the woods from. The darkness also blocked out the scene of horror that was to his right. It was still there, he didn't doubt that. Just couldn't see it, which, with the dead silence that surrounded them, made it that much eerier.

After another forty minutes, the mechanical crank and firing of an older eight-cylinder big block broke the silence. It stuttered at first as it warmed up after the cold start. Jacob knew what this meant. They would leave shortly. His heart sank when he thought Father Lucian would just be another statistic added to the body count. A count that his family was responsible for. No matter how many ways he tried to think about it, he couldn't avoid that fact. They were responsible for everything that had happened. Directly, with Sarah at the center of it, but also indirectly. As Father Lucian explained to him earlier, it was their responsibility as keepers to protect this location, and they failed.

Jacob turned to walk back toward the car, but before he completed the turn, something appeared down the road in the headlights. Whatever it was slowly emerged out of the shadows and onto the road surface. His mind finally recognized the form and took off running toward it. To his right, there was a thunderous crash. A gust of dust rushed at him. He could only assume the objects that had been hanging in the air most of the afternoon had finally fallen back to the ground. It wasn't something he gave too much thought to. His attention was on the individual that crawled out on the road on their hands and knees and now collapsed.

When he finally reached them, he recognized it was Father Lucian. He was barely conscious and in obvious pain. A crimson curtain of blood poured down his face. The blood oozed from punctures that lined his forehead. His white eyes looked up through the curtain at Jacob, while his body shook.

6

Jacob followed Father Murray and Lewis Tillingsly as far as they would allow, but as soon as they pulled the green curtain shut around the emergency room bay, he could follow them no further. Behind the curtain, doctors tended to Father Lucian. He was still conscious but in immense pain. Deep scratches covered his body. They were in rows of three. Each oozed blood. With every movement as they loaded him in and out of the back of Lewis's car, he'd screamed and writhed in pain. His left hand grabbed at the sources of his pain, a crown of thorns clutched tightly in his right hand that neither Father Murray nor the nurses that met them at the door could pry out.

The moans and screams that emerged from behind the curtain were horrifying and blood curdling. The dread that had consumed Jacob for the last several days descended further down into the depths of despair. So many had been hurt and lost, and now another lay behind the curtain. As the pain-filled sounds stopped, and the parade of nurses and doctors ceased, Jacob assumed the worst. When Father Murray emerged and pulled the curtain back, Jacob felt an explosion of relief. Behind the curtain was Father Lucian, sitting up in the bed. Bandages covered the exposed areas of his body, but he was up, alert, and talking with Lewis and a doctor. His expression looked to be that of a man in good humor, not one in pain. His right hand still hung on to the crown of thorns tightly. It seemed to glow slightly. Something Jacob attributed to the lights that hung over the bed.

"All right, Father, I am a believer," said the tall doctor in green scrubs. He passed Father Murray as he exited through the gap in the curtain. Father Murray appeared to smirk at that revelation.

"Is he okay?" Jacob asked.

"Oh yes, and getting better all the time. His faith is healing him," Father Murray said and then pointed to the man's right hand.

"That is a relic? Like the cross?"

"Jacob, that is not any relic. That is the crown of thorns that Jesus wore when he was crucified. It is the most sacred of all. That is why Father Lucian wields it."

"The one?" Jacob asked. The revelation that his father possessed a cross made from the crucifix was hard enough to swallow. It had taken him a few days until he was brave enough to pick it up and hold it. Each time he did, he treated it as an antique, holding it on top of his open palm. Never brave enough to close his hand around it. The fear of dropping it and it shattering on the ground was ever present in his thoughts, even though he had seen his father and Sarah deposit it rather harshly on a table from time to time without damage. Now he found himself in the presence of the actual crown of thorns that was depicted in every image of the crucifixion. He took a step backward to give it more space.

"Father, a little help please…" Lewis called from inside the curtained area.

Jacob turned his attention from Father Murray and back to the hospital bed, where Father Lucian was attempting to stand up and get dressed. Father Murray rushed to the side of his bed and looked for an unbandaged area to grab hold of and restrain him in the bed, but every surface was covered.

Father Murray pleaded, "Lucian, please. Stay still. You have been through a lot."

"Nonsense," he said as he stood up beside the bed.

Lewis stood there with his arms out to catch the battered priest, but he was steady as a rock on his feet. Not a wobble or waver. He brushed away his attempt to assist with his left hand. Then he reached over and grabbed the bandage that covered his right forearm.

"Leave it alone, Francesco, please," Father Murray pleaded again. The last syllable wasn't out of his mouth before the bandage was dangling by a bit of adhesive tape. The flesh of his forearm completely exposed, only three red scratches remained where enormous chunks of flesh had been missing before. The scratches faded by the second, right in front of Jacob's eyes.

The remaining bandages were removed with care, the last of them coming off as a nurse walked back in to check on the patient. Shock was written all over her face and in her eyes as she saw the pile of bandages on the hospital bed, and the man brought in on the brink of death just half an hour ago now standing and adjusting his black hat.

Father Lucian walked out of the area and past the nurse, who stood there with her mouth wide open. "Thank you for the wonderful care," he said.

"His faith healed him," Father Murray said as they passed her.

All she could say in response was, "I see."

Lewis followed Fathers Murray and Lucian, Jacob falling in behind them, back outside. A light rain shower had started when they were inside, driving the chill that accompanied the late hour on this fall evening. Jacob shoved his hands as far as he could into the pockets of his jeans. The nip still bit at him through the sleeves of his sweatshirt.

"Father, do you mind if we retire to the church to talk?" asked Father Lucian.

"Not at all. We can set you up in the guest room."

"Father, why don't you two go ahead," Lewis said. "Jacob and I will retrieve Father Lucian's bags from upstairs and be along shortly."

"All right. My car is over this way," Father Murray said, and he and Father Lucian walked out into the gloomy night.

Lewis headed back upstairs to Jacob's father's room. Jacob just followed blindly. He knew the way like the back of his hand now, but that wasn't it. His mind was elsewhere. It struggled with what he had just seen. The stories he had heard his father and Father Murray tell talked of amazing events. Some he had just begun to accept as real, and others he accepted as just that, stories. This was the first time he had seen anything like this with his own eyes.

When they got up to the room, Wendy was still at her post in the chair, watching TV. Jacob looked at his father for any sign that something had changed, but to his disappointment, there was nothing. His father lay there just like he had for the last several days. Arms and legs showing no signs of moving or even adjusting to get more comfortable.

"Anything?" Lewis asked Wendy.

"Nah, he has been quiet. Not a movement or sound," she reported as she looked back at Jacob's father with a look of disappointment. Then she looked at Jacob with a half-smile and mouthed, "Sorry."

"Take the night off and go get some sleep. I got junior. He won't be giving me any trouble," said Lewis.

There was no hesitation or question if he was sure. Wendy grabbed her purse and jacket and headed out. Jacob saw her give Edward one last look before she exited the room.

"Jake, grab the father's bags and let's go before it gets too late."

Without a word, Jacob grabbed the two simple black leather bags, both tattered and well worn but still sturdy as he picked them up. From their weight, Jacob could imagine what was in both bags. One probably had a night shirt and a single change of clothes. The other had objects that shifted around more. Probably toiletries, and the larger item he felt move as he lifted it might be another pair of shoes.

On the drive over, Jacob's thoughts continued to stay focused on what he had witnessed. He was a believer in the spiritual. He had to be with the life they lived, but this was beyond that. This was biblical. This was something the best screenwriter wouldn't dream up. He struggled. He struggled a great and deal and finally opened up.

"Mr. Tillingsly, how did Father Lucian heal so fast?"

There was a big gulp followed by a cough from the man who sat in the driver's seat of the car. He stumbled and stammered for a few seconds before he finally said, "Jacob, I am not really sure. I know what we saw, and based on things I have seen with your grandfather and your dad, there are two explanations I can offer. Sometimes, a demon does something that is just temporary. Like a wasp stinging you if you get too close to their hive. That is the easier explanation, and something I have seen a lot. Then I have seen things that I can't explain. Things that go beyond what I can explain."

"Which do you think this is?" Jacob asked.

"Well, this time I'm not sure. Probably leaning more toward the things-I-can't-explain side. I know what my eyes saw, but my brain can't explain it."

"Same here. I'm still not sure if I saw what I think I did. Maybe my mind was playing tricks on me," Jacob said.

"Jake, buckle up. You're going to experience a lot of that. Sometimes you can't question everything and try to explain it. Sometimes you just have to believe."

7

"How is he doing?" Lewis asked as he walked in through the back screen door of Father Murray's home.

It struck Jacob that with all the time Father Murray was around his family, it was always at their house or the church. He had never been inside Father Murray's house. He also couldn't decide if his surroundings surprised him or not. It was simple. Not overly large-looking from the outside. Inside, the kitchen was just large enough for a single table with four chairs. Neither was particularly fancy, just plain unfinished wood. A single gas stove, not of this decade or the previous one either, with a matching white refrigerator. A white porcelain farmhouse sink sat under the window with bleached white curtains hanging over it.

"Eh, he is doing fine. Just cleaning himself up a bit," Father Murray said. "I'm making some coffee. Would you like some?"

Lewis nodded.

"Jacob, coffee?" he asked.

Jacob shook his head at Father Murray's offer. Coffee was not a taste he had acquired yet. His version of caffeine came in more sugary sources of various colors. Not that he didn't need some. A large yawn was an indicator of that.

Father Murray handed Lewis a cup and then grabbed two more and led them into a dining room. Like the kitchen, it wasn't anything remarkable. Dark wood molding, white walls, and a similar but larger table. Up against the opposite wall sat an old bureau with a large book on top of it. It was open, with an ornate bookmark.

Lewis took a chair on one side, and Father Murray placed a cup in front of one chair and then took the one next to it for himself. Jacob looked around and took the one on the side with Lewis. The sound of water running came from the only two doors in the room. Both doors were open and appeared to lead to bedrooms. Jacob had to assume there was a shared bathroom, something he once heard called a Jack and Jill on a home improvement show his father watched. Behind him, through an archway, was a sitting area. It was too small to truly call a living room, but it had a small sofa and a television. That was not like the appliances he saw in the kitchen. It was a modern high-definition flat-screen. No smaller than fifty-two inches. Not a surprise. The father liked his football, as Jacob heard him and his father talk about on more than one occasion.

"So, what now?" Lewis asked in between sips of his coffee.

Jacob swung his attention to Father Murray to hear the plan but saw only a shrug. That was not the answer he hoped for. He didn't really know what precise answer he hoped for. What to do next escaped him. He had hopes on the drive over that either Father Murray or Lucian would know exactly what to do. Those hopes were a little less than they were earlier in the day. Seeing Father Lucian crawl out to the roadway was a serious blow to them. Now, seeing Father Murray shrug was another serious gut punch.

"Father Lucian said after he cleaned up he would discuss what he saw. I can only hope he has some ideas." Father Murray stopped to take a drink of his coffee. When he placed it back on the table, both hands reached up and made a slow drawn-out rub down the sides of his face. "I don't know what to do next."

The sound of the water stopped, leaving the men in silence, draped under a darkness that covered the whole town. Jacob looked back and forth between the two men at the table with him. Both appeared lost in thought. There was a lot to think about. He knew that. His mind never had a lack of topics to ponder. Front and center were his father and sister. When he wasn't thinking of one, he was thinking of the other. It was his sister he was thinking about when he dipped his head down and laid it on his arms, folded on the table.

Darkness surrounded him. It was peaceful and serene. He knew he was asleep. Exhaustion had gotten the better of him again, and he had nothing in him to fight it. One wonder of the universe that had always fascinated him was how time seemed to stand still while you were asleep. Now when he dreamt, he had a sense of the passage of time, but that was it. When he didn't dream, he closed his eyes and woke up what seemed to be just moments later. It could have been fifteen minutes, an hour, or eight hours. It was always the same. At the moment, he could have been asleep for minutes or hours. He didn't know. There was no dream or anything to give him a sense of time when he heard a voice in the darkness. It cried. No, it sobbed, remorsefully. "Jacob, tell him I am sorry. I couldn't stop it from hurting him."

"Sarah?" he asked.

"Jacob, please. Tell him I am sorry."

"I will," he said, and then a thought hit him. "Or you could tell him yourself. Tell him how to help you."

"Oh no! I couldn't dare," she said. "It would know. It is risky enough to reach out to you."

Hearing her voice sound so lifeless and desperate broke Jacob's heart. He ached as he looked around for any sign of her. There was nothing. Just darkness.

The pangs radiated through his subconscious. He needed to see her. To talk to her. To help her.

"Sarah, how can we help you?" he asked.

"You can't," she said.

"There has to be something we can do!" he exclaimed. His own voice echoed in the space. There was no reply. There was nothing. It was different now. He could feel the emptiness. "Sarah!" he cried, but there was no response.

She was gone.

"Sarah, come back. Come back please. Don't go."

A hand shook him on the shoulder with a light touch. Jacob rustled awake and lifted his head. Father Murray was returning to his chair, and the other two men were sitting at the table. Father Lucian sat across from him with a towel around his neck, hair still damp, and a pleasant smile on his face as he gazed at Jacob.

"You were having a dream," said Lewis.

Jacob looked around at the three sets of eyes that looked at him. He had to rub his own to try to clear the blurriness from them. Was it just a dream? He wasn't sure. Probably so. Now that he was awake, it seemed so far away and faded more with every second. "What did I miss?" he asked, his voice still scratchy.

"Not much. Father Lucian just sat down," Lewis said. "So, what happened out there?"

Father Lucian leaned forward and rested his forearms on the table, after a single wipe of the towel across his forehead to take care of drips of water that escaped his hair and headed down his face. "I found the shed. No animals or creatures until I reached it. They were inside with her. Sarah was still there, floating above the symbol, like you said." He gave a simple nod to Father Murray. "It let me walk right in. No resistance at all. It put her and the creatures on display. Like it was proud of what it had done. Proud of what it created. It turned Sarah around for me to see. I saw the girl I remembered, and then I saw a creature in her place with marks that emerged from under her skin. Eyes the blackest black I have ever seen. It was then I felt it probing at me through her glance. Like a punch with a blunt instrument, but in my mind. It tried to enter my thoughts, but it couldn't. Each failure angered it. I could tell. The creatures took notice of my presence. They moved closer to me, growling and snarling the whole time. I felt it try again. That is when I really felt it. It couldn't enter my thoughts, and the entire shed filled with an evil I have never felt before. Even the light of my faith couldn't cut through." He stopped and rubbed his forearms with his hands. It reminded Jacob of how he rubbed his arms once after a pitch on the funny bone beamed him. "One creature dragged me out of the shed and into the woods. The others bit and clawed at me until I was outside the trees. Then I crawled back to the road."

"Do you know what we're dealing with?" asked Father Murray.

Father Lucian's head nodded. "Yes, I know. Not the particular entity or type, but I know what we are dealing with. It is an evil unlike anything we have ever seen before."

8

"So, what now?"

"That, Sheriff, I don't know. It is more than I can handle alone," Father Lucian said.

His voice didn't sound defeated, as Jacob might have believed it would speaking such a statement. There was a sternness to the sound and to his expression. He was a man deep in thought, underneath a great weight. The weight wasn't crushing him. Instead, it caused every step to be measured and careful. Inside, that gave Jacob hope. That hope contrasted with what little patience his teenage emotions could muster at the moment. There was a need to explode at any second and demand to know what they could do.

The only things stopping it were the expressions plastered on the faces of the others at the table. They were defeated. Each searched Father Lucian for hope. Whether they found it, Jacob couldn't be sure. He only glanced at them as he kept his focus looking for his own hope, to quell the eruption brewing.

"I hate to ask this," said Sheriff Tillingsly, "but is there any way to contain it?"

Father Murray and Father Lucian shared a look.

"If we can't get rid of it, our next priority needs to be protecting the town."

"I don't know," Father Murray said. "I really don't know, Lewis. I mean, I understand where you're going, but I'm not sure if we can."

"Even just keep it contained out there. We can keep everyone away from them and try to get back to something similar to normal."

"Normal. Will we ever be normal again? That is the question," Father Murray said.

Lewis sat back from the table and rubbed his brow. "Seems we've had this conversation a few times before. Things returned to normal."

"True, but that was because Edward came home," Father Murray said.

That was enough to uncap the volcano that brewed under the surface inside Jacob. The topic of returning to normal reminded him that no matter how *normal* the town returned, his life would never be normal. They wanted to contain his sister, not help her. And they completely forgot about his father. His father who lay, now alone, in a hospital room. His father, who they credited with returning the town to normal. His father, who no one had talked about how to help. "Come on!" he shouted. "There has to be something you can do for my father and sister." Both hands hit the table, hard. It was more of a reflex than an intentional move.

It startled all but one, and that one wasn't Jacob. He was just as surprised by it as the other two. Father Lucian, on the other hand, was not, or at least gave no indication he was. He appeared lost in thought and didn't say a word as he stood up and walked around the table and back to the bedroom. He just passed the doorframe when he paused and asked, "Father, do you mind if I make a phone call?"

"Well… of course. No need to ask," Father Murray responded.

His tall and thin frame disappeared through the door, which he pushed slightly closed. While he was out of the room. Father Murray and Lewis resumed their conversation about next steps, much to Jacob's continued disappointment. It was building up in him again and was about to explode when a moment of maturity overcame him, and he pushed up from the table to walk into the kitchen. Just removing himself from the situation helped a little as he stood and stared out the window over the kitchen sink. There wasn't anything he looked at that calmed him. It was night, and outside the window all he saw was a slight shadow where the woods edged the property and then the night sky above them.

Being so far away from any major metropolitan location gave those who lived in Miller's Crossing a perfect view of the night sky. That was something Jacob learned to appreciate. In Portland, they saw the moon and a few stars, but that was it. On their first night in Miller's Crossing, his father took him out into the pasture and told him to look up. There he saw an ocean of stars, more than he ever imagined could exist. Edward had pointed out a few stars that he remembered his father pointing out to him as a child, then others he later learned about as a cub scout. He told Jacob he felt bad for the other scouts. Even on the camping trips, the lights from the nearby cities robbed them of the views he remembered. On that night, after he pointed out the North Star and the Big Dipper, he told Jacob that his own father had told him to look to the stars when you were confused, worried, or stressed. "Look to the heavens for the answers" was the exact phrase he said. Then he explained, there won't be a magical voice that gives you the answer, but if you let your mind wander among the stars and realize how insignificant your problem is compared to the size of the universe, it puts everything into perspective. Jacob remembered giving his father a funny look at that, to which his father responded, "I didn't get it either at your age, but I did later in my life. My father said the same thing when I looked at him like you're looking at me now."

As he looked at the stars visible through the parting clouds, his mind didn't struggle to realize how large the universe was and how small a part of it he was, but that didn't seem to make his problems seem small. In *his universe* they were huge and all-consuming. There would be nothing that would minimize it or make it go away for him. No matter where they set up the roadblocks Lewis was talking about in the other room. No matter who they moved out of danger. The problem still existed. His world was still destroyed. His family was still... gone.

"Jacob."

Jacob spun away from the window and saw Father Murray leaning in through the doorway. "Father Lucian is back. Care to join us?"

Jacob walked back in and retook his seat at the table. Father Lucian sat across from him, back board-straight, face confident. He began when Jacob settled into his chair.

"I have conferred with my superiors. All agree. What is happening here is not just a danger to this location but to the entire world. That is not to be taken as being overdramatic. Remember, this a significantly spiritually active place in the world. An area where the two realms overlap. If a demon were able to get control of it, they could open a portal with little difficulty and let others in. The fact that it has control of your sister, with her knowledge and abilities, is more of a danger. That may have already happened. Left unchecked, evil will spread out from here, endangering others and, what may be the worst fear of my superiors, letting a part of the world we have worked very hard to keep private become very public. The greater world is not ready to realize that the evil they flock to see in movie theaters really exists. We do have an idea, but I need each of you to understand there is no guarantee this will work." He paused and leaned onto the table. His forearms rested flat on the surface, eyes looking right into Jacob's, which made Jacob uncomfortable. "Mr. Meyer... Jacob, I want you to know we will do everything we can for your sister and father, but I can't make you any promises beyond that. Our focus is ending this. Do you understand?"

Jacob swallowed hard to digest what that meant. It was something he wasn't ready to accept, but he didn't see any other option. "Yes, sir," he said wearily.

Lewis reached over and put a hand on his right shoulder.

"As each of you are aware, I am sure, there are six other places in the world like Miller's Crossing. We have assigned each a family to keep it safe. Each of those families have been serving that post for hundreds and in some cases thousands of years. They have seen things I can't even fathom. We are bringing a member of each of those families here to assess the situation and to help."

"When will they arrive?" asked Father Murray.

"Two days. They are each being contacted now and will travel immediately."

9

Jacob spent the next two days where he'd spent the previous six, the hospital room next to his father. Deputy Wendy Tolliver gave him a ride back to his home twice to take a shower and get a fresh change of clothes. That was the first time Jacob had stepped foot back in his home since what happened. It was weird. This was not the first time he came home to an empty house. That was a rather common occurrence. It was knowing that neither his father nor his sister would be coming home later tonight that was different. Knowing that made the entire house feel empty and unfamiliar.

He never turned the television on or anything for any noise. It was just in and out. Wendy's radio echoed updates on the happenings in town through the house. This gave Jacob a more detailed view of what was going on than either Sheriff Tillingsly or Father Murray were telling him. Deputy Tony Yale was spending his day running hourly patrols through town. When not driving through town, he was camped out on State Road 192, watching the single grove of trees in the distance for any activity, which there hadn't been for a few days now. Ted Barton used his spot in the storeroom of his grocery and mercantile store as a lookout and called in updates pretty regularly. Most of the times were just to say nothing had happened or to ask if anything was happening elsewhere since it was so quiet in town. Others were as well. That seemed to be an overwhelming theme to the radio traffic. Nothing was going on, and people were getting nervous. Jacob shared that feeling.

Back in the hospital, all was quiet, but unlike the world outside those walls where quiet was a good thing, Jacob would give anything for something to happen inside. Anything would be better than nothing. Visitors stopped by often. Father Murray had left his normal perch to assist Father Lucian in preparing for their visitors. His home was far too small to accommodate seven more people, so he reached out to members of his parish and arranged housing. Many were close friends of the Meyer family and offered to do anything they could to help. Charlotte Stance took in two, as did her family. Mark Grier offered to take one in, along with Jacob. He had attempted to get Jacob to come stay with him and his wife instead of spending every day and night at the hospital. His son's old room was still set up and available. Jacob had considered it but so far refused. It was an offer he might break down and accept soon, though. The last two would be the houseguests of Lewis Tillingsly.

When Jacob heard they would fly in, he imagined they would be picked up and brought in on a chartered aircraft, but by the middle of the second day, it was clear that was not the case. Each was flying in on separate commercial flights. Each required multiple connections before arriving at Dulles International, just about an hour away. Their arrival times were split all throughout the day. Jacob overheard that those who volunteered to let one of the arriving guests stay with them were leaving around eleven a.m. that morning to go meet them all at the airport. He didn't know for sure what time they got back, he could only assume it was late since Father Murray stopped by the hospital at just after nine to check on him and Edward.

The question was the same as it always was. "Any change?"

Jacob's response was the same too, and almost robotic. "No. No movement."

Father Murray walked toward the head of Edward's bed, crossed him, and said a prayer like he had every night.

"Jacob, we are all getting together at the church in the morning. I'll pick you up. Why not come home with me, or let me drop you off at the Griers, so you can get a good night's sleep?"

"Nah. I'm good here," Jacob responded.

"You sure?"

"Yes, sir."

"All right. I will be here around eight," Father Murray said as he turned to walk out of the room. On his way out, he patted the red recliner he had spent the better part of the last week in. "You should try this one. It's more comfortable."

Jacob didn't respond, but his mind considered it. His body waited to react until the father had left. The cushions molded around his body as he sat down. A shift of his weight backward reclined the chair to almost flat. His back appreciated the comfort of the chair, as did his neck, shoulders, and hips. It wasn't long before the darkness in his mind matched the darkness outside the room. He hadn't felt tired before he sat in the chair. The momentary comfort that came over his body allowed his consciousness to seek a similar comfort. His breathing slowed, and he was out.

The calm of his sleeping state didn't last. Jacob's mind wandered in and out of various topics and images. Each involved his father and sister. Each carried a feeling of loss and pain with them. He called out several times for Sarah. Still unsure if what he had experienced twice before was real or a dream, his subconscious still tried. There was no answer. Just the images and darkness. When he gave up, a part of him accepted that when all this was over, he would just be left with images and darkness, nothing else. The family he once had would be no more. His soul felt alone.

The feeling was enough to stick with him when he shook awake, just after four in the morning. His eyes caught a nurse leaving the room as he sat up, and he could only assume she bumped the chair while tending to his father. The chair was close to the bed. Something he remediated with a few scoots backward and a twist to put it parallel against the wall. That created a wide space for anyone who needed to tend to his father.

Jacob leaned it back again, hoping to slip back into sleep. Instead, the feeling that lingered played deeper in his mind while he was awake. It wasn't pictures of his father or sister this time. It was thoughts about the future. His future. Could he still live here? That was the question his mind didn't have a problem answering. Too many memories were a big part of that answer. The larger part was about the people he would have to face daily. The people his family hurt and devastated. Where would he go?

Jacob rolled on his side. The new position didn't chase the thought away. Nor did it invite in sleep. He got up and walked out into the quiet hall. They dimmed the lights so only every third light was on. He followed the alternating pools of light and darkness down the hallway to the sunroom, which was not lit up by the sun at the moment. The lights were all off, bathing it in darkness. From there he had a good view of the night sky, with their town of Miller's Crossing below. The town he would need to leave.

That was his last thought until he heard, "Jacob. Jacob. Time to wake up."

Jacob opened his eyes and looked up at Father Murray. At some point after he sat down on the ratty sofa in the sunroom, his body and mind finally both agreed, and he slipped away. He had no intention of falling asleep down there. It was just a change of scenery to clear his mind. It had obviously worked. Or so he hoped.

"What time is it?"

"Half past seven."

A big stretch preceded, "Give me just a few, and I'll be ready." Jacob felt surprisingly refreshed. The sofa looked like it would be hard and lumpy, with springs sticking you through what was left of the cushions, but it was rather comfortable. Something he would have to remember for tonight and the rest of the time he stayed up here.

"You got time."

Jacob didn't need a lot of time. He was more expedient than his sister at getting ready. Instead of the several-hour routine she went through, he just threw a splash or two of water in his face and ran his fingers through his hair. Before he left the bathroom in his father's room, he brushed his teeth, a must, and then threw on a fresh change of clothes. Jeans, plain white T-shirt, and his school hoodie. A constant wardrobe choice between the months of September and March, when there was enough chill in the air to need sleeves.

Jacob rode with Father Murray over to the church mostly in silence. Being one of the few times Jacob had seen these areas of Miller's Crossing during the day since, he was astonished by how much it had changed. The normally busy sidewalks in the center of town were empty. Shop after shop showed every sign of being not just closed but boarded up. The wind had piled up leaves and small bits of debris against sides of buildings and in the gutters. Something the city refuse department would never let happen under normal circumstances. They cleared the streets and sidewalks by dawn, every day.

Weeds were visible above the carpet of leaves in front of the high school. The small baseball diamond next to the elementary school was just a patch of dry clay. No white lines, which were always visible from the twice-a-week games and practices held there. An orange cloud of dust rose up from it as the wind crossed it. No one had tended to it by watering it down.

The sign on the elementary school advertised the upcoming "Fal_ Festi_al." The second F hung on for its life to the bottom rail of the sign against the breeze. Jacob knew what it was. It was the highlight of his years at that school, and a must-attend for everyone else in town regardless if you had a child of school age or not. The date was next Saturday. At the moment, chances seemed bleak for that happening.

The lack of cars on the road was obvious. Not that there was a traffic problem in Miller's Crossing, but you always passed a few cars on the road everywhere you went. Being the only car sitting at a traffic signal at this time of morning was a rare occurrence. Not seeing another car anywhere, up and down both of the roads Jacob could see, was beyond rare. The only thing keeping the scene from classifying as desolate was the lack of tumbleweeds blowing down the pavement. The leaves dancing in a whirlwind would have to do.

They pulled into the church's gravel-covered parking lot. Several cars were already there, but no one was outside. Jacob assumed everyone was already inside waiting on them. He looked at his phone. They weren't late. The others were possibly just early.

Father Murray brought the car to a stop and opened the driver's side door. He placed one foot on the gravel when Jacob opened the passenger side door with a squeak that sent several birds fleeing from a nearby oak and its colorful red and orange foliage. They climbed rapidly away from the noise, which had ceased, leaving just the sound of their own wings against the air and their bodies.

"Jacob," Father Murray called.

Jacob stopped with one foot already out of the car and turned back toward the father.

"Two things."

"Yes, Father," Jacob said with a hint of question in his voice.

"These visitors are going to ask you a lot of questions. Father Lucian said the more they know about you, your father, and Sarah, the better. Just answer them. Hide nothing. There is no reason to. Think of these people as family. You all share a similar responsibility and bond."

"Yes, sir," Jacob said. The thought of playing twenty questions with people he didn't know was not appealing. It was a game he had been playing himself twenty-four hours a day.

"Second... and I'm not sure how to explain this. Try not to stare. Some of them are... well, not used to being around people and are a little... different."

Jacob followed Father Murray up to the church. He stopped after his first step up the front stairs and let his head roam to his right to take in what he saw out of the corner of his eye. Off to the side of the church, nestled back among the trees, was a single round structure. It resembled a tent, but not one covered by the typical vinyl or canvas he was familiar with. It was something more rustic, more raw. Smoke still rose above the remnants of a fire pit constructed just in front of the doorway.

10

Jacob had walked into the church several hundred times since returning to Miller's Crossing. On top of every Sunday and holiday, this was a regular place for his family to visit to sit and talk with Father Murray. Waiting on their father as *he* talked to Father Murray was more like it. Sarah had had conversations, more so after she returned from the Vatican. Jacob never had more than a handful. Mostly just attempts by a family friend to reach out to the younger generation and talk. It fascinated him how much the father knew about sports, something that didn't fit his impression of a priest.

Walking in this time was different. Completely different. He stepped into a whole other world, in the confines of something familiar. He wasn't the only one. Mark Grier and Lewis Tillingsly stood in the back, just inside the door. Both were taking in the scene of the guests assembled at the front. Jacob paused by them and let Father Murray go ahead up to the front. Father Lucian warmly greeted him and then made introductions.

"Is that them?" Jacob asked.

"Yeeep," Mark Grier said.

"What are they like?" he asked, his eyes going over them one by one. Taking in their appearance. Their dress. How they stood and moved.

"Well... it might not be polite to say, but odd," Mark said. "See that guy in the black waistcoat with brass buttons?"

"Yes."

"He's staying with me, along with the woman there in the long dress. The guy slept standing up, all night long."

Jacob looked at Mark as if he was pulling his leg. "You're just messing with me."

"No lie." His right hand sprang up like he was taking an oath. "When I went to wake him this morning, he was asleep, standing, in the dark, pressed into the corner."

"Trade ya," Lewis said. "That chap there in the Doctor Dolittle hat, a Mr. Lionel James Halensworth. When we got home, he asked if I would like to share a drink. I obliged. Then had another, and then another. Each round began with a challenge aimed at me and the one in the bow tie, Mr. Nagoti, to a drinking contest. I haven't felt this hungover since I was," he paused and looked at Jacob, "your age. Mind you, times were different back then. You need to wait until you're older."

"Jacob," Father Murray called. "Come on up here. We have some people you need to meet."

His beckon silenced the hum of several individual conversations and caused every eye in the building to focus on him. Jacob took one step, and then a second. The second step was followed by another one that lacked confidence, but he proceeded in putting enough steps together to reach the gathered mass up front, and he only looked back at the two familiar faces at the back half a dozen times.

At the front, several walked forward with their hands extended toward Jacob. Their movement overwhelmed him and sent him a step backward. That prompted a similar response for those who approached him. But only in their movements. Their facial expressions hadn't changed. His reaction didn't shock or surprise them. Neither were their expressions warm and welcoming. To Jacob, they looked curious. That was the word he felt best described how they looked at him. They looked at him with the curiosity of a medical student studying a lab rat for his reaction when exposed to a new maze, smell, or drug.

"Jacob, I would like for you to meet Madame Catherine Stryvia, from Bulgaria. Her family takes care of the Rila Lakes." The woman, a raven-haired beauty in her mid-thirties, looked like something straight out of a gothic horror movie. Pale white complexion, long black dress, and a red cape completed the look.

She extended her hand again. This time Jacob took it. Her grip was firm but dainty at the same time. The curious look she had on her face a few moments ago hadn't changed. She studied him. Again he felt like that lab rat.

"I had the honor of meeting your sister at the Vatican," she said. Her accent was thick, and her tone cut through the air, but there was a hint of warmth and compassion in it.

The man in the bow tie, Mr. Nagoti from Japan, was the next introduced. He said nothing. Just shook Jacob's hand and bowed slightly. Jacob wasn't sure if he should do the same at first. He started, then stopped, and then finished it rather awkwardly. The man's stony expression cracked ever so slightly.

Jacob had barely released Mr. Nagoti's hand when two beefy hands grabbed and yanked him in for a tight and uncomfortable embrace against the girth of the man in the Doolittle hat. "How you doing there, Jacob?" said the voice of Mr. Halensworth. The embrace had plastered Jacob's ear against the man's chest such that he could hear it echo inside his frame. The aromatic scents of the drink, or drinks, of choice from the night before were still present with every word.

"I'm okay," he croaked. Which was all he could do.

"Chin up, lad. We're here."

Next up, behind Mr. Halensworth, stood a small-framed man. Bald, with a pleasant smile. He moved forward briskly and took Jacob's hand.

Father Murray handled the introductions. "Jacob, this is Tenzein Mao, a monk from Tibet." The man shook his head up and down when he heard his own name. "He is the most experienced in the room, besides Father Lucian, that is. Mao took over for his father when he was a few years younger than you. He is now eighty-three."

Jacob hoped he didn't act as surprised on the outside as he was on the inside. There was no way the man in front of him was any older than forty. Not a wrinkle on the man's face, not even a smile line. Not from a lack of smiling either. He had that kind of face that looked like it was always smiling and pleasant. A man who always looked to the brighter side of life.

"This is Lord Marcus Negiev, from Lithuania."

The man who reached forward for Jacob's hand with both of his was the one in the black waistcoat and brass buttons that Mark Grier had pointed out. Jacob thought his father's friend was pulling his leg with the story of the man sleeping standing up in a dark corner. Now, face-to-face with the mysterious man, he believed every word. His features were pale and gaunt under a mob of jet-black hair combed straight down on all sides. Eyes sunken in, but not lost for life. They examined Jacob and the rest of the assembled visitors.

"It is good to meet you, Mr. Meyer," he said, without the lisp that Jacob had expected.

"It is good to meet you too," was all he could muster, while his mind repeated over and over Father Murray's earlier warning. *Don't stare. Don't stare.* Easier said than done, as the man standing before him probed Jacob's essence with his eyes.

Jacob pulled his hand away from the man's clammy two-handed shake. He then moved out of their way. There was no one left to meet, or so Jacob thought. He now stood at the front of the church, through the mass of people who stood around the first two pews. Father Murray made several nods to Jacob's right. Neither of which Jacob understood and looked at him curiously. The next motion, the point of a finger, was a clearer signal. Jacob followed the direction of the finger to see a single person sitting at the end of the first pew. The mass of people had previously blocked his view of her presence. The person, a woman covered in what appeared to be furs, looked uncomfortable and out of place, pressed as far to the other end of the pew as she could get. Her head and face hid behind a mass of wild hair, gaze locked on the floor. Her body swayed ever so slightly forward and back.

Jacob started her way, but Father Murray grabbed his arm. "We can meet her later. She is from a tiny village in Brazil that she has never left before. She is not that comfortable around people. Best to just leave her be for now."

"Is she..." Jacob paused and pointed in the direction of the tent and fire he spotted outside.

"Yep, that's where she slept. She brought her own tent. Wasn't comfortable inside the house."

11

"Thank you all for coming," announced Father Lucian. The normally calm and quiet priest raised his voice to break up a few of the conversations still going on among the group. "Let's take a seat," he said, again louder than he normally spoke.

A few of the party were being stubborn, but they now heeded his call as silence descended over the sanctum.

"Jacob, you come up here with me."

Jacob joined Father Lucian, a man he towered over by almost half a foot. This added to his feeling that he was on display. It didn't help that every set of eyes in the room watched his every move.

"Again, thank you all for coming such a long way. There is not much more I can tell you than I did over the phone. One of our own keepers has been possessed and put this town under siege. She may have been possessed by the demon even at the time we were training her."

A murmur once again broke the silence as each of the people sitting in the pews turned to comment to the person next to them. Each had lost the look of curiosity they had earlier and now shared one of concern.

"I know. I know. I am not sure if that is the case, but I do know what it means if it were true. I believe we need to proceed believing that whatever has her knows everything we do. She may be strong enough to resist and guard our secrets, but we won't know."

"Father," Mr. Negiev said as he stood up. He tugged at the bottom of his waistcoat before speaking. "If it is true, and it knows everything we do, what can we do?"

Jacob's despair that had been deepening by the day dropped to a depth he didn't believe it could. It made him realize there was no bottom to that pit.

Father Lucian replied, "It would know what we are taught, but not our experiences. That is why I called each of you. We share a similar background, but that is where it stops. Each of us has a wealth of experience from our own lives and what our ancestors handed down to us. It is that which we need."

Everyone seated seemed satisfied by the answer. They nodded at one another.

"Here is what I can tell you from what I have been told and seen for myself," Father Lucian continued. "She is out there trapped by a creature that either has opened or is trying to open the portal. There are several creatures as well as some animals with it under its control. From what I can tell, those beings have been here for a while, so they haven't come through recently, which is why I am not sure if it has opened a portal yet. I have been told they stay in that shed most of the time but have come out and roamed through the town at least once."

Father Murray held up three fingers from his seat in the front pew.

"Three times before. Each time, they sought out and attacked anyone they encountered," Father Lucian said. The last statement sounded like more of a question, each word said with a slight pause between it and the next as Father Murray confirmed the statement with a nod, one word at a time. "It is not scared of us. When I went out there, it actively probed my thoughts to see if it could get in. It wants to control." He paused and took a breath that was long and deep. Jacob could hear the air moving through the man from where he stood next to him. "I believe it is Abaddon."

"Psh," said Mr. Halensworth, his lips upturned and puckered. "We have all dealt with one of his minions before. I have lost count."

Mr. Negiev and Madame Stryvia both laughed. She turned her head away from her counterpart from the United Kingdom. Mr. Negiev snipped back, "I seriously doubt that, my friend. If you have, I could count the text messages you sent me every time you've dealt with anything."

"Yeah, yeah. You owe me a few drinks for some of those," dismissed Mr. Halensworth. The shot didn't appear to harm his pride any. "Father, what makes this one so dangerous? We have all done battle with one of those before."

"Because this time, it is him," Father Lucian said frankly.

The jovial banter that preceded this announcement stopped, and for the first time since he entered the church, Jacob believed the others in the room looked how he felt.

"You mean, the actual demon?" Mao asked.

"Yes, he was released several decades ago and not put back in."

"And we were not told?" stammered Madame Stryvia.

For the next fifteen minutes, Father Lucian recapped the details of how Abaddon was released by Father Murray years ago. The story caused several disapproving looks in Father Murray's direction. Each of which appeared to make him uncomfortable.

Nothing appeared to bother him more so than the eruption by Lord Negiev. "A keeper's post was abandoned? There are rules about this. Why was it not reported? Why was another not placed?" Each question directed at Father

Murray. Each question delivered harshly. Each question left there in the air with no definitive answer.

Father Lucian did his best to dismiss it, but the realization caused a stir.

Jacob stood there and listened to the story. Some of which he had heard, but much he hadn't. His father had only told him his grandparents had died. It was something they talked about when he was younger. Jacob couldn't remember why anymore. Probably some random question his four- or five-year-old self asked. It came up again when they returned to the family farm. Each time he was told, he was too young for his mind to consider any reason for someone to die other than illness or old age. Since then, it had never come up. His gaze wandered, as did those of the rest of the room when they figured out Father Murray was responsible for their deaths. This added to the darkness that had hung over Jacob for the past nine days. What it added wasn't more despair and loss, it was fear.

"We should not dwell on the past. Our focus needs to be on why we are here," Father Lucian explained in an attempt to calm and refocus the group. It worked. The room was instantly silent. "We need to perform an exorcism, one I believe will take our combined skills and experiences. This won't be easy. There should be no illusions of that. I must be truthful. I'm not even sure it is possible, but we must try. This concerns all of us. If this town is lost, it poses a threat to each of yours, and everywhere else too."

"Father." Lord Negiev stood up. "We need to know, does it have the relic?"

Father Lucian turned to Jacob. The attention of the room followed. His hand reached inside his right pants pocket. It felt the object. The one that was so familiar to his father but so foreign to him. Just two pieces of wood put together in a shape. Out he pulled it, and when the first bit of wood breached the top of his pocket, there was a collective sigh in the room. With it fully out, he placed it flat on his hand and offered it to Father Lucian. The old priest reached over but didn't take the object. Instead he closed Jacob's fingers around it.

"Jacob, have you?" asked Madame Stryvia.

The precise "what" was not asked, but Jacob had an idea what she meant and answered. He knew the twenty questions would start at some point. This was probably it. "My father hasn't trained me or involved me in this side of his life, but I do feel and see ghosts. I have for the past several years."

"So, you have never felt the cross?"

"No. Not in the way I think you mean. I have held it and read through the book, but that was it."

"But you know about it? Have seen it used, correct?" asked Mr. Halensworth. His body leaned forward while his right hand rubbed his chin.

The answer was clear in his mind. The first and only time had occurred just a few weeks ago outside the homecoming dance. Before that, he had heard about it from both his father and Sarah but had never seen it. "Yes, just a few weeks back. I saw my father use it against a group of demons at our homecoming dance. That was the one and only time."

"And your sister? Ever see her use it?"

"No," Jacob said, but before he finished the answer, something flashed in his mind. It only took another second for him to make sense of its importance. "I never saw her use it, but I do know she didn't always take it."

"What do you mean? She doesn't need a relic?" Madame Stryvia asked, a question that seemed to surprise many of the group. They all leaned forward and mouths fell open. Some covered them with a hand, but others didn't. Leaving them gaping open below raised eyebrows.

"It is true," interjected Father Lucian. "Sarah does not always need the relic. Many times during training, she showed the ability to deal with spirits and even demons without the relic. I took her to observe the exorcism of an eleven-year-old boy, as a purely educational endeavor. I instructed her to just stand off to the side and not say a word. She did exactly as I asked until both me and the attending priest were thrown against the wall. She stepped forward and spoke to the boy. Before we were on our feet, she had dismissed the demon. The boy sat resting comfortably in the chair, alone. When we returned to her apartment, I noticed the cross still sitting on the nightstand."

"Not possible!" exclaimed Lord Negiev.

"Actually, it is." Mr. Nagoti spoke for the first time. He was the only one to this point who hadn't responded or reacted to anything he had heard. He sat straight and unemotional the whole time, which stuck out to Jacob amongst the reactions of everyone else. The only other person who hadn't reacted at all was the one who sat at the end of the pew away from everyone. The dignified man from Japan adjusted his bow tie and continued, "In my culture, there are stories of those in past generations who showed such abilities. It was said they tapped into dark energy and entities to aid them. I believe they partnered with some of the very beings they fought against to use their abilities to help them."

"There are examples of that in all your pasts. Some good, and some bad," Father Lucian said. Jacob fought the urge to look at Father Murray after what he had learned a few minutes ago. "I now believe that explains some of Sarah's capabilities."

"Sheriff? Sheriff? You there?" asked a voice over the radio fastened to the hip of Lewis Tillingsly, standing in the back. The sound forced six heads to twist around, like a cell phone call in a quiet theater. Much like the people who receive those calls, Lewis walked back toward the door to answer. To his disadvantage, they'd designed the church to amplify sound no matter where you were.

"What is it, Tony?"

"They're back. Just getting to town center."

"How many?" Lewis asked.

"Seven. No sign of Sarah though."

With that Mr. Halensworth stood up and declared, "What are we waiting on? Let's go." He scooted past the others and headed toward the back. "Sheriff, please lead the way."

The others were now behind him, as Lewis looked past them and up to the front.

Father Lucian nodded and joined them. "Come on, Jacob."

They stepped outside into a world that reminded Jacob of a horror film. The cool sunny morning that had existed when he entered was gone. Replaced by layer after layer of black clouds, wind that screamed as it passed by, and rolling thunder with every eye-blinding flash of lightning. He didn't remember rain being in the forecast for the day or any weather alerts on his phone.

"It knows we are here. I felt it as soon as I arrived," said the final, and eremite, member of their party with a hiss. A quick tug at the fur she wore pulled it tighter around her shoulders before she strolled off toward her tent in the woods.

12

Jacob was in the second of four cars that sped through the backroads of Miller's Crossing. Sheriff Lewis Tillingsly drove the lead car, but there were no lights or sirens. It was his personal Plymouth, not a cruiser with the light bar. That didn't stop them from blowing through several traffic signals on the way. No other cars were out on the road. The only factor that made it dangerous was how dark it had gotten. It was a little before ten in the morning, but it was already as dark as ten at night. Streetlights were on, and their headlights led the way. Dark trees lined the route, trees they only saw during the brief and blinding strikes of lightning that seemed to follow them from the church along their trek.

In the car with Jacob and Father Murray were Tenzein Mao and the mystery lady whose name Jacob had yet to hear. Both sat in the back behind them and were praying to themselves silently or in their own native language.

"Young Meyer, you have seen demons only once, yes?" asked Tenzein after he completed his prayer.

"Twice," Jacob answered.

"Oh, so not just with your father?" he asked.

"I snuck out a few nights ago and saw them," Jacob responded, and then added, "and my sister."

"You saw your sister?"

"Yes, sir."

"Did she see you?"

"No." Then Jacob remembered his dream and corrected himself. "Yes. Maybe. I'm not sure."

"This is a confusing time for you, I am sure. Lots of emotions rolling around in you," Tenzein said. He leaned forward against the back of the front seat. "Emotions are strong energy, but you have to control them. Uncontrolled, they will betray you. The secret is you need to have a calm mind. Can you do that?"

Calm was not the word Jacob would use to describe his emotional state at the moment. At best, he was a hurricane that was still gaining strength, and he ricocheted between anger, depression, despair, hopelessness, and back again, over and over, every minute of every day.

"Probably not," the monk answered his own question. "Do this. Imagine the calmest body of water you have ever seen. The glassy surface of a clear lake.

No waves, no wake. Then imagine yourself floating on it. Only your face is above the water. The water filters everything from the universe around you, leaving you with the serene peace of nothingness. The water has done its job, now you have to do yours. Ignore everything you are feeling, everything you are thinking. Focus on one purpose. No ripples in the water. You disturb the water, you disturb the balance of the universe and invite chaos. You no disturb the water, you are in control of the universe."

Jacob's mind wandered through the scene Tenzein described. He remembered the feeling of swimming and lying in the tub with his head submerged but his face still above the water. Every sound around him—the screaming and yelling of the other kids at the community pool, the music his mom played during his bath time—all of it muted. It was there, but he was in a peaceful place. A world he could easily become lost in. The rest of it he had his doubts about. His body and mind felt jittery and unfocused. "Does it work?" he asked.

"Yes. I meditate using that image twice a day, every day. I also do it before I confront anything. I didn't always. I was a few years younger than your age when my father died and left me this responsibility. A village two mountains away sent for me, and I rushed in, unfocused." Tenzein stopped and, with his right hand, rolled up the sleeve on his left arm. A large scar stretched from his wrist up past his elbow. It was jagged, not clean and surgical. Obvious gaps in the muscle under the skin created craters. "I was foolish and paid the price. I sought wisdom from my elders. They turned me to the teachings of our religion beyond those about the spiritual world that they taught me. My religion taught me to center my mind, body, and soul. Through that wisdom, I have been able to overcome all challenges. It tells me we will overcome the danger we both feel now."

He was right. Jacob felt it. He had for the last few minutes. It started as just an icy chill but progressed to a shiver that traveled up and down his body. Pins pricked the surface of his gooseflesh skin. The shops and buildings in the center of town were visible far ahead of them. No signs of anything else. At least visually. They were there. No question about that.

Lewis pulled off to the side of the road about a quarter of a mile before the buildings. The rest of the cars pulled in behind him. It wasn't long before their occupants all stood outside the cars, all facing the buildings.

"They're there. That is for sure," announced Mr. Halensworth.

They all knew it and nodded. There was something else too. Jacob felt it but wasn't sure if anyone else did. He was being watched. Not by anything close, but by something far away. Its attention was on him and him alone.

13

Lord Negiev and Mr. Halensworth took the lead. Neither appeared to take the danger too seriously. Each took turns and called out whatever was there.

"Come on. Where are you?" Mr. Halensworth bellowed.

"Are you hiding from us?" Lord Negiev asked. His tone taunted the air.

The rest followed several feet behind them. Each acted as if they took their surroundings with a level of reverence the other two had forgotten.

"Come on. I wanted to see how big and bad you are," the brash Englishman bellowed.

Jacob heard Madame Stryvia retort, "Idiots" just under her breath. It was easy for him to hear her, even as quietly as she said it. There wasn't a sound coming from anywhere. No crickets. No wind. Even the thunder had subsided. In the horror movies he enjoyed, the lead character would say, "It's quiet, too quiet," and eerie music would play in the background to foreshadow the impending arrival of whatever evil the story was about. He now found himself in that same setting, except without the eerie music. It wasn't needed. The stillness combined with the cold chill and the feeling of being watched was more than enough to give Jacob the biggest case of the creeps he had ever felt and put his head on a turnstile. Left, then right. Nothing. Even behind him, nothing around them except darkness and an empty street he had been on hundreds of times before, but never like this. It was mid-morning but appeared to be the middle of the night.

Up ahead of him, Mr. Halensworth had stopped and taken off his brown sport coat, folded it up and placed it neatly on one of the several park benches that lined the shopping district. On a normal day, with the sun out like this day started with, it would be uncommon to find these benches empty. People would stop to sit and talk, and others made special trips with their morning coffee to sit there and read the paper while greeting everyone who walked by. The Doctor Dolittle hat joined them on the bench. Then, he pushed both sleeves of his starched, white button-up shirt to his elbow, displaying the forearms of a man who had been in a few fights throughout the years.

His compatriot at the front removed nothing but did spread out slightly toward the other side of the road. A quick tug of his waistcoat and a pop of his neck to the right preceded the plunging of his hand into his right pants pocket. It came out as quickly as it went in. With it, a long string and a cross that looked oddly familiar to Jacob. An instinctual glance down at the one still in his right hand confirmed it.

"In case you are wondering Jacob, they all have one. We divided the original crucifix up into crosses for each site. Yours being the last," explained Father Murray from just behind Jacob. "The assignment of a keeper used to be reserved for a member of the clergy, a priest, but your family broke that tradition. Since then, assignment followed ability."

Mr. Halensworth had his out in his hand as well and was now whistling, as if calling a dog.

"So childish," Madame Stryvia mumbled under her breath, just in front of Jacob. Her pace quickened, quickly leaving the others behind, and she joined the two she just admonished. Her red cape fell to the ground with a flourish, revealing the cross hung around her neck.

"Don't antagonize them, you fools," she admonished them again. "Can't you feel their angst?"

"Of course I can. We all can. I just don't like not being able to see them," answered Halensworth, his voice less brazen than before. "I would rather they come on out than this stupid cat-and-mouse game."

"That I agree with," she said.

"Same," agreed Lord Negiev.

The three walked further ahead of the rest and then all stopped, midstride, on the same step.

"Which side?" Madame Stryvia asked, her gaze locked straight down the road.

A chorus of "left" and "right" answers emerged from the assembled keepers. All except Jacob, that was. He was late with his answer. He felt it, and he knew what he felt. There was no way he could miss it. It started as a soft chill on one side, then the other. Then it built, fast, and rampaged through his essence with the ferocity of a speeding freight train until it exploded out. "BOTH!"

Jacob's voice pierced the silence of the night just as two large creatures jumped from the roofs of the buildings on either side of the road. They landed mere feet in front of the trio that took the lead. None backed up and gave any ground. Instead they adjusted their stance and held the ground. The creatures, a combination of human and animal that nightmares were made of, both stood at least ten feet tall and snorted and snarled.

"Watch it, they are not alone!" exclaimed Mr. Nagoti.

"Where at?" Lord Negiev asked. His hand shot forward. The cross dangled in front of him toward the beasts. They recoiled against its presence but didn't flee, didn't retreat.

He didn't have to wait long before they answered his question. Two more leaped in from the same buildings, and another emerged from a side street. All three strolled forward. No urgency in their unnatural gait. Snorts and snarls accompanied their breathing. Puffs of smoke emanated from their nostrils. Two pairs of clawed hands dragged against the pavement, producing sparks. Another claw dragged against the glass of a storefront window. It made the sound of fingernails on a chalkboard sound like the sweetest aria. The glass above the line created by the claw fell from the window frame and shattered on the sidewalk. They left trails of flame behind every step. This was something Jacob hadn't seen that night at the high school, nor when he snuck out. It drove a fear deep inside of him. One thought jumped into his mind, *This is Old Testament fire and brimstone stuff.*

A crumpled metal trash can crashed and slid to a stop on the pavement in front of him. The creature that had thrown it stood and screamed in a hundred voices while it watched the can fly through the air.

"Mark, Lewis, you might want to go get behind the cars," warned Father Murray.

"No objection, Father," responded Lewis. He was already several steps away, and Mark had already reached the bumper before the father had completed his suggestion.

"Is that all of them?" Mr. Halensworth asked.

"I think so, but not sure," responded Madame Stryvia. "There is such an evil feel to this place. I can't tell if there is anything else."

"I know," he replied. "So, guys, what do you say about returning to your area of the woods and we all get together to do this later? No need for you to get hurt now."

The offer to walk away was refused, as one creature swiped at Lord Negiev. He dodged and rolled to the ground.

"That would be a no," Mr. Halensworth said with a grunt as he charged the beast directly in front of him. A wild swing of his cross missed. "Foul creature, you do not belong in our Lord's world..." he began. The longer he spoke, the brighter the light that resonated from the cross.

Lord Negiev was now back to his feet and made his own swipe at his foe but missed as well. The creature returned the favor and connected. The impact sent him rolling back on the road. He jumped up and slapped at the spot on his waistcoat where it made contact. It smoldered with small black flames emanating out from the center. The slaps did nothing to extinguish the flames, only producing sparks with every whack. Quickly, he threw off the coat, leaving it in a smoking pile on the road. Then, after he adjusted his red velvet vest, he marched forward and declared, "This one is mine."

His counterpart couldn't hear him, he was too busy sliding on the asphalt after another thunderous strike sent him flying to the ground. The sound of it echoed around them and rumbled the ground they stood on.

"Let's not let them have all the fun," said Mr. Nagoti. He, Father Lucian, and Tenzein Mao moved forward. Each pulled out their own crosses.

Tenzein Mao looked back at Jacob and said, "Remember, Jacob, peaceful mind. Imagine the water."

The last member of their party followed the others forward but remained a few steps behind. She observed everything around her carefully, cautiously. Jacob did the same. The sensations overwhelmed him. He could no longer feel a single entity or even the five he saw. There was an overbearing evil. Both in his mind and in his physical being. Acid crept up his throat, and his legs shook but stayed locked to the ground. Several attempts to step forward resulted in a buckle in his knees that he caught before anyone else noticed. A voice in the back of his head reminded him this was his town, and his family caused this. The voice nagged him and ate away at what was not consumed by fear and that feeling of evil all around him. It was down to its last bite when he gave himself the talk. It wasn't a pep talk or an inspiration speech. Nothing the climactic scene of a movie could be made from. It was guilt. The guilt he felt as he watched several strangers now sprawled across the roadway as they attempted to confront the demons in his town. The demons his sister, possessed or not, let out and sent into town to confront them.

One wailed in the depths of his consciousness as Mr. Halensworth made firm contact with the cross and sent it back where it came from. "That's one," he exclaimed. "How many for you, Negiev?"

Jacob stepped forward. One step. Really it was less than a step, more of a half of a step, which was all he could muster under the weight of everything he felt and what was in his mind. Father Murray voiced a warning, "Jacob..." from behind him, but a supernatural event interrupted the rest of the message. A single bright white lightning bolt shot from the sky and struck a spot about an inch in front of Jacob's right foot. The foot that had taken the step. An explosion rocketed through the air with the blinding light, stopping both keepers and creatures in their place. Both Mr. Nagoti and Tenzein Mao took advantage of the distraction. Light shot from both of their crosses and froze two of the creatures in their tracks. They dismissed both quickly in a flash of blue flame and smoke.

The rest weren't having as easy of a time. Lord Negiev chased his target down the road. It fled from him, not on the road itself but along the front of the shops. Its claws crashed into the bricks on the front of the buildings with each step, sending piles of debris raining down.

Madame Stryvia had avoided any contact but had failed to trap or dismiss the one she had targeted. With each attempt she made, it swung at her or moved, forcing her to stop and get out of the way. She yelled, "Enough!" and a flash of light shot from her cross, sending the creature crashing to the ground. It stayed there until it disappeared in a flicker of blue flame and smoke, after she finished the rite of dismissal.

That left two. Both were trying to get away. They could let them and deal with them again, out there, or end it now. A decision that would be made for them, when a tandem wheel pickup, Ted Barton's truck, flew at them from the darkness. A parting gift from one beast, or was it? As the mangled truck bounced past and over them, its friend charged them. Jacob watched, helplessly, as the scene unfolded before him. All were on the ground, where they landed to avoid the truck. None would have time to get up to avoid the approaching creatures who, along with Jacob's pulse, were picking up the pace at an astonishing rate. Their steps, and every beat of his heart, echoed in his head like explosions.

A scream, a primal scream, unlike anything Jacob had ever heard, rocketed through the air with a flash of light. The sound and light knocked both creatures to the ground, where they wailed in pain. The scream came from the silent member of their group. The one who had yet to be introduced. She knelt on the ground and watched the others finish the creatures off before she got up and walked away into the darkness.

14

"Everyone all right?" Father Murray asked.

"No worse for wear," Halensworth said. He examined the scrapes on his arms and then rubbed the trickle of blood coming down his forehead, which he hit on the ground while avoiding a wild swing. "Well, maybe a little wear."

"I'm okay," Lord Negiev said.

Madame Stryvia helped him to his feet. Jacob saw scrapes on him as well, but what really got his attention was the mark that was still smoldering on his shirtsleeve. There were no visible flames, but there was smoke. Smoke that slowly rose from the spot and lingered just above him for an unnatural amount of time. His jacket still sat in a pile on the ground and smoldered with the same unsettling smoke. Both Madame Stryvia and Lord Negiev attempted to smother the spot, but it continued to smoke. Neither appeared to suffer any burns from the contact.

Jacob walked over to the piled-up waistcoat on the ground. He ran his hand over it and through the smoke. There was no heat. This was not like any fire he had ever experienced. It was cool and icy the closer he moved his hand to it. The texture and tone of his skin changed the longer he left it in the smoke. It took on a gray shriveled-up appearance while in the smoke, and normal peach skin returned after it passed through to the other side.

"Let me help you with that," Father Murray said. With a vial he retrieved from his pocket, he walked over.

"Ah yes," remarked Lord Negiev as Father Murray flipped the top of the vial up and dripped a single drop on his sleeve, and then another small drop on his coat. Both stopped smoldering in an instant.

As the keepers regrouped, more scrapes and bruises were evident. Some from impacts with the ground. Others from punches and swipes by the creatures. Luckily none suffered any gashes from the large claws.

"That was a test," Mr. Nagoti stated. "They gave up too easy."

"Agree. It wanted to see who was here. It can undoubtedly feel us, just like we can feel it," said Father Lucian. "Next time won't be so easy."

Everyone seemed to agree, which explained the lack of any collective exhale of relief. They knew this was just the beginning, and it would only get worst. Jacob knew it, too, but what was worse than this? His mind couldn't make that leap. Things had already passed what Hollywood had loaded his adolescent mind with.

"So, what are we waiting on? Let's go take care of this. They won't be expecting that."

"Slow down, my English brother," Tenzein Mao said with a voice as steady and calm as the very water he asked Jacob to imagine. "That may be exactly what they are expecting. This was a test, and also a way to call us out. If we rush forward, there is no surprise in that move. There is also no logic in that move either. Lack of logic and clarity will only lead us down the path to failure."

There was no nod or verbal agreement. The agreement with his statement stood strong in the group's silence. The group still nursing their wounds. The group that had already moved back toward the row of cars they came in.

"Should we wait for her?"

"No, I have a feeling she will be back at the church before we are," responded Father Lucian as he ducked into Lewis Tillingsly's car.

Jacob looked at Father Murray quizzically over the top of his white Cadillac. The look continued in the car as Father Murray started it and pulled off. Tenzein Mao was alone in the back. They U-turned right there in the road and headed back to the church the way they came. Jacob kept watch along the road for the mysterious member of their group but never saw her. Not until they pulled into the parking lot of the church, and he spied her sitting outside her tent by the fire. When she saw the cars enter the gravel lot, she started her trek toward them.

"How is that even possible?" Jacob mumbled. It took them a good ten minutes to cover the distance by car. There was no way someone could travel on foot and beat them back.

"You are thinking too linear," responded Tenzein. "The road has a lot of curves and turns in it, but that is not the only path from there to here. Remember, the shortest distance between two points is a straight line."

"What do you mean?"

"She didn't follow the road," interjected Father Murray. "That is Manuela Borio. She is from a little village outside Pisco, Peru. They travel everywhere by foot. Excellent sense of direction. I have no doubt she could cut through the woods and find her way back here."

"Odd," commented Jacob.

"Oh, that isn't the oddest. Do you know what is special about her assignment? Pisco, Peru?"

He shook his head. The town's name was not one he was familiar with. The only town he knew in Peru was the capital, Lima, thanks to his World Geography class.

"Her family has two assignments. The first conquistadors that marched through the Peruvian jungle encountered a tormented soul that approached with a whistle that increased the closer it got to you. It would lure its victim with the whistle, then either devour them or take them deep into the jungle to let them starve to death as it watched. At first, they thought it was just one, but after talking with several villages, they learned there were more, maybe hundreds, that stormed through the villages each night looking for victims. They were called Tunche, *fear* in their language. The Borio were a family with the gift that was selected from one of those villages to contain them and protect the villages. The story goes, they spend every night listening in the jungle for the whistle and then race to stop them before they can harm anyone. Then about a hundred years ago, they were given an additional but less involved assignment. In 1913, Sarah Ellen Roberts was brought to the city and buried in a tomb. They executed her under suspicion of being a vampire. Now, she isn't the first person executed for that reason. She was the one the church most believed it to be true of. So much so, they assigned the Borio family to watch over her tomb to ensure she never rose again. Nothing has happened yet." Father Murray opened the driver's side door and got out before he continued. "I don't believe it ever will, but someone does."

Jacob and Tenzein followed Father Murray and the others back into the church.

"Nice of you to join us," Mr. Halensworth sniped as Manuela reached the stairs before him. He paused as she entered, and in very broken English she said, "Imbecile."

From two people behind, Madame Stryvia snarked, "I like her."

15

Jacob collapsed in a pew in the back and allowed the others to gather up front. To say there was a disagreement around tactics would be an understatement. It was no surprise to him that Halensworth and Negiev wanted to charge right out there and follow the creatures back to the building and take the fight to them. Both made expert use of a first-aid kit Father Murray had retrieved from his residence to nurse their wounds. Quite a sight for Jacob though. Bandages covered their arms, knees, and one on Lord Negiev's forehead, yet they were demanding to go out there for more.

The others were more conservative in their approach, wanting to talk about how to proceed and when, to avoid walking into an ambush. Three were more subdued than the rest. Manuela was not a surprise. She kept her distance as she always seemed to. Madame Stryvia stood back, more lost in thought than ignoring the disagreement. This wasn't much of a surprise either. Jacob only met her a few hours ago. From what he had observed so far, she was calmer, almost logical. At least from what he could see. Something that reminded him of his sister, not a comparison he should mention out loud in present company under the circumstances. She offered a few points of view, more on the side of those wanting to plan than rush, but that was it.

The one who was a surprise to Jacob was Father Lucian. He stood at the front, not consulting either side of the discussion. He offered nothing, and most striking, he didn't try to stop it. Jacob didn't know if this meant he lost control of the group or if he was just letting each side work it out on their own. He had to consider that regardless of his position in the church, he may not be the senior here, the person in charge, or the person with the most experience. Who that was, he didn't know. They didn't wear uniforms or present a resume. Jacob had to imagine that each family had their legendary and storied accomplishments that would qualify them at one time or another as the better to lead, or the most experienced and capable. He hoped so, at least. Most of all, he hoped it wasn't his family that was the most experienced. That would be the worst irony in the history of the word. They needed a hero or a group of heroes now. He hoped this was them.

The bickering continued for a good half hour. During which they applied the last of the bandages and dressed the remaining wounds. It wasn't until they were in the church's light that Jacob could see the scalded marks on Lord Negiev's arm. If he was in any pain, he didn't let on. He continued, unabated, to attempt to convince the others they needed to press on with the battle.

Terms and phrases whipped past Jacob. Nothing was a complete sentence or even a complete thought. Just words that made little sense. His attempt to put a few together and hear exactly what was being said resulted in words from different voices combined in a confusing mishmash of nothingness. A few words individually made sense, like: evil, dangerous, threat, kill, and death. They could mean anything. Alone they were just words. Combined with other worlds they would have more meaning and context. That was the puzzle piece he was missing.

A steamroller delivered the first two-word combination he picked out: "kill her." It knocked the wind out of him. He had to sit and listen more while he tried to recover. The impact of the words sent him into a state of hyper-focus. Able to pick one or two voices out of the jumble. They were as clear as if they talked straight to him. No other voices were present. What they discussed sent his normally calm and reserved demeanor into a full rage. Something he had never felt before. Not that one time his father grounded him for talking back when he was thirteen. Not the time the Valley Ridge pitcher beamed him right between the shoulder blades with an inside fastball. And not any of the times his sister made him the target of some good-natured ridicule taken way too far. This was much worse than any of that, and before he even knew it, he was on his feet and stormed forward with two confident steps and then a mad sprint at his target. He only stopped when he had two good handfuls of red velvet vest. The aggression must have fueled his strength more than he expected, as he held Lord Negiev several inches above the ground. Jacob shook him while he screamed, "That is my sister you're talking about killing!"

Father Murray and Lewis Tillingsly grabbed hold of Jacob and pulled him back. Lord Negiev slipped from his grip and fell to the floor. His leather-soled shoes slapped against the surface when he landed. The sound coincided with another word his brain picked out of the ether: "don't." A word that could have meant anything, but what clouded its mystery more was whose voice it was, Sarah's. That was all she said. He didn't see her like he had the other times. All he really saw was a host of shocked faces that were trying to comfort and calm him, and others that just stood around and gawked at his explosion. Father Murray and Lewis managed to pull Jacob across the aisle and sit him in a pew. Both were talking to him, but he didn't hear them. Just a jumble below the anger and hatred that coursed through his veins. He sat there, semi-restrained by a single hand of Father Murray's on his shoulder that, if he wanted to, he could pull away from in a second. His gaze scanned the crowd for a new target, but the conversations about what to do had stopped. There were no more threats against his family. The only words spoken were, "Jacob, it's all right," or "Mr. Meyer, we will do all we can for your sister," and "It's okay, Jacob. We won't hurt her."

The one person who said nothing, neither before the outburst nor immediately after, left her lone perch away from the others and approached Jacob. Manuela walked calmly over to Jacob and sat down beside him. No words were spoken as she looked deep into his eyes. He hadn't noticed until that moment, under that mess of hair, she had nice green eyes and pretty facial features. Her right hand reached out and took his left, then her left reached out and took his right. A smile crossed her face as Jacob felt the heat of his anger leach out of his body and down his arms. He could feel it as clear as the sleeve of a shirt sliding down his arm. A feeling of calm came over him, and it transported him back to a memory of his mother singing him to sleep in his bed back in Portland, his clown night-light projecting its shape high above on the ceiling. His father's voice said, "Night, champ."

The rage was gone when she let go of his hands. So was much of the despair. Instead, his mind felt focused, for the first time in days. There were no random thoughts. No radical emotions bouncing around in his mind. Just a single purpose. How can we end this?

"No bottle up," she said in a calming tone. The smile, still on her face, was nurturing. "Remember water."

From over her shoulder, Tenzein Mao repeated, "Clear mind, Jacob."

Manuela got up and walked off. Nothing else was said as she went back to the same spot she sat in before.

Jacob looked up at Father Murray. "How? What did she do?" His expression was that of a child who just watched a magician not only pull a dove out of his hat but also made it disappear in a burst of flame right before his eyes.

"Jacob, people have all different abilities and gifts," was the only answer he gave.

As vague as it was, Jacob understood. The world in which he lived meant he needed to have a great deal of faith. Not in the religious sense but in the possibility that anything could be true.

Madame Stryvia was next to approach him. As she left the crowd, their looks gave him the feeling the others elected her as the peacemaker. She sat next to him, still with a somewhat fearful look, and reached over tentatively with her right hand and placed it on his leg. Her touch was warm, but her hand trembled.

"Jacob, we will do everything we can—"

A loud clap of thunder interrupted her, the source of which wasn't a cloud outside, or it didn't sound that way. It sounded inside. Just above their heads. Another one sent the church into darkness as the sound shattered the stained-glass windows that lined the walls. The ominous clouds still hung over the town and blocked out any sunlight that should be up at this time of day.

A flash of flame illuminated the pitch-black interior of the church. Jacob threw up a hand to block his eyes. Behind it, a cross burned above the altar. It wasn't the one positioned there in the church that had hung steadfast for decades since its construction. No, this was one of flame. As it turned, Jacob saw a figure suspended against it. It didn't move, just turned along with the cross until it was upside down. The sight drove a stake straight through Jacob's heart. It was his sister, or her image, but at the same time, it wasn't. The black marks he saw before covered her skin again, and her eyes glowed yellow like lumps of amber.

The illumination of the flames revealed visitors around them. They stood up and down every aisle and pew, covering every inch of the floor. They were human, or so Jacob thought. They appeared human, but some were missing limbs, others skin. Men, women, and children charred black. Burnt pieces flaked off them and fell to the ground. Faces expressionless, eyes hollow. The stench of burnt death and rot billowed from them.

"I know who each of you are. I know what each of you are. I know what each of you don't want anyone else to know," cackled a voice high above them.

The hundreds of scorched bodies opened their darkened mouths in unison and screamed, a blood-curdling scream that raped the silence and sanctuary of the church. The scream lasted for several painful seconds, sending Jacob's hands up to cover his ears. That did nothing. Nothing blocked the sound. It was in his mind, in his thoughts, in his body. Then, as sudden as it all appeared, it was gone. No boom of thunder or flash as when it arrived, just silence and nothingness. The lights flickered back on, revealing a cloud of smoke hovering in the rafters and the shards of colored glass lining the walls. The smell remained.

"What the hell was that?" asked Lord Negiev. His words were strong, but the croak in his voice let on to the shock everyone still felt.

"An invitation to an old-world ass-kicking, that's what," stated Halensworth. One fist pounded into his palm, but his tone had lost the edge it had had moments earlier.

The display and visitor took the wind out of everyone's sails and left them in a state of malaise and confusion. No one more so than Jacob. The image of his sister, or what seemed to look like his sister, burnt into his brain. The hundreds of bodies that surrounded him, their sound, their smell, their presence were still there with him, even though they were gone. Every moment of this world became stranger than the next, and it was well beyond a world he recognized. Thoughts in his mind tried to organize themselves to make sense of it all, but the logical constructs met blockades of emotions like fear and depression. If they had breached through, he wouldn't have found much clarity, as the thoughts were more focused on acceptance of what he was seeing as real, nothing fake or dreamt up. Which was a far reach for him, but it was something he would need to accept. Each attempt rammed into that hard wall fortified by disbelief.

The wall had blocked out the outside world and forced Jacob to withdrawal within himself. Inside a safe cocoon where he could be protected, at least emotionally, from further damage. Madame Stryvia, who still sat next to him, tried to break through. Jacob saw her and knew she was there, but to his damaged psyche, she was miles away through a door at the end of a dark hallway. For the moment the door was still open and allowed him to hear her ask, "Jacob, stay with us. Stay with me." Her touch on his arm was a muted sensation. The other conversations in the room dissipated behind the wall in Jacob's mind. He was going, and somewhere deep inside he knew it, but he lacked the will to pull himself out. Lacked the will to grab hold of a waiting hand to be pulled out. Lacked the desire to return to this world. There was a peace to all this. Jacob was still sad, extremely so, but he may be able to live with that. If he could stop the pouring of salt in his open emotional wounds, and additional moments of shock.

There it was again, that muted sensation. Someone was touching him. His eyes moved to change his view down the dark hallway that was his mind's view of the outside world. He saw the hands of Madame Stryvia, both of which were crossed neatly on her lap. It wasn't her. The feeling was around his legs, where her brown eyes looked. He followed her gaze down. Fingers moved in his pocket. Whose fingers were they? Were they his? The question was only fleeting though. He wasn't sure it was important enough to care. The fingers pulled something out of the pocket. *Oh, that*, he thought.

He followed it as it moved toward his right hand, which Madame Stryvia had grasped and was opening. They placed the object inside, almost with care, and she wrapped his fingers around it again. Slowly. The object was familiar in his hand. As his fingers wrapped around it, he recognized the shape. It felt warm. Not just Madame Stryvia's hands, now wrapped around his, but the object. The world grew larger in his vision. The corridor descending away from the actual world grew smaller. The end of it that led to the outside world came closer. Sounds were no longer muted. His name called clearly by several voices. Each dripped with compassion.

"Jacob, come back to us."

"Jacob, don't give in."

"Jacob, we need you here with us."

His eyes searched their faces as they spoke, but they finally settled on the woman in front of him. "Welcome back, Jacob."

She released his hands, and his fingers opened. The object in his palm emanated a slight glow that delivered comfort. A feeling he hadn't known in some days.

"Jacob, don't worry. We will do everything we can for both Sarah and your Father," Father Lucian said, his hand on Jacob's shoulder to provide a fatherly comfort.

The comfort he already felt grew into something else. Something he couldn't put his finger on. A feeling he couldn't describe welled up inside him. It gathered speed within, combining with thoughts and questions. Like a tidal wave picking up debris, every little bit added to its strength until it finally crested.

"What exactly are you going to do?" he asked, his voice firm and edged on demanding while remaining respectful of those gathered around him. It even appeared that they appreciated the question and echoed it as they all turned their attention to Father Lucian.

"We go get her and bring her back here. We have to work in our world. Not its. That is the only way," Father Lucian said.

"We go get her and bring her back? Just that simple?" asked Mr. Nagoti.

There was no pause for consideration before Father Lucian replied with, "Yes."

Jacob, nor any of the others, appeared to share his confidence in that simple plan.

"I have always performed an exorcism where the person was. To confront the beast there and make them let the person go."

"To cleanse the place," added Lord Negiev. Worry filled his words.

"This is far different from anything any of us have ever encountered," Father Lucian said. "I see no other way, and it will take all of us."

"But how? How can we get her back here?" Tenzein Mao asked. His calm and clear mind he spoke of several times to Jacob now seemed to be clouded with worry and concern.

"I have an idea on that."

16

The dark clouds still hovered over the town like a blanket of pain holding in the grief. They were lower than normal rain clouds. The lightning strikes that exploded from them were brighter and bluer than normal too. The rain drops pinged off the windshield with a thud instead of the usual splash or ping. Nothing about this "weather" event appeared natural as they pulled up to the bridge across Walter's Creek.

When they got out of the cars, the air felt foreign to them. It was heavy, dank, and evil. Jacob tasted sulfur and smoke. He closed his mouth and swallowed to clear the taste, but it didn't, it got worse. Burning his eyes and sending streams of tears down his face. He wasn't the only one. Madame Stryvia fashioned her red cape into a mask up over her nose and mouth, allowing only her eyes to peer over the top edge of it. The others attempted to use the arm of a shirt or jacket. The image inspired Jacob, who pulled his hood up and then pulled hard on the drawstrings, closing it off to only a small hole for his eyes to see through. It wasn't perfect, but it helped.

"We aren't in Kansas anymore," remarked Lewis.

"No, we aren't. You and Mark stay here with the cars," said Father Murray.

"Now, Father," Lewis tried to object, but Father Murray cut his objection short.

"Absolutely not. Not this time." His voice cracked while delivering the impassioned plea. "We lost John last time. This will be worst. Much worse."

Jacob, within earshot of the conversation, swallowed hard to try to force down the lump that had developed in his throat. The scene before him was worse than anything he could have imagined. Removing the dark clouds that hung over the landscape and the bright white lightning that struck all around them, the landscape before him was that of a foreign world. Something out of a wartime movie, with piles of debris all over the place and stripped of anything that made the area look like planet Earth. Small fires burned all around, probably from lightning strikes that hit the downed trees. Smoke spewed up and mixed with the clouds. His eyes watered, and his throat wretched with every breath. There was a rumble under his feet. Not in waves, like he heard others describe. A constant one. Like a great beast growling.

The first to enter was Mr. Halensworth. He made no great speech. No proclamation. He simply wiped his brow with his handkerchief before his first step. Lord Negiev was next to follow, but not without taking another long look at the scene he was about to step into.

"Fathers, I am not sure about going in alone. Shall we?" Madame Stryvia asked.

Father Murray and Father Lucian both agreed with a nod.

"Jacob, stick close by," said Father Murray. It was a direction he didn't need, and one he had no intention of disobeying. He closed ranks and walked in with them.

Madame Stryvia gripped his right hand again, forcing his fingers tighter around the cross, which hadn't left his hand. "Keep this and your faith held tight. Both will protect you," she said. What Jacob wouldn't give to feel the comfort he felt earlier right now.

To the left of them, Mr. Nagoti, Tenzein Mao, and Manuela entered, tentatively, as did the two in front of them. Caution now replaced the bombastic statements of earlier. Every step was an exploration. What was on the ground below them? What was ahead of them? Would they run into any creatures like they saw earlier? Jacob didn't know. He didn't believe any of them did, but in they walked. Past burnt piles of broken trees, and others that had already burned themselves out, blackening the surrounding ground and adding their own charred aroma to the air.

There was something else in the air. Something burnt and rancid, it leached through the fabric of his hoodie and turned his stomach. The turning continued, and its contents raced upward. His hands barely pulled the hood away from his face before his body convulsed forward, spewing the fluid on the ground. After the second heave, he opened his eyes and gasped, almost choking. His reaction was so violent he fell backward. His gaze still locked on the severed human head, wedged between two downed trees, eyes open and looking at him, but now covered with vomit.

"You're all right," Father Murray said as he reached down to help Jacob up.

As he walked past the head, his eyes watched. Its eyes watched back. A reminder to Jacob of all the people who had lost their lives out here. He felt the urge to look down where he stepped, but didn't. He didn't want to see anything else like that.

Ahead of them, Halensworth and Negiev had stopped and were studying a spot on the ground. As they came closer, they could see the two men were rubbing at it with their shoes. Jacob's stomach turned again. He didn't want to see another human body part, and not one these two men kicked at. He walked around them and kept moving forward. The others stopped at the spot and looked at the object that had grabbed the attention of the two men. Several asked, "What is that?" There was a chorus of, "I don't know," from many of them.

One voice, the one that belonged to Tenzein Mao, had an answer. "I know what it is. Jacob, come here." He waited until Jacob joined them before he answered, "It's a fulgurite."

"A what?" asked Lord Negiev.

Manuela bent down and ran her hand over the object, and Jacob bent down for a closer look. It was beautiful. A clear round crystal, sitting on the ground, reflecting each of the blinding lightning bolts like a flash cube.

"You're right," Manuela said.

Jacob reached over and ran his hand across the crystal. It was smooth, perfectly glass smooth.

"Jacob, use your hands and dig around it," requested Tenzein Mao.

Jacob hesitated for only a second, but that was long enough for Manuela to scrape dirt and sand away from the edge. As she did, Jacob noticed it was not just a flat piece sitting on the surface. It went down. He worked on the other side, and after a few moments, they had a couple inches of it exposed. He reached down with both hands, grabbed it, and gave it a little tug.

"Careful," she muttered, and covered his hands with hers to help.

Slowly he pulled it and its branches free from the ground. It was beautiful. A tree, with a trunk and branches, of clear crystal that glimmered with every flash of the surrounding horror.

"It happens when lightning hits a spot of sand. There is a dry lakebed close to my home. I have seen many of these. A few are on my nightstand."

"Ironic," Father Lucian said.

"No, Father. It's nature. In everything, there is beauty. You just have to find it."

The object was beautiful. It was one of the most spectacular objects Jacob had ever seen. There was no questioning that. What was ahead of them was not. It was hell on earth. A hell they trudge on toward.

Father Murray stopped the group a few times. Each time, he explained he thought something moved ahead of them, but then he released them and kept moving. Jacob saw nothing, except a monochromatic desolate no-man's-land, leading up to a lush green thatch of trees that loomed head. Every step closer, the air felt heavier, denser, and eviler. What was in there knew they were coming. Jacob felt it. They probably all did. It was powerful. That much was sure. Its presence radiated out and pushed against his conviction. Dread rushed into his body. From the look of the others, he wasn't the only one.

Their steps looked laborious and painful. Jacob felt something, something strange. A small headache developed. He couldn't put his finger on where though. It was everywhere. Thoughts were interrupted midstream, not by pain, but by a distraction. Other images and thoughts flooded in front of them. Things pulled from deep in his childhood. Horrifying memories of his mother, not as he remembered her but as the chemo- and cancer-ravaged skeleton she was just before she died. Things he hadn't thought of in years. Others were thoughts he wasn't sure he had ever had. Images of him throwing punches and wielding a weapon. Neither of which he had done. They were created images and struck an emotional chord down deep, but why? That quick question was the first thought of his own he had completed since the headache started. Just as quick as that thought was, he was pulled back down, but by what? Then the word *probe* flashed into his head. Father Lucian said it tried to probe his thoughts. Could this be it?

Wait, my dad isn't dead, he thought as he saw himself standing over a casket. *Maybe it's Sarah*. If she knew they were coming for her, she may be reaching out to help.

When did his home burn down? he asked himself as he stood in front of its burning remains.

If it was Sarah, why would she be showing him these images? It made no sense, but that sensation of illogic didn't last more than a fleeting second. The image of his sister standing over him with a stake replaced it. With an evil but satisfied grin, she thrust it down into his chest. His hand shot to a spot of searing pain. There was nothing there, but that didn't stop the pain. A pain that pulled him out of the malaise he was falling into. The trance that was overcoming him. This wasn't Sarah. This was *it*. This was the demon that had her. Just like Father Lucian told them, it probed at him and was now probing at Jacob. Scratch that; Jacob looked both left and right. They were all fighting it, in their own way, but some were losing the battle. His fingers tightened around the cross. It was clear to Jacob. It had begun, and they weren't even there yet.

17

Lord Negiev was the first to scream and fall to his knees. His hands reached and clawed at some imaginary force in front of him. Mr. Nagoti tried to help him but caught a flailing hand against his cheek, sending him falling backward to the ground. Jacob went to help him up, but the man was frozen where he lay, muttering to himself the entire time, faster than Jacob had ever heard anyone talk. The others weren't any better off. They just stood and watched, or appeared to. Their gaze was directed at him, but to Jacob they looked to be anywhere but in the here and now. This included both Father Murray and Father Lucian, who Jacob looked to for help. Help was something no one was in a position to give at the moment.

All he could do was watch as he stood in that desolate nightmare that used to be full of majestic pine and oak trees. Where small animals like squirrels and foxes made their home. There was no life here anymore. Not that it was all death, which there was plenty of all around. All he had to do was look. There was evil. An evil that attacked any signs of life and drained them, until there was nothing left. It wore on them physically, using fear. The fear of the setting. The fear of the unknown that was out there. What it didn't tear down through those means, it moved in and tried to rip to shreds from the inside out. It played with their thoughts, toyed with their emotions. Struck fear that produced genuine pain. Jacob still felt that pain. A spot on his chest still felt burned and skewed. But it was inside. Not the skin or muscle. Deeper than that. The others were obviously going through the same thing.

While the others were battling, Negiev was writhing on the ground. His hands dug in the dirt. He shoved handful after handful to the side as fast as he could. Words gushed out of him between wails and shrieks. Jacob looked at the ground Negiev was digging for any sign of why. There was nothing, just dirt. Just dirt and the tip of his own cross, poking out of a mound of dirt. Another shove threw more dirt over the top of it. Jacob bent down quickly and picked it up. Remembering the incident at the church, he attempted to shove it into one of Negiev's hands. They moved without pause and knocked the cross out of Jacob's hand twice. A third attempt also failed.

He knelt over him, with both crosses in hand. He felt hopeless and called out to the others.

"Madame Stryvia, help me," he implored.

She stood there locked in her own world, mouth moving, but no sound escaped. Twitches and shudders consumed her body. To her side, on the ground, lay her cross, the red rope she wore it on still looped around it. How it had been removed, Jacob didn't know. He didn't see when it happened.

"Tenzein, I need your help." But again there was no reply. Like the others, he was unresponsive and not present, his cross just inches from his foot.

As a last-gasp effort, Jacob touched Lord Negiev on the back with his cross. On contact, a light exploded from it and the skin sizzled underneath. He collapsed flat on the ground. Jacob pulled it back slightly, but he heard a muffled response. "Jacob, don't. Press it harder."

He did, and the form on the ground bucked and twisted. Hands clawed in the dirt. Boots kicked. Then it all stopped. Lord Negiev lay there silent and still. *Is he breathing?*, Jacob wondered. He didn't have to wonder long, as a hand raised up. It motioned and grasped in the air. Lord Negiev said nothing, but Jacob knew exactly what he wanted and shoved the cross in the waiting hand. Lord Negiev rolled over and looked straight up at the nightmarish sky above them. The ordeal exhausted him.

"Are you okay?"

"No, but will be," he panted.

"What happened?"

"Hell. Hell happened. That thing is pure evil," he explained as he sat up. "Where are we?"

"You don't remember?" Jacob asked. This question made him feel alone. He was back with him, or was he?

"I do. The woods, or what used to be. I was back home. Inside a small cottage I visited seventeen years ago. A child," He wiped the dirt off his face with his sleeve. It did little more than smear it more than it already was. "Just a child, no more than six years old, had been taken by a demon. I came to confront it and began the rites. This thing toyed with me for three days. I thought I had finally cracked it." Lord Negiev sighed, and tears ran down both cheeks from eyes that avoided direct contact with Jacob. "I thought… I was wrong. It was just toying with me again. A river of blood rushed in and around the child. I couldn't lift him out of the bed. I tried to keep the blood off his face. Keep him alive as I prayed and continued. Nothing I said or did stopped it. He drowned, right there in front of me. I remember the last cough as the child tried to gasp a breath. At that moment, the demon left the child. Allowed that innocent creature to suffer the horror of dying."

"It's probing us and messing with our thoughts."

"Not probing. It's going inside, scrambling your brain, and then rearranging everything to put your worst horrors up front. I think…" He paused to wipe the tears from his eyes, which smeared more dirt across his cheeks. "I think it made me an offer. I remember a voice telling me it could make it all stop. It could save the child. I just have to allow it."

"Father Lucian said it did the same to him. It probed him and tried to turn him," explained Jacob.

Looking ahead of him toward the grove of trees ahead of them, Negiev said, "Good God. It's doing that and we are still way out here. We are in trouble, Jacob. We are in trouble. Help me up. We need to help the others."

18

"Who do we start with?" Jacob asked.

"Why did you start with me?"

"You were the first to fall to the ground. Digging at it with your hands."

Lord Negiev waved his hand at Jacob, and he stopped providing details. It was a good question. Who was next? No one appeared to be in any more distress than anyone else. All were battling the demon inside.

"Father Lucian," Jacob said.

Both men were already looking his way before Jacob said anything. To him, it was both the logical and only choice. They ran over to him, passing up Mr. Nagoti and Manuela on the way. Jacob almost tripped on downed branches twice, both stumbles caused by a distraction in his head. Something was still there. It wasn't flashing images to him anymore, but it was there all the same. His grip tightened on the cross. Its corners, rounded by centuries of handling, hurt as if they were sharp and splintered under the force of his grip.

"Okay, where is it?" Lord Negiev searched the ground around the priest but found nothing.

Jacob stopped and studied the priest and how he stood. He was hunched over, one hand up as if to protect himself from a strike that never arrived. The other folded across his chest. That alarmed Jacob. "Oh my God!" It looked like he was grasping at his heart.

"What?" Lord Negiev asked, but saw what Jacob did. "Father? Father? Is it your heart?"

The old priest didn't move, didn't respond. His face was distressed, but he was alive. Jacob wondered if the demon could keep Father Lucian alive if his heart stopped. There was still a lot he didn't know or understand. There was more than a lot. He understood nothing. It had come close to killing him the first time, but he watched him heal right before his eyes. Could they be locked in a battle between the evil of Abaddon and the faith of Father Lucian? They could be. Maybe this time the demon would take his prize.

"He still has a pulse. I don't see his cross. Jacob, help me find it."

Then Jacob saw a single finger twitch, just a millimeter further than it had been before, and he remembered. "Wait!" he exclaimed. His hand thrust into the father's jacket. He immediately found the object and pulled it out from inside his jacket.

"Oh my. Is that... Is that what I think it is?" stuttered Lord Negiev as he dropped to his knees and crossed himself.

Jacob didn't answer as he loosened two fingers from the cross in his hand. He needed those to support one side of the object as it and his other hand lifted it up and placed it on Father Lucian's head. On contact, there was picture of instant release on his face. His old, withered lips mouthed "Thank you." Both hands came up in prayer.

One by one, Jacob and Negiev went around and did the same for each of the keepers. They found each keeper's relic and put them in their hand. If they couldn't force the person to grip it, they placed it on them. Each time, the person fell to the ground, a jumble of humanity that contained an emotional wreck. Some wept. Some just kneeled silently, unable to shake the images and feelings it stirred. All except Father Lucian, that was. He was the picture of calm and walked around tending to the others. A simple prayer and a calming touch before moving on to the next person. If it was comforting to them, they didn't show it outwardly. Most never acknowledged he was there, just focused on the ground as he leaned over them.

"You all right?" he asked as he made his way to Jacob.

"Yes, sir. How are they?"

"Worse for wear. They will be okay. Just need time."

"Okay," Jacob said. His voice sounded timid even to himself. He expected this would mean they would have to turn back, diminishing the glimmer of hope he had about saving his sister.

"Can I ask, what did it show you?"

"Father, what do you mean?"

"Have a seat here on this tree. We have time. It's not going anywhere, and as long as we hang on to our faith and these relics, tightly, it can't harm us. Not for a while at least. I feel it took a lot out of it to do this."

"Was this what you experienced when you went in the first time?"

"Yes, Jacob. It is. He looked around in my thoughts. In my memories. In my fears. That is what it wanted. Fear is a powerful weapon. It can make even the most pious person betray their faith. So, Jacob, what did it find in you?"

Jacob thought. What he saw was a jumbled mess that came in and out of various thoughts. There wasn't a theme. "Lots of things, Father."

"Like what?"

"The death of my mom and how she looked just before she died. A casket being lowered into the ground. Our home burnt to the ground. And Sarah."

"What about Sarah?"

"She stood over me with a stake and drove it into my heart."

"Let me guess, you felt that like it really happened?"

"Yes! How did you know?"

"How can I say this," Father Lucian started, and then paused as he thought. "You were lucky. Being so young, it had so little to pull from as it searched for your most painful memories. What it settled on was trying to destroy the hope you held for saving your sister. That was its best weapon. The pain you felt was that strike at hope itself. How do you feel now?"

Jacob held up the cross and replied, "Better."

"Your faith is strong, just like your father. The cross only helps amplify that and signifies your faith. It's a tool, but not the source. You need to remember that. As long as you hold your faith tight and close to you, nothing can harm you."

"Mind if I pull up a log?"

"How you are feeling, Lionel?" Father Lucian asked Mr. Halensworth.

"You know. How are you, Jacob?"

"I'm okay, sir."

"Jacob and I were just talking about what happened. So how many times has it been for you?"

"You mean how many times has a ghoulie poked around in my noggin?" He blew out a lengthy sigh. "I've lost count."

"Is it always the same?"

"Nah. This was one of the worst, but they are all a little different. I guess it depends on what they want. This one wasn't playing around, I can tell you that. A far departure from the time one had me in between a buxom blonde and redhead. Now that demon wanted something different, not that I wanted it to stop, mind you." He caught himself and took notice of the company around him. "But you are too young for that."

"Yes, this one wanted something different than that," Father Lucian added. "Nothing pleasurable."

"Father, what was it for you? If you don't mind me asking."

"Not at all, Jacob." He chuckled, which Jacob found odd considering the situation and the setting. "You both might find it silly. I had lost my faith. To me, that is akin to losing my life and myself, and is the most painful experience I could have."

"Father, for it to have pulled that up, is it safe to assume it had happened?"

"Yes, Lionel, once. It is a moment that still haunts me. I was thirty-one, not long out of seminary school, and working in a little church outside Vienna. Father Montegue, my senior, assigned me to the counseling of our parishioners. You know, family and marital matters. Not the most religious task you could imagine. This young family came in with problems with their teenage son. Both parents were previously divorced, which added to the conflict as you can imagine. I, looking at this from a therapist lens and not a theologist, saw a blended family that was struggling to get along. I saw the teenage son having a true crisis of identity, not a crisis of faith. The more his parents pushed the family into our church and into my office for counseling, the deeper his crisis became, causing the problems to escalate at home. I didn't see it, correctly, until after his parents found him hanging from the shower. Just moments before I received their call, I was shown a vision of him, hanging from a shower with a smile on his face. A voice said, "He is mine now." It was then I knew. I reached for the phone to call them, but it rang with the news as soon as my hand hit it. I missed it and failed them. I was too busy being a therapist. I ignored their spiritual health. His family's situation upset him. I dismissed it as just being a teen. That emotional state created an open door for a malevolent being to make a promise and pull him in. That is what I believed happened. When I look back on it, I saw signs. He became more reserved with the family, but challenged me openly, even violently, during our sessions. One time he even mocked me and asked what I would know about a family. That I was too busy... how should I say this? Too busy being God's lover to ever produce any children. It took everything I had to make it through the funeral. Everyone's eyes were on me. I felt their blame, their anger. For the next three months, I went through my own crisis of faith. I had lost it. Lost everything. I was just an empty shell with no direction. It may not seem like anything big, but to me, this is my life, my purpose. All of that was gone. On a Tuesday afternoon in April, I stood up on the windowsill of my fifth-floor apartment. My foot had moved its last inch toward the edge. The next step would have sent me off, but there was a knock at the door. That sound, that simple knock, drew me more than my despair did. My neighbor, a sweet woman, Lauren Gabriel, a teacher, needed me. Her mother had just been diagnosed with terminal cancer and wanted me to say a prayer with her. Seeing the pain in her face and the comfort her faith brought her as I led her in prayer gave me the smallest of hopes my faith was still there."

"Well, Father, I am sure glad you found it. You have helped me more than once through the years, and you're a mentor to me."

"Yes, Lionel. We have known each other a long time, haven't we? I believe I know what it pulled up for you. Elizabeth Beets in Salisbury?"

Mr. Halensworth coughed, then swallowed. He stumbled a bit to get the first words out before he agreed. "Yes, that day."

"Was it your worst day?" asked Jacob.

"By far. One that I never want to remember. Jacob, my boy, exorcisms are skirmishes in the everlasting war. Some days you win. Some days both forces leave the battlefield in a draw. Some days you lose. I lost big that day. A town elder knew who I was and approached me about his wife. She had been acting off. His priest told him there was something ungodly going on. I knew what it was a quarter mile away. I should have known I was in over my head. Stupid me didn't realize that until she let out a blood-curdling scream as it ripped her body in two right down the middle."

"In two?"

"Yes, Jacob, in two. I told it there was only room for one entity in there. Just before the scream, the most horrific voice you ever heard told me, 'Then let's make two of her.'"

19

The others wandered over, one at a time. Each had composed themselves the best they could. They still showed remnants of what had happened. It had taken a toll, a large one. Jacob expected Father Lucian to gather and announce they would turn back and hopefully try again another day. There was no way they could continue, but stopping and going back never came up. Each member told Father Lucian they were okay to continue. He explained to Jacob this was just the first or second, if you counted what happened in the church, of many things that would happen to them. The statement didn't appear to shock anyone, except Jacob.

Father Lucian led the group in a prayer to secure their faith. The others did their best to put themselves together and then moved forward, their steps strong, not tentative. Instead of multiple groups like before, they were a single unit walking just behind Father Lucian. No chatter among them, just the wind and thunder overhead echoing across the barren landscape. Smoke from the fires swirled above them, but they were buried among the burnt smell of hell itself.

At the edge of the grove, they stepped in without even a pause. As soon as Jacob's second foot stepped in, the world changed. The burnt hell cleared, replaced by the sweet smell of pine floating on the crisp fall air. Rays of sunlight blasted in through the trees from above. Jacob looked up, shielding his eyes from the glare. Not a single cloud crossed his vision. Birds even chirped in the distance. He felt an uneasiness by this setting. More than he did in the world they just left. The others must have, too, as their progress slowed as everyone not only took in their surroundings but looked ahead cautiously for what was next to come. This was no time to let down their guard. They needed them up.

"This way?" Father Lucian turned to Father Murray and asked.

"Yes," he said, then exclaimed, "Stop!"

Up ahead, a single fox emerged from behind a tree. Its tail up, bushy, and almost wagging. Its fur was clean. Too clean for Jacob's comfort. It looked like something out of a Disney movie, not an animal that had been living out in the wild its entire life. Beyond it, flowers sprung up from patches of green grass. Something you wouldn't ever see in the later days of October. A fawn pranced along in front of them between two rows of trees. Jacob watched it bounce away as he walked through that same gap in the trees. Blades of grass sprang to life right under his feet, and the chirp of birds echoed in the trees above them.

All unnatural for this time and place. All added to the eerie and unsettling feeling that had risen in Jacob. All made each of his steps a repeat of the last. Step forward, look left, look right, then step again and do the same. He was young and hadn't experienced much of this world, but he didn't have to be a keeper to realize none of this was real, and it created all of this for one purpose, to put them off balance. It did.

Green leaves sprouted from the trees, and the last of the fall foliage that lined the ground disappeared below a carpet of green grass. They passed the fox, who kept his distance but stayed ever watchful. Like a guard. It wouldn't be long before they spotted another one. This one Father Murray again recognized and knew for sure he had seen it before. The telltale white stripe on the top of its gray head was a dead giveaway. Absent was any evidence of the arrows Laurence Moultry put in him or the slugs deposited by Lewis. There was no outward look of aggression. Its head up and alert, not cowered down below its shoulders. The muscles in his shoulders looked relaxed, and its tail flopped down behind it.

Not taking any chances, Father Murray led the others around in a wide arch, but they were cut off from going too wide by another familiar visitor, a small black bear cub. It was more interested in rolling around on a patch of flowers than coming after them, but Jacob couldn't avoid feeling its placement was important.

"We are being funneled somewhere," Father Murray said.

"I agree," Mr. Nagoti said.

"But where?" asked Madame Stryvia.

"I have a feeling I know where."

"Father Murray, care to share?"

"The shed. It shouldn't be much farther."

"Like lambs to a slaughter," Halensworth uttered under his breath.

"What was that?"

"Nothing."

"Clear mind, gentlemen. Clear mind," said Tenzein Mao with the calmness of a glassy lake.

"Lock your emotions away and stay focused on why we are here," ordered Father Lucian. He stepped forward and took the lead now, away from Father Murray.

There were no more tentative steps. No more animals to direct them. It didn't take long for the shape of a shed to appear in the distance between the rows of trees. What Jacob saw didn't match the horrifying descriptions he had heard about a rundown dilapidated shed. What was coming in to view more and more with each and every step was serene and peaceful. It was white, with colorful flower boxes under the windows. Blue drapes hung behind them. Scalloped molding lined the edge of the roof. Twirls and twists of smoke drifted, not billowed, out of the clean redbrick chimney.

Father Lucian and Father Murray were the first to emerge from the trees into the clearing that surrounded the shed. "This isn't right," Father Lucian said.

They all spread out, taking in the surrounding area. Father Murray appeared to focus on a single spot. He knelt down, crossed himself, and said a prayer. "No, this isn't. John's body was right here when we left."

"He was still here when I was," Father Lucian said. "I feel he still is, we are just not allowed to see it."

"So, none of this is real?" asked Lord Negiev.

"There is much deception here," Tenzein said. "I can feel it. The world around us is clouded."

"Yes, Tenzein, I feel it too. All of you," called out Father Lucian, "clear your minds and stay alert. Trust your feelings and instincts, and not your eyes. It is trying to fool us."

Trust your feelings and instincts, and not your eyes. That statement resonated in Jacob, who until that moment didn't realize how calm and relaxed he felt. Much like he would on a walk through the pasture on his family's farm. The warm sun and fresh breeze added to the confusion around this place that his brain remembered as containing so much evil. He closed his eyes and attempted to block out the outside world. The world fought back. The breeze felt brisker, cooler on his skin. Each chirp of the birds became louder, more cheerful in tone and melody. Even the grass beneath him felt like it was massaging the soles of his feet, sending him reminders of what it felt like as a child to run through the pasture barefoot. The harder he tried to block it, the more this world kept hold. Then Jacob turned his mind to an image. His body floating in a lake. Ripples emanated out at every thought. He focused, *slow the ripples, slow his thoughts. Force out everything.* Each chirp he heard created a ripple. First large, then smaller and slower. The world around him gave, but it allowed the despair back in. The thoughts that were forced into his mind earlier. The sight of his mother just before she died, the scenes of town for the last few days. His sister stretched over a cross of fire in the church. The darker the image, the more pain and despair he felt, but even those he was able to smooth out into just small rolls in the water. Then, one by one, the pin pricks started. First in the small of his back, and then they ran up his spine. Like a shot of lightning that provided clarity. By the time it hit the bottom of his neck, he felt it. The true depths of the evil that consumed this place. The hatred and despisal of this world on the other side of the walls from them. The intent to kill and enslave all and take this world from his master. He felt it all, in a level of clarity that was clearer than his own thoughts.

His eyes opened, and he peered into the window. Behind the blue drapes sat his sister, on a chair in the center of the room. A well of emotion surged forward, to rush in and grab her, but the calm water in his mind drowned that thought. He knew that would be exactly what it wanted, and he had no intentions of giving him that.

20

"She's in there," announced Jacob, a statement that caused each member of the group to whip their head in his direction in unison. All shared the same expression. This struck Jacob as odd. *Didn't they expect her to be there?* he asked himself. He walked along the exterior wall, avoiding the bed of rose bushes planted along the side, and then around the bed of petunias to the front porch. The plantings had a similar appearance as the fox. They were all too perfect, like a newly planted bed. Nothing was out of place, not even a single petal or leaf had fallen on the freshly placed pine straw. He stepped up on the porch toward the drab green door.

A floral wreath hung on it. His eyes only stayed there for a second before moving toward the bright brass doorknob, also too shiny for something exposed to the weather. He looked back at the assembled keepers behind him and then back at the doorknob, then back at them again. He needed confirmation, someone to tell him it was time to go in. The calm demeanor was still there, no ripples. So, emotion was not driving him to yank it open. He knew going in too fast or before everyone was ready could be dangerous. All he had seen over the last week, hell the last twenty-four hours, cemented that realization in his head for the rest of his life.

"Jacob, go ahead, but do it slowly," said Father Lucian from right behind him.

His hand reached out and touched the knob. It felt cool. Jacob turned it slowly with ease until he heard the click of the lock opening, then he stopped and paused. With a single breath in and single breath out, he pushed the door in. The only thought in his head as it opened was, *No ripples*. It opened smooth and quiet, not a single squeak from the hinges. Inside he found a glossy light-oak hardwood floor and a single rug covering the center. On the rug sat the only piece of furniture in the one-room building, a simple wooden chair. Sarah sat on the chair, her feet flat on the floor, and dressed in her Sunday best with perfect hair and makeup, and a pleasant smile on her face.

"Hi, Jacob, Father Lucian, Father Murray. Come on in," she said.

A hand on the small of Jacob's back eased him forward. He obeyed the encouragement and stepped in, but moved to the side to allow the others to enter. Her eyes followed him as he entered, ignoring the others, or so he thought.

"Welcome, all of you. I don't recognize you, but I am told I know everything about you."

It sounded like his sister, but what she said didn't. Other than the few times in his dreams, this was the first time he had heard his sister since she left the house that morning over a week ago. She looked good, not like the time he saw her in the street with the markings all over her skin and wild hair flowing behind her, but like how she sounded, something was different. Her posture was upright, too straight, kind of how everything else looked. It was all too perfect.

They all entered and gathered in front of her. Not a person said anything as her head turned slowly to look at each one. Her gaze inspected them, and the pleasant smile took on a slight smirk.

"So, Father Lucian, how is this going to work?"

Father Lucian crossed himself and stepped forward. "Come now, Sarah, you should know. You were my top student." His tone was steady and superior, like a teacher talking to a student.

"Oh, but I do, Father. I do know. Do you really think you can walk in here, show your little crosses at me, and I just let her go?"

Father Lucian walked around her. His hand reached inside the pocket of his black pants and pulled out a vial. He flipped it open. As he walked, a few drops hit the floor with every step he took. Sarah watched him as far as her head could turn. Then it whipped back in the other direction to catch Father Murray doing the same toward Father Lucian. They created a complete circle around her. As they did, the rest of the keepers crossed themselves. With their crosses held out, each knelt around her in an arch.

"Lord, have mercy," Father Lucian started.

"Lord, have mercy," repeated the keepers.

"Lord, have mercy," Father Lucian said again.

"Lord, have mercy," repeated the keepers.

"Christ, hear us."

"Christ, graciously hear us."

"God, the Father in heaven."

"Have mercy on us."

"God, the Son, Redeemer of the world."

"Have mercy on us."

Sarah cackled in three distinct voices. She grinned wildly, as if this amused her. "Keep going. This is just getting good."

Father Lucian didn't stop. "God, the Holy Spirit."

Neither did the keepers. Each head still bowed in prayer, they repeated after Father Lucian's prompt, "Have mercy on us." Their outstretched crosses began to glow. The one Jacob held did as well, even though he hadn't joined in on the prayers yet.

"You know who used to have his mercy? Our kind. My master was the Son of Dawn. A powerful being. Because he wouldn't submit to your"—she coughed as if gagging on the word itself—"God, he turned his back on us. He will do that to you too," barked Sarah.

"Holy Trinity, one God."

"Blah, he is not the only god, fools."

"Have mercy on us."

"Holy Mary, pray for us."

"Pray for us," beseeched the keepers.

"Holy Virgin of virgins."

"Pray for us."

The spots of holy water Father Lucian and Father Murray dropped on the floor around Sarah sizzled.

"Saint Michael."

"Pray for us."

"Are you going to ask all of those so-called saints to pray for you? I can tell you some things that will prove to you that your faith is in the wrong beliefs. I know you know what I mean, Father Lucian. I took your faith once before. And Father Murray, I have to thank you. If it weren't for you and your dive into the dark side, neither of us would be here." She looked at the keepers that knelt around her. "See, kids. Even the most righteous of you all can be tempted to switch sides. Just like lovely Sarah here."

The entire time Sarah, or the creature within, taunted the group, Father Lucian continued to list the names of saints, and the keepers asked them to pray for them.

"We have tempted you at one time or another. Some are just ashamed to admit it. Mr. Yato Nagoti, nice to see you again. You were once tempted to bring back your own son, after you failed to keep us from taking him. If I remember, you tried to burn your own cross as a sacrifice. Too bad for us, it doesn't burn so well. By the way, how is your wife? We had a lot of fun talking to her after her loss, right up until she leapt off the top of that building. It really doesn't take much to talk someone into such a thing after such a painful loss. It must torture you to know it wasn't really the loss of her son that did it. It was the disappointment she felt toward you, for not being able to free him from our grasp."

His cross shook, and his voice skipped one refrain before he rejoined the group, but now with a slight tremble.

"All holy saints of God," said Father Lucian as he and Father Murray completed another circle of holy water around Sarah and the chair she sat in.

"Oh, that is enough," exploded a voice from the bowels of hell itself. The light breeze that followed them in through the door disappeared. As was the bright sunlight that pushed in through the window and door. Darkness replaced them as a violent wind swirled outside.

The evil toothy grin that had been in place since they started grew wider, beyond the natural limits of what Sarah's face could produce on its own. Her arms threw outward away from her. A blast of heat erupted outward with the force of a hurricane. The shed exploded, sending shards of wood everywhere, knocking the keepers to the ground. Each attempted to block themselves from the blast of heat that hit them. Each struggled to their feet under a red sky.

The peaceful and serene setting they entered was all a distant memory. The surrounding trees were ablaze. Ominous clouds swirled above them in a high-speed vortex that screamed and wailed at them. Jacob could feel their combined will being sucked up toward it. In front of them, Sarah was no longer his sister sitting in a chair. Marks pressed through every exposed area of her skin, and she now floated above a pentagram of fire. To her left, outside where the shed used to stand, was the headless body that wasn't there before. Jacob looked around and accounted for Father Murray and Father Lucian and the other keepers. When he searched, he saw another body slouched on the ground. He recognized Kevin Stierers right away.

The heat continued to pulsate out toward them in waves. One after another. Each hotter than the previous. The gap in between was just long enough for Jacob to catch his breath before the next wave knocked it out again. Each wave encountered a flash before it pushed right through. The keepers had not lost their purpose, nor their faith. They resumed their prayers as soon as they hit the ground. Light shot out from their crosses to confront the waves. Father Murray and Father Lucian stood strong, each praying furiously into the swirling storm. The sound of the wind blocked Jacob from hearing them or the response from the keepers. They threw in dashes of holy water. Most never reached their target, and instead vaporized in the heat of an approaching wave, now as intense as a blast furnace. Others were blown away by the wind. The ones that made it through boiled on contact with their target. Sarah jerked, writhed, and distorted in pain as the cry of every undead creature in the universe escaped her mouth. Each scream rumbled the ground, several sending Jacob to his knees. After the last, he stayed there with his hands held up to block his face from the heat. While his face didn't bear the full brunt, his hands and arms did.

Even though Jacob had nothing to compare this to, he knew they were losing. Everything around him told him that. Sarah, or it, had the upper hand and was on the offensive. Burning branches flew at the keepers, not from above but from trees some distance away, giving them more room to build up speed. Each exploded in a ball of fire as bodies rolled out of the way. The tails of Lord Negiev's coat caught fire, again. He tossed it to the ground, where it burst into flames.

"Jacob!" he heard, just under the howling wind and explosions. He turned his head to the right and saw nothing but Madame Stryvia and Manuela, knelt down in prayer. To his left, he could see the others doing the same, flames all around them. Embers blew in the air everywhere, and columns of hot air rose from the ground, distorting his vision.

"Jacob!"

He looked around again. Beyond Madame Stryvia and Manuela, in a column of dark black smoke, stood Father Lucian. He looked right at Jacob, mouth moving. A prayer, Jacob assumed. His right hand pointed to Sarah. Jacob turned and looked at her. She was directing the firebombs of branches with her hands. Two towers of smoke appeared on either side of her. Each took the shape of an ungodly creature. Long arms and claws formed. Her yellow eyes glowed as bright as the embers that floated in the air. Jacob looked for any sign that it was still his sister, and saw none, but it didn't matter. He had a job to do. One Father Lucian gave him after he told them about what he thought were his dreams.

His eyes closed. *No ripples,* he thought, before he called out to Sarah in his thoughts. It didn't take long before the world around him disappeared in a bright flash, the vessels in his eyelids clearly visible.

21

"Jacob, you can't be here. He will kill everyone," Sarah cried.

"We're here to save you, sis." His voice disappeared into the black abyss. This wasn't the family kitchen or other friendly surroundings like the last couple of times they talked. He couldn't see her, but he could hear her talk, and worst of all, he could hear her cry.

"I can't be saved. Get away. Run. Run now!"

"Don't talk like that. Father Lucian has brought all the keepers here to help..."

"Jacob, I know," interrupted Sarah. "I know. So does he. There is nothing they can do for me. If they try, he will just kill me and move on to the next person. Father Lucian has to know that. I know he does. You, all of you, need to leave. I might be able to protect you long enough to get away."

"I am not going anywhere. I am here just like Dad would be. You are my sister."

"Jacob, you know what happened to Dad. He wanted to kill him. I protected him the best I could. Don't you understand?" she sobbed to the point of almost being unintelligible.

"I have his cross. I won't fail."

"Jacob, you are so infuriating," she screamed in between sobs. "You do not understand how any of this works! No clue what any of this is! All you will do is get yourself killed. I can't protect you. What don't you get about that? You need to leave. Now! I don't care if the others stay. Maybe it's better if they do. They can force him to kill me and end all this. Then all of this will end. That's it. Jacob, tell Father Lucian to kill me. Stab me right in the heart. Take away its host. That will end all this. That's the only way you can help me. It has to be done. Go now. Tell them. Tell them to kill me and release me. I beg of you."

"Not going to happen," Jacob said. Hearing the grief in his sister's voice more than tugged at his heart strings. It struck terror deep inside. The image of the lake he held in his mind had more than a few ripples at this point, but he fought to stay level, just like Tenzein Mao told him and Father Lucian insisted he would need to while doing this.

"Jacob!" she shrieked. "This is the only way. If you don't, then I will do something myself that will force it to kill me, but you have a chance to end my pain, make it quick. Have them kill me. Now!"

The darkness in his mind took on a hue, almost blue, but Jacob ignored it and kept talking to his sister. "Sarah, stay with me. Come to my voice and let me help you."

There was no reply, but the darkness again lightened.

"Sarah, are you still there?"

Still no reply, and no crying, but there was a sound. A sound that came from everywhere. In front of him, behind him, under him, and above him. "Sarah, can you hear me?"

"Run, Jacob! Get away!" she screamed, barely audible. There was a great distance between them now that hadn't been there before. They weren't in the same room anymore, if this was a room.

"No, Sarah! I am not going anywhere. We are here to help you. Resist it. Use what you know from the inside. Can you do that?" he insisted.

There was no response. He was about to ask her again, but a noise sounded in the distance, where he last heard his sister's voice. It started soft but grew into a great roar that vibrated the surrounding space. Water splashed up around his ankles. Until then, he wasn't aware he was standing in water. The darkness lifted to expose his surroundings. He was standing ankle deep in a large pond with a rock-lined shore just feet behind him with a dense forest just beyond. Coming at him was a wave, a large tidal wave as tall as a multi-story apartment building, blocking out the light and casting him in shadow.

Jacob tried to run, but the water wouldn't release his feet. He tried again, but still they were held firm. The water sucked out toward the wave, adding to its mass and exposing his feet as he tried to run again, but they were stuck to the pebbled bottom of the lake. He looked up just as the crest of the wave broke. It landed on him with the force of that apartment building, knocking him free from the bottom and sending him tumbling head over feet in the churning of the tidal forces. It spun his body over and over. The force of the water squeezed the air out of his lungs to the point of burning. He needed to breathe but couldn't break free. Even if he could, he didn't know which way was up. His legs and arms painfully whacked rocks on the bottom or other debris in the water, causing him to scream. One scream let a bit of water in his mouth and nose and down into his windpipe. His body began to cough and choke, and he fought every instinct he had to open his mouth. There were no moments of his life flashing before his eyes. No flash of memories. Just two thoughts: she was right, and this is how I will die.

His right arm smashed into the trunk of a tree, and his body fell to the ground as the water receded. It was broken, and pain forced another scream. This scream expelled the water he'd swallowed and led to minutes of uncontrolled gags and coughs. He wheezed in his first breath of fresh air and rolled over. The break in his arm, just below the elbow, sent shocks through his body and out in the form of another scream.

High above, a voice boomed, similar to how the voice of God is portrayed in movies he had seen. "How is the calm lake now, Jacob? Still able to control the ripples? You are not in control here. Your sister is mine, as is your world."

A dark spot developed in what he thought was the sun, eventually blocking it out and casting everything in the same blood-red hue he saw after the shed exploded. The spot appeared to be getting closer. It had features of a face that he could make out. Someone human, but not. Things were out of proportion and grotesque. Yellow eyes that were not level, with hints of flames burning in the centers. A mouth with jagged, animal-like teeth scrawled across the face. There was no nose he could make out. It grinned as it came closer and appeared satisfied.

Jacob used his good arm to pull him further up the shoreline to get away, but the more he crawled, the further away from him the trees became.

"I have been waiting for you, Jacob. I have known your family for centuries. Most recently your father, and now your sister. It was time we met." It cackled. "Too bad it was just before your death."

Jacob's body shook. The pain of his arm was blocked by the fear. Heat emanated from the creature and singed Jacob's skin, but he didn't feel the burns. The fear of what he saw, what he heard, what he felt was all-consuming. While his mind yelled to run, his body did not try to flee and stayed right there on the rocks, with the woods the same distance behind him as they had always been.

A breeze came out of nowhere and carried a message on it. It was meant for just Jacob's ears, but Abaddon noticed and looked up and sneered in its direction. The message was nothing more than a whisper, but it was as clear as if it was said right in Jacob's ear. "Jacob," Father Lucian's voice said. "It's time. Let's go."

Jacob took in a breath and then declared, "We will meet again." Then he opened his eyes.

22

What he opened his eyes to was a scene from hell itself. The red sky and burning trees were still there, but the rain of burning blood and tornados of flame that chased them were new. Jacob stumbled the first few steps as Father Lucian pulled him along by his right arm, which was not broken. When he gathered himself, he could run on his own. Adrenaline had driven fear into his veins, and he felt he could sprint at a world-record pace back to the cars, but he didn't. He stayed with the group, to help. Not all of them would have been able to keep up. Some were quite older than he was. Another, the brash Englishman, was carrying Sarah over his shoulder.

Sarah was unconscious, and her body alternated between her normal appearance and the strange markings from second to second. The other keepers continued their prayers amidst their huffs and puffs of exertion.

Once clear of the burning grove of trees, they headed straight for Walter's Creek, where it was flatter and easier to move, no downed trees on the shore. Halensworth had slowed considerably by the time they reached the edge of the creek. Jacob moved forward to take his burden. He helped him set Sarah down on the ground. Her eyes were glazed over and unresponsive. She was alive, but panted like an animal.

"We need to keep moving," yelled Father Lucian. He and the others were still moving to the cars. The ground under them rolled and heaved, much like Jacob felt ten days ago.

Jacob reached down to pick up his sister and carry her the rest of the way, but Tenzein Mao stepped forward and grabbed his arm. The man, who couldn't be more than one hundred twenty pounds soaking wet, reached down to grab her.

"I can carry her," insisted Jacob.

"I have run across mountains carrying something heavier," he said as he hoisted her up over his shoulder and took off in a sprint.

What he said must have been true. He moved effortlessly along the creek, and Jacob followed close behind. Even the rumbling and twists of the slick blood-rain-soaked ground that sent Jacob on a misstep here and there didn't slow the Tibetan monk. He made haste to the road, where three cars waited. Two sat running with their headlights and wipers on. The wiper blades slung the blood off the side, only to repeat this task as more steaming red rain coated the glass.

Through the streaked, cleared sections of glass, Jacob saw the faces of Lewis and Mark. Their expressions were beyond words. Lewis threw open his door and got out wearing a large black poncho.

"Come On!" he ordered, and three members of their party made a beeline straight for his car. Three more headed for Mark's car. He did not get out, just sat inside looking out at the others as they ran through the storm of blood with a horrified look on his face. Jacob couldn't blame him. He would rather be inside the dry car himself.

"Mao, take her to my car," Father Murray yelled.

Tenzein followed Father Murray to the Cadillac and loaded into the back with Sarah and Father Lucian. Jacob jumped in the passenger side, and both cars behind them honked wildly. He had shut the passenger door when Father Murray dropped in and slammed his door with a fearful scream. The impact into the passenger side sent the oversized car spinning across the road. Father Murray had it started before it came to a stop. The wipers sprang into action and gave Jacob a good look at what had hit them. The two creatures that appeared in the smoke next to Sarah in the shed had followed them out, and one had thrown his grotesquely shaped form into the side of the car. It sat on the road and gave its head a shake before charging again. Father Murray pulled down on the column shifter, threw the car into drive, and floored it.

He swerved the less than nimble car to avoid the impact, resulting in a glancing blow down the driver's side. It sent them into a slight skid on the blood-soaked asphalt. Father Murray kept the pedal down on the floor and sped away, following the taillights ahead of him. Jacob looked back. Through the smeared back window he saw the creature giving chase. Its claws scraped on the road surface as it ran. Its speed surprised him, as it caught up with them and swiped an enormous claw at the back of the car. It missed. The second swipe hit the trunk deck, driving the claw through the sheet metal. The car lurched left and then right and slowed down thanks to the demonic anchor that was hanging on. Its claw cut through the sheet metal with a nerve-rattling scrape that each of the occupants heard above the throaty roar of the straining V8. Each looked back. They wished they hadn't.

The Cadillac slowed more and more, and Jacob was afraid it would stop altogether. In his mind, he saw it stopping and then being pulled backward while the creature destroyed it piece by piece and killed everyone inside. It tried. Snarling and snorting the whole time, with apocalyptic ear-shattering screams, it failed, and the old American sheet metal tore through, letting them pull away. It followed again, but their acceleration was too fast, and it disappeared behind the curtain of the blood-red rain.

The rain stopped just a few miles beyond Walter's Creek, but the storm intensified. The lightning and thunder seemed to voice Abaddon's protest all along their path back to the church. Jacob expected the three cars to be struck at any moment, but none were. There were close calls, but no direct hits. He hoped that meant something was protecting them. If that was true, that meant they might have a fighting chance. The sight of the church spire appeared above the trees, adding to that hope. As little as it was.

Mao rushed Sarah into the church and placed her on the altar. Her body convulsed and shook uncontrollably.

"Help me hold her down," he cried.

Jacob rushed to the front with Halensworth. Each grabbed an arm and a leg and held it down as firm as they could. Her skin was burning hot, and Jacob grimaced at the pain but didn't let go. Nothing would make him let go. Not the burning pain. Not the heaves as her body jerked up and down. Not the phasing in and out of the odd markings on her skin.

Father Lucian took a position at her head. With his thumb he drew a cross on her forehead while reciting, "In the name of the Father, Son, and Holy Ghost."

Sarah screamed, rattling what remained of the stained-glass windows from their frames, and then collapsed flat on the marble-covered altar.

Father Murray returned from his residence, handing towels to the keepers to clean the blood off. Then he handed two large white sheets to Jacob and Halensworth.

"What do we do with these?" asked Halensworth.

"Roll them up length-wise, tightly, and tie her down."

Jacob knew what he meant and went to work. He tied it across her legs and under the top and around each leg of the altar. He pulled on it to check, and it was tight. Halensworth did the same around her chest.

Father Lucian checked both sheets. "Now begins the hard part."

23

Father Murray carefully removed a folded-up red stole from a drawer in a table hidden off to the side in the vestibule. Jacob watched with amazement at the care the priest took as he unfolded it and let the ends drop. His hands held on at the center. His head bent down slowly, reverently, and kissed the stole at its midpoint and slipped it over his head, allowing it to slide in place around his neck. The man, his face still stained from the rain, looked at peace as he stood there. Behind him, the large stained-glass window was nothing but a gaping hole with colorful shards of glass dangling from it.

Father Lucian had also donned a red stole and joined Father Murray in front of the altar. He carried a silver chalice. Father Murray carried a silver plate. Both priests carried out a ritual Jacob had seen every Sunday morning, but they usually performed it at the altar. It was impossible now, with Sarah strapped to it.

Father Murray prayed in Latin as he held the wafers high above his head and then broke them in half before he placed them back on the silver plate. Then he took the silver chalice from Father Lucian and held it high above his head and prayed. Latin was something Jacob never learned. Not that he had an interest to. In high school they forced him to take a foreign language. His choice, French. No particular reason. Well, that was not entirely true. Lynn Edwards, that was the reason. He had a crush on her and watched her step into the French class across the hall from the Spanish class he was enrolled in. The next day, he requested a schedule change. Just a year later, he couldn't remember much French, but he knew every inch of her smile.

It was a good thing his father had seen the future and knew his choice of foreign language before it happened. One Sunday when he was eleven, he leaned over during this portion of the service and translated, loosely, what was being said. He told him his father did the same for him years ago, ruining the awe he felt when he thought his father could speak Latin. What he told him Father Murray said was, "At the Last Supper, Jesus took a loaf of bread and broke it into many pieces, and gave one to each of his disciples and said, 'Take, eat. This is my body. Do this in remembrance of me.' Then he took a cup and filled it with wine and passed it to each of them and said, 'This is the cup of the new covenant and my blood. Do this in remembrance of me.'" He was sure this was the eleven-year-old version of what was being said, as what Father Murray said was much longer.

With both tasks complete, Father Murray motioned for each of them to come forward. One by one he and Father Lucian gave communion to the keepers. As the father leaned over Jacob, he crossed himself and accepted the wafer in his hand. Father repeated the same line he had said six times already. Once again in Latin, but Jacob knew it to be, "This is the Body of Christ." He slipped it in his mouth. Father Lucian was right behind him and presented the chalice. Jacob sipped the wine, and Father Lucian repeated his line, which Jacob knew as, "The Blood of Christ. The Cup of Salvation."

When they were all done, the six keepers and Jacob stood where they had knelt. They were battered, bruised, and stained, but renewed.

"All right. All right. We shouldn't expect this to be easy. It will probably be the hardest thing we have ever done. I think we need to divide up into shifts," Father Murray said, and then he seemed to stammer a little before chuckling. "Um, Father Lucian. Why don't I let you take things here? I just realized. I have never done an exorcism before."

"I agree with Father Murray. This will be trying. We should take shifts. I will start. Lord Negiev and Mr. Nagoti, you can join me. Father Murray will then take Jacob and Manuela. Madame Stryvia, with your extensive experience, would you mind leading the others?"

"Not at all."

"Okay, good. Now, this is important. If you are not involved at the moment, you need to stay back. I want to say you need to be out of the church, but you might be needed. Do not respond or engage it at any time. If you feel you are being affected or compromised, remove yourself. And I cannot stress enough, don't let your experience make you complacent. This is nothing like any of us have been involved in before." He turned to make eye contact with everyone. Each person agreed silently. Then Father Lucian turned his attention to those who stood in the back of the church. "Sheriff, I need a favor."

"Sure, Father, what is it?"

24

Jacob moved to the back of the church. As he took each step, he kept his head turned to the side to keep an eye on what happened at the front. Much like the ceremony Father Murray and Father Lucian performed before they administered the communion, Father Lucian was going through one now. This time, a purple stole replaced the red one. He kissed the middle point, just as he had done before. The others knelt before him. Using his thumb, he marked them with crosses made of oil on the forehead. Then they took up positions around Sarah on the altar, Father Lucian at her head. He marked her forehead as he had the others.

The movement, the protest, that Jacob expected never arrived. Her body stayed still. The air above her did not. It swirled, rustling the edges of her skirt that hung off the altar. It continued to pick up speed, gathering pieces of glass. First just a few pieces, then larger and larger shards, all staying on the outside of the flow, around Father Lucian, Lord Negiev, and Mr. Nagoti. The debris rode the current and coalesced above them. Spinning, combining, and forming a cloud of color. The sound of the clattering and crashing pieces was deafening. Slowly each piece was reduced to nothing more than a speck of dust due to the hundreds and thousands of collisions it suffered with other pieces.

The dust became a dark cloud. One that swirled and rolled and grew. Flashes, first just a flicker, and then great blinding ones, like those on a camera, began. Rumbles of thunder rattled the structure. It didn't come from outside. It came from within. The longer Father Lucian prayed and chanted, the louder the thunder became. When he sprinkled his holy water on her, she lay still, but the clouds above her seized and shook. Large claps of thunder forced Jacob to cover his ears. When he took his hands away, he heard a woman wail. It was not his sister. Madame Stryvia sat in a pew at the back of the church. Her hands had reached up and gripped her head. A horrifying scream emanated from her open mouth. It was followed by screams of, "No! No! No!"

Tenzein moved toward her, as did Father Murray; Jacob was close behind. She said nothing intelligible. Just mumbled repeatedly, syllables, no words, except for "No!" Jacob looked on, helpless as the others attempted to calm her, but nothing they did could reach her. She swayed back and forth, with her eyes rolled back in her head.

"The damn thing is in her head again," Father Murray said.

Tenzein searched her for her cross, but before he could find it, Manuela said, "Wait." She scooted in between Tenzein and Madame Stryvia and took her hands, much like she had with Jacob earlier. The screams stopped, and her body fell limp in the pew. Tears streamed from her eyes as she sat there. Manuela said nothing, just like with Jacob. She got up and left, but this time rushed out of the church. The eyes of Jacob, Father Murray, and Halensworth followed her. Tenzein Mao still tried to comfort Stryvia.

She leaned forward in the pew, supporting her head in her hands. "That thing was inside me again. Search and pulling at every horrible memory I have."

"It's going to keep trying," Father Murray said. "You have to stay strong. Don't let it."

Just then, the surrounding room changed. They were no longer in the church. They were no place Jacob recognized. The sights, sounds, and even smells were all foreign to him. It was musky and old. The walls were covered in some kind of torn wallpaper. What was there was dirty. Where there was none, water spots and lines of black mildew dotted the wallboard. Lamps on either side of a bed flickered on and off. She cried, "No! Not this!"

In the bed lay an old woman, covers pulled up to her neck and eyes fixed on the ceiling. Her chest heaved up and down with each hollow raspy breath. Hands that were nothing more than bones lay at her side. The fingers twitched, as if to point at something in the room, but they lacked the muscle to raise off the white comforter. The woman mumbled to herself in a language Jacob didn't recognize.

"We need to get out of here. Now!" exclaimed Madame Stryvia.

"Why? What is it Catherine?" Father Murray asked.

The room took on a heavy feeling. Jacob couldn't explain it. A tingling sensation exploded inside him. There was no slow start that worked up his spine to the back of his neck like he normally experienced. This was there, and there now. His head whipped around toward the altar, but there was just another filthy wall with peeling wallpaper. The sensations consumed and controlled him. Madame Stryvia stood up from the pew, and it disappeared. She backed up, brushing him as she passed. With even that momentary contact, Jacob could feel her shake. Her hand attempted to grab his to pull him backward with her, but missed.

In front of him, the woman lay in peace and just breathed. Behind him, the normally calm and stoic keeper banged like a lunatic on the door to get out. The others just stood where they were when the world around them changed. No other sound but the banging and the breathing. Not even the continuous praying and ritual at the front to remove the demon from his sister could be heard. As far as Jacob knew, they were taken someplace far away. Someplace overwhelmed by a paranormal evil he had never experienced before, but what was it? He saw nothing to match what the sensations in his body felt.

Whimpers and half screams accompanied the banging on the door.

"Catherine, what is wrong?" Father Murray asked.

"We need to get out. Someone help me with this door. Please," she pleaded.

Father Murray stepped toward the bed and looked at the woman. His movement caused a shriek from behind them, and then another plea.

"Father! Stop! Don't take another step!" The sheer fear in her voice sent additional chills up Jacob's spine. The banging stopped, but whimpering replaced it. "That is Alina Ravula. Possessed by a demon that I could never identify. I know where and when we are, and we need to get out now. Help me."

Just then the woman sprung up and sat in the bed. Her neck creaked and popped as her head turned to look at each person on the room. Not a muscle moved on her face. Not even a twitch. Her empty and unblinking gaze stared right through Jacob and Halensworth to Stryvia behind them. The straight line of her pale lips curled up ever so slightly at the edges. They parted just enough to display the jagged and rotting teeth inside. Her body leapt up and stood on the bed, rigid straight.

Each of the keepers stepped back. Jacob took more than one and bumped into Madame Stryvia at the door. Her hand grabbed for his again, and this time found it. Alina Ravula jumped over the foot of the bed. Her frail and decrepit fame didn't bend at the knees or anywhere else to perform the jump. It just moved, still board-straight. Now she was only feet away from the keepers, and they took another step backward.

Halensworth pulled out his cross and held it at her. "By God's grace, back away and release that woman."

She hissed at him.

"This isn't real. It is him, Abaddon, trying to get to us," Father Murray said.

To Jacob, the fear felt authentic enough for his hand to have gripped his own cross. Halensworth must have agreed. His hand stayed steadfast with the cross in between her and him.

Her hand swiped out at him, passing under the cross. At first it looked like she missed, but slowly a dark crimson line appeared on his button-up white shirt. He looked down in disbelief. A swipe Jacob dodged, as he jumped back and forced Madame Stryvia into the door with a thud. Father Murray rushed back to join the huddled group. Tenzein Mao did as well and perfectly timed his move to make an attempted attack on him miss. He pushed through to the back to help open the door. Jacob could hear the pounding and constant turning of a creaky door handle, but it never budged.

Alina Ravula stepped closer to them and then bent at the waist, projecting a stream of blood from her mouth at them. It came out with the force of a fire hose, sending most tumbling to the slick floor. For the second time in a matter of hours, Jacob found himself covered in the metallic stench of blood. Halensworth gathered himself to a knee, and with the power of a football fullback exploded up and put his shoulder into the door. It splintered around the hinges and collapsed to the floor. They each ran through it and into another room, a different room. Behind them, the door disappeared into a flat beige-colored wall.

25

A strange and horrifying sense of déjà vu set in on Jacob. They were now in another room. Different smell. Different walls. Different bed with someone lying in it, but the same spine-tingling fear controlled his body. This room lacked the filth of the other room. It was clean and orderly. The bed was nicely made around the person, and the nightstands and chairs were all positioned neatly around the room. Almost too neatly. Everything was square to a corner. The sun of a new day shone through the window. Jacob leaned his head forward and peered through it. He saw vast mountain ranges. They weren't in Virginia anymore.

"This will not make me afraid," Tenzein Mao said. He stepped forward and to the side of the bed. "It showed me this before, out there. It didn't affect me then, and it won't affect me now."

Jacob believed him. His voice was firm, resolute. Too bad Jacob didn't feel so strongly. An unknown fear crept in from his feet. It wasn't the tingle of something paranormal, that was already there. It started as twitches in his calves and then moved up through his thighs. They wanted to run, jump, do anything to get the hell out of here before whatever happened next happened.

"Tenzein, I take it this is your memory?" Halensworth asked, his arm across his stomach attempting to stop the bleeding.

"Oh yes. I remember this clearly. I was eight. This is my grandfather just before he passed. He will die before the sun goes down. He lay like this for a great number of days, while he was eaten alive on the inside."

"Cancer?" Jacob asked. His voice shook, a combination of fear and remembering his mother in her last days.

"No. That would have been easier. He couldn't—"

"I made a choice," the old man interrupted. His eyes looked up in a sightless stare. Each breath he took rattled inside his chest.

His words startled the group, but no one more than Tenzein Mao, who was stopped midsentence. His normally calm and steady appearance took on a more fearful look for the first time Jacob had seen since he arrived. "That was not my grandfather's voice," he said, "but he is right. He made a choice. There was a small child, two villages over. It was possessed. He tried for weeks to free the child, but couldn't. See, the mind of a child is innocent and willing to accept anything. A demon can't possess someone who doesn't accept them in, making a child the perfect target."

"It also makes them the most difficult to free," added Madame Stryvia.

"Yes it does. My grandfather found that out. When he saw no other option, he sat my father down and explained that he had a great life, no regrets, and needed to make a choice." He paused to look at the body of his grandfather, who had just uttered that word. "Said he could free the child, giving it a chance at having a good life too, but he would have to sacrifice himself. I sat around the corner from them as he told him. My father argued with him, but my grandfather was a stubborn man. Nothing my father said could have changed his mind. Many times he let my father believe he won, but he still went on and did what they were arguing about. This time, though, it ended in an agreement, and my grandfather passed his cross and book to him before he walked out. The next time I saw him, he was lying here, like he is now. See, my grandfather saw only one way to free the child and allow it to have a chance at a full life. He had to give himself to the demon and let it take him. He wasted away over the better part of a week until he passed."

"I am sorry for your loss, Tenzein. He made an honorable sacrifice."

"Yes, Mr. Halensworth, he did. I would like to think if presented with a similar situation, I would do the same."

"Now is your chance. For all of you," the old man said, once again startling the group.

"What do you mean, Grandfather?"

"I will never give her back to you. One of you can save her," he rattled again. This time the words came out faster than his mouth moved.

"So that is what this is about?" Father Murray asked. "This is an offer, not an attempt to break us down."

"Maybe both. You are all weak. I could manipulate any one of you, anytime I wanted. I have played you all like a fiddle. Monk, you never felt like you measured up to the honor of your family. Here is your chance. Take the girl's place."

"Tenzein, don't even think about it," Father Murray insisted. "It wants us to give up. No one will have to make that choice. No one," he added while he looked everyone in the eye.

Jacob knew if it came to that, it would have to be him. He couldn't let anyone else do that.

"Shut up, priest. You don't know what you are dealing with. You never did. You walked around under some veil of faith, assuming you are protected and righteous. You are just as flawed as that God you put your faith into." The body of Tenzein's grandfather shook and swelled up like a party balloon. It continued, pushing the sheets and sending them falling to the ground before it popped, splattering them and the walls with a mixture of blood, torn tissue, and other biological matter.

The room started to shake, and the walls moved back. The window disappeared along with the mountain landscape. The wood floor under his feet pulled back, and a familiar floor slid in under him. Cabinets lined the walls. A kitchen island he had eaten breakfast in several hundred times took shape, as did the breakfast nook he should have sat at to eat. As familiar as the kitchen in his home was, it was different. Things were in different places, and it looked, well, dated. Like something out of the seventies. Stacked in the sink were yellow dishes. A large radio sat on the island, playing music. The sound was not clear, it was distant. Like background music in a faded dream. A woman dressed in jeans and a shirt with rolled-up sleeves moved back and forth from the island to the sink with stacks of dirty dishes. She hummed to the music as she worked.

The back door flew open, and in walked something not human. It was a distorted creature that Jacob had seen before. Father Murray ran toward it and tried to stop it. The creature passed right through him and sneered as it did. The woman screamed, and Father Murray dropped to his knees. Jacob watched it plunge its claws into her flesh. Crimson rivers ran down her body and pooled where she fell to the ground. A man who looked a lot like his father did now stormed in the same back door just as she hit the floor. He held up the cross and proclaimed, "In the name of the Son, Father, and Holy Ghost, I banish you from this world." A glimmer of a glow developed in the center of the cross, but that was it. There wasn't time for anything else to happen. A swiping claw slashed across the man's neck while he stood just feet inside the door. His body collapsed, partially decapitated, through Father Murray, and landed on the floor. Father Murray wept and reached down to touch the man, but his hand passed right through. Another figure emerged in the back door, a much younger Father Murray. Everything happened so fast, leaving the group stunned by what they saw. The only sounds they heard were the sobs of Father Murray and the music that played on. A single tear rolled down Jacob's cheek as the realization set in that he just watched the death of his grandparents.

"Take me! Take me! I have blood on my hands. Let me sacrifice myself and repent," Father Murray bawled.

"No," barked Tenzein Mao. "Don't let it manipulate you."

"No. It's my turn. Let me fix my wrongs. I can help this family. I owe it to them after all I have cost them."

The beast turned and walked toward Father Murray, then stopped. The surrounding walls faded, and scenes of the church seeped in. Slowly, and then more predominately, until that was all they saw. They were still in the same row of pews they were in before. Manuela had returned and was completing a circle of salt around them.

"Splendid thinking, girl," said Halensworth.

The scene Jacob saw at the front of the church was not as peaceful as it was when they were taken away. The black cloud continued to swirl and heave above his sister, but now her body struggled against its restraints, bucking and yanking with every second. Father Lucian continued to command the demon to release her. After each command, Lord Negiev and Mr. Nagoti repeated his line. In between lines, Father Lucian alternated pressing crosses into her flesh or anointing her with oil or holy water. A shriek or a howl met every gesture. The clouds above repeated her objection. The dark symbols that pressed through her skin phased in and out of view.

"I will never let her go, priest. You know that," it objected through Sarah's voice.

Father Lucian ignored the challenge and continued, "Unclean demon, I cast you from this body."

"Praise be to God. Through him, all sins are forgiven," repeated both Lord Negiev and Mr. Nagoti.

"Why do you praise God, priest? Your faith is fake. You have doubted him," it said, and added virulently, "You still do."

Father Lucian pressed a crucifix into her forehead one last time, then stumbled away from the altar. He collapsed into the first pew, and Lord Negiev and Mr. Nagoti sat on the single step that led up to the altar. Their heads dropped into their hands.

"Lucian, are you all right?" asked Father Murray as he rushed to the front. Jacob and Madame Stryvia followed.

"Yes, just tired. It has been an exhausting ten hours."

Jacob was astonished at the statement. Had it really been ten hours? To him and the others, it seemed they had only been gone a few moments. He reached into his pocket and pulled out his cell phone. It was almost dead, but the clock read 11:48 p.m. A gaze out the window still showed the same world that was there before. Whether it was from cloud cover or just the darkness of night now, he wasn't sure. There was no way to be sure.

"Okay, you guys get something to eat and rest. We'll continue it," said Father Murray. He looked to the back and motioned for Manuela. As she walked forward, Lord Negiev and Mr. Nagoti got up and dragged themselves out the side door toward Father Murray's personal residence. He offered to help Father Lucian up, but his friend waved him off.

"Just give me a moment. I will be fine."

"Jacob, this is very important. If it tries to engage you, or if Sarah tries, ignore them. You must stay focused on what we are here to do." Father Murray picked up a book, opened it to a page, and handed it to Jacob. "Here are the prayers I will be using. You and Manuela are the respondents. You must read the line under the line I read immediately, without delay. If I say anything you don't see on the page, just say 'Praise be to God. Through him all sins are forgiven.' If I hold up my hand, you say nothing. We will start with the Lord's Prayer. Got it?"

"Yes," he said as Manuela walked past and took her position at the foot of the altar. She poured a single drop of holy water from her own vial onto her left hand. With the index finger of her right hand, she retrieved the drop and crossed herself across her chest.

"Doesn't she need a book?"

"Oh no, dear boy," chuckled Father Murray. "You and I are probably the only ones who do. We are significantly underqualified compared to everyone else here. Now, stand straight."

Retrieving his own vial, Father Murray blessed Jacob and then approached the altar. Jacob stepped up the single step that led to the altar and entered a different world. The hot and steamy air around him buzzed and shook, rattling his teeth. Ominous clouds above him rumbled and flashed every second. He watched as Father Murray took his position, paying no attention to his surroundings. Jacob pushed through the thick air to his spot next to Manuela and knelt. The buzz and rumbling around him intensified. In front of him, Sarah appeared to be having a horrible nightmare while asleep. Her body twitched and twisted in the restraints.

"Our Father, who art in Heaven."

Sarah's eyes fluttered open. They were bright yellow, with black centers that contained burning embers. Jacob's body jumped when he saw them, but the only reaction he saw from either of the others was a look of admonishment from Father Murray. Jacob joined back in with the prayer.

"Are you back for more, priest?" a horrifyingly raspy voice asked. Thunder rumbled above their heads. "Why not go ahead and kill her? Solve the problem by killing off another generation of the family. Something you are good at," the voice taunted.

"Amen." They completed the prayer, and Father Murray placed a cross on Sarah, the first time of many. Jacob watched Father Lucian do this earlier, but he was not close enough to hear the sizzle of her skin under it, or the growl that resonated deep in her throat. There were marks, cross-shaped, burns all up and down her arms. This fresh one left a similar mark on her shoulder.

"The glory of God commands you," repeated Jacob and Manuela. His attention was so focused on his sister, he almost missed it, but at the last minute he looked down at the book and recognized the words he heard Father Murray say.

The growls and hisses continued from Sarah as the storm grew above their heads. It was a brisk swirling wind that tousled Jacob's hair to one side. Small pieces of debris still became airborne, but little to nothing threatened them. Any threats they felt were from the rumbles of thunder and flashes of cloud to cloud lightning above them. All of which were frightening in their own right in a normal storm, but having it happen just feet above your head felt biblical.

Jacob watched the skin of his sister change from normal flesh color to the black symbols and back with each verbal objection or scream. From his close vantage point, Jacob could see the dark markings were in fact symbols. They were not merely markings on her skin but were raised areas pressed up and through it. Each smoldered slightly when it appeared. When it went away, it left no evidence of its presence.

26

Hours later, they continued to drone on with prayer after prayer. Each resulting in a reaction. Some were simple growls with thunder and lightning. Others were of a more personal nature. One of which included an hour-long diatribe of how Father Murray's parents were disappointed in him, delivered by the voice of his own father. Jacob watched in awe as he powered through, unfaltering, as insult after insult was fired at him, including several minutes of being called a murderer repeatedly. He continued through, never wavering in his duty or the conviction in his voice. It was only hours later that any effects showed. Jacob thought it was probably exhaustion. He knew he felt it, both physically, from not having slept since the previous day, and emotionally. Seeing his sister there, watching how she reacted, continued to tear at him. He'd hoped they would have seen some sign of her emerging through and the demon leaving. She hadn't gotten any worse, but she hadn't gotten any better.

Father Murray was sprinkling holy water on her again, which still sizzled on contact. Jacob had lost count of how many times he had done this. This time, her body bucked hard again against the restraints, and she gasped. Then she convulsed and gagged as a fountain of green vomit exploded from her mouth. It stopped just as quickly. Father Murray and Manuela both rushed to her. Jacob started, but Father Murray ordered, "Stay there." Father Murray turned Sarah's head while Manuela cleaned her mouth out, restoring her airway, which a gasp for air confirmed. Manuela tore a piece of the sheet that restrained the top half of Sarah to the altar. She used the piece of material to clean off her face the best she could.

A vibration and sound coming from Jacob's pocket caused him to jump. His body recovered with a natural reaction and reached into his pocket to retrieve it. What he saw on the screen was equally as shocking as when it went off. It was his father's number. His thumb couldn't move fast enough to hit Accept. A brief shake from the excitement and anticipation caused it to miss the first time, but the second time, it hit the green check and he answered, "Dad, is that you?"

"Yes, Jacob. It is," his father said. "You need to stop. You're killing your sister. Do you understand me?"

"Dad, we are trying to save her," he screamed back into the phone.

"You are killing her. There is no way to save her, but if you keep doing this, you will kill her," he said, emphasizing the last few words as if to command him.

"Jacob, who are you talking to?" Father Murray asked. He looked over Sarah's body with a stunned look in his eyes.

"It's my Dad. He says we need to stop."

"You have to stop. You will kill her if you don't. Listen to me son," his father directed again.

"Jacob, that can't be your dad. He is unconscious in the hospital. You know that. It's the demon. He is trying to manipulate you."

Jacob knew that was his state when they left, but that was yesterday. A lot could have happened. He hadn't had a chance to check in to see if his father's condition had changed. Then a moment of rationalization hit him. Sarah woke him up. She put him in that state in the first place. She probably reached out to him like she had Jacob, and it woke him. That had to be it. There was no other explanation. He beseeched Father Murray to understand. "No, Father, he woke up. He had to. He probably felt what was going on with Sarah and woke up. He and Sarah could probably communicate like she could with me. We need to listen to him."

"Watch her, please," Father Murray said to Manuela and rushed down the steps, away from the altar and to his overcoat, still stained red from the rain of blood. He reached inside and pulled out his own phone.

"Jacob," his father's voice summoned through the speaker. "Trust me. I can sense what she is going through. He will kill her if we don't stop. They mean no harm. Let her be, and we can live as a family."

"But, Dad," Jacob said. His father's words confused him. "What do you mean? They mean no harm. Who are they? The keepers?"

"No, Jacob, Sarah and the others. They mean no harm. It's all just a misunderstanding. One we can all work through together. Now get Father Murray and Father Lucian to stop. They will only harm her."

"Wendy? It's Father Murray. Any change in Edward's condition?" Father Murray asked to his own phone. His voice sounded stressed. "None at all? I will have to explain later." He put his phone down on the pew and walked toward Jacob.

"Dad, I don't understand."

"Jacob, put the phone down," requested Father Murray, his voice calm and soothing.

Jacob did not comply. "Dad, I don't understand. How can we all work through this? Sarah is controlled by a demon."

"No, son. She has talked to me. She is in control of it."

An overwhelming hope caused his heart to skip a beat. He didn't know how to respond other than to ask, "What do we do?"

"Jacob, put the phone down."

Jacob didn't put the phone down, but he pulled it away from his head a few inches. "Father Murray, it's good news. Sarah told my father she has control of the demon."

"Jacob, you are being fooled," Madame Stryvia exclaimed from the back.

"Jacob, that isn't your father," Halensworth said from the front pew.

Jacob's eyes looked back and forth at each of them, and he couldn't believe his ears. He was talking to his father. There was no doubt in his mind. It was as clear as the last time they talked. The phone was still in his hand, but now hung down around his waist. A voice from the other side pleaded through the speaker. It was too far away for Jacob to hear their words.

"Jacob, I just talked to Wendy. He is still unconscious. He hasn't woken up yet."

Father Murray stood just feet away from Jacob as he stated that, allowing him to see his eyes, facial expression, and body language clearly. It created a massive conflict in him. It battled the hope he had felt from his father's words and created doubt if that was his father at all.

"Jacob, you need to listen to me," Father Lucian said as he walked in. Halensworth walked in behind him. Jacob never noticed him leaving but assumed he went to get help. "That is not your father on the phone. Your father is still in the hospital. What you are talking to is Abaddon, and it is only in your head. It is playing on your faith, which is so very strong. Your faith in your father. Your faith in your sister. Your faith in being able to help her and save the day. Look down at your phone. Look at the screen. Trust me on this."

At that moment, Jacob held up the phone and looked at the screen. What he saw, or what he didn't see, on the display caused a few fast blinks. His fingers frantically moved to unlock the screen. Then he checked the call history for the call that might have become disconnected. There was nothing. The last call he had received from his father was the day of the event when he was searching for Sarah. His hand dropped again with the phone down to his waist. His jaw dropped as he searched the others for answers.

"Jacob, it is playing that faith you hold. Come, sit with me. Lionel, can you replace him?"

"Father," Manuela spoke up. "Father Murray and I can handle this. We only have an hour left."

Jacob stumbled away from the altar. He took one glance back as his feet landed off the step. An evil grin adorned his sister's face. Was that related to what had just happened to him? He didn't know. The evil image stuck with him though.

The smile was evil and distorted. Her eyes were still closed, her body still. There was a quiet satisfaction to how she lay there.

27

Father Lucian walked Jacob out of the church and back to Father Murray's residence with a fatherly arm around his shoulder. Jacob staggered there, exhausted and confused. A few moments of clarity had him wondering if it was the exhaustion that was causing his confusion. There was no way his father would call him. Like Father Murray reminded him, his father was still in the hospital and very unconscious. If anything had changed, Wendy would have called Lewis. What was he thinking? How could he have ever believed it? Even though he sounded very awake and alert to him.

They stopped in the kitchen, where Father Lucian took a bottle of soda from the refrigerator and put it on the table in front of Jacob. He turned back to the counter next to the sink and asked, "Like ham?"

"What?"

"Ham. We have turkey too. You need to eat something."

"Uh... yeah... Ham is fine," he stammered. Jacob was only half aware that he had pulled out the chair, sat, and taken a swig from the bottle. The coolness of the liquid felt like the serum of life itself as it slid across his tongue and down the back of his throat. Not as refreshing as the smiling models show on the commercials, but to him it was close. He felt he had emerged from a barren wasteland after weeks of being deserted. His mind still lingered in that place, with a heavy dark cloud and fog hanging over any rational thoughts. He wasn't sure what would clear it. Attempts to think about it, or what he had just experienced, left him in the same spot with no resolution. A clink of porcelain plate landing on the table drew his eyes. There was a new sensation. He was hungry. Something he didn't realize until that ham sandwich landed in front of him.

His arms reached for the sandwich and picked up half. They were weak and strained as he pulled it back to his face and took a bite. *How could this be?* he wondered. He just stood there, praying and repeating lines from a book Father Murray had given him. Not even a double header made him this weak. The food helped. It felt normal. Something that was odd in itself at the moment.

"Better?" asked Father Lucian.

Jacob just nodded.

"I have to admit. I am impressed. This was your first, and you lasted far longer than I had ever expected. This is not easy, by any means."

"What do you mean?"

"Oh, I gave you maybe two hours before you became too exhausted to continue."

"Glad to see you had such faith in me," Jacob sniped back.

"Jacob, I didn't mean that as an insult. You misunderstand me. Most people turn and run after twenty minutes in their first exorcism. The feelings. The constant mental challenges. The questions their own mind runs with about their own faith. It is exhausting. Only someone with a focused mind can do this, and you did quite well. Tell me what you felt."

Jacob had to think about that question. He was exhausted, but nothing really came to mind. He experienced nothing like he did while out in the woods or what he went through with the others in the church. He just knelt, reading or reciting, every thought on helping his sister and his father. Then it hit him. "Committed, Father Lucian. My thoughts were on doing my job and helping my sister and father. That was it."

"Then that explains it, Jacob. Your focus and your strong love and faith in your family drove you, keeping anything else from interfering." Father Lucian leaned back in his chair with a smile. "You may find it hard to believe, but that demon spent hours trying to get to you. Do you remember seeing me in the church before, when I came in and got you?"

"No," Jacob said. He saw no one other than Manuela, Father Murray, and Sarah. Everyone else was outside of his field of view, and he never attempted to look around.

"I was in and out the whole time. I was there when a fire burned around the three of you. I was there as bolts of lightning exploded everywhere. I was even there when the ground rumbled, threatening to bring the whole church down while voices from every language known to man echoed around the building. Do you remember any of that?"

Jacob was about to take in the last bit of the ham sandwich but stopped with it halfway into his mouth. With a quick gulp, he responded, "No."

"Well, it all happened. All to try to influence you. It took Abaddon over nine hours before he finally realized what I already knew. The only way to reach you was through your family. You are an amazing and impressive young man. Now I need you to be strong once more. Okay?"

There wasn't even a question about that for Jacob. If it was for his family, he would run through a wall. "Of course."

"We can't separate Abaddon and Sarah, not without killing her. I realized that the first time I went out there. What I have experienced since confirmed it, but that doesn't mean she is lost. We can still help her. In fact, we are doing that now, and you helped."

Jacob felt the cold sweat of panic develop on his brow. "Father Lucian, if we can't get it out of her, how does that help her?"

"We can give her a life. There are ways to contain it and give her control back. It will require constant monitoring and care."

"Anything. I will do it. Just tell me what to do," Jacob eagerly requested.

"Jacob, I know you would, but this goes beyond you, your father, or even something myself or Father Murray can do. I have called those who can help. They will be here tomorrow. Until then, we need to keep this up. It will all be all right."

"Father, I don't understand," Jacob said. The food and drink had replenished his body, but his mind felt the fog creeping back in. His thoughts, his hopes, were lost in the circles Father Lucian spoke in. They would help his sister by leaving the demon where it was. How would that help her? It made no sense to him. This he knew for sure and didn't question if his exhaustion played a factor.

"Jacob, the proper answer I should give you is, there are things we are not meant to understand, but being who you and your family are, that is not the case. You are meant to. We cannot always separate the demon from the soul of the living, but there is an order of sisters who specialize in basically flooding the demon in faith where it is held at bay. That allows the living soul to have as normal of a life as possible, under the circumstances. It requires a level of discipline far beyond what I have. They will help your sister, you will see. She will be awake and talking to you just like she always has."

"Father, what will happen then?"

"Let's not get too far ahead of ourselves. We have a lot of work yet to do. I want you to get some rest. We can talk about that once they arrive. Little victories, Jacob. Cherish the little victories in life, and you will never be dismayed."

With that, Father Lucian stood up from the table and walked out of the kitchen, leaving Jacob to his thoughts. For the first time in over a week, not a single thought ran through his mind. Not a single attempt to make sense of this. What was the use? Nothing made sense, except the darkness that fell as his eyelids closed. An arm as a pillow on the table, the great empty blackness absorbed the tired teen.

28

Jacob was not alone in the kitchen when he woke up. Lord Negiev was in there fixing a cup of coffee, his back to him. The sun shone in behind him through the window over the sink. It was an unfamiliar but welcome sight.

"How long have I been out?" croaked Jacob.

Lord Negiev, startled, turned around and said, "Oh, hey, Jacob. Did I wake you?"

"No, sir. How long?"

"Maybe six hours. How are you feeling?"

"Confused."

Lord Negiev laughed an abrupt laugh. "I would get used to that feeling. It is common in this world."

"Anything change while I was asleep?"

"A ton. Why don't we go check it out? Want some coffee?"

Jacob shook his head, then stood and opened the refrigerator. He pulled out another bottle of soda and held it up for Lord Negiev to see. He smiled at Jacob and walked out of the kitchen.

Jacob followed him out, across the small grassy patch that separated Father Murray's residence and the side entrance to the church. A pleasant cool breeze blew across him. It felt as if the town had just exhaled. Just a hint of warmth from the sun made it through the chilled air, causing his skin to break out in gooseflesh. That wasn't the first time in the past many days, but it was the first not caused by something evil. In fact, he felt nothing evil at all as he walked into the church.

Seated in the front few rows of pews were Father Murray, Father Lucian, and the rest of the keepers. Voices echoed in the rafters. They were female, gentle but determined. "Sit laus Deo."

His eyes followed his ears up to the altar. Kneeled at each of its four corners were habit-wearing nuns. That was something he had only seen in movies. He stood and gawked at the sight, focusing on their new visitors. So much so, he never noticed his sister had been cleaned up and dressed in a habit herself. She was not motionless like before. The breathing was regular and smooth. Not the rapid raspy breathing of before. There was color in her cheeks. Before then, he hadn't realized how pale she had looked, but lying there she looked alive.

"Jacob, come have a seat with me," requested Father Lucian.

As his name hit the air, Sarah's eyes opened and looked as far to the side as they could. Jacob saw them watching him as he walked toward Father Lucian. A simple but pleased smile developed on her face. A far cry from the smile of sneering satisfaction he saw when he left.

"Is she okay?" he asked.

"She will be. Have a seat."

Jacob sat next to Father Lucian. The keepers were spread across the pews behind them. Some were asleep. Some watched what was going on in front of them. Jacob's eyes stayed forward the entire time. The scene was surreal. The four sat like statues. Each word they prayed was perfectly synchronized with one another. The same tone. The same speed. So much so, they sounded like one voice.

"Jacob," Father Lucian started. His tone had a professional, almost consoling but compassionate tone. Much like Jacob imagined he might use when giving a family unpleasant news. "Your sister will be just fine, but I need you to understand something. She can never come home."

Jacob's jaw and heart dropped, and he leaned back hard against the pew's back with a bang.

"We cannot separate her and Abaddon without killing her. The only option left is to contain and control the threat. The sisters you see are from San Francesco, a monastery in Tuscany. Lauren is quite familiar with them."

An uh-huh of agreement came from behind him.

"The sisters in this order are very devoted and disciplined. Far more so than you, me, or anyone I have ever met. They have what it takes to maintain a watch over her."

Jacob attempted to interrupt, but a hand on his arm created a pause that Father Lucian took advantage of.

"And, Jacob, before you say you can watch over her too, you need to understand what I mean. This is not just watching over and taking care of her. One nun will pray by her side at all times, to keep the beast controlled and allow Sarah to live. If they stop for the briefest of moments, it will take over again."

The wind, and hope he felt when he saw her smile earlier, had just been punched right out of him. A hopelessness and despair replaced it. This was different from before. His sister was safe, and the terror that had gripped the town would end now, but he lost his family. His father was still in the hospital, unconscious, and now his sister would never return home.

"Where will she go?" he asked.

"Back to the abbey with them. You can rest assured, she will be well taken care of and have as full a life as possible. In fact, she and I talked about working together on some of the more difficult cases I have to deal with."

"Wait! You talked to her?"

"Yes, Jacob. The sheriff returned from the airport with them just after you fell asleep. It didn't take them long to do their work, and she emerged. You can go talk to her now if you want."

Jacob's body lurched forward, then paused. "You sure?" he asked. "I won't disturb them?"

"Not at all, Jacob. Go. Go talk to her."

He ran, covering the distance in just four steps. She lay there quiet, but smiled as he approached. "You always thought I was evil," she said with a tone of sarcasm that was most definitely his sister.

"Sarah, stop that."

"Jacob, I am so sorry. So sorry for everything I did. Everyone I hurt..." Her voice trailed off as tears began to run from her eyes.

Jacob reached over and wiped the tears away with his hand. "Sarah, stop. It wasn't you. It was that... thing."

"I know, Jacob, but I still feel responsible. While he was doing all that, I was still here watching it all, unable to do anything about what I saw myself doing. You don't understand how helpless and frightened that makes me feel. And Dad. What I did to Dad." She gulped. "I will fix that before I go. I promise you that."

"Sarah, it's okay."

"No, it's not. Not by a long shot, but I can let some good come out of this. Father Lucian believes its presence in me is why my abilities are so strong, and I can use that to help others, so they don't go through this." She sniffed, and for the first time her own hand moved and wiped the corner of her eyes, where some tears had formed again. "It is what I have to do, Jacob."

"I understand," he said, and he did. He could see the determination in her eyes. The same determination he saw when she told him about making Myrtle's her own. "Is it still there?"

"Oh yeah, and he is not happy."

"What is it like? I can't even imagine."

"You know those days you don't know why but you just feel you're in a bad mood?"

Jacob nodded.

"It is exactly like that. So watch out for my moods." She flashed him a quick grin, which again to Jacob seemed more like his sister.

Jacob sighed, a deep and remorseful sigh, that released everything that had been pent up and built up in him over the last week. He knew it wasn't over but could see the light amidst the shadows.

She sat up and let her legs dangle off the side of the altar. The sisters from the San Francesco didn't move, didn't stop. Their prayer had a rhythmic chant to it and even felt soothing to Jacob.

"Father?" she asked.

"Yes, my dear." Father Lucian stood and walked toward her.

"I want to see my father now. I want to help him."

Father Lucian looked at the nun who was to the right of where Sarah's head was when she was lying on the altar. The woman's head raised, showing Jacob her face for the first time. She was older than he first imagined. Her face was weathered and aged, but kind, almost grandmotherly. She didn't pause her prayer and kept rhythm with the other three but responded all the same with a simple nod.

"Okay, I will drive," Father Lucian said.

Sarah hopped down and walked through the decimated church toward the front door she had walked through many times. This time, though, she led a train of habit-wearing nuns, who followed her, praying the whole time.

29

Father Murray allowed Father Lucian to borrow his Cadillac to transport Sarah and her escorts to the hospital. Lewis followed them with Father Murray and Jacob. On the way, he told the story of picking them up at the airport. He explained he considered himself a religious man but felt rather humble in the sight of those four walking through Dulles International Airport and out to his car. None of them said a word during the entire trip. He wondered if it was an oath they had taken, but explained to Jacob that Father Lucian said they just weren't used to being outside of their abbey. The one part of his story that stuck with Jacob was when he explained, "I felt like Moses though. Walking through with them caused the large crowd to part like the Red Sea." Jacob glanced back to Father Murray quick enough to catch a roll of his eyes.

When they arrived at the hospital, Jacob saw exactly what Lewis had joked about. As they walked in the hospital, which wasn't crowded in any sense of the word, the doctors and nurses that mulled around parted to either side to allow Sarah and her entourage through. Father Murray greeted each as they passed. A few had shocked looks on their face as they recognized Sarah.

Sarah strolled into her father's room, sending Wendy clamoring for the corner. "It's okay, Wendy. I will explain later," Lewis yelled into the room from the outside. It was crowded. Too crowded for all of them to fit. At the door, the older sister reached out and touched Sarah, and she paused just in the doorway. She then turned to Father Lucian and said, "I can handle this alone. We won't be long."

"Yes, Mother," Father Lucian replied.

She reached around Father Lucian and grabbed Jacob just below the elbow. It was a firm grab, and she pulled him forward. "Come on in. You need to be here," she said with pleasant and calm eyes before rejoining the prayer. They walked in and let the door close behind the three of them. Only her prayer could be heard now. As they rounded the corner where the bathroom was, Sarah rushed toward her father, leaned over and hugged him.

"Daddy! Daddy! I am so sorry!" she wailed.

Jacob walked to the other side of the bed and watched as his sister composed herself and sat in the red vinyl chair. Her hand held on to her father's hand. Her eyes closed, and the room grew quiet. The constant prayer was there, but softer than before, leaving just the constant pump of air in and out by the machine that kept his father breathing.

She stayed like that for what Jacob felt was forever, but it was at the most several minutes. He looked back at Wendy several times, who still looked on at the scene in wonder and surprise. Then something that really surprised both happened. A jerk under Edward's eyelids. His eyes were moving back and forth. A few more minutes passed, when first the left eye popped open and then the right, and he turned his head as far as the ventilator tube let him to look at his daughter. He turned to look at his son.

"Hey, Dad," Jacob said.

"Let me get a doctor to get that tube out of him," Wendy said with urgency and then rushed out of the room.

A doctor rushed back in to check Edward. First, he checked his eyes, then his pulse before he listened to his breathing. He turned off the machine and listened again. Sarah kept hold of her father the whole time.

"Mr. Meyer, can you hear me?" the doctor asked.

Edward looked straight up at him and nodded.

"Well, I'll be…" he whispered as he removed the hoses and straps that held them in place. "Give me just a moment, and I will have this out of you." He finished disconnecting the machine.

Edward's breathing wheezed in and out of the tube that was still down his throat.

"Okay, Mr. Meyer. When I say, I want you to blow hard. This will be uncomfortable but won't take long. Ready?"

Edward nodded again.

"Blow," said the doctor. Out he pulled the long tube that had spent the last week down Edward's throat delivering the air needed to keep him alive.

Edward coughed once it was out. Something that was expected by the doctor, who quickly poured him a cup of water and handed it to him, asking him to drink it slowly. He listened to his breathing once more and then said, "Good. Sounds strong."

"Daddy, you understand, don't you?" Sarah asked.

"Yes," he croaked. "I do."

"Understand what?" asked Jacob.

The doctor, who looked as comfortable as someone who just walked in on one of the great secrets of the world, slipped by and out. His eyes locked on the praying nun as he left.

"Everything," Sarah said. Her eyes never left her father. "I told him everything that has happened and everything that needs to happen. Just like I reached out to talk to you. To warn you to stay away and leave me." She paused and slowly looked up at her brother. "Something I see you ignored."

"You're welcome," said Jacob.

"Jacob, that was both very brave and dangerous," admonished his father.

"I know, but I had help. Lots of help."

"I heard," said Edward. "How much time do you have left?"

"Our flight leaves tomorrow."

"Then I have until then to get my strength up enough to go with you," replied Edward.

"Oh no. No way, Jose. You are in no shape to travel. I wish I could stay longer so you could, but they explained they can only do this for so long away from the abbey, but Jacob, if you wanted to accompany me, I would like that."

The three of them, and their spiritual escort, spent the rest of the afternoon and into the night talking. Not about what happened, but everything else. Sarah made a few brief mentions of "I am going to miss that" when subjects like Myrtle's or the Fall Festival came up. Each pulled the spirit of the conversation backward a tad, but not for too long before a funny remember-when story pulled them back up. The whole time, the nun who knelt behind Sarah never moved and never stopped. Father Lucian told Jacob they were dedicated, but no words could match what he saw and finally understood. This was a life assignment, a mission, that they had chosen and threw every ounce of their essence into.

When the early hours of the morning arrived, the fatigue of what Edward had been through finally took hold, and the doctors and nurses insisted he get some sleep. It wasn't a long goodbye between him and his daughter, but it was a tearful one, from both her and him. She reminded him many times that he could come to visit anytime he wanted. By that time, Father Lucian and Father Murray had joined them. Lewis was in and out. Father Lucian not only agreed but encouraged Edward to visit often. "It would be good for both you and her to see each other and spend time together. It would also be good for you to meet with Mother Demiana. She has a lot she could teach you."

Early the next morning, Lewis and Father Murray drove the party to Dulles International. The keepers had agreed to stay longer and visit with Edward. Mr. Halensworth didn't hesitate, insisting he loved sitting around and sharing stories. What Jacob heard before he departed was the request from Father Lucian to stay and keep Edward company. It was important to him that Edward knew he was not alone and didn't feel like he was out on an island, being the only one who hadn't had the opportunity to train with or meet any of the others. They were a family like no other in the world, comfort would come from recognizing that.

When they arrived at Dulles, Jacob expected to walk into the terminal and out to one of the commercial gates. The excitement about his first international flight nearly doubled when they were escorted down a private set of stairs and out onto the tarmac itself. It doubled again when he saw the sleek and clean business jet with the papal keys on the tail waiting for them. Father Murray gave Sarah a long and warm hug, and then a handshake for Father Lucian. They spoke no words. Jacob wondered what one might say in this situation. They don't really make an *'It has been nice knowing you. I hope the demon inside you lets you enjoy life'* hallmark card.

Inside, the jet was spacious but still very much like a commercial airliner, not like the private jets he had seen pictures of that sport stars used. He sat in a seat on one side of the aisle with Father Lucian. Sarah sat on the other side, her escorts behind her. At no time were any less than two of them praying. Mother Demiana took her shift to pray, but other times talked with Sarah. Some of it was instructional discussion. Sarah had a lot to learn. Others were stories Mother Demiana shared with Sarah of experiences when she was a girl.

It was dark when they landed in Italy. Jacob found it amazing the days were shorter during the fall just like back at home. They rushed into a row of black SUVs that sped through the gates of the airport. Father Lucian made sure Jacob sat with Sarah for the thirty-minute ride from the airport in Florence to the convent just north of the city in Fiesole. The two sat mostly in silence on the drive. Jacob felt a dread settle in. It was much lighter than what he had felt before, but still there. He knew there were just moments before he would have to say goodbye to his sister. She would still be alive and just be a phone call away, but he wouldn't see her every day, every week, every month, or even every year for that matter. There would be a great distance between them, one that seemed to grow as he sat there. He couldn't let it, and for the first time since he was probably five, he leaned over and grabbed her, and held her close. He hid his tears from her, but he knew she could hear the shake in his breathing as he cried. It was okay, though, he could hear the same in hers.

They pulled into the Piazza Mino da Fiesole, and the SUVs came to a stop. The convent was at the top of a long and winding stone walkway. He walked Sarah up it, holding her hand the whole way. At the top, he thought he needed to stop, but Mother Demiana told him to go on, they would show him around, that he was "family." She gave them a tour of the building Jacob could only describe as Tuscan. It reminded him of an Italian restaurant they stopped at in Newport City three summers ago. Wood eaves and beams, stucco walls. A simple courtyard with fresco paintings and reflection ponds, and woods all around the complex with paths for walking.

At the end of the tour, Father Lucian approached Jacob. "Why don't we let your sister settle in. You can come see her again in a couple of days."

"A couple of days, Father? I'll be back home then."

"Well, not exactly. Your father and I discussed you staying here with me for a little while to start your formal training. What do you think? Want to come with me and spend the night in the Vatican?"

"Go, Jacob," urged Sarah. "It's wonderful there. Enjoy it, but don't let Father Lucian work you too hard. He really put the screws to me."

Jacob seemed unsure.

"You can come walk with me on Thursday. It's your time now."

WHAT'S NEXT FOR THE MEYER FAMILY?

There is more coming in the Miller's Crossing series. To be notified when the next books are released, join my mailing list at - https://authordavidclark.com/

Meanwhile, read what's next for Sarah Meyer in the series, "The Stories of Sister Sarah". This series is the re-telling of Sarah's life covering the adventures of her and Father Lucian as they investigate and solve some of the world's most legendary paranormal mysteries.

DAVID CLARK

THE STORIES OF
SISTER
SARAH

1

"First, I want to thank you for agreeing to meet with us."

The old woman sat upright in a simple wooden chair with a pleasant look on her face. A man, only a few years younger than her, sat off to her left. He was apprehensive and sat on the edge of his chair as if he were ready to pounce on some great evil at any moment. Looking at the tone of his senior-citizen body, it was obvious he could still do that if needed. He had every appearance of someone who knew a life of manual labor. Maybe a craftsman or a farmer. On either side of the woman's chair, two nuns knelt and prayed silently.

"Oh, not at all. I am more than happy to talk about my life. You will have to excuse my brother, he is a bit protective of me."

"Well, I hope to put him at ease. We are here with all due respect, and hope to conduct this interview as such. Your Mother Superior gave us an hour, shall we begin?"

The young man who had been speaking leaned forward just a bit further and placed a microphone on the floor in front of the elder nun. His black-rimmed glasses almost slipped off his nose when he bent over, prompting a quick push back into place with his forefinger. The hand continued to brush a mop of straggly-length dark hair out of his face.

"Any background?", he asked the blonde twenty-something to his side. The man gave him a thumbs up.

"First, can you introduce yourself and tell us who you are?"

"Sure, I am Sarah Meyer. Daughter of Edward Meyer."

"And, you are a nun here at San Francesco?"

"In a way of speaking. They take care of us, and I follow their beliefs and life. I must admit, I found the life very pleasing and finally took the oath when I was thirty-three."

"And how old are you? If you don't mind me asking?"

There was a great pause between the six people in the room, only the two nuns continued. Their prayers nothing more than a whisper.

"Not at all, I am 85 years old, and IT is 3184 years old."

One of the two nuns gasped out loud and paused her prayer for only the briefest of moments. Sarah looked in her direction and said with a calm voice,

"Please don't stop child. I don't want it to make a mess of these nice men. I have a story to tell."

There were two audible gulps in the room, and Jacob leaned forward further in his chair. Sarah extended her hand out toward her brother and placed it on his knee. She smiled rather mischievously. Not like someone who was evil, but more like someone who was having a little fun. Which was the case. At this moment, she felt in complete control of herself. The two younger nuns, both relatively new when compared to her length of stay, were doing a fine job of keeping Abaddon hidden, as did all the sisters that had served at Sarah's side. There were only brief moments where she lost control. All brought back under control without any world-ending catastrophes. A welcome improvement over the first time he took control of Sarah.

"You gentlemen can relax. We are perfectly fine at this moment, but let's not waste time."

"Yes ma'am. We don't want to cover what happened before you arrived here. We have already spoken to your brother about that, and that has been well documented many times over once the story came out."

Sarah chuckled, almost a grandmotherly laugh as if a grandchild amused her, but it came across as disturbing and, once again, set the tense room on edge. "Oh, I am sorry," she apologized. "I don't know why, can't really explain it, but thinking about how our secret was let out still amuses me. Maybe it was how hard everyone worked to keep it a secret, but in the end the Vatican published a book on us all. No investigative exposé or anything, just a book all on our own."

"Yes," he stumbled. "It is a wonderful book. I have read it many times. The section on you and your family is fascinating."

"I have read it too. The missed quite a bit, but that is expected. Please continue."

"What we are most interested in are the stories once you arrived here. The, I guess, cases you helped Father Lucian and the other keepers with through the years, using.. ITs power."

"I imagined that was what you would want to hear. I helped him with a great many, up until his passing, and then Father Domingo took his place and we continued our work. Is there a particular one you want to hear about first?"

He consulted his notebook, flipping through several pages of scribbled items. Sarah thought, *how old school of him, he still writes notes.* Most of those that have come and talked to her walked in with a digital notebook or robotic camera. Not these two. The main interviewer, a man in his mid-thirties she would guess, in a brown sweater almost has that documentary film student look, with his pad full of notes. She bet, and before she finished the thought, her eyes found the pencil stuck behind his ear. During the vetting process, something Jacob always did, he verified these two were not just students, or anyone that might be there to exploit her. They were professionals, two of the best. Ralph Fredricks, and two-time Golden Globe winner, and his cameraman Kenneth Lloyd. Sarah hadn't had a chance to watch any of the films they produced, but she trusted her brother. She was aware of the sheer number that he had turned down since the book came out fifteen years ago.

The book, something no one warned anyone about, was aimed at trying to return the world's faith in the spiritual. Pope Mark, a priest from Columbia, said he felt like he was watching the world walk away from God and toward the digital spark of technology, forgetting who they really were and where they came from. It was a theme in every sermon he gave. It was also dead center of his policies and directions from the Papal office. A media campaign, unlike any the church had undertaken, began to show the world the spiritual side they had forgotten. Movies and shows about religious sites and figures. The reception was lukewarm. His critics within the church said the stories were old and worn. Everyone knew the figures. Everyone knew the sites. None of them had any appeal.

Then, through several edicts and Papal papers, he began to acknowledge the church's belief in the paranormal, and the truth about its support in the practice of exorcisms. Both were expected to make a splash, but they didn't do much more than create a ripple. Popular culture movies and themes had desensitized the entire world to those topics. In what some called an act of desperation, he outed the Sites, the Keepers, and all their stories. To Sarah's horror, there was no warning when it was released. Mother Francine woke her early one morning and told her as soon as she had heard herself. That was the first. She lived in fear for a while, and stayed secluded in her room. Not even taking the walks out among the trees in the courtyards to listen to the birds, an activity she had grown very fond of through the years. Sarah knew some details of her story were not as glorious as others, and might even make her the target for both those wanting to grab a piece of story, and those that would fear her and want to protect the world from her, but no one came. No one inquired. The public dismissed the stories as works of fiction. Then little by little, a few interviews with keepers here and a documentary there, credibility grew. That created a ground swell which turned into a tidal wave of requests. All of which the Abbey diverted to Jacob, who eagerly volunteered so they wouldn't be bothered. It was a burden he explained he needed to do after all they had done for his sister.

"Sister, how about the first time?" Ralph asked, after closing his notebook.

"How did I know you would ask about Poveglia?"

"It is called the most haunted place in the world, and it was your first time," he responded.

"Well, then. Let's get to it."

You can find the first book in the novella series at the links below:
Amazon US
Amazon UK

You can also find the Boxset of the first 3 stories – The Unholy Trinity #1 at the links below:
Amazon US
Amazon UK

THE DARK ANGEL MYSTERIES

Meet Lynch, he is a private detective that is a bit of a jerk. Okay, let's face it he is a big jerk who is despised by most, feared by those who cross him, and barely tolerated by those who really know him. He smokes, drinks, cusses, and could care less what anyone else thinks about him, and that is exactly how the metropolis of New Metro needs him as their protector against the supernatural scum that lurk around in the shadows. He is "The Dark Angel."

"The Blood Dahlia", is book one in this new series.

THE BLOOD DAHLIA

A NOVEL OF THE DARK ANGEL MYSTERIES

DAVID CLARK

1

"So, what did you end up doing last night?", Detective Lucas Watson asked.

"Stayed in. Watched a movie," his grizzly ex-partner said while he nursed his second scotch, no rocks.

"Really? What movie?", asked the detective, who then slammed his glass down on the bar. "Can't shoot worth shit."

"Haven't been able to shoot all season, not when it matters."

"So, what movie?", the question marks dripped from his voice.

"Eh, I don't know. Some old war flick I found clicking around after I got bored with the game. They couldn't shoot last night either."

The question marks that had dripped from his question now shot forward out of his narrowed eyes. Lynch had seen this look many times in their past. Each time, though, he was on the same side of the table as the detective. This was his first time on the other side. He could see why suspects could feel unsettled. "Why do I feel you aren't just curious?"

"Some friendly curiosity, since you blew off coming over to watch the game, and some professional curiosity. We found the three most notorious gang-bangers in town tied to a fire hydrant."

"Really? Well, that should make your job easier. You don't need to chase them," Lynch said. He held up the glass for the barkeeper to see. He needed another one while he and his old friend sat and caught up. "They can't hit anything," he said as the whole bar moaned behind him. The New Metro Barons just missed their ninth shot in a row on the television positioned over the bar.

"You know I don't care if that was you."

"That's good. I don't care whether you care or not. Never did, and still don't give a shit, but remember, I am fifty-four years old, retired from the game. Way too fucking old to do anything like that anymore. The day is a good day if I can get up and take a crap in the morning." That may have been a bit of an exaggeration. Lynch wasn't twenty anymore, but he wasn't out of shape. To the contrary, he was rather built for a man of his age, but most couldn't tell it under the tweed suits he wore almost everywhere. The clothing made him look husky, still imposing, but less than an intimidating figure. Where his stature left off, in that regard, his face filled the gaps. The chiseled jaw of his aged and pitted face, littered with battle scars, was enough to make most shudder with a just a simple look from him. Not that he cared what people thought, one way or the other.

"If it wasn't you, and I still have my doubts, we still need you out there."

"Go find one of those cape wearing freaks or guys in the spandex to help you. I am not the hero type. You should know that better than anyone."

Detective Lucas Watson slapped his old friend on the back. "I got work tomorrow, and those losers show no signs of life." He stopped and pulled on the jacket that hung over the back of the bar stool. "Do me a favor, call an Autoride. You have had a few of those." The hand holding his hat pointed at the fresh scotch, no rocks, the barkeep just placed down in front of him.

After two more scotches, and the end of the 111-82 loss by the home team, Lynch grabbed an Autoride. The driver, Ahbdan, talked the whole way home. Luckily, he wasn't the type that waited for an answer. He just continued on with his point. A few strategic nods and hums kept the one-sided conversation going all the way home.

Lynch staggered in the door and into his study. The television was already on when he hit the sofa flat. His hand searched the floor for his scotch glass, but then he remembered he hadn't stopped at his private bar, just inside his study. One leg threw itself to the floor, to start the motion of getting up to remedy the situation, but the other leg protested and stayed right where it was.

In reach of his hand was the remote, which he grabbed and clicked, pausing just a second on each channel. Not to digest what was on and decide whether to watch it or move on. It was more of a rhythm thing. Like the drumming of fingers on a table or desk, just a natural timing. The world was built on a natural rhythm. Most never slowed down long enough to realize it. Lynch had long enjoyed the melodic drumbeat of rain in the darkness of the night. It was his percussion concerto. Like the clinking of ice cubes in a shot glass, not that he would be all that familiar with that sound, he takes his drinks without. A person's life and behaviors were rhythmic, too. Most felt more at ease when life followed a certain pattern, a common everyday mundane drone, every day like the next. Upset that pattern, and some will go crazy. The universe likes order. The bad assumption was order meant good. Order just meant order. Good and bad. The yin and the yang.

Lynch often asked himself, *what kind of God would create a world where good and bad had to even out? One with a sick sense of humor, that is what kind.* If he let his finger pause more than a second on any of the channels he clicked by on, he would see plenty of examples of that littering the evening news. He didn't need to see that to know it happened. It was something he could feel in his bones after all the years out working the streets. Every refreshing breeze carried a scream, just like the ones that haunted him every night he closed his eyes. Either it was the six-year-old he'd arrived just a little too late to save as the bastard that was abusing her in the basement of the rundown row-house just north of city center slashed across her throat, or the married mother of three who was held for ransom to sway her senator husband as she took a bullet to the temple just as he entered the door, or any number of other failures that stained Lynch's life.

The phenomenon that was this mysterious savior, worked under the cover of darkness, was never stained, or tarnished. They lauded it in the public; he was a hero. Not a soul knew about all the misses, all the times he never found them or was late, or missed. Well one soul did, and it was tortured.

"Are you in for the night?"

Lynch coughed to clear his voice, but it didn't help much. The smoke of the bar and the damp night air left him congested as he answered his robotic butler, "Yes."

"Good, I won't have to clean any blood out of your clothes tonight."

Lynch snapped back, "It wasn't mine, and you need to shut the hell up and get me a scotch before I make you a glorified toaster."

"Like I haven't heard that before, and you have had too much already," it said as it wheeled out of the study, back into the hall. Its metallic frame had a little sassiness to it as it rounded the corner.

Lynch sent the remote flying in its direction but missed. It only took a moment for him to regret not throwing something different. The television was now stuck on the news, with the mugshots of the three gang-bangers who were mysteriously found tied to a hydrant last night. After they took the mugshots down, the reporter rolled through the photographs of all of those believed to have been killed by them. People Lynch had missed on again, he had no doubt that a terrifying scream was part of the last sounds they'd made.

Faced with a choice of retrieving the remote or a scotch, he chose the scotch, a double, and managed to take it up the stairs, where he fell into bed. The screams would take him now, unless the scotch beat exhaustion to the punch.

Want to read more? Download using the store links below:
Amazon US
Amazon UK

Have you read the whole Miller's Crossing series?

Miller's Crossing Book 1 – The Ghosts of Miller's Crossing
Amazon US
Amazon UK
Ghosts and demons openly wander around the small town of Miller's Crossing. Over 250 years ago, the Vatican assigned a family to be this town's "keeper" to protect the realm of the living from their "visitors". There is just one problem. Edward Meyer doesn't know that is his family, yet.

Tragedy struck Edward twice. The first robbed him of his childhood and the truth behind who and what he is. The second, cost him his wife, sending him back to Miller's Crossing to start over with his two children.

What he finds when he returns is anything but what he expected. He is thrust into a world that is shocking and mysterious, while also answering and great many questions. With the help of two old friends, he rediscovers who and what he is, but he also discovers another truth, a dark truth. The truth behind the very tragedy that took so much from him. Edward faces a choice. Stay, and take his place in what destiny had planned for him,or run, leaving it and his family's legacy behind.

Miller's Crossing Book 2 – The Demon of Miller's Crossing
Amazon US
Amazon UK
The people of Miller's Crossing believed the worst of the "Dark Period" they had suffered through was behind them, and life had returned to normal. Or, as normal as life can be in a place where it is normal to see ghosts walking around. What they didn't know was the evil entity that tormented them was merely lying in wait.

After a period of thirty dark years, Miller's Crossing had now enjoyed eight years of peace and calm, allowing the scars of the past to heal. What no one realizes is under the surface the evil entity that caused their pain and suffering is just waiting to rip those wounds open again. Its instrument for destruction will be an unexpected, familiar, and powerful force in the community.

Miller's Crossing Book 3 – The Exorcism of Miller's Crossing – Available Fall 2020
Amazon US
Amazon UK
The "Dark Period" the people of Miller's Crossing suffered through before was nothing compared to life as a hostage to a malevolent demon that is after revenge. Worst of all, those assigned to protect them from such evils are not only helpless, but they are tools in the creatures plan. Extreme measures will be needed, but at what cost.

The rest of the "keepers" from the remaining 6 paranormal places in the world are called in to help free the people of Miller's Crossing from a demon that has exacted its revenge on the very family assigned to protect them. Action must be taken to avoid losing the town, and allowing the world of the dead to roam free to take over the dominion of the living. This demon took Edward's parents from him while he was a child. What will it take now?

Miller's Crossing - Prequel – The Origins of Miller's Crossing
Amazon US
Amazon UK
There are six known places in the world that are more "paranormal" than anywhere else. The Vatican has taken care to assign "sensitives" and "keepers" to each of those to protect the realm of the living from the realm of the dead. With the colonization of the New World, a seventh location has been found, and time for a new recruit.

William Miller is a simple farmer in the 18th century coastal town of St. Margaret's Hope Scotland. His life is ordinary and mundane, mostly. He does possess one unique skill. He sees ghosts.

A chance discovery of his special ability exposes him to an organization that needs people like him. An offer is made, he can stay an ordinary farmer, or come to the Vatican for training to join a league of "sensitives" and "keepers" to watch over and care for the areas where the realm of the living and the dead interaction. Will he turn it down, or will he accept and prove he has what it takes to become one of the true legends of their order? It is a decision that can't be made lightly, as there is a cost to pay for generations to come.

ALSO BY DAVID CLARK

The Dark Angel Mysteries

The Blood Dahlia (The Dark Angel Mysteries Book #1)

Amazon US

Amazon UK

Meet Lynch, he is a private detective that is a bit of a jerk. Okay, let's face it he is a big jerk who is despised by most, feared by those who cross him, and barely tolerated by those who really know him. He smokes, drinks, cusses, and could care less what anyone else thinks about him, and that is exactly how the metropolis of New Metro needs him as their protector against the supernatural scum that lurk around in the shadows. He is "The Dark Angel."

The year is 2053, and the daughters of the town's well-to-do families are disappearing without a trace. No witnesses. No evidence. No ransom notes. No leads at all until they find a few, dead and drained of all their blood by an unknown, but seemingly unnatural assailant. The only person suited for this investigation is Lynch, a surly ex-cop turned private detective with an on-again-off-again 'its complicated' girlfriend, and a secret. He can't die, he can't feel pain, and he sees the world in a way no one ever should. He sees all that is there, both natural and supernatural. His exploits have earned him the name Dark Angel among those that have crossed him. His only problem, no one told him how to truly use this *ability*. Time is running out for missing girls, and Lynch is the only one who can find and save them. Will he figure out the mystery in time and will he know what to do when he finds them?

Ghost Storm – Available Now

Amazon US

Amazon UK

There is nothing natural about this hurricane. An evil shaman unleashes a super-storm powered by an ancient Amazon spirit to enslave to humanity. Can one man realize what is important in time to protect his family from this danger?

Successful attorney Jim Preston hates living in his late father's shadow. Eager to leave his stress behind and validate his hard work, he takes his family on a lavish Florida vacation. But his plan turns to dust when a malicious shaman summons a hurricane of soul-stealing spirits.

Though his skeptical lawyer mind disbelieves at first, Jim can't ignore the warnings when the violent wraiths forge a path of destruction. But after numerous unsuccessful escape attempts, his only hope of protecting his wife and children is to confront an ancient demonic force head-on... or become its prisoner.

Can Jim prove he's worth more than a fancy house or car and stop a brutal spectral horde from killing everything he holds dear?

Game Master Series

Book One - Game Master – Game On

This fast-paced adrenaline filled series follows Robert Deluiz and his friends behind the veil of 1's and 0's and into the underbelly of the online universe where they are trapped as pawns in a sadistic game show for their very lives. Lose a challenge, and you die a horrible death to the cheers and profit of the viewers. Win them all, and you are changed forever.

Can Robert out play, outsmart, and outlast his friends to survive and be crowned Game Master?

Buy book one, Game Master: Game On and see if you have what it takes to be the Game Master.

Available now on Amazon and Kindle Unlimited

Book Two - Game Master – Playing for Keeps

The fast-paced horror for Robert and his new wife, Amy, continue. They think they have the game mastered when new players enter with their own set of rules, and they have no intention of playing fair. Motivated by anger and money, the root of all evil, these individuals devise a plan a for the Robert and his friends to repay them. The price... is their lives.

Game Master Play On is a fast-paced sequel ripped from today's headlines. If you like thriller stories with a touch of realism and a stunning twist that goes back to the origins of the Game Master show itself, then you will love this entry in David Clark's dark web trilogy, Game Master.

Buy book two, Game Master: Playing for Keeps to find out if the SanSquad survives.

Available now on Amazon and Kindle Unlimited

Book Three - Game Master – Reboot

With one of their own in danger, Robert and Doug reach out to a few of the games earliest players to mount a rescue. During their efforts, Robert finds himself immersed in a Cold War battle to save their friend. Their adversary... an ex-KGB super spy, now turned arms dealer, who is considered one of the most dangerous men walking the planet. Will the skills Robert has learned playing the game help him in this real world raid? There is no trick CGI or trap doors here, the threats are all real.

Buy book three, Game Master: Reboot to read the thrilling conclusion of the Game Master series.

Available now on Amazon and Kindle Unlimited

Highway 666 Series

Book One – Highway 666

A collection of four tales straight from the depths of hell itself. These four tales will take you on a high-speed chase down Highway 666, rip your heart out, burn you in a hell, and then leave you feeling lonely and cold at the end.

Stories Include:

- Highway 666 - The fate of three teenagers hooked into a demonic ride-share.
- Till Death – A new spin on the wedding vows
- Demon Apocalypse - It is the end of days, but not how the Bible described it.
- Eternal Journey - A young girl is forever condemned to her last walk, her journey will never end

Available now on Amazon and Kindle Unlimited

Book Two – The Splurge

A collection of short stories that follows one family through a dysfunctional Holiday Season that makes the Griswold's look like a Norman Rockwell painting.

Stories included:

- Trick or Treat – The annual neighborhood Halloween decorating contest is taken a bit too far and elicits some unwilling volunteers.
- Family Dinner – When your immediate family abandons you on Thanksgiving, what do you do? Well, you dig down deep on the family tree.
- The Splurge – This is a "Purge" parody focused around the First Black Friday Sale.
- Christmas Eve Nightmare – The family finds more than a Yule log in the fireplace on Christmas Eve

Available now on Amazon and Kindle Unlimited

GET YOUR FREE READERS KIT

Subscribe to David Clark's Reader's Club and in addition to all the news, updates, and special offers available to members, you will receive a free book just for joining.

Get Yours Now! - https://www.authordavidclark.com

ABOUT THE AUTHOR

David Clark is an author of multiple self-published thriller novellas and horror anthologies (amazon genre top 100) and can be found in 3 published horror anthologies. His writing focuses on the thriller and suspense genre with shades toward horror and science fiction. His writing style takes a story based on reality, develops characters the reader can connect with and pull for, and then sends the reader on a roller-coaster journey the best fortune teller could not predict. He feels his job is done if the reader either gasps, makes a verbal reaction out loud, throws the book across the room, or hopefully all three.

You can follow him on social media.
Facebook - https://www.facebook.com/DavidClarkHorror
Twitter - @davidclark6208

The Miller's Crossing Series © 2020 by David Clark. All Rights Reserved.
All rights reserved. No part of this book may be reproduced in any form or by any electronic or mechanical means including information storage and retrieval systems, without permission in writing from the author. The only exception is by a reviewer, who may quote short excerpts in a review.

This book is a work of fiction. Names, characters, places, and incidents either are products of the author's imagination or are used fictitiously. Any resemblance to actual persons, living or dead, events, or locales is entirely coincidental.

David Clark
Visit my website at www.authordavidclark.com

Printed in the United States of America

First Printing: September 2020
Frightening Future Publishing

Printed in Great Britain
by Amazon